The Complete

QuickSilver

series

KILL ME QUICK

A QUICK STUDY

QUICK AND THE DEAD

PLUS ALL SIX QUICKSILVER SHORT STORIES

Josie Jaffrey

CONTENT WARNINGS & SERIES RECAPS

There is a full list of content warnings at the back of this book, and also available at Josie's website at the link on the left below.

Recaps of the Silverse books are available on Josie's website at the link on the right below.

CONTENT WARNINGS

SERIES RECAPS

www.josiejaffrey.com/content-warnings www.josiejaffrey.com/series-recaps

By Josie Jaffrey

Stories from the Silverse: the World of the Silver

The Seekers Series
Killian's Dead (short story prequel, free to Josie's
subscribers)
May Day
Judgement Day
Winta's Day
Valentine's Day
Dark Days
End of Days

The QuickSilver Trilogy
Kill Me Quick
A Quick Study
Quick and the Dead
QuickSilver Omnibus Edition

The Solis Invicti Series
A Bargain in Silver
The Price of Silver
Bound in Silver
The Silver Bullet

The Sovereign Trilogy
The Gilded King
The Silver Queen
The Blood Prince

Silverse Serialised Stories
Dead Box
Dead Road

Silverse Short Stories
Encounters: Silverse Short Stories

Other Fiction

The Deluge Series
The Wolf and the Water

Short Stories
Broken Wings (collection)
Ring The Bell

CONTENTS

PART ONE

KILL ME QUICK

I

'NO,' KULIKA SAID, crossing her arms over her chest.

'Kulika—'

'Sir, with respect, you're a bastard for even asking.'

'With *respect*?'

Kulika cringed; *bastard* might have been putting it a little strongly.

Kulika Yadav owed her life to her boss. Before he'd come along, her tortured existence had been worse than death. This life that she had now in England, full of freedom and laughter and actual friends, that was the life that she owed to Killian Drake, Baron of Oxford. Yes, they were both immortal Silver – vampires, for the uninitiated – and practically indestructible, so it wasn't as though she'd been at imminent risk of death when he'd found her in that Charleston mausoleum. But she hadn't been *living* either.

In every way that mattered, he'd saved Kulika.

She never took that for granted. She'd die for him, she'd kill for him, and then she'd bury the bodies where no one would find them. In fact, if you'd asked her yesterday, she would have told you she'd do anything at all for Baron Drake, but that was only because she'd never imagined that

3

he'd send her back to the very hell he'd pulled her out of a century ago.

'Sir, I can't,' she pled. 'You know what'll happen if I do.'

'And you know what will happen if you don't.' He said the words softly. They weren't a threat, they were a statement of fact.

Kulika knew the truth as well as he did: if they didn't find a solution to this problem, and soon, then Baron Drake was going to die. *Really* die.

'There must be another way,' Kulika said desperately.

'I can't think of one,' he said, then he sat down in his chair, rested his elbows on his desk and put his head in his hands. 'It isn't as though I haven't been thinking about it. I never *stop* thinking about it. If she doesn't come back to me…'

She was Jack Valentine, the unlikely love of Baron Drake's life. Unfortunately, she was also a chaotic mess of a person who made terrible decisions in every sphere of her life, including those that involved her personal preservation. Long story short: she'd managed to infect herself with a poison, and now she was slowly burning to death from the inside out. There had been an antidote in production, but to make it they needed the blood of one particular Silver – Dr Jahan Khalyed – and he'd recently burned to death himself, along with every remaining trace of his blood.

Basically, Jack was fucked.

There was a muffled little *tap*. It was so quiet that Kulika wouldn't have noticed it at all without her Silver hearing. She couldn't be sure, since the baron still had his head in his hands, but she thought it might have been the sound of a teardrop hitting the blotter on his desk.

If Kulika had still been the delicate waif she'd pretended to be in her youth instead of the body-building badass she'd turned herself into, she might have fainted from shock.

Baron Drake was an island. He was a model of self-containment. If he had any vulnerable feelings at all, he never expressed them, at least not in front of other people, and he absolutely, positively didn't cry. In all the centuries of their acquaintance – friendship, even, if that wasn't too presumptuous – Kulika had never known him to loose a single tear. And now, seeing him raise his face from his hands again and rearrange his hair into its former tidy state, she saw no trace of tear marks on his face.

Perhaps she had been wrong.

But there had been that tiny *tap*.

'I'm sorry,' he said, shuffling some papers around on his desk. 'You're right. I shouldn't have asked. I'll let you get back to work.'

'Doesn't Dr Ross have any other ideas?' Kulika asked.

'This *is* her idea. We've traced the bloodlines, we've done the testing, and Dr Khalyed's only possible viable descendant went missing in Charleston in December.'

'*One* living descendant?' Kulika said incredulously.

'That's right,' he confirmed. 'Just one.'

Bugger.

Kulika had been so hoping there would be another option. Dr Ross thought it was possible – not likely, but *possible* – that the blood of one of Dr Khalyed's human descendants could be substituted for his to make the antidote Jack needed to survive. That descendant would have to be turned Silver before their blood was usable, and even then the genetic similarity might not be sufficient, but it was the only hope Jack had. It was a long shot, either way, but there was at least *some* hope.

But why did the only viable candidate have to be in Charleston, of all places?

'And you're *sure* Bartholomew took her?' Kulika asked. 'If she went missing over six months ago, then—'

'No. I'm not sure of anything.' Baron Drake pulled a file from the top drawer of his desk, then pulled a photograph from the file and stared at it for a moment.

'That's her?' Kulika asked.

'It is.' He swivelled the picture so it faced her way.

The photo showed a dark-haired, red-lipped, brown-skinned woman. She looked about thirty, maybe a little younger, and she was standing in a park, squinting into the afternoon sunshine, next to a pale-skinned woman of about the same age who was only half in the photo. The half-there woman had the kind of orangey red hair that glowed in the sunlight. It reminded Kulika of countless sunsets across the water of the open Caribbean seas. The image took her back to memories she both avoided and longed for, often at the same time.

'Perhaps I can talk to Bayly,' Baron Drake said, interrupting her reverie. 'Perhaps he might recognise her.'

'Sir,' Kulika said discouragingly. 'Job Bayly won't even talk to *me* most days. He's definitely not going to talk to you.'

'Then what do you suggest?' the baron replied, desperation edging his tone into anger. He pulled himself together quickly and said, 'You're right. I'm sorry, Kulika. This isn't your problem. You just… Carry on.'

It was a dismissal.

Kulika should have taken it. Frankly, Jack had brought this on herself. She was reckless, and impulsive, and it had only been a matter of time before she'd landed herself in the shit. If it had been just Jack's life on the line, then Kulika might have been inclined to wash her hands of the whole business and walk away.

The problem was that Baron Drake was in love with Jack, and when the Silver fell in love, it had frankly terrifying consequences. The moment he fell for Jack, Baron Drake's life became bonded to hers. If she died, then through the operation of that bond, the baron would die also.

Kulika struggled to understand why any Silver would engage in romantic shenanigans at all when the stakes were that high, particularly a Silver as powerful and important as the baron. It seemed entirely too risky to be worthwhile. As the baron's head of security, Kulika avoided those kinds of entanglements on principle, so it seemed particularly unfair that she'd become embroiled in this debacle regardless. Through no fault of her own, she was now in the unenviable position of having to protect Jack, someone who tended to hurl herself headfirst into trouble, all in order to protect the baron, her sworn master. Apparently, that also required Kulika to walk voluntarily back into her own personal hell.

'Give me the photo,' she said with a sigh.

'No, Kulika,' the baron said, covering the snapshot with his hands. 'You're right. I can't ask you to—'

'Just give me the damn photo. Sir.' Kulika snatched it from under his fingers and took a picture of it on her phone before returning it to him.

'I can't ask you to do this,' he said.

'And you're not asking, sir. But if I'm not back in a week, send Hugo, will you?'

'Kulika, I… I don't know what to say. Jack and I—'

'I'm not doing this for Jack,' she said, then she turned and left the office before she could change her mind.

If it were just for Jack, Kulika would have told the baron to go swivel. Not in so many words, perhaps, but she would truly rather have let Jack die than go back to that dark-cornered, godforsaken mansion in South Carolina.

But for Baron Drake, after all he'd done for her, after all the pieces of himself he'd sacrificed to give her this life that she loved...

She couldn't just let him die.

2

PATIENCE QUICK COULD claim neither of the attributes that formed her full name. She'd never understood the point of delaying gratification, and although she was a keen runner, she rarely paced above a jog, particularly in the heavy heat of a Charleston summer. *Impatience Steady* would have suited her better. Really, she had no idea what her birth parents had been thinking.

It could have been worse, she supposed. At least she wasn't called Chastity or, god forbid, Temperance. Neither would have served her well in her current situation.

'Get you another?' the bartender offered.

'Why not?'

He took Quick's empty glass, then smiled at her in a way that made her feel a little floaty. Or maybe that was the two pints of beer she'd already sunk.

'Here you go,' he said, setting another beer on the bar with another of those smiles.

Quick's cheeks heated, even though the room was blissfully air-conditioned. She idly wondered how soon she'd be able to get him back to her hotel. Then she reminded herself that he was barely old enough to be tending bar, and certainly too young for Quick, who was fast approaching thirty and feeling every year of it, particularly after the fruitless heartbreak of this last one. But he was also inhumanly gorgeous, with dark hair and dark eyes, mid-brown skin that shone like gold, and the most alluringly friendly voice Quick had ever heard. It wasn't just his accent, either. Quick had been in South Carolina and its surrounding states for nearly six months now and had developed some immunity to it, but then the bartender looked her right in the eye and called her *sugar*, and she was lost.

Faced with that kind of seductive artillery, any English woman used to stiff upper lips and cold shoulders could be forgiven for melting a little, even one whose resistance hadn't already been shattered by grief.

'Hot out, huh?' he said, smiling again as he leant on the bar.

It was, indeed, hot out. It was the kind of hot that made Quick grateful for chub-rub shorts and breathable cotton, but somehow she didn't think that was what he was talking about.

He gazed at her intently, still smiling that smile, and she gazed right back.

The confidence of the man was infectious.

'Yeah,' she replied dreamily. 'Hot.'

It wasn't her best work, flirting-wise, but then she'd already put in the groundwork. They'd flirted before, though not as intensely as this. The circumstances had been different earlier in the year, but now... Well, now she had nothing left to lose.

Quick hadn't come to Charleston for pleasure. Her best friend had gone missing on a work trip before Christmas, and this bar was one of the few places her bank records confirmed she'd been. Over the past half year, as Quick's search efforts had become more and more impatient, she'd linked up with the families of other missing people and the bar had become ground zero for coordinating the search parties. She'd been here enough times that the guy always recognised her when she walked in, and said, 'Hey, you're back. How are you doing, sugar?' in a way that made her feel completely welcome.

Quick hadn't given him more than casual consideration until now, because she'd been focused on more important things, but now that her money had run out, she'd been forced to abandon her search. She was flying home tomorrow, and she felt like burning some bridges on the way.

The bridge in question leaned over the bar towards Quick, then lowered his voice to say, 'So. What are you doing later?'

Quick laughed. Everything in her life had gone wrong, over and over again, but sometimes things just lined up perfectly. Shame it never happened when it actually mattered.

A patron at the other end of the bar called the beautiful young man away, but he gave Quick a look as he left that told her to stay put, so she did. She paid another server for her shrimp dinner, then sat at the bar playing patience with the deck of cards she always carried in her handbag. She liked the game, despite the unfortunate name, and it had become a frequent habit this year. Tonight, though, on the day before she left the country, the game felt symbolic. It was a way to say farewell to each of the cards before she left her unsuccessful six-month-long mission behind her and retreated back home as a failure.

She shuffled and dealt out the cards on the bar.

King of Clubs, Jensen Mardh.

Three of Hearts, Danny van Brugen.

Eight of Diamonds, Mairead Carlisle.

They hadn't found a single one of them, or any sign of the forty-nine other missing people whose photos and descriptions adorned the cards in the deck.

She dealt them. She flipped them. She built her columns of beautifully descending suits. And then, staring up at her from the latest card she'd turned onto the bar, there was the reason she'd come out here on sabbatical in the first place: *Jack of Spades, Evita Khalyed.*

Quick played one round, then another, and another, but Evita's photo was always a shock when it first appeared, and once her card was face-up, Quick's gaze kept being drawn back to it. She knew it was only her imagination, but the more she played, and the more she drank her beer, the more she felt like Evita's dark eyes were watching her sadly, with disappointment.

Why didn't you find me? Quick could almost hear the straightforward, irritated tone of her voice. *It's only been six months. Are you really giving up so soon?*

'What are these?' the barman asked.

His sudden return made Quick jump, though a decent amount of time must have passed while she was playing and getting lost in her farewells, because there were no other patrons demanding his attention now.

'Cold case cards,' she said, shuffling the pack quickly back together.

'What, now?'

'You haven't heard of them?'

He shrugged and smiled, but then his gaze narrowed on the pack, trying to get a peek as she collected the cards.

'The cold case squads here in the States print them up with details of missing people or unsolved murders,' Quick explained, 'then they give them out to inmates in local prisons. The idea is that one of the prisoners will see someone they recognise, or hear about a case from a cellmate or whatever, and then they'll snitch.'

'Interesting strategy,' he said, plucking the King of Clubs from between her fingers and looking hard at the face of Jensen Mardh.

'This is a special deck we had made,' said Quick uncomfortably. 'You must have heard about all the disappearances in and around Charleston, right?'

The barman furrowed his beautiful unlined brow and shrugged. Apparently he hadn't paid much attention during her previous visits here.

'Well, yeah,' said Quick, taking the King of Clubs back and shuffling it into the pack. 'That's sort of the problem. The missing people are all tourists, most of them moving through Charleston rather than planning to stay here, and no one's found any evidence that anyone's actually been hurt, so there's been hardly any press. But I swear it's happening. People really are going missing. Some of us clubbed together and had these cards made for the local prisons and police departments, trying to get the word out.'

'*Us*?' the barman asked.

'Friends. Relatives. Loved ones of the missing. You know.' Quick tried to order her thoughts at the same time as she shuffled the unruly deck back into a shape that would fit in the card box. 'Thing is, back in December—'

She stopped herself. She didn't want to talk about this tonight. She'd promised herself she wouldn't, that for one night she'd have some fun without thinking about what had happened. It was a downer, and she and the beautiful barman been getting along so well that she didn't want to dampen the mood.

'That's why you're here?' he asked. 'I thought you were just… I don't know. Seeing the sights.'

'Let's not talk about it.' She pasted a smile on her face.

'Okay,' he said, with more readiness than she'd expected. 'Want another beer?'

'Sure,' she replied, glad of the subject change. She'd expected intrusive questions about the things she was trying to forget tonight, but there was none of that from the barman. Probably it came with the job, that pleasant superficiality. When she mentioned Evita, most people wanted to get right into it and start digging, so it was refreshing when he just presented her with a new beer and another of those smiles, then disappeared into the back room to fetch a box of bottles to refill the bar fridges.

Was he closing up?

'Um… Barman?' she called, which felt rude, but she had no idea what else to call him.

'Yeah, sugar?' he replied, emerging with another box.

'I'm sorry, I don't know your name,' she said awkwardly as she got off her barstool.

'Well, Monteiro's my surname,' he said, smiling, 'so everyone just calls me Monty.'

'You can call me Quick.'

His eyes twinkled at her. 'Sounds exciting.'

'It's not.'

He smiled again. God, that smile. Those eyes. And actually, now that Quick came to look at them more closely, those *lips*. She could stare at them for hours. As she watched, he licked them deliberately, and Quick just about melted to the floor.

'I didn't realise how late it was,' she said, picking up her handbag, wondering whether he'd bite. 'I should really go.'

'Why?' Monty asked. 'You got somewhere to be? Got a

boyfriend?'

'Nope,' she laughed. 'But you're casting your net a little narrow, there.'

It took a moment for him to work that one out, then he asked, 'Girlfriend? Other exclusive romantic relationship?'

'Not right now.'

'Then stay,' he said, coming out from behind the bar. 'A friend of mine is having a party tonight at his place, and it's amazing. There's a pool, and this huge old house. Let me finish up here, and we can go together.'

'I don't know, Monty. It's late.'

I'd rather take you back to my hotel, is what she was thinking. She couldn't party all night. She needed to get some sleep, then fly home fresh and sober tomorrow, so she could get back to work the following day. The university had been very understanding about the sabbatical, but they wouldn't keep her position open forever. She needed to show them she hadn't been broken by Evita's disappearance, or she'd risk losing the confidence of the faculty.

But the past six months had been *hard*, hard enough to make her hesitate. She'd had her eye on this beautiful man for months. It was her last night in this beautiful city. Hadn't she earned a night of abandon? Even, perhaps, a one-night stand?

'I'll make it worth your while,' Monty promised, then he leaned down and kissed her.

She was drunk, and she wasn't quite ready, but all things considered it was a pretty good kiss. Good enough that she was willing to put in the effort to try for a better one.

'Just give me five minutes,' he said a little breathlessly. 'Will you wait? Let me settle you down here.'

She hadn't said yes, but somehow she was sitting at a low table by the door in a soft chair, with a beer at her elbow and the buzz of alcohol numbing its way along her veins. She really should say no, but Monty was back behind the bar now, clanking around as he talked to someone on the phone. She couldn't hear the words, but after a moment he raised his voice in a kind of pleading tone that made her feel uncomfortable. He sounded like a kid asking his parents to let him go out and play, which for all she knew could have been exactly what he was doing.

He was *so* young.

Abruptly, Quick didn't want to be here anymore. She gathered her things as quietly as she could, then made her way to the door, but it wouldn't open. She rattled the handle, but it was locked tight.

That was worrying.

Quick started panicking, but she vaguely remembered Monty fiddling around over in that direction as he sat her down. Of course he would have locked up for the night. Perfectly normal. There was nothing weird about that.

He was laughing in the back now, whatever disagreement he'd been having on the phone forgotten, but the incident with the door had made Quick reassess her situation. As he ended the call and swaggered back to the door to fetch her, she was already preparing her excuses.

Then he said, 'Look, I didn't want to say anything and get your hopes up if I'm wrong, but you know the guy on that card?'

'The card?' Quick struggled to pick up his train of thought. 'You mean the King of Clubs?'

'Yeah. Jensen… Jensen whatever.'

'What about him?'

'I think he'll be there. At the party.'

For a moment, Quick thought she'd misheard. 'You *know* Jensen?'

'He's not calling himself that, and I might be wrong, but yeah. I think so. Maybe.'

'Oh my god. I need to call his family.' Quick started fumbling in her handbag for her phone. 'I need to get his mum and—'

'The thing is, I'm not sure,' Monty said, stilling her hands. 'I don't want to get their hopes up, if… Look, just come to the party.' He started guiding her through the restaurant. 'My car's parked out back. I can drive us.'

Quick laughed. She might have been a little drunk, but she wasn't an idiot. She knew she shouldn't get into a car with a virtual stranger, in the middle of the night, in an unfamiliar city from which tourists had been disappearing with shocking regularity over the past six months. She knew it was dangerous.

But then, *Monty* wasn't dangerous. He wasn't just a random stranger, he was the guy who worked at the seafood bar, the same guy she'd seen there every time she'd visited. He had roots in this place.

And Quick knew Jensen's parents. She'd met them, and his sister, and his boyfriend. They'd been one of the most active families in the search party group, working around the clock to find their son, but also never hesitating to contribute their time and support to all the other families who were trying to find their missing loved ones. They were kind, and generous, and so open that the thought of raising their hopes unjustifiably twisted her stomach. Someone needed to check this was real before getting them involved.

But she didn't know exactly where Monty was proposing to take her, and it was late, and she'd already drunk more than enough, and she had a flight to catch tomorrow, and a hangover over the Atlantic would be *brutal*…

Then Monty took her face in his hands and kissed her

again, and she forgot to care.

Maybe she was an idiot after all.

3

KULIKA FOUND JOB Bayly at a beachfront bar in Jamaica overlooking the sunken pirate city of Port Royal. The term *beachfront bar* might conjure up images of white sand and palm trees and sun loungers, but this particular bar was a stark breeze-block box surrounded by rickety metal chairs and tables, set on top of the concrete promontory that reclaimed the edge of old Port Royal from the sea.

Great view, though.

'I wouldn't have thought you'd want to come back here,' Kulika said as she took a seat at the table beside Bayly.

'Wouldn't have thought you would either,' he replied, then he took a long drink from his bottle of beer, his eyes trained on the sunset out over the darkening turquoise water. 'You picked your moment, didn't you? Can't even allow an old sailor a little holiday.'

'You don't get shore leave unless you're sailing, and from what I hear you're not doing much of that these days.'

'And you are, are you?'

'Not unless you call punting on the Cherwell *sailing*.'

'I do not,' Bayly said, looking affronted.

Kulika just laughed. They sat quietly side by side for a

moment as she tried to find the right words to get him to open up, which was always a challenge with Bayly.

'Look,' she said, 'I didn't want to come to the mansion.'

'And I can guess why.'

'You don't have to guess, Bayly. You know.'

'Hmm,' he grunted.

They'd been stuck in that vile place together, at the end. Bayly had made it out before she had. He hadn't come back for her, and she'd never blamed him for that. If she'd got out first, she wouldn't have gone back for him, either.

But now…

She'd done some asking around. She knew Bayly had been living at the mansion for months now, even though he'd always sworn he'd never put down roots on land, not unless someone forced him. And to go back to Bartholomew… Well, that made no sense at all.

'I heard you're living there,' she hazarded.

'Hmm,' he grunted.

'I heard you're running errands in town, like a lackey.'

This time, Bayly made no sound at all, he just stared at the water as though he was out there riding the waves instead of sitting here, baking on the concrete.

'Why are you even involved? That's what I don't understand. You hate him as much as I do. You hate the mansion. You hate dry land. You hate all of it.'

'Maybe,' Bayly hedged. 'But I know enough that I can feel which way the wind is blowing.'

'Don't give me that.'

A kid came out to clear the table and move them on now that the dinner rush was coming in, such as it was. Bayly got a pack of beers to go, then headed down towards the harbour wall to walk along the waterfront. Kulika followed him, though she was sure he'd prefer she didn't. After a few minutes, Bayly cracked a couple of the beers open and handed one to her. They walked for a while in silence, out towards Fort Charles, and Kulika waited. Bayly would talk when he was ready, she knew, and soon enough he was.

'I have someone now,' he said quietly. 'He's involved.'

'How involved?'

'Too involved to come out here with me, even for a day.'

'Fuck. Well, that's not good.'

'And now you're here, getting yourself involved in something I know you'd rather be well clear of, which I'm guessing means that the playboy buccaneer you choose to work for—'

'*Baron* Killian Drake is not a playboy,' Kulika said. Then she thought for a moment and added, 'Anymore.'

Bayly scoffed. '*Killian* now, is it?'

'Yes. It is.'

He scoffed again.

'Come on, Bayly. You, of all people, should understand the need to leave your past where you buried it.'

'Don't know what you're talking about,' Bayly said, taking a swig from his bottle.

'Denial.'

'Says you.' They reached a makeshift bench at the waterfront and Bayly took a seat, putting the cardboard carrier of beer bottles down on the ground at his feet. 'Now,' he said, 'don't you think you'd better tell me what exactly your *baron* thinks you're doing here?'

Kulika sat beside him, stretching her long legs out in front of her in the evening sun. It warmed her in a way the sun in England never seemed to manage, seeping into her joints and sinking into her skin.

'You remember Dr Khalyed,' she said.

'Old Jekyll?' asked Bayly.

'He died.'

'I thought the poison from that lab accident of his killed him decades ago,' said Bayly.

'As it happens, no.'

Bayly sat up a little straighter on the bench. 'But he was a monster. He was biting and killing other Silver. Burning them up to ash.'

'Only because of the way the poison mutated his blood. It wasn't his fault, Bayly. He wasn't a bad man, and he's dead now, anyway.'

'Well,' Bayly said, settling down again. 'Good.'

'Not good, actually. Before he died, someone… else was infected with his blood,' Kulika said, deciding it would be best to leave Jack and the baron's connection to the problem out of it entirely. 'We can cure them, but to do that we need to track down Khalyed's last living human descendant, turn her Silver and use her Silver blood to… I don't know, do something clever and scientific. We've got a team for that. I just need to track the girl down, turn her and get her back to Oxford. As quickly as possible.'

'And that's why you're here?' Bayly asked.

'Yes,' Kulika replied. Then she noted the suspicious look on his face and said, 'You were expecting something else?'

'No,' he said, but he didn't elaborate.

'Her name's Evita Khalyed,' Kulika said, showing the photo on her phone to Bayly. As she did so, she caught a glimpse of Evita's half-there companion and confirmed that she'd been right about the colour of the woman's hair: it was the exact same shade as the fiery reflection of the sunset on the water in the bay.

Bayly looked at the screen for a moment, looked away, looked again, then looked away for good. 'Hmm.'

'Well?' she said. 'Have you seen her?'

'Seen her?' Bayly shook his head. 'She's familiar, perhaps, but then her face isn't unusual. She could be any number of women.'

'But she isn't. That's the point, Bayly: she's the only one of her kind. I need to find her, and her specifically, and I need to do it now. She came to Charleston for a speaking engagement in December, her university says.'

'I wasn't even here in December,' Bayly replied, fixing his gaze back on the waves. 'I came through earlier this year and got… stuck. But not in December. It was just Bartholomew here then. Him and a couple of his pets.'

'That's what I was afraid of.' Kulika sighed. There was no getting around it: she would have to speak to Bartholomew himself, which meant digging up all the memories she'd hoped to keep buried for good. 'The things we did back then, Bayly,' she whispered. 'The things Bartholomew did at Whydah. The things he buried in that mansion.'

'I haven't forgotten,' he said tersely. 'I was thinking maybe you had, if you were planning to go back there.'

'But you've already gone.'

Bayly was quiet for a moment as he finished his bottle of beer, then he put the empty back in the cardboard carrier and screwed the top off another. 'It's too late for me,' he said. 'I don't have a choice anymore. It's not too late for you.'

'I'm not sure I have a choice, either,' Kulika said quietly. 'We've exhausted all our other contacts. We've called in all our favours. This is our last chance.'

Bayly took a long swig of his drink, then he said, 'He won't let you go again, you know.'

This wasn't news to Kulika, but if she acknowledged it then she'd never be able to make herself go back to Charleston, so she pretended she hadn't heard.

'What surname is he going by these days?' she asked.

'Roberts, sometimes. Mostly he doesn't bother with it.'

'Ah,' Kulika said. 'A man who doesn't exist has no need of a name?'

'Precisely.' Bayly finished his bottle in several large swallows, then returned the empty to the box with its friends. 'Returning to the mansion will be... an adjustment.'

Kulika knew what he was saying. The baron was a modern vampire, but Bartholomew was the kind of old school that the modern ones left behind, over time. Baron Drake's mansion and Bartholomew's mansion were separated by more than just the Atlantic Ocean. In terms of their rules and attitudes, they were whole worlds apart.

'It's more crowded than it once was,' Bayly said.

'We've heard rumours,' Kulika replied. There'd been whispers for months about the rising number of new Silver in Charleston, but that wasn't the only spot they'd been multiplying. There had been more in London lately, too, and elsewhere on the continent. All the Silver in the world seemed to be preparing for something, and Kulika had a good idea what it was. 'Bartholomew always wanted to come out of the shadows, didn't he?' she said.

'But your ruler, Solomon,' Bayly said. 'He doesn't.'

'The Primus, you mean,' Kulika corrected him, using his proper title. Solomon was somewhere between a king and a god for the Silver of the UK and beyond, so she wasn't about to go around disrespecting him.

'He'd still prefer we all stayed hidden from humans?' Bayly said, ignoring the correction.

'Until someone forces his hand.'

'Well, that's going to be a problem. Does the Primus know what Bartholomew has been doing? Does he know how many Silver have been turned this year alone?'

A thought occurred to Kulika then. 'Is that why you

thought I was here? To… what? Negotiate an alliance with Bartholomew?'

Bayly shrugged as he twisted the top off his penultimate beer. 'If anyone was going to mutiny against the Primus, it would be your baron,' he said. 'He never took kindly to being ordered. He likes giving orders himself too well.'

'That doesn't mean he's stupid enough to ally himself with a psychopath like Bartholomew.'

'But he *is* stupid enough to send you right back into Bartholomew's cage?'

Kulika couldn't defend Baron Drake without spilling his secrets, secrets that she couldn't trust with Bayly, so instead of replying she sat quietly and finished her beer as the sun dipped beneath the sea.

'They're fishing for them like sharks going after seals,' Bayly murmured into the night. There were no street lamps in this spot, so it was illuminated only by the ambient light from the bar and businesses behind them, and now the moon reflecting off the water. 'Bartholomew's sending all his pets out to pick off the weak ones at the edge of the pack, the ones no one will miss.'

'How many, Bayly?' Kulika asked, wondering what she was about to walk into.

'More than you'd think. He sends the new ones out again when he thinks they're ready, to fetch more, and the new ones… They treat it like a game. They're playing with the humans, romancing them to try to make the turn stick. Then afterwards, when it goes wrong…'

Bayly didn't finish his thought, but he didn't need to. Knowing what went on in that mansion, Kulika could fill in the blanks.

It was old lore, the trick about turning humans Silver by seduction, but it was deeper than the Charleston Silver seemed to appreciate. If you wanted to make absolutely sure that turning a human Silver would actually work, the Silver who turned the human needed to feel some affection for them, and ideally the human should reciprocate that affection. It was connected with frequencies, or absorption rates, or the body's innate ability to heal, or something like that. Kulika had never paid much attention to the science. When Baron Drake had first explained it to her, she'd listened as far as she needed to get the confirmation she'd prayed not to hear: Bartholomew would not have been able to turn her Silver successfully if some part of him hadn't loved her, at least at the start, at least a little.

How much easier it would have been if the truth had been otherwise.

'You're seeing a lot of... failures?' Kulika asked, as delicately as she could.

'Too many.'

'And what's he...?'

'Doing with them?' Bayly laughed darkly. 'Feeding them to the gators.'

Kulika winced.

Until recently, she had never seen the evidence of a failed turning with her own eyes, but now she knew exactly what kind of mindless zombie was created when a Silver tried to turn a human and got it wrong. She also knew from experience that the kindest thing to do for someone in that zombie state was put them out of their misery, and quickly.

Being eaten by alligators did not sound like a quick or merciful death.

'Are you sure about this?' Bayly asked her. 'You're absolutely certain you want to come back?'

Kulika just laughed. Bayly knew as well as she did that she wouldn't even be suggesting a return to the mansion unless it was a last resort.

'It's messy,' said Bayly. 'You know I don't like it when things get messy. It's going to end badly.'

'Then give me another option.'

He looked at her for a moment, then with his gaze fixed back on the water, he screwed the top off the last bottle of beer and handed it to her.

'That's what I thought,' she said quietly.

4

MONTY HADN'T BEEN kidding: the old house did have a pool, and both it and the house itself were enormous.

'My god,' Quick said as she got out of the car and shrugged her handbag onto her shoulder. 'What is this place?'

Monty slammed his door shut and joined her in the darkness. 'It used to be a plantation or something.'

'Oh.' She winced, thinking about how much blood money would have gone into building it. Although Colonial American history wasn't her field of study, she'd read enough on the Elizabethans and the Stuarts to know how the plantations had worked. 'I thought these houses were mostly museums now?'

Monty shrugged and grabbed her hand, then pulled her towards the music that was coming from behind the building. As they approached, Quick was surrounded by an ethereal blue light that cast strange waving patterns onto the canopies of the trees at the back of the property, and onto the Spanish moss that hung from their boughs. It wasn't until they turned the corner that she realised the glow was coming from lights set in the walls of the pool, which refracted through the water in swirling blue patterns to illuminate the back yard. If you could even call something the size of four football pitches a garden.

The space was enormous. In the centre of a large paved area was an Olympic-sized pool, further expanded by the addition of hot tubs and plunge pools and cascading rock-pile waterfalls that surrounded it. A little further out, where the trees and flowerbeds clustered in, there were water lilies and ponds filled with koi carp – god knows how they kept them away from the chlorine – all of which turned the back yard into a kind of grotto. It might have been magical, were it not also heaving with people. There must have been at least two hundred scantily-clad bodies frolicking in the pool, lounging on the benches around it or dancing on the lawn off to one side, where a stack of speakers blared music out across the party.

Within a single second, Quick knew she didn't want to be here. Within two, she was feeling out of place in her floor-length, long-sleeved cotton dress. Within three, she was ready to turn back the way they'd come. She might have done it, too, were it not for Jensen Mardh.

'Monty!' a high voice cried. 'You made it! But you're cutting it fine.' The voice had a British accent, but Quick couldn't pinpoint its source in the crowd.

'Yeah, well,' Monty replied, which gave Quick no information at all.

Then the source of the voice emerged from the mass of bodies chatting and drinking and dancing around the pool, and Quick had a moment's fleeting suspicion that she was being pranked. The woman had hair and skin of a similar colour to Quick's own, but that was where the similarity ended. Where Quick's freckles bunched together across her nose and cheeks as though they were afraid to leave the safety of the herd, this woman's were dusted lightly across her skin with a touch so uniform and delicate that it looked almost artificial. Her hair shone, her nails gleamed, her cheeks pinked attractively with blush instead of burning crimson red like Quick's did. She was wearing a bikini, showing off every curve of her body with a confidence Quick had never managed to embrace, and not a single inch of her looked sunburnt. If she'd been out here all day, then either she had access to the kind of sunscreen Quick could only dream of, or she had magic skin. Seeing her was like being confronted with a vision of everything Quick had the potential to be, if only she didn't insist on being quite so much herself. Unlike Quick, this woman belonged here.

'Well, you might as well join in for the next hour, at least,' the woman said, giving Quick a discouraging look up and down. 'If you're staying, that is.'

'I'm not,' Quick said, at the same time as Monty said, 'We are.'

They looked at each other, while the woman looked at each of them in turn, then Monty said, 'Look, Quick, I told you I'd find your guy if I could, and I will. I just need to go and speak to a friend and find out where he's at, then I'll be right back. In the meantime, why not enjoy yourself? This is Penny. Penny, this is Quick.'

'Quick?' Penny said sceptically.

'Surname,' Quick explained, before turning back to Monty. 'And really, I'd rather just come with you and look, and if he's not here I can call a cab—'

'Five minutes,' Monty said, then he disappeared into the crowd and Quick lost track of him before she could follow.

'Shit,' she murmured.

'Yeah,' agreed Penny, 'he is, sometimes. Hot, though. He's looking for someone for you? Did I hear that right?'

'A friend of a friend. Monty said he'd be here, but I'm starting to wonder if maybe that was a line.' The surroundings weren't filling Quick with confidence. Back at the bar, Monty had seemed like the answer to all her prayers wrapped up in a pretty package, but here amongst his peers he seemed more like a frat boy whose lies were catching up with him. She should never have let him bring her out here in the first place. 'Look, I've got a plane to catch tomorrow. I don't suppose you have the number of a local cab company?'

'You're going home?'

'Yeah. All the way home, ideally.'

Penny looked at Quick more closely and asked, 'Where are you from, exactly?'

'Leicester, originally. You?'

Penny glanced around quickly, then lowered her voice and said, 'I always tell people London, but honestly? Staines.' She smiled, and Quick found herself smiling back. 'Silly, isn't it?' Penny went on. 'Imagine lying about something pointless like that. It seems so immaterial now.'

'Why's that?' Quick asked.

'Oh, you know.' Penny shrugged one shoulder in a shy way that Quick found rather endearing, then she added, 'It's nice to hear a familiar accent. Comforting, you know?'

'How long have you been here?' Quick asked.

'A while,' Penny said. 'Too long, really. But then it's too late to go back now.' Her expression was haunted. It discouraged further questions. Whatever had happened to Penny to keep her from home, it was dark. And for all the superficial decadence of their surroundings, there was a darkness to the party too. It didn't feel like a spontaneous gathering of people who wanted to spend time together. It felt like a group of strangers connected only by their common desire to forget themselves and escape the world outside.

The whole situation made Quick uneasy.

She should just tell Jensen's family about the lead in the morning, and maybe send them out to follow it up themselves in the daylight. Impatient though she was for answers about Jensen's disappearance, which might in turn lead to answers about Evita's disappearance, she was getting a bad feeling about this place, and she'd been through enough that she'd learned to rely on those instincts.

'Anyway,' Penny said, brightening up, 'forget the past. Let's enjoy the *now*, at least until Monty comes back. Did you want to get a drink?'

'I don't think—'

'Come on,' Penny insisted, leading Quick away from the house and around the pool, towards the bar on its far side.

Quick didn't need another drink, but she was certain that Penny needed one even less. As Penny walked across the paving stones on her bare feet, she was weaving in an irregular dancelike motion, out of time with the music and even with her own step. Whatever she had been drinking, she'd clearly already had enough.

'Penny,' Quick said, catching the other woman's hand in her own. 'Do you just want to get out of here?'

'Get out of here?' Penny asked, looking at Quick as though she'd just asked if she wanted to fly to the moon. 'No one leaves the mansion.'

'What do you mean? You absolutely could,' Quick insisted. 'I could call us a car and we could just… go.'

Penny squeezed Quick's hand, then let it go and turned back towards the bar, insisting, 'Just have a drink.'

There was definitely something off about this party. The laughter was too manic, the music was too loud, the expressions around her were too close to crossing over from ecstasy to agony. It occurred to Quick that maybe Penny was trying to take her somewhere quieter, somewhere she could ask for her help. The currently-deserted bar would be a good place for confidences to be shared, so – reluctantly – Quick let herself be led.

The bar was a permanent installation set inside its own powered gazebo. It was a C-shaped structure, marble-topped and brick-built, with cupboards and fridges inside and a tall central plinth ringed with optics and glasses.

'They must throw a lot of parties to need a bar this big,' Quick commented.

Penny didn't reply, she just walked inside the embrace of the gazebo to pour a chilled glass of beer for Quick before shaking up a cocktail for herself, something thick and red that looked fruity and sickly sweet. The glasses were real, which seemed like bad planning at a drunken pool party. When Penny walked back out of the gazebo again and onto the grass, there was a sheen to her eyes that Quick didn't like.

'Are you all right?' Quick asked.

'I haven't been all right for about five months now,' Penny said with a hollow laugh. It was a bleak sound.

'You just look a bit—' Then the light filtering up from the pool hit Penny's face. Quick stared into Penny's eyes for a moment, sure she must be seeing things. But no: there was silver in her eyes. It was like liquid mercury, forming fine silver filaments that followed the path of the tiny blood vessels in the whites of her eyes. 'Your eyes,' Quick said.

'Oh, right.' Penny laughed. 'Yeah, I mean, look around.'

Quick did. At first, she saw nothing, but then she started to spot more glinting eyes across the party, just here and there, perhaps one in every fifteen or twenty of the partygoers.

'Is it drugs?' Quick asked, not having much firsthand

experience to draw upon. Could drugs mess up your eyes like that?

Penny said, 'Something like that.' Then she added darkly, 'You'll see.'

'See what? It's not...' Quick looked down into her drink. 'Is this spiked?'

'No! I only meant that you're here on a kind of important night. You've got about half an hour to make up your mind, but if you decide to stay here with Monty after that... Well, you'll see.'

'See *what*?' Quick asked again, but Penny just sipped at her drink and started moving back towards the pool. 'Look,' Quick said, holding her beer in one hand and fishing in her handbag with the other as she trailed after Penny, 'I only came because Monty said this guy would be here.' She pulled out the missing persons deck, shuffled clumsily through the cards one-handed until she found Jensen Mardh, then held his card up in front of Penny's face. 'His name's Jensen, but Monty said he was calling himself something different. Have you seen him? He's missing.'

'Oh, sweetie, we're all *missing*,' Penny said cryptically, pushing the card away. 'The question is: do you want to be *found*?'

Then she downed her drink, chucked the empty glass onto the grass with an impossibly-long throw, and dived into the pool, leaving Quick alone in the shadows at the far edge of the porch.

For a moment, Quick just stood there, wondering what the hell she was supposed to do now. She could wait for Monty to get back, which seemed increasingly futile, or she could go looking for Jensen herself, which seemed about as promising as waiting for Monty, or she could get out of this unsettling place and try to find some way of calling a cab.

Unfortunately, her phone had no signal, and she was fairly sure that none of the scantily-clad drinkers had theirs to hand right now. That seriously limited her options. She was just contemplating venturing inside the house to see if she could find a landline – the place looked old enough to have one – when the party crowd rippled outwards as though someone had dropped a stone in its centre, then parted to reveal a woman walking towards the steps at the other end of the porch.

Walking wasn't the right word, though. The woman was planting her feet down into the earth as though she was setting her stance for a fight, holding her arms slightly tensed at her sides, poised for action. She reminded Quick of a leopard, all coiled energy and strength, lean muscle and long limbs. She didn't look at all like she was here for the party, and that wasn't just because of her bearing. Not only was she wearing practical clothes – dark jeans, dark boots, sleeveless T-shirt that showed off the natural muscle of her arms – but her expression was focused. One side of her short blonde hair fell over her face, but the side facing Quick was shaved short enough to show her scalp, so Quick could clearly see the look in her eye, and it meant business.

The woman was like a strong breeze blowing in off the river. It took a second or two for Quick to catch her breath.

The woman was heading into the house, and although that had been Quick's destination too, she was absolutely not going to get in her way. Everything about her felt dangerous.

Maybe, Quick decided, she should wait for Monty just a little longer.

5

BARTHOLOMEW WAS HAVING a party.

Kulika shouldn't have been surprised, but it was nearly two in the morning when she and Bayly arrived back at the mansion, and it was a Tuesday night – well, Wednesday morning, now – not the weekend, but the back garden was absolutely heaving. It looked like they were planning to go all night.

'Children,' Bayly muttered under his breath. If it hadn't been for Kulika's Silver hearing, she wouldn't have been able to pick up his words over the thumping music.

'Are these all new Silver?' Kulika asked as she wormed her way through the mass of pulsating bodies. 'This many?'

'No,' Bayly replied.

He wasn't having to push people out of his way; they parted in front of him like water splitting around a rock, then closed up again just in time to rub against Kulika's bare arms. It was making her feel claustrophobic and irritable, and that wasn't a good state of mind in which to walk back into Bartholomew's mansion.

But she could do something about that.

'Move!' she yelled, in the same tone she deployed to bark

36

orders at the baron's security team back home. It had exactly the desired effect, in that the crowd jumped back and stopped bloody touching her, with the added *undesired* effect that it opened up a clear path between her and Bartholomew, who was leaning just inside the open glass doors that led out onto the porch, speaking with a young man with mid-brown skin and dark hair. When Bartholomew's eyes locked with Kulika's he waved the young man off, despite his protests, and gave her his full attention.

She'd forgotten how imposing he could be. He was tall with soft, tanned skin, long dark hair, and pale eyes that changed their shade to match the sea. He dressed casually, in faded jeans and a dark henley that was unbuttoned just low enough to show a peek of the copper coin he wore on a leather thong around his neck, but his demeanour was far from casual. His face was all hard angles and unyielding edges, his expression cold and avaricious. Perhaps he intended it to be welcoming, but instead he just looked hungry. After all these centuries, he was practically salivating to have Kulika back in his domain.

She almost turned around and left then. The last place in the world she wanted to be right now was here, walking back towards him, but this wasn't just about her anymore. She had the baron to think about, too.

'Kulika,' he whispered, and each syllable felt like a chain wrapping around her throat. 'You're back.'

'Briefly,' she said.

He just smiled, as though she had already surrendered to him, but this time Kulika knew better. She would do a lot of things to save the baron's life, but never *that*.

Bartholomew believed in the power of the written word. Once upon a time, he'd thought the things he wrote could change people's minds, but that belief didn't outlast his transformation into one of the Silver. Now, he just used words to chain people to him, like a devil with a blood-soaked pen. If Kulika gave him the slightest opening, he'd find a way to make her sign her name to his Articles. That would be the end of her freedom, the end of her life, and the end of Baron Drake's too.

Whatever else happened here in these haunted corridors, Kulika Yadav would not sign her life away. Not again.

'I'm looking for someone,' she said. 'She disappeared in your territory at the end of last year. Evita Khalyed, her name is.'

Was Kulika imagining it, or had Bartholomew's composure slipped for a fraction of a second when he'd heard the name?

'I've got a photo,' she pressed on, reaching into her back pocket for her phone. She knew she was rushing this, and probably making a mess of what should have been a delicate negotiation, but if there was any chance that she could get the information she needed and leave without even stepping foot inside the mansion—

'Come in,' Bartholomew said, waving away her phone at the same time as he waved Kulika inside. 'Tell me what you've been doing with your life. Thank you, Bayly. You can go.'

Bayly grunted and turned to leave as ordered, and it was then that Kulika *really* started to worry. Bayly had never been the obedient type. If he was being this compliant, Kulika had to wonder exactly what it was that Bartholomew was holding over him, and how this "someone" of Bayly's was "involved". Bayly had refused to talk about it on the way here, so she could only speculate. She really didn't want to linger long enough to find out the details.

'I'm not staying,' she said.

'I'm sure you have time for one drink,' Bartholomew replied.

He cupped her elbow with his hand to guide her inside, sending shivers of horror over her skin and up the back of her neck. She wanted nothing more than to shrug him off, but that would cause a scene, which was hardly going to get her the information she needed, so instead she bit down her revulsion and let herself be led along the corridor to the other side of the house, then into one of the leather armchairs in Bartholomew's library. She'd been in this room plenty of times before, because it was the place from which Bartholomew ran his empire, but she had rarely been invited to sit. She'd been on her feet, or on her knees, or facedown on the floor, but so rarely in the armchair.

The seat of honour should have made Kulika more comfortable. It did not.

'Have you seen her?' Kulika asked, turning her phone towards Bartholomew once more.

He wasn't sitting. Instead, he closed the door to the room, then leaned against the shelves in a posture that looked relaxed, but felt contrived. It put him above her, over her, peering down at her from a great height.

Just as he always liked to be.

'Rum for you?' he asked, ignoring her phone screen as he pushed off from the shelves and turned to the cupboard where he kept his liquor.

'I don't want a drink, Bartholomew.'

'But you do want my help, Kulika.' He raised his eyebrow at her.

So this is how it would be: she would have to trade a piece of herself for every ounce of cooperation she managed to wring from him. If she'd had time to waste, she might have been able to talk her way to what she wanted without conceding at all, but she couldn't afford to play the long game. In the circumstances, some sacrifice on her part was inevitable. But if she was careful, perhaps she could make it a small one.

'I don't drink hard liquor anymore,' she said.

'Then blood,' he offered.

She swallowed her laugh. She was absolutely not accepting a cup of blood from him, not when she didn't know where it had come from. 'A beer?' she countered.

Bartholomew pressed his lips together, unimpressed. He said, 'Very well.' Then he balled one hand into a fist and, maintaining eye contact with her, slammed it into the wall beside the cupboard, three times, fast.

Kulika heard the footsteps outside immediately, and they were running. When they reached the library door, Bartholomew barked, 'Beer,' then they disappeared back down the corridor again without their owner opening the door, and returned just as quickly as they'd left. The man who let himself into the library was human, surprisingly, and he carried a bottle of beer on a tray next to a chilled glass. As he went to pour it out for her, Kulika saw the black tattoo in the palm of his hand: the mark of Bartholomew's covenant.

She took the bottle quickly from the tray, ignoring the glass. The man bowed and backed out, shutting the door quietly behind him without ever raising his gaze to Bartholomew.

'You have humans sign your Articles now?' Kulika asked once the man's footsteps had rushed away again down the corridor.

'Why not?' he said lightly. 'Those who sail with me have always signed.'

Which was technically true, because all the pirate crews had signed Articles in the old days, but they weren't sailing now, and *the old days* had ended centuries ago. The Articles Bartholomew used now, on dry land, were different. The mark on that man's palm – the one that mimicked the pattern of the copper coin Bartholomew wore at his throat – he gave that only to people he thought were worth binding to his new covenant.

Kulika had worn it, once. To her knowledge, it had never before been tattooed into human flesh, because Bartholomew had never seen any value in humans on land beyond the sustenance of their blood. She had to wonder what had happened to make him change his mind about their worth.

But her curiosity would have to wait. Right now, she needed to be careful how she chose to spend his goodwill, so Kulika just sat and drank her drink. Bartholomew poured himself a rum, leaned against the bookshelves again and drank *his* drink. After maybe a minute had passed in silence, Kulika finally broke it by asking, 'Will you look at the photo?'

'Come now,' Bartholomew replied rebukingly. 'It's been decades since we last spoke.'

'Over a century, in fact.' Which still wasn't long enough for her.

'All the more reason for us to spend some time reacquainting ourselves with each other before turning to business.'

Kulika wanted to say that she had about as much desire to get reacquainted with Bartholomew as she did with the abusive father who'd sold her into marriage in the New World, thus putting her into Bartholomew's path in the first place. But not only would that have been inflammatory, it would also have been untrue. In fact, she'd happily trade the two centuries she'd spent under Bartholomew's flag for ten times that with her father, if only that were an option.

Her father, at least, was dead. With every year that passed, it looked increasingly unlikely that she'd ever be able to say that of Bartholomew.

'I'm not here to talk business,' she said instead.

'Everything is business. Everyone and everything has a price.'

'A woman is *missing*,' Kulika said.

Bartholomew gave her a level look. 'And I'm sure you wouldn't be here searching for her if it wasn't somehow the business of you and your new captain.'

Which, to be fair, was bang on.

'Perhaps we can come to some kind of arrangement,' Bartholomew offered, then he wandered over to his desk in the corner of the room and pulled a large leather-bound book from the top drawer.

He didn't have to tell Kulika what it was; she recognised it well enough. Once upon a time, her name had been between its covers, signed in her own hand and in her own blood: a promise to obey Bartholomew in word and deed, and in heart and soul.

That was his offer, then, for the knowledge Kulika sought.

A small sacrifice indeed.

Bartholomew must have seen the horror on her face, because he said, 'We both know that you wouldn't have come here for any trifling matter, my girl. Whatever this missing woman is to Drake, she must be of paramount importance for him to gamble with his best piece.'

'You don't know what you're talking about,' Kulika said dismissively.

'Don't I? If it were a matter of protocol, he would have sent someone less central to his operations. If it were a matter of force, he would have sent someone he thought could scare me. But instead, he sent the only thing he has to offer that I actually value.' Bartholomew crouched down in front of her with the old book resting on his knees, looking up into her eyes as though he were looking into her soul. 'He sent me *you*.'

Even if Kulika had wanted to reply, her throat was too tight to squeeze out a word. She felt like a fly tangled in a web that spread wider than she'd thought.

'So,' Bartholomew continued, opening the book and turning it so that a fresh new page lay under her hand, 'are we going to talk around in circles all night, or can we just cut to the chase and seal the covenant now?'

'No,' she said, finally finding her voice, though quietly.

'No?' he replied with amusement.

'Never. I will never swear myself to you again.'

He pulled the book back towards himself and snapped it shut before rising to his feet. 'Shame,' he said. 'I thought you wanted to find this missing woman, but if you're sure you can't be persuaded...'

'You *have* seen her, then?'

'Perhaps, perhaps not.'

God, how Kulika wished she could walk away. How she wished she could tell him he was wrong, and that Evita Khalyed was nothing to her, just a random missing woman, not the difference between life and death for the man to whom she owed more favours than she could count.

Instead, she took out her phone again, pulled up the photo and turned it to Bartholomew. 'Which is it?' she asked.

He plucked the phone from her hand and squinted at the photo, as though he were genuinely trying to remember, instead of just leading her on. 'I'll have to think on it,' he said noncommittally, then he disappeared her phone somewhere about his person. 'In the meantime, you must stay. I'll have them make up one of the suites for you upstairs.'

'No, thank you,' Kulika said, putting her half-drunk beer to one side and standing from the armchair. 'I should get going, so if you'll just give me back my phone…'

'Oh, Kulika,' Bartholomew replied with a feral grin. 'You misunderstand me. When I said that you must stay, I meant you truly *must* stay.'

'As your prisoner?'

'As my guest.'

Kulika forced out a laugh, pretending that she wasn't starting to panic. 'You may as well drop the act now, Bartholomew,' she said lightly. 'I'll never give you my oath again. You'll have to take it from me by force, and I warn you: I'm not the same weak, broken lackey who left you a century ago.'

Then his hand was around her neck, her back was against the shelves, and her feet were kicking in the air. She could get out of the hold easily enough, she knew – for all his superhuman strength, she had a measure of her own, along with a whole heap of training – but something was wrong with her throat, and for some reason she couldn't seem to move. Instead of fighting back, she'd frozen in Bartholomew's grip like a kitten held by its scruff in its mother's mouth.

'I won't force the covenant on you,' he whispered against her cheek. 'You know that's not how it works. But however strong you think you've become, you know that I *could*. Soon enough, you'll be begging me to take it from you, just like you did on the *Onslow*. You'll be fighting to get me back under your skin. I *know* you, Kulika. Did you forget that I'm the one who made you who you are today?'

'I'm who I am today in spite of you,' she gasped out, 'not because of you.'

He laughed and let go of her, throwing her back down into the armchair. 'What a tired cliché you've become. You're an empty thing without me. You do realise that, don't you? That void you're trying to fill in the centre of yourself, that thing you've spent the past century searching for, has it not occurred to you that the piece that fits inside that space is *me*? Or are you still in denial about your proper place?'

'You're wrong,' she coughed.

'Denial it is, I see.' He sighed. 'I'd give you the whole world, Kulika. I did, once. He can't give you that.'

'He doesn't have to give me anything. He gave me freedom from you, and that was enough.'

'Until today, when he sent you right back to me.'

There was nothing she could say in the baron's defence that wouldn't make the situation worse, so she said nothing at all as Bartholomew dropped the book back into his desk drawer and slammed it shut.

'If you want information about this missing woman,' he said, 'then you'll stay. Make yourself comfortable. Try to remember why you chose to wear my covenant on your skin in the first place.'

'And if I try to leave?'

'Go, by all means,' he said, smiling that feral smile again, 'if you've decided that she's no longer of any importance to you. But know this: you'll never find her without my help.'

He could be lying. Kulika had seen him lie before, repeatedly and convincingly, but he'd always been honest with her. Unlikely though it sounded, the covenant between the two of them had been one of trust, as well as one of blood. With Kulika, he had always told the truth.

'One night,' she said. 'And only one night.'

'Excellent!' He grinned like a hungry wolf. 'Go on outside. Enjoy the party. You might even like it so much that you decide to stay.'

'I'm leaving tomorrow.'

Bartholomew just continued to grin.

Kulika could only hope that her words would prove as true as his had always been.

6

QUICK STOOD BY the porch as she drank her beer. She was waiting for the beautifully muscled woman who'd gone into the house to come out again, but only so that she herself could slip inside to find a phone. It wasn't that Quick wanted to see her again, to see if she really was as beautifully muscled as she remembered. That would have been ridiculous, because not only was she a complete stranger, in an unfamiliar place, but she was also palpably dangerous.

Quick was just… drinking her beer. Slowly. Once she'd finished it, if the woman still hadn't reappeared, and if there was still no sign of Monty, then she'd just have to go inside and find a phone. And if she happened to bump into the woman while she was in there, maybe that wouldn't be the worst thing in the world.

She'd just about convinced herself that this was the only reasonable course of action when the glass doors opened and the woman stepped outside again. She didn't look happy, her bottom jaw jutting in a way that made it clear she was gritting her teeth. Somehow, that made her even more alluring.

Without conscious thought, Quick took a step towards the

doors, but with her eyes fixed on the woman, she wasn't paying attention to where she was going and barrelled straight into a man coming from the opposite direction.

Her nearly-empty beer glass was knocked from her hand and smashed on the paving slabs, followed by her handbag and all its contents. Her phone skittered across the ground and away into the darkness under the porch, her wallet was kicked between the dancing feet of the partygoers and into the pool, and the cold case playing cards – still loose from their packet – were scattered in a wide circle around her, surrounding her with the faces of all the people she had failed to find.

She had come here for Jensen, she reminded herself with a pang of guilt. *Not to ogle at terrifying yet attractive women.*

She crouched down to collect the cards with new resolve: she would gather them up, track down Monty, get an answer from him about Jensen – one way or another – then get the hell out of here.

'What are these?' asked the man she'd bumped into, crouching down at her side. He looked like one of the buccaneers that Evita had portraits of in her office, with an anchor beard, long chestnut hair and dark lashes framing dark eyes. And he was not happy.

'These?' Quick repeated, still a little dazed from the collision, then she saw that he was holding a couple of the cards between his fingers. 'Oh. These. Playing cards.'

'Why have they got photos on them?' he pressed. 'Why have they got *her* photo on them?'

'They're cold case playing cards,' Quick started to explain. 'They've got pictures of missing people…' Then she saw that the buccaneer was holding Mairead Carlisle's card in his hand. 'You know her?'

'Do *you* know her?' he asked.

'Sort of,' Quick replied. 'I know her family.'

For some reason, that just seemed to make him angrier. Quick was about to enquire further, but Monty chose that moment to finally reappear.

'Monty,' she said, looking up at him, not sure whether or not to be relieved to see him.

'Are you kidding me with this?' the buccaneer asked him, then he grabbed Quick by her arm and hauled her to her feet, making her drop all the cards she'd gathered.

'Hey!' she said.

'With what?' Monty asked the buccaneer. 'What happened?'

'Where have you been?' Quick asked Monty. 'Where's Jensen?'

'Have you seen these?' the buccaneer asked Monty, holding out a handful of the cards.

'Yes,' Monty replied, ignoring Quick entirely.

'Then what the fuck?'

'What?'

'I mean,' the buccaneer said, turning Mairead's card to face Monty, 'what the fuck?'

'So you *do* know her?' Quick asked the buccaneer.

The buccaneer looked at her, then back to Monty, saying, 'Is your girl going to be a problem? Because this,' he picked up a handful of playing cards and broken glass, 'looks like a problem.'

'Jesus, Brandon,' said Penny, coming up behind him. She must have just emerged from the pool, because she was dripping wet and wearing a towel. She unwrapped it from her body to press against the buccaneer's – Brandon's – palm. 'You're fucking bleeding. *Again*. And that's your marked hand.'

'I just want Monty to tell me if this is going to be a

problem,' he said, ignoring Penny and his bleeding hand entirely, as though he didn't even feel it. Quick checked his eyes and saw the same silver in them that she'd seen in Penny's. Maybe whatever they'd taken to make their eyes go like that also made them numb to pain.

And rude.

Monty rolled his eyes and started gathering the cards up himself. 'This isn't going to be a problem,' he said to Brandon.

'I hope not, because I don't want to have to tell Bartholomew—'

'Like he'd ever give you the time of day,' Monty said. 'Let's not forget who was here first, all right? I know what I'm doing.'

'But you've never actually done this before, have you?' Brandon said, glancing at Quick in a way that felt significant.

'Done what?' Quick asked, then she turned to Monty. 'What exactly is going on here?'

But Monty had frozen. He was staring at one of the cards he'd been in the process of gathering up, and he looked like he'd seen a ghost.

The card was Evita's.

'Now you look like he did when he saw Mairead,' Quick said to him, gesturing at Brandon. 'Just how many of the people in this deck do you recognise? And how do you know Evit—'

'Stop,' Monty said, holding up a hand.

'Tell me what you know, Monty,' Quick insisted. 'She's my best friend. You recognised her.'

But Monty just shrugged and said, 'We see a lot of people here.' He had shuffled Evita's card out of sight now, slipping it into the centre of the pack as he snatched the whole lot from the glass on the floor and from Brandon's grip. He moved faster than Quick would have thought possible, if she hadn't just seen it with her own eyes.

'Take her to the block,' Monty said quietly.

'What are you—' Penny and Brandon were holding Quick's upper arms, manhandling her. 'Monty,' she said.

'I'm sorry,' he said quietly, stepping towards her as he slipped her missing persons deck into his pocket. 'This didn't go the way I planned it, but it's the way it's got to be.'

When they were toe to toe, he reached out to touch her face. She thought for a second that he was about to kiss her, so she turned her head to the side, because there was no way she was going to let that happen.

What actually happened was worse.

She should have left when she'd had the chance. If Jensen had ever been here, he was beyond saving, and Penny obviously didn't want to be saved. She was right here, helping Brandon to hold Quick in place with a grip that felt like a vice squeezing tighter and tighter around her arms.

And the woman who walked like she was spoiling for a fight... Well, she wasn't the kind of person who needed saving from anything, but Quick looked around for her desperately, wondering if there was any chance she might be willing to save Quick. From Monty and his friends, from failure, from a life hollowed out by loss after loss, and never filled up again.

Too late now.

Monty's hand covered Quick's nose and mouth, then his teeth found her neck. If she could have breathed, she might have screamed. She did neither.

In her last moments of consciousness, as her vision dimmed, she thought she caught a glimpse of sunshine in the darkness. The pain faded into panic, and panic faded into

nothing at all.
Just emptiness and cold.

7

KULIKA STEPPED OUT onto the porch and into the night air with a measure of relief, but no pleasure. Then Bayly joined her, and her discomfort flared into irritation.

'You didn't tell me it had got this bad,' she said accusingly. 'What's going on here, Bayly? This party, the pool, all these people, and don't think I didn't notice those new buildings over on the far side of the property. What are they? Dorms? And you let me walk in here without warning me that he's marking humans now. *Why* is he marking humans?'

Bayly didn't reply to any of this, he just stood beside her as the two of them looked out across what had once been the dirt training ground on which they'd wrestled, and was now a pool party filled with teenagers and twenty-somethings. It had been important, that space. Back in the day, they'd established the pecking order of the mansion on that dirt. The better you fought, whether clean or dirty, the higher your rank in Bartholomew's crew. It looked as though those days were long gone. Now, Bartholomew's followers seemed to be establishing their hierarchy through drinking games, wet T-shirt contests and drunken brawls.

Maybe that wasn't such a change. After all, they had been pirates, once.

A splash of ethereal colour drew Kulika's gaze to the far side of the porch. There was a group of four people there, two men and two women, standing apart from the rest of the party. The colour she'd seen was the red hair of one of the women, shining like fire in the dark. Kulika caught only a glimpse of her soft face, transformed into an eerie kind of beauty by the undulating light filtering up through the pool, before she walked away arm-in-arm with her friends, crossing the grass towards the new modern block that lurked beyond the trees.

Her hair shone like sunset on the water. Like the hair of the woman who was standing in the photograph next to Evita Khalyed.

'Who's that?' Kulika asked Bayly, but Bartholomew was the one who answered. She hadn't realised he was there, but then he always had been beyond-supernaturally stealthy. She would have to remember that, along with so many other things that she had hoped could stay forgotten.

'The redhead?' Bartholomew asked. 'If you want her, she's yours.'

'All I have to do is sign, right?' Kulika scoffed.

Bartholomew just smiled. Kulika turned back to Bayly, meaning to ignore Bartholomew, but Bayly had already slipped away.

Lucky him.

'She's a person, not your property,' Kulika said, turning back to Bartholomew.

'She's both,' he replied. 'She took the deal: we turned her Silver and she signed the Articles. She wears the mark of my covenant. If you want, I can have her in your bed within the hour, ready and waiting.'

'Aside from the obvious objections,' Kulika said, putting herself between Bartholomew and the retreating vision of the woman with the sunset hair, 'do you really mean to convince me to sign your Articles by gifting me a woman who's made herself your property by doing exactly that? You're not going to tempt me into slavery by offering me one of your slaves.'

'Not slavery, Kulika,' he said, reaching out to caress her cheek. She caught his wrist before he could touch her skin, tossing his hand away, and he laughed. How he loved to laugh. 'You are not her,' he whispered, leaning in closer than she would have liked. 'The terms of our covenant would be different.'

'Different how?'

'Better. For you, that is. Worse, for me. I'd do that for you, Kulika. That's how much it would mean to me to have you return home, my prodigal daughter.'

It was true that Bartholomew had been like a father to her three hundred years ago, but by the authoritarian standards of the time, it was a hollow title.

'This isn't my home,' she said. 'It never was.'

Bartholomew looked like he was about to make her another offer, but then the young man who'd been trying to speak to him earlier returned, saying, 'Sir, I'm sorry, but—'

'You'll be sorrier in a moment, Mr Monteiro.'

'Sir, please, I wouldn't interrupt if it wasn't important. It's just that…' The young man glanced at Kulika, then looked back to Bartholomew. 'Sir, I really need to speak with you. *In private.*'

Bartholomew glared at the poor kid for a moment, then turned to Kulika and waved her off into the party, saying, 'I'll catch up with you later. In the meantime, feel free to make whatever enquiries you like of my guests.'

Which was as good a suggestion as any, she supposed, but she wasn't likely to get very far without her phone and the photo of Evita Khalyed that it contained. She wasn't likely to get anywhere at all without Bartholomew's cooperation. He'd recognised the woman's face, Kulika was certain. He knew her, or had seen her at least, but he wasn't going to give up that information easily. Maybe, between now and the morning, she could come up with some way to bargain it out of him. Maybe she could track down Bayly and get him to explain exactly what plan of Bartholomew's required this many new Silver and humans carrying Bartholomew's black mark. Or maybe she'd be better off getting out of here right now, before the water got too deep for her to stand in it.

She stepped off the porch towards the pool, meaning to find some answers, but slowed as she heard the young man start talking to Bartholomew behind her.

'Sir, we've got a problem,' he said.

'Then deal with it, kid,' Bartholomew replied.

'It's about the girl I brought in tonight. She's being… uncooperative.'

'And whose fault is that, hmm?'

Kulika's hearing had improved since she'd left Bartholomew. Either he'd not considered the fact that the abilities of the Silver improved with age, or he'd underestimated the effect that a century would have on hers, because he didn't make any attempt to move their conversation further into the house.

'Surely by now you know not to bring someone new so late in the cycle,' he continued. 'Just let her go.'

'That's the problem, sir. I can't.'

'And why not?'

'The thing is, the reason I brought her in the first place was that she was looking for some of the people who've gone missing, and it seemed like the fewer questions there were the better, you know? But it turns out there's a whole bunch of families looking for a whole bunch of missing people, and she had these and—'

Kulika peeked over her shoulder just in time to see the kid handing a stack of small cards to Bartholomew, who began to leaf through them.

'And what exactly are these?'

'Missing person playing cards, she says. The thing is, sir, if you look at the card on the top of the pack...'

Bartholomew flipped the card so he could see its face, then he became very still indeed. From this angle, Kulika couldn't see anything except the back of the card.

'She was looking for Jensen,' the kid said. 'But she said this name, and I think... I think she knows Jane.'

Bartholomew looked up, in what appeared to be shock. As he did so, he noticed Kulika's attention and realised his mistake. He nodded her an irritated farewell, then drew the young man back into the house and out of earshot.

Shame. He wouldn't underestimate her so easily next time.

But the endeavour hadn't been entirely fruitless. She had more information now than she'd had at the beginning of the night. She was more convinced than ever that Evita Khalyed was here, or had been here, and it sounded like she was just one of many. Mr Monteiro had spoken about *the missing people* as though there were a lot of them, maybe enough to fill a whole deck of cards. On top of that, there was one that was important to Bartholomew, important enough to drag him away from tormenting Kulika.

Jane.

His reaction to that name, to the picture on that last card... Maybe that was something Kulika could leverage to get the information she needed. If only she could get her hands on those cards.

First, though, she needed to find Bayly and make him spit out some answers.

She waded out into the party, letting the conversation flow over her. Drinks. Hook ups. Fights. Drugs. Competitions between all the young idiots to see who was the strongest, even though they all now had more strength than they could wield responsibly. What on earth was Bartholomew thinking? There was a reason that the Silver were turned slowly, one by one, then ushered gently and carefully into immortality under the supervision of their creators and elders. This kind of mass expansion meant that there were precious few experienced Silver to guide them through the transition, or to curb their excesses when they stepped out of line. If a bunch of them all decided to go rogue at once…

Kulika felt like she was walking into a powder keg with a fuse of indeterminate length. There was no telling when it might go off. The only sure thing was that, sooner or later, it would.

8

WHEN QUICK WOKE up, her tongue felt fuzzy in her mouth, her throat was dry and her back ached. Sitting up was an effort. It was dark, or near enough. There was a faint light seeping through a long, straight crack in the ceiling above her, but not enough to fully illuminate the space she was in: a rectangular room about twenty feet wide with a low ceiling, no windows and a dirt floor. A cellar, then. It smelled damp and vegetal, and she could hear a drip echoing from what sounded like a long way off. Beyond that sound, there was nothing.

No birdsong. No traffic. No thumping party music.

The world had been taken away.

Then her ears popped and she heard a noise that made her jump back against the wall: the scuffling sound of feet on dirt. There was someone, or something, in here with her.

'Are you still human?' a voice asked from the darkness at the far end of the cellar. Feminine, North American accent, but not local.

Quick wasn't sure whether to be relieved or concerned to have company. And the question was... odd.

'Excuse me?' Quick replied with a dry voice that broke

into a whisper.

'Human,' the voice said, but this time it was quieter, as though the word had been spoken in the opposite direction.

'What do you mean *human*?' Quick asked. 'What else would I be? And who are you? And where are we? And what the fuck?'

'That about sums it up. You want water? There're faucets in the corner over here.'

Abruptly, Quick realised that she was parched. But she was also wary of the voice luring her into the darkness, and aware that the person who owned it had yet to answer any of her questions.

Quick stood with difficulty, and not just because she was feeling unsteady. She was five foot nine and her head was grazing the ceiling, even though her feet were bare. Who knew where her sandals had gone, or her handbag.

Then she remembered: the missing person playing cards, Brandon and Penny holding her arms, Monty leaning down and biting—

Her hand flew to her neck. She could feel the tender wounds there, scabbed with dried blood.

'He bit me,' she said in disbelief.

'Yeah, the vampires do that,' the voice said. 'Just be grateful you're not a zombie.' Then its owner walked into the faint light leaching through the crack in the ceiling. She looked like Lara Croft after she'd fought her way out of a particularly filthy tomb, only she had light brown skin, bleached blonde hair with long black roots, chipped silver nails and a nervous energy that gave Quick the impression that she was both unpredictable and unsafe to be around.

'Excuse me?' Quick asked politely, wondering how far she'd get if she started running. The room felt big, but there was no guarantee she'd be able to find a way out of it. She couldn't run forever, and likely not long at all in this dehydrated state.

'You said you got bitten,' the woman said.

'Yes,' Quick replied tentatively.

'Show me your eyes.'

Quick backed away as the woman stepped closer.

'I will pin you down and pull your eyelids up myself if you make me,' the woman growled.

'Jesus, Xiaoyu,' said another voice from the shadows, then a young man was standing at the woman's side, tugging her back by the arm. He was tall and gangly, hunched over in the low space, with dark skin and a scraggly little beard that made Quick think he was probably younger than he looked. She couldn't place his accent, but it wasn't purely American; there was at least a bit of French in there. 'She just woke up,' he said. 'Give her a chance.'

'A chance to murder us all?'

'All?' Quick asked, looking between the two of them. 'How many of you are there?'

There was a click and suddenly the room was flooded with light. Quick had to look away, blinking the strobing brightness out of her eyes for a few seconds before she could bear to look back. When she did, she saw that the room was much larger than she'd first imagined, stretching easily a hundred feet away from her, supported at regular intervals by concrete pillars. Breeze-block walls. The far corner had been screened off with ratty sheets hanging between the pillars. It was clearly some kind of flood cellar, but it looked like an unusually low parking garage, lit at irregular intervals by fluorescent strips across the concrete ceiling.

Quick's side of the space was empty except for her, Xiaoyu and the young man, but the other side was a patchwork of people laid out on makeshift beds on the dirt floor, mostly fashioned from blankets and clothing. There must have been a hundred people down here, easily, and every single one of them was looking at her.

'We watch,' the young man explained. 'When they open the hatch and throw someone down,' he said, indicating the space on the ceiling where the line of light had now disappeared in the glare of the fluorescents, 'we turn out the lights and we wait to see what wakes up.'

Which explained why everything had been so silent when Quick opened her eyes. The people in the cellar hadn't been sleeping. They'd been keeping guard.

'And now I need to see your eyes,' Xiaoyu said, then she grabbed Quick by the hair and dragged her directly under one of the fluorescents. Quick yelled and elbowed back, but by the time she'd started fighting in earnest, Xiaoyu had already let her go. Quick ended up flailing into an undignified heap on the floor.

'She's clean,' Xiaoyu declared.

Only then did the people watching from the other side of the cellar make a sound, as though they had been collectively holding their breath until that moment.

'Louis,' the young man said, holding out his hand to Quick. She shook it without thinking, because it was just what you did. 'I'd say *welcome*, but...'

Quick looked at him, at Xiaoyu, and at the hundred-odd people beyond them. They were diverse in appearance but mostly young, either teenagers or kids in their twenties. There were some older adults in the mix too, but none of them looked older than fifty. A few were looking at her with curiosity, but most of them had lost interest now that the excitement was over.

'You were looking for the silver,' Quick said as she put it together. 'Weren't you?' she asked Xiaoyu. 'You were looking for silver in the whites of my eyes.'

'You noticed they have that, huh?' Xiaoyu jutted her hip out to one side and rested her hand on it, a gesture that was more cocky than sassy. She was clearly the one calling the shots in this hole in the ground.

'So it *is* drugs, then?' Quick asked.

'Drugs?' Xiaoyu laughed dismissively. 'What drugs do you know that make your eyes go weird, give you super speed, super hearing and super strength, make you immortal and give you a thirst for human blood? Come on.'

'But…' Quick said. 'You mean you were serious about the vampires?'

'You got bitten and you still don't believe me?'

'No. Yes. I don't know. *Vampires*?'

'Look,' Louis interrupted, 'this is going to be a long conversation, and I can't stand all hunched up like this forever, so can we get away from this damned hatch and sit down?'

Xiaoyu glanced up at the covered hole above their heads then started backing up towards the far side of the room. 'Right,' she said. 'The night's not over yet. There could be more.'

'More what?' Quick asked.

'Just…' Xiaoyu glanced up, then away, then up again, getting jittery now. It looked like her anxiety was back, and then some. 'Just get away from the fucking hatch, okay?'

They'd barely taken a step when there was a *clank* from right above their heads. Neither Xiaoyu nor Louis said anything, they just grabbed Quick by the arms – still tender from Brandon and Penny's manhandling – and dragged her to the far side of the cellar in a crouched and panicked run, coming to rest behind a pillar about halfway along the space.

Louis pressed a finger to his lips, then the lights went out.

The clanking came again, followed by the rasp of something hard scraping across the floor above, then the hatch was lifted open. Quick peeked around the corner of the pillar as a square of warm light shone down onto the dirt floor below, bringing with it the sound of conversation.

'You're zero for five,' a man said, braying so loudly that this words were clear to Quick even though she was some distance from the hatch. 'When are you going to call it quits? None of these girls fancy you, Bub. Give up already.'

'Right, yeah,' came the reply, 'and remind me, what are you on? One for seven? Doesn't seem to me like you're doing much better.'

'Um, hello? I have *one*, at least. You got none, buddy. None.'

'Yet,' the second speaker said. Then, as if to punctuate his speech, a bundle of something person-sized – probably a person, Quick forced herself to admit – dropped through the hatch and onto the cellar's dirt floor with a sickening, cracking crunch. The hatch shut a second later, blocking out the conversation from above and leaving them in the darkness. Her eyes had become accustomed to the brief light, so now Quick couldn't see a thing, but she could feel the reassuring press of concrete at her back, and the warmth of Xiaoyu and Louis pressed on either side of her.

'What now?' Quick whispered.

'Now we wait to see what they turn into,' Louis whispered back.

'You mean they could turn into a vampire?' Quick said, horrified. Then the implications filtered through her panic and she clapped her hand to her neck. 'Am *I* going to turn into a vampire?'

'If you haven't yet, then you won't,' Louis said. 'And you haven't, because there's no silver in your eyes. It shines like crazy under those fluorescents, and yours didn't. You're clear. You're no vampire, I promise. Going by what they were just saying, though, this latest one's going to turn, one way or another.'

'And most of the time they go quickly,' Xiaoyu muttered quietly. 'So shut up and watch.'

Quick wanted to ask more, but Xiaoyu shushed her down before she could get the words out, so instead she sat between them in the darkness and peered around the pillar, waiting for her eyes to acclimatise again. By the time they did, the bundle underneath the tiny crack of light coming through the ceiling was starting to move.

There was a stomach-churning *snap* and everything was suddenly utterly silent. Where Quick's arm pressed against Xiaoyu's side, she could feel Xiaoyu's heartbeat thumping against her ribcage, but she couldn't hear her breathing. It felt like the whole room was holding its breath, unbidden, as though this were a practised routine.

Except the person who had fallen through the hatch. There was a loud, rasping breath coming from that direction now. It had an unpleasant, gurgling quality to it that made Quick think of the last drops at the bottom of a milkshake. The person didn't move, though. Not at first. To begin with, they just gurgled and sniffed. The noise lasted long enough to make Quick uncomfortable, because surely they should be going to help the poor person if they'd hurt themselves falling into the cellar, shouldn't they? It sounded worryingly like they might have punctured a lung, and if that was the case then shouldn't they be putting them on their side or doing something to help them breathe before they drowned in their own blood?

Quick opened her mouth to suggest this, but she only managed to say, 'Shouldn't—' before the person beneath the hatch snapped their head up from the ground. Their face was snarling, twisted and feral, and they were looking directly at Quick.

'Idiot,' Xiaoyu muttered, then she scrambled to her feet and yelled, 'Blankets! Back to row three, ready to bundle on my mark!'

'Run!' Louis said to Quick, so she did, following Xiaoyu to the far side of the cellar, where people were already on their feet and lining up between the columns across the width of the space, holding out coats and blankets and sheets between them. Louis and Quick squeezed between two people to get behind the line, then turned in time to see the figure under the hatch rising unsteadily to their feet.

It was a white man, Quick thought, though with the dirt, loose clothes, twisted features and mid-length hair falling over his face, it was difficult to be sure. He was tall, too tall to stand upright in the cellar without bending over, but he didn't even try to reach his full height. Instead, he held his body in a poised, forward-leaning stance, back hunched and arms hanging down loosely from his shoulders. When he raised his head, his attention snapped to the blankets and he started to move towards the crowd, slowly at first, then quicker, until he was running full pelt at them with an inhuman, guttural roar.

'Lights!' Xiaoyu yelled, and the fluorescents snapped on.

The man screamed, losing momentum and direction as he ploughed into the blanket fence and was bundled up like a burrito. But he recovered quickly, too quickly, his limbs flailing free of their constraints and taking out several of the people who were trying to pin him. Quick lunged into the fray without thinking, grappling to snatch a piece of the blanket and secure it around his arms.

'Mind his mouth!' someone yelled, too late. The man's

teeth had already sunk into Quick's forearm.

She screamed – this was fifty times more painful than it had been when Monty bit her – then she started pounding him around the head with her other fist until, finally, his jaw released its grip. The release was abrupt enough to take her off balance, toppling her down on top of him as she wrestled to get the blanket over his head. He pinned her, his grotesquely twisted face snarling inches from her throat as the others held him back.

No, she decided.

The panic flowed out of her body, replaced with a calm sense of purpose. Leveraging her not-inconsiderable weight against his, she flipped him, then straddled his body with her knees on his shoulders, forcing his back to the ground. She reached for a nearby blanket and bundled it around his head so he wouldn't be able to bite again, then it was just a matter of holding him in place while the others got him wrapped up tight.

'Knock him out!' Xiaoyu yelled.

A big white guy who looked like a football player raised his fist above the snarling man's swaddled head, then brought it down with a force Quick hadn't managed herself. Suddenly, the bundle went still.

For a moment, Quick just sat there in shock, then Louis came up behind her, helping her off the man and to her feet.

'Zombie,' he explained.

'Zombie,' Quick repeated, numbly.

'It happens sometimes,' he said. 'When they try to turn one of us into a vampire and it doesn't take, this is what you get.'

'Oh no,' Quick said, looking with horror at the unconscious creature at her feet, at the bite on her arm, then feeling for the crusted bite at her neck. 'Please tell me I'm not going to—'

'Relax,' Xiaoyu said. 'Zombie-ism isn't catching, and I already told you the vamps didn't try to turn you. One of them just drank from you a bit. No big deal.'

'No big deal?' Quick was reeling. 'I just got bitten by a zombie, and found out Monty's a vampire—'

'They call themselves the Silver,' Louis chimed in unhelpfully.

'—and that he drank my blood, and it's *no big deal*?'

Xiaoyu pulled aside her shirt collar, displaying a roadmap of scars and half-healed scabs snaking down her neck and onto her shoulder. 'Yeah,' she said. 'No big deal. Why else do you think they keep us down here? We're the blood bank. Stop being such a fucking drama queen about it.' Then she grabbed the unconscious zombie by one ankle while another woman grabbed his other, and together the two of them dragged him back towards the hatch.

'Don't mind Xiaoyu,' Louis said, kneeling at her side to spare his back. 'She's been here longer than most of us. A lot of people die in this place. It hardens you up, you know?'

'How long?'

Louis shrugged. 'I don't know. Months? I've been here since March, and Xiaoyu'd already been here a long while before then.'

Months.

Quick remembered the way Monty had frozen when he'd seen Evita's face on that card, and the way he'd shut Quick down when she'd tried to say her name. He'd recognised her, or her name. And if he knew her, then maybe…

'My best friend has been missing since December,' Quick said. 'I came here looking for answers about another missing person, then I thought I was onto a lead about my friend, but the moment I started to ask around at the party—'

'You ended up here,' Louis finished for her.

Which was exactly where Evita could have ended up.

'Evita Khalyed,' Quick said. 'Do you know the name?'

Louis shook his head.

'Evita Khalyed,' Quick said again, raising her voice as she looked at every face in the cellar, one by one. Between the panic and the zombie and the shock, she hadn't been paying attention to them earlier. She might have missed her friend in the crowd. The hope surged in her chest like a hot, sharp splinter of desperation. 'Evita Khalyed! Are you here?'

'Keep your voice down!' Xiaoyu whisper-yelled at her. 'They can hear you upstairs.'

'They have their dorms up there,' Louis said. 'If they think you're causing trouble…'

'This place is like cold storage,' muttered a man behind her. 'We're fast food. Disposable.'

'Has a woman called Evita been through here?' Quick asked him.

'No Evitas,' Xiaoyu said, as though that were the end of the conversation. She and the other woman had reached the hatch now, and they unceremoniously dumped the zombie underneath it.

Quick looked around, appealing to the rest of the crowd as she said, more quietly this time, 'Has anyone else met an Evita here?'

'No,' Xiaoyu said. 'They haven't.'

'Why don't you let them speak for themselves?' Quick snapped back.

'Why don't you try using your brain, noob? Far as I know, I was the first one they put down here, so if I don't know Evita, no one else will either. Now shut up while I get rid of this guy.'

Then she reached up and thumped on the hatch with her

fist.

'Jonah! You're zero for six,' she yelled. 'Jonah! Come and clean up your own damn mess!'

The hatch opened wide and Xiaoyu took a few big steps back.

'You want to be number seven?' said a man from above, one of the same voices from earlier.

'Fuck off, kid,' Xiaoyu spat. 'And if you don't want your blood supply to dry up, maybe you could try feeding us, huh?'

Instead of answering her, he jumped into the cellar, scooped the unconscious zombie up into his arms, then leapt back out again in a single bound. If everything that had happened that evening up until this point hadn't already convinced her of the truth, that simple physical impossibility put it beyond question. These people were not human.

The hatch thumped down again, sealing Quick and the other prisoners into the vampires' larder.

'What will they do with him?' Quick asked Louis.

'I don't know,' he murmured. 'And I'm pretty sure I don't want to either.'

It was only then that Quick's adrenaline wore off enough for her to feel the pain in her arm. She winced.

'Let's get that clean,' Louis said, standing into his hunched crouch as he led her through the drift of blankets to the corner of the cellar that had been sectioned off from the rest with hanging sheets. Quick had expected some kind of praise or thanks for her bravery with the zombie, because she had literally thrown herself into danger to help the others, but most of the cellar inhabitants barely looked at her. Like Louis had said, being down here seemed to harden people up, as though they'd grown protective shells over their feelings.

'Friendly bunch,' Quick murmured.

'Don't judge them too harshly,' Louis replied softly. 'The truth is, people don't last long down here. You don't tend to make friends, because you'll only lose them.'

'You're friendly,' Quick pointed out.

'Well, look out for yourself and don't make me regret it. Through here,' he said, ushering her around the corner.

There was a line of stainless steel sinks, a couple of shower heads set in the wall above a drain in the middle of a small concrete area of flooring, and a couple of grungy-looking steel toilet cubicles. Louis helped her wash the wound as clean as they could get it in one of the sinks – which wasn't as clean as Quick would have liked – then bind it up with a strip of cotton torn from the sleeve of her dress.

'Right now, it's the most sanitary thing down here,' said Louis apologetically as he ripped it into pieces. 'Sometimes they let us shower and change clothes when they take us up to feed, so hopefully someone will bandage this up for you properly then.'

'When's that likely to be?' Quick asked, desperate to get out of the cellar, but none too keen to get bitten for the third time in as many hours.

Louis just shrugged.

'Xiaoyu was right under that hatch when the vampire opened it,' Quick said quietly, trying to understand the strange dynamic between her and the one she'd called Jonah.

'Yeah,' Louis replied.

'But we were all clearing away from the hatch earlier.'

'Because of the zombie. The vampires are bad, but they're rational, and they need us alive for our blood. The zombies are bad too, but they're pretty easy to take down if we work together, like you saw. The problem is that sometimes the vampires do manage to turn someone into one of them, and when those wake up down here all blood-starved and crazy… Well, that's the scary shit. That's when people die.'

'But if the newly-turned ones are so dangerous, and the vampires care so much about keeping us alive, why do they put them down here?'

'Because feeding them is what we're for,' Louis said darkly. 'That's *why* they want to keep us alive. If we die doing it… Well, to them, that's a fair trade.'

'Lights out,' said Xiaoyu from beyond the bathroom curtains. 'Let's all get some sleep while we can. I'll watch the hatch with Reynolds.'

Louis rushed Quick back out into the main cellar, settling them both onto a blanket on the floor as the room plunged into darkness once more. Quick should sleep, she knew, because if today was any indication of what was to come, she'd need to be well-rested for tomorrow.

Instead, she opened her eyes into the dark cellar and replayed the moment the zombie had pinned her to the dirt and snarled into her face. Over and over again.

She was going to die down here, and there was not a person in the world outside this hell hole who knew where she was.

9

KULIKA HADN'T BEEN able to find Bayly that night. She'd thoroughly searched the party and the mansion before following his scent to the parking area out front, where it disappeared. The traitor had driven away and left her here.

By that time, it had been late enough that Kulika would normally have been getting up for her dawn training session, but between the jet lag, the all-nighter and the nocturnal hours they kept at the mansion, she'd decided to pack it in and go to bed instead. That was when she'd discovered that the suite that had been prepared for her was not only one of the grandest in the house, it was also the suite neighbouring Bartholomew's.

His and hers.

Kulika couldn't imagine what Bartholomew thought he was playing at. There'd never been anything romantic between the two of them; he was a paternal figure to Kulika, quite apart from the fact that she was gay, and he had been celibate since the sixteenth century. It was inconceivable that he had carnal designs on her, which could only mean that he wanted her under his control in other ways.

For Bartholomew, that was not out of character.

As a general rule, control freaks didn't make good pirate captains, but Bartholomew was the exception to that rule. Piracy was supposed to be a democratic institution, as set out in the common Articles.

ARTICLE I. Every man shall have an equal vote in affairs of moment.

There was a share of the loot for each man according to his contribution, there was compensation paid to those who were injured during the course of their duties, and there were harsh penalties for those who broke faith with their crewmates. That was how the Articles had started out: as a code of conduct to govern buccaneer – and later pirate – civilisation. They weren't intended as chains to wrap around the crew, to twist them and press them into committing horrific depravities, all in the name of loyalty to their captain, to the exclusion of all others. Piracy was supposed to be about freedom, not cultism.

Bartholomew did things differently.

If it had been anyone else wearing the fancy hat, the crew would have mutinied, but Bartholomew wasn't just anyone. He'd always had that intensity about him, too unsettling to be called charisma and too intriguing to be repellent. The balance had been different at the beginning, when Kulika had first been thrown into his orbit. Now she felt more horror and less awe. Still, even she had to admit that there was an undeniable majesty in the dramatic way he burned the world down. Part of her understood why so many people had gathered to watch, then and now. What she couldn't understand was why Bartholomew was so keen for her to be amongst their number.

She was contemplating this mystery as she lay in the four-poster bed she'd been allocated, fully-clothed and unwilling to let her guard down enough to do anything about that, staring at the canopy above her head. It was fitted with mosquito netting to keep out the worst of the bugs that congregated on the marshy areas of the property that slipped down towards the Cooper River, but to Kulika it just looked like a spider trap. She imagined them all up there, spinning their webs and multiplying in the dark, waiting for the right moment to strike, just like the Silver of Bartholomew's mansion.

She must have dozed a little, because she was jerked awake by a knock next door, muffled voices, footsteps running, smashed glass and yells. She went from sleeping to awake to out of the door within a second.

'What?' she asked Bartholomew as he hurried past along the corridor, pulling a henley on over his head.

'Go back to bed, Kulika.' He headed down the wide, curving staircase without stopping. A human woman was at his heels, rushing to keep up. 'How far out are they?' Bartholomew asked the human as he descended one flight and made for the next.

'Ten hours, they say,' she replied.

'Ten *hours*? Where the hell are they?'

'Oklahoma, sir.'

'Well, get Jessamy back on the phone now. They definitely have the footage?'

'And the bodies, sir.'

'Good. It's time to put out the call.'

'Yes, sir. All of them?'

'All of them,' he said. 'I want them here on Sunday, after we've finished this cycle. The last cycle.'

Then Kulika didn't hear anything more, but she had a bad feeling. Whatever it was that Bartholomew was planning to do here with all these new Silver, it was starting now.

She quietly closed her bedroom door behind her and

headed down the stairs after Bartholomew, moving as silently as she could. She followed the sound of his voice to the back of the house, past the library, through the old kitchen to the door that led down to the wine cellar. It was shut, and there were two Silver standing guard beside it.

Then a voice from beyond the door called, 'I can hear you out there, Kulika. Go back to bed.'

So much for her attempts at subterfuge. He wouldn't say a thing while she was standing out here, so she decided to take her snooping elsewhere. Maybe she'd find a lead from somewhere – or someone – else on the property.

She passed the library on her way back to her rooms, then quickly doubled back as she realised it was open, and unoccupied. With Bartholomew shut away downstairs, she couldn't imagine a better opportunity to go through his private sanctuary, so before she could think too hard about everything that might go wrong, she slipped inside and closed the door silently behind her.

The shelves and cupboards were a waste of time, and she quickly discounted them as containing only books and booze and memorabilia from their old days on the high seas. His desk, though. That was where he'd always kept his secrets.

The leather-bound book was in there, of course. That was no surprise. The shock was the number of new signatures that Bartholomew had accumulated since Kulika left. If her quick count was correct, and assuming all the recent signatures were of Silver who were still alive and serving him, then he already had an army. There were hundreds of names in that book, all drawn in the blood of the signatories, reeking of death and rot. If Bartholomew chose to marshal them all for whatever insurgent purposes he had in mind, then with the power even a new Silver had in their body, that many of them collected together would leave nothing but destruction in their wake.

Shuddering, Kulika sealed the book silently back in its drawer and continued her search, but there was little else of interest in the desk. Until she opened the very last drawer, and reached right to the back, where she found a deck of playing cards she recognised from the night before.

Jensen Mardh. Carolyn Villiers. Valencia Khan.

Photos, descriptions, last known whereabouts. With a sinking feeling in the pit of her stomach, Kulika realised that she was holding a missing persons deck in her hands. She flicked through it quickly, looking for a Jane, the name that had thrown Bartholomew so much when the kid had mentioned it to him last night. She didn't find one, but she did find that there was one card missing from the deck. Whoever this Jane was, Bartholomew had taken her picture from the stack, which only confirmed Kulika's suspicions: she meant something to him.

It wasn't much, but it was a start. And it was time to make herself scarce.

Putting everything back the way she'd found it, Kulika left the library and went searching for a way to get a message out to the baron. First, she looked for a phone, but apparently they were banned from the mansion, along with any other connection to the outside world. There was no hum of an internet router, no distant ringing, in fact nothing electronic at all beyond the lights. As far as Kulika could tell, the mansion had barely been upgraded since she'd been here last.

Next, she tested her exits: the road, the river, the woods. If she could get to Charleston, or even as far as a phone someone would let her borrow, then that would be enough. No such luck. It seemed that she could wander the property freely, but the moment she approached the boundary line, two or more Silver appeared and politely, but firmly, reminded her that Bartholomew would like her to remain at the mansion. She could fight her way out, in a pinch, but then she'd leave empty-handed.

In the end, she went back to the house. She didn't feel as though she had much choice.

It was still early enough that the heat of the day hadn't yet filled the inside of the house. In the breakfast room, the airy space that opened out onto the porch, the sun was slanting low through the closed glass doors. Kulika flicked the catch and slid them open, letting in the breeze.

She remembered the times when she would stand here alone in the dawn light, before. She'd done it often. The glass doors were new, but the porch had been here when she'd first arrived, three hundred years previously. She'd slept in the attic back then, in a box room that had been subdivided into little more than a cell that filled up with insects and wet heat in the summer. She'd wake before the rest of the mansion and come down here to sit out and enjoy the cool breeze coming off the river. Sometimes, she'd go to the water to fish or swim with Bayly, the mansion's only other early riser. They never talked, they just sat and existed in the freedom of the morning before Bartholomew woke and his covenant snapped back into place. It was the only time Kulika had ever felt free at the mansion, always with Bayly at her side.

'Morning.'

Kulika turned to see Bayly standing there, lounging against the wall on the other side of the doors, in the same place he had always stood. Something tight loosened in her chest, then. She'd been counting on his help in her search. To find herself abandoned last night, and to think herself abandoned again this morning... It had been a blow.

'You came back,' she said.

'I'm sorry I left,' he replied, his eyes fixed on the horizon, as always. 'I had business.'

'Bartholomew's business?'

'Who else's?'

Kulika stepped out onto the porch, and only then did the pool come into view, together with the detritus of last night's party. Whoever's job this was to clean up, they were clearly still asleep. There were empty bottles all over the grass, on the paving, even in the water, and smears of blood stained everything.

Too many humans around too many new Silver, all of them drinking. Of course it had ended badly.

'Is it like this every night?' she asked Bayly.

'Some nights,' he replied. 'Tuesdays get messier than most.'

Kulika leaned back against the porch railing and crossed her arms over her chest, waiting for Bayly to elaborate. When he didn't, she said, 'Don't you think it's time you told me what's going on here?'

'You know what's going on,' he replied.

Kulika had a terrible feeling that she did. She thought about the number of Silver she'd seen around the pool last night, the number of covenant tattoos on palms human and Silver, the number of signatures in the book, and the size of the new buildings that looked like nothing so much as barracks.

'He's preparing for war,' Kulika said.

Bayly didn't reply, but then, he didn't need to.

'Why the humans?' she asked.

Bayly shrugged. 'Every army needs a supply train.'

'And your involvement? I can't help but notice that you're not wearing the tattoo.'

Bayly looked at his boots, tapping one heel contemplatively against the opposite toe. It was clear from his body language that he wasn't going to tell her.

'That would be me,' said a voice from beyond the porch. The man came up the side of the house from the driveway. He was neat-looking, wide-shouldered, white, with sandy-blond hair, a square jaw, and bright blue eyes. 'Hi,' he said to Kulika, climbing the porch steps and offering her his hand, tattooed palm and all. 'I'm Enzo.' His accent was Italian, but his smile was all American: big, too-white teeth and oozing charm.

'Kulika,' she said, shaking his proffered hand. She was reluctant to touch the tattoo, but that was pure irrationality. There was no magic to it, she knew. She just hated the fucking things.

'I guessed who you were,' Enzo said, still smiling like a white-toothed shark. 'Bayly's told me a lot about you, though apparently he hasn't told you very much about me.' As he said this, he turned to Bayly with a wry smile. 'He's protective.'

'Uh-huh,' said Kulika.

Bayly said nothing at all.

'Well, I'm not here long,' said Enzo. 'Just dropping by to check in with Bartholomew, then I've got to get back to the lab.'

'Bella's still here,' said Bayly darkly.

'And I'll be gone before she sees me.' He turned to Kulika and explained, 'She used to be my assistant, at the lab.'

'What lab?' Kulika asked.

'BioSilver,' he said. 'I'm a research student there.'

'*BioSilver*?' Kulika repeated, but before she could ask anything else, Bartholomew called for Enzo from inside the house. For a second she wondered how he'd even known

Enzo was here, but if there were enough guards to chat with Kulika every time it looked like she might be leaving, there were surely enough to report on new arrivals.

'Got to go,' Enzo said, then he dropped a kiss on Bayly's cheek on his way into the house and was gone.

'He looks like a used car salesman,' Kulika said to Bayly once Enzo was out of earshot.

'I didn't ask for your opinion,' Bayly replied angrily.

'Well, you're getting it anyway. What kind of mess have you got yourself into? *BioSilver?*'

'It's the Primus's research lab.'

'I know what it is,' Kulika replied irritably. 'I work for Baron Drake, who works for the Primus, and I know what his fucking labs are called.'

'You asked,' Bayly harrumphed.

'No, I didn't. I was questioning whether you're *really* doing what I think you're doing, because if you were somehow involved in a plan to steal research or even Silver bioweapons from the Primus's lab, we both know that would be suicidally stupid.'

Bayly shrugged. 'If they want a war…'

Kulika gaped at him for a moment, not quite able to believe what she was hearing. 'Jesus Christ. When you asked if I was here to start a mutiny against the Primus, I didn't think you were serious.'

Solomon was technically only the Primus of the UK, but in reality he ruled a large chunk of the Silver population of the globe. The younger Silver outside of Britain didn't pay much attention to him, but that was only because they didn't know his history. If they had any idea of the carnage he'd wrought in his many millennia on the Earth, or how he'd clawed his way through blood and rebellion to position himself as the progenitor of the Silver in the first place, maybe they'd reconsider bending the knee. It was true that Baron Drake wasn't as deferential to the Primus as he might have been, but the baron was about as close to a peer as the Primus got these days. Even then, the current situation with Jack had raised tensions between the two right up to the breaking point.

If Kulika was going to stay loyal to the baron, she was resigned to the fact that she might have to defy the Primus one day. But preemptively sending spies into his facilities to steal his secrets? That was bold.

'Whose plan was it?' Kulika asked.

Bayly said nothing, he just turned his gaze back to his feet.

'Is Bartholomew making him do this?' Kulika pressed on. 'Or was this your idea?'

'I told him it was reckless,' Bayly said finally, clenching his jaw.

It was Enzo's plan, then. That made more sense. 'Trying to impress Bartholomew, was he? He must be new.'

Bayly didn't reply.

'You don't have to stay,' Kulika pointed out. '*You* haven't signed the Articles.'

'I sired him,' Bayly said.

'So? Bartholomew sired me. It doesn't mean anything.'

Bayly looked at Kulika sharply, dead in the eye.

Any human looking at him would have noticed nothing unusual, just as anyone looking carefully at Kulika or Bartholomew would have assumed they were nothing more than mortal. The silver tracery that patterned the whites of the eyes of the Silver was a signature they could learn to suppress, with focus and patience, and all the old pirates had been blessed with centuries in which to practice the skill. It was how they hid their existence from humanity, and it was yet another reason that Kulika was concerned that Bartholomew was turning so many new Silver at once. Either they were going to have to learn to hide their silver *extremely* quickly – even the luckiest among them would still take at least a few months, and some many years – or Bartholomew would have to keep all of them isolated on his property. Or, the third and most worrying option, perhaps he had no intention of keeping them hidden at all.

Then Bayly did something that was considered crass, or threatening, or even flirtatious amongst the Silver, depending on the context: he flashed his silver. Just for a second, he released the control that he held over the silver and allowed it to flood back into the tiny blood vessels in the whites of his eyes. It didn't stop there, though. Instead, it flooded into his irises, filtering through their natural brown colour like spokes before circling his pupil. Then the silver was all gone again, erased as Bayly exerted his control over it once more.

'Shit,' Kulika said.

Bayly had silvered for Enzo. That extension of the silver into the irises was something that happened when the Silver fell in love. It was the physical mark of Bayly's bond to Enzo, the same mark that Baron Drake had in his own eyes, representing his love for Jack. Bayly could no more abandon Enzo to Bartholomew than the baron could abandon Jack to burn to death from the poison in her veins. If Enzo died in this house, Bayly would die too. Their lives were tied together, forever.

'I feel like I should be giving you my condolences,' Kulika said. 'Could you not just take him and get out of here?'

'Because it was so easy to leave the first time,' Bayly scoffed.

'It's not going to get any easier, and if you're taking on

the Primus then you're all going to end up dead. You do realise that, don't you?'

'Things have changed since you left. Since we both left.'

'I can see that.'

'Well, you can't see everything.'

'I could help, Bayly,' Kulika said, exasperated. 'Maybe we could even help each other. I'm sure Bartholomew recognised Evita Khalyed from the picture, and I can tell you're holding back on me. So how about you give me some information to help me track down Dr Khalyed, then I get the two of us *and* Enzo out of here safely.'

'Right,' Bayly laughed dismissively. 'I can't help you, Kulika, any more than you can help me. You just look out for yours, and I'll look out for mine. All right?'

Then he walked away, down from the porch and around the side of the house to the driveway. A few minutes later, Enzo followed him out, waving to Kulika as he passed. She heard an engine start up on the other side of the property as he moved out of sight. It was a short visit for both of them, apparently.

She understood Bayly's reluctance, really she did. She wasn't unsympathetic. Leaving Bartholomew the first time had not been a simple matter. She wasn't sure how Bayly had done it, but back in the days before ubiquitous car ownership and women's rights, Kulika had needed to dress up in men's clothing just to get out of Charleston and onto a ship back home to England. Not that the concept of cross-dressing had been alien to her; it was how she'd become a pirate in the first place.

When Kulika had been young, the world had been different. Back then, you couldn't make your own way as a woman without earning it first. When Bartholomew and his pirates had boarded the *Onslow*, the ship that was supposed to be taking her across the Atlantic to her new husband, she'd seen it as an opportunity to rewrite her future. If she'd known just how dark that future would be, maybe she would have opted for the same route as her cousin Charlotte and just poisoned her husband instead. When Kulika counted up her sins under the black flag, she had to admit that a single straightforward murder would have been a quicker and less bloody path to independence.

But that wasn't the path she'd chosen. Instead, she'd disguised herself as a man before Bartholomew and his crew breached the cabin of the *Onslow*. She'd signed his Articles. She'd been tattooed with the mark of his covenant. Then she'd realised what he really was, and he'd made a different mark on her entirely. He must have known she was a woman all along, but he'd still broken his own rules to bring her onto the crew.

ARTICLE VI. No boy or woman to be allowed amongst them. If any man shall be found seducing any of the latter sex and carrying her to sea in disguise he shall suffer death.

Bartholomew hadn't died for breaking the terms of his own Articles. Escaping him, Kulika nearly had.

But she and Bayly were older now, stronger, cleverer. The world was different too, with fast transport and enough people to get lost in. Surely it wouldn't be so difficult to escape a second time, particularly since Enzo was the only one who'd actually sworn the oath. Bayly had to be exaggerating.

Kulika was turning this over in her mind, worrying at its edges, trying to see what she'd missed, when she noticed an unusual scent. She followed her nose to the edge of the porch, to the spot where she'd seen the sunset-haired woman with her friends the night before. There was blood on the paving slabs there, spilling from their edge into the grass.

She was pretty sure that the scent was coming from the blood, but she needed to get closer to be sure, so she hopped over the porch railing and landed in a crouch next to it, then took a sniff.

Sunshine and oranges. Rosewater and crushed ivy leaves. Blackberries in hedgerows on cold autumn mornings.

It was the richest scent Kulika had ever encountered, layered and complex and a little bit different every time she breathed it in. That wasn't a characteristic of Silver blood. Usually, the Silver had a distinct personal scent that was easily recognisable to anyone who knew them well. This was different: a kaleidoscope of the seasons filling her nostrils.

It could be a mixed drink, she supposed. Maybe there was the blood of several different humans in this single spill. One thing was certain, though: the intoxicating scent couldn't belong to the woman with the sunset hair, because she was Silver.

Irrelevant, Kulika told herself, unsure why the memory of that woman kept distracting her. Then she caught that shifting, seasonal scent on the breeze, pulling her in the direction of the trees beyond the pool.

She followed it.

10

IN THE BLOOD cellar, the day was heating up fast, and Quick's stomach was beginning to grumble. She should be packing up her hotel room now, getting ready to catch her plane this evening. It looked as though she was going to miss her flight, but right now that was the least of her worries.

'There'll be food soon,' Louis reassured her quietly.

She hadn't realised he was awake too. 'Sorry,' she whispered as her stomach grumbled again. 'Hope I didn't disturb you.'

'Nah. I woke up when Xiaoyu did.'

The lights were off, so there was only the faint glow from around the hatch to see by, but it was enough to illuminate Xiaoyu sitting alone on the floor between the sleeping area and the hatch.

'Didn't she take a watch shift?' Quick asked, thinking Xiaoyu would surely have needed a lie in to catch up.

'She did,' said Louis. 'Sometimes she doesn't sleep much, and then she gets like this.'

'Manic?'

'Let's say "vigilant".' Quick raised her eyebrows sceptically, and Louis added, 'Her instincts when she's like this are right more often than I can explain.'

As if to prove his point, there was a clunking noise from above, then the hatch was lifted clear.

'Breakfast!' a voice yelled. 'Get the fuck out the way, Xiaoyu.'

Then a man and a woman jumped down into the cellar. Vampires, Quick guessed; they treated the five-foot drop like it was an inch, barely even bending their knees to take the impact. The woman was blonde, busty and beautiful, and the man was the male version of her. They could have been twins, or Ken and Barbie, immortalised perfection. Seeing the two of them now, and thinking back to meeting Penny and Brandon last night at the party, Quick couldn't believe she hadn't picked up on the truth sooner.

'Who's doing the Casting this week?' Xiaoyu asked the man.

'Getting jealous, are we?' the woman replied.

'I didn't ask you,' Xiaoyu snapped at her. Then she turned back to the man to ask, 'How many?'

'Not you,' the woman said, 'that's all you need to know. And anyway, we've got a little surprise lined up for you before then.'

The man pulled paper bags down from the edge of the hatch, one after another, and slung them into the cellar as the woman walked over to the bathroom corner to collect a pile of full bin bags, three in each hand.

'Well?' Xiaoyu pressed.

'You'll find out soon enough,' the man replied.

The woman laughed on her way back to the hatch, saying, 'You tease.'

Then they jumped back out again, taking the bin bags with them, and shut the hatch behind them. Quick had the unsettling feeling that she was a hamster whose cage had just been cleaned out.

'Watch out for that one,' Xiaoyu said ominously as Quick and Louis joined her.

'The guy?' Quick asked.

'The woman. Bella, her name is.'

'Why?'

Xiaoyu sighed. 'Just watch out.'

The others were crowding close now, coming to collect their bags of food. Someone turned the lights on. There was no pushing, no fighting, no squabbling over who got what. When Quick opened her own bag, she understood why. Inside, the rations were basic: apples, bread, raw carrots, crackers. There was nothing here to fight over.

'Bella was down here for a while,' Louis said as he munched on a carrot.

'But she's a vampire,' said Quick.

'She is now, but back when I first got here, she was just one of us. She was nice, too. Scared, like all of us, but kind of sweet. A bit naïve, maybe.'

'But she lost it when they turned her?' Quick guessed. It made sense, because how else could you convince yourself to drink human blood when you'd so recently been a human yourself? The only way she could make it add up was if the transformation did something to the brain.

So she was surprised when Louis said, 'No. Not then. Thing is, she was head over heels for this guy, sure he was going to be rescuing her any second. She didn't realise he was the one who put her down here in the first place. Then after he turned her, they both disappeared for a while on some secret mission no one talks about, and she came back alone. She's been waiting for him ever since. *That's* what broke her.'

'She's got a broken head, not a broken heart,' Xiaoyu

scoffed.

'Maybe they're not all that different,' Louis replied.

'Whatever. I've had enough,' Xiaoyu said. 'Everyone's got a fucking love story, and it's boring as shit. I'm showering.'

Xiaoyu walked off to the bathroom corner, passing everyone else who'd gathered back in the sleeping area. Some were breaking open their bags, some weren't even bothering.

'Is it the same food every time?' Quick asked Louis.

'More or less. We only get the good stuff when we go upstairs to feed them. That's the carrot, you could say.' He huffed a bleak little laugh and took a bite of the literal carrot in his hand.

'How often does that happen?'

'The feeding? At first, a couple of times a week. After that, it takes longer to recover. Sometimes we get injections and stuff, but people get worn out after a while, and they bring in new people to replace them.'

'You mean they just kill us when we *wear out*?' Quick asked with horror.

Louis shrugged. 'Some of us they turn, like Bella, and we get to see those ones again. Most of them, though, they just don't come back.'

'Bloody hell.'

Some great detective Quick had turned out to be. She'd come to this place hoping to find Jensen, maybe even Evita, and now she was going to die here. Which made her wonder.

'Maybe my friend was here, once,' Quick said quietly. 'It was December when she went missing.'

'Maybe,' Louis replied, but he didn't sound convinced.

Quick didn't want to believe it either. If Evita had been turned into a vampire, she would have been at the party last night. If she had come to this place but remained human, she'd be in this room right now. The inescapable truth was that if Evita had indeed come this way – and Monty's reaction to her picture suggested she had – then she was dead.

But it would be an answer, at least, and the end to a six-month-long mystery that only Quick had cared enough to investigate. And look where that had got her. Quick would be the mystery, now. The difference was that no one would come looking for her.

Evita and Quick were both lonely souls. They'd found each other at university, bonding over the losses that had isolated them in the first place – abuse, random violence, illness – and the university itself had become a shared refuge. Not the university where they'd studied, because they'd outgrown that, but the institution of scholarship itself. With the bickering, the infighting, and the pettiness of intellectualism, the world of academia was like the dysfunctional family they'd never had, and they had it together. Their disciplines might not have been identical, but their shared sense of kinship was.

Then Evita had disappeared. Their colleagues had noticed she was missing, but only Quick had felt her absence like a wound. They would doubtless notice that Quick was missing now, and they'd wonder. Maybe they'd wonder enough to worry whether the same fate had befallen her as had caused Evita's disappearance, but they wouldn't worry enough to do anything about it. Maybe they'd comfort themselves by imagining that Quick had found Evita, that they'd rekindled their college romance – a brief liaison back when Quick was still realising she was bi and Evita was still realising she wasn't – and ridden off into the sunset together.

Maybe, if she worked hard at it, Quick could imagine a

happy ending for Evita too. If she worked even harder, she might be able to imagine a world in which Evita was found, alive and well, and came looking for *her*.

But in the reality of this hot, dank hole, that was a stretch.

'No one's looking for me,' Quick murmured into her paper bag.

'Nor me,' Louis said. 'None of the others, either. It's part of how they pick us.'

'They *picked* us?'

'The people no one would notice,' Louis said bitterly.

'People who'd stay at a party until two in the morning on a Tuesday night 'cause they got nowhere else to be, and no one waiting on them,' said a man who was chewing sadly on a slice of worthless white bread. 'None of us got no one.'

People around him murmured their agreement, then settled down quietly to their rations. They were all quiet. Over a hundred people in this cellar, and there was nothing but quiet compliance. That was strange, wasn't it?

Quick left her bag of food on the ground beside Louis and started walking around the room, feeling the walls, digging at the dirt in the corners, prodding at the ceiling in the places where it cracked.

'What are you doing?' asked Louis.

'Looking around,' Quick replied. Between the blood loss and the zombie, she hadn't taken the opportunity to scope it out last night, but now that the lights were on and she was starting to think clearly, she knew exactly what she had to do.

Scope out the terrain. Work out the best exit. Plan an escape. Even if it meant taking on the vampires and going out through the hatch, there had to be a way out of here, and Quick was going to find it.

A lot of hours later, Quick had a sore back, sore knees, dirt caked under her bloody fingernails, and a load of bug bites she'd rather not think about. She knew all too well that if she got bitten by some deadly American spider in this cellar, help would not be coming, but she'd kept searching nonetheless: pulling at the plumbing in the bathroom area, pushing at the hatch in the ceiling, digging a yard down into the dirt by the wall before she unexpectedly hit rock. She didn't know much about geology, but she knew from listening to Evita's research that Charleston was built on sand and clay. The rock only made sense when she cleared a little more dirt away and found that it was in fact part of a large stone slab. Whatever this building was, it had been built on the ruins of something else, ruins that she had no chance of shifting.

She yelled in frustration, then Xiaoyu threw a handful of dirt at her.

'Shut up,' she said. 'Don't attract attention.'

'So that's all you do all day?' Quick asked, brushing the dirt from her face as she looked from Xiaoyu to Louis, who was lounging next to her on the floor, then to all of the other cellar inhabitants who were dozing or talking quietly in their own little groups. 'You just sit around and wait for them to come for you?'

'Yep,' said Xiaoyu.

'And none of you are going to help me find a way out?'

'Nope.'

Quick yelled again. Xiaoyu threw more dirt. Most of it landed in Quick's hair and wouldn't shake out again.

'Stop it!' Quick yelled.

'You stop it,' Xiaoyu replied calmly.

'Look,' Louis said, 'everyone goes through this stage.'

'What?' Quick blinked the dirt out of her eyes.

'Idiot,' Xiaoyu said irritably. 'Do you think we've just been sitting down here for months with our thumbs up our asses? If there was a way out, we would have found it by now. We've all tried, and now we're all tired, and literally drained. There's no way out except through the hatch, which is locked tight from the other side. When it's opened, the vampires are there, and they kill anyone who tries to get out. No one is coming to save us. No one gives a shit. So sit down, shut up, and eat your damn carrots.'

Tired and out of options, Quick went and rinsed her hands under the tap, then did as Xiaoyu said.

'Feel better?' Louis asked as Quick bit into an apple.

'Not really.'

'Yeah. Well.'

'We're all going to die down here, aren't we?'

'Not necessarily,' Louis replied cautiously. 'Some of us'll go to the Casting on Friday, and who knows? We might get lucky and survive it.'

'Oh, right,' Quick said, recognising the word from Xiaoyu's conversation with the vampires. 'What is that?'

'The Casting?' Louis said. 'It's the ceremony where they try to turn people into vampires. Every Friday they do it, up at the house.'

'You've been?' Quick asked, curious.

'If I had, I'd either be a vampire or a zombie or dead.'

'And you call that *lucky*,' Xiaoyu chipped in sardonically.

'Sure, if you get turned,' said Louis. 'Better vampire out there than dead down here.'

'Is it? One way or the other, no one comes back from the Casting,' Xiaoyu said darkly, then she walked back towards the hatch, leaving Quick with Louis.

'Is she expecting something?' Quick asked.

'No,' Louis replied. 'The hatch won't open again until dinnertime, so you might as well rest while you can.'

Then the hatch cracked open, making a liar of him. It

panicked Xiaoyu. She was in her defensive stance between the hatch and the rest of the humans before the thing was even half-raised.

'Shit,' said a quiet voice from the floor above, then a face peeked into the gap left between the half-open hatch and the ceiling.

It was the woman Quick had seen last night at the party, the woman who walked like she was walking into battle. Her platinum-bleached hair fell over her eye as she peered down into the cellar and looked at them all one by one. Was it Quick's imagination, or did she hesitate for just a moment longer when she saw Quick's face?

'You're all human down here?' the woman asked.

'What's it to you?' Xiaoyu asked. 'Who are you?'

Not one of the vampires, then, Quick thought. Or perhaps she only hoped.

Praying she was right, she looked closely at the woman's eyes in the lights of the fluorescents, taking a few steps closer to make sure, until she was barely six feet away. By that point she was certain: there was no silver in her eyes. The woman who moved like a warrior was not a vampire. Perhaps she might yet prove to be Quick's salvation.

'I'm… I'm sorry,' the woman said. It felt for a moment as though she was speaking only to Quick, but then her gaze moved on to Xiaoyu and the others. Her accent was English, her voice iron-hard and rich. 'I can't get you out. Yet,' she added. 'They haven't gone far.'

'But you are *going* to get us out?' Xiaoyu asked.

The woman looked uncertain for a second. She said, 'I'll try,' then froze, listening. 'Got to go,' she said, and she closed the hatch again.

Quick looked around at the dirty, drawn faces in the cellar. They looked back, and at each other. No one seemed quite sure what to make of what had just happened.

'What was that?' someone asked.

'False hope,' Xiaoyu said with exhaustion in her voice. 'Go back to your nap.'

Some of them did, but despite her aching body and the energy drag she was starting to feel deep in her bones, Quick couldn't sleep. Unlike Xiaoyu, she still had hope.

II

MORE THAN A hundred humans in the cellar beneath the
new block. Kulika had spent hours carefully searching the
mansion and its surroundings before the newly-turned
vampires had finally cleared out enough to give her a route
into the building. Some kind of meeting at the house, it
looked like. Kulika was torn, trying to decide whether her
time would best be spent eavesdropping at the mansion or
poking around in the new block, but the beguiling scent was
still drawing her on, and it made the decision for her.

She found the cellar hatch in a double-locked cupboard
hidden behind what looked for all the world like an ordinary
wall. She wasn't sure what she'd been expecting to find
beneath it – vanquished enemies, feral vampires, pirate
treasure – but Bartholomew had sealed the cellar up tightly,
with soundproofing and god knows what else, so Kulika had
gone in practically blind. All she'd been able to tell was that
there were things moving around beneath her. Then she'd
seen far too much, too many starved bodies, and in the
middle of them all: the sunset-haired woman.

Not Silver, after all. She was human, and captive.
Bartholomew's captive.

Kulika knew from personal experience just how traumatic that could be, but she'd still walked away and left the woman in the cellar with the others. Now she was dealing with the aftermath of that decision.

More than a hundred humans Kulika had just abandoned to god-knew-what fate, all to preserve the faint hope that she might be able to save her baron and his reckless lover. The maths didn't add up, but it was what she had chosen. She consoled herself with the fact that it hadn't been much of a choice at all. If she'd tried to get the humans out, then the minute they'd got close to the boundary line, Bartholomew's goons would doubtless have jumped into action. Then Kulika would have lost any chance she had of getting the answers she needed, and the humans would have been herded back to the cellar, having gained nothing.

So many of them trapped down there, and for what? For food, for turning, or for fun? Bartholomew could be sadistic, but that many victims?

And she'd left them all to die.

Just like Bartholomew had done at Whydah.

The memories spun in her head, too similar for comfort.

The *Porcupine*.

It had been three centuries ago now, 1722. Just six months after she had been turned Silver, they had found the ship at anchor with ten others off the African coast of what was now Benin. Bartholomew had had only three ships of his own, one of which was just a supply ship, but they'd all arrived when the captains and traders were ashore conducting their business. Those left behind on the merchant ships surrendered readily enough to the pirates. Bartholomew sent a boat to shore with his ransom demands – gold dust for the safe release of the merchant ships at anchor – and ten of the captains agreed to his terms. The captain of the *Porcupine* did not.

In retaliation, and to prove that his threats were serious, Bartholomew set the ship alight.

The *Porcupine* was almost fully-loaded with a cargo of eighty enslaved Africans. Some jumped overboard in an attempt to escape, but they were chained in pairs, and there were sharks.

Despite all the lives he'd taken before that day, and all the terrible sins he'd committed since, it was the *Porcupine* that had finally broken Kulika's trust in Captain Bartholomew Roberts. But by then it had been too late: she had signed his Articles. She was his until he discarded her, or she would answer to the rest of the crew.

ARTICLE VII. He that shall desert the ship or his quarters in time of battle shall be punished by death or marooning.

Under Bartholomew's flag, they had always been in time of battle.

Judging by the shouts that were coming from the mansion when Kulika emerged from the block, not much had changed in the past century. She had thought it was odd when every Silver in the place headed up to the house together, giving her the run of the block. It was as if they'd been responding to some silent signal. Kulika hadn't heard anything, and she'd been listening, so she could only imagine that this was a congregation they'd been waiting for. Perhaps, she speculated, it had something to do with the phone call Bartholomew had taken this morning.

She followed the noise up the porch steps, through the breakfast room to the large open hall where the staircase swept gracefully down from the upper storeys. That was where she found the mob, crowded thick around the edges of the room and baying, like a pack of dogs held back only by the fear of their master. In the centre, lying at the bottom of the stairs, was a young, tattooed man with dark hair long enough to cover his face, but not the blood that pooled on the floorboards around it. Kulika had no doubt that Bartholomew was behind the beating, though she was just as certain that he hadn't personally laid a finger on him. That honour belonged to the young woman who was standing over him with a bloody knife in her hand.

Kulika could smell the blood. That wasn't unusual, but the way it clawed its way into her nostrils and thudded into her chest was. It was like inhaling a drug. That was the moment Kulika realised she'd allowed herself to become too thirsty, and too hungry. She was in no shape for a fight.

'This isn't your business, Kulika,' Bartholomew said from the first floor. He was standing at the mezzanine railing that overlooked the hall, gazing down at the carnage, pulling the strings of the Silver below like a puppeteer in his fly tower.

At his words, the crowd stilled.

Kulika stopped at the edge of the room and looked around. There were scores of Silver there, all apparently happy to participate in whatever this was. There hadn't been even a fraction of that number in residence in the days of Kulika's covenant to Bartholomew. She didn't recognise any of the congregation from back then, but she could pick out at least fifteen of them who were old enough to hide their Silver, and who were maybe even older than Kulika, judging by the sensitivity with which they reacted to their surroundings. Kulika had expected the newbies, but it was an unpleasant surprise to find this many experienced Silver allied with Bartholomew. Their presence wouldn't be enough to control the new ones, but it was definitely enough to start a war.

'Your crew's grown a bit,' Kulika said to Bartholomew, breaking the silence while the others warily watched her, watched the bloody scene at the foot of the stairs, and watched their glorious leader presiding over it all.

'You're naïve to think this is the full complement,' he replied. 'But this is their justice to exact, not yours.'

'Article seven?' she asked, stalling while she tried to work out how best to play the situation.

'You're not crew,' said the woman with the knife. It was dripping blood onto the back of the man's head, but he wasn't reacting to the sensation. From what Kulika could hear from her spot by the door, he wasn't even breathing. Whatever the woman had done to him with that blade, it was serious enough that he hadn't healed yet. Hearts could take hours to heal, brains sometimes a day, and that was if the Silver was older and stronger. If the guy on the floor was a new convert, it could take a week, if he ever woke up at all.

This is how Bartholomew enforced his power. He didn't get his hands dirty; he let other people dirty their hands for him. That was how he liked things. It was in all the books, that quote of his.

Since he had dipped his hands in muddy water, and must be a pyrate, it was better being a commander than a common man.

Kulika was certain he'd never said those words himself – he would never be so straightforwardly supercilious – but they were the kind of words other people could put in his mouth easily. They suited him well.

'You're not a part of this,' said the woman with the knife.

'Unless you want to be,' Bartholomew invited from the balcony above.

Kulika felt her lip curl involuntarily with disgust. 'I don't want any part of this.'

'He broke the covenant,' Bartholomew said, gesturing to the broken and bloody man on the floor. 'He was *disloyal.* You've done much worse than this to people much less deserving than him.'

She couldn't deny the accusation, because it was true. Back on the *Royal Fortune*, Bartholomew's flagship, she'd spilled enough blood to drown them all. Some of that bloodshed had been ordered by Bartholomew, but Kulika would be lying if she said that she hadn't wanted the carnage. Revelled in it, even. She'd learned the craft of death at Bartholomew's feet, and she'd learned it well enough to yearn for it when she was denied her fill. Perhaps she'd developed an appetite for it over time, or perhaps she'd simply recognised – as all the crew had eventually – that they could buy Bartholomew's favour with brutality.

'You used to understand what loyalty meant,' Bartholomew continued, turning his back on the mob to make his way down the stairs. 'Then the great Baron Drake came along, a guest in my house, and you stole away with him in the middle of the day, abandoning your captain and your crew.' He turned the corner of the staircase so he was walking towards them now, descending the stairs with the grace of a debutante at a cotillion. 'Back on ship, we used to have a word for that.'

'It's not mutiny if you've served out your commitment,' Kulika said.

'Oh, yes. Article nine. *No man shall talk of breaking up their way of living till each has a share of £1,000.*'

'I made you a thousand times that amount, at least.'

'But how much more did you owe me for what I made you?' Bartholomew asked. He was at the bottom of the stairs now, stepping carelessly over the unconscious man as though he were a sleeping dog, then crossing the floor to stand face to face with Kulika. 'Look at you,' he breathed, standing too close, so close that she could feel the heat of him. She wanted to step away, but that would be the worst kind of surrender in front of his followers, so she stood firm. 'Without me, you'd be three hundred years dead in childbirth for the whelps of some grey-bearded coloniser. With me, you are a finely-honed weapon of teeth and muscle and bone. Are you truly so ungrateful for what you've become?'

'I became what I had to in order to survive,' she said quietly. 'But you take more than you give.'

Bartholomew snatched her hand up in his own, turning her palm to the sky so he could trace its lines with his fingertips. He pressed his thumb gently to the spot where his black mark had once been inked and whispered, 'Only because you always discard what I give you. I'm offering you the whole world. We're taking it, Kulika, and I want you at my right hand when we do. Don't dismiss that without giving it some consideration.'

The words sounded as though he meant them, which threw Kulika. She'd expected threats, she'd expected recriminations, but she hadn't expected sincerity, nor had she expected such a bald statement of his intentions. She'd worked out that he was building an army, because that was hard to miss, and she'd guessed that he was going to force a revelation of the Silver to humanity, because that was exactly the kind of chaos on which Bartholomew had always thrived. What she hadn't anticipated was that he would have set his sights so wide. When he'd offered her the world, she hadn't taken it literally.

That had clearly been a mistake.

'Think on it,' he said. Then he stepped back and surveyed his followers with a smile, raising his voice to address them. 'In the meantime, we have business.'

The crew cheered.

'Read the charges, Bella,' said Bartholomew.

A curvy blonde, dressed for a ball in a floor-length red

satin gown, stepped forward and started reading, incongruously, from a couple of bright yellow sticky notes that had been stuck together. 'Alex – the accused of this crew – turned Leo Silver, but he didn't take responsibility for him in accordance with Article fifteen. Instead, he allowed him to leave the property in breach of Article fourteen, and Leo then used his Silver abilities off the property and in front of a human, in breach of Article twenty, all of this being done without the approval of the captain that's required by Article twelve.'

'Jessamy,' said Bartholomew. 'Your testimony.'

The woman with the knife turned to Bartholomew. 'It's like I told you, Captain,' she said, pushing her hair away from her eyes with the back of one bloody hand. 'I thought Alex got your permission to have Leo leave the property. I think Leo even thought he had permission, because me and Alex were supposed to go and drop off some bottles of blood with him this morning so he could stay home in Oklahoma a while. Then it looks like he was crushing on the girl next door, and he bit her, then tried to heal her and… Well, you've seen the bodies. You've seen the video, even.'

'And luckily for you,' Bartholomew said to her, 'I've seen you on the security video as well, so I know that you're telling the truth. Otherwise, I might find that story a little hard to believe.'

Jessamy visibly relaxed, her white-knuckled grip on the knife slackening as her shoulders fell.

'And the sentence?' Bartholomew asked, looking around the room now, his gaze touching briefly on the face of every single person gathered there.

All except Kulika. Bartholomew might be pretending that she wasn't in the room, but she suspected that, now that she was here, at least some of this performance was for her benefit.

Join us, or watch what'll happen if you don't.

'Death,' said an anonymous Silver in the crowd.

'Death,' said another.

Bartholomew smiled, and it wasn't long before the entire room was chanting the word, loud and demanding.

'As you've spoken,' he said, 'so it shall be, by the code. Jessamy, if you please.'

The woman with the knife grimaced momentarily before hiding her expression – not quickly enough – then crouched down with the knife in her hand beside the unconscious man. At least, Kulika hoped he was unconscious, given what happened next.

First, Jessamy rolled the man onto his back. Next, she pulled up his bloodied T-shirt to expose his naked stomach. Then, with the practised skill of someone who had done this before, she sliced into his abdomen, stuck her hand in up to the wrist, rooted around a bit, stuck the knife in again, and finally emerged with her bloody hands full of what Kulika judged to be about a third of his liver, which Jessamy brought over and presented to Bartholomew.

The others piled in on the body then, each drawing a knife from somewhere about their person or borrowing one from a friend. For a while, there was nothing but a huddle of people surrounding a nexus of wet, sawing sounds that Kulika wished she wasn't hearing. When they all pulled back and returned to their places at the edge of the room, each of the crew was holding a bloody mass in their hands and there was nothing left of the body but a smear of blood and hair on the floor.

'What now?' Kulika asked Bartholomew, covering her nausea with bravado. It turned out that, after a hundred years away, she was no longer hardened to such bloodthirstiness.

'You feed him to the alligators?'

'Not the gators, no,' he said. 'We're more frugal than that. Waste not, want not. Blood is blood, after all.'

With a savage smile, he raised the dripping fistful of liver to his mouth. Then, with his eyes locked on Kulika's, he bit down. Apparently this was the cue that the rest of them had been waiting for, because now they raised their own excised pounds of flesh to their mouths, with varying degrees of relish. But still, whether they held muscle or sinew, organ or bone, they followed Bartholomew's lead without question.

Piece by bloody piece, they ate him.

12

THE NEXT MORNING, Kulika was still at the mansion, though not by choice. She'd tried to make an exit after seeing Bartholomew's new cult in action, but then he'd said, 'Stay another night,' and the scores of cannibalistic, blood-smeared Silver who now comprised his crew had taken that as an order. She hadn't been offered the opportunity to refuse.

It wasn't until she woke that she discovered that not only was her suite in the mansion right next to Bartholomew's, but the two shared a connecting door. She'd flopped straight into the grand four-poster bed without washing or changing her clothes, not because she was still keeping vigil – though she probably should have been – but because she couldn't find the duffel bag she'd brought with her. When she went looking for it that morning in what she'd thought was a cupboard, she found something worse.

The door didn't lock from Kulika's side.

'Good morning,' Bartholomew greeted her as he pulled the inner door to his suite open. His, Kulika noticed, was fitted with a lock and key. 'Did you sleep well?'

'I did,' she said with irritation, 'but only because I didn't know about this door.'

He laughed dismissively. 'You'll feel better when you've eaten. Come down to the dining room and grab something from the buffet.'

'You lay on a buffet breakfast, now?' When she'd lived here a century ago, in much more modest quarters, it had been all porridge and rice and help yourself to a ladleful from the pot on the fire, and count yourself lucky if you get there before it's all gone. Yesterday, she'd eaten only a cereal bar from her jacket pocket for breakfast, then a sandwich that she'd scrounged from the kitchen of the new building for lunch, and nothing for dinner. After the theatrical demise of Alex, she'd found she'd rather lost her appetite. This morning, it had come back with a vengeance.

'You might have noticed that there are more of us to cater for nowadays,' Bartholomew said.

'I wouldn't have thought they'd be hungry after yesterday, after all that protein,' Kulika replied darkly, her stomach churning again at the memory.

'Oh, don't be like that,' he laughed. How was he *still* laughing, after everything she'd seen?

'I came here for information about Evita Khalyed,' she said. 'I don't know what you were trying to prove with that display last night—'

'So sanctimonious,' Bartholomew laughed again. 'As though meting out justice isn't your entire purpose. I've heard the whispers coming out of the old country about what happens to Drake's prisoners. Those captives in his basement, the ones that are supposed to be under his protection during their sentences, how many of them live long enough to serve out their terms? He's nothing more than a rogue executioner, and you're his enabler.'

'The people he punishes are serial killers,' Kulika said, in a more defensive tone than the one she had been aiming for. It made her sound weak, and weakness wasn't something she ever wanted to show to Bartholomew.

'Silver serial killers, who've openly killed humans, yes?'

'Yes.'

'But that's not their *crime* in the eyes of the Primus and your baron, is it? Their crime is that by openly killing humans, they've risked revealing the existence of the Silver to humanity. What they really are is oath-breakers. So my question is: how are their crimes any different from the breaches of the Articles that Alex committed? Didn't he deserve his punishment more, not less, than the edict-breakers that your Drake murders cold-heartedly in their prisons beneath his mansion?'

'What the Primus and the baron consider their crimes aren't necessarily the same,' Kulika said, too defensively again.

'Different means, same ends?' Bartholomew asked.

'It's too early for sophisms,' Kulika replied irritably.

This was the problem with Bartholomew: he'd knot you up in your own arguments until you found yourself agreeing with him by accident. Then he had you trapped.

He laughed. *Again.* 'The point is that you've done worse to crew members who've done less, if not under Drake's orders then under mine.'

'But I'm not your enforcer anymore.'

'Just answer me this,' he insisted. 'How is what happened last night any different to the deaths you dealt to mutineers back on ship?'

'We didn't use to eat them!' Kulika yelled.

'Then we were wasteful,' he replied lightly, as though that were the end of the discussion. Kulika was left with the uneasy feeling she always had at the end of a debate with

Bartholomew: he'd won, and she'd lost, but she wasn't sure how or what. 'Come and have breakfast,' he said, heading past her to her bedroom door, then out into the corridor. 'No hunks of dead meat, I promise.'

She couldn't believe he was joking about it. No, actually, she could believe it. It just chilled her blood.

'You've forgotten who you are,' he said, then he turned his back to her and started walking down the stairs.

'No, I'd forgotten who *you* are,' Kulika said quietly. She'd been so focused on not becoming trapped here again, bound by Bartholomew's covenant, that she'd forgotten about the slow creep of immorality that infected everyone in close proximity to him. She'd forgotten how thoroughly you could lose yourself in the example of the people around you, and end up unconsciously following their lead. When the person leading was Bartholomew, that influence was beyond dangerous. As last night had demonstrated all too clearly, it could be fatal.

If Kulika could have picked up Evita Khalyed's trail from anyone else, then she would have done. As it was, she had no other options, so she followed Bartholomew down to the ground floor, intent on making him surrender the information she needed, and hoping desperately that she wouldn't have to follow him any further than that.

There didn't seem to be anyone else around in the mansion, but then it was late, the heat of the day already pervading the mansion. Anyone sensible, who hadn't been sleeping off days of overexertion and undernourishment, would have taken their breakfast hours earlier.

'I don't know why you're keeping me here,' Kulika said, close on Bartholomew's heels, 'but if you think that what you did last night is going to make me stay, then you're wrong.'

'Am I though?' he said, stopping at the foot of the stairs and turning to meet her as she reached the bottom step. 'Don't you remember what it was like on the ship? The fire, the fury, the blood. You loved it, Kulika. You can't pretend that you didn't. You know what it's like to yield to your soul's call to savagery, and you know the acceptance you can find from being around other people who hear it too. Or have you forgotten that I was there when you came into your strength?'

It was a day that Kulika had tried very hard to forget. Sometimes – not always, but sometimes – newly-turned Silver could go a bit... wrong. Most of them, if cared for properly, and if attentively fed with blood by their makers, could transition to life as one of the Silver with minimal danger to themselves or others around them.

Bartholomew had been neither proper nor attentive. That wasn't the way he'd run his ship.

When Kulika had wakened from Bartholomew's draining bite and found herself ravenous for blood in the middle of a boarding action in the waters off Sierra Leone, the crew of the prize hadn't stood a chance. She'd blazed through them like a hurricane, a mindless creature using powers she hadn't realised she'd had without any thought at all, driven only by her thirst. Bartholomew liked to say that the crew hadn't even had time to surrender, but Kulika knew that wasn't true. She remembered their pleas. She hadn't heard them in the moment, but they'd come back to her later, and every night since when she closed her eyes and tried to sleep. She knew full well that she'd killed unarmed men who'd offered her no resistance at all.

'And that was just the beginning,' Bartholomew whispered, leaning close. 'You forget how well I know you, and how well I know your vices. All I want to do is let you fulfil your darkest desires.'

'Why, Bartholomew?' she asked. 'Why do you even care?'

'I made you,' he said. 'You were mine. I lost you, and I have lost too much in recent months. Then here you are, falling into my lap again like a gift in the hour of my greatest need.' He reached out to cup her jaw with his hand, caressing her cheek with his thumb like a mother would her child's. His eyes were drinking in every inch of her, shining with hungry pride. 'I would have you back at my side,' he whispered. 'I see your reluctance, but you don't see my determination. You will be mine again, Kulika, not because I'll force it on you, but because you know that only I have the power to give you everything you want.'

'And if what I want is freedom?' she asked, stepping away and out of his reach.

'Do you have freedom now?' Bartholomew asked derisively. 'You haven't broken free, Kulika, you've just traded one captain for another. You'll have a better life on my crew than on his.'

'I like my life fine the way it is.'

'And when the Revelation comes?' Bartholomew asked softly. The bottom dropped out of Kulika's stomach. 'You know it won't be long now. We're prepared. Drake is not.'

'You're not prepared,' Kulika spat. 'You've just filled your mansion with untested new Silver who can't control themselves.'

'But they do, and they will, or they'll answer to me. They bear my covenant. They know what that means; you saw it yesterday. They're loyal.'

'I have my own loyalties,' Kulika said.

'And when the Silver are known to the world, how is an alliance with a washed-up baron who's defied his king going to protect you? The Primus will kill him, along with everyone who follows him, including you. You know this as well as I do.'

'Baron Drake has never defied the Primus.'

'Now you're lying to me?' Bartholomew said with disappointment. 'I can always tell when you're lying, Kulika.'

She looked at Bartholomew, at the intensity of his gaze and the determined set of his jaw, and she knew that her own matched his. He was as determined to keep her here as she was to leave.

'I'm going back to Baron Drake,' she said.

'He called this morning,' Bartholomew replied casually.

Kulika's stomach twisted. The baron had probably been trying to get hold of her, but of course he couldn't, because Bartholomew was holding her phone hostage. Probably for the best, because what would she have told him? That she was going to let both him and his lover die because she couldn't bear to be back under Bartholomew's thumb again? Now that she imagined relaying that to Baron Drake, it sounded terribly selfish. She was his head of security. It was her job to give her life to protect his. She had a duty to him, and she was failing it.

'We came to an arrangement,' Bartholomew said.

Kulika was surprised, perhaps even a little scared by that. Bartholomew might have been happy to barter with the lives of his crew, but that had never been the baron's style. He understood the value of autonomy. At least, Kulika had thought he did.

'What kind of an arrangement?' she asked.

'If you stay until Monday, I'll tell you everything I know about Evita Khalyed. Otherwise…'

Otherwise, she knew, she would get nothing at all.

It was Thursday. She could manage four more days for the sake of the baron's life, couldn't she?

'And what do I have to do during those four days?' Kulika asked suspiciously. 'What do I have to sign?'

'Nothing at all,' Bartholomew said, walking to the breakfast room doors on the other side of the hall. To get there, he crossed the bloodstained spot on the floorboards from the night before – one of many, Kulika saw. He flung the doors open and said, 'Just enjoy my hospitality for a few days. That's all.'

She hadn't agreed to Bartholomew's deal, not in so many words, but – tentatively – Kulika followed him.

In the breakfast room, the glass doors that opened out onto the porch were shut now, keeping out the heat of the day. Fans spun lazily from the ceiling, but there was no air conditioning to cool the breeze, and the old house was hot.

'Help yourself from the buffet,' Bartholomew said, sweeping an arm towards the wall to their left. On one side of the space, a table was stacked high with pastries, cut fruit and bread. On the other, a line of a dozen humans was being arrayed against the wall by a few of the young Silver. The humans all had their hands behind their backs. It took a moment for Kulika to spot the restraints bolted into the wall and understand their purpose.

'This isn't how we do things,' she said, backing away.

'Isn't it?' Bartholomew asked blithely. 'Well, with so many mouths to feed, it's how *we* do things.'

'Then you can do them without me,' Kulika said, walking clear through the room and out through the porch to the pool. Maybe a few laps would clear her head.

'You can't hold out forever,' Bartholomew called after her.

But that was where he was wrong. Since she'd left the mansion, Kulika had taught herself the one thing that was beyond Bartholomew's understanding: self-discipline. She could keep her appetites in check, and until she could find a more ethical blood source, that was exactly what she would do.

IN THE BLOOD cellar, time passed slowly, and Quick was growing impatient.

The bags of food kept coming, filled with the same fare every time. Quick kept looking for exit routes, but finding none. No one wanted to talk to her, too conscious of lost friends to risk making any more.

No one except Louis.

To pass the time during the long, empty hours, he lay next to her and whispered outrageous stories about his huge family, spread all across the South. Quick was sure they were more fiction than fact, and maybe that was why she liked them; the truth felt too bleak in this hole in the ground. In return, Quick told Louis how she'd met Evita, and recounted all the escapades they'd had travelling around the world together. Eventually, though, even those stories became infected with the knowledge that Evita had likely died in this place, and that the same fate would claim Quick before too long. When that reality struck her, Louis just slung an arm around her shoulders and pretended he didn't notice that she was crying.

Then the vampires came for him, and eleven others. At

first, Quick thought maybe Louis had got his wish, and they were taking him to the Casting, but that wasn't it. That wouldn't happen until tomorrow, he said. They needed blood, they said. There was a system, he said, and it was his turn, so he let them take him up through the hatch.

An hour later, the others came back.

Louis never did.

After that, Quick didn't make any more friends.

The blood cellar was disturbed on Thursday evening by the screaming thuds of a hell of a lot more people being flung down through the hatch. It was early enough in the evening that Quick had not yet managed to fall asleep, though that probably had less to do with the hour and more to do with the fact that she was lying on dirt in a stifling hot basement with a hundred other people, at least half of whom snored or screamed in their sleep.

When the proper screaming started, Quick sat bolt upright and prepared to run towards the blanket line – though god knew that wouldn't be enough to catch so many zombies – but Xiaoyu grabbed her arm and pulled her back to her sleeping spot.

'It's the Casting tomorrow,' she said. 'All of them are human.'

'So many, though?'

'There are always a lot on Thursdays,' said Xiaoyu, but she looked increasingly worried as more and more people were pushed into the cellar, wearing flimsy outfits or underwear or, in some cases, nothing at all. 'They have the big party in the middle of the week, then they sleep it off with the humans in their rooms, party some more on Thursday, then they need somewhere to put them all to cool down before Friday.'

'That happened to you?' Quick asked.

'To most of us,' she said, which didn't really answer the question.

The newcomers were being tossed in on top of each other now, some rolling across the dirt floor to thud against the walls, some trying to push their way back up through the hatch, but most of them just trying not to get crushed in the wide heap that was forming under the hatch.

'Not this many, though,' said Xiaoyu as she stood from her watch. 'Something's up.'

Without discussing it further, the existing cellar-dwellers got to their feet and shifted into a line that cut the cellar in two, with the bathroom area and bedding behind them, and the newcomers in front.

For the next little while, they did nothing but watch. The fluorescents had been off when the hatch opened, and the newcomers were making enough of a racket to mask any sounds of movement from the far end of the cellar, so they hadn't noticed that there were people already in residence. All of their attention was focused on the hatch as more and more people poured down on top of them. It took maybe ten minutes of solid, frenzied activity before the people who were inclined to try and fight their way out off the hatch had been subdued, and the rest had realised there was no point in following their lead.

There was a whole crowd of new additions by the time they were done. It was just as well that Quick had sworn off making new friends, because none of them looked like they would welcome it.

The hatch slammed shut, plunging them all into darkness. After a few seconds, someone in the far end of the cellar flicked the light switch on.

One of the newcomers, a college-age man who looked like he spent too much time in the gym, said, 'Who the fuck are you?'

One of the existing cellar residents squared up to him and said, unhelpfully, 'Who the fuck are *you*?'

Then the fighting started. Xiaoyu ended it with a whistle that was loud enough in the echoing space to have everyone covering their ears.

'Knock it off!' she yelled. 'Food's there,' she said, pointing at the stack of paper bags in the centre of the cellar. 'Bathroom's there.' She pointed to the corner. 'Welcome to the blood bank. Now settle the fuck down.'

And that, more or less, was the end of that. There were other questions – how do we get out of here (you don't), are we going to die (almost certainly), and who put you in charge (don't fucking start with me) – but soon enough, the newcomers stopped fighting.

As Quick had learned, there was no point.

14

KULIKA SPENT THE rest of Thursday in frustrating inaction. She couldn't get back into the block, because it was full of new Silver. She couldn't leave the premises, because Bartholomew's guards were on high alert. And she couldn't get information from any of the Silver about even the most innocuous thing, let alone the identity of the mysterious *Jane* whose card was apparently missing from the deck in Bartholomew's desk, because each and every one of them ignored her when she tried to talk to them. It was becoming clear that an order had been issued by their captain, and the crew was determined to obey it.

Having run out of other options, she even tried speaking to Bartholomew himself, *voluntarily*, but he was locked up in the mansion's wine cellar again on some secret business that Kulika couldn't get even a sniff of, however hard she'd tried, both metaphorically and literally. Her sense of smell was pretty good for a Silver her age, but she still couldn't pick up on any unexpected scents in the mansion, in its kitchen, or around the door to the wine cellar.

Feeling frustrated, and more than a little thirsty for the blood she was trying to pretend she didn't need, she grabbed

120

a can of beer from the unnecessarily extravagant bar in the back garden and cracked it open on the porch.

It helped her to be somewhere familiar, however much the view had changed. Out here, in the place she had often retreated to think during the bad old days, maybe she could come up with a plan.

'Heard you've been asking around about Jane,' said Bayly, surveying her as he came out of the house to join her on the porch.

'How long have you been here?' she asked. She'd been searching for him all day with no luck, and she hadn't heard a car pull up.

'Stayed over last night,' he said. 'Got a room upstairs, same as you. Not as grand, of course.'

'You could have come to find me earlier.'

'No,' Bayly said quietly, looking down at where his elbows rested on the porch railing. 'I couldn't.'

Which was as good as saying that Bartholomew wouldn't have let him.

Kulika asked, 'Do you know who this Jane is that Bartholomew's being so secretive about?'

'Nope,' Bayly replied.

'Are you saying that because Bartholomew told you to?'

Bayly just shrugged.

'We didn't use to lie to each other, Bayly.'

'We used to be on the same crew,' he pointed out.

Which meant Kulika would get no more from Bayly than she had from any of the other Silver on the property. That was irritating, but not unexpected. After all, he had Enzo to think of.

There was noise coming from the mansion behind them now, voices calling to each other and music cranking up in the anticipation of some kind of party. They seemed to happen most days here.

'You were here last night, then,' Kulika said. 'For the… whatever that was.'

She hadn't seen Bayly in the cannibalistic crowd, but she'd felt him there. She'd hoped she was wrong, that Bartholomew wouldn't have been able to induce Bayly to take part, but she knew their erstwhile captain wouldn't have accepted anything less. One way or another, he made his followers follow him.

'That Silver, he was just a kid,' said Kulika.

'They're all kids, the new ones,' Bayly said. 'Alex was stupid.'

'Explain.'

Bayly sighed, and the sound was heavy. 'Kid's a barman in town. He turned this other kid called Leo, just a teenager. Too young for all this.' He waved a hand over his shoulder at the mansion, but it was unnecessary. Kulika knew what *all this* was. She'd been barely out of her teens when she'd lived it for herself, and still she hadn't lived long enough to enter Bartholomew's world. She wasn't sure that anyone could. 'And Leo was in love,' Bayly added.

'Silvered?' Kulika asked.

'The minute he went home to see his girl,' Bayly confirmed. 'So now Bartholomew's got a fresh Silver out of the mansion without his leave, still so new he has to wear sunglasses to hide his eyes, and Leo loses control. Bites the girl, drains her, tries to heal her and fails. She dies. He dies, killed by the bond to his love, so *now* Bartholomew's got two bodies, one of them Silver and the other human with a silver palm print on her skin, from where the kid tried to heal her through the bond.'

'Oh, god,' Kulika interjected. 'Is that why he's down in the wine cellar?'

Bayly tapped his nose, which as good as confirmed it.

'And, to top it all,' he went on, 'he's got surveillance video from the house, inside and out. The kid moving at Silver speed outside when he snatches the girl, the two of them inside the house, him biting her and trying to heal her. The whole thing. *Assets*, he says, but he's pissed off about it all the same, and someone has to pay for it, to keep order. With Leo dead, Alex gets the blame for letting him off the property, as if we don't bend that rule all the time. So here we are.'

For a man of so few words, it was a long speech, rapidly spoken. That was just one indicator to Kulika that Bayly was more than a little upset about it.

'You knew the kid?' she asked.

'I knew Alex. They're shits, these new ones. All of them, running around poking their sunglasses where they don't belong. But, just marginally, Alex was less of a shit than the others.'

'You ate him,' said Kulika. 'Part of him, anyway.'

Bayly's face shuttered. 'It's so they can't come back from it,' he said with a shrug.

'He wasn't coming back anyway, Bayly. We both know that. And even if he did happen to be some miraculously regenerative youngster, there's no reason *you* had to be the ones to eat him. You said they feed the mistakes to the alligators.'

'He says eating them makes us stronger.'

'What it's making you all is *insane*.'

'He says the power is in the blood, and consuming our dead keeps the power in the crew.'

'Of course he does,' Kulika said, throwing up her hands. 'He's just building a new vampire mythology on land to replace the pirate mythology he had on the water. You do realise that, don't you?'

'I'm older than you, Kulika,' Bayly said gruffly. 'I'm not part of the sunglasses brigade.'

It was true that Bayly's transformation pre-dated Kulika's own – he'd actually been there when the old pirate capital of Port Royal sank in the earthquake of 1692 – but apparently wisdom and age weren't that closely linked, because he was being an idiot.

'Get out of here,' Kulika said quietly. 'If you can see what he's doing so clearly, then just go.'

'And have them do to me or Enzo what they just did to Alex?' Bayly said incredulously. 'Bartholomew has them all believing that if one of us leaves without being consumed, it'll diminish our power. And he has trackers, good enough to find us anywhere in the world and bring us back to him. You saw them in there yesterday.'

'I saw some older Silver, but I didn't recognise them.'

'You wouldn't. A couple of them came up in the Gold Rush and stayed out west until Bartholomew started calling people this way. The rest came over from Japan and Russia, or down from Canada.'

'But why?' Kulika couldn't understand why so many ancient vampires would be flocking to join Bartholomew. 'It's not as though he's got anything special to offer.'

'Hasn't he?' Bayly asked.

'Has he?' Kulika asked.

But Bayly didn't answer. He just said, '*You* should get out of here, though.'

'Not without finding Evita Khalyed.'

'The longer you stay here, the harder he'll make it for you to leave.'

'I'm here until Monday, and that's it.'

'He's holding out on you until then?' Bayly asked.

'Yes,' Kulika admitted.

'It's not in your nature to sit and wait.'

'It's not in your nature to *eat people*, Bayly. I'm just doing the same as you: what I have to.'

'No, you're giving him time to change your mind,' Bayly said irritably. 'Just go. While you still can.'

'If I didn't know any better, I'd think you were trying to get rid of me.'

Kulika had been joking when the words left her mouth, but they landed in a way she hadn't expected. Bayly's lips twitched, then he looked down at the porch railing as though he were hiding his face.

'What aren't you telling me?' she asked.

'Nothing,' he replied defensively. 'Nothing you don't know. It's just… This is the line, Kulika. If you stay for tomorrow night…'

'Why? What's so special about tomorrow?' Bartholomew had been doing weekly Castings, she knew. She'd picked up that much from the chatter around the mansion. As rare as Castings were on her side of the world, they seemed almost run-of-the-mill here, so that couldn't be it.

'Everyone's here,' Bayly said, lowering his voice to a whisper. 'Everyone who has humans to bring is bringing them now, either to turn or to add to the blood bank, and Bartholomew's sworn humans are going the same way. He's tying up loose ends, then the rest of the crew is coming this weekend after… Look, that's what this is all about,' he said urgently. 'It's happening, and it's happening now.'

'What is?'

'He's got *assets*. The recordings.'

'What are you talking about?' Kulika asked, not following his train of thought at all.

'We're coming out. *Now*.'

A heavy weight settled in the pit of Kulika's stomach as she finally caught on.

They'd been fighting this battle in the UK for years now, half of the Silver wanting to reveal themselves to humanity and take charge, and the other half wanting to stay in the dark, where they felt safer. Over there, the Primus had always won out and kept them hidden, but if Bartholomew forced the point here in the States, the rest of the world wouldn't have much choice but to follow.

Wasn't that what Bartholomew had always wanted? More Silver followers.

If Bayly was right, he was about to have all the followers in the world.

15

NO ONE IN the blood bank slept well that night, which is to say that they slept even worse than they usually did. With the influx of new people, the atmosphere was restless. They were fighting over blankets, and food, and the crying and screaming just seemed to get louder and louder as the night went on.

When the hatch was flung open on Friday morning, Quick felt like she'd barely slept at all, but neither the newcomers' sleepless night nor their injuries were slowing them down. They crowded under the opening, clawing for it and shouting to be let out, as though the night had never intervened between their arrival and now.

'Quiet!' someone yelled from above the hatch. The voice sounded depressingly familiar. 'We need bodies. Where's Xiaoyu?'

In the spot beside Quick, Xiaoyu went very still. She'd taken Louis's place beside Quick without either of them discussing it, but that meant she'd had to abandon her watch of the hatch. She clearly hadn't been expecting it to open so soon.

'Back!' the guy yelled from upstairs. 'Move away from

the hatch or I'll break bones when I push you. Got it?'

The newcomers backed away slowly. They were shortly replaced by a single familiar vampire jumping down into the space, his gaze roaming through the darkness until it landed on Xiaoyu.

It was Monty.

'Shit,' Xiaoyu murmured, then she got quickly to her feet and asked, 'How many?' walking towards Monty as though by doing so she could shield the others in the cellar from his scrutiny.

'Twelve, for starters,' Monty said. 'Full house today.'

'Are they here for the Casting?' she asked.

'Sort of. Look, less questions, more volunteering. The redhead from the other night,' Monty said. 'She needs to go up.'

Quick's blood ran cold. He was talking about her.

'You already fed from her,' said Xiaoyu.

'She still needs to go, her and anyone else new this week who hasn't gone up yet. Make up the numbers with whoever. You pick them. None of last night's lot, though, not yet.'

Xiaoyu turned and walked back towards Quick, grim-faced. 'Sorry, Red,' she said quietly.

'He's going to bite me again, isn't he?' she asked, her hand flying to the still-raw wound at her throat.

'Probably not him, but one of them will. Nothing I can do except come along for the ride.'

It didn't take long for Xiaoyu to find enough people to make up the full dozen Monty demanded, picking those who were most able to spare the blood. By the time they made their way to the hatch, two vampires Quick didn't recognise were in the hole keeping the newcomers back, while another stood under the hatch ready to help Quick and the others up. Monty had disappeared.

'It's not so bad,' Xiaoyu said reassuringly – which would have been more convincing if Quick wasn't still sore from the first bite – then the vampire hoisted her out of the hatch. The others followed, leaving Quick until last.

Upstairs, it was quiet. Maybe the other vampires were sleeping it off, or maybe they weren't home. Either way, there were just the three of them there to corral Quick and her cellar-mates through the communal showers on the ground floor – there was no regard for modesty in the blood bank – then into the walk-through wardrobe next door. The clothes were mismatched and worn, chucked in disordered piles, but they were at least clean, and after a little sifting Quick found a loose cotton dress in a size that would fit her. There were no shoes.

When they emerged from the building, blinking in the morning sunshine, the grass was dry and prickly under Quick's bare feet. It had to be mid-morning, judging by the angle of the sun, and it was already hotter than Quick could bear. More than a couple of minutes out in this and her skin would be lobster red.

'Hurry it up,' said one of the vampires in the back, then Monty reappeared from around the side of the building and took Quick's upper arm in a firm grip.

'Look, Quick,' he said in a hushed voice. 'I'm sorry about —'

'*Sorry*?' Quick replied incredulously, twisting as he marched her across the lawn so she could look him in the face. 'What for, Monty? For biting me? For lying to me? Or for throwing me in a cellar with a hundred other people so you and your friends can slowly drain me to death?'

He changed, then. He was one of those men, at his core. Before she'd snapped back, he'd been all apologies and reconciliation, but the moment he saw she wasn't going to buy it, he brought out his teeth.

'I am more dangerous than you can possibly imagine,' he said softly. His words carried all the more threat for the gentleness with which they were delivered, but Quick was tired and sore and she'd been pushed to her limit.

'If you're going to kill me,' she said, 'then do me a favour and kill me quick.'

'I probably will tonight,' he said irritably. 'You're going to the Casting.'

If Monty hadn't been holding Quick up, she would have fallen.

'I'm what?' she asked.

'You're going to the Casting,' Monty repeated.

Nausea tugged at the back of Quick's throat. She remembered everything Louis and Xiaoyu had told her about her chances of turning vampire or zombie, and suddenly being slowly bled to death over a period of weeks didn't seem like such a bad way to go. At least it meant she wouldn't have to die tonight.

'I'm sorry, Quick,' Monty said, 'but you haven't given me much of a choice.'

'Really?' she said incredulously. 'So when you lied and told me Jensen Mardh had been here, that you could help me find him, that wasn't a choice? Because I was ready to leave that bar and get right on my plane back to the UK until you *chose* to tell me that.'

'Jensen was here,' Monty said. 'I didn't lie about that.'

'What?'

'We tried to turn him. It didn't work.'

'You mean he turned into a zombie?'

'Don't use that word,' he said, shushing her as he looked around at the others to check if they'd heard. From the pissed-off looks on their faces, Quick guessed they had. 'I mean he's *gone*, like a lot of the people in your little pack of cards.'

'And Evita?' Quick whispered, tears pooling in her eyes. She'd known her friend was most likely dead, and had almost resigned herself to it, but now that she was having it confirmed—

'*Don't* say that name,' Monty said under his breath. 'Ever. I mean it. It'll get you killed here.'

'If I'm dying tonight anyway, then what does it matter?'

They'd reached the house now, but Monty pulled Quick to a stop as the others filed inside.

'I'll be there in a minute,' he told them, then he pushed her back up against the porch railings and held her there, pinning her upper arms with his hands.

'Look, Quick,' he said. 'I know this hasn't exactly gone to plan, but the boss says either you're going to the Casting tonight or you're dead. I'm trying to save you here, but I need a little cooperation. The others who are up for the Casting, they've had time with the people who're sponsoring them. They've built some kind of relationship, at least. But we don't have that, and without it I won't be able to turn you Silver. So either you get stubborn about it and die, or you try to find some kind of positive feeling for me so you at least have a chance of living through the Casting, because that's what it takes.'

'What are you talking about?' she said.

'I know you've seen what happens when we try to turn someone Silver and it goes wrong. You just said it.'

With a grimace, Quick remembered the zombie in the cellar.

'Yeah, well,' Monty continued. 'That's what happens when there's not enough, shall we say *tender feelings*, between the Silver and the person they're fixing to turn.'

Quick's grimace increased.

'Sure, look at me like I'm a monster,' Monty said. 'It's your funeral. Or not, because you've probably guessed by now that we're not really in the business of bothering with last rites. Either way, if you decide to hate me, the Casting won't work, and you'll be *gone* by the weekend.'

'I didn't decide to hate you,' she said acidly. '*You* decided when you brought me here.'

Monty shook her, thumping her head back against the porch railings before pinning her there once more. 'It's my neck on the line here, too, you know,' he hissed. 'You think I'm not going to look a fool if I can't turn you? So just drop the hostility, all right? You were practically drooling at me back at the bar, so why can't you just do that again?'

'I didn't know you were a vampire back then. Or that you were… like this. And I was drunk.'

'I can get you drunk,' Monty offered.

'But you can't take back the rest.'

'Then what *can* I do?'

Quick looked at his beautiful face, his flawless skin, his shining eyes, but she could no longer find in his features the friendly barman who'd served her three nights ago, and for so many weeks previously during her searches for Evita. A few days ago, she'd looked at him and seen a way out of her misery, if just for a moment. Perhaps he had been no more than a consolation prize to her, but Quick had *wanted* the man she'd thought he was. Now that man was just… gone.

But he did still have one thing she wanted.

Needed.

'You can tell me about Evita,' she said.

Monty went still. He glanced at the porch door, then looked around carefully before lowering his voice even further to say, 'Gesture of goodwill?'

'At the very least, it might make me hate you less.'

'And that would be good for both of us,' he said calculatingly.

'Right.'

He licked his lips nervously, clearly caught in indecision, and Quick was reminded how young he was. What an idiot she'd been to follow him out here. Really, what had she been expecting? Not a vampire, certainly, but the idea that this kid would have anything useful to tell her, or any allure that was worth risking her flight home over, let alone her life—

But she couldn't think that way. If she did, apparently she was dead.

Then Monty whispered, 'You should be asking about Jane.' He spoke so quietly that Quick found herself involuntarily squinting to make out the words, as though that was going to help.

'Pardon me?'

'Jane,' Monty repeated. 'Not Evita. *Never* Evita, not in this house. Got it?'

'I don't—'

But then he was dragging her away from the railing, up the porch steps and through the house's glass doors, following the others into what appeared in the light of day to be a large and rather quaintly-appointed breakfast room. There were spindly little chairs arrayed next to spindly little side tables, and along one side of the room there was a breakfast buffet laid out on a table that was polished to such a perfect golden sheen that it had to be an antique. But none of that was dazzling enough to distract her from the line of people chained to the wall next to it.

'Monty—'

He shoved her up against the wall, knocking the breath out of her lungs, then she felt the metal click around her wrists.

By the time she recovered herself enough to do more than bend over and gasp for air, Monty and his fellow vampires had gone, leaving her and the others chained to the wall in a line. Xiaoyu was standing next to her.

'Don't fight it,' she whispered.

Quick blinked up at her through watering eyes, not understanding what she meant.

'Whatever happens next,' Xiaoyu clarified. 'Don't fight it.'

'*You're* telling me not to fight?'

Xiaoyu shrugged a shoulder. 'It goes easier if you don't.'

Over the next couple of hours, Quick was able to observe the truth of that in gruesome detail. People came into the room regularly, sometimes humans who took fruit and pastries from the buffet, sometimes vampires who ate their fill of the food, then pinned one of the chained humans back against the wall and bit into their necks with a chillingly casual directness. When her fellow offerings let it happen without protest, it was brief and efficient. When they fought – and only one did, a young man who was as new to the cellar as Quick – the protracted, screaming struggle finally ended with blood on the walls and a mauled wound at the boy's neck that was even more ragged than Quick's zombie bite.

The others looked away. That was the worst of it, and the thing that turned Quick's stomach when she remembered it later. As the boy screamed and thrashed against the wall in the grip of the vampire's jaws, the rest of the humans – Quick included – did nothing at all. *It was his own fault*, they muttered afterwards. They'd warned him not to fight it.

Every time someone new entered the room, Quick flinched, anticipating her own turn. She dipped her chin, hiding her face, trying to put off the inevitable, but there were only so many humans chained to the wall, and the vampires were avoiding those who'd already been bitten. After an hour, most of them had taken their turn; it was just Quick, Xiaoyu and one of the younger women at the far end of the line remaining. Odds were one in three that she'd be next.

'Fresh meat,' Bella yelled, coming in from the porch with a line of people following on behind her, including a few Quick recognised from the cellar. Bella and a couple of other vampires guided them into the room, then started unchaining the people who'd been brought in along with Quick. For one beautiful, shiny moment, Quick thought maybe they'd all get a reprieve, that she'd be allowed to return to the relative safety of the cellar unbitten, but when she looked at Xiaoyu, she was shaking her head. *Not until we're bled*, she mouthed.

And so it proved to be. The vampires were just switching out the people who'd already been bitten. The rest of them – Quick, Xiaoyu and the young woman at the other end of the line – stayed put as the others were unchained around them. A door opened across the room during the shuffle, and there was the noise of someone entering the space, but Quick's view was blocked by the exiting humans. It was only when they finally parted like clouds that she could see who had come in: the woman with the sunshine hair who walked like she was ready for a fight.

And Quick began to hope.

However fondly Quick was supposed to be thinking of him, she knew that Monty had precious little to offer her. If her fate rested on being able to conjure up the feelings she'd had for him on Tuesday night, then she was fucked. Monty was not Quick's way out of this place.

Her, though? The woman with the undercut and the determined look in her eye? She was an outsider here, too.

Quick could tell from the way she'd held herself at the party the other night. She hadn't been here to socialise, she'd come for a fight. Now she was Quick's last hope of salvation. Maybe somehow, Quick could appeal to her humanity and—

Then Quick met the woman's eyes, and she saw nothing but silver.

<h1 style="text-align:center">16</h1>

KULIKA WAS HUNGRY.

She'd ignored the thirst yesterday, and she'd made it through the night without losing too much sleep over it, but when she'd woken that morning and looked up at the spider-infested canopy above her head, she'd felt the weakness in her muscles and started to despair. For Kulika, who had practised discipline religiously since leaving this house a century ago, the sensation was a shameful surprise, but even her self-awareness couldn't stop the wanting.

She needed blood. She shouldn't, not so soon, not when she'd been using so little energy, and yet. Maybe it was all the bloodshed she'd witnessed two nights previously at the ritual. Maybe it was the constant state of fight-or-flight, or the memories swirling around her of the blood she'd spilled in this place, but all at once her devolution felt inevitable. Even her silver was slipping, the concealment of the colour in her eyes becoming impossible to sustain.

That hadn't been a problem for centuries. It would have been embarrassing in other circumstances. As it was, every Silver she encountered on her way from her suite to the breakfast room took the flashing of her silver as a threat, and got the hell out of her way, fast. She wondered then what they'd heard about her. Bartholomew wouldn't even have had to lie to make them fear her. They should. Right now, thirsting for blood in a place where drinking from the vein was her only option, Kulika feared herself.

As she barrelled into the breakfast room, she could smell the sugar on the pastries, the sweetness of the fruit, and the rich tang of blood flowing in the veins of the humans who were being chained along the wall. Now, the thirst was becoming irresistible in a way she recognised far too well, here in the very place where her thirst had plagued her most. She could feel her control slipping, inch by inch, in a way that would never have happened at home.

She could hear anxious hearts racing. She could smell the heat of blood rushing. If she looked very closely, she could even see arteries pulsing under the skin of the humans gathered against the wall, some already bitten, some bleeding from cuts that were more savage than they should have been. The new Silver led the drained ones away, shutting the porch door behind them.

Then Kulika saw her.

There, at the end of the line, was the woman with the hair like sunset. The woman who smelled like all the seasons kaleidoscoping into one. The new Silver had been blocking Kulika's view when she'd first entered the room, otherwise she would have noticed her immediately. She couldn't help herself from noticing her now, or from staring at her uncontrollably. Someone had already bitten her, judging from the marks on her neck. Then Kulika saw the mangled wound on the woman's arm and realised it must have been more than one someone. The Silver didn't bite like that.

'Who did this to you?' Kulika asked softly, stepping towards the woman.

She banished her weakness in a second, suppressing her silver, feeling her control locking into place once more.

It was too late, though. The woman had seen the silver.

'You're one of them,' she said with disgust.

Kulika's heart sank.

'One of *them*?' Kulika repeated stupidly, hoping against hope that the sunset-haired woman thought she was one of Bartholomew's crew. That, she could deny. And god, how she wanted to deny it. Anything not to be whoever *them* was.

But then…

'The vampires,' the sunset-haired woman said. 'You've got the silver veins in your eyes.'

There was no denying that.

'What did you think she was?' asked another of the chained-up humans, the woman from the cellar beneath the block, the one who'd spoken to Kulika the other day. Then the woman turned to Kulika and said, 'Are you going to tell us who you are, or what?'

'Kulika,' Kulika said.

'Xiaoyu,' the woman replied. 'This is Quick.' She went on to introduce the others, each by name, but Kulika had stopped listening the moment she'd heard that word.

Quick.

Even her name was an imperative. Kulika wanted to take it as an order. She could hear the thudding of Quick's heart — *Quick* — and she could feel the heat of her skin, even from across the distance that separated them. Kulika wanted to close the gap between them so keenly that it made her ache. Maybe it was just the thirst, and the exhaustion, and that beguiling scent of citrus and forests and frost, but she was now finding it impossible to restrain herself. Her gaze raked Quick's body uncontrollably, from the roots of her sunset hair to the tips of her bare toes, drinking in everything in between just as hungrily as Kulika wished she could drink in her scent, her taste, her blood.

Just a drop.

Without meaning to, Kulika took a step, and another, and who knew where she would have stopped if Xiaoyu hadn't interrupted by saying, 'I wasn't asking your name, though.'

Kulika blinked, and found Quick looking back at her with something close to horror, a horror that Kulika shared.

'I was asking who you *are*,' Xiaoyu continued. 'What you're doing here. When you're going to get us out of here, and why exactly you want to do that since you're one of *them*.'

'I'm not one of them,' Kulika said numbly. Her mind flashed back to the bloody carnage of two nights ago and her stomach churned. 'I'm Silver, yes,' she clarified. 'But these aren't my people.'

'They're feeding you,' Xiaoyu pointed out. 'And not just pastries.'

'Us,' Quick said quietly.

Kulika couldn't stand the vitriolic look on her face.

'He doesn't do that for just anyone,' Xiaoyu added.

'He?' Quick asked.

'Bartholomew,' Xiaoyu explained to her. 'The guy in charge. Head vampire. Coven leader. Whatever.'

'Captain,' Kulika said, then for reasons she couldn't explain even to herself, she told them the truth. 'Captain Bartholomew Roberts. I'm not sworn to him anymore, but a long time ago, a very long time ago, he made me part of his crew.'

'His *what*?' Xiaoyu asked, but Kulika paid little attention to her question because Quick was laughing.

Laughing.

'Bartholomew Roberts?' she asked, her eyebrows raised in

disbelief. 'Barti Ddu? You're telling me this place is owned by Black Bart, the infamous Golden Age pirate, and not only is he still alive, but he's a *vampire*?' Then she started laughing again, then crying, and finally she slumped back against the wall with her face hidden behind her sunset-red hair.

'Don't mind her,' said Xiaoyu. 'She's new.'

But Kulika did mind. She minded a lot.

The confused scent coming off Quick wasn't so much frost and sunshine now as it was bitter leaves and wet earth, muted and fallow, as though her scent were an extension of her mood. Kulika had never come across a scent that changed like that before, and she wasn't sure what it meant.

'Are you okay?' Kulika asked, taking one restrained step closer to Quick.

'Is it true?' Quick asked, her face still hidden by her hair.

'Yes,' Kulika said, standing in front of her, but still a good six feet away, for everyone's safety. 'Didn't you know? You signed his covenant, so I thought—'

Then Quick tossed her hair away from her face and looked up at Kulika. Her eyes were so green. Green like grass, but not the grass here in the baking summer of South Carolina, the grass back home where only the hottest days of the hottest summers parched it from rich to dull.

'What are you talking about?' Quick asked.

'The Articles,' said Kulika. 'He said you signed the Articles.' Then Kulika glanced around Quick's body to where her hands were chained to the wall, and saw her unblemished palms. 'You're not wearing his black mark.'

'What are you talking about?'

'The ones in the blood cellar don't sign until we get turned,' Xiaoyu said.

Which meant Bartholomew had lied to her, Kulika

realised. The night when she'd arrived back at the mansion and Bartholomew had offered Quick to her, saying she'd signed his covenant... Well, she hadn't. Quick wasn't wearing Bartholomew's mark, and she wasn't Bartholomew's to trade with. Which meant she wasn't Bartholomew's to claim, either.

Oh, Kulika thought.

Oh.

The ramifications of that knowledge were dangerous. *Very* dangerous.

Perhaps it was just the thirst talking, but Kulika *wanted* Quick. She could break her chains without effort, even blood-starved as she was. She could walk out of here, fight her way through the guards and take Quick with her, and Bartholomew wouldn't be able to do a thing about it.

Not a single thing.

Except deny Kulika the knowledge that had brought her here in the first place, knowledge that would save the woman Baron Drake loved. Knowledge that would save him too, the only man who had proved himself worthy of the loyalty she gave him.

Kulika loved him. It was a platonic, dutiful, unspoken kind of love, but it was real. That was what she was weighing against the freedom of a single human she'd just met.

It was an easy reckoning, or at least it should have been.

'You're thirsty,' Xiaoyu said, interrupting Kulika's muddled thoughts.

'What?'

'I said, you're thirsty. You need blood.'

'I... No, I'm fine,' Kulika insisted, ignoring the way her muscles twitched with need. It came over her like this sometimes, the thirst, when she'd been over-exerting and under-consuming. It felt like acidosis shaking and tingling through her thighs, making them spasm ever so slightly beyond her control.

'If you were fine, then you wouldn't be looking at Quick like you're an alcoholic and she's a fifth of bourbon. Here,' Xiaoyu said, turning her head to tip her hair away from the side of her neck. 'Drink.'

'No,' Kulika said, horrified, but whether the horror stemmed from the idea of the act itself, now it came down to it, or from the identity of the donor, she wasn't sure. She couldn't remember the last time she'd drunk from the vein. Well, actually she could, and that was rather the problem. 'I don't—'

'You said you were going to get us out of here,' Xiaoyu said. 'Right?'

'I said I would try,' Kulika replied carefully.

When she'd made that promise, she'd had no idea how she'd keep it, and that hadn't changed. Sneaking out of here with Quick was one thing, but there were more than a hundred humans in that cellar, and she was just one Silver against Bartholomew's entire empire. She had no chance.

'Well, on the off-chance that you're telling the truth, you can't help us if you're shaking like that, can you?' Xiaoyu said.

'Shaking?' Quick asked, looking at Kulika with concern. Kulika saw her attention settling on Kulika's fingers – steady as a rock – before settling on her thighs. She looked down to see that there was a faint, but unfortunately visible, twitching in her legs.

'I'm fine,' Kulika said again, because quite apart from the memories she was trying to suppress, she could see the many overlaid scars patterning Xiaoyu's neck. She could hear the erratic faintness of her pulse, too, and scent the sickly deficits in her blood. She had been fed from too much, and for too long. 'You're not, though. You can't spare the blood.'

'I'm fine,' said Xiaoyu brusquely, but she leaned forward so her hair curtained back over her shoulders, hiding the scars at her throat.

'I can spare it,' said Quick resolutely, offering her own neck.

Kulika's mouth went dry. Her eyes traced Quick's freckled skin with her gaze, from the soft curve of her shoulder, along her collar bone, to the point where the vein thudded in her elegant neck. Kulika would kill to taste her blood, but in this urgent state she might end up doing exactly that.

'No,' Kulika finally croaked, with effort.

'Then one of the others,' Xiaoyu said, nodding towards the humans lined up beside her. Some of them were watching the three women with mild interest, but others were eyeing up the buffet, or slumping against the wall as though lost in thought, but probably just too exhausted to move. They were all grim, they were all dirty, and none of them spoke a word except Quick and Xiaoyu.

It was eerie.

Kulika hesitated. Maybe she could go out into the city somehow, maybe find a blood bank or—

The door opened behind her, and she turned to see Bartholomew leaning casually in the doorway. She wondered how long he'd been hanging around outside, listening, waiting.

'Still not drinking?' he asked. It was a taunt.

'Not thirsty,' she lied.

He barked a single, sharp laugh. 'Still so hesitant, Kulika? Chasing ghosts? I thought you'd have put them to rest decades ago.'

He knew exactly what was haunting her. He'd been here

when Kulika had taken her last bite, and there when she'd taken her first bite, and present for every one in between. He'd always been there, watching, and here he was still. She'd been naïve to expect anything else.

She turned to face him, trying her best to mask the muscle spasms in her legs, but of course he saw. He *always* saw.

Then his gaze passed along the line of humans and he saw Quick. His eyes widened, just slightly, so slightly that most Silver probably wouldn't even have noticed the reaction, but his surprise and displeasure was clear enough to someone who had known him as long as Kulika had.

He was trying to hide it from her, but he was angry.

He turned and yelled out into the hall: 'Get the kid in here. Now!'

When "the kid" arrived, he proved to be the same boy who'd interrupted her conversation with Bartholomew on her first evening at the mansion: Mr Monteiro.

'What is this one doing here?' Bartholomew asked him, pointing at Quick.

'She's new,' the kid said, bewildered. 'The new ones do the feeds.'

Bartholomew grabbed the kid roughly around the back of the neck and pulled him close, pressing his forehead against the kid's, staring down into his eyes. The old pirate whispered, 'Why must you disappoint me like this?'

'I didn't— I thought—'

'Did I not make your duty clear?'

Kulika could see Bartholomew's grip tightening around the kid's scruff, his fingers whitening as they dug into his flesh. The kid's mouth screwed into a line of pain, but he didn't try to escape. He was wearing Bartholomew's mark on his palm, and there was no escaping that.

'I'm sorry,' the kid gritted out. 'I'll fix it.'

'See that you do,' Bartholomew said. He stared into the kid's eyes for one last second before letting him free, dropping the kid from his grip as though he were a louse he'd picked out of his hair.

The moment he was released, the kid ran for Quick and started fumbling with her chains. Kulika wanted to stop him. She wanted to scream and fight and stand in his way, but with Bartholomew standing right there, she couldn't afford to show any emotion at all. If he saw a crack in her defences, he'd slip his fingers inside it and twist until it broke her open, so instead of going after what she wanted, she stood and watched impassively while the young Silver freed Quick from the wall and started dragging her towards the porch doors, dragging her away from Kulika.

Then Quick lunged. The kid couldn't have been expecting it. With his Silver strength, it should have been laughably easy to keep a human under control, but nonetheless Quick's wrists slipped from his grip, and his surprise gave her enough time to launch herself at Kulika.

Quick thudded into Kulika's chest like a key thrusting into the lock it was made to fit. Her sudden presence in Kulika's arms was overwhelming – her warmth, her scent, the softness of her skin – so overwhelming that Kulika lost her breath along with her mind, and found herself unable to say anything at all. She should have been pushing her back, pretending Quick's proximity did nothing to her, but instead she just looked down into Quick's green eyes and began to swim.

Until Quick spoke.

'I need to ask you about Jane,' she whispered urgently, as though the name was one Kulika should recognise.

'Jane?'

'Jane. I need to find her, to find—'

Then the kid grabbed Quick by the wrist and jerked her back, out of Kulika's arms, out of the porch doors and away. The abruptness of it was numbing, leaving Kulika with nothing but the twitching of her muscles and the cold, sick sensation that something that was part of her had been lost.

The strength of her reaction was an unwelcome surprise, one she tried to cover by asking Bartholomew, 'Who's Jane?'

Kulika hadn't forgotten what she'd overheard the first night she'd been here, or how Bartholomew had reacted when the kid had told him, *I think she knows Jane*. She wondered now if he'd been talking about Quick. Bartholomew had certainly been unsettled to find Quick here, in exactly the same way he had been unsettled when he'd heard her say Jane's name, however much he was trying to hide it now.

'She's just one of the many new Silver we've welcomed to the mansion over the past six months,' Bartholomew replied dismissively, but he was schooling his expression in a way that just made Kulika more suspicious. 'No one special. And there are more to come tonight. You'll attend the Casting ceremony, of course.' It was an order, not an enquiry.

'And the human you just had taken away?' Kulika said, prodding. 'You seemed a little upset to see her here.'

'If I am upset,' Bartholomew replied, 'then it's because a member of my crew failed to follow orders. The girl is irrelevant.' He smiled. It put Kulika on edge. 'Unless you were planning to make a meal of her yourself? But perhaps I can offer you an alternative.'

He walked to the wall and snatched one of the young women out of the line, breaking the chains that held her in place. She hadn't been bitten yet today, or at all in fact, if her unblemished throat was any clear measure. She was a redhead, but her hair was more strawberry blonde than auburn, with none of the sunset fire of Quick's.

'Get the other humans out of here!' Bartholomew yelled into the hall, and a couple of young Silver rushed in to do as he demanded, leaving just the three of them behind in the breakfast room: Bartholomew, Kulika and the strawberry blonde.

Bartholomew pushed the woman into Kulika's arms, pressing in behind so she was trapped between the two of them. Kulika tried to move back, but Bartholomew chased her every step of the way, until her back was against the wall and there was nowhere to run. With the woman's vein thrumming so close to her mouth, she was no longer certain that she wanted to.

'Do you think I can't see the need in you?' Bartholomew whispered to Kulika over the young woman's shoulder, leaning in so close that Kulika could feel his lips moving against her earlobe. 'You can't hide your appetites from me. I know your hunger too well. You remember what happened the night you left?'

As if she could ever forget.

It had been months of deprivation, months of punishment for what Bartholomew had termed her *little mutinies*, all designed to push her to the edge until she snapped. *I can't be lenient with you just because you're my second*, he'd explained over and over as he drained and starved her of blood. *If I don't discipline you for your little mutinies, when you're supposed to be the most loyal of all my crew, then what will become of my authority? You brought this upon yourself.*

She'd nodded, and apologised, and begged his forgiveness for being late to answer his call, or for failing to pass on every tiny piece of gossip she overheard from the crew, or for punishing them more leniently than he would have liked for their transgressions. In those last months, there had always been some new crime for which he demanded her atonement. She could see now exactly how he'd manipulated her into that final crisis, but that awareness did nothing to limit her shame.

When she'd bitten the girl, and the many others that had followed in her rampage, she hadn't been in her right mind. Not that it mattered. Bartholomew would have used her guilt to tie her to him ever more inextricably, and if Baron Drake hadn't been there to get her out when he did…

He'd barely known her back then, but he'd seen enough during his visit to the mansion to know that Bartholomew had broken her and, for some reason that Kulika still didn't fully understand to this day, he'd decided to help her instead of condemning her. Maybe he'd seen something of his own savagery in her and felt a kinship there, because he was certainly capable of savagery himself. Or maybe he'd seen someone who needed to be rescued, and decided to play the white knight for once. Either way, he'd cleaned up the mess she'd left in her wake, forcing Bartholomew to relinquish his claim on her under threat of mortal retaliation. In doing so, he'd put his position and his life on the line, irreparably fracturing the uneasy alliance between the Silver of the UK and those of the USA in the process. It was a debt she could never repay, but she could at least try, and god knew she'd been doing a crap job of that so far.

'I see you shaking, Kulika,' Bartholomew said, grabbing the human between them by the back of her head to tilt her chin back and bare her neck to Kulika's bite. 'You're weak. If you mean to last through the weekend and get the information you came here for, then you need to drink. So drink. I know you like a redhead. I haven't forgotten the way you looked at Penny on the night you arrived.'

Kulika had no idea who Penny was, but with the young woman's blood just a breath away, she was struggling to remember her own name, let alone anyone else's.

'It's the only way we feed in this mansion,' Bartholomew said. 'Not from bottles or bags, stored and tainted with plastic. My crew drinks only the best, fresh and warm and straight from the vein, as we always have. You can feel the power in it, can't you?'

To her shame, she could. She remembered it from every dream she'd had since she left this mansion. Sometimes they were nightmares, but sometimes…

Kulika's vision was beginning to strobe, narrowing her senses so that when Bartholomew leaned down to the young woman's neck and sank his teeth into her throat, opening a vein that dripped tantalising streaks of red down over her skin, all Kulika could see, smell, feel, *taste* in the air was the blood.

Bartholomew pulled back, then he reached out his free hand to wrap around the back of Kulika's head, settling it at the base of her skull as though it belonged there, guiding her to the thing that – in that moment – she wanted more than anything in the world.

Kulika was lost before her lips were even wet, drinking as though her thirst were just as acute as it had been back then, after Bartholomew had starved her, instead of being a minor inconvenience she could have controlled with enough discipline. She told herself that drinking the woman's blood was a concession she was making to save Baron Drake's life, that if she didn't then she would weaken into uselessness, or Bartholomew would evict her from the mansion with no information at all about Evita Khalyed's whereabouts. But the truth she knew in her heart was that she should have been able to last days, weeks, perhaps even months without drinking again and still function well enough to fulfil her purpose, which was simply a matter of remaining in the mansion until Monday arrived. The truth was, she'd allowed Bartholomew to influence her, just as he had done a hundred years before, and for all the hundreds of years before that.

She was weak, and she had allowed him to break her. Again.

As she pulled away from the young woman's neck, leaving behind a double bite mark that was as clean as she could make it, but still not clean enough, Kulika felt the blood settling in her stomach like a rock.

Bartholomew smiled wolfishly and said, 'It's good to have you back.'

17

'JANE,' QUICK SAID desperately, 'I need to find her, to find—'

But then there were hands around Quick's wrists, shoving her out through the doors and down the porch steps, hurrying her bare feet over the flagstones around the pool, leaving her with nothing but the memory of Kulika's baffled expression.

She hadn't recognised the name. Whatever Kulika's true purpose was in this house – and Quick realised then that she never had told them – she clearly had no idea who Jane was.

'You're a liability,' Monty hissed at her as he dragged her to one of the poolside chairs and sat her down in it.

'And you're a liar,' Quick replied.

'You couldn't wait more than a couple of hours before blurting out that name? If I'd known you were that impatient —'

'What was that about in there?' Quick asked. 'What did you do wrong? I wasn't supposed to be bitten, was I?'

'Please, just… stop,' was the only reply she received.

Moments later, the other human captives were hurried out of the breakfast room behind them, and Monty handed Quick off to the vampires who were escorting them, as though he

152

couldn't wait to be rid of her. He barely looked at her. It didn't bode well for tonight.

'Jane?' one of the humans whispered as they were all shepherded across the lawn on their way back to the block. The speaker was a man walking just ahead of her who looked to be about her age, with matted shoulder-length hair that might have started out in braids. 'Why was the new girl asking about Jane?'

'Shut up,' Xiaoyu whispered quickly, and he duly shut up. Not quickly enough, though. Between one step and the next, Bella – who was among their escort – aimed a kick at his knee, an economical gesture that looked like nothing at all, but ended in a stomach-churning snap that had the man pitching forward and onto the ground with a scream that made Quick's skin shiver.

'We don't talk about Jane,' Bella said, then she walked off ahead with the others, leaving Xiaoyu and the woman she'd called Reynolds to pull the injured man to his feet and help him, still yelling, across the lawn. Quick fell in step beside them, hovering there in case she was needed, but feeling utterly useless as the vampires and the other humans walked swiftly back inside the distant block, leaving them behind.

Quick saw Reynolds's fear as she looked anxiously towards the door of the building, and guessed this would not end well for any of them. The man was still screaming.

'Shh,' Xiaoyu said urgently to him. 'Come on. We've just got to get you inside—'

'I'm sorry,' said Reynolds, then she dropped the man's arm from around her shoulders and made a break for the block at a flat run, slipping through the metal side door as Quick scrambled to take her place.

'For fuck's sake, shut up,' Xiaoyu said as the man screamed.

'Xiaoyu!' Quick rebuked her.

'If we don't get him inside quickly and quietly then we're all— Too late,' she said, her eyes widening as she looked beyond the trees.

The vampires were coming back. Three of them, striding out of the building towards Quick, Xiaoyu, and the man who couldn't walk even with their help.

'We've got him,' Xiaoyu insisted. 'We can take him.'

They ignored her entirely. One scooped the man into his arms while the other two held Xiaoyu and Quick back. What happened next was the work of a moment: a bite, a twist, and then the vampire was carrying the man's body across the gardens towards the river that glinted at the distant edge of the property.

'For the gators,' the vampire who was holding Xiaoyu explained, grinning at Quick's dismay.

'Fucking Bella,' said the other from behind Quick. 'Someone's got to get her under control. Isn't this one Monty's?' He shook Quick a little, as though she were nothing but a prop.

'Want me to go get him?' asked the other.

'I'll go. You got them in the meantime?'

The other laughed, as though the idea of him being unable to control a couple of humans was ridiculous.

'Yeah, okay,' said the one holding Quick as he passed her to the other. 'Be right back.'

He rushed off to the block, moving so fast that Quick could barely see him. She caught her breath and whispered to Xiaoyu, 'Is that speed normal?'

Then there was a clatter from the mansion behind them, the porch doors opened and the last human stumbled out, a redheaded young woman, holding her neck. She collapsed on the porch steps.

'Fuck's sake,' the last Silver muttered. 'Not another one.' He pushed Quick and Xiaoyu down onto the grass, said, 'Sit. Stay,' then rushed off to fetch the redhead while Quick and Xiaoyu looked on silently from their spot on the lawn.

'Well,' whispered Xiaoyu. 'There goes our last hope of getting out of here before tonight.'

'What?' said Quick.

'Kulika, or whatever her name is. The point is, she was lying.'

'Because she drank from that girl? Come on, Xiaoyu. You offered her your blood, didn't you? Just because she bit her, it doesn't mean—'

'Look at her neck,' said Xiaoyu as the girl was carried past. Quick did, reluctantly, and what she saw made her wince. The girl's throat had been mauled with more than one bite, breaking her skin in a way that reminded Quick of the boy who'd struggled. It was a mess.

'Face facts: she's not here to save us,' Xiaoyu said quietly. 'She's just another one of them. If we're going to get out of here, then we're going to have to do it on our own.'

'I don't suppose there's any point in running?' Quick said.

'From here? In the daylight? With vamps all around us? No. We do it when they're not expecting it, at night—'

'Because that worked out so well for you last time,' said a sarcastic voice from behind them. Quick turned to see Monty coming around the pool from the far side of the house, trailing a couple of other Silver in his wake. 'You're not going anywhere, Xiaoyu. You've tried, like, twenty times. Give up.'

Xiaoyu was glaring at Monty. The fierceness in her eyes suggested there was more to their past than Quick had realised.

'But as it happens,' Monty continued, 'Quick *is* going

somewhere.'

'Oh?' Xiaoyu asked. When Xiaoyu glanced her way, Quick could see the concern in her eyes.

'Come on, sugar,' Monty said to Quick, grabbing her by the wrist and pulling her to her feet. 'We're going upstairs.' Then he wrapped his arm around Quick's shoulders with a casualness that suggested she should welcome it.

There were wolf whistles and laughs from the Silver, but Quick was left with little doubt that she *absolutely* did not want to go upstairs with Monty. She made to push him away, but he sank his fingers into her shoulder and held her close, whispering into her ear, 'Am I really worse than turning zombie?'

In that moment, with shivers of disgust travelling up her spine, Quick honestly wasn't sure. She looked at Xiaoyu's anxious face and the words she'd said to Quick earlier that day returned in a dark echo.

Don't fight it.

It goes easier if you don't.

For better or worse, Quick didn't. She let Monty take her inside the block with Xiaoyu and the others trailing along behind, and tried to find the strength to make herself yield.

18

THE ONSLOW.
>*The Royal Fortune.*
>*The Porcupine.*

So many names tattooed down Kulika's spine, across her heart and into her bones. Bartholomew might have forgotten them, but Kulika would not. By the time this trip was over, if indeed it ever ended, she would have many more names to add to the list.

>*The cellar.*
>*The redhead.*
>*Quick.*

So many people she'd failed. So many lives she'd traded to get what she needed. But what was the alternative? Do nothing? Just walk away empty-handed and let the baron die?

That she could not do.

Just three more nights. She just had to wait until Monday, then Bartholomew would give her the information she came here to get. Just three more nights, then she could track down Evita Khalyed, turn her Silver, and take her back to Oxford, where the science bods could use her blood to make an antidote to save stupid Jack's stupid life, ensuring that Baron Drake's rather more precious life would continue for centuries to come.

That was why she'd come here, she reminded herself. That was why she was enduring Bartholomew's games. She just had to concentrate on her own mission, instead of letting herself get distracted by the allures of... other things. She was a soldier now, not some rebel pirate who could follow her own whims.

Discipline, that's what she needed, for tonight and everything that would follow. *Discipline*, she repeated in her head as she leaned on the porch railing and tried to steel herself against the carnage that would surely come at the Casting that evening.

She could still taste the woman's blood in her mouth, sharp and fearful. In her muddled senses, it leaked into the tantalising scent of four seasons rolled into one, souring to bitter leaves. Her mind was filled with memories of a soft body pressed against her own, memories of her teeth sinking into flesh she didn't want to bite, that had already been bitten by another, marred by the saliva of the person she hated more than anyone in the world. She'd tasted him in the woman's blood. Part of him was inside Kulika now, not just the blood that had turned her into what she was today, but his *spit*.

After all the violations Bartholomew had perpetrated against her, how strange it was that her mind had latched onto that one to stoke her outrage.

'You drank from the vein, then,' Bayly said, coming to stand beside her in his spot, just as he always did. 'Wasn't sure you would.'

Kulika didn't want to talk about it, particularly not with Bayly. What business did he have judging her, with the mess he'd gotten himself into? But she knew his judgement wouldn't chafe were it not for the fact that she agreed with his censure.

It had been... undisciplined, and that worried her. If Bartholomew was set on breaking her down piece by piece, then so far he was succeeding. Kulika knew that he would only stop when she'd signed his Articles, and Baron Drake wasn't here to bargain her out of them this time. She couldn't afford to let Bartholomew mark her with his covenant again.

She'd burned the first black spot out of her skin in the bowels of a ship bound for England, holding her palm against the boiler until it puckered and smoked as she'd screamed into the din of the engine room. When she'd ripped her hand away, the scalding metal had claimed the tainted skin. It was a rebirth in fire, even if that fire was blackened by coal dust and soot.

Kulika was a phoenix, she reminded herself. A hundred years ago, she'd bid good riddance to those ashes and – whatever Bartholomew thought her biting that woman symbolised – she would rise from them once more.

'It's no concern of yours what I do,' she said to Bayly as she pushed away from the railing and headed back into the house. 'You said it yourself: we're no longer on the same crew.'

19

FROM THE ROOF of the block, the view over the river was beautiful. Quick and Monty were up above the shade of the trees, but there was a covered deck that faced east, sheltering them from the worst of the afternoon sun and giving them as much privacy as they could have wished for. In other circumstances, it might even have been romantic, but not now, not here, when Quick knew exactly what was going on in the building beneath them.

In the cellar in the bowels of the block, she knew that Xiaoyu and the others were waiting to see which of them would get dragged out for the Casting and which would stay in the blood bank until they were used up. Monty had walked her through the rest of the block on their way up here to the roof, giving her the tour. The ground floor was innocuous enough: the wash rooms, the kitchen, store rooms, the wardrobe, and some messy common areas that were filled with vampires watching TV, playing video games and generally hanging out. They could have been plucked out of any college campus across the country. The dorm rooms on the upper two floors of the building would have had a similar college feel to them, had it not been for the rampant orgy going on within them. Quick hadn't known where to look.

'It can be fun here,' Monty had said to her unabashedly.

Quick had squinted along the corridor filled with half-naked people spilling from one room to another, laughing and screaming and moaning, and thought it didn't *sound* fun. It sounded like intoxication and mania and desperation.

'Are they on drugs?' she'd asked.

Whatever he'd expected her reaction to be, it hadn't been that.

'They want to be here, Quick,' he'd said irritably. 'Most of these people begged to be allowed up here. They're desperate just for the chance to be like us. Do you not understand that? Do you not understand how lucky you are? It's here or in the cellar. You can be up here and enjoy yourself, or you can die down there in the dark.'

'Lucky?' she'd said incredulously. 'Lucky that you kidnapped me and bit me and brought me here against my will to bet my life for the chance to become a monster? Why would I *want* that?'

That's when he'd lost it, dragging her up the concrete staircase at the end of the hall and through the fire door that led out onto the roof. For a moment, she'd thought he was going to throw her right off it, but then he'd stopped and sat down on the deck, huffing like an overly-dramatic teenager. Which was practically what he was, Quick realised.

'I didn't choose this either, you know,' he said now. 'I didn't ask to be this way. Well, I did, but not in the way you might imagine.'

Quick sighed, because of course Monty was going to make this about himself. Worse, he was going to make her drag it out of him like he was some brooding, reluctant love interest and she was his fawning admirer. Well, she didn't have time for that. She didn't have time for any of this nonsense, not if she was going to find a way out of this mess before the end of the night.

She plonked herself down next to him unceremoniously and said, 'Spill it.'

That was all the encouragement Monty needed to launch into his tragic story. He'd been the first of the new vampires, he claimed, turned by a man who was centuries old, yet apparently not wise enough to avoid falling head over heels for Monty. He'd promised Monty the secret of eternal life, a secret Monty desperately needed in order to save his poor dying mother, but when Monty had woken to his undeath and realised that eternal life came with the curse of drinking human blood, he knew his god-fearing mother would never accept it, or him, so here he was, doomed to live forever, unloved and bereft of family.

The whole story felt hollow and rehearsed, and Quick didn't believe a word of it.

'You didn't have to drag me into it,' she said when he was finished.

'We have to make more Silver,' he replied with a shrug. It was a nonchalant dismissal, which as good as acknowledged that he'd never taken her feelings into consideration, and he certainly wasn't about to start now.

'Why?'

'Bartholomew says so.'

Quick remembered everything she'd half-learned that morning about the vampire in charge – the *pirate* in charge – and wished she'd had a chance to ask more than the most cursory questions about who he was and why he was keeping them here. Then she remembered the imposing man who'd grabbed Monty by the scruff of his neck, and she started to put two and two together.

'You're talking about the man who made you unchain

me?' she asked.

'He really wants you to be Silver,' said Monty. 'Don't ask me why, because I don't have an answer for you, but he wants you to turn and he wants it to happen tonight.'

'Or else?'

Monty just shrugged again, but his expression said enough. He wasn't simply scared of Bartholomew Roberts, he was petrified.

'They killed that man,' Quick said.

'What man?'

'When we were on our way back here from the house, one of the guys who heard me talking about Jane mentioned her name, and Bella broke his leg. Shattered it, more like,' she added, remembering the noise it had made with sickening clarity.

'Oh,' Monty said. 'Yeah. I heard they took someone to the river.'

'Just for saying her name. You're the one who told me to ask about her.'

'I didn't tell you to ask *Bella*,' he said. 'She's out of her fucking mind. Just… stay away from her, okay?'

'No problem,' she said. 'Because I'm not going back down to the dorms.'

'You might want to,' Monty replied with what seemed like reluctance.

'Why?'

'It doesn't have to be me, Quick.'

Quick looked at him, puzzled, examining his face for some clue as to what he meant and finding none.

'There are a lot of Silver downstairs,' he said. 'Take your pick. I want it to be me who turns you, but it doesn't have to be. It can be any other Silver in this building.'

'Why on earth would you want it to be you?' Quick asked,

bewildered. 'After all this?'

'I'm the one who chose you,' he said, looking into her eyes as though he were trying to impart some deep feeling with his words. 'I didn't do that for nothing. I *like* you.'

'I liked you, too, Monty,' Quick replied. 'But then—'

'But then nothing,' he said, reaching out to cup her cheek with his hand. 'Forget the rest. Can we just go back to that night in the bar? Just for tonight, can you try to forget everything that happened after, for both of our sakes? We've only got until midnight.'

Quick hesitated, wanting to peel his palm from her cheek, but also realising that he was talking some twisted kind of sense.

'People stay together, you know,' he whispered. 'Afterwards.'

'You mean there are *couples* in that mess downstairs?'

'Not downstairs,' Monty admitted. 'They normally move out, into the city or around here. The boss is always happy to make arrangements for people to live close, once they've paid their debt, and if I turn you then my slate will be clean. He's got deep pockets, you know.'

'Is that what this is?' Quick asked, finally taking his hand from her cheek to trace the black mark on his palm with her fingertips. 'The mark of your debt?'

'No,' he replied. 'This is something else.'

'The covenant?'

He nodded, swallowing. 'That's… That's forever. But if I can turn you Silver, then he'll buy us a place together. Let us leave. Set us up in style, you know?'

'And that's a life you *want*?'

'Given all the choice in the world, maybe I'd choose different. But it's better than dying in the cellar, isn't it? And when you're Silver, I can tell you everything. Maybe we can even go looking for your friend together. How about that?'

That caught Quick's attention. It was the most attractive offer she'd had from him since they'd left the restaurant, and she couldn't imagine why he was making it.

'*You're* not going to die in the cellar,' she said, still trying – and failing – to understand what was motivating him.

'Maybe not down there, but...' He looked away for a moment, as though he were washing a thought from his mind. 'There are other ways to die in this place. That's why we're all doing this, Quick. We just want to get out alive. So I guess the question is: do you want to get out with me, or not? If it would help,' he said, pulling a small bottle of rum from his back pocket, 'I can even get you drunk.'

When he put it like that, with his eyes locked on hers in a way she remembered viscerally from that night in the bar, the offer was hard to refuse.

Don't fight it.

It goes easier if you don't.

Quick grabbed the bottle and drained it half empty, then handed it to Monty to finish. When he'd downed his portion, he threaded his fingers through Quick's and looked at her for a moment, waiting.

This was it, then.

Quick closed her eyes, picturing someone else beyond the shield of her eyelids, leaned in, and kissed him.

Don't fight it.

To save her own life, along with any hope she had of saving Evita's, she could force herself to yield.

AS MIDNIGHT APPROACHED, Kulika found herself in the middle of a full-blown, bells and blood, candles and incense Casting ceremony. Perhaps she shouldn't have been surprised, but somehow she hadn't expected the new crew to keep to the old rituals. They weren't actually necessary. All you needed to turn someone Silver was a blood exchange and an emotional link between the couple involved, so why bother with the chanting and the processions and all the bloody Latin? Kulika had assumed that a confirmed rebel like Bartholomew would avoid all the pomp and circumstance, as he had in his days of high seas piracy, so she was surprised when she left her room that night to find one of the human servants standing outside her door, offering her a robe.

And a phone.

'It's for you,' the man said.

Kulika looked at the screen and saw that there was an open line to an unlisted number. She took it suspiciously and held it to her ear.

'Hello?' she asked.

'It's Jack,' Baron Drake said, with no preamble. His voice

was shakier than she would have liked.

'What about her?' Kulika asked.

'She's running out of time.'

Kulika's grip tightened around the phone hard enough to make it creak. She took a deep breath, got herself under control and asked, 'How long have I got?'

'I don't know. The Primus, he… Look, I just need you to hurry. Are you getting anywhere?'

'Yes,' she lied. 'I should know where Khalyed is by Monday.'

'That's days away,' the baron said.

He let everything he'd left unsaid hang in the air between them.

It's too long.

Jack doesn't have time.

If Jack dies, then I die.

After a few empty seconds, Kulika said, 'I'll see what I can do,' then the line went dead.

Under normal circumstances, Kulika would have considered that suspicious, or at the very least a little rude, but then Bartholomew walked out of his own room next door, wearing his own robe, with a look on his face that was too innocent to be believed. Kulika was sure he'd at least been listening to her conversation with the baron, and in all probability he'd been controlling the line, waiting until he had what he wanted before cutting the call dead.

He knew how desperate she was now. Kulika had just given him a bargaining chip, and from the look on his face, he couldn't wait to play it.

'Something wrong?' he asked her lightly.

'You know what's wrong,' she replied, thrusting her hands into the arms of her robe and pulling up the hood. 'I can't wait until Monday. I need you tell tell me where Evita

Khalyed is. Now.'

'Oh dear.' Bartholomew's sincerity was entirely fake. He was a better actor than that, but he wasn't even trying now. 'Well, if you want to move up the schedule, perhaps you'd consider...' He pulled the large leather-bound book from within the folds of his voluminous robe and opened it to a new page, proffering it like a platter of delicacies.

'I'm not signing the Articles,' Kulika said.

'Not even for Jack?' Bartholomew asked with twinkling eyes. 'Yes, I know about her. I think the entire Silver world knows about Jack Valentine by now, the young fool who poisoned herself trying to kill the Primus and yet somehow, unaccountably, finds herself forgiven.'

Kulika winced inwardly. It was inevitable that the news would get out eventually, with the splash Jack had made with that particular piece of idiocy. Kulika could only hope that it wasn't yet common knowledge that Baron Drake had silvered for Jack, because once that news leaked, she'd be out of time. They all would be.

'What I don't understand,' Bartholomew went on, 'is why *you'd* care enough to try to save her, or what the woman you're searching for has to do with any of it. But if you'd care to explain to me—'

'This has nothing to do with Jack,' Kulika said, too quickly.

'Then why are you looking for her?'

'I do what I'm told.'

Bartholomew laughed. 'For *him*, perhaps.'

'And for you!' Kulika yelled, snapping. 'For hundreds of years, I did everything you told me. I buckled down, and buckled under, and tied myself in knots following your orders. All I'm asking for is a little grace. Give me the information I need, and I'll come back here after I've done what needs doing. You'll have the three days I owe you.'

'And you expect me to take your word for that? When you abandoned me and my covenant?' Bartholomew said, shaking his head like a disappointed parent. 'You know there's only one thing you can do to repair my trust.' He held out the book again, pulling a sharp-nibbed quill from his robes to lay across its pages. 'You want to surrender yourself to me just as much as I want you to,' he said, leaning in close. 'You belong here, Kulika. With me.'

The terrible thing was, part of her believed it, and every time he told her so, she believed it a little more. After everything she'd done, all the blood she'd spilled, and the blood she'd drunk from the vein of an unwilling human only that morning…

Didn't she belong here more than she belonged anywhere else?

That was the power Bartholomew had always wielded over her. He validated the darkest parts of her, the parts she kept hidden from the baron and everyone else in her neat little life across the Atlantic, and by validating them he turned her shame into his strength. He *knew* her. He knew the memories that plagued her, the urges she laboured under, and the way she would break if he pushed her in just the right way. Worse, he enjoyed those parts of her. He gloried in the wreckage she knew no one else would even tolerate if they knew it was there.

It would have been easier if he'd just wanted to destroy her. Instead, he wanted to release her darkest self and worship it. He had always loved the way she fell apart.

'Sign,' he whispered. 'And I'll give you everything you ask of me, for the rest of time.'

'No orders?' she asked.

'No orders,' he agreed. 'Except the ones you may give to

me. Do as I ask, and I shall be your slave.'

'No restrictions?'

'You leave Drake and stay here with your crew, where you belong. Other than that, no.'

'But you'll let me complete the mission I started for him?'

Bartholomew looked into her eyes for a long moment. She could see his reluctance, but it was matched by his hunger. Eventually, he said, 'Yes. Then return to me, and I will make you a pirate queen worthy of this crew. Worthy of *any* crew.'

Kulika weighed his words, and felt the truth in them.

The feelings they were holding between their locked gazes took on a dreamlike quality. He *wanted* her. Not romantically, not physically, but still so intensely that he – the fabled dread pirate Roberts – was was prepared to humble himself at her feet just to have her at his side. It was intoxicating. When she saw herself through his eyes, Kulika saw a goddess drenched in blood.

For a moment, she forgot that she had abandoned that self centuries ago. Trapped in the heat of his awe, Kulika picked up the quill and held it against her fingertip, poised to prick her blood onto the page.

Then a gong rang through the house, and the quill fell from her fingers, unbloodied. By the time Bartholomew had collected and returned it to her, Kulika's uncertainty had crept back in.

She hesitated, and the gong rang again.

'Sir,' said a young Silver Kulika didn't recognise, long-haired and anchor-bearded, like a knock-off Bartholomew Roberts from his pirating days.

'Not now,' Bartholomew said irritably, not breaking eye contact with Kulika.

The knock-off pirate cringed, but persisted. 'The thing is, sir, there are a lot of them tonight, and if we're going to get through them all before—'

'This can wait,' Kulika said decisively, laying the quill back across the pages of the book. She needed time to think, and the ceremony would give her that.

The gong rang again.

It was tolling midnight, Kulika belatedly realised.

With one last, frustrated glance at Kulika, Bartholomew closed the book with a snap, sealing the quill inside. He turned to the knock-off pirate. 'Go, then,' Bartholomew said brusquely. 'Get back downstairs.'

Then he pulled up his hood, offered Kulika his arm, and escorted her down the staircase into the candlelit darkness below, trapping her hand against his body where it looped around his arm.

Kulika had a horrible suspicion that now he'd got this far, he wasn't going to let her go until her blood was on the page.

21

IT WAS LATE when the crowd assembled in the largest common area of the block. Quick remembered thinking it was a huge, sprawling space when she'd first seen the room during Monty's brief tour, but now they were packed in here like sardines between the sofas, side tables, bean bags and chairs that littered the room, it felt tiny.

Judging by a quick count of the shining eyes amongst those immediately surrounding her, about half of the crowd were vampires, and most of those were women. Most of the humans were men. It was easier to get the boys here, Xiaoyu had told her down in the cellar. All the vampires had to do was stick a pretty picture on a dating app, say they were up for anything and give the address, then the young idiots came rushing incautiously to their doom. Most women were more circumspect, more suspicious. It took trust to get them to the mansion, which meant a time investment from the vampire looking to lure them.

Not from Monty, though. All he'd had to do was bat his pretty long eyelashes and bait her with the promise of finding one of her missing people, and Quick had come running.

Like an idiot.

Looking at Monty now, standing beside her with a proprietorial gleam in his eye, she was struggling to think of anyone she loved less.

She'd tried. She'd kissed him up on the roof, danced with him in the dorms, and even attempted a bit of a fumble, but it had been clumsy and wrong and it made her feel like dirt. Quick was fast realising that she just didn't like Monty that much. In fact, after everything that he'd done, she thought she might hate him. Evita used to say that love and hate weren't all that far away from each other, that the true opposite of love was apathy, but now Quick knew that was bollocks. She'd gone from being indifferent about Monty, to being mildly attracted to him, then straight to utter contempt for him as a person and a vampire. That was a one-way track that she didn't see any hope of reversing back down, not while there was so much more contempt already rushing down the line behind her, pushing her along.

It didn't matter that her life was at stake, and any hope of finding Evita with it. It didn't matter that Monty was the only vampire in this room who even knew her name. She was starting to think that anyone else might be a better choice for the Casting.

'Right, listen up,' said Brandon, the long-haired pirate-looking guy from the night of the pool party, the bastard who'd conspired with Monty to start this nightmare. He was standing on a table, raising his voice to get the attention of the room, who were mostly ignoring him.

Until Bella hopped up beside him.

'Shut the fuck up!' she yelled. 'Listen carefully or you fucking die!' She glared around the room, daring anyone to so much as whisper, then hopped back down to the ground when she was satisfied that they wouldn't, ceding the table to Brandon again.

'Crazy,' Monty whispered to Quick, making an unkind gesture as he did so. 'Like I said.'

'Right,' Brandon said from his perch. 'There's a lot of us tonight, so here's how it's going to go. We're going in one line, single file, from here through the wardrobe – humans first and Silver behind, except I'll lead us out. When you get to the wardrobe, you find a cloak that fits and put it on with the hood up, then follow me over to the house. When we get there, you pick up a candle from the stack by the door and light it from the candle of the person in front of you. When we're in the hall, the Silver line up against the wall by the door, humans by the wall on the other side of the room. Questions?'

There were none, or at least none that anyone was brave enough to ask.

'Good,' said Brandon. 'When you're all lined up, Bartholomew's going to call you forward one by one. When he says your name, you move to the foot of the stairs and take your hood away from your face. He'll ask you who's going to try and turn you, you point out the Silver you want, and that's your bit done. Questions? No? Off we go, then.'

Monty pushed her towards the door, and there was no time to think after that.

The wardrobe was a scrum, with people grabbing and snatching and all the time the rest of the queue pushing them from behind. Quick ended up with a robe that she was sure was intended for a man, if the width of the shoulders was any measure. Despite her height, the hem trailed on the floor to be trodden on – frequently – by the person behind her. At least the walk to the house was mercifully short.

It was lonely, walking hooded and single file, strongly suspecting she was the only human in the line who didn't want this. She felt isolated in the darkness. She thought about running, just legging it across the grass to the river. Then she remembered the man from that morning, and the alligators. Which probable death would she prefer, one by Monty's teeth, or at the teeth of an alligator?

It's just a bite, he'd told her earlier that evening. *You drink a taste of my blood, then I drink yours, and it's done. It'll be over in no time. You'll see.*

Or, she supposed, she wouldn't. She was almost certain, in fact, that after Monty bit her she wouldn't be seeing much of anything at all, not with any kind of sanity. If she let Monty bite her, she'd be waking up as a zombie. In those circumstances, maybe she'd be better off trying her luck with the gators. She might have done exactly that, but they were already at the house now, and there were vampires everywhere.

She'd missed her chance.

There were more robe-clad humans waiting for them by the pool, about the same number again as those coming from the block. When Brandon had said there were a lot of them tonight, he wasn't kidding. Quick couldn't imagine how they were all going to fit into one room.

That became clear the moment they stepped inside, through the main door at the front of the house. The hallway was enormous, more a ballroom than an entrance hall, lit only by candles placed here and there on the walls and in standing candelabra. The ceiling stretched up three floors above their heads. To the left, a grand staircase swept up to the first floor, where a mezzanine ran around every side of the room, wider on the wall opposite the staircase than it was along either side. From the banisters at that wide edge, a dimly-lit cluster of figures dressed in dark robes looked down on the gathering.

'Candle,' someone said, snapping Quick's attention back down to ground level. She'd been staring up, she realised, and she'd forgotten what she was supposed to be doing. It seemed like ages now since she'd last slept, and she was starting to panic, so concentration was in short supply.

The woman in front of her was holding out her lit candle, gesturing Quick to the pile of unlit tapers on the table to her side. Quick grabbed one and, after a bit of confusion, managed to light it off the one the woman was offering. That done, Quick made to follow her across the hall to the far wall where a crowd of hooded, candlelit figures was already arrayed, only to be jerked back by her robe. At first, she thought the person behind her had stood on the hem again, then he said, 'You have to give me a light!' and she realised her error.

By the time that was all sorted out, Quick was flustered and shaky and sweating under her robe. The crowd of humans waiting opposite parted in front of her as though they were worried they might catch her lack of poise, which was fine by Quick. It gave her a clear path to the wall, where she could lean and think and try to come up with a way out of this mess.

She could only hope that her name was called somewhere close to last.

22

FROM THE BALCONY on the first floor mezzanine, Kulika had a clear view of the floor below. Bartholomew had insisted that she stay there, by his side, hooded at his right hand like a dark bride. *This is what I'm offering you*, the gesture said. *All my power, all these Silver under your control, and more to come.*

Kulika couldn't deny that it was impressive in its scope, if repugnant in its conceit. She'd never seen a Casting ceremony with so many candidates. It was going to take all bloody night. The humans were moving one by one to the centre of the hall beneath them as Bartholomew called their names from a list he pulled from the back of his covenant book. Once the human had called out the name of the Silver they'd chosen to attempt their turning – a novelty, since usually the Silver did the choosing – the matched pair moved to a side room and didn't return.

Kulika didn't want to imagine what was going on in that side room any more than she wanted to remember what she'd nearly agreed to upstairs, but the long ceremony gave her plenty of time to reflect on both.

She'd nearly signed her life away, and she wasn't at all

certain that she wouldn't actually go through with it before the night was over. Right now, she couldn't come up with a better plan.

'Patience Quick,' Bartholomew intoned beside her.

Kulika's spiralling thoughts slowed abruptly, as though they'd been caught in treacle.

Quick.

Kulika twitched, barely suppressing the impulse to step up to the railing for a better look. But she didn't have to get any closer to recognise Quick once she'd pulled the hood away from her sunset hair, shaking it free so it glimmered in the candlelight.

Kulika felt sick. She could feel eyes on her too, and turned to Bartholomew to see him looking at her with an interest he didn't try to hide. He'd seen her twitch, and he'd probably sensed more besides: the racing of her heart, the tensing of her muscles, and a thousand other tiny signs that her attention was hooked on the woman who stood in the centre of the floor beneath them, waiting for the question Bartholomew was about to ask.

'Whom do you select to turn you Silver?'

Down below, Quick looked like she was scrambling. Her gaze was searching the crowd of young Silver opposite her, looking for something she couldn't find. Even from across the space that separated them, Kulika could feel the nervous energy rolling off Quick in waves, infecting her with the same anxiety.

She should have realised Quick was going to be a candidate tonight; why else would Bartholomew have dragged her out of the buffet line this morning? And now it was too late for Kulika to do anything about it. Quick was going to get bitten, and if what Kulika had heard from Bayly about the mansion's success ratios was true, she was probably going to die. No wonder she was nervous.

Kulika hadn't had a chance to be nervous about her own turning, because she hadn't seen it coming. There had been no Casting ceremony, no ritual, just a visit to the captain's cabin that ended with his blood in her mouth and his teeth in her throat. Perhaps that had been a mercy. Quick would have none of that, but Kulika prayed at least that the bite she received would be less brutal for it.

The hall was quiet as Quick delayed her choice. None of the other candidates had been like this. They'd all walked through the door with a name already on their lips, ready to declare themselves. Quick was different, though. Unlike the others, she didn't seem excited to be here. Her gaze was darting around like that of a startled deer, trying to latch onto something, and failing.

Finally, she looked up at Bartholomew with despair in her eyes, and stilled. Then she pointed at the balcony and said, 'I want her to do it.'

It took a second for Kulika to realise that Quick was pointing at her. During that second, all hell broke loose.

23

QUICK WAS PANICKING. There was no other word for it. She gripped her candle in sweating, shaking hands, worrying at the wax that spilled down over her fingers. She'd known this was coming, known she'd have to choose someone, known that anyone would be better than Monty, but *who*? She didn't know any of these other vamps. She hadn't even exchanged a word with almost all of them. The only names she could remember were Brandon's, who was a bastard – besides which, he'd already been chosen and left the hall – and Bella's, but she seemed like an even worse option than Monty.

She could just point, she supposed. Randomly, into the crowd of vampires, and see where her finger landed.

But was no connection at all *really* better than the unwanted connection she had to Monty? She didn't know, she couldn't work it out, and she was running out of time to decide.

Everyone was waiting.

She had to say a name.

Any name.

Just as Quick had opened her mouth to say 'Monty', her

gaze flicked hopelessly up to Bartholomew, but it landed on the briefly-candlelit face of the woman next to him. The woman Quick had once considered to be her only hope of salvation in this place.

Maybe she'd been right: maybe Kulika would be the one to save her, just not in the way she'd hoped.

So she pointed at her.

It was impulsive, but really, what did she have to lose?

Across the hall, Monty was now the one looking panicked. By contrast, a strange calm was settling over Quick.

'You can't choose from the balcony,' he stage-whispered to her. 'You have to choose from us.'

'Why?' Quick asked.

Monty spluttered for a moment, before saying, 'Because,' which seemed like a stupid reason to her. If she was most likely going to die tonight, then Quick was going to play the cards she'd been dealt the best way she knew how, and she knew in her bones that Kulika was her best way out of here alive. She'd known it from the way her stomach had flipped the moment she'd caught sight of her candlelit face.

If only Kulika was willing to try.

Up on the balcony, what Quick could see of Bartholomew's face didn't look pleased. Kulika was looking at him with open confusion, her hood pulled away from her face now, as the ritual required. Then her eyes found Quick's, and Quick felt the spark.

There was something there.

Wasn't there?

Maybe it was just her desperation talking. Maybe she was kidding herself, but if Kulika would only try…

Bartholomew said something to Kulika, then turned and walked from the balcony. After one more glance at Quick,

Kulika followed him. From the floor above, a door slammed. And they waited.

24

IN THE UPSTAIRS parlour, Bartholomew threw his book onto a spindly little side table with such force that it rocked, then he put his hands on his hips and stared out of the window into the dark night.

'Do you know her?' he asked.

'Barely,' said Kulika, as surprised by what had just happened as he seemed to be. 'I met her for the first time this morning. You were there.'

'And there's nothing between you?' he pressed.

'Nothing,' Kulika replied, but her mind wandered unbidden to sunset hair, grass-green eyes, and the scent of the frosted earth in winter, releasing a knot in her chest that she hadn't known was there.

Kulika felt Bartholomew's attention sharpening on her. He turned to face her.

'You could do it,' he said, clearly sensing more than Kulika had wanted to reveal. 'Couldn't you?'

'No way,' Kulika said. 'I'm not doing to her what you did to me.'

'Because that was the worst thing that ever happened to you.'

'It's up there,' she said acidly.

'I gave you immortality.'

'You *cursed* me with immortality,' Kulika yelled. 'I didn't ask for it. All I wanted was freedom, a life where I could travel and be something other than a wife to a tyrant.'

'And that's exactly what I gave you!'

They were shouting at each other now, voices raised and fists clenched.

'No, you just made me first mate to a tyrant instead!'

'You're the one who chose to disguise yourself and run off to a life of piracy,' he argued. 'Without the power I gave you by turning you Silver, you would have been a wife to the whole crew! I didn't want to subject you to that.'

'But you'll subject me to this?' she asked, pointing towards the hall. 'You'll make me bite that girl, risk her life, and—'

'You like her,' Bartholomew said quietly.

'Enough that I don't want to kill her. You know that's exactly what will happen if I try to turn her.'

'I don't think so,' he said, watching her carefully.

Kulika watched him right back.

'Do this for me,' Bartholomew said, 'and I'll give you what you want.'

Kulika stilled. She must have misheard, or misunderstood, because what he'd just offered her made no sense.

'Let me get this clear,' she said slowly. 'If I try to turn Quick Silver, then you'll give me the information you have on Evita Khalyed.'

'Yes,' he said, gritting the word out like the concession pained him, though he made it nonetheless.

'Even if the turning isn't successful?'

'Yes.'

'I won't have to sign anything?'

'You won't have to sign anything,' he said reluctantly. 'I'll let you leave tonight, and all you have to do is attempt to turn one human Silver.'

'And you'll confirm that in writing?' Kulika said.

Bartholomew hesitated for the briefest second before saying, 'In writing.'

'In your own blood.'

He tutted impatiently. 'In whoever's blood you wish.'

It didn't make any sense at all.

'What's your stake in this?' she asked.

'I want to make more Silver. As many as possible. You know that by now.' His words were light, but the look in his eyes was intense.

'But why do you care so much about turning *her*, in particular?'

'Does it matter? You'll get what you want, and I'll get what I want.'

It wasn't explanation enough. Quick *meant* something to Bartholomew, that much was clear. If she didn't, then why would he be willing to give up his strongest bargaining chip – Evita Khalyed's location – when he'd had Kulika on the verge of signing his Articles just hours before?

But, as he'd said, did it matter? Kulika had come here to do one thing: find Evita Khalyed. She couldn't do anything about the fact that Quick's life was on the line, and the woman had made her choice. Quick wanted Kulika to attempt the turning, Bartholomew wanted Kulika to attempt the turning, and if Kulika wanted to save Baron Drake's life – which she absolutely did – then she *needed* to attempt the turning.

So why was she hesitating?

Perhaps her pride was pricked, she thought. Perhaps it hurt that Bartholomew's gaze, so intently focused on her earlier that night, had switched so easily to a new target.

But the more she prodded at Bartholomew, the more likely he was to recant his offer. She couldn't give him time to reconsider, not over something so trivial. Her pride wasn't worth Baron Drake's life.

'All right,' she said, picking up the book and throwing it at Bartholomew. 'Then write it down. A new section, in the back. *Kulika's* covenant.'

25

NO ONE WAS moving in the hall below. Quick heard shouting from upstairs. She couldn't make out the words, but the vampires opposite her were exchanging looks that suggested they could. When they weren't glaring at Quick, that was.

Then a door on the mezzanine above slammed open and Bartholomew returned to his perch. Kulika didn't follow him.

'Patience Quick: return to the line,' Bartholomew said.

Confused, and more than a little scared, Quick did as she was told. None of the other humans had been sent back to the wall, but then none of them had chosen a vampire who wasn't in the diminishing crowd opposite them.

'Phoebe Perrin,' Bartholomew said.

A girl stepped forwards, taking down her hood, then gave the name of her chosen vampire, and the ceremony continued as though nothing had happened. It was as though Quick had never been called on at all, as though Bartholomew had pressed a reset button and erased the previous five minutes.

Did that mean Kulika had rejected her? That Quick would

end up back in the blood bank with the others, feeding the vampires day after day until they bled her dry? Or would she get the chance to make a different choice when the others had made their selections?

No one said anything about it, or even acknowledged what had happened, so she guessed she'd just have to wait and see.

For the next hour, Bartholomew called name after name until the hall was practically empty. At the end, there were just three other humans left in the line with Quick, and ten vampires opposite, including Monty. He was still glaring at her, relentlessly.

When the next girl stepped forward, she glanced nervously back at Quick for a moment before saying, 'Monty.'

He looked at the girl. He looked at Quick. Then he crossed the floor, wrapped his arm around the girl's waist and left without a backwards glance.

That option was off the table, then.

The last two made their choices, one after another, and then it was just Quick on her side, still unhooded, with seven hooded vampires she didn't know facing her across the hall.

Quick looked up at Bartholomew, waiting for him to call her name, but instead there was a rush of air and all the candles went out – including the one Quick was holding – plunging the hall into darkness.

Quick stepped slowly backwards until she could feel the wall behind her shoulder blades, waiting for her eyes to acclimatise to the dark.

She waited.

And waited.

Still, all she could see was black.

There was movement on the other side of the hall. She

heard the door to the outside world opening, caught a brief glimpse of a handful of figures silhouetted against the starlit doorway, then the door closed again and the darkness returned. But at least she knew where the door was now, so she had something to aim for.

Carefully, holding her arms out in front of her, she pushed away from the wall and struck out across the hall, bare feet scuffing along the floorboards. It shouldn't be too much further, she thought. Maybe forty paces in total, so half as much again as she'd already travelled, but every step felt like a mile in the dark.

Then her outstretched hands hit something warm.

She stopped.

The other person snatched.

26

IN THE ROOM upstairs, Kulika was pacing.

The ceremony was interminable. So many candidates. So many Silver. And, she imagined, so much blood in the room beneath her where the turnings were taking place.

She'd watched from the window for a while, counting the bodies coming out through the mansion's back door. With some of them, the ones who were being carried unconscious back to the block, they wouldn't be able to tell for hours whether the transformation had been successful or not. With others, it was clear already. A few of the former humans walked themselves happily back across the lawn with their partners, as newly-transformed Silver. A lot more were dragged, biting and growling, off to the river to feed the alligators.

It was efficient, Kulika had to give him that. Bartholomew had never been one for wasted effort, which was exactly why this situation with Quick was such a puzzle. Kulika had the contract, signed in Bartholomew's blood. She just had no idea why he'd given it up in return for so little from her.

When the door to the room finally slammed open, revealing Quick struggling vainly in Bartholomew's arms,

Kulika was still no closer to an answer.

'Put her down,' Kulika said.

'She's all yours,' Bartholomew replied, plonking Quick into the nearest armchair. She looked flustered, pink-cheeked and wild-haired. It affected Kulika more than she liked to admit.

Bartholomew closed the door, but he was still on the inside of it.

'Leave us,' Kulika said.

'That wasn't part of the deal,' he replied.

'I thought you wanted this to work?'

Kulika stared him down, hands on her hips, feet planted firmly, braced for a fight. For a moment, she thought she might get one, but eventually he reached for the door again.

'I'll be right outside,' he said, then he left.

Kulika knew he hadn't gone far. She could hear him out on the mezzanine, listening and waiting, which meant she would have to be careful how she played this.

'What's happening?' Quick asked her, combing her unruly hair back from her face.

Kulika wished she could help, but she held herself back.

'He wants me to give you what you asked for,' she said instead.

'But you...' Quick looked away for a moment, then looked back at Kulika nervously and said, 'But you don't want to?'

'Irrelevant,' she lied. 'He made me an offer I couldn't refuse.'

An offer that was still suspicious enough to have Kulika on high alert, but she'd been in that state for hours now, and it was grating on her. She was tired of fighting, tired of scheming, tired of pouring all her energy into staying one step ahead of Bartholomew. Whatever he wanted from

Quick, he'd got it, and Kulika was about to get what she wanted, too. What she needed now was to stop fighting and get the job done.

Kulika dropped down into the armchair opposite Quick, tracing her features with her gaze. She looked younger tonight, not physically but in the youthful innocence of her wide, shining eyes. She had no idea what she'd landed herself in the middle of, that much was clear.

'Why would you put me in this position?' Kulika asked, almost plaintively. 'You don't know me. We aren't anything to each other.' Kulika blinked as the realisation settled heavily in her stomach: they were nothing to each other, which meant…

'If I try to do this, then I'm going to kill you.'

'I'm sorry,' Quick replied firmly, 'but you're my best chance.'

Kulika shook her head, but there was no way out of this now. Quick was set on this course of action, Kulika had already agreed to it, and the blood was on the page.

'Let's get it over with, then,' Kulika said, getting to her feet.

'First, tell me what it'll be like,' Quick asked, looking up at Kulika with something close to desperation. She needed something to cling to, Kulika realised. An order of things, a process that she could follow so she didn't have to concentrate on the bigger truth looming at the end of the line.

Kulika tried to put the process into words, but the reality of her own turning was distorted by trauma and time. The pieces she remembered were the ones she wished she could forget, the moments of clenched fists and lost dignity and a pain that was so intense that it had felt distant only hours after the event, not to mention centuries. So instead she asked herself: what would she have wanted to know before her turning, if she'd had the choice? But again, she'd suppressed too much of the experience to have any idea what to say.

There was one thing she could offer Quick, though. She'd learned enough since her own transformation to know that you didn't have to turn someone the way she had been turned, with violence.

'It won't hurt,' Kulika promised, taking Quick's hand to pull her to her feet.

Quick looked confused. 'But, the biting,' she said, letting herself be pulled.

'It can be painful, sometimes. It doesn't have to be, if you'll let me…'

'If I'll what?'

But Kulika couldn't bring herself to say the words. Ever since she'd first seen the sunset-haired woman three nights ago, shining across the grotty squalor of Bartholomew's pool party, she'd been drawn to her. She'd wanted to run her fingers through her fiery hair – no, she'd wanted to bury her face in it and inhale. Now that she was beginning to learn the kaleidoscopic scent of English hedgerows, Scottish summers and Spanish orchards that belonged to her, she could barely think straight. She wanted to press her hands into the small of Quick's back and pull her close. She wanted to lean in until her lips were touching Quick's own. She wanted to taste her so badly that her hands hurt with the tension of holding herself back.

Kulika's gaze flickered over Quick's face, pinging like a pinball between the freckles scattered across her cheeks, the generous curve of her lips, the shining hint of dark desire in the dilation of her eyes, until Kulika was dizzy with it.

Then, without Kulika saying a word, Quick reached out a

hand and curved it around Kulika's neck, stroking her fingers behind her ear so they came to rest against Kulika's undercut, rasping through the short hairs. She shivered involuntarily with the pleasure of it and Quick's face froze, then she started to draw her hand away.

'No,' Kulika said, snatching Quick's hand with her own so she could return it to its place. 'Don't stop.'

Then, tentatively, she ran her own fingers into the strands of sunset that had been haunting her for the past three days. They felt like silk, warmed by the heat of Quick's body. Kulika wondered how they would feel pillowed on her shoulder, fisted in her hungry hands, draped across her naked chest.

She looked into Quick's eyes, trying to find a moment of hesitation. If this wasn't what she wanted, if *Kulika* wasn't what she wanted, then she'd drop her hands, step back and break her bargain with Bartholomew. If this wasn't what Quick wanted…

'Yes?' Kulika whispered, leaning in close.

'God, yes,' Quick said.

And Quick kissed her.

27

KISSING KULIKA WAS like… Quick had no idea what it was like. She'd never experienced anything even remotely similar, except for maybe that one time she'd been trying to fish a bagel out of the toaster with a knife and accidentally electrocuted herself. It was overwhelming, and shocking, and she wouldn't have been surprised to find that she'd burned herself in the process.

Then Kulika had started kissing Quick back, her tongue making the briefest contact with Quick's lips, and Quick forgot to breathe. Kulika tasted of the sea, clean and fresh and beckoning her beneath the waves.

She wanted her.

Kulika actually *wanted* her. Quick could feel it in the pressure of her lips, and in the way she'd grabbed for Quick's hand, then run her fingers through her hair… There was no way to misread that.

Was there?

Unless what Kulika really wanted was Quick's blood. She was a vampire, after all.

Oh.

Quick knew she had a long-practised habit of assuming

she was unwelcome, but in her defence her assumptions had often proved true. First there'd been her stepfather, who'd alienated her from her mother during the last years of her illness; then her aunt and uncle, who'd changed their minds about formally adopting her the moment she got into a fight at school; then the entire foster system, which passed her around one negligent home after another, each of them interested only in the cheques they got for keeping her. In fact, ever since she'd been four years old, no one in the world had seemed genuinely pleased to have her in their lives, not until Evita. It felt naïve to imagine she might ever find another person who cared.

But maybe that didn't matter. If Quick was a vampire, she'd be strong. She'd be fast. She'd be immortal. With all that power, maybe she could finally find Evita, or at least find out what had happened to her.

'Are you ready?' Kulika asked.

Even if Kulika only wanted Quick for her blood, maybe that was okay, if she was only willing to make Quick strong, like her.

Quick looked into Kulika's grey eyes and said, 'Yes.'

While Quick watched, keeping eye contact all the time, Kulika very deliberately bit her own lip, until beads of blood formed around her teeth.

'Still ready?' she asked through bloody lips.

'Yes,' Quick said, and if her reply was more tentative this time, it didn't stop Kulika from lowering her lips back to Quick's, filling her mouth with copper and her mind with confusion. This felt… wrong, yes, but better than it should. Quick found herself licking her lips when Kulika pulled away, which puzzled her, but then Kulika's mouth was at her neck, kissing a trail across her throat, and Quick stopped caring if any of it was wrong, or strange. She wanted to feel it, and feel it all, the kisses and licks and nibbles all culminating in the tantalising scratch of Kulika's teeth as they grazed her skin and—

When Kulika bit, the world exploded into fireworks of pleasure, and Quick exploded with it.

28

SOMETHING HAD GONE wrong. Something had gone terribly, horribly, awfully wrong, and Kulika didn't understand how.

She'd needed to kiss Quick, not just because she'd wanted to, but because that was how the process worked. The Silver kissed the human, which produced a scent mark that clung to that human and shielded them from the pain of the bite. Kulika didn't understand the science behind it, but she knew that it worked in practical terms, so that's what she'd done.

What she hadn't expected was her reaction to smelling her scent mark mingled with the seasonal delights of Quick's personal perfume. If Kulika had thought that turning Quick Silver would change the alluring variability of her scent, she'd been wrong: it had done nothing but intensify it. It was overwhelming, and despite her intention to be careful, Kulika had lost control entirely. She kissed, she grabbed, she bit. It spun her around and muddled her mind, the mixed aroma of land and sea, as though between the two of them they could contain the whole world. The thought was grandiose and ridiculous, but it settled in her chest like an incontrovertible truth.

When she felt the tingling in her eyes as she tasted Quick's blood, it was barely a surprise. She'd spent the past few days following Quick's flame-red hair like a beacon through the labyrinth of this dark mansion, so was it really any wonder that Quick had turned out to be the object of all her desires?

In short: Kulika had silvered.

She didn't know what it was supposed to feel like, and stories of the sensation were few and far between, but she didn't need to look in a mirror to know that the silver in the whites of her eyes was now suffusing the grey of her irises. She *knew* it, the same way she knew up from down, and she knew where her hands were when her eyes were closed. Kulika had found the missing part of herself, and it was in her arms. *She* was in her arms.

Kulika released her bite and drew back to find Quick looking up at her with silver in the whites of her eyes. God, she was beautiful. With their new silver surroundings, her irises twinkled like emeralds set in white gold, gleaming in the candlelight.

'Did it work?' Quick asked.

'It worked,' Kulika replied.

More than worked, she thought. Though she needed no confirmation of her new feelings, Kulika found that too: in the bite mark at Quick's neck. It wasn't bleeding, because the wound had been sealed with silver, healed by Kulika's new bond to Quick. Her other wounds were gone, too: the bite mark on the other side of her neck, and the bite on her arm.

'You got lucky,' Kulika said. *We both got lucky*, she thought. If Quick hadn't survived the transformation, then the bond would have dragged Kulika to the grave along with her.

'I want you to know that this isn't why I came here,' Quick said, a little bashfully. 'I didn't even know— I came here looking for a friend who went missing last year.'

'I came here looking for someone too. Then I found you.' Kulika smiled, tucking a strand of hair behind Quick's ear, then whispered impulsively, 'Do you want to get out of here?'

She didn't want Quick in this place, with its demons and its ghosts and its bad memories, not to mention Bartholomew lurking outside every door. She could find another way to track down the information she needed for the baron, but right now her priority was getting Quick as far away from the mansion as possible, beyond Bartholomew's reach, before he convinced either of them to sign his covenant.

They could go out of the window. Kulika could carry Quick if she needed to, and fight her way past anyone who tried to stand in her way. If they could make it as far as the river, they could steal a boat and get to Charleston proper, then there were planes and ships across the ocean and, hell, she'd *swim* it if that would get Quick safely back to Britain and away from him.

He would have heard their discussion. By now, he would know that the transformation had worked. And that meant they had to leave now.

Right now.

29

BEING BITTEN BY Kulika was nothing like being bitten by Monty. For starters, Monty had savaged her neck like a wild animal, while Kulika sunk her teeth into Quick's skin in the same way she kissed: with focus and precision, as though she meant to do it well.

And the kiss.

When Kulika had told her being bitten didn't need to hurt, she had told the entire truth. It hadn't hurt at all. Instead, it had burned through Quick like lightning, setting every nerve alight in the most pleasurable, outrageous way imaginable. For a moment afterwards, she could do nothing but catch her breath. Then, all she could do was watch.

Kulika's eyes were sparkling with silver, gunmetal threaded with platinum. If Quick looked into them for very much longer, she was certain she'd be so thoroughly hypnotised that she'd do anything the woman suggested.

But not this.

'Come on,' Kulika whispered, tugging her towards the window.

Quick had come here to find Evita. That had not gone to plan, admittedly, but she'd picked up some clues along the way. She knew that missing kids ended up here, and she knew how. She knew that more than one of the vampires had recognised the faces on her playing cards, including Evita's. She also knew, if Monty was to be believed, that this all had something to do with someone called Jane – or maybe that Evita had been going by a pseudonym – and that the mere mention of *that* name was enough to make Bella lose her mind entirely.

An hour ago, Quick hadn't been in a position to do anything with that information. Now, things were different. She could feel a new strength suffusing her body, and feel the new sensitivity she possessed. Sounds were louder, lights were brighter, and scents were heightened in a way that seemed to draw her inexorably towards Kulika. She could hear the other woman's slow pulse. She could see the twitching in her muscles as she waited impatiently for Quick to follow her, and part of her wanted to do exactly that. The rest knew that, with this newfound strength, and with the authority that being a vampire would provide her in this place – at least compared with the impotence she'd had as a human – she could surely find the answers she'd come here searching for.

'I can't leave,' Quick said, pulling reluctantly away. 'Not until I find Evita.'

Kulika turned, her gaze sharpening. 'Evita?' she said. 'Please tell me you don't mean Evita Khalyed.'

Hope leapt in Quick's chest. 'You know her?'

'No.' She lowered her voice to a pitch Quick shouldn't have been able to discern, and yet she could. 'Does he know you're looking for her?'

'He who?' Quick asked.

Kulika nodded towards the door.

'Bartholomew? I don't know.' Then Quick finally put her

finger on the change that had been staring her in the face since she'd first opened her eyes after Kulika's bite. 'Your eyes are different,' she said. 'Is it because of what just happened?'

'In a way.'

'What way?'

Kulika threw open the window and said, 'Long story short, it means I'm not leaving this mansion without you. So come on.'

Quick was still trying to work out what that *really* meant when the door opened.

'Leaving so soon?' Bartholomew asked, sauntering inside. He seemed almost friendly to Quick, but then she turned to Kulika and revised her assessment. Kulika's grip on the window ledge was so tight that she was warping the frame, splintering it under her fingers.

That was the first sign of trouble. The ones that followed would be worse.

30

'WE'RE LEAVING,' KULIKA said, striding forward and taking Quick's hand again to pull her out of Bartholomew's reach. If Kulika had any say in the matter, he would never touch her again.

'Oh, I don't think so,' he replied.

'We had a deal,' Kulika pointed out, 'written in your own blood. I did what you wanted, now give me the information you promised me and let us go.'

'You've got it,' he replied nonchalantly, infuriatingly.

'What are you talking about?'

'Dr Khalyed was here,' he conceded. 'Briefly. But I don't have any idea what happened to her after she left, or where she went. The best information I have is sitting in your new girlfriend's pretty little head. She's her best friend, you know. Knows everything about her, inside and out.'

Kulika turned to Quick and looked at her, numbness spreading through her limbs.

'Why are you talking about Evita?' Quick asked, looking between the two of them.

Kulika cracked. All this time she'd been hanging around the mansion, waiting on Bartholomew's pleasure, wasting days on the promise of knowledge he didn't even have. He'd never had anything to give her. He'd bluffed on an empty hand, and she'd gone all in.

'You had nothing. All this time,' she said to him softly, dangerously, then she yelled, 'Nothing!' and kicked out at the nearest side table, splintering it into kindling.

Quick jumped away, putting an armchair between them. Kulika was scaring her, she realised. She should calm down, *discipline* herself, but she couldn't calm down, not now she'd worked out what he'd done. This whole time, he'd been playing her.

Of course he'd been playing her.

'What was the point?' Kulika yelled at Bartholomew. 'I would have signed,' she said, knowing in her heart that it was true: she would have signed his Articles in return for the information she'd thought he held. 'You could have had me, but instead you've just delayed me by days, for no reason at all.'

'You know me better than that,' he replied, leaning casually against the door, pushing it back into its frame until it clicked shut. 'Everything I do is for a reason.'

'Then why even bother? For fun?'

'Please, Kulika. I'm a businessman these days, not a pirate. I work for the rewards that profit me, not merely for my own amusement. But I've fulfilled my part of the bargain. You have your information. Pick Ms Quick's brains as much as you wish, and then you can leave.'

'I'm not staying here another minute,' Kulika said.

'Then you'll leave with nothing,' Bartholomew replied. The first hints of a smile began to tug at the corner of his mouth. 'Because, you see, Ms Quick is staying here with me.'

'No, she's not,' Kulika replied with equal assurance. 'I

turned her, and I'm claiming her. She doesn't belong to you, Bartholomew. She's not wearing your mark. She hasn't signed your covenant.'

'Hasn't she?' Bartholomew asked, his smile becoming ever more evident. Then he pulled a new leather-bound book from his robes, one that Kulika didn't recognise, and opened it to a page covered in red signatures. 'They all sign on their way into the mansion for the Casting,' he said, adding with mock sincerity, 'Oh, dear. Did you not know?'

Kulika looked at Quick as the bottom fell out of her world.

'Outside the main door,' Quick whispered. 'They said we had to. They said—'

'So you see, Kulika,' Bartholomew said, crossing the room to snatch Quick's hand before Kulika could stop him, 'she does, indeed, belong to me.'

He pulled a new object from his robes, a weapon Kulika recognised with a sharp chill of fear.

Kulika yelled, 'No!'

But it was too late. Bartholomew had already uncurled Quick's fingers and slammed the stamp into her palm, while Kulika stood by hopelessly and watched.

Quick screamed.

Kulika's blood froze.

It was a crude thing, that stamp: a vicious cluster of needles fed by a well of ink at their base, designed by Bartholomew himself with utility rather than comfort in mind. Kulika remembered all too clearly how it had felt when he had ground the pointy end into her own skin, leaving behind a dirty black wound that had bound her to his crew for all eternity. At least until Baron Drake had come along.

Kulika rushed to Quick's side, wrapping her arms

protectively around her as Quick cradled her bleeding palm. It would heal soon enough now that she was Silver, but Kulika knew from experience that the stain would remain, Bartholomew's black mark sealed deep under the skin.

Quick was bound to Bartholomew.

Kulika felt sick.

Quick, the woman Kulika had just turned, had just silvered for and, undeniably, had just fallen for, pitching headfirst into a love from which the only possible escape was death.

'That's why you wanted me to turn her,' Kulika whispered to Bartholomew. Even to her own ears, her tone sounded like an admission of defeat. 'You knew I would silver.'

'I guessed,' Bartholomew conceded, sheathing the stamp. 'You were showing… How to say this delicately? Signs of partiality?' He was smiling like a wolf now, no longer bothering to hide his triumph. He opened the book to the page of signatures once more, and pointed at one in the centre that read, *Patience Quick*. Even from this distance, Kulika could scent that it was written in Quick's own blood.

'As it turns out, I didn't need you to sign my covenant,' Bartholomew said to Kulika, tapping the signature with a grin. 'Not when I already have your heart right here.'

He slammed the book shut, and the noise was like a chain wrapping around Kulika's throat.

Then he laughed.

And laughed.

PART TWO

A QUICK STUDY

I

IN THE MANSION on the Cooper River, Patience Quick was sleeping off a belly full of blood in the big four-poster bed of the grandest guest suite the house had to offer. It was occupied currently – and for the foreseeable future – by Kulika Yadav. The guest herself sat in an armchair by the bed and stared at the resting Silver she had just created.

She'd done the best she could for her. She'd bitten with all the gentleness she could offer, she'd caught Quick in her arms when the exhaustion of the turning and the covenant began to break her, then she'd stepped outside to find a human to drain into a glass so Quick wouldn't have to do any biting of her own.

Bartholomew decreed that all his crew drank from the vein, but…

Not yet.

Let her take it slowly, just this once. Let her not tear her way wildly into this new life the way Kulika had been forced to do, with hungry teeth and flesh beneath her fingernails.

Kulika watched the gentle thudding of Quick's pulse at her throat as she slept peacefully, counting every beat as a gift.

One thousand, eight hundred and fifty six. One thousand, eight hundred and fifty seven. One thousand, eight hundred and fifty eight.

Still her heart beat, thud after gentle thud, and Kulika's heart beat with it.

In the master suite next door, Bartholomew Sometimes-Roberts was flicking through the ledger of signatories to his Articles, counting each life as his due.

Two hundred and fifty six. Two hundred and fifty seven. And there on the final page – *two hundred and fifty eight* – the blood-inked signature that had finally brought Kulika back to him and sealed her place at his side forever.

Patience Quick.

With Quick bound to his covenant, and Kulika bound to Quick, she would never be able to leave him again, and that was everything his dark heart desired.

At least, it had been, until six months ago when *she* walked into his life and—

But he had vowed to himself that he would not remember that day, and didn't he have a solution to that particular problem right here at his fingertips? So instead he directed his mind back to the page, and forced a smile onto his lips. After a couple of seconds, it was not so very hard to keep it there.

Let Kulika have a few hours with the girl. Let her reflect on what she'd gained, and what she stood to lose at his merest whim. Let her have just enough time to realise how much was she was entirely in his power, then he'd demonstrate it in a way she would not forget.

His smile widened.

Over two hundred and fifty signatories, and Kulika besides. With that many Silver at his beck and call, he would have his war, and win it too.

* * *

On the Palisadoes – the narrow strip of land that connected Port Royal to the rest of Jamaica – Job Bayly crouched beside the road in an unremarkable spot and counted his buried treasures.

This stretch of sand had been a graveyard once, back before the earthquake of 1692 had sucked the old pirate capital under the sea. The island was sand all the way down, and that was what had doomed it. When the earth had shaken sand and water together, rocking and roiling on the join of two tectonic plates, it liquified the land until the whole peninsula was nothing but a gurgling morass of quicksand, swallowing everything in its path and spitting out only the bits it couldn't chew.

Bayly wouldn't have believed it himself if he hadn't seen it with his own eyes. When he looked out now along the dark expanse of the new quayside and closed his eyes, he could still remember exactly how it had looked more than three centuries ago. Port Royal hadn't just been a ramshackle collection of pirate huts and taverns along the shore, not like some of the old Caribbean settlements. Instead, its buildings had been raised ill-advisedly high on floor after floor of fine stone, with wharves and storehouses, churches and synagogues, and not just one but five stone-built forts to guard the harbour. The place had teemed with British soldiers and ships, both military and merchant vessels, and besides that the streets had been filled with buccaneers and privateers of every kind. It had been a bustling and licentious paradise, catering to every secret desire a pirate might harbour in their breast, or their belly, or below their belt. The locals used to brag that there was one tavern for every three residents, and the papers afterwards were full of stories about heavenly punishment, crowing that their god had seen fit to swallow Port Royal into the earth as a judgement on its wickedness.

Bayly thought that probably wasn't far from the truth. His own days in that port had been filled with drinking and debauching, but he'd been wickeder than most and yet here he was, still walking the earth in whatever kind of soulless form the clergy would condemn him and the rest of the Silver as inhabiting. Bayly didn't care much for their opinions either way. He'd never been one for moralising.

He liked the sunken city. He'd always been drawn here, enough that he came back often, and not just to check on his treasure, either. The place called to him like the ghost of a life half-lived, echoing through the centuries with memories of what might have been, pulling on him like an anchor tethering a ship to the sea floor. He dragged it along behind him in the sand, but it dug in deep, caught and held.

This graveyard called to him most of all. It had once been the final resting place of buccaneer supreme Henry Morgan. The gravestones were gone now, along with every other marker that might have led Bayly to the right spot, but he didn't need any guide beyond his own senses. He knew well enough where the 'X' was, no "digs" required.

He chuckled to himself at the private joke.

They were still down there, his secrets. He could sense them. Hear them, almost. They were fifteen feet under the sand, locked away in a lead box that had been dug up three times since it was first buried here, and only once by Bayly himself. That was the problem with treasure: everyone was always going hunting for it, like they had a right to what wasn't theirs. These treasures, though, Bayly would guard with his life – had guarded, in fact – and with good reason. One of them was enough to buy Enzo out of Bartholomew's covenant, if he reckoned it right, and that was a bargaining chip he wouldn't be surrendering to anyone.

Ever.

No matter who they were.

In the darkness, the sea looked like blood. Everything reminded Bayly of blood these days. The tide was gentle that night, each wave rolling in across the sand as softly as a breath, but when it withdrew it left the scrubby beach stained in ways that called unpleasantly on Bayly's more recent memories.

Not that he minded the bloodshed. He'd never flinched, not once. What he minded was the way the captain used that bloodshed to tarnish his crew, then polish them up afterwards into something that was shinier to his eye, more valuable.

Kulika saw the way of it clearly enough. Bayly had seen it just as clearly himself, but Bartholomew had tied him up in knots just the same, the way he did with everyone. There was no escaping it, no way except by blackmail and bribery, which was the way he'd got out the first time, or by overwhelming force, the way Kulika had.

It was her own damn fault that she was stuck there again. He'd warned her, more than once. She was the one who'd chosen to come back. Let her find her own escape hatch, because he wasn't giving up his. He had a neat solution to his own problems, and he was keeping it.

But oh, he did so hate it when things got messy.

Bayly laid a hand against the scrub-pitted, rocky sand and felt the pulsing call of the treasure beneath his fingertips. It would be time to dig soon. Soon, but not yet.

First, he had to do what he had been unable to accomplish in all these long months trapped in Bartholomew's net: convince Enzo that it was time to cut free.

2

IT WAS STILL dark when Quick was dragged unceremoniously from Kulika's bed and thrust out into the corridor beyond, where Monty was waiting for her. She got only a brief glimpse of Kulika's outraged expression and Bartholomew's dark smile before the door was slammed in her face.

She blinked the fog from her mind, trying to get her thoughts in order.

She'd been turned by Kulika, as evidenced by her overwhelmed senses.

She'd been marked by Bartholomew, as evidenced by the tattoo on her palm.

Then…

What?

She remembered the room spinning, and there'd been a glass of something she'd rather not think about at her lips – which she must have drunk mindlessly for all she could recollect it – and now here she was, bewildered in the corridor. There'd been no time to talk, or to ask any of the hundreds of questions she needed answered, right now.

What's going on in this mansion? What's going to happen

to us now? And, pressing on her with an urgency that Quick couldn't deny, *Does this mean that there is, in fact, an* us?

She wasn't going to get any answers from Monty, either, because the only thing he would say to her was, 'Back to the block,' before shoving her on ahead of him and falling into a sullen silence. When she started to talk, she just got another shove between the shoulders.

She could have run. She had the power now, didn't she? But then, where would she have gone? She couldn't just abandon Xiaoyu and the others in the blood cellar. Besides which, she needed to be here to find out what had happened to her best friend.

Kulika was looking for Evita too, she'd said. And whatever Xiaoyu said, Quick was sure she'd been trying to get her and the others out of the cellar. That meant Kulika was on their side, didn't it?

Then there was the covenant to consider. She'd signed the book, but she had no idea what any of it actually meant. It wasn't as though she'd been given the opportunity to read the terms and conditions, or to refuse them if she'd objected. None of it had been presented as though she had any choice in the matter.

It all came down to this: Quick had too little information and no plan at all. She obviously wasn't going to get anything out of Monty, so she decided she might as well do as he demanded and go back to the block. With any luck, she'd find someone there who was feeling more talkative.

But once Monty had directed her to the twenty-bunk dorm room she would apparently be sharing, initial signs weren't good.

'Here she comes,' a girl whispered quietly into the expectant hush.

Quick wasn't sure she would have been able to make out

the words twelve hours ago. Now that she was one of *them*, with her senses turned up to the maximum, every sound pinged around in her head like an angry scream of static. Her own footsteps sounded as harsh as a snare drum, even barefooted, and her heartbeat was so distractingly loud that she wasn't sure she'd ever be able to ignore it.

And the scents. Better that she didn't think too much about them, or she'd be dragged back into the memory of the fresh rush of Kulika's perfume through her sinuses when she took her first breath as one of the Silver, and forget herself all over again.

Kulika.

The few brief lucid moments they'd had together were torture to remember. Quick wanted so much of her, and she'd been allowed barely a taste. Now, with no idea when she'd see her again – if ever – she wondered if it might be better if last night had never happened at all.

'Who is she?' one of the girls asked, looking directly at Quick as she stood hesitating in the doorway where Monty had abandoned her.

'I'm Quick,' she spoke into the dim light. It probably should have been more than dim, perhaps entirely dark, but Quick could see better now, too.

'Not you,' the girl said again. '*Her*. The one who turned you.'

'Kulika?' Quick asked, and a sigh went around the room.

Kulika.

Quick knew she'd been hedging her bets when she'd chosen Kulika at the Casting, but she hadn't appreciated quite how much she'd overreached until that moment.

'I told you it was her,' a voice said from over by the window, then so many conversations started up that Quick lost track. She caught snippets: *pirate code... ran away and broke the covenant... definitely going to choose her.*

They recognised Kulika's name, that much was clear. What any of the rest of it meant was beyond Quick's comprehension, and she wasn't comfortable enough with her audience to start asking questions to clarify, or any questions at all. Instead, she made her way over to the first unclaimed bed she could find – a bottom bunk – and sat there, wondering what the hell she was supposed to do now. When they'd been climbing the stairs to this floor, Monty had said, 'Training starts later. Sleep now or don't sleep.' Those were the only words he'd spoken to her since leaving the mansion, so she should probably have taken them seriously, but the dorm was loud – *everything* was loud to her new senses – and she was haunted by memories that wouldn't leave her alone.

A kiss.

A bite.

A blissful moment of joyful release, like the surging chords of an anthem reverberating in her chest, then Bartholomew had stamped his covenant into her hand and the dream had ended.

This was the nightmare, now.

She stroked the black tattoo that sat in the centre of her palm. The skin had already healed, another ability her new being possessed, but the ink was trapped in there now.

She counted fourteen of them in the dorm room, including herself, and they all seemed to have the same mark. She recognised a few of the others from the Casting, but there'd been so many people in the hall that she couldn't be sure they were all new, like her. One of them she was sure about, though: by some miserable twist of fate, she'd ended up sharing a bunk with the girl who'd chosen Monty to turn her. Apparently, he'd been more successful with her than he would have been with Quick. She was hanging over the edge of the top bunk now, staring down at Quick with huge, brown, silver-threaded eyes. She had sharp cheekbones, tan skin, and long, straggly brown hair pulled into a messy ponytail that was draping straight down into Quick's face.

'Hi,' Quick said tentatively, brushing the girl's hair away. 'I'm Quick.'

'Oh, I know,' the girl said, 'Monty didn't stop bitching about you the whole way over here from the house.'

'Oh,' said Quick, because what was she supposed to say to that?

'Seriously,' the girl went on. '*I'm* the one who chose him. *I'm* the one who finally gave him a win. You'd think he'd be a little grateful or, I don't know, flattered at least, but oh no, he's all pissed off about you leaving him hanging instead.' She paused for a moment with a peevish look or her face, then added, 'I'm not, by the way.'

'Sorry?' Quick asked, having lost the thread entirely.

'Pissed off with you. I mean, obviously. I got what I wanted out of it. No complaints. About you, anyway.'

'Sorry?' Quick said again, still feeling like she wasn't really part of this conversation.

'I came here to turn Silver, and now I'm Silver, so even if Monty's going to obsess over you and ignore me like we didn't spend the past week fucking each other's brains out, then whatever, right? His loss.'

The girl's face disappeared and there was a *flump* from above, the bunk shaking as the girl settled onto the mattress. Apparently she was done talking, along with the rest of the dorm. They were quiet now, which gave Quick the distinct impression they'd been listening in to the conversation she'd just had.

It was an inauspicious start to Quick's time in the dorm,

but she had an ominous feeling that things were about to get much worse.

3

THE MORNING AFTER Kulika turned Quick Silver, the news broke. It started in Oklahoma, but it wasn't more than an hour before the rest of the country picked it up and ran with it. Now video of Cara Alton's Silver-speed abduction was playing nonstop on news channels, websites and social media worldwide.

The first clips hadn't given Kulika much cause for concern. The comments said it all.

I thought you were serious journalists, and now you're falling for crappy AI deepfakes? Give me a break.

Who's got their finger on the fast forward button?

Usain Bolt goes slower than this.

Nice try. Jog on.

But now, less than an hour later, speculation was surging out of control. Someone reputable had analysed the tape and declared it genuine. *Look*, one commentator said, *you can see vehicles moving in the background and they're going at normal speed, so how do you explain that if there's no doctoring?*

Then someone put Cara's parents in front of a camera. They'd already been badgering the local media to pay more attention to their daughter's abduction, which they'd always claimed was the result of a supernatural event. They'd been right there, they said. They'd seen it all. Or, rather, they *hadn't* seen it. One minute she'd been there and the next: nothing. Just her lemonade glass smashing on the paving and an empty space where she'd been standing just a millisecond before.

They were crazy, everyone had said. But now, four days later, with video evidence to back up their story, people were finally starting to take them seriously.

Bartholomew's opening volley had hit its mark.

Kulika was staring at the videos on her newly-returned phone when Bartholomew summoned her to the library. It wasn't a surprise. She'd been expecting the summons ever since he'd breezed through the connecting door between their rooms while it was still dark that morning and ushered Quick out with a brisk, 'Take her, kid.'

Kulika had protested, of course. She'd screamed and fought, for all the good it had done her. As Bartholomew had already demonstrated recently, he was more than capable of overpowering her.

'Settle down,' he'd said as he pinned her to the wall by her throat. As she'd thrashed hopelessly against his grip, her gaze had been drawn irresistibly to the copper coin he wore around his neck, the glinting token a shiny version of the tattoo that now scarred Quick's palm.

She'd stilled, then.

'You see how it is.' A gloating smile had tugged at Bartholomew's lips. 'You could have been my queen, Kulika,' he'd said, as though he were the one who'd been disadvantaged by her failure, and not Kulika. 'I would have been your slave,' he'd said. 'But instead…'

He'd let Kulika fill in the blanks.

'So fragile, these new Silver,' he'd said sadly. 'One little slip of the wrist, and—' Then he'd slammed his empty fist against the wall, punching a hole right next to Kulika's head. 'You understand the delicacy of the situation, don't you?'

Swallowing against his grip, Kulika had nodded awkwardly, her eyes fixed on his.

He'd released her, then. There would have been no point in holding her any longer; he'd already got her under control, broken and trained to his word.

'Stay here for the time being,' he'd said, as though it were an invitation rather than an order. 'I'll call for you in a while.'

The phone was a consolation prize, and a reminder: *everything you have is mine to give or take away.*

The photo of Evita Khalyed was missing from it now, along with every other bit of information Kulika used to have stored on it. He'd wiped it clean. She could still access the internet, though, so at least there was something to distract her while she waited for his next move.

If only the distraction hadn't been quite so cataclysmic in its implications.

Oklahoma Teen Snatched into Thin Air!

President Denies Military Tech Responsible for Teen's Disappearance

Supernatural Creatures in Our Midst?

The Silver were coming out, whether they wanted to or not. Maybe that wouldn't have bothered Kulika so much yesterday, but now that the Silver included Quick, she felt the threat of it jumping in her chest.

There was a knock at the door and a voice called, 'Bartholomew wants you in the library.' It sounded like the guy Bartholomew called "the kid", and everyone else called Monty. Kulika raced to the door, hoping to find out where he'd taken Quick, but the corridor was empty when she got there.

The coward had run away.

'Kulika,' Bartholomew greeted her as she walked into the library without knocking. 'How nice to see you, even if your arrival is a little… abrupt.'

'You were expecting me,' she argued in her defence, but even to her own ears the words sounded petulant.

Bartholomew's face softened into that look of paternalistic tolerance that she so hated, the one that said, *This child of mine is such a trial, but I am a caring and gentle parent, so I will weather it.* Kulika knew very well what Bartholomew really was, and she resented the gap between the persona he projected and the one he inhabited. She could see the width of that gulf, even if none of his followers would acknowledge it.

He was no father to her.

'Sit,' Bartholomew said.

Kulika made her way to one of the leather armchairs she'd occupied during their last discussion in this room, but Bartholomew stopped her before she could sit with an, 'Ah-ah-ah. I don't think so. Do you?' He raised an eyebrow at her, then held her gaze for a moment before looking regretfully at the bare floorboards.

This was how it would be, then. He'd welcomed her back into this house as a peer, and he'd offered her more than that besides. Now he wanted her to feel just how far she'd fallen, as though her loss of status were an unfortunate result of her own decisions instead of a punishment he was inflicting on her.

You could have had all this, he was saying, *if only you had appreciated what I offered you.*

Kulika reminded herself that he held Quick's life in his

hands.

She sat on the damn floor.

Bartholomew sat in the armchair and looked down at her like a master looking down at his dog, then he grinned his shit-eating grin.

Kulika wanted to punch it off his face, but instead she breathed deeply. She had borne this before. For Quick, she could bear it again.

'Can I see her?' Kulika asked.

'The crew are training until this evening,' Bartholomew replied dismissively. 'In the meantime, I've got a job for you.'

'You said no orders,' she reminded him, as ridiculous an assertion as that was while she was sitting on the floor at his feet. 'You said I could complete the mission I started for the baron.'

'Those were the terms of a different bargain though, weren't they?' he said condescendingly. 'As things stand, our deal has been completed, and we have no bargain at all between us now. But then we don't need one, do we?'

'No,' she agreed. They both knew she'd do exactly what he asked, whenever he asked, so what was the point in denying it? 'Would you let us leave?' she asked desperately, trying not to let her voice break over the words.

'Of course, *you* may leave,' he said magnanimously. 'You're not a member of my crew. You haven't signed the Articles. You're free to go whenever you wish.'

Kulika sat in silence, waiting for the rider she knew would inevitably follow.

'But why would you want to go when your heart is here?' he asked.

'Will you let *her* leave?'

'Why would she want to, when her crew is here? It's been

too long, Kulika,' he said, sitting back in his chair as though he were an old man reminiscing over fond memories, instead of a youthful immortal counting his victories. 'You've forgotten how strong the ties between a crew can be. Our Patience doesn't want to leave, does she?'

Kulika wanted to object to the *our*, but the truth was that, right now, Quick belonged more Bartholomew than she did to anyone, perhaps even more than Quick belonged to herself. That was what the covenant did, as Kulika knew from personal experience: it erased you and replaced you with the person Bartholomew wanted you to be.

'She refused to go with you last night, as I recall,' he added. 'When you wanted to leave?'

Even though Kulika knew he was twisting the event to his own purposes, she felt that barb land sharply in her chest.

'Only until she's found her friend,' Kulika argued weakly.

'Is that what she told you?' Bartholomew asked, with what sounded like pity. 'Did she say she'd be willing to go with you afterwards, or did you simply assume so? My dear girl, does she even know how you feel?'

'Yes,' Kulika insisted, but it sounded like the lie it was. They hadn't had the time to talk. There'd been the bite, and then she'd tried to get Quick to leave, and then Bartholomew had been there with his covenant stamp and she'd had to rush out to get blood for Quick to drink before she went feral and then…

Then it had been too late to tell her anything at all. 'If you'd just let me talk to her, then—'

'As it happens,' Bartholomew interrupted, 'I *am* willing to let you complete that little mission of yours.'

That had Kulika sitting up a little straighter, which irritated her; in her head she imagined herself as a pointer pricking up its ears.

But it was suspicious. Why, when his position was so strong, would Bartholomew grant her any concession at all? She was almost afraid to ask, for fear that the question would chase his generosity away, but she knew him better than that. If he was offering her even the tiniest crumb of consolation, there was a reason for it.

'Why?' she asked. 'Why do you care?'

'I care for all of my crew.'

'And Evita Khalyed was part of it? You didn't tell me that before.'

'Because you weren't crew before.'

'I'm not crew *now*. You just said so.'

Bartholomew just smiled at her.

As good as, she thought. She'd come back to this mansion swearing she wouldn't sign her life away again, and she hadn't. She'd let Quick do that for her, in ignorance of what her blood on the page would mean, and in ignorance of what would follow afterwards. She was still ignorant, in fact. She didn't know that Kulika had silvered for her. She didn't know that Kulika's life was now bonded to hers, or that Kulika was tied to Bartholomew just as surely as Quick was. More so, because he knew she'd do anything to protect Quick, even if it cost her everything in the world: her freedom, her pride, even her life.

Kulika was in love, and that love would be her undoing.

She couldn't say Bartholomew hadn't warned her. Back on the *Royal Fortune*, he'd always stressed that Article six was the most important one.

No boy or woman to be allowed amongst them. If any man shall be found seducing any of the latter sex and carrying her to sea in disguise he shall suffer death.

'Women, they're nothing but trouble,' he'd said to her. He'd said it loudly and often, not least every time they'd executed another crew member for breaking the code; more times than she could count. 'Let them under your skin and they'll sink you.'

And she'd nodded along, hanging on every word, believing to her bones that they were true.

No wonder he was crowing now.

'Tell me the rest,' she said now with a sigh.

'You asked me about Jane,' he said.

Kulika remembered. She'd heard the name from Quick, and—

'I told you she was one of the new Silver here at the mansion,' Bartholomew went on. 'And that's true, but the notable thing about Jane was that, unusually, she lost her memory when she was turned.'

'I've never heard of that happening before,' Kulika said, curious now.

'Me neither, but there it is. Apparently she had a sense of humour about it, though, because she called herself Jane Doe. She couldn't remember her real name, or where she'd come from, or how she'd come to turn Silver, but there were other things she could remember, like the geography and history and Charleston, especially as it related to the lives and deaths of the pirates who raided it.'

'That was Evita Khalyed's area of study,' Kulika said.

'Exactly.'

It was a subject Kulika had researched before she left Oxford. The whole reason Dr Khalyed had come to Charleston in the first place was to make a presentation to a bunch of academics and pirate fans about her research on the sinking of Port Royal. The 1692 disaster had happened before Kulika's time – she hadn't even been born to her human life back then – but she'd heard about it from Bayly and some of the others they'd sailed with. Apparently Dr

Khalyed had a theory based on relics recovered from the ruins of the sunken city. She theorised that some pirates were taking aliases throughout the buccaneering days of the late seventeenth century and the Golden Age of piracy that followed, reinventing themselves as new characters to evade capture. It was a pretty insightful theory, though she'd missed the essential detail that most of the pirates who did so were Silver, and they were reinventing themselves so no one would notice they weren't aging or dying like they should.

Now she'd lost her memory, she'd never know how right she'd been.

'So Jane and Evita Khalyed are the same person?' Kulika asked.

'It seems that way,' Bartholomew replied.

'And she was crew,' Kulika said.

'Yes.'

That made sense of so many mysteries that Kulika had puzzled over since arriving at the mansion. She'd known from Bartholomew's reaction to Jane's name that she was important to him. She'd also suspected from her snooping in his desk that he was keeping the missing person card with her picture on it somewhere close to him. And then there'd been that moment in the breakfast room when Quick had thrown herself at Kulika, saying, *I need to ask you about Jane*. She must have worked out that Evita had been going by that name while she was at the mansion.

So much made sense now.

'And she's already Silver?' Kulika asked.

'Yes,' Bartholomew replied.

'Since when?'

'She arrived here at the beginning of the year.'

'When exactly?' Kulika pressed, 'And how exactly?'

But Bartholomew just shrugged, as thought it were

irrelevant. Kulika didn't like that. It left too many questions unanswered. Maybe Bartholomew just hadn't paid attention, and he was certainly trying to give that impression, but it wasn't like him not to notice everything that happened on his property. It wasn't like him at all.

'The point is that she's gone,' he said. 'And you're going to find her.'

'Where did she go, then?' Kulika asked. 'Who saw her last?'

'Those are questions that no one seems capable of answering,' Bartholomew replied, with more than a little frustration. 'She was here, and then she was not.'

'When?'

'A few weeks ago.'

'That recently? Was she living in the house, or over at the block?'

'In the dorms,' he said. 'The others can show you her things. I don't know the details.'

He was becoming dismissive now, as though he wanted her to go away and do the task she'd been set instead of sitting here asking more questions, but he didn't tell her to go. Maybe he didn't want her to notice his discomfort, but she did. She noticed every glance away, every twitch of his fingers, every tiny slip of his smile. Those little observations were the only reason she'd survived as long as she had in this house the first time around.

She'd learned her master well, and she knew him well enough to know that if she threw him off his guard, she might provoke him into revealing more than he intended.

'Do you think she's dead?' she asked abruptly.

There it was: a slight widening of his eyes. It was evident for only the tiniest fraction of a second before he covered it, but Kulika saw it.

'She means something to you,' she said.

'I don't know what you're implying,' he replied calmly.

Kulika didn't know, either. She knew from the photo she'd seen that Dr Khalyed was a beautiful woman, but she also knew that her beauty would have had no effect on Bartholomew. In all his long centuries of celibacy, not a single person of any gender had raised any kind of romantic feeling in him. The question then became: what did she have that he wanted?

'Is it something to do with her research?' Kulika asked.

'Her work was of no consequence,' he said dismissively. 'I lived those years, along with the centuries before them, as well you know. I don't need some academic to tell me what pirates were like through the lens of three centuries of romanticisation. We *were* pirates, Kulika. Or have you forgotten?'

As if he would ever let her.

'Then why is she so important to you?'

'She's a missing piece,' Bartholomew replied with an innocent shrug. 'She's part of the crew, and when she left she took a piece of their power with her.'

Kulika raised her eyebrows at him.

'You might disbelieve it, but they can feel it,' Bartholomew insisted. 'They're part of each other, and they aren't complete when they're separated. Why do you think they all stay here? Her absence is like an ache in their blood. Either she needs to return to us or, if she's no longer alive, we need to recover her body.'

'So you can eat it?' Kulika asked, remembering the spectacle she'd witnessed earlier in the week.

Bartholomew gave her a disapproving look that made her reconsider her tone. She was pushing it, and the line he had drawn was not a flexible one.

'You disdain them without understanding their pain,' he said. 'Ask our Patience when you see her next, and she'll tell you. It eats at them. It drives them. You could let it drive you, too, if you would only surrender to it. You could join us, properly. It could be just like it was before,' he said, reaching down to caress Kulika's cheek. 'The two of us, together again.'

Kulika was confused, no longer understanding what place Bartholomew had ordained for her in his plan. Why, if he intended to elevate her, did he have her grovelling on the floor in front of him? He'd wanted to humiliate her, that was clear enough, but she'd assumed that humility was all he'd want from her now. He had Quick. He could give Kulika nothing but the dirt on his boots and he knew he'd have her at his command.

But he seemed to be offering her more than that: a place on the crew, as his first mate, at his side.

'Is that what you want?' Kulika asked.

'Of course,' he said softly. 'When I told you I wanted to give you rein to fulfil your darkest desires, that was more than just words. You have such unrealised potential, bottled and corked by Drake and the repressive mansion he runs back in the old country. Old indeed. Old-fashioned. Outdated, Kulika. All I've ever wanted is to set you free you from him, and now that you're home... I have so much to offer you, if only you would embrace your true self again.'

It would have been easier to dismiss his words as rhetoric if they hadn't struck her so deeply. Her sense of self had been on shaky ground ever since her return to Bartholomew's mansion, and now that she'd silvered for Quick – fallen in *love*, something she thought she'd never do – she could feel her identity splintering into pieces that were too fragmented to force back together again.

And the person Bartholomew remembered from their century together, that blood-soaked pirate who had cut down crew after crew in their never-ending quest for treasure? Kulika remembered her too, and with fondness, like a seductively comfortable cloak that she could step back into whenever she wanted, and find herself cradled in the anonymity of the dark. That was the persona into which Kulika had been birthed as one of the Silver. She was nostalgic for her in the way that most people are nostalgic for their youth: with envy for the power that rose-tinted memories attributed to her, but with equal scorn for her mistakes, believing rashly that she could not make them again.

Kulika understood well enough why that memory was so seductive to her. She understood less why it preoccupied Bartholomew.

'Why offer me anything at all?' she asked.

'I made you Silver,' he said, cupping her face in both of his hands, then he leaned down to press his forehead against hers. Kulika couldn't look away, and not just because he was holding her in place. His gaze was like a cage, trapping her attention. Her eyes watered as she stared into his. 'You are mine,' he whispered, 'and I am yours.'

'And Quick?' she whispered back shakily.

'Is crew,' Bartholomew replied, 'and the crew is ours. Yours and mine.'

'Ours,' she repeated.

'Always.'

Then Kulika blinked, and the moment broke. Bartholomew released her face and relaxed back in his chair as though it had never happened, smoothing the sleeves of his henley.

'So, you see,' he said briskly, 'you won't be finding Evita

Khalyed for Drake's sake at all. You'll be doing it for the crew.'

For the crew.

The words were painfully familiar.

'All right,' Kulika said heavily. 'For the crew.'

'That's my girl.' Bartholomew smiled, and three hundred years melted away.

That's my girl, he'd said as she blinked back to consciousness after slaughtering half the hands on board their prize during the thirst of her turning.

That's my girl, he'd said as she savaged her way through blades and gunfire to get to his body and hurl it overboard, as they'd agreed, on the day the pirate Bartholomew Roberts had apparently died taking grapeshot in the neck during sea battle with the *Swallow*.

That's my girl, he'd said as she finally sank her hand into his chest and brought it out holding his heart, on the night she'd left the mansion behind her for what she'd vowed would be the last time.

For the crew, she'd spat back at his unconscious body, but what she'd meant was, *for myself*.

Now, Kulika had no crew any longer, nor any self that was worth saving. There was just Quick, and *her* crew, and the captain they all served.

4

'EVERYONE UP!' CAME a shout from the corridor, accompanied by what sounded like someone hitting a saucepan with a spoon. 'Out of bed, you lazy fucks!' the shouting continued along the corridor. 'Training starts and ends today, so get your butts downstairs!'

'Language!' someone shouted back.

'Oh, fuck off, you puritanical shit.'

'Lord, listen to the mouth on you.'

'And look at the ass on you. You don't hear me complaining.'

'He don't get no complaints about that ass!' a third voice joined in, then the block echoed with brittle laughter bouncing off the empty walls.

It wasn't the way Quick would have chosen to wake up, but right now she didn't want to wake up at all. Given the alternative, she supposed, she should be grateful. So many of the people who had walked into the hall last night weren't alive to see this morning.

Quick had overheard the women in the bunk next to hers talking about it during the night.

'I heard fifteen percent,' one had whispered. 'That's what

Josh said, anyway.'

'Your sire?'

'Right. Good numbers, he said.'

'Eighty-five percent of us dying is *good*?'

'According to him. Guess we should count ourselves lucky.'

'Luckier than most, sounds like.'

A few more people had joined the dorm overnight. Some of them cried. That was a surprise. Quick had thought she was the only person who didn't want to be part of the Casting ceremony last night, so she wasn't expecting anyone else to be sad about turning vamp. Maybe they'd lost people they'd come here with, she thought, or maybe she'd just been dead wrong to think she was alone in her unwillingness. Either way, she couldn't see any red eyes once the curtains were flung open to let in the dawn sunlight, so she couldn't pinpoint her possible allies. Right now, surrounded only by eyes threaded with silver, she couldn't trust anyone at all.

Quick had slept in her clothes, covered only by the robe she'd worn to the ceremony last night. She wasn't sure what this training would entail, but a loose cotton dress didn't seem like ideal attire. Looking around the room at bikini tops and suits and ball gowns, none of them with any shoes at all, it seemed like Quick wasn't alone in being unsuitably dressed. They weren't given an opportunity to change. Instead, the long-haired, anchor-bearded man that Quick knew as Brandon came to the door and yelled, 'Downstairs, now!'

Her bunkmate jumped down from above and walked out without giving Quick a second glance. The others followed her, whispering as they went, filing out of the room in pairs and threes. It all gave Quick the feeling that she was the odd one out. She merged into the pack quietly, watching, listening. The others were mostly younger than Quick, and they all seemed to know each other. Beside them she felt grey and dirty, because compared to them, she was. None of them had come here from the blood cellar, she was sure now, and that showed not just in their appearance, but in their attitudes too. They weren't terrified captives, too scarred by loss to allow themselves to make new friends, or even idle conversation. They'd come here from the poolside, or from the house, or from parties where they'd gone with styled hair and tight clothes, expecting a good time. Their hair was messier now, their make up a little smeared by pillows and sheets, but they tidied each other up on the way down the stairs so that by the time they'd all traipsed through the common area on the ground floor and out into an open space behind the building that Quick had never seen before, they looked ready to go out all over again.

'Line up against the wall!' Brandon yelled, pacing away from the building so he could get a good look at them all.

Quick inserted herself somewhere in the middle of the crowd as more people poured out of doors in other parts of the building, doors she hadn't even realised were there. The whole structure was C-shaped, with two wings about half the length of the main section projecting off the back to cup around this wide area of open dirt.

All in all, there were about sixty of them lined up against the bare breeze-block walls when they'd all finally congregated, enough that they couldn't all have been turned Silver the previous night. There had only been a couple of hundred people in the hall, and at a success rate of fifteen percent, the maths wasn't hard: there were double the number there should have been. As was evident from the more comfortable clothes that some of those who'd arrived later were wearing, part of their number had been expecting this.

'Training time!' Brandon yelled, settling a pair of plastic sunglasses onto his nose. He was wearing bright, multi-coloured Bermuda shorts slung low on his hips and a lilac tank top that bared his tanned arms to the early morning sunshine.

In the shade of the building, it was cold enough to make Quick shiver, but Brandon's next words made it clear that she wouldn't be shivering for long.

'Running, jumping, fighting,' he said. 'Now that you've all turned, you can move super fast, jump super high, and hit really fucking hard. You've got the day to mess around out here teaching yourself how to do all that, then you're out of time. Some of you who were turned earlier have had a week or two to practice already,' he added, which explained the extra numbers, 'so you can show the others how it works.'

'Most of you are going to suck,' said Bella from the sidelines. She was leaning in the doorway of one of the wings, dressed in a patterned satin robe with pyjamas underneath. She had her hands wrapped around a steaming cup of what Quick would have bet anything was coffee. Quick watched enviously as Bella sipped it.

'Nice of you to get out of bed and join us,' Brandon said to Bella. 'You going to help?'

'Nope, just here to heckle,' she said.

Brandon looked like he was going to argue, but then a handful of other vamps came out of the door behind her, with Monty in the lead.

'I'll take it from here,' he said to Brandon, who raised his hands and stepped aside. The dynamics were strange. Either there'd been some kind of hierarchical rearrangement amongst the vamps, or turning that girl Silver had done more for Monty's status than Quick realised, because for now he seemed to be absolutely in charge.

'Angelina,' he said, holding out his hand towards them.

Along the line a few yards to Quick's right, the girl who had the bunk above hers – the girl Monty had turned – stepped forward with a smile and jogged over to take his hand.

'Show them what you can do,' he said to her.

Angelina smiled again, smugly this time, then she moved. And Christ, did she move. One moment she was standing calmly at Monty's side, and the next there was a whirlwind-raising blur along the line of spectators before she reappeared on his other side, having circled the entire training ground in a fraction of a second. Quick was barely recovering from that disorienting sight when Angelina moved again, this time jumping in a single massive leap from the ground until she stood on the far corner of one of the wings of the building, looking down at them from several storeys above Quick's head.

'That's what you're aiming for,' Monty said.

Angelina landed gracefully on the ground and sauntered over to join him once more, then he turned to her, dropped a kiss on her cheek and whispered something that not even Quick's new senses could pick up. She heard Angelina's answering giggle, though, so she could take a pretty good guess.

'Once you've mastered that,' Monty said, 'you can start sparring. Get to work.' He didn't need to shout, as Brandon had. By the end of Angelina's demonstration, it was quiet enough that when everyone started muttering, the whispers crashed over Quick like waves.

Some kind of prodigy.

Why her?

Thought it took months to learn.

All the while, Angelina stood in the sun and beamed.

Quick didn't rush to compete with her. Instead, she stood by the wall for a while and watched as the others ran around the perimeter of the packed-dirt space. A few grasped the skill immediately and moved on to jumping, with less success, but most of them were still running around aimlessly at normal speed when Quick decided she couldn't put it off any longer.

She had things to do, namely finding Evita and rescuing the people in the cellar, somehow. If she was going to have any hope of doing those things, then she'd need all the powers she could muster, and soon.

She took a deep breath and pushed away from the wall.

The moment Quick stepped out from the shadow of the building, her skin began to burn. It wasn't just turning pink, either; it was puckering and spitting, like it was sizzling against direct flame. For a second, she just stared at it, unable to process what was happening, then someone slammed into her in a waist-high tackle, shoving her back into the shade. Her head cracked back against the wall, leaving her ears ringing and blood in her mouth. She must have bitten her tongue, she guessed.

Then the screaming pain of the burns rushed in, boiling along her bare arms, up her neck, across her face. There was a shrieking noise that sounded like a dying animal, which she soon realised was coming from her. *She* was the animal, and it certainly she felt like she was dying. She tried to look down at her arms, imagining she'd see only a blackened and charred mess of bones and immolated muscle, but she couldn't open her eyes. Her eyes were sealed shut. Her eyes had been *burned* shut.

She shrieked again. She could hear Monty talking, yelling

at her, but she couldn't make out the words between her own screams. Her skin was peeling off her body in sticky wet strips and she was going to die like this, in the worst way she could imagine, melting into a puddle of pain and ash in the dirt.

Then a quiet voice said, 'I'm here,' and her body stilled of its own accord.

She was still in pain – incredible amounts of pain that blazed along every part of her exposed skin, then tightened at the places where her dress rubbed against it – but it was as though the pain had been moved into a different box, off to one side. She knew it was still there, and she could feel every bit of it, but it wasn't occupying her mind the way it had moments before. Instead of imagining her arms burning away in front of her sightless eyes, she became a breeze riding over the ocean, breaking across the bow of a wooden-hulled ship to chase up into the rigging and pull strands of blonde hair across welcoming sea-grey eyes.

'I need to touch your skin,' the voice said.

Quick should have protested, because her skin was *on fire*, but as her mind's eye skipped through the salty air, she was distracted by the gentle cresting of cold dawn light over the horizon, and she surrendered to it.

She felt a hand slip around the back of her neck, sliding beneath her hair to cradle her head, then her mouth filled with fresh water. She swallowed, and a relieving cold pooled at the back of her neck at the point of the hand's contact, then broke over her, cooling her skin, rolling her into its undertow in an embrace that gathered in her chest and burst out through her body in rush of sea spray.

When she sat up and opened her eyes, she did so with a gasp, like a diver coming up for air.

'Are you okay?' Monty asked. He was crouching beside

her on the ground, his face a mask of concern, but no one else in the crowd gathered around them was looking at him. They were looking at the woman on Quick's other side, the one who was staring intently at a canteen as she screwed the top back on.

Kulika.

'Better?' she asked, her gaze still fixed on her task.

'Better,' Quick replied with disbelief.

And she was. She looked down at her arms and saw only clean, unscarred skin. She touched her face and eyelids to find them smooth and painless under her fingertips. If it wasn't for the layer of ash that now surrounded the spot where she was sitting, she might have thought she'd imagined the whole thing.

'Good,' Kulika said. 'Pale skin? You get sunburnt easily?'

'Yes…'

'It happens this way sometimes. You'll be sensitive for a while, until your body adjusts,' Kulika said softly, then she stood and turned to Monty. 'Cover her up and get her some sunblock. Do not let her burn again.' The threat in her tone was understated, but it was there.

Then Kulika was gone. She just disappeared, leaving a susurrus of whispered gossip in her wake as the crowd dissected Kulika's brief cameo.

'What happened?' someone whispered.

'Must have been blood in that bottle,' someone whispered back. 'Healed the new girl up. Kind of reassuring, right?'

'Makes me want to carry a bottle of the stuff around.'

'Captain says we only drink from the vein.'

'But *she* doesn't have to? What gives?'

'That was Kulika Yadav,' a third voice chipped in. 'Keep your voice down.'

'Shit,' the first voice whispered, and it sounded fearful.

Whatever status Kulika had to these people, it didn't fill Quick with confidence. In fact, it sounded like it should make Quick wary.

But hadn't Kulika come to Quick's rescue? Hadn't she saved her from the fire? It was more than any of the others had done.

Yet all the while, she hadn't even looked at Quick.

Not once.

'Shit,' Monty breathed. 'Do you need more blood? Are you hurt, or—'

'I'm fine,' Quick said, a little confused.

The whisperers had mentioned blood, too, but Quick was sure it had just been water she'd drunk. Hadn't it? She struggled to untangle the threads of what had just happened, because there had been a distinct hallucinatory quality to it all. One minute she'd been burning, then there'd been the breeze and the sea and the water in her mouth…

But she must have been mistaken. In the trauma of the moment – she had nearly *burned to death*, after all – perhaps it wasn't surprising that her mind had taken her away somewhere else, somewhere that transformed fire into a breeze and blood into water. It must have been blood she'd drunk or she wouldn't have healed. That was just how vampires worked.

'You could have warned me about the sunburn,' Monty said to Quick.

'I think you mean that *you* could have warned *me*,' Quick replied, snapping at him because she was too jittery to control her tone. 'What else is suddenly going to be life-threatening now? Should I be avoiding garlic and crosses, too?'

'Very funny,' he sneered, before getting to his feet and ambling off into the block.

Quick hadn't been joking. She was shaking from the adrenaline rush and crash of the last ten minutes, so instead of going back to training with the others, she just sat against the wall and tried to calm herself down while she waited for Monty to come back with some suncream. She assumed that's where he'd gone, anyway. She hoped it was, because the sun was getting higher all the time, and she wouldn't be in the shade much longer.

None of the others tried to talk to her, about Kulika or the burning or anything at all. In that respect, at least, it looked like she would be remaining in the dark.

5

'KULIKA,' BARTHOLOMEW CALLED out of the porch door.

Kulika hadn't asked his leave to go and help Quick before running out of the library, but really, what had he expected her to do? She'd felt Quick's pain rip through the bond, burning through the cord that tethered Kulika to her until it threatened to snap entirely. Bartholomew had said it himself: the new Silver were fragile. An injury like that, to so much of her body, with flames that were still burning when Kulika had—

She didn't want to think about it. She didn't want to remember the image of Quick lying on the ground like that with fire dancing up her limbs, black smoke rising and blood spitting, but she knew she'd be seeing it in her nightmares from now until the day she died.

Which could so easily have been today. If Kulika had reached Quick a few seconds later, they would both have burned up in that fire.

'Kulika,' Bartholomew called again and, like a faithful mutt, she came to heel.

'I had to,' she said, running up the porch steps. 'She

would have died.'

Bartholomew didn't reply, he just gave her a disappointed look and turned away, walking back into the house.

Bayly was leaning against the porch rail drinking his coffee, as he usually did at this time of the morning, and probably wishing he was anywhere else. Kulika caught his sympathetic eye for a moment before she hurried inside after Bartholomew.

'You know I had to,' she insisted. 'You *know*.'

He didn't turn around, he just kept walking until they were back in the library, with Kulika trailing at his heels the whole way. He shut the door behind them.

When he moved towards Kulika, at first she thought he was going for her neck again, so she flinched and backed up until her shoulder blades hit the door. Instead, he reached out to touch her face, trailing his fingers across her cheek as though they belonged there, then pressing his thumb gently to her forehead as though in benediction. It was a gesture she'd received a hundred times or more, on the ship, before.

'We have some trust still to rebuild between us. Don't we?' he said.

Bartholomew had been a priest once. He'd known how to make his congregants feel like the eye of god was watching over them, in the same way that he knew how to make his crew feel like their captain's eye was watching now, and not always benevolently. He blessed and cursed with equal iniquity, and all they could do was count the blessings when they got them. Kulika knew she should take this one and run.

'I'll do whatever you want,' she said desperately. 'You know that. You can trust my feelings for her.'

'But I need to trust your feelings for *me*,' he said mournfully. 'I need you to believe in what I'm trying to build here.'

'Which is?'

He turned to the side for a moment, clenching his jaw, as though he was trying to find the right words, as though he hadn't had every one written and rehearsed in advance. Kulika thought it was an act at first, but when he spoke again, he did so with such emotion that she found herself doubting her own assumptions.

'I know you hate this place,' he said, gesturing around at the book-lined shelves of the library. 'This hemmed-in building, and the walls of words I have to write to keep us all together here as a crew. My god, we were *pirates*. There was nothing *but* the crew, and the plunder, and the open waves. I know you resent being beached in this mansion, and that you always did, but do you really imagine that I don't resent it too?'

In truth, Kulika had never considered it. Bartholomew was the *captain*. He was in command. He told them what to do, and when to do it, and although he'd always told them he was acting for the good of the crew, only an idiot would have failed to see the glint of megalomania in his eyes. She'd just assumed that he was following his own whims, doing whatever he wanted and dragging them along for the ride, because it had always appeared that way. He'd never given the impression that he wasn't completely happy in his lordship of this mansion, but then coming here hadn't exactly been a choice either. The Golden Age of piracy had ended, the great protagonists of the time had either been hanged or forced into hiding, and the crew of the *Royal Fortune* had little choice but to do the same.

'We did what we had to do, to survive,' Kulika said, echoing the words that Bartholomew had spoken to her so many times during those first days on land in the Carolinas.

'I want to do more than just survive,' Bartholomew said.

'Yes, the world changed, but now we finally have the power to change it back again. Don't you see?' He took her hands in his, clasping them as though they were a lifeline in a storm. 'Haven't we waited long enough to become again the people we have always been? *Pirates*, Kulika. *Vampires*. We don't settle, we roam. We don't ask, we take. We don't hide, we *ambush*. It's time that you remembered who you are. Who we all are. I only want to remind you.'

'I remember, Bartholomew.' She remembered so vividly that it scared her. Those memories should have turned her stomach – once, at the end, when she'd left here with Baron Drake, they had done exactly that – but now they gave her a thrill that uncomfortably straddled the space between horror and desire.

And was that really such a bad thing? She was bound to Quick, and so bound to Bartholomew. If he was going to use her as his instrument of destruction either way, then perhaps it wasn't so terrible an idea to harden herself to his violence, just a little. Not enough that she would cross the line into savagery, just enough to shield herself so that she didn't end up breaking herself in her efforts to shield Quick. She could allow herself that much free rein.

'I want to give you that again,' he said, looking into her eyes. 'A life where we don't have to compromise on who we are, where we're not fettered by having to hide our needs and desires. A life of freedom; for you, and me, and for our Patience, too. Isn't that something you want as much as I do?'

'I...'

'I remember that night on the beach in Hispaniola,' he whispered seductively as he squeezed her hands in his. 'Washing off the blood in the shallows, piling the fire high on the sand, then drinking our fill and more from the prisoners we took from that prize off the Windward Isles. And then, when the embers smouldered down…' His eyes locked with Kulika's, and they burned.

She burned too.

She'd forgotten that night. Repressed it, even.

Heat shivered across Kulika's skin, bringing incongruous images of Quick flooding into her mind, muddling them with the memories of Hispaniola. Her recollections of Quick's accident that morning should have been unpleasant – the fire, the burning – but instead Kulika remembered the moment she'd healed Quick with her touch. She felt again Quick's smooth skin pressed against the palm of her hand, and the teasing softness of Quick's hair as Kulika slid her fingers into it, connected to their bond, and unleashed herself in a wash of healing energy. There had been catharsis in that moment, the same kind of catharsis she'd felt that dark night on the beach in Hispaniola as she'd taken that willing woman in her arms, as they'd pulled each other out of their clothes and, finally, for the first time, Kulika had slid her fingers into—

She'd known Bartholomew had been watching, somewhere out in the darkness of the dunes.

Back then, Kulika hadn't objected; he'd always had his eyes on her, and she'd found comfort in his omniscience. She'd known later – much later – that she should have objected, because it wasn't right, was it? But so much of what they'd done in those days was wrong, and no one had been keeping score. They were *supposed* to do wrong. Like Bartholomew said, they were *pirates.* They roamed, they took, they ambushed. They *lived*, and they made no apologies for it. Bartholomew had certainly never made any, and Kulika hadn't felt he owed her them.

She'd known he was watching that night, and she'd

undressed her prize on the beach anyway. Maybe that was even why she'd done it, because – god help her – she'd *liked* it.

'Every night could be Hispaniola,' he whispered, and her skin burned where his breath touched her cheek.

When Kulika saw that night in her mind again now, the person in her arms wasn't the anonymous woman who'd taken her virginity, every detail about her forgotten in the haze of blood and rum and time. Instead, it was a woman with lips that tasted like autumn berries, skin that smelled of freshly-cut flowers, and sunset-red hair that glinted in the firelight as it spread across the sand.

As Kulika lay back against the door to the library with past and present flickering together in her mind, she knew Bartholomew was watching, tracing her reactions by the flush of her cheeks, the scent of her arousal and the sticky touch of her palms as she lost herself somewhere between fantasy and memory. Still, she didn't want him to stop. The truth was, she'd missed having his eyes on her.

'All I want is to see you take what you desire,' he whispered, and some part of her that she'd been denying for a hundred years stretched and twisted in her core.

There was a knock at the door behind Kulika's head.

'What?' Bartholomew barked angrily, his gaze still locked with hers.

'Um,' a voice mumbled from the other side. 'You wanted me to bring Jane's stuff?'

Finally, Bartholomew released Kulika's hands and broke eye contact so he could guide her gently away from the door and wrench it open. She was still trying to get a hold of herself when he dismissed Monty and turned back to her with a small cardboard box in his hands.

'Go on,' he said, his annoyance at the interruption spilling over as he tipped the box out onto the table. 'Look through her effects. Talk to the newer crew. Find out what you can.'

His rapid change in mood made Kulika want to reclaim the charged atmosphere of a few moments before, however uncomfortable it made her. The switch had been so abrupt it shocked her, but it didn't surprise her. Bartholomew had always been a mercurial creature.

'In here?' she asked.

'You can use this room. I've got business elsewhere,' he said dismissively, as though he hadn't just given her free rein of his inner sanctum. It was a mark of trust, however casual he made it seem.

He gives and he takes, Kulika reminded herself, but it was hard not to feel the approval in the gesture, as he no doubt intended that she should do.

It was enough to make her hope, recklessly.

'And afterwards?' she hazarded.

Kulika waited for a moment, praying that he'd reward her with something more, so she wouldn't have to ask for it herself. He was not so magnanimous, though. He liked to feel the power he had over people. He wanted them beg.

'Surely you're not asking to see our Patience again, so soon?' he said, with what sounded for all the world like real concern. Then he chuckled. 'Have patience, and you will have *Patience.*'

It was a hollow joke. Kulika didn't laugh.

Bartholomew sighed, disappointed with her again.

'Search the girl's things,' he said irritably. 'When you're done, the kid can get the crew to come and speak to you in turn, and perhaps you'll be able to learn something he couldn't. I'll be back this evening, and then we'll talk.'

'And if I find something?' she said. 'Where will you be?'

'Away,' he said, then he left her alone in the library,

slamming the door behind him.

6

QUICK COULDN'T DO it. She'd run and jumped in the meagre shade of the building all day, until her feet had bled and healed fifty times over, but she still couldn't get faster than a normal sprint or higher than a normal jump. She hadn't even tried sparring; everyone else had paired up without her. Maybe that was for the best. Given the way things were going with the running and jumping, she would only have ended up pummelled to pieces anyway.

The others had all given up and gone inside by now, half of them having successfully mastered at least one of their powers, but Quick was going nowhere. Now that the sun had dipped beneath the horizon, she could finally stop worrying about staying in the shade and concentrate properly on what she was trying – and failing – to do.

The door to one of the common areas opened behind her and a familiar voice called out, 'Hey, you thirsty yet?'

Quick turned, panting, to see Penny standing in the doorway dressed in sweatpants and a strappy T-shirt. She hadn't forgotten that Penny was one of the vampires who'd helped Monty throw her down into the blood cellar that first night, so no wonder Penny's demeanour was tentative now.

She hovered by the door, her expression somewhere between hope and concern.

'I'm fine,' Quick said, turning back to her drills.

'The others are refuelling,' Penny said. 'You know. With blood.'

That got Quick's attention. 'From the blood cellar?' she asked.

'They're in the big common room. They're nearly done, so we'll be putting the humans back down through the hatch soon, but I saw you hadn't come in yet and... Thing is, if you don't drink the blood, you're never going to make this work. You need it to power the Silver speed and all the rest, and you're not always going to get the chance to fuel up, so I'm just saying.'

'Saying what?'

'Take it.' Penny pushed the door open wider, holding it open for Quick.

Quick didn't trust her. She couldn't, not after Penny had so happily participated in her incarceration, but no one else in this place seemed willing to speak to her at the moment. At least if she went with her, she might get some answers.

'After you,' Quick said as she reached the door, not wanting to let Penny get behind her. She got a hurt look in return, but Penny did as Quick asked anyway.

'It happened to me too,' Penny said as they picked their way through the furniture, empty beer bottles and snack detritus carpeting the small common room on the other side of the door. 'I'm not saying that makes it any better, but I didn't ask for this either. I was in the blood cellar too, in the beginning.'

'I think that actually makes it worse,' Quick said quietly.

'And I'm not...' Penny trailed off as they reached the corridor, then turned back to face Quick. 'I'm not going to apologise, because I didn't have a choice in what I did, any more than you do now.'

Quick laughed at how ridiculous that sounded. 'You're a vampire. I was human. You put me in your *blood cellar* so you could drink my *blood*.'

'I drink the blood because without it, I'll die. You'll die without it, too. I put you down in the cellar because that's what I was ordered to do, for the crew, and because we have to get our blood from somewhere.'

'Just following orders?' Quick asked sarcastically.

'Don't be facetious,' Penny hissed. 'You are *one day old* in this place. You have no idea what it's like here. What it's been like, for months.'

'Then tell me.'

'I'm not sure I can even put it into words,' Penny said, looking hopelessly into Quick's eyes. 'We're all prisoners here, one way or another. It's not just that if any of us left, the others would track us down and drag us back, dead or alive. There's something else, too. I don't know if it's something in the blood, or something about *him*—'

'Him?'

'Bartholomew,' Penny said in a voice that was little more than a whisper. 'He never comes over to this block, but then he doesn't have to, because you can almost feel him watching anyway. And Kulika...'

'What about her?'

'Well...' Penny raised her eyebrows at Quick.

'What?'

'You've got to be wondering why none of the others are talking to you.'

'They're cliquey bastards.'

'*You're* the cliquey bastard. You got turned by Kulika Yadav. Don't you even understand what that means?'

'Last call!' came a shout from along the corridor.

'You'd better go,' said Penny. 'Third door on the left.'

'What does it mean?' Quick asked.

'Later. Go on.'

'Last call! Going in ten, nine, eight, seven…'

'You're not coming?' Quick asked.

'I can't be seen talking to you,' said Penny, horrified. 'Now go.'

'…three, two…'

Penny pushed Quick off along the corridor, then disappeared in the opposite direction, leaving Quick to walk through the door just as the countdown reached zero.

Brandon had been the one doing the counting.

'Here she is,' he said, flicking his hair over his shoulder as she walked in. 'Always making an entrance.'

'Making a scene, more like,' said Angelina.

Juvenile, Quick thought. The block might feel like a college dorm, but she didn't have to act that way. Didn't they have enough to worry about?

'Hello, Angelina,' Quick said cordially as she walked into the room, determined to be friendly. Then she took a proper look around and froze on the spot, just a few steps from the door.

The "big" common room was certainly that. It had floor-to-ceiling windows along one wall, and was filled with groups of Silver gathered on sofas and beanbags, drinking and chatting and laughing. There was one enormous television on the wall on this side of the room, showing a first-person shooter game that the nearest group of Silver were whooping at, and another at the far end, displaying some kind of list on the screen. The party mood became uncomfortable the moment Quick noticed a handful of bedraggled humans arrayed against the side wall to her left, bleeding from the neck.

Xiaoyu was amongst them.

'Shit,' she said to Quick. 'It worked, then?'

'It worked,' Quick replied quietly.

'Okay, back downstairs,' Brandon said to the humans, then he added to Quick, 'You drinking?'

'I don't…' Quick looked around the room, noting all the people looking on with barely veiled interest, then looked back to Xiaoyu and the line of humans. What did they expect her to do? Just pounce on someone and bite them while the others played video games in the background, like that was a perfectly normal and not at all surreal thing to do?

'Performance anxiety?' Angelina teased her.

Brandon gave Angelina a long-suffering look, then turned to Quick and said, 'You can drink in there.' He pointed to an open door, close to the other end of the space, which led to a small room with another television. 'You, snarky girl,' he said to Angelina. 'Help me get the others back downstairs. You two as well,' he added, beckoning over a couple of spectators from a nearby sofa.

They groaned.

'Get used to it!' Brandon yelled at them. 'Fresh meat does the chores. Now get off your asses so I can go sit on mine.'

It was only when they started leading the humans out of the room that Quick realised they were leaving her with Xiaoyu.

'Wait, I can't—'

Xiaoyu sighed. 'You can,' she said, then she turned and led the way to the little room Brandon had indicated.

Quick looked at the faces of the other Silver, watching her blithely and with only half an eye as they lounged around on sofas and beanbags, drinking and playing games and relaxing. It felt incongruous. They'd just been biting people in here and drinking their blood, and now they expected Quick to do the same. Did they not realise how utterly wrong this all felt to her? Did they not feel it too?

'Come on,' Xiaoyu called. She was already inside the little room, waiting.

Quick felt unbalanced by the whole experience, like she was walking on marshmallows, but she followed anyway. As soon as she was inside, Xiaoyu closed the door behind them, sealing them in together. It was a strange space, maybe designed for taking video calls, because although the television screen on the wall was large, the room was filled with a small conference table and six office chairs that were crammed behind it, all facing it. There were office supplies scattered over the centre of the table as though a meeting had just ended: notepads, a pot of pens and other stationery, even a speaker phone.

'Let me take a look at you,' Xiaoyu said, grabbing Quick by the shoulders and squinting at her.

While Xiaoyu assessed her, Quick assessed Xiaoyu. In the short time that had passed since Quick had last seen her, she looked thinner and even more drained. Maybe that was something to do with the contrast between Xiaoyu and Quick's current company, because all the Silver looked so bloody healthy, or maybe it was something to do with the lights up here, but Quick didn't think so.

'You look tired,' Quick said.

Xiaoyu ignored her and asked, 'What's that on your throat?'

'What?' Quick tried and failed to get a look at her own neck.

'It's like two little silvery lines. Let me...' Xiaoyu scooped up Quick's loose hair, pulling it across her back and over her opposite shoulder. Then she leaned in closer. After a second's pause, she grabbed Quick's chin and yanked it down and to one side, then with her other hand she ran her fingers into Quick's hair at the back of her neck, parting it at the base of her skull. 'It's all up in your hair. It looks like you've got silver paint on your scalp, but there's none on your hair. Like it's stained the skin or something. Shit, it's…' She jerked away abruptly, letting Quick's hair fall back into place. 'It's all shiny and weird.'

'Must be a Silver thing, I guess,' Quick said with a shrug. 'I haven't looked in a mirror since… I never really thought about what it would do to me physically. I'm not suddenly going to drop a hundred pounds and start wafting around like an eternally consumptive teenager, am I?'

'I don't think it works like that,' Xiaoyu said. 'The reason they age so slowly is the same reason they heal so quickly: their cells repair themselves as they age or get damaged, by replacing the damaged ones with bits extracted from the blood they drink. Basically, stuff that's broken gets fixed. But fat isn't a defect in your body that gets healed – fat storage is a function your body performs in order to give you reserves in times of need. It's perfectly normal and healthy.'

'Said no doctor to me ever.'

'Well they just did,' said Xiaoyu, her attention back on Quick's neck.

'You're a doctor?' Quick asked.

'Was. Probably won't get the chance to be again. You haven't drunk yet, have you? Blood.'

'What? No. Yes. From a bottle, just after I got turned.'

'But not from the vein.'

'No,' Quick said quietly.

'Well, you're going to have to. If you don't, we're both going to suffer the consequences, and I'm on my last fuck up before gator town.'

'I can't—'

'You'd be surprised how easy the others find it. Just do it before I lose my nerve.'

'If you lose any more blood you're going to fall over.'

'Then I'll sit down,' Xiaoyu said. 'Just get it the fuck over with, will you? Or have you forgotten how much it hurts?'

'I don't want to—'

But Xiaoyu interrupted her by grabbing a pair of scissors from the pot of pens and jamming one of the points into her own wrist, making any further argument impossible. It wasn't just that there was no point in protesting now the blood was already flowing. Instead, Quick's problem was that, with the scent filling the small space, she couldn't hold herself back. She was on Xiaoyu in seconds, pushing the woman down into a chair as she fell to her knees at Xiaoyu's feet and dragged her wrist to her mouth, sucking ravenously.

She hadn't even realised she was hungry.

7

AFTER SPENDING MOST of the day interviewing the new Silver from the block, Kulika was simultaneously bored of talking and horrified by the grief they'd casually shared with her. Each life had been decanted into pills that would be easier for her to swallow, but they all amounted to the same thing in the end: desperation. Everyone came to the mansion in desperation, whether because their need made them easy prey for the Silver or because they came here willingly to escape something worse.

It was more than Kulika had wanted to know.

Looking at the never-ending pool party that was once again gearing up outside the porch, it was so easy to discount these kids as just that: kids. Young people who didn't understand anything about the world or the gravity of their situation, and who only cared about getting wrecked. It was a shallow view, but it was so much easier to believe that than to imagine that these new Silver might have as many terrible reasons for being here as Kulika and her own crew'd had for being on board the *Royal Fortune* three centuries ago. People had thought the pirates were dangerous, immoral, hedonistic raiders, and they had been, but they'd also been terribly damaged people who were each trying to escape whatever haunted them.

You didn't sign up for the precarious, hard-working, perilous world of piracy if you had any other way of making a living. With the picture he painted of unbridled freedom, Bartholomew was remembering it through rose-tinted glasses, though not without some justification. When you were practically immortal, it was truly a life in which there was pleasure to be found, but for the human members of the crew, piracy was a death sentence, sooner or later: scurvy or gangrene or grapeshot or drowning. Believe it or not, in those days most of them couldn't even swim.

It had been worth it, though. Back home they'd had nothing but poverty, starvation, abuse and slavery to look forward to. At least out on the sea, they'd had a chance at making a fortune. That had been enough.

These new Silver were really no different. Some of their incentives to escape were the same, some new. There were more addictions to different drugs, in their families and in themselves, but otherwise Kulika might have been talking to her old crew for all the troubles they shared with her, some more willingly than others.

She was exhausted by it.

All day, and all she had to show for it was a belly full of other people's pain. No one had recognised Evita's name. Most of them knew Jane Doe, but no one knew who had turned her Silver, how she'd come to be at the mansion, or where she'd gone. One day she'd been there, the next not.

The whole thing was an exercise in futility.

It was approaching dark when Kulika finally allowed herself a break. She slipped out onto the porch to find Bayly already there, basking in the evening's heat.

'Party time again,' he muttered into his beer bottle. His

gaze was fixed on the new Silver congregating around the pool.

'Been here all day?' Kulika asked, recalling the last time she'd seen him, in this very same spot that morning with his coffee.

He laughed dryly at that, which she assumed meant no, but with Bayly there was really no telling.

'Heard you got the same bug in your eye as me,' he said.

He meant the silvering, Kulika assumed.

'Seems like,' she said.

'So you're staying.'

It was a statement that didn't need a reply. They both knew that neither of them was going anywhere while the people they loved were still part of Bartholomew's crew.

Forever, probably.

'Strange, that,' Bayly said.

Kulika didn't follow. It wasn't strange to her that she was staying; it felt inevitable.

She looked at Bayly in enquiry.

'It's strange how many new Silver there are here,' he said significantly.

'Yes…' Kulika agreed, but she still wasn't following.

'And back in the old country, I hear. More people silvering too, like you and me.'

It was true: there had been more new Silver in London recently, and more Silver falling irrevocably in love. Before this last year, Kulika couldn't remember hearing about anyone silvering at all, ever. There had always been stories, of course, so she'd known it was technically possible, but it was all so remote that the whole concept had taken on the tone of myth. Maybe it had happened to the friend of a friend of a friend, hundreds of years ago, but never to anyone she actually knew. The fact that it had actually happened to *her*...

Kulika, and Bayly, and that kid Leo who was on the video abducting Cara Alton, and Baron Drake, too. It was like an epidemic.

'Love is in the air,' Bayly said, with a bitter laugh. 'Almost like someone worked out a way to make the turn stick. Chemically.'

That was when Kulika put the pieces together. Enzo working at BioSilver, Enzo joining the crew, then so many new Silver being created at the mansion, and silvering. It was a sequence that started with BioSilver and ended with a Silver army for Bartholomew.

'Enzo took something from the lab,' she guessed.

'Yep.'

Then the implications hit her. 'You mean, me and Quick —'

'Not you,' Bayly interrupted, his tone resentful. 'You don't eat with the crew. Those who do, though.'

'Like you and Enzo.'

'Like us.'

'Fuck, Bayly.'

He nodded. 'Same result, different means. Kind of sours the love connection, though, doesn't it? It's supposed to mean something.'

'It does mean something.'

'Not enough,' Bayly said darkly, looking out towards the horizon, where the Cooper River flowed inexorably to the sea. 'Not when he doesn't feel it, too. It isn't even real.'

'I'm sorry,' Kulika said, because what else was there to say? Bayly was chained to Bartholomew's crew by a love that had been chemically induced.

Forever, probably.

Suddenly, her own situation didn't seem that bad.

'Um, Ms Yadav?' Two of the new Silver were standing at the foot of the porch stairs, looking up at Kulika. 'Monty said you wanted to speak to us?'

The young man was the buccaneer lookalike from the night before, with long, dark hair and an anchor beard. He was dressed colourfully in shorts and a tank top. The young woman wore what looked like pyjamas, as though she'd just been dragged here off the sofa. She had pale skin and long, reddish blonde hair, like a pale imitation of Quick. She was familiar, but Kulika couldn't quite place her.

'All right,' Kulika said, pushing away from the porch railing with little enthusiasm. 'Back to the library, then.'

Bayly nodded in farewell, but he had a look in his eyes that Kulika didn't like: distant, empty, hopeless.

No, she didn't like it one bit.

8

'I'M COMING FOR you,' Quick had told Xiaoyu when she'd finally managed to snap herself out of her bloodlust and relinquish the poor woman's wrist. 'As soon as I can.'

'I'll believe that when I see it,' Xiaoyu had replied.

'I *will*,' Quick had promised.

Xiaoyu had just laughed. There'd been dark circles under her eyes by then, and she'd not been entirely steady on her feet when the others had come to fetch her back to the cellar. She'd been trying to hide it from Quick, but her shoulder still thumped into the doorframe as she left the television room, wobbly and uncontrolled.

Quick felt wretched about it for the rest of the day, but she felt even more wretched now as she lay in bed and tried to imagine how she could have played things differently. She'd never known anything like the complete loss of control that had overwhelmed her when the scent of blood filled the air, not as an adult anyway. She'd felt something like that hunger when she was younger, a starving child left alone in an empty house full of empty cupboards and a padlocked refrigerator. Every time she remembered that feeling, which was constantly now, the shame poured into her stomach and spiralled out through her body in hot curls of horror.

She had to get down into that cellar. She had to know if Xiaoyu was okay, if only for her own peace of mind.

Maybe she could come up with a way of busting all the other humans out of the cellar while she was there, or maybe a quick reconnaissance trip would give her some ideas about how to bust them out later, but that motivation wasn't at the forefront of her mind. All Quick could think as the others finally fell snoring into their beds around her, drunk and messy, was: *Did I kill her?*

Angelina was the last one to sleep. Quick had practically given up waiting for her when the girl stumbled in, jumped straight up from the floor to her top bunk and fumbled the landing in the dark, heedless of the way the impact shook the entire bed frame. If Quick hadn't been awake already, she would have been awakened then.

'Night,' Quick said.

Angelina didn't reply.

Quick was tempted to head down to the cellar right then, but she chose caution instead. Lying back in her bed, she stilled her own breathing and tried to listen for the breathing and heartbeats of the vampires sleeping around her. It was yet another skill they should be able to master, Brandon had told them all, and yet another that had eluded Quick.

It wasn't that she couldn't hear more if she concentrated, because she could. The problem was that letting one sound in meant every other sound came in too, in a rushing cascade at high volume, flooding her brain with so many noises that she couldn't tease them apart. How was she supposed to hear a single heartbeat over the roar of her own? How was she supposed to zero in on a single source from one direction when she was surrounded by cacophony from all around? It was impossible.

After several long, frustrating minutes, Quick gave up trying to be cautious and decided the coast was probably clear. Whatever. She couldn't wait any longer. She slipped out of bed and padded out of the dorm on bare feet.

There were people still partying outside. The stairwell had windows that faced in the direction of the house, and although they were set too high for Quick to see out through them, the eerie blue glow of the pool lights filtered in to illuminate her path. She could hear them, too. There was no music tonight, but there were voices and laughter and the kind of hoots and screams that marked out drinkers who'd gone too far down the bottle to have any volume control. She could only hope that none of them would choose to stagger back this way.

Pausing a moment to make sure the block itself was quiet, Quick padded down the stairs to the bottom floor, and started searching for the cellar hatch. It should have been easy to pinpoint the place, because it wasn't as though she hadn't been there before. The problem was that she'd not been entirely conscious when she'd been dumped down the hatch in the first place, and when she'd come up it had been with a bunch of other humans on their way to be blood donors, so she'd had her mind on other things. She remembered that there'd been a sort of alcove space off the main corridor about twenty feet from the front door, and the hatch was in that alcove, but she couldn't find it now. She was sure the alcove was on the right hand side of the corridor, but there were no doors set in that wall for a clear thirty feet from the main entrance, and the only ones she found led into full rooms. It was the same story on the other side of the corridor.

Quick was bewildered.

Maybe her memory was playing tricks on her. Maybe it

had been a different corridor, next to a different entrance. Or maybe it had been in one of the other wings entirely? Perhaps she could get her bearings better if she came in from the outside, instead of trying to reconstruct her route from the inside out.

She was contemplating this, her hand on the front door, when a bolt of warm air blasted past her, swirling the skirt of her dress and throwing her hair into her face. By the time she'd pulled it back enough that she could see again, she realised she wasn't alone.

Monty and Angelina were standing beside her. Monty had his hand on the door over her own, stopping her from opening it, while Angelina stood behind him looking smug.

'Where are you going?' Monty asked her.

'Outside,' Quick replied.

'Why?'

'Just for some air,' Quick lied, but apparently not very well, because Monty wasn't buying it.

'Oh, Quick, Quick, Quick,' he said sadly, shaking his head.

'Oh, Monty, Monty, Monty,' she parroted back childishly, giving him a dirty look.

He wasn't much impressed with that, either.

'Come on,' he said, grabbing Quick's shoulders and steering her back along the corridor to the big common room. 'I think it's time the two of us had a chat.'

'Monty?' Angelina said sweetly. 'My points?'

'I'll mark them up,' he said over his shoulder. 'Go back to bed.'

'Your bed or mine?'

'Yours,' he said emphatically.

Angelina huffed, then glared at Quick as she stalked past them on her way upstairs.

'What points?' Quick asked Monty.

'There's a hierarchy in the mansion,' he replied, 'and you're fucking up my place in it.' He sat Quick on the nearest sofa, then crouched down in front of her so they were looking at each other eye to eye. 'I was the one who brought you here, so everything you do reflects on me. The fact that the great Kulika Yadav turned you? That works in my favour. The fact that you're being such a giant pain in the ass? That counts against us both.'

'I was just going out for a walk, to look at the stars, you know,' she said.

'No, you weren't,' Monty replied. 'You were looking for the hatch to the cellar.'

Quick's blood ran cold.

'No, I wasn't,' she said.

'Yes, you were. Look, I'm not as stupid as you seem to think I am, and I hear better than pretty much everyone in this block. I know you're planning to break Xiaoyu and the others out, so let me just say: you can't, you won't, and if you try again then shit in here is going to get even hotter for you than it did this morning.'

The memory of fire crawling up her arms made Quick shudder.

'You're crew, now,' Monty went on. 'You don't just get to walk away. You signed the covenant.'

'Yeah, I'm hearing a lot about this covenant,' she replied. 'But I didn't get to read it, or really have any choice about whether or not to sign it, did I? So I'm not sure how you expect me to know what I can and can't do according to it.'

'Then look.' He grabbed her by the arm, dragged her off the sofa and pulled her over to the wall, where a poster-sized laminated list shone in the moonlight that was spilling through the windows. The writing was archaic and incongruous in the context. 'Or let me summarise. No leaving the building without permission. No drinking blood without permission. Do what you're told by your superiors, which to you is everyone.'

'Or?'

'You die,' he said simply.

'I'm a vampire,' Quick replied, confused. 'I'm immortal.'

'No,' Monty replied impatiently. 'You're *Silver*. You're strong, but you can still die, especially when you're this new, and especially if it's other Silver trying to kill you. And trust me, if you break the covenant, the rest of the crew *will* try to kill you. They'll succeed, too.'

'Is that what happened to Evita?' Quick asked quietly.

'*Jane*,' Monty corrected her. 'Her name is *Jane*. And no. I don't know what happened to her, but I'm pretty sure she isn't dead.'

'How do you know?'

Monty looked away and said, 'Just call it a gut feeling.'

'No, Monty,' Quick said irritably. 'I'm going to need more than that.'

'We're looking for her, okay?' he said quietly. 'We want to find her as much as you do.'

Quick looked at him suspiciously, examining his face for the lie. She didn't find one, but she still said, 'I don't believe you.'

'Okay, then don't,' he replied plainly. 'It's not like you can do anything about it either way, sugar.'

'Don't call me sugar.'

'Sugar,' he said antagonistically.

Quick shouldn't have risen to the bait, but she was tired and raw and she couldn't help herself. She swung for his face, but he caught her wrist in his hand and had her pinned facedown on the sofa so quickly that it took her a second or two to understand why she was suddenly lying on her stomach.

'It's that easy for me,' he said, leaning down to whisper into her ear. It felt like he had his knee pressing into the centre of her back, but it could just as easily have been his hand. 'All I have to do is push.' He did, putting enough strain on Quick's ribs that she was certain something was about to snap. 'I can hear your heart thumping, sugar,' he whispered, leaning close as she moaned and struggled for breath. 'That's not a good sign, you know. Just a bit more pressure, maybe a little twist, and I'd crush your heart in your chest.'

'Monty…' she pleaded.

'You think you can't die? That'd be enough, believe me.'

Then the pressure lifted, Monty moved away, and Quick groaned as her strained ribs shifted back into their proper positions. Those seconds of dislocated pain were worse than the pressure itself had been, but they were only seconds. Afterwards, there was no pain at all.

'You made your point,' she breathed, carefully sitting upright.

'Yeah, I did.' He looked at her for a second, then said, 'But you're still not done, are you?'

'I have questions,' she said cautiously. 'All I have is a list of things I'm not supposed to do, but what *am* I supposed to do? Why am I here? Why was Ev— *Jane* here? What's the point of it all?'

Down in the blood cellar, the rules had made a twisted kind of sense. The vampires needed blood, so they imprisoned the humans to provide it for them. They also wanted to turn more people into vampires – *Silver* – and they needed humans for that, too. So far, so sensible.

But what didn't make sense to Quick was why the Silver

would have all these rules for themselves too. Why were they imprisoning themselves? What were they waiting for?

'You don't have to understand,' Monty replied. 'You won't get to understand either, not unless you move up the ladder.'

'You mean like a pyramid scheme? Like a *cult*?'

'Like a *government*,' Monty countered. 'You understand?'

'Not really.'

Monty sighed. 'Go back to bed, Quick.'

'You know I'm sharing a bunk with your new girlfriend, right?'

'Yes.' He closed his eyes and rubbed his temples. 'She did mention it once or twice. And she isn't my girlfriend.' He paused for a moment, then dropped his hands and looked at Quick contemplatively. 'You know,' he said, 'if you don't want to go back to the dorm, you could always come up to my room. We could... talk some more.'

Quick looked at him for a moment, said, 'I think I'd rather sleep with Angelina,' then headed back upstairs to her miserable little bunk.

She still couldn't sleep when she got there, though, and not just because of Angelina's indignant huffing from the bunk above. Her brain wouldn't stop spinning.

Bartholomew and Monty and the others were doing *something* in this place. There was a purpose to all of this, because there must be, and from all that she'd seen it didn't seem possible that their purpose could be good.

Somehow, Evita had escaped it, though. That was enough to give Quick hope.

9

KULIKA COULDN'T SLEEP.

She was fixating on those last two interviews of the day – Brandon and Penny – trying to pull their stories apart in her head and put them back together again in a way that didn't make Bayly look guilty as hell.

There'd been a treasure hunt, of all things. According to Brandon and Penny, they'd been spending a furlough day at one of Charleston's many museums when they'd seen a roster of Stede Bonnet's old crew, and they'd recognised a name: Job Bayly.

He was an idiot to have kept it, really. Kulika was, too, if it came to it. They made fun of Bartholomew – behind his back, of course – for changing his surname all the time, but with the benefit of hindsight, Kulika could see the sense in it. When people tried to trace his history, at least they had to work at it.

Brandon and Penny had already known by then that they were living amongst bona fide pirates, and when they'd made the connection between the gruff man in the mansion and the name on the crew roster, they'd hatched a plan to use Bayly to find Stede Bonnet's pirate gold. Apparently, Jane

275

Doe had gone along for the ride, at least as far as a cruise ship bound for Jamaica. They'd all boarded separately, each treasure hunter out for themselves, and they'd seen Bayly on board too, but that was where the trail went cold. Brandon and Penny had partied on the ship all the way to the island, poked around Kingston for a day or two without finding anything much, then partied all the way back again. It turned out that Jane – Evita – had been the brains of the operation, which was hardly a surprise given her academic background. Without her, the other two had been entirely at sea.

After they left Jamaica, they'd never seen Jane again. Bayly had already been at the mansion when they returned, and Jane wasn't due home until the end of the week anyway, so they hadn't thought much of it at the time. It was only later, when she missed her curfew, that they began to worry. They should have said something – they both acknowledged that to Kulika – but it turned out that Bayly's reputation was only marginally less scary than her own. When the call had gone out to find Jane, he'd glared, and they'd kept their mouths shut.

Even though it pained them. Even though they felt Jane's absence like a half-forgotten grief in the pits of their stomachs that roused them sweating from their sleep. Bartholomew was right about that: this crew didn't just miss their missing crewmate, they *keened* for her.

After hearing their story, Kulika was conflicted.

There was no pirate gold, of course. There had never been any. They'd collected a lot of plunder in those days, because that's what pirates did, but they'd spent it like water, too. Why bury it in a hole and go hungry when you could have a hot meal and a hot wench every night for as long as it lasted? They hadn't been the kind of people who engaged in sound financial planning. As far as they knew, they'd all be dead before they took the next prize anyway. Might as well make the most of it while they could.

Bayly had been a little different though, hadn't he? A little more secretive than the others, always going off on his own. And then there was Port Royal. He'd haunted that sunken city as much as it had haunted him, always returning as though the ghosts he'd buried there were calling him back.

Kulika had asked about that once, when they'd both been here before. Bayly hadn't told her much, just that the man who'd turned him Silver had been there during the earthquake that swallowed the place whole. He hadn't spelled it out, but Kulika could fill in the gaps: Bayly's maker had died when Port Royal sank.

Was he sad about that? Or relieved? Kulika had never been able to tell either way, which was so often the way it went with Bayly. He felt something, Kulika was sure, but what it was? Only Bayly knew. She hadn't wanted to pry. She'd had her own problems. Still did, but now it looked uncomfortably as though their personal concerns were about to collide.

Maybe it was time she pinned Bayly down and got some answers.

Kulika gave up on sleep, pushed herself out of bed, pulled on her clothes and strode across the room with purpose. But when she reached the door, she found it locked.

What the hell?

She grabbed the handle and rattled it, trying to work out what had gone wrong. When she bent down and squinted through the jamb, she could see that a lock had been thrown on the other side of the door. Several locks, meshing across the threshold to secure the opening, as though she was a wild beast that needed to be caged.

She could have broken the door. Come to that, she could

have just gone out through the window and saved her strength. In the end, she knocked on the connecting door between her rooms and Bartholomew's. If he was going to have the discourtesy to lock her in like an animal, the least she could do in return was interrupt his sleep.

'You locked me in,' she said incredulously when he opened the door.

'No,' he replied, brushing his hair out of sleepy eyes. 'I locked *them* out.'

'*Them* who? The crew?'

'You have some admirers, apparently.'

Kulika stared at Bartholomew, speechless for a moment. 'Why?' she asked eventually.

Bartholomew looked at her quizzically and asked, 'Why not?'

Kulika shook her head, shaking off the irrelevancy, and said, 'I need to speak to Bayly. Now.'

Bartholomew was quiet for a moment, tipping his ear towards the floor as though he could hear straight down to Bayly's room on the storey below. Maybe he could, because the next thing he said was, 'He's not here.'

'What? Where is he?'

'He'll be back tomorrow,' Bartholomew assured her. 'They'll all be back tomorrow.' From the tone of his voice, it was clear there was an implication in those words that Kulika didn't understand.

'What's tomorrow?' she asked. 'Is this about Cara Alton?'

Bartholomew laughed. 'It's never been *about* her,' he said. 'She's just a tool. You'll see, tomorrow.'

'Can't you just tell me? If you want me to support you, don't you need me to know—'

'Tomorrow,' he said, turning to face her, which effectively stopped her from following him. 'I'll send for you.'

Kulika didn't want to wait until tomorrow. She wanted to follow up on every piece of information she had immediately, so she could find Evita Khalyed and bring her back here to Quick and the crew—

No. Bring her back for *Dr Ross*, so she could save Baron Drake and Jack.

Right?

Either way, the end result would be the same, and her mission hadn't changed: find Evita Khalyed. It was simple. She didn't need to let Bartholomew make it complicated.

'I know you're impatient,' he said, 'but it's late, and you need to rest. And before you do that, I need you to make a call.'

'A call?' Kulika asked, thrown. 'Who am I calling?'

'Your old mansion.'

'My old…'

'It'll be morning there by now.'

She'd stayed up so late that it was tomorrow, and it would be later still back in Oxford.

'I'll see you at breakfast,' Bartholomew said, then he smiled encouragingly at her before closing the connecting door between them. He didn't lock it, though, because he didn't need to lock himself away from Kulika. Not now he had her on such a short leash.

Kulika stood there for a moment, staring at the door. Then she crossed the room, pulled her phone out of her back pocket, and lay down on the bed.

Bartholomew was right, of course. She had to make the call. Kulika might not have any numbers stored in her phone, but fortunately she knew Baron Drake's office number by heart.

'Hello?' he answered on the second ring. Even with the time difference, it was still early enough in Oxford that the

Baron wouldn't normally have been at his desk.

'It's Kulika,' she said.

'You've seen the news, I suppose,' he said, with the kind of exhaustion in his voice that suggested there'd been no rest for him since it broke. Probably not since long before then. Without the antidote Evita Khalyed's blood would provide, Jack was getting closer to death every day, along with Baron Drake himself. 'Bartholomew's work?' he asked.

'Yes.'

'And he's listening in?'

'Safest to assume that, yeah.'

'Then I'll keep it brief. The Primus is… No. I'll keep it briefer: find Evita Khalyed and come home.'

'I'm working on the first part. The second might be harder to swing.'

'Kulika—'

'What I'm saying is that it might be a good idea to get Dr Ross out here,' Kulika interrupted, 'if you can spare her. Then she can bring her formula with her and take what she needs from Dr Khalyed's blood the moment I track her down. That way, you won't have to rely on me to bring the antidote back for you if I'm… delayed.'

He paused for a beat, then said, 'Should I send Hugo?'

'No,' Kulika said quickly.

Adding more of the baron's people into the mix wouldn't help at this point. She was going to have a hard enough time extracting the doctor when the time came without having to worry about anyone else.

The doctor would have to come, though. There was no getting around that. Kulika was certain that, even if she did manage to find Evita Khalyed, Bartholomew wouldn't let the girl leave the mansion any more than he'd let Kulika herself leave. After all, they were both crew.

'All right,' the baron said. 'I'll send her. When?'

'I'll be in touch.'

'Make it soon.'

'I'll do my best,' she replied, but he'd already hung up.

Kulika hated to put Dr Ross in danger, but if the doctor had proved anything over the past year, it was that she could look after herself. Besides, this was the best plan available in the circumstances. If Khalyed couldn't go to the doctor, then the doctor was going to have to come to Khalyed, then take the antidote back to Oxford, leaving Kulika behind.

This was the truth that Kulika knew in her gut: by bribery or by choice, she would be at Bartholomew's side from now until the end of it all.

However soon that day might come.

IO

IT WAS LATE on Sunday morning, the atmosphere sticky and hot, before Quick and the rest of the dorm finally woke from their exhausted sleep. When they did, they woke dramatically.

First there was a crash and a scream, a couple of bunks away from Quick's. Then a splatter of something wet and warm hit her face. By the time she'd sat up and rubbed the liquid away with her sleeve, the whole room had descended into chaos. She saw the colour on her sleeve: blood red.

'Holy crap!' someone yelled.

'Fire!' yelled someone else, then everyone was hopping out of their beds and thundering towards the dormitory door in a single, unrestrained mass. They were bunched around the doorway, kicking and clawing as they tried to get past each other.

Quick looked towards the window at the other end of the dorm, which was currently aflame, trying to find another way out. That was when she noticed that the man in the bottom bunk next to hers wasn't moving. His sheets were starting to char around him, the result of an unbroken Molotov cocktail that sat smouldering on his pillow, but still he didn't move. There was something wrong with his head. In the spot above his ear, where there should have been tight, short braids of dark hair to match the ones covering the rest of his scalp, there was a long furrow of white, pink and red. No wonder he wasn't moving.

Quick should have run with the others. She should have just got out. The fire was raging around the window and the room had already filled with smoke. Besides, she didn't know these people, and they'd shown little enough consideration for her – and each other – that surely she didn't owe them anything. But the man's sheets were starting to burn properly now, and Quick couldn't help but think back to her sun-related accident on the training field yesterday. She knew how it felt to have fire licking up your limbs, and that gave her a pang of sympathy for the man who was probably already dead.

Only probably, though. The whisper of a chance was enough to have her dragging the sheets off her bed to smother the flames on his, then dragging his inert body off his own bed and towards the door. By that point, it wasn't crowded anymore. From what Quick could see through the smoke, it looked as though the others had disappeared entirely.

'Someone give me a hand, here!' she yelled into the thick air, but no one called back. All she could hear was crackling and roaring as the fire took hold behind her. With so many Silver in the building with extraordinary powers, could they really not organise a bucket chain?

Which is when she remembered: she had those powers too. Allegedly. She had yet to activate any of them successfully, but didn't people always say that you could do amazing things when fuelled with adrenaline? If humans could lift cars off human children, then surely Quick could carry one unconscious Silver out of a burning building.

And maybe she would have done, had it not been for bloody Monty.

Quick was halfway down the block's many stairs with the unconscious man slung over her shoulder when Monty rushed up from the ground floor and nearly knocked her flat.

'Leave him!' he yelled at her over the sound of the roaring fire.

'No!' Quick yelled right back at him.

'You're going to get yourself killed!'

'You're going to get *him* killed!' she said, shrugging her shoulder to indicate the man she was carrying with surprising ease. But then the smoke caught in her lungs. Brandon had told them yesterday that they didn't technically need to breathe anymore, but Quick's body disagreed. She started coughing and she couldn't stop, every heaving breath dragging more toxic particles into her lungs so that she had to cough again, then heave in another breath, in a terrible endless loop. It didn't stop until Monty flung her over one shoulder and the man over the other, then carried them both outside to the training ground. Quick made sure to keep to the shade.

'He'll live,' Monty said, dumping the unconscious man onto the ground.

'We've got to get the others out,' Quick said, turning to go back into the building. 'There are hundreds of people in the cellar, and if we don't open the hatch they'll all—'

'They're fine,' Monty said, looking unconcerned. In fact, as she looked around the crowd that had gathered outside the block, Quick noticed that no one looked particularly concerned. Some of them were even heading back inside, as though Quick hadn't just barely staggered out.

'What—'

'Fire's out,' one of the others said as they walked past Quick. 'Two minutes forty three. Looks like one of the bottles didn't smash, so I'm docking you twenty points.'

'*Twenty*?' the woman next to him said incredulously.

'You're still a hundred and ten up on the day. Just take the win.'

Quick looked at Monty, expecting an explanation, but he avoided her eyes, then walked off as soon as he spotted Angelina.

Quick looked down at her ragged cotton dress, now stained with blood and soot to add to the general dirtiness it had already acquired. She grabbed a handful of her hair and sniffed it: charred plastic and grease.

'What the hell was that?' she asked no one in particular.

'Fire drill,' Bella said with a shrug. 'If you want to move up the board, maybe next time don't stop to drag out a corpse.'

'What board?' Quick asked, but Bella had walked away too, heading back inside the building.

Quick followed her, in search of answers. It seemed like most of the crowd was heading the same way now, filing towards the big common room. But instead of gathering at the end nearest to the doors, where Brandon had been holding the humans the day before, everyone was clustered instead around the large television on the wall at the far end of the room, the one that showed the list Quick had noticed previously. As she got closer, she saw it was a list of names next to a load of numbers she couldn't parse. It scrolled down, the numbers changing, flicking red and green as they went up and down, apparently controlled by a young woman hunched over a laptop beneath the screen.

'Plus twenty for mine!' a guy yelled. 'She came out first.'

'No, mine did,' a woman argued back.

'Twenty each,' Monty said, pushing to the front of the crowd. 'And ten for each sire.'

The numbers changed, and the names and lines shuffled up and down the board.

'Hundred and ten for me,' someone else shouted, the woman Quick had seen outside. 'Duke agreed.'

'Fine,' said Monty, and again the board shifted and updated.

There were a few more shouted numbers, and a few more adjustments from the woman on the laptop, but by that time Quick wasn't paying attention anymore, because she'd worked out what the screen actually was.

They were *ranks*, like this was some kind of gameshow, and not just for the newcomers. Everyone was on the screen somewhere. As the list was finalised and began to scroll in a continuous loop from top to bottom, Quick saw Monty's name in the very first slot: Angel Monteiro. That explained why he was suddenly swaggering around like he owned the place. She couldn't find Kulika's name, though, not anywhere.

Quick's was easy enough to spot, though.

'You started off at the top of the newbies,' said Penny, coming up beside her. 'But the others crept up on points yesterday when you couldn't do Silver speed or jumping, and you actually lost points today because Monty had to rescue you from the fire.'

'I lost more points than the guy I pulled out of there?' Quick said incredulously.

'Well, you made some pretty stupid choices. Kaiden just had the misfortune to get hit in the head with a Molotov cocktail, which wasn't really his fault. So, yeah. You're coming in dead last.'

'I don't understand,' Quick said, looking at the scrolling

board as though she could decipher the deeper meaning behind it if she simply squinted harder. 'They set our dorm on fire to win *points*?'

'This place is boring,' Penny said, as though that were explanation enough.

'Excuse me?'

'We're out in the middle of Bumfuck South Carolina, and there's nothing to do. Playing with the board passes the time, and it means fewer arguments in the long run. Trust me. I was here in January, back before they put it up, and it was fucking awful.'

'*This* is awful,' Quick said, horrified. 'That guy nearly died.'

'Yeah, but at least he was the only one. People used to get into death matches every hour, fighting over who got first pick from the blood cellar, or who got the nicest bunk. Petty shit, but then petty shit feels big when there's nothing to distract you from it. This way, we always know who's on top.'

Quick felt sick about the whole thing. The board wasn't based on merit. Instead, from the little she'd seen, the people who topped the pack were the ones who were the best at behaving like dicks, either because they were the strongest or because they came up with stupid pranks like setting the dorm on fire. If those were the requirements to succeed in this place, then Quick was going to fail miserably.

But she was stuck here. Last night had made that abundantly clear.

'I guess I'm screwed, then,' Quick muttered.

'Oh, don't be like that,' Penny replied. Quick hadn't been talking to her, but Penny didn't seem to realise that. 'You won't get up to the top, but if you worked at it you could hit close enough to the middle to earn some privileges at least.'

Quick's interest sharpened. 'Like what?' she asked.

'Like more blood, better food, better rooms.'

'Showers?'

'What?' Penny screwed up her pretty little nose. 'Don't tell me you've been mouldering in that dirty dress since the Casting ceremony?'

The disgust in her voice just made Quick angry.

'No one told me I had another option! I thought we had to get permission for everything around here.'

'And you didn't think it was weird that everyone else was wearing clean clothes?'

'How was I supposed to know that? It's not like any of them actually talk to me,' Quick said, her temper snapping. Then she added sulkily, 'None of them came here from the blood cellar. I just thought they'd been wearing better things when they arrived.'

But now she came to think about it, Quick realised that the dresses and suits and swimwear had been replaced over the course of the past day with more practical clothing. It was just that she'd been concentrating on other things. She might have been around the others nonstop since the Casting, but she'd been pretty much alone the whole time.

Penny's expression softened along with her tone. 'You're not in the cellar anymore. You can shower whenever you like. Get new clothes from the wardrobe, too, and there's always something to eat in the kitchen, even if it's crap. The board's just for the big ticket items like dinner with the captain, furlough for trips off the property. Stuff like that.'

'We *are* stuck here, then?'

'Not forever.' Penny smiled awkwardly. 'But I'd be lying if I said people don't get points for hunting down deserters.'

Shit.

How was she ever going to get herself and Xiaoyu out of

here, or find Evita, if she had power-hungry Silver dogging her every move?

Quick thought for a moment, then asked, 'How high do you need to get for the big-ticket things?'

'Dinner with the captain? Top ten, I'd say. The rest, top half maybe? Look, don't worry about it. You'll get there. Just go get cleaned up, all right? Today's a big day.'

Quick wanted to ask what that meant, but everyone was leaving the common room now that the board had been updated. Penny slipped away with them, leaving Quick with a lot to consider.

She took her time in the shower, and in the wardrobe afterwards, mulling things over as she did so. There was another matter of concern, too: when Quick checked her neck in the bathroom mirror, there was no silver on it or – as far as she could see – at the base of her skull. Had Xiaoyu been mistaken yesterday, or was she losing it? Either way, Quick couldn't leave her down in the cellar much longer without checking on her. She had to find a way out, and she had to do it fast.

In the wardrobe, Quick chose clothes that would cover as much of her skin as possible, whilst also being light enough for the heat and sturdy enough to work out in. When she returned to the dorm, at first she thought she'd walked into the wrong room. There was no blood, no ash, no fire damage at all. She walked back out and realised there was no damage in the corridor either, even though the whole building had been filled with ink-black smoke half an hour before.

It was unsettling, to say the least.

There was a bottle of sunscreen on her bed, along with a parasol. An actual parasol. It had a wooden handle, and the frame was covered with black material and trimmed with lace. It looked *quaint*. Quick was not quaint. She would never be quaint, but apparently she was about to spend the day leaping and running around the training ground looking like Mary fucking Poppins.

'Hurry up, newbie!' someone yelled from down the hall.

Quick didn't realise it was her they were yelling at until an angry woman popped her head around the doorway of the dorm and said, 'Hey, newbie! Get your ass in here!'

'Excuse me?' said Quick.

'You're bottom twenty on the board, am I right? Well, *bottom* bottom.'

'Yes…'

'Then you're on clean up duty. Did no one tell you?'

'I… No, I—'

'Then *hurry up*. You're already late, so if you could get any lower on the board, you already would be. If you want to earn any points at all today, you'll shift it! Now!'

Quick obeyed.

In the dorms further along the corridor, people were scrubbing and painting and replacing furniture, some at Silver speed and some at the only speed Quick could manage. Someone gave her a paintbrush and pointed her at a section of stripped wall. No one spoke, they just worked with the kind of concentration that told her they were serious about getting more points for the board.

Over the course of the morning, Quick realised she should get serious too.

Furlough for trips off the property, Penny had said.

Off the property.

Which gave Quick a new objective: get up the bloody board, and do it fast.

II

THE MANSION WAS busy this morning. Kulika had woken to the noises of engines in the driveway, furniture being moved in the rooms below hers, and laughter in the hallways. It was as if the crew was congregating for Sunday church. Kulika wasn't sure she'd like the object of their worship.

Frustratingly, Bayly was not amongst the newly-returned crew. She'd checked the porch, where he would normally be drinking his coffee, and found it empty. She'd checked his room on the floor below hers, and found only a stripped single bed surrounded by no personal effects at all.

That was when she really began to panic.

'Bartholomew,' she said, pushing her way into the library without an invitation. 'Where's Bayly? You said he'd be back today.'

'No,' Bartholomew said, slowly rising from his desk chair. 'I said he'd be back tonight.'

'You said today.'

'Tonight is today. Either way, I don't think it's enough of an emergency to justify this intrusion. Do you?'

It was only then that Kulika realised they weren't alone in

291

the room. Monty was on his knees at the far end of the room, his face pointed into the corner of the bookshelves like a naughty child paying penance for talking in class.

'What's going on?' she asked.

'Oh, nothing,' Bartholomew said, walking around the desk to join Kulika at the door. 'Just a little misunderstanding about fire safety. Walk with me, won't you?'

Kulika glanced at Monty, still motionless in the corner, then looked uncertainly back at Bartholomew. 'All Bayly's things are gone from his room,' she said. 'I don't think he's coming back, and I need to talk to him now.'

'Oh, he's coming back,' Bartholomew promised her. 'Don't you worry about that. Now, come with me.'

Reluctantly, Kulika let herself be led to the door at the far end of the mansion's kitchen, the one she'd followed Bartholomew to the other day after the unlucky Alex came home. He opened it to reveal a set of brick stairs leading down into a space lit with bare, dim bulbs. From the doorway, Kulika could see nothing except the corner in the stairwell below them where the steps turned to the side, leading down deeper.

She didn't want to go down.

'What are you showing me?' she asked, trying not to sound as hesitant as she felt.

'Part two of the grand revelation plan,' Bartholomew said with a smile, then he stepped up close behind her, forcing her to move down the steps so she didn't end up falling down instead. He shut the door behind them.

Kulika turned to look where she was going, resigning herself to the descent. She took a step, and another, and with each one the temperature dropped so perceptibly that she was sure the space must have been artificially cooled. But there were no wires, no hum of air conditioning, nothing except the bare wires tacked to the walls, trailing power to the bulbs above their heads as they descended into the frigid space below.

She'd never been down here in the bad old days, but then she'd never gone into the kitchen at all. The old cook would have thrown his meat cleaver at her. He'd been precious about his domain. Besides, they all knew Bartholomew had buried things under the mansion, things both living and dead. No one went underground except him, not just because it was forbidden, but because only an idiot would go digging up the skeletons Bartholomew had accumulated over five hundred years of sin. Some secrets are best left buried.

'What is this place?' she asked.

'Cold storage,' Bartholomew said, with an edge of amusement in his tone that chilled Kulika's blood.

She suspected she wasn't going to enjoy the joke. Her suspicion was confirmed when she turned the corner and saw the body laid out on a large stone plinth raised up from the centre of the dirt floor.

'Leo, I presume?' she asked, breathing through her mouth.

She could smell the rot from here. It might have been cool in the cellar, but they were still in South Carolina in high summer, and the poor kid had been dead five days. There was only so much that could be done to preserve a body without the benefits of proper refrigeration and embalming fluid.

'Tell me you're not going to eat him,' she added, her upper lip curling back involuntarily.

'Not all of him,' Bartholomew replied, stepping past her on the stairs so he could circle the plinth. 'Jessamy knows her work well. When she and Alex went to find Leo, she drained and chilled his blood before arranging to transport him back here. Poor Alex,' Bartholomew added, shaking his head sadly as though he wasn't the one who'd incited his execution. 'The blood may not be entirely fresh, but it's fresh enough for the Convocation.'

'The Convocation?'

'Tonight,' Bartholomew said with a gleeful smile that made Kulika uneasy. 'You'll see.'

'This is the thing you wouldn't tell me about yesterday,' she guessed. 'This is why everyone's coming back to the mansion today.'

'Exactly. Think of it as a crew meeting, where the old guard will have a chance to welcome the newcomers. And what a meeting it will be. We're celebrating, Kulika,' Bartholomew said. His joy felt out of place in the cellar that had become a crypt. 'The number of Silver we created on Friday night was unprecedented. *Unprecedented*. Not in all his years as Primus, and god king, and whatever else he wants to hold himself out to be, did Solomon achieve anywhere near the numbers we're pulling in. Do you have any idea how long it's been since Silver were made and gathered in a single group the size of our current crew?'

'No,' Kulika said. She still thought it was reckless to leave so many new Silver practically unsupervised, but she knew this wasn't the moment to say so. Bartholomew was in speech mode now, and all he wanted was for her to play along with the call and response.

'Never,' he said. '*Never*, not in all the millennia the Silver have been walking the earth. We're a new breed, and we're stronger than any Silver that have come before us.'

Kulika didn't like the way this was going. She'd heard that kind of talk before, and she knew just how insidious could be. Hearing yourself talked about in those terms made you feel special, a blessed part of the elite. It might even make you feel sorry for the people who weren't so fortunate, in the beginning at least, but once you heard it often enough you'd slip into disdain and start to feel that your specialness entitled you to more than those who were not like you. After all, weren't you *worth* more than them? Weren't you better? Once you became nicely embedded in those ideas, it was just a slow, incremental slide towards thinking that the world would be better off if it didn't contain anyone who wasn't as special as you.

In Bartholomew's words, Kulika could hear the first wave of the storm that would sink the ship.

'And then there's this,' he said, crossing the cellar to a second, sheet-covered plinth Kulika hadn't noticed before, because it was tucked into an alcove like a sarcophagus would be in a crypt.

'Cara Alton?' Kulika asked.

'The very same.'

'But why bring her back here? She's not crew.'

'No, but that doesn't mean she can't be useful to us,' he said. 'You know the old stories about silvering, I suppose?' He walked the length of the plinth slowly as he spoke, trailing his fingertips along the covered body like he was a car salesman tempting Kulika with a shiny new Porsche.

'I know some.'

'Well, a lot of them are fantasy, obviously. There's this romanticised idea that when the person a bonded Silver loves dies, the life bond disintegrates that Silver into a pile of twinkling dust and they just… blow away on the breeze. To counter that ridiculous theory—' Bartholomew turned and gestured expansively at Leo's very solid, un-dusty corpse. '—I present Exhibit A.'

'And your point is?'

'My point is that although some of the myths are hokum, not all of them are. Which brings me to Exhibit B.'

He ripped the sheet off Cara Alton's body with gratuitous drama, the material snapping through the air like a whip. The poor girl was half-naked underneath it, her skirt bunched up around her hips, her T-shirt pushed up to reveal her bare stomach. Bare, that is, except for the silver handprint that glimmered on her stomach.

'You know what that is?' Bartholomew asked in a low voice.

He must have seen the silver mark Kulika had left on Quick's neck when she'd healed her bite. It wasn't worth denying that she recognised the peculiar shine, glinting like frozen mercury beneath Cara Alton's skin.

'It's a healing mark,' she said.

'Wrong,' he replied with a grin, pleased that she'd remained on-script. 'It's the straw that's going to break the camel's back. The sceptics can dismiss the Silver speed video as doctored or fake, but when they have this girl's body? When they open her up and look at what's inside her, do you know what they're going to find?'

'No.'

'Nothing,' he said emphatically. 'No blood, no exit wound through which the blood could have been drawn, and an indelible silver mark that's penetrated the skin far deeper than any stain would go. It'll be on her cells, you know. It goes right down to the bone, a mark like that.' He smiled as though he were remembering something funny, then said, 'I opened one of them up once. Even the *blood* was silver.'

A sharp rush of fear skittered across Kulika's skin.

'Not our Patience,' Bartholomew said with a laugh. 'You'd know if it had been her. You'd feel it, the way *he* felt it when I— But I'm becoming distracted, aren't I?'

Bartholomew's smile did nothing to reassure her, but then it wasn't intended to. It was intended as a threat.

Then the smile softened, and Kulika was left wondering if she'd imagined the menace she'd seen in it just a moment before.

'I want you beside me tonight,' he said, taking her hand in his. 'For the Convocation.' His words felt sincere, but Kulika could no longer follow the emotional thread of their conversation. Was this an order, or a request? Was he threatening to hurt Quick if she didn't, or had he genuinely been sharing a twisted memory with her and expecting her to appreciate it? Given her history, that wasn't beyond the realms of possibility, but she no longer had any idea of Bartholomew's angle.

Perhaps *that* was the intention.

'Is this a test?' she asked suspiciously.

'Call it an offer,' he said.

'An offer of what?'

'Just be ready when I come for you at midnight,' he said.

On the off-chance that it was neither test nor offer, but threat, Kulika resolved to make sure that she was waiting.

There had been no sign of Bayly all day. Instead, Kulika had spent her time talking to all the returning Silver to discover what they knew about Dr Evita Khalyed, AKA Jane Doe. She'd been hoping to find something – anything – to point her away from Bayly, but the returning Silver knew even less than the Silver from the block. Most of them didn't even remember "Jane", beyond the tugging ache that her absence created in each of them.

That, it seemed, was more real to them than Evita herself had been.

All too soon it was midnight, and Bartholomew appeared at her door with a robe in his arms and a smile on his lips, neither of which seemed like good signs. Still, Kulika followed him downstairs into the candlelit silence of the hall, where hundreds of other robed Silver waited for them.

This time, Bartholomew didn't stop at the mezzanine, not like he had done at the Casting. Instead, he led Kulika right down to the foot of the staircase, where he stood and addressed his crew.

Their crew.

'Tonight is the last night that we'll come together like this in darkness,' he said, holding his robed arms open wide like a priest inviting them all to take the sacrament. 'The next time we gather, the Convocation will be in daylight, in the open, and we will no longer need to hide our power. In anticipation of that revelation, I'm making a revelation of my own.' He paused dramatically, then turned slightly towards Kulika and added, 'I trust that my Second requires no introduction.' The gesture was enough to make his meaning clear.

Half of the crew had already seen Kulika with Bartholomew since her return, at the Casting ceremony if not at the demise of Alex, and it didn't seem to surprise any of the new Silver that she'd been returned to her former position, no more than it surprised Kulika herself.

He gives and he takes.

But the older Silver in the congregation *were* surprised, though their shock at Bartholomew's words had less to do with her elevation than it did with the title he'd given her.

Second.

The Latin word for that was *Secundus*, the name given to the Primus's second-in-command.

No wonder the older Silver were shocked. Some of them were as old as Bartholomew himself, and they'd see the title he'd given Kulika as an indicator of his own intentions. America had never ascribed to the rule of Solomon, or to any of the other Primi around the world who pretended they were his peers, but now Bartholomew was using the language of the Silver kings.

That couldn't have been unintentional. Every single thing Bartholomew did was deliberate. He had the power already, and now it seemed he was snatching the title too. He was setting himself up as a new Primus.

Despite their shock, not one of the convocants objected.

Bartholomew looked around the Convocation, assessing their reactions. No one was stupid enough to show him anything but acceptance, not amongst the crew.

Later, though.

Kulika wondered about later.

There was a table placed at the foot of the staircase and off to one side, tucked slightly behind the banisters, so Kulika hadn't noticed it at first. Bartholomew walked over to it now and lifted from it the most ornate cup Kulika had ever seen. It was a large and fierce thing, double-handled and rounded at the bottom like a bowl. Between the two handles, looping over the top of the vessel like an arched bridge between its two edges, was a curved blade. There was something odd about the inside of the bowl too, because when Bartholomew took it in his hands, his face was suddenly illuminated from below, as though the mirrored surface were concentrating and directing the light from all the meagre candles that lit the hall and turning them into more than the sum of their parts. It felt like a religious item, a cup that really deserved to be called a chalice.

Seeing its construction, Kulika had a pretty good idea what it was for.

Bartholomew passed it to the first Silver on his left, holding it reverently by both handles as he lowered the base into the man's palms. Now that his face was illuminated by the inside of the cup, Kulika saw that it was Monty. He didn't mess around. He brought the wrist of his free hand right down onto the curved blade, opened the vein so it bled a little into the bowl, then shifted his grip to hold the cup by both handles as he passed it to the next person in line. By the time it had made its way halfway around the hall, the light reflecting up from the inside of the bowl was distinctly dimmed, and the entire outside of the cup was darkened and dirtied with smeared blood.

Then it came into Quick's hands.

Kulika had been aware of her since the minute she walked in the door. How could she not be? Every gesture Quick made, every tiny shift of her clothing, sent her perfume rolling in waves across the hall to Kulika. She could feel her nostrils flaring, desperately trying to catch every facet and intricacy of Quick's scent, but she couldn't stop it. She didn't *want* to stop it. With the kaleidoscopic aroma filling her head, Kulika was transported back to that kiss, that bite, and away from this dark cabal.

When Quick opened her vein into the cup with a hesitant grimace, Kulika felt the pain as though it had sliced through her own wrist. She smelled the blood too, and it sparked a protective fury in her stomach that she hadn't expected. She wanted to rush across the hall and knock the cup from Quick's hands. She wanted to pull Quick's wrist to her mouth and heal her wound, but then everyone would know that Kulika had silvered for her. Given her new status as Bartholomew's Second and all the competition that would provoke, it seemed ill-advised to advertise the fact that bumping off just one vulnerable new Silver – Quick – would be enough to take out Kulika too.

Stupid.

Seeing Quick bleeding across the hall, there was nothing

Kulika could do about it except watch and worry and yearn.

'Steady,' Bartholomew whispered to her, so softly that she imagined she would be the only one to hear it.

It shouldn't have worked.

One word, and from *him*.

He touched her hand, and the word spread through her body like a command.

Steady.

It really shouldn't have worked.

Nonetheless, the fury rushing through Kulika's body settled immediately. Her fists unclenched, her jaw relaxed, and she couldn't even smell the blood so much anymore. It was as though Quick's scent had dissipated into the air, banished at a single word, a single touch from Bartholomew.

Perhaps it was just conditioning from all those long years serving beneath his flag. Either way, Kulika didn't like it, and she was riling herself up to get angry about it, but then Bartholomew released her hand with a smile and the world came rushing back in. By then, the danger was gone. Quick had passed the cup on to the next Silver, who started the whole grim business up again. Round and round the circle, until the cup returned to them, full now.

Bartholomew took the cup and put it back on the table, next to a stoppered vial Kulika hadn't noticed before.

'Our crewmate, Leo,' he said, raising the vial up high before emptying its contents into the cup and swirling it around. Next, he held the cup out towards Kulika and nodded at the blade. Reluctantly, she cut herself on it and contributed her own blood. Finally, Bartholomew cut his own wrist and added his blood to the mix, then sent the cup around the hall again.

This time, they all drank, Quick included. There was no way for Kulika to intervene, and no good reason that she should. After all, it was just a little blood. What could it hurt?

She wondered then whether Bartholomew had been deliberately trying to emulate a religious event. It was fitting, because here they were taking communion, only the blood was their own, and Bartholomew's. For a girl born when Kulika had been, raised to be a good Catholic, there was a twisted and solipsistic symbolism in it that crept unpleasantly into her mind.

Bartholomew didn't drink, she noticed, so Kulika didn't either. When the cup reached her, she turned to offer Bartholomew the nearly-drained vessel instead. His gaze lingered on hers as their hands met around it, and for a moment she thought he was going to hold it up to her lips, but instead he just held her fingers in place beneath his so she couldn't let go of the cup.

He was waiting for something, and Kulika had a terrible suspicion that she knew what it was. *This* was the test.

'Your chalice, Primus,' she said, loudly enough that her voice rang out across the hall.

Bartholomew smiled his approval and released her hands, then turned to place the cup down on the table behind him.

The candles snuffed out, the ceremony apparently over. The crew departed quickly and quietly after that, leaving Kulika and Bartholomew alone in the dark.

'How do you do that?' she asked him, feeling grateful and violated all at the same time. 'The way you steadied me like that.'

'I made you, Kulika,' he said plainly. 'Blood calls to blood.'

Kulika didn't know how to feel about that, or what it meant for the ceremony she'd just witnessed. Taken part in, even. It didn't sound good, though. It sounded like

Bartholomew had an influence over her that she'd never fully appreciated.

'I could do more than just that for you,' he went on, 'if you'd only drink.'

'From that?' Kulika asked, looking askance at the dirty, bloody cup.

'Or from a purer source,' Bartholomew said, offering his healed wrist to her.

It was one hell of an offer. The Silver didn't drink each others' blood, not under normal circumstances. It was done only when new Silver were made, or in dire straits when a Silver was injured and there was no other blood available, or if the Silver were in a sexual relationship and were feeling kinky. The Convocation tonight had been irregular enough, but the offer Bartholomew had just made to Kulika?

It was intimate enough that it probably went against his vow of celibacy.

'I can't accept that,' Kulika replied, backing up a little. If he could settle her with a word and a touch through the connection his blood had forged between them three hundred years ago, what control would he gain over her if she accepted now?

'I would allow your lips on my skin, Kulika,' he said softly.

'And what would you demand of me in return?' she asked.

He gives and he takes.

He smiled and pulled the sleeve of his robe back down over his wrist. 'Not tonight, then. Later, perhaps.'

'Perhaps,' Kulika said, while silently vowing to herself that it would be *never*.

'You did well tonight. In fact, I think you've earned a little trust.'

Then he took her hand in his, raised it to his lips, and

finally delivered the words of benediction she'd been waiting for.

12

THE SILVER OF the block were partying. Quick hadn't earned the right to join them yet, Monty told her, but since this was a special night – the Convocation to end all others – the top rankers were willing to make an exception.

'Do we have to?' someone asked Monty as they passed on their way to the pool.

Belatedly, Quick realised it was Kaiden.

She was a little surprised to learn that he was now amongst the top rankers, but not as surprised as she was by his attitude towards her. She'd saved his life. She'd got herself demoted on the stupid board to drag his body out of a burning building and not only did he not seem particularly grateful, he seemed to be actively resenting her help. Quick hadn't expected effusive thanks or anything – to her mind, she'd only done what any decent human being would do in the same circumstances – but then they weren't human anymore, were they? Rules of common decency no longer applied.

Kaiden's attitude didn't make the invitation to the pool party any more appealing. Quick felt out of place and useless so, not being the type of person who was inclined to accept a bad hand without drawing again to see if she could get something better, she made some desultory excuses to Monty, then dragged herself outside to the training ground to try the running and jumping drills again.

After an hour, it wasn't going well. Her stomach was roiling, but she couldn't tell whether that was because she was hungry, or because she was feeling sick from the blood cocktail she'd drunk at the Convocation. Just a sip, as she'd been instructed, but still, she was beginning to regret drinking it at all. She hadn't been given a choice, but then she probably wouldn't have refused even if she had been, because of the stupid board. Despite her connection to the apparently-famous and ever-absent Kulika Yadav, she was still on the bottom.

Kulika hadn't been absent tonight, though, had she? She'd been right there next to Bartholomew. She'd probably been at the mansion this whole time, only Quick wasn't allowed to leave the block to see her and Kulika apparently had no inclination to come and see her. Quick had thought – naively, she now realised – that it meant something that Kulika had come to rescue her yesterday. She'd even imagined – naively again – that she might have Kulika on her side when she came to make her daring escape, however she managed it.

No such luck. She was on her own, which meant there was only one course of action she could follow: she needed points. If she wanted to be given enough leeway to find Evita, free Xiaoyu, and get them all the hell out of here, she needed more status than she had right now. Otherwise, she was going to spend every day in the block like she had spent today: painting the walls, cleaning the toilets, carrying supplies, and generally tiring herself out so much that even on the rare occasions that she was allowed a blood ration to regain her strength, she'd be too exhausted to do anything but sleep.

That was another reason she'd chosen to come out to the training ground and practice rather than party the night away: this might be the only chance she'd get to score some points for her abilities.

If only she could get a single bloody one of them to work.

As Quick was trying and failing for the hundredth time to jump more than a foot in the air, a voice said, 'Let me try,' from the sidelines.

Quick thought she recognised the voice, but she didn't believe that Kulika was really there until she turned around and saw her leaning up against the wall of the block, watching. Her robes were gone now. She was dressed in dark trousers and a black racer-back top that bared her arms and showed every muscled inch of her shoulders.

Quick said, 'Um.'

Kulika smiled to herself and pushed away from the wall, stalking across the training ground towards her. 'It's easier if you try it in action, sometimes,' she said. 'Have you tried sparring yet?'

'No.' Quick didn't want to admit that she was such a pariah in the block that no one would partner with her.

'Do you want to?' Kulika asked, looking at Quick with a wicked glint in her eye.

Quick swallowed. Her mouth was suddenly dry. Now that Kulika was closer, all Quick could smell was the salty scent of her skin. She wanted to lean in and sniff it, but she held herself back, because that would probably be weird.

Correction: it would *definitely* be weird.

Kulika came to a stop just a step away from Quick. She was smiling.

'Well?' she prompted.

It felt like a dangerous proposal. Not only was Kulika

apparently a dangerous person, but Quick's reaction to her was dangerous as well. Quick had seen Kulika side by side with Bartholomew, so she knew just how involved she was with this place, but she still wanted Kulika with a fierceness that scared her. If she actually *touched* her again, even if they were fighting, Quick wasn't sure what would happen.

But she *really* wanted to find out.

Kulika had only been away from her gym in Oxford for a few days, but it felt like longer, to her mind and to her body. Having the chance to stretch out the kinks would have been welcome in any circumstances, but when Quick was her opponent, when every kick and punch she blocked would bring them thudding into contact with a joyful burst of uncontrolled impact?

From the first hit, she loved it so much that she already knew she'd never want to stop.

'I'm no good at this,' Quick said after her first swing.

Kulika had asked her to aim a punch at her face, and she'd thrown herself off balance and ended up falling into Kulika's arms. Her ready, waiting arms. It had been all Kulika could do to let Quick go after she'd put her back on her feet.

'Try again,' Kulika said, 'but this time, plant your feet a little wider, like this.'

Kulika demonstrated, and Quick imitated the stance perfectly. That was a good sign, but Kulika would have been lying if she'd said that a part of her hadn't been hoping Quick would need some adjustment. Her fingers were itching to touch her.

But no. She didn't want to force this. She would initiate contact only when strictly necessary for teaching purposes. Or when invited. God, she wished she would be invited. Quick hadn't tied up her hair, so it flowed loosely around her shoulders in a waterfall that Kulika longed to stroke. She wanted to run her fingers through it and see how it moved in the moonlight, how the colour changed when the light hit it at different angles. It was... distracting.

'Like this?' Quick asked, snapping Kulika's attention back to her stance.

'Right,' she said, clearing her throat. Why was her mouth suddenly so dry? 'Just raise your hands a little more. You're trying to guard your face.'

Quick lifted her arms in a way that pressed her cleavage together, drawing Kulika's gaze inexorably downwards.

'Better?' Quick asked.

When Kulika's attention snapped back this time, she found Quick looking at her with amusement. Seeing her smile, Kulika couldn't help but smile back. That was when Quick swung again, trying to take advantage of Kulika's distraction, which just made Kulika smile more.

This girl was *ruthless*.

And Kulika loved it.

Quick was eighty-five percent certain that Kulika had just been checking her out. Granted, this T-shirt scooped a little lower in the neck than Quick would have preferred, and when she raised her fists the effect it had on her body was eye-catching, but Quick was pretty sure she'd caught Kulika's eye in a good way.

Ninety percent certain.

It still wasn't enough, though. In the circumstances, she would have to be absolutely one hundred percent sure that Kulika was into her before she made a move, because the circumstances were dire. Quick was at the very bottom of the pile, trying to escape this place and take her friends with her, and Kulika was standing next to the man who seemed to have power of life and death over them all.

No, she couldn't be too careful. Perhaps she had distracted Kulika for a moment – ninety-five percent certain, given the way Kulika was looking at her now – but Quick herself couldn't afford to be distracted.

However alluring the distraction might be.

'I'm not very good at any of this,' she said apologetically.

'Because you're trying to force it,' said Kulika. 'It's tensing you up through the shoulders, so you're holding yourself back instead of reacting naturally. You're Silver, now. You're built for this. You've got the potential for enormous speed; you just have to let it fly. Look,' she said, then she put her hands on Quick's shoulders and Quick forgot to breathe. She wished suddenly that she'd picked a top from the wardrobe that was more like Kulika's, so more of her skin could have been bared to the other woman's touch. But then it was distracting enough to be touched by her like this, through the shoulders of her T-shirt.

If Kulika wanted her to relax, this was absolutely not the way to go about it.

Quick was absolutely letting herself get distracted.

Fuck.

'Guard up,' Kulika yelled as Quick swung again.

She was getting the hang of it surprisingly fast. Satisfyingly fast. It sometimes happened like this, usually with no warning. Kulika'd had a suspicion, though. These days, most people went through their adult lives never even throwing a punch. They didn't know how to do it, or how it felt, and they'd certainly never dream of doing it in polite society anyway, so why learn? Which meant they never found out if they were any good at fighting. But Quick had a natural affinity for it.

After a few more bouts of fist-fighting, Kulika introduced her to some basic kicks, and that was when the rest of her power finally unlocked. One minute Kulika was blocking a jab, then Quick stuck out a leg and tripped her up, rolling Kulika onto the ground. She wouldn't have caught Kulika out under normal circumstances, but Quick had done the whole thing moving at Silver speed. Unfortunately, she appeared to have caught herself out with it too, overshooting so she pitched face-first onto the ground.

On top of Kulika.

'Um,' Quick said.

They were chin to chin, nose to nose, close enough to kiss, and Kulika was oh so willing.

For one brief, joyful second, their eyes locked and Kulika thought Quick might actually be about to close the meagre distance that remained between them, but then Quick scrambled back to her feet, muttering, 'Sorry,' and Kulika could only regret the missed opportunity.

'Don't be sorry,' Kulika replied, jumping to her feet. 'You're getting it. You just moved at Silver speed on that last kick.'

'I did?'

'Did you not realise?'

Quick looked puzzled for a moment, then frustrated, then she looked away. Kulika wished she knew what had just happened inside her head, but Quick was giving nothing away.

'You can do this,' Kulika promised her. 'Just reset, and come at me again.'

The next time Quick started punching, it was serious. Having tapped into her power once, she was brimming with it now. She sped impossibly fast into dodges, she leapt impossibly high into kicks, and she hit Kulika so hard that it was almost a fair fight.

Kulika felt like yelling with the joy of it. She thrilled to it. She was an instrument of muscle and force, and Quick wasn't holding back. She didn't need to – yet – but Kulika was surprised by her strength, given how recently she'd been turned. It wouldn't be long before Kulika wouldn't need to hold back either, and the thought of that was enough to bring a grin to her bleeding lips.

She was *so* strong.

'I'm not sure I can carry on much longer,' Quick panted eventually.

'You need blood,' Kulika said. 'Using the speed burns through it.'

'Then I guess I won't be using it much.'

Quick wandered back over to the building and sat down with her back against the wall, leaning her head back against it as she caught her breath. The silver mark was gone from her neck, Kulika noticed. Probably the one in the roots of her hair too, though the waves were cascading so abundantly over Quick's shoulders that it was impossible to tell for sure.

God, Kulika wanted to reach out and touch it. Instead, she sat herself down beside Quick and looked up to the stars, trying to calm her hungry eyes with the sight of anything else.

'We need to talk about Evita,' Kulika said into the darkness.

'Do you know where she is?' Quick asked, her voice full of hope.

'No,' she replied. 'I'm looking for her, though.'

'Why?' Quick asked suspiciously.

Dammit. She was clever too.

'To bring her back here,' Kulika said.

'To him? For Bartholomew?'

'For all of us. She's crew.'

'Right,' Quick scoffed. 'You say that as though you expect it to reassure me.'

'This won't be forever,' Kulika whispered, with more hope than truth.

'People keep saying that, too, but again: not reassuring. *Why* won't it be forever? Because we're all going to get out of here and go back to our lives, safe and sound, or because we're heading towards something that's going to kill us all? The way people are talking around the block, it sounds to me like none of us are making it out of here alive.'

'*We* will,' Kulika said, with conviction she didn't feel.

'And Evita?' Quick asked.

'Her too. I'll find her. I'm good at finding people.'

'But you don't know her, not like I do.'

'She doesn't know herself,' Kulika countered. 'She lost her memory when she got turned. She's been calling herself Jane Doe.'

Quick laughed.

'I've been speaking to everyone who knew her when she was here,' Kulika went on, 'learning what I can. Have you heard anything that might help?'

'They won't talk about her,' Quick said. 'Last time I said the name Jane around here, I got someone killed.'

'Well, they talked to me. Not that Bartholomew gave them much choice about it. Do you know who Brandon and Penny are?'

'Yes,' Quick said, then she made a face.

'You don't like them?'

'Penny's being friendly enough, but she's part of the reason I ended up in the blood cellar. Brandon too. I don't like either of them much,' Quick admitted.

'Well, apparently Evita – or Jane – did,' said Kulika. 'The

three of them went on a cruise to Jamaica together, and only two of them came back. I can't find anyone who saw her again after the cruise left the island.'

'So she's still there?'

'We'll see. I'm flying out tomorrow. Well, later today.'

Kulika had booked the tickets the moment she'd realised Bayly was a no-show at the Convocation. It had been dark, yes, but Kulika was sure that he hadn't been there. She'd known Bayly for hundreds of years. She would recognise the scent of his blood from literally a mile away, and it had been nowhere in that hall this evening.

Which meant trouble, particularly since Kulika had definitely seen Enzo. She'd spoken to him before coming to the block, and he'd sworn up and down that he had no idea where Bayly had gone. She could think of no good scenario that explained Bayly's absence, on a night when Bartholomew had insisted all crew members be present. *The full complement*, he'd said, but he'd got at least one less than that. Two, if you counted Evita.

Maybe Kulika was worrying unnecessarily, but her gut told her that she'd find their two missing crew members together.

13

JANE DOE.

That was just like Evita, with her dark sense of humour. The familiarity of it made Quick's chest ache.

'I'm flying out tomorrow,' Kulika had said, which meant that she was allowed to leave the property, unlike Quick. She'd had to get special dispensation from Monty just to use the training ground.

It reminded Quick how little she knew about the woman sitting next to her in the dark, and how little she should trust her.

'I'm not sure I should even believe you,' Quick said quietly.

'About what?'

'About finding Evita, about getting out of here. About anything. I don't know you.'

'I suppose not,' Kulika replied quietly.

'But I *want* to trust you. So who are you?' Quick asked.

An awkward expression flitted across Kulika's face. 'I'm Kulika Yadav,' she said.

'Yes, I know,' Quick replied impatiently. 'But who *are* you? You said you were going to help us escape the cellar, but then you were standing next to Bartholomew at the Casting and again at the Convocation. He called you his Second. They say that makes you... Well, put it this way, if they knew you were here with me right now I'm pretty sure they'd bump me up the board by about a hundred points.'

'The board?'

'Forget it. The point is, you made me into *this*, then you saved me yesterday and suddenly you're training me... But the others act like they're scared of you, and it sounds like that's with good reason, and I don't understand how you can be that and this at the same time. You said you were part of Bartholomew's crew. *Were*, past tense, but it doesn't look like that from where I'm sitting, and I don't understand any of it.'

'What are you asking me?' Kulika's expression was almost offended, and Quick didn't understand that, either.

'I just want to know where you stand. Where *I* stand.'

Kulika pushed her hair away from her face in a gesture that looked to Quick like she was buying time.

'You kissed me,' Quick said. 'And it was—'

'It takes away the pain,' Kulika explained quickly. 'If I hadn't, it would have hurt when I bit you.'

Quick's mouth went dry. The way Kulika described the kiss, it was as though she'd just injected Quick with a little anaesthetic, but the effect of it on Quick had been far from numbing. She hadn't trusted her feelings at the time, barely daring to believe that Kulika might actually want her. From the way Kulika was talking now, it seemed Quick was right to have been cautious. She hadn't been cautious enough, though, because the realisation that the kiss had been merely practical – the last thing a kiss should ever be – crushed Quick's fragile psyche into a paste on the dirt.

Stupid, she thought.

Then she cleared her throat and said, 'I see,' because she'd been sitting in silence for a while now and she had to say *something*. 'And what about being Bartholomew's Second?'

'What about it?' Kulika was getting defensive now, in a way that twisted something in Quick's stomach. She didn't want to think about what might be causing that defensiveness, but at the same time, she had to know. If this was it, if Kulika and Bartholomew were involved, then she'd rather know now so she could put to rest whatever feelings were still trying to sprout their way out of the broken mess of her heart.

She only had herself to blame. There was a very good reason that she only did flings and never relationships: all her life people had abandoned her, starting with her parents, so she'd learned to be careful with her feelings. In fact, she'd become so good at protecting them over the years that pushing people away had become more instinct than choice.

But Kulika was somehow different. Without even meaning to, Quick had started to let her in. On the night of the Casting, Quick had reminded herself of all the reasons that Kulika didn't actually want her. It made perfect sense from a practical standpoint: Kulika was a vampire, and she'd wanted Quick's blood. Now Quick knew there was a further layer of practicality: Kulika had kissed her so the bite wouldn't hurt, so she wouldn't make a fuss about it. Now that Quick had further context for how the Silver in this place worked and the twisted games they played with each other for status, it was clear that Kulika had a practical reason for turning Quick Silver, too: it would bump *her* up the hierarchy. If her recent promotion to Bartholomew's Second was any indication, that ploy had been very successful indeed.

But none of that explained why Kulika was here now,

sitting in the dirt with Quick. Could Quick really have imagined the tension between them as they sparred? Had it truly only been her who'd felt the press of their bodies together in the scrum and wished they could be closer still?

'Why are you here, Kulika?' Quick asked, a simple question to stop the rest of her thoughts from spilling out.

'I don't…' Kulika was drawing patterns in the dirt with her fingers. Evasive. 'It's complicated.'

'Then tell me something that isn't,' Quick said desperately. 'But tell me *something*. Tell me where you're from, what your favourite colour is, how old you are.'

'I've been Silver since 1721.' Kulika said the date so casually that it took Quick a while to process the fact that she'd said *seventeen* twenty-one instead of *twenty* twenty-one. It shouldn't have been a surprise, given the brief details Kulika had already let slip, but it knocked the wind right out of Quick's chest.

'1721?' she parroted back.

'Bartholomew turned me,' she said, looking down at her hands as they drew in the dirt, away towards the horizon, then back at the dirt. She never looked at Quick. 'I'm the only person he's ever turned. He cares about that.'

'So you're…' Quick scrambled for a way to phrase things delicately, while a stone settled heavily in her stomach. 'You and Bartholomew, you're a couple?'

'No,' Kulika said immediately, looking at Quick now. 'God, no. Never.'

Which stamped down the last shreds of hope that Quick had been harbouring for her and Kulika. The way Monty had talked about it before the Casting, she'd come to believe that turning someone Silver was kind of… sexy. It had certainly *felt* sexy, and Monty'd said you had to feel something for the person you turned, or vice versa, and then there'd been the kiss, so had she really been so wrong to assume that Kulika might have felt about her the way that Quick had begun to feel about Kulika?

But if there had been nothing between Kulika and the person who'd turned her Silver...

God, no.

It all made Quick feel naïve and ashamed.

'We were never involved,' Kulika added. 'I guess you could say I was Bartholomew's Second back then, too, as I am again now.'

'You support what he's doing here?' Quick asked, trying not to let the pain creep into her tone. She didn't want to believe that Kulika was on board with everything that had happened to Quick in this place, and to her and Xiaoyu in the cellar, and with everything Bartholomew was planning to do. She didn't want to believe that Kulika really was one of *them*.

'I didn't say that,' Kulika replied.

'But you're not going to stop him, either.'

'It's complicated,' Kulika said again, looking frustrated now.

'It looks pretty simple from where I'm sitting.'

'Is it?' Kulika asked, looking into Quick's eyes. 'Really? Why are you here, then, if you don't want to be part of his crew?'

'I need to find Evita.'

'I told you: I'm working on that.'

'And get Xiaoyu and the others out of here.'

'Then go open the cellar. I'll run interference while you free them,' Kulika said, with every indication that she was absolutely serious.

'But... I can't just...' Quick sat and scrambled for a moment before saying, 'I need an actual *plan* first. I signed the covenant, apparently. The others would find me and kill me before I got out of the county.'

'Right,' Kulika said. 'So maybe we're both stuck doing bad things for good reasons.'

Quick didn't know what to say to that, but apparently they were arguing now. Kulika's expression had become stern, her jaw set and her brow furrowed. She was looking up at the stars as though she bore them a grudge.

'You should get some rest,' Kulika said after a minute or so of silence. 'Refuel with blood.'

'Rest, yes. Blood, no. I'm not allowed,' Quick said. Kulika still looked bewildered, so Quick explained the points system and the board. 'I have to earn it,' Quick finished, 'and I'm failing miserably at that.'

'Then I'll get them to give you some blood.'

'Don't bother,' Quick said. 'They'll only dock me even more points that I don't have. I can manage on my own.'

'You don't have to.'

'No,' Quick said, feeling more convinced of it than ever. 'I think I do, actually. That's how things work here. But you *could* show me where the blood cellar is,' she added grudgingly. 'I can't remember the way.'

Kulika obliged, silently leading Quick through the ground floor of the block to a hidden cupboard set into the wall. No wonder she hadn't been able to find it by herself; she'd been looking in the right area, but unless you knew exactly where to look, it seemed like just an ordinary stretch of wall.

'How did you know it was there?' Quick asked Kulika.

Kulika tapped the side of her nose and said, 'Silver senses improve as you age.'

'And you're three hundred years old,' Quick remembered.

'Right.'

It was a hell of an age gap, just one of the many reasons

that pining after Kulika was a terrible idea.

'Well, thanks,' Quick said. 'I guess I'll go to bed now.' That was a lie, obviously. She fully intended to crack open the hatch the moment Kulika left so she could check Xiaoyu was all right. Then she could make some kind of a plan to come back here later when she knew she wouldn't be interrupted.

'He won't let you take them,' Kulika said quietly.

'Excuse me?'

'You might be able to break into the place and snatch some blood if you're quick, but you'll never get more than a few seconds before they realise what you're doing and stop you.'

'Why? Are you going to tell them?' Quick asked, revving up to get angry.

Kulika didn't match her energy. Instead, she said, 'No, but Bartholomew knows everything that happens on his property. He's watching me, so he'll be watching you.'

'Cameras?' Quick looked up into the corners of the corridor ceiling. She should have thought of it earlier.

But Kulika just tapped her nose again and said, 'Silver senses. They're stronger than you seem to realise.'

'Strong enough for you to know what's going on down there without opening the hatch?' Quick asked, as an idea occurred to her.

Kulika raised an eyebrow, and Quick took it as an invitation.

'I drank from Xiaoyu, and she was already weak, but they took her away before I could check she was okay, and now I'm worried I might have killed her,' Quick said, the words rushing out like water. 'Can you…? Do you think you could just…?'

'The cellar's soundproofed,' Kulika said. 'Sorry.'

'Makes sense,' Quick replied. 'I guess Bartholomew didn't want the Silver in the dorms to be disturbed by the noise.'

Kulika's expression changed, then. 'How bad was it down there?'

'Bad.'

Quick didn't want to elaborate. She didn't want to remember the zombie, and the broken bones when the new humans were chucked in, and the terror in the dark when she hadn't known what was coming down through the hatch next. Most of all, she didn't want to think about the fact that she was now part of the reason the blood cellar existed. She had to get her blood from somewhere, however rarely she was allowed it, and it was coming from down there.

'Night, then,' Quick said abruptly.

'Oh,' Kulika said, looking like she wanted to talk more, but she still said, 'Night.'

Quick smiled a tight smile and walked away down the corridor towards the stairs that led to the dorm. With every step, she felt the urge to turn back and repair things with Kulika, or just throw herself into her arms and kiss her, but all of those urges were proposed by her body and vetoed by her brain.

She needed to be on her own. She needed to think, and she couldn't do that around Kulika, surrounded by so much uncertainty and mistrust. Part of Quick wanted so much to open up to her, but the part of her that had kept her alive this long was begging her to count up the red flags and run in the opposite direction.

Belatedly, that's exactly what she did.

She couldn't trust Kulika, or anyone else in this place. The only people she could ever trust were herself and Evita. Maybe she'd revise that opinion if Kulika came up trumps and actually did find her friend, but if not, then Quick would get out of here and do it herself.

Not without Xiaoyu and the others, though.

If Bartholomew's senses were strong enough to surveil the block from the house, then that was a serious spanner in the works. But just because he had the ability to point his senses out here, that didn't mean he *would* if his attention was directed elsewhere. Which meant the only way Quick had any hope of getting into the cellar was to create the kind of distraction he wouldn't be able to ignore.

Maybe it was time to take a cue from the Silver further up the board, and start setting shit on fire.

14

AFTER SUNDAY NIGHT'S party, which continued until well after dawn on Monday, none of the higher-ranking Silver were awake to crack the whip. Most of them were lying around unconscious in the big common room, spilling through the glass doors out onto the deck by the training ground, and generally making a mess of themselves.

But not all of them were asleep when Quick ventured downstairs from the dorm, which was going to throw a spanner in her quest for fire-lighting materials.

'It's too fucking crowded in here,' Bella was complaining, kicking an unconscious Silver off the sofa by the deck so she could sit down.

When that Silver landed on the floor, he groaned and rolled over to look up at Bella. It was Brandon.

'Then find us somewhere bigger,' he shot back at her sleepily. 'You were supposed to be looking.'

'I have been. Everywhere's too small and shitty and there's not enough space to build.'

'Then look harder. Christ, Bella. Anyone would think you wanted to stay here forever.'

'Just shut up, will you?' Monty said. Quick hadn't noticed

324

him immediately, but she recognised his voice and followed it to an armchair facing the deck, where he sat rubbing at his temples. 'I'm trying to think.'

'And I'm trying to find a suitable headquarters for a hostile takeover of the whole fucking world,' said Bella. 'What makes you think your job's more important than mine?'

'The fact that it fucking is!' Monty snapped. 'You're window dressing. I'm doing the actual work. Just get the hell out of here and go find a place with a big enough pool house or whatever bullshit thing will make you happy. I'm trying to build a dynasty, here.'

'With your one little successful Silver disciple?' Bella said mockingly. 'Angelina's not much of a dynasty.'

'With Bartholomew's whole fucking army!'

'Will you both shut up?' Brandon groaned.

He wasn't the only one who was disturbed by their argument, if the moans coming from around the room were any indication.

'Some army this is,' Bella said, turning to survey the partied-out Silver who were filling the floor. In the process, she caught sight of Quick hesitating in the doorway. Her eyes narrowed. 'Oh, look,' she said to Monty. 'Here's one of your many failures now.'

Monty glanced up, saw it was Quick, and replied, 'Not exactly a failure when she got me on the top of the board, is she?'

'Because of Kulika Yadav,' Bella argued, 'not because of you.'

'I'm the one who brought her here, aren't I?'

'And dumped her just as quickly.'

'Like Enzo dumped you, you mean?' Monty said acidly.

'He didn't dump me,' Bella replied. 'He's back, isn't he?

He came back for me.'

'Sure about that, are you? Where did he sleep last night?'

Bella went still for a moment, her eyes narrowing further as she glared at Monty, then she snapped out of it abruptly, crossed the room towards Quick, grabbed her arm and said, 'Come on, Failure. We're going house-hunting.'

'She hasn't earned the points to go off-base,' Monty said.

'Well, does anyone else want to come with me?' Unsurprisingly, there were no volunteers. 'That's what I thought. Maybe this way she can actually start earning her way up the board.'

'Okay,' Monty said speculatively. 'Two-fifty for you if you find us a place. A hundred for Quick if she helps.'

'Three hundred for me,' Bella countered.

'Fine. Now get out of here.'

'Gladly,' Bella said, exiting the room backwards with a mocking bow, dragging Quick along beside her. When they were halfway down the corridor, she muttered, 'Prick.'

'Yeah, he is,' Quick agreed.

'I wasn't talking to you,' said Bella. 'Go shower and find something classy but sexy in the wardrobe. Fast. Do your hair and make up too. You can't go house-hunting for multi-million dollar properties in sweats, looking like someone pulled you out of bed through a hurricane.'

Quick did as she was told, doing her best with the tools she had to work with, which were a limited selection of clothing and a make up bag she found in the wardrobe containing products that did not suit her colouring at all. She tried, but she had to smother on the sunscreen if they were going outside to avoid going up in flames, and it didn't play well with the make up. Bella was quicker with her own transformation, shedding her slept-in party dress for a classily understated skirt and jacket combo that showed off her curves to their best advantage. When she saw Quick with her pink dress and black parasol, she sighed.

'New plan,' Bella said. 'Find a plain suit and wipe off the clown make up. You can be my chauffeur.'

Quick went back into the wardrobe, and came out again having made the required changes. The skirt suit was a little snug around the waist, and she couldn't button the jacket, but if she was staying in the car then it would do.

'Acceptable,' Bella confirmed, looking her up and down. 'You need sunglasses to hide the silver in your eyes, though,' she added, sending Quick back into the wardrobe to find a pair. When she emerged once more, Bella said, 'You drive, right?'

'Yes.'

'Automatic or stick?'

'Manual transmission,' Quick said. 'Stick, I guess.'

'That's not what I've heard,' Bella said, then she laughed like this was the funniest joke she'd ever heard.

It wound Quick up enough to make her reckless. 'Who's Enzo?' she asked.

Oh, she should not have asked that question. For a moment, Bella looked angry to the point of going feral, but she pinned her lips shut and instead gestured sharply for Quick to follow her out of the block, into the muggy morning heat, and over to the mansion.

Where they found a man standing on the porch, drinking coffee. He was freshly-showered and stylishly-dressed in chinos and an ironed shirt. Everything about him looked expensive. Even from across the lawn, Quick had a suspicion he would smell amazing.

Seeing him, Bella's entire demeanour changed. The tension went out of her shoulders, the fierce grimace disappeared from her face, and her entire body inclined towards him like a sunflower bending towards the sun.

'Enzo,' Bella called to him softly.

When he looked their way and saw Bella approaching, his eyes widened a little and he moved back from the rail, almost as if he was scared of her. That did not bode well.

'Were you waiting for me to wake up?' she cooed at him in a tone more saccharine than Quick had ever heard her use before. 'God, I was starting to think you'd abandoned me here forever. When you said you were coming back, I thought you meant in maybe a week, not in *six months*.' She laughed, a sound of pure relieved joy, but stopped abruptly when she realised that Enzo wasn't smiling back at her. 'What's happened?' she asked solicitously.

'I'm…' He looked over his shoulder into the house, then back at Bella. 'I can't talk right now.'

'Enzo.' Bella smiled at him in incomprehension. 'What do you mean, you can't talk? You haven't seen me in half a year. You could at least say hello. Can't you?'

But he was looking back over his shoulder again. 'I—'

'You came back for me, right?' Bella said, getting angry now as she strode towards the porch. 'You had to be away to finish your mission for Bartholomew, but it's over now, and you came back for *me*, because you love me. Don't you?' There were angry tears in her eyes.

Quick didn't know what to do. It felt wrong to be standing here witnessing what was clearly a lovers' tiff, but she also didn't feel like she could just go off on her own unsupervised, so instead she stood by the edge of the pool like a lemon with her parasol, looking at her feet and trying not to feel Bella's pain.

That was when Bartholomew sauntered out onto the porch, his eyes directed down at the phone in his hands as he went to join Enzo.

'My Second is on her way to Jamaica,' he said without looking up, 'searching for your boyfriend. You'd better hope she can find him, because if she doesn't then it's bad news for you.'

'Boyfriend?' Bella asked in a small voice.

'Oh.' Bartholomew finally looked up. 'I didn't realise we had company.' That was surely a lie. If his senses were as powerful as Kulika had led Quick to believe they were, he would have known they were headed this way the moment they left the block.

'Boyfriend?' Bella asked again, turning a wave of wrath on Enzo. 'You have a *boyfriend*?'

'He does,' Bartholomew said with a blithe smile. 'Bayly. How long has it been now, Enzo? About seven or eight months?'

'About that,' Enzo said quietly.

'*Bayly*?' Bella screeched.

But Bartholomew was already heading back into the house, calling Enzo along behind him like a dog. He went running, leaving Bella to gape after him.

For a few long seconds, she didn't move.

'Are you okay?' Quick said.

For a few more seconds, Bella still didn't move, then she turned sharply and strode off around the side of the house. Quick had to run to keep up. When Bella reached the driveway, she walked to the mansion's front door, slammed her way through it and into a small utility area behind it, then started rifling through a rack of car keys until she found the one she wanted. Just as Quick had managed to scramble into the room behind her, she turned and slammed her way back out again, letting the door close in Quick's face. Quick scrambled back outside again, chasing hurricane Bella.

'Fuck him,' Bella muttered as she crossed the drive. 'I've

been waiting in this shithole for six months. *Six months*. He said he loved me, you know. They always *say* they love you, but that's just because you have something they want, isn't it? And I had the keys to the lab. I thought, when I let him do this to me,' she said, gesturing at her silver-threaded eyes, 'I thought, hey, a whole lifetime together sounds fun. *Romantic*. I was a fucking fool,' she spat. 'He was fucking that grumpy old pirate the whole time.' Bella laughed then, the kind of laughter that might so easily have tipped into tears.

That was when Quick started to worry, because it was clear that none of this was directed at her. In fact, it was as though Bella had forgotten Quick was there.

Quick followed Bella to the car that matched the keys Bella had selected, an unnecessarily large SUV that was so high it would challenge the stretch fabric of Quick's skirt to get into the damn thing. Bella was headed for the driver's seat until Quick said, 'Didn't you want me to drive?'

Then Bella blinked and turned back towards Quick, looking at her as though she'd just appeared from nowhere.

'Chauffeur,' she said.

'Right,' said Quick.

'Yes,' Bella agreed, then she tossed Quick the keys and circled the car to hop into the passenger side, muttering to herself the whole way. 'Into Charleston, then, to the first realtor's office,' she said distractedly. 'I'll tell you where to turn.'

Quick hopped into the driver's sear, closing the parasol only after she was in the safety of the filter glass, then she put the car into gear and rolled it down the drive. She had a suspicion this outing was going to be more trouble than it was worth, even for a hundred points. Even for a thousand points. But she was committed now, and she didn't have much choice but to see it through.

15

WALKING AWAY FROM Quick the night before had been one of the hardest things Kulika had ever had to do. It was clear that Quick didn't trust her, and no wonder. They'd only known each other a few days, and during those few days they'd only met on a handful of occasions. On half of those occasions Kulika had ended up biting someone, and on half of *those* occasions the person she'd bitten had been Quick. Really, they weren't the kind of statistics that inspired trust.

Kulika had no such qualms about Quick. She loved her, from the top of her sunset hair to the bottom of her dirt-caked toes. Whatever happened at the mansion while she was away, whatever Quick did, *who*ever she turned out to be once Kulika had a chance to get to know her, it would make no difference. Kulika was in it for the long haul, regardless. Quick would be her person from now until the day one of them died. Either way, Kulika wouldn't survive Quick.

She was in exactly the same situation as Baron Drake now, and look where that had landed him. If she couldn't find Evita Khalyed and get Dr Ross to make this antidote, then Jack would die, so the baron would die, creating a power vacuum she was sure Bartholomew would be only too happy to fill.

Kulika meditated on that as she drove to the airport and caught her plane to Jamaica. It didn't take more than five minutes of flight time for her to realise that, even if she was Bartholomew's Second, allowing him to achieve world domination wouldn't be good for any of them. That knowledge made her a restless traveller, fidgeting in her seat all the way to Kingston. She needed to find Dr Khalyed, and she needed to find her now, but she couldn't run over water, so here she was stuck in a metal box in the sky, painfully aware that by the time she arrived Bayly would have had a least a day's head start.

Longer than that, as it turned out. The plane landed in the early afternoon, but it took Kulika until long after dark to track Bayly's scent to the right spot. She'd assumed he'd be somewhere in Port Royal, maybe even in old Port Royal itself, off the edge of the current harbour line, digging around in the remains of the sunken city. Instead, she finally ran Bayly's scent to ground in the old graveyard on the Palisadoes, a thin stretch of land that was now little more than rocky, scrubby sand to either side of the highway, a meagre bulwark between the road and the sea.

She should have come here first. She alone of all the crew suspected what Bayly had buried here in the earthquake of 1692. Or, rather, *whom*. He'd told her once, and only once, when he was sunk deep into a bottle. The mention was so brief that she hadn't been sure he meant what he was saying, or how seriously she should take him. Just six horrific little words: *Buried Digs alive with old Morgan.*

Digs, she knew, had been his lover once, the man who turned him Silver. And Morgan… Well, every pirate worth their salt knew who Henry Morgan was. But Bayly had never mentioned it again, and Kulika knew enough not to go digging up other people's buried treasure.

Evita Khalyed hadn't been Bayly's to bury in the first place, though. The Silver could technically live forever locked away like that, without light or air or blood, just withering slowly into dust and madness. But Khalyed was new, and Kulika had no idea exactly how long she'd been underground. A month? Two months? She could only hope that she wasn't too late.

Bayly was nowhere to be seen, but his scent dead-ended at the water's edge and pooled there, as though he'd lingered for some time. She found the exact spot easily enough. It had been disturbed recently and cleared of scrub, so the sand and rocks sat awkwardly amongst each other with only a few uprooted weeds for company. Kulika started digging.

She wasn't alone for long.

'Kulika,' he said, stopping in the surf.

'Bayly.'

'You worked it out, then.'

'Eventually,' she said, getting to her feet. 'I heard a couple of the kids decided to take a cruise out here and I thought to myself, *why Jamaica, of all places?*'

Bayly shrugged. 'It's a nice place.'

'It's a hot, sticky place in high summer, and they were already in a hot, sticky place with its own blood bank. No, I don't think they came here on holiday. Then I thought, I know someone who likes to spend time on this island in particular, because he's got history here, and it turns out that you went on a little holiday of your own around the same time that Brandon and Penny and "Jane" took theirs.'

'They told you about the treasure, then.'

'Neither Brandon nor Penny is very good at keeping a secret, and they're more scared of me than they are of you.'

'With good reason. They've heard enough about you.

Bartholomew tells them,' Bayly said. 'Bedtime stories for the crew. Something to give them nightmares.'

'Where's Evita?' Kulika asked.

Bayly said nothing, but he was edging slowly up the beach and around to one side as he spoke, trying to put the land at his back instead of the sea. This would end in a fight, then. It would be a fight that Bayly would lose. He'd never had the upper hand on Kulika, and she wasn't about to let him get it now. He didn't have her edge, or the anger she used to sharpen it.

'You buried her here with Digs, didn't you?' Kulika asked.

She could tell from the look on his face that she'd guessed right.

'You could have told me where she was whenever you liked,' Kulika growled. 'You knew, Bayly, all along. You knew what it meant to me, going back to that mansion. You knew that the moment I walked through that door I'd be surrendering my life, my freedom, everything I've worked so hard to build over the past hundred years, and *still* you said nothing. We were right there,' she said, pointing back towards Port Royal. 'You sat on that harbour wall with me before I'd even set foot back on the mainland. You knew full well where I was going, and why, and still you let me go. You let me go, knowing all the time that the person I was looking for was buried right here, not even two miles away from where we sat.' Kulika's fists clenched at her sides, her fingertips digging into her palms.

'You're too late, anyway,' Bayly said quietly, edging further around. 'I moved her.'

'No,' Kulika said as cold washed over her skin.

'I knew you'd work it out sooner or later. You're not stupid, but then neither am I.'

His back was almost to the highway now, and Kulika's

was almost to the sea, but she couldn't bring herself to care. It didn't matter where he manoeuvred himself. She'd fight him underwater if she had to, but one way or another she would make him pay for delivering her back into Bartholomew's hands.

She wasn't sure who moved first. Probably her, but with Silver speed and Silver reactions, there wasn't much to choose between a fraction of a second here or there. They crashed together in the centre just the same, punching and head-butting and brawling in the dirtiest of dirty fights. Kulika got her knee in Bayly's crotch, and he got his fist wrapped around her hair, and after that it was a melée of teeth and nails that ended with both of them broken and only half-healed, but Kulika on top with her fingertips digging into Bayly's throat.

'You've only got yourself to blame for this,' she said, spitting blood. 'You're the one who let him get me on a chain again.'

'I only let you fall in love, same as me,' he gasped out through gritted teeth.

'I'm *crew*!' she yelled into his reddening face. 'You were supposed to look out for me!'

'You *were* crew!' he yelled back. 'You're not anymore!'

'I *am*!' Kulika yelled one last time, then she abruptly released her grip and fell back on the rocky sand, staring at the man who had once been – and was, she realised, once more – her crewmate. 'I am, Bayly,' she said quietly. 'I'm crew. Again.'

He looked at her hopelessly, and she looked hopelessly back, one caged animal to another. At that, their fight was over, as quickly as it had begun.

'Where is she?' Kulika asked eventually, wiping the blood from her mouth.

Bayly just looked at her through helpless eyes. He wouldn't tell her.

'Will you at least tell me why?' Kulika asked.

'For Enzo,' Bayly replied.

'*For* Enzo? Does Khalyed mean something to him?'

'She means freedom,' he replied simply, but he wouldn't elaborate. He just shook his head and fell silent.

'You know you've broken the covenant,' Kulika said. 'You know Bartholomew won't let it slide.'

'Article two,' Bayly murmured.

'At least. *If any man rob another he shall have his nose and ears slit, and be put ashore where he shall be sure to encounter hardships.*'

'We're already ashore, Kulika, and I've encountered hardships enough.'

Hadn't they all?

That was when it had all started to go wrong, on the day Bartholomew had sold his ships to buy the mansion. It had put them so tantalisingly close to the sea, and yet a whole world away. None of them had wanted to settle down, but the British had been cracking down on piracy, and there was no way to be subtle about a crew as large as Bartholomew's, or to muscle their way through. Bartholomew and a few of the others might have had the strength, but the rest were only human, and turning them Silver en masse hadn't been an option. Without the formula that had just been developed by BioSilver, their odds would have been about one in a hundred for each attempt, and that was with generous estimates. Three hundred years ago, turning people Silver just hadn't been that simple.

Kulika supposed she should be grateful for Bartholomew's success with her.

'The old punishments don't hold, anyway,' Bayly said

with resignation. 'You know that. With the new Articles, it's death every time.'

'I'll still have to take you in.'

'He'll kill Enzo,' Bayly said, looking at Kulika with pleading eyes. 'I'm too old and too hardened for him to bump me off any other way. He'll kill us both.'

'And if I don't bring you in, what do you think he'll do to Quick when he finds out?'

Bayly licked his lips nervously. 'Maybe he doesn't have to find out.'

Kulika gave Bayly a dubious look, because really? He knew as well as she did that Bartholomew would *always* find out, then he'd make them all pay for it.

'No, listen,' Bayly said quickly. 'What if you gave me a week? Just… give me a few days to get my business straight. The crew can wait that long to get her back, can't they?'

'Baron Drake can't,' Kulika replied flatly. 'He needs her blood so the doctor can make his antidote, and he needs it now.'

'Blood I can do,' Bayly said excitedly, as though Kulika had already agreed. 'Look, I'll get Jane's blood and bring it to you. You can give it to your doctor. Hell, I'll even ask Enzo to lend her his lab space so she can work.'

'Bartholomew'll find out.'

'He won't,' Bayly insisted. 'How could he? Just—'

'He will find out.'

'How, unless you're going to tell him? Or are you all in on this plan of his? You back to following Captain Roberts, pretending like he gives a shit about any of us?'

Kulika nearly went back to punching him. 'Of course he doesn't give a shit!' she yelled, throwing a handful of rocks at her crewmate. 'Jesus, Bayly. You really think I'm buying it?'

'I think it looks a lot like that lately.'

Which touched a nerve with Kulika, maybe because she knew he wasn't entirely wrong. 'Well, it isn't,' she insisted. 'I know him, better than even you do. He's not doing any of this for us. He just wants to have the world fit his idea of what it should be. He sees imperfection in everything around him, and because it can't be exactly the way he wants it to be, he wants to burn it up and start again. Assuming, of course, that he'll survive the burning. The annoying thing is,' she said, tossing a stone at the road, 'he's probably right.'

'Then give me a little grace, would you?'

She shook her head. 'It's too risky.'

'Please, Kulika. I'm begging you. One day.'

'I can't just—'

'I'd do it for you if it was Quick on the line.'

Kulika shouldn't have hesitated. She should have dragged Bayly back to Bartholomew, kicking and screaming if necessary. She should have dragged Enzo out of his rooms, then threatened him until Bayly gave up Evita Khalyed's location. It's what the old pirate Kulika would have done. It's what the baron's bodyguard would have done too, just a week ago, knowing that the baron's life was on the line.

But it was Bayly, and he was in exactly the same situation with Enzo that she found herself in with Quick. She softened, and he saw it.

She *softened*.

That wasn't like her at all.

'I'll get the blood,' Bayly said quickly, already backing away to the road. 'Just meet me in Waterfront Park, down on the pier. Midday. I'll bring it to you.'

Then he was gone, disappearing in a blur of Silver speed. She could have followed, she supposed. Probably should have done, but she'd burned a lot of energy today searching for him, it had been too long since she'd last drunk any blood, and she wasn't ready to put on the speed.

She'd have to get a flight back to Charleston, and even then she'd barely make it back in time to meet Bayly the next day. Doubtless that was exactly as he'd planned it. He always had been more cunning than he looked.

Kulika sighed and pulled her phone out of her pocket. It was the middle of the night in the UK, the early hours of Tuesday morning, but he picked up on the third ring.

'Send Dr Ross,' she said without preamble.

'You've found her?'

'Not exactly,' Kulika replied, 'But I'll have her blood tomorrow.'

'Good enough,' the baron said.

Kulika hoped like hell that it would be, for all of their sakes.

16

KULIKA HADN'T INTENDED to ask Bartholomew's permission for Dr Ross to work in Enzo's lab at BioSilver. She hadn't intended to tell him anything at all, but circumstances conspired against her.

Dr Ross arrived earlier than expected the next morning, while Kulika was still making her way back to the mansion, somehow managing to fly across the Atlantic in less than the time it had taken Kulika to hop back to Charleston from Jamaica. If Kulika'd had her way, Dr Ross would never have set foot on Bartholomew's property, but clearly Baron Drake hadn't briefed the doctor about how dangerous his rival could be – or at least, not sufficiently – because she was sitting in the library drinking tea with the man himself when Kulika returned.

'Ah,' Bartholomew said as Kulika rushed into the library, anxiously following Dr Ross's scent to the very heart of the mansion. 'You know my Second, I think?' he said to the doctor.

'Your Sec— Kulika?' Dr Ross said, looking between the two of them, bewildered.

She hadn't known, of course. Kulika hadn't told the baron

341

about her recent promotion when she'd spoken to him on the phone, for obvious reasons. If she was supposed to be anyone's Second, it was his, not Bartholomew's. There'd be no stopping that particular piece of treachery from spreading now. When Tabitha Ross went back to the UK – *if* Bartholomew let her go back to the UK – she'd take with her the news that Kulika had defected. It had been inevitable that Baron Drake would find out sooner or later. If Kulika was lucky, maybe she could persuade Dr Ross to give her time to call him so she could break the news to him herself. She owed him that, at least.

'I wasn't expecting you so soon, Dr Ross,' Kulika said, lingering in the doorway. 'I would have met you at the airport if I'd known when your plane was getting in.'

'Oh well,' the doctor said, forcing a smile. 'No harm done. I'm here now.'

The doctor was a small, round woman dressed in a colourful skirt and T-shirt. She had a mess of long brown curls that she kept pinned up in a bun using whatever utensils came to hand – today it was a coffee stirrer and a disposable toothbrush that she'd probably got on the plane. Her face was round and expressive, which made it difficult for her to hide her discomfort. Dr Ross clearly didn't want to be in this room any more than Kulika wanted her here.

'Did you find Bayly and the girl?' Bartholomew asked Kulika.

'Not yet,' she said. 'But I know where he'll be at midday.'

'Then go and bring him in. I can look after the doctor.'

'Actually, sir…' Kulika was trying to be deferential, to get on Bartholomew's good side for the favour she was about to ask, but she could see from the look on his face that she'd already made a serious misstep. 'Primus,' she corrected herself, then she watched as Dr Ross attempted to control her shock. 'I thought perhaps Enzo could allow Dr Ross some lab space at BioSilver. Just for a day or so, for her work.'

'And what work is that, precisely?' Bartholomew asked.

Shit.

It had been arrogant of Kulika to think that she could play both sides and get away clean. Bartholomew was *always* watching.

'You told me I could complete my mission for Baron Drake.'

'But I didn't tell you that you could compromise Enzo's cover at BioSilver in the process. What exactly do you expect me to say to Solomon if he discovers that Dr Ross is working at his facility, in my territory, in the office of a man he believed to be a human research student?'

'That you know nothing,' Kulika suggested. 'Besides, Enzo already has everything you need from BioSilver. Doesn't he? Does it really matter if we burn him? It's just for a day or two.'

Bartholomew thought on this a while, then said, 'Fine. I'll let Enzo take Dr Ross to the lab, but you bring him and Bayly back here before the end of the day.'

'Yes, Primus. Thank you, Primus. If you're ready, doctor?'

Kulika ushered the doctor out of the library and through the mansion as quickly as she could.

Dr Ross started talking before they'd even reached the door, saying, 'What was that all—'

'Shh,' Kulika interrupted her quietly. 'Not here.'

Enzo was waiting on the porch, just where Kulika had expected to find him, wearing a linen suit and lounging like a catalogue model with a tiny espresso cup in his hand. Kulika had no idea where he'd got it from; the house didn't have a machine.

'Enzo!' she yelled at him. She'd hoped to startle him

enough to stain that fancy suit of his with coffee, but all she managed to do was burn his fingers. It was something, though.

'Kulika,' he said quickly. 'I didn't know what Bayly was doing. I promise, I didn't—'

'You can shut up right now,' she said. 'Get the keys to the truck and meet us out front.'

Enzo scuttled off through the house, leaving Kulika and Dr Ross alone on the deck. Dr Ross was carrying an old-fashioned doctor's bag, but nothing else. No suitcase, no other hand luggage. She obviously wasn't expecting to stay long.

'You've got the formula in there?' Kulika asked, nodding at the bag.

'In a little cooler, yes. I had a devil of a time getting it through customs, I can tell you. Baron Drake had to put in a call.'

There was an awkward silence, which Kulika broke by saying, 'I'm sorry I wasn't there to meet you.'

'It's okay,' Dr Ross said sadly, looking down at her patent plum flats.

'I would have been there if I could, but—'

'It's okay,' she said again. 'You've got a lot going on here, I can see.' The words sounded sympathetic, but her tone was snippy and judgemental.

'I have,' Kulika said. 'But it's not what you think.'

'I think Jack's going to die without this antidote, and you've chosen to spend your time manoeuvring yourself into a better position instead of trying to save her life.'

'It's not what you think,' Kulika said again.

The doctor ignored her, her expression set somewhere between sadness and extreme ire, so Kulika grabbed her by the hand and started leading her down the porch steps.

'I don't——'

'Just come with me,' Kulika insisted, so the doctor let herself be led past the pool, across the lawn, through the trees to the cleared space where the block stood. Kulika had picked up a variegated scent on the breeze, and she knew what they'd find when they circled the block to the training ground enclosed behind it.

Quick.

She was kneeling at the edge of the building inside the shaded curve of its wings. Every so often she plunged a sponge into a bucket of soapy water, then used it to scrub the breeze blocks clean, muttering to herself irritably the whole time.

Kulika pulled the doctor to a stop at the corner of the building, where they could peek around into the courtyard without being seen themselves.

'Why are you——'

Kulika interrupted Dr Ross by revealing her silver, letting the doctor see how the silver in the whites of her eyes had extended into her irises: the physical mark of her feelings for Quick.

'Oh,' Dr Ross said. Then she nodded towards Quick and said, 'Her?'

'Her,' Kulika confirmed. 'I wouldn't still be in this place if she could be anywhere else.'

'*Oh,*' Dr Ross said again, her expression pained now. 'The baron mentioned something about a covenant?'

'She signed it,' Kulika confirmed. 'Under duress.'

Dr Ross was a clever woman. She understood the rest without Kulika having to spell it out.

Standing across the training ground from Quick without being able to approach her was an exquisite kind of torture. Kulika could smell the scent of lush blackberries, sharp spring daffodils and frost-rimed rose-hips rolling across the space towards her, making her wish for nothing more than to carry Quick back across the Atlantic with her and undress her underneath the first convenient hedgerow. She'd settle for undressing her under the Spanish moss hanging from the mansion's oak trees if that option was available to her, but the doctor was standing right beside her, and besides, she didn't have permission from Bartholomew to be here right now. If he found Kulika with Quick then she was certain he'd make her pay for that liberty, in blood or in shame.

'Come on,' Kulika said quietly to the doctor. 'I'll walk you to the truck.'

In that moment, Quick's head snapped up and froze in place, like she'd just heard something. She couldn't have heard Kulika speaking, though. She'd pitched her voice so that it would only carry to Dr Ross, and anyway Quick was so new that her hearing wouldn't be that sensitive yet. Would it?

Then Quick turned her head a little to the side and sniffed the air. God, could she *smell* Kulika? Even from across the training ground, with the breeze moving away from her?

Quick turned a little further around and locked eyes with Kulika, before shifting her gaze to the doctor, then back to Kulika.

'Kulika,' Quick said. There was something bleak in her eyes, but Kulika couldn't afford to hang around and find out what it was. She'd already lingered here too long.

'Quick,' Kulika murmured, then she nudged the doctor back towards the drive, where Enzo would be waiting with the truck.

She should never have come out here in the first place. Bartholomew would know, as he always knew, and would always know.

Perhaps it was time Kulika did something about that.

17

QUICK'S EXCURSION WITH Bella the previous day should have been more exciting than it had proved to be. Mansion-hunting around South Carolina was certainly better than scrubbing the toilets in the block, but Bella hadn't been kidding when she'd said that Quick would be her chauffeur. Quick had driven up to the grand gateways of any number of gorgeous houses, but she'd been ordered to stay in the car every time. Given her sun allergy, perhaps that had been a blessing in disguise.

Bella had thrown her sunglasses onto the console angrily the moment she'd sashayed her way back into the SUV after the third viewing, and said, 'You know they all do this, right?'

Quick'd had no idea what she was talking about.

'Everyone back at the house who's ever turned someone Silver has done it by pretending to be someone they're not,' Bella had continued. As she'd spoken, she'd twisted the silver locket she'd been wearing, tightening its fine chain around her own throat. 'Enzo, Monty, Kulika, all of them. And because they all do it, they pretend like that makes it okay. Maybe it *does*. Maybe the only way to deal with that is by following their example.'

Bella's anger had mellowed as she'd talked her way through this, apparently not requiring any input from Quick, who might as well have been invisible.

Quick should have worried more about that at the time, but instead her mind had got stuck on the first bit of what Bella had said: *Everyone back at the house who's ever turned someone Silver has done it by pretending to be someone they're not.*

Driving back from Charleston on her own that evening, Quick had been sorely tempted to barrel straight past the mansion and never turn back. It had been a fleeting thought, the spontaneous impulse of a second, and she hadn't needed more than a couple of breaths to banish it.

They would find her. They would drag her back here. They would kill her, leaving Evita and Xiaoyu with no one fighting their corner at all.

So she'd discarded the idea almost as soon as it had occurred, turned sedately onto the long driveway and parked the SUV neatly in the line of vehicles that was arrayed in front of the house. Then she'd returned obediently to the block, where a long list of chores had already been awaiting her attention. She hadn't given another thought to Bella and the greasy realtor whose house she'd left her at. They'd had a tedious day driving from one tacky mansion to another, with one tedious realtor after another. Why Bella had decided to take that last one to a bar, of all the sleazy bastards they'd met that day, Quick had no idea.

But Bella had insisted she'd be fine, and Quick knew she was more than capable of looking after herself with a single middle-aged human, so she'd driven away and left Bella to her revenge sex, assuming she'd make her own way back to the mansion when she'd got it out of her system. Nothing to worry about.

Until now, that was.

'You're *sure* she hasn't been back today?' Quick asked Monty, who was glaring at her like she'd just lost a beloved pet.

'You think I don't know where my own people are?'

'I think Bella doesn't think she's one of *your* people,' Quick argued. 'I think she probably wanted to feel like her own person for a while. I'm sure she'll be back soon. She just needed some time on her own.'

'Because of Enzo,' Monty said.

'Right.'

'But otherwise she seemed perfectly fine to you yesterday?'

'Well, she wasn't *happy*,' Quick admitted.

Monty gave her a frank look. 'Bartholomew was there. From what he told me, she was more than *not happy*.'

'Okay, she was fucking livid,' Quick snapped. 'What do you expect me to say?'

'Enzo says she's crazy.'

Quick laughed. 'Right. You know what they say about men who tell you their exes are crazy?'

'What?'

'You should ask what the guy did to *drive* them crazy. He told her he loved her, then turned her Silver, dumped her and went off with his boyfriend without telling her. So is she crazy, or is she justifiably pissed off and paranoid? She wanted to blow off a little steam. I didn't see any harm in that, plus she outranks me, so what did you expect me to do?'

'Drop fifty points and go scrub the training ground walls,' Monty replied without missing a beat. '*That's* what I expect you to do.'

'But I haven't done anything wrong!' Quick protested.

Monty disagreed.

It wasn't like Quick had a right of appeal in this place, so she trudged off to the cleaning cupboard and dragged out all the supplies she'd need. While she was at it, she searched the cupboard for matches and solvents and firelighters. After checking every precariously-packed nook, she gained a Bic lighter and a nearly-empty can of lighter fluid from a box of barbecue equipment on the top shelf. It wasn't much, but it would do.

The weight of the fuel was heavy in Quick's pocket as she scrubbed away the blood that had congealed on the breeze blocks outside. They'd be able to smell the solvent on her, probably. If she wanted to use the stuff, she'd either have to stash it somewhere safe until she was ready to start the fire, or she'd have to do it immediately. The problem was, to create the distraction that would divert Bartholomew's attention away from the block long enough to get Quick into the basement, she'd have to create *another* distraction that would divert Monty and the others long enough to get Quick up to the house to start the fire in the first place.

And it would have to be up at the house, she'd decided. It was old, there was a lot of wood and polish inside, and Quick was pretty sure it would go up like kindling. It was also Bartholomew's home, so the stakes would be high enough to get everyone involved and away from the block, so she could do her thing. But with higher stakes came higher punishment, so she'd also have to make it look like an accident.

It had to be tonight, then. There'd doubtless be another pool party, and if Quick could wangle an invitation then maybe she could accidentally arrange for a cigarette to get knocked under the porch and onto an area that had somehow become soaked in lighter fluid. With any luck, the porch would hide the first flames from sight, and the party would keep anyone from noticing that anything was wrong until the fire had already properly caught hold.

Was it a great plan? Probably not. Was it the only one Quick had? Absolutely, so she was going to go with it and hope like hell it didn't blow up in her face.

Kulika.

For a moment, Quick didn't understand why the echo had suddenly popped into her mind. She'd been obsessing over the woman since… Well, since Quick had first seen her last week, if she was being honest, but usually the little pangs of want that struck her from time to time came on the heels of a thought about Kulika. They didn't just appear out of nowhere when she was in the middle of planning an arson attack.

But there it was again, that little pull, like sunshine on seawater.

Then Quick realised it was a scent that was calling her. She put down her sponge and sniffed the air, trying to work out whether the scent was real or imaginary.

Oh, it was definitely real, and it was stronger now, licking up Quick's nostrils and down her throat, making her shudder in ways she'd rather not admit, even to herself. She turned from her work, trying to track the scent.

'Kulika,' Quick said.

She was standing at the far corner of the training ground next to a short woman Quick didn't recognise, but they didn't stay. The moment Kulika locked eyes with Quick, she turned and escorted the other woman away, leaving Quick bewildered and a little hurt.

It was a nothing encounter.

Was she being surveilled? Was Kulika keeping an eye on

her?

There was no way to know.

Quick wanted to wallow in the uncertainty of it. She wanted to dissect every interaction she'd ever had with Kulika and pin down her reactions, in a vain attempt to work out where she stood. Instead, she forced her mind back to the wall, to the blood, and to the lighter fuel in her pocket. These things were tangible and real, and one of them would get Xiaoyu out of the cellar, even if Kulika Yadav would not.

18

IT HAD BEEN a mistake for Kulika to see Quick. Bartholomew gave Kulika a stern look when she returned to the house after leaving Dr Ross in Enzo's hopefully-safe hands, then he grilled her on the baron's plans and what she'd found in Jamaica. Kulika obfuscated on both, with limited success.

No, she didn't know exactly what Dr Ross was doing in the lab or why. No, she hadn't brought Bayly in, but someone had told her where he'd be at midday. Those statements weren't technically lies, but they weren't the whole truth either, and Bartholomew could tell. He let her leave for the meet with Bayly, though not without reminding her that he held Quick's life in his hands.

'You're lucky that I'm preoccupied with arrangements for phase two today,' he told her. 'I'm choosing to trust you, as my Second, to deal with these matters appropriately. Don't betray that trust, Kulika. You know what the consequences might be.'

Under the circumstances, that was more than she'd hoped for, but it meant the deal Bayly had offered her was off the table. Evita's blood wasn't enough. She needed to bring him and Evita in, and she needed to do it today.

There was still an hour before midday, so she headed to BioSilver to make sure Dr Ross had everything prepared for when Kulika returned with the blood. Kulika had been here a couple of times before, on business for the baron, which gave her the credentials to get inside. It was where the man Kulika couldn't stop thinking of as *the* Primus – Solomon – conducted the kind of research he'd rather not allow in his own territory: bioweapons, Silver poisons, and more idiosyncratic formulae like the one Enzo had stolen. The lab's distance from London gave Solomon plausible deniability, and a twelve-hour buffer in case something dangerous got loose. It was attached to one of the local universities, masquerading as a science block on a campus that didn't offer undergraduate science courses. That was an oddity, but there were enough postgraduate students that the facility passed under the radar. Solomon was good at keeping it that way.

Enzo's own lab was enormous. No wonder he didn't mind sharing with Dr Ross; there was enough white space filled with enough strange machinery to keep a whole team of biochemists busy. The door had a little plaque on it that said *Dr Enzo Cappelli*, so he'd clearly got his feet properly under the table at BioSilver. That was incredible when you thought about it, because surely a lab run by the Silver would have protocols in place to make sure they knew who they were hiring, or at the very least whether they were human or not. Somehow, Enzo had slithered his way through the net.

Kulika suspected he had form for that.

'Hi, Dr Ross,' Kulika said as she pushed through the doors to the lab. 'Are you settling in all right?'

'Oh, yes,' the doctor said. She was sitting at a work bench, looking through what Kulika assumed was a microscope at what she assumed was the formula Dr Ross had brought with her. There was an open vial on the bench next to her, in a rack holding four other identical vials. 'The lab is remarkably well equipped,' the doctor added, then she rattled off the names of a few machines that she hadn't expected the lab to have, but it was like a foreign language to Kulika. She couldn't make head nor tail of it, but then she'd never had the patience for that kind of work.

'Okay, well,' Kulika said, 'I'm going to collect the blood sample and bring it right back here. Do you have everything you need to start making the antidote?'

'I should do,' Dr Ross said, shifting a few things around on her work surface, as though she were counting things off in her head. 'Yes. I think we're ready. Has the sample been refrigerated?'

'I don't know,' said Kulika. 'Does it matter?'

'Maybe, maybe not. Hard to say without knowing how long ago the sample was drawn, or how Dr Evita Khalyed's particular pathology works, and that's if she even carries the same traits as Dr *Jahan* Khalyed did. It's a bit of a gamble. Here,' Dr Ross pulled a small cooler out from under the bench. 'Put it in this as soon as you have it. I don't suppose...' The doctor hesitated.

'Suppose what?'

'Is she okay?' Dr Ross said, looking up at Kulika with big eyes. 'Evita, I mean? I knew her grandfather, and... Well, this situation where you're bringing me a blood sample instead of the woman herself. It doesn't fill me with confidence.'

'I know. I'm trying my best here. I've got a lot of reasons to find her and see her safe, believe me.'

'Okay,' Dr Ross said after a moment.

'I'll get going, then.' Kulika held up the cooler in farewell, and made for the door.

'Oh,' Dr Ross said, 'by the way, your friend came by.'

'You mean Enzo?' Kulika asked. 'I hate to break it to you, Dr Ross, but he's not my friend. In fact, I'm pretty sure that Enzo's only real friend is Enzo.'

'No, not Enzo. The woman. The one with the generous… um, assets.' At first, Kulika thought maybe the doctor was talking about Quick, but then she added, 'The blonde one,' and Kulika started paying attention.

'What blonde one?' she asked.

'The lab assistant. Emma?' Dr Ross said vaguely, her attention half on her computer screen. 'No, Bella. That was it.'

'Bella is not my friend,' Kulika said, remembering the woman who had read the charges at Alex's execution.

The doctor looked up from her work then.

'She isn't?' Dr Ross asked.

'No. In fact, I've never even spoken to her. Are you *sure* it was Bella?'

'Long blonde hair, curvy, well-endowed, you know. Conventionally attractive, if you like that sort of thing,' Dr Ross added, in a tone that suggested she didn't, though her pink cheeks told a different story.

Oh, god.

Kulika could see how it would have been. Bella used to work at BioSilver, didn't she? That was where Enzo had met her, if Kulika remembered right. She'd been his key into the place, and now she'd waltzed back in here, charmed the eminently charmable Dr Ross, and used that access to… what?

'Are you missing anything?' Kulika asked, looking around to see if anything was out of place. 'Did she take something from the lab?'

'No, of course not,' the doctor replied, affronted. 'She was barely in here five minutes. We just had a little chat and then — Oh.' Her gaze had landed on the vials at her elbow. 'Um.'

'Um?' Kulika said sharply.

'Well, um. There were six of those, and now… But surely not. I must have knocked one out of the holder, or left one in the cool box when I lifted them out. Check the— Check the cool box.' Dr Ross was getting jittery now, her hand shaking a little as she pointed at the cooler Kulika was holding.

Kulika opened it, emptied it out, turned it upside down. 'Nothing,' she said.

'Oh, dear,' Dr Ross said, taking off her glasses and chewing at one of the arms. Then she popped beneath the work bench, searching the floor, and popped up again with her hair half undone and anxiety written all over her face. 'Oh, dear,' she said again.

'Remind me what that formula does?' Kulika asked, as calmly as she could.

'It, um.' The doctor licked her lips. 'If injected into Dr Evita Khalyed, it would probably turn her into the same kind of monster that Jahan became. He, um, whenever he bit one of the Silver – which the formula seemed to *make* him do – the people he bit went up in smoke, burning up instantly from the inside out.'

'And if anyone else took it?'

'Someone human? I don't know. We haven't done the tests. But someone Silver? They'd probably…' The doctor pushed the hair out of her eyes and put her glasses back on. 'They'd just die, I think. The same way as when Jahan bit people. Burned up.'

Kulika took a deep breath and let it out again slowly.

'So what you're telling me,' she said, 'is that Bella has her hands on a vial of poison that will kill any Silver she chooses to give it to.'

'Yes,' the doctor said in a small voice.

'How long ago did she leave?' Kulika asked, already packing the cooler up again and heading for the door.

'About half an hour, I suppose?'

'I have to go and get the bloody blood sample. You keep looking for the vial, just in case. I'll call Bartholomew.'

Dr Ross paled. 'Do you have to—'

'There's a rogue Silver out there with a Silver-killing weapon. She's a member of his crew. She's signed his covenant. Yes, I have to call Bartholomew.'

The doctor nodded hopelessly.

'I'll be back with the blood sample,' Kulika promised, 'then we'll sort this out. Sit tight.'

Bloody newbies.

Kulika had told Bartholomew that it was a bad idea to have all these new, untested Silver running around barely supervised. It wasn't just the physical changes either, it was the mental ones. Turning into what they were could change your whole perception of the world and your place in it, and the way Bartholomew was gathering them all together into this cult of his was enough to fuck anyone up. It certainly seemed to have fucked Bella up, good and proper, but saying *I told you so* wasn't going to get Kulika very far right now, particularly when she'd been the one who'd brought Dr Ross here with the killer formula in the first place.

When she called Bartholomew, she stuck to the facts, and they were bad enough. He didn't yell. Kulika would have felt better if he'd yelled.

Christ.

If it wasn't one disaster, it was another.

And then, inevitably, another.

Bayly wasn't waiting for Kulika on the pier at midday.

Instead, she found Enzo there, sitting on one of the wide wooden benches and looking across the harbour to Fort Sumter.

'He's not coming,' Kulika said.

'No,' Enzo agreed. 'He gave me the blood, though. Here.'

Enzo passed over a large, conspicuously un-refrigerated vial. Kulika sighed and stowed it away in the cooler.

'Where is he, Enzo?'

'I don't know,' he replied, his eyes fixed on the dolphins cruising through the harbour.

'I don't believe you. You know I have to take you both back to the mansion. I have to bring Evita too, sooner or later, but if I show up with you on your own then Bartholomew's just going to kill you to wipe out Bayly. He's ruthless like that, and he doesn't like being messed around. I don't either, especially by people who are supposed to be my friends.'

'We're not friends,' Enzo said, in a horrified tone that Kulika might have found it offensive if she wasn't so angry.

'I wasn't talking about you, you pillock. I was talking about Bayly. Now where is he, and what's he done with Evita Khalyed?'

Enzo still said nothing.

'I don't know what he sees in you,' Kulika said. She turned to face Enzo, then rested one foot on the bench where he was sitting, so she loomed over him. 'I can understand what you would see in him, if you actually gave a shit about him at all, which I think is unlikely. I think you're a slimy little opportunist, Enzo. I think you're under the impression that you're going to walk away from this, but let me set you straight on that.'

Kulika moved her foot quickly, landing it squarely in Enzo's crotch and pinning him to the bench with the heel of her boot. The noise he made was satisfyingly high-pitched. He wriggled and squirmed and tried to break free, but Kulika knew her craft and she was significantly stronger than him.

'If you don't tell me where Bayly is right now, I'm going to drag you back to the mansion and hand you over to Bartholomew. He will not be kind. I might not be either,' she said, grinding her heel a little to reinforce her message.

'He bought a boat,' Enzo squeaked.

'Where?'

'The marina by the aquarium.'

'Name?'

'*Buried Treasure.*'

'Of course it is. Christ, Enzo,' Kulika said, finally removing her foot, 'you could have told me this yesterday. You knew I was going to Jamaica looking for Evita.'

Enzo hunched over and moaned for a moment before replying. 'I do have some loyalty, you know.'

Kulika scoffed. 'You could've fooled me.'

'Yeah, well, I was dealing with problems of my own yesterday. Bella got all emotional on me. Apparently she thought me turning her meant more than it did. She got upset. You know.'

Kulika's temper flared.

'You know she's stolen a vial of formula from the lab now?' she said.

'What?' Enzo asked. 'Why?'

'Not the formula that makes turning Silver easier – you already stole that out from under BioSilver's nose. I'm talking about the formula Dr Ross brought with her from the UK.'

Enzo blanched.

'I guess you know what it does, then?'

'Look,' he said evasively, 'how could I have known she'd

react like that? I didn't expect her to go all cuckoo on me. I needed her to trust me so I could get into BioSilver, so I needed to turn her Silver, which meant, you know…'

'You led her on.'

'Barely,' Enzo insisted. 'I'm gay.'

'Did you tell her that?'

'Of course not.'

'Then what does it have to do with anything?'

'Why are you looking at me like this is my fault? Maybe I gave her a slightly false impression so I could get into BioSilver like Bartholomew wanted, but none of this is on me. How was I supposed to know she was a fucking maniac?'

Kulika couldn't believe what she was hearing, but she knew from her long experience dealing with killer Silver – mostly men, mostly narcissistic, never willing to admit their mistakes – that a man with so little conscience couldn't be made to see the error of his ways. Her time and irritation would be better spent focusing on the immediate problem: Bayly.

Bartholomew had assured her he'd deal with Bella – possibly the worst call Kulika had ever had to make – but he'd also assured her that there'd be trouble if she wasn't back that afternoon with Enzo and Bayly in tow.

'Come on,' she said, dragging Enzo to his feet. 'We're going for an afternoon out at the aquarium.'

19

SOMEONE WAS BANGING pans together inside the block. At first, Quick thought it was just bad cookery, but it soon became clear that the noise was meant to be an alarm call of some kind. She could hear people filtering through the corridors, so she abandoned her sponge and bucket and followed them to the big common room to find out what was going on.

Brandon was standing on a chair by the board.

'We need volunteers!' he yelled as everyone crowded into the room. 'Two hundred points up for grabs!'

'For what?' someone shouted.

'We got a rogue,' Brandon replied. 'One of the crew's gone missing.'

Quick's stomach sank. She was pretty sure she knew who he was talking about.

'Who?' someone else yelled.

'Bella,' said Monty. He was standing beside Brandon's chair, and he was looking directly at Quick.

Shit.

'Fuck, no,' someone said, turning and leaving the room. He wasn't the only one, either. As soon as the crowd heard that it was Bella who was missing, half of them made a swift exit.

'She's crazy,' one of the remaining Silver said. 'Where's the danger money?'

'Four hundred, then,' Brandon said.

The guy who'd spoken considered this for a moment, then said, 'Nah. The others are right. It's not worth it,' and walked away.

Quick made to follow him and the others out of the room when Monty caught her wrist and dragged her back.

'Not so quick there, Quick,' he said, with little humour. 'Something tells me this is the perfect job for you. After all, you're the one who lost her.'

'I didn't lose her,' Quick replied, trying and failing to snatch her hand back. 'I told you: she's just blowing off steam. Where's the harm?'

'Where's the *harm*?' Monty said patronisingly. 'The harm is that this morning, Bella walked back into the BioSilver labs using her old security pass, and into the office where Enzo works.'

'Oh no,' said Quick, getting a bad feeling in the pit of her stomach.

'Where Bella found a visiting doctor using Enzo's equipment,' Monty continued as if she hadn't spoken, 'and pretended she was his lab assistant to get into the lab and lay her hands on, well, whatever she could find.'

'Oh no,' Quick said again.

'Which happened to be a formula that the visiting doctor had brought with her to develop an antidote for a dangerous and contagious Silver virus. Or poison. Or whatever. I don't exactly know, but the point is that Bella's now out there, running around pissed at Enzo and Bartholomew and probably the rest of us too, and she's got her hands on a vial of stuff that could actually kill us. So yeah. *Oh no.*'

'And you're trying to blame this on me?' Quick said incredulously. 'I'm three days old, remember? And bottom of the board.'

'You could go lower,' Monty said threateningly. 'So where is she?'

'How the hell am I supposed to know?' Quick said irritably. 'She had me drive her from one realtor's office to another, and we looked at some properties, but apparently none of them were right. Then she asked me to drive her and this one realtor to a bar, which I did, and then I dropped them back at his place in North Charleston. She said she was going to get a lift home.'

'Where's the house?'

Which was a reasonable question, to which Quick had no answer. She'd used the satnav, and she didn't know that area well. She couldn't remember exactly where they'd been.

'Can you check the trip history on the SUV's computer?' she suggested.

'No, but I'll tell you what: *you* can.'

For a moment, Quick didn't understand what he was suggesting.

'You want me to go after her?' she asked. '*Me?*'

'Well, you can use Silver speed now, and if what I saw the other night is anything to go by, you're pretty good with your hands, too.' He smirked.

Quick seethed. 'You were *watching* us?'

It wasn't as though she and Kulika had done anything out on the training ground except fight and talk, but the idea that Monty had been spying on them was unsettling and intrusive. It had Quick running through her memory of the night in her head, trying to find anything he might have misconstrued, and she hated that. It had been *her* night with

Kulika, maybe the last one she'd get. However badly it had ended, there'd been parts of it that she'd cherish for as long as she lived. It didn't belong to Monty. She didn't want his grubby little fingerprints on any of it.

'*Everyone* was watching,' Monty said. 'How do you think you got bumped up the board ten places?'

'I didn't know.' Quick hadn't looked at the board since she'd first found out about it. 'I didn't think I'd earned any points.'

'Well, here's your chance to earn some more,' Monty said.

'Come on, Monty,' said Brandon, hopping down from the chair. 'It's not like the newbie's going to be able to overpower Bella.'

'And then you're wasting our only lead,' Penny chimed in, the only other Silver who'd hung around. 'She'll tip Bella off, then it'll be that much harder for us to find her later.'

'Four hundred, if you bring her in,' Monty said to Quick, ignoring the others. 'Another two hundred if you bring back the vial, unopened.'

'The vial that'll kill me?' Quick asked. 'No way.' Then she thought for a moment and said, 'Not on my own.'

Which was how she, Brandon and Penny ended up on a road trip to North Charleston. Quick was playing chauffeur again while Brandon lounged in the passenger seat and Penny sprawled in the back.

There was a buzz, and Brandon pulled his phone out of his pocket.

'Message from Monty,' he explained. 'He's spoken to Bella on the phone.'

'Did he find out where she is?' Penny asked.

'No, but he warned her about the vial thing being a poison. Apparently she thinks it's some kind of cure. That's what the doctor told her.'

'A cure for what?' Penny asked.

'Not sure. Monty says she hung up on him, and now her phone's off.'

'So the plan stays the same?'

'I guess.'

The plan, such as it was, was to use the satnav to return to the last place Quick had seen Bella, then have a poke about. It shouldn't have worked. It had been nearly twenty-four hours ago that Quick had left Bella here, and she could have gone anywhere with that long a head start, but when Quick parked up in front of the realtor's quaint little house and they all spilled out of the SUV, the first thing Brandon said was, 'Her scent's here.'

'How recent?' Penny asked.

'Recent. Like, maybe she's still here. Let's send the newbie to knock on the door and see.'

Quick didn't like being called *the newbie*, but she disliked the vibes surrounding the house even more. She really, *really* didn't want to knock on the door, but they were going to have to do it sooner or later. Pulling the band-aid off as fast as possible had always been Quick's preferred approach, so she opened her parasol before she could talk herself out of it and went to knock on the pretty stained-glass-windowed door.

Part of her had been expecting it to swing open, but that didn't happen. She tried the handle.

'Locked,' she called back at Brandon and Penny, but they'd already moved to the side door next to the garage.

'This one isn't,' Penny called back.

When Quick joined them, she saw that not only was the door not locked, but the lock had been pushed clean through the doorframe.

'Well, that's not good,' said Brandon, hanging back to

examine the door while Penny went into the garage. The space was L-shaped, with enough room for a car up front, and a work bench along the back wall. The section that continued off to one side to join the main house looked like a utility space, but because of the shape of the room, Quick couldn't see much except the edge of a chest freezer from where she was standing with Brandon. Penny had walked all the way to the back wall though, so she could see plenty.

She screeched and jumped back.

'What?' Brandon asked, but Penny didn't pay him any attention. Instead, she was backing slowly away from the utility area, her eyes wide and fixed on the hidden area in front of her.

'Penny!' Brandon yelled sharply, to get her attention. 'What gives?'

Finally, she looked at Brandon with haunted eyes, pointed into the utility space and said, 'What the hell are *they*?'

20

THE *BURIED TREASURE* was an unassuming little motorboat with a single small cabin. Kulika had imagined that, after all his centuries, Bayly might have been able to afford a yacht, or even a super-yacht, but then he'd always refused to invest in property because he didn't want to be tied to dry land. If all you did was buy boat after boat, assets which depreciated over time, then your bank balance sank along with them. It was clearly a lesson Bayly had resolutely failed to learn.

It made Kulika's job easier though, as did the fact that the marina was deserted.

'Bayly!' she yelled, dragging Enzo out of the backseat of the car where he'd sat obediently the whole way from Waterfront Park. Now that she'd shown him what she could do, he wasn't even trying to challenge her physically. It was clear that Enzo's arsenal – such as it was – was entirely emotional: he was a lover, not a fighter.

'If you want to live,' Kulika yelled, 'you'll step out of the boat and into the car without a fight.'

'You wouldn't kill me, Kulika,' came a voice from inside the cabin. 'I'm crew.'

'And Bartholomew has Quick,' Kulika reminded him. 'I think what I'd do for her might surprise us both. Do you want to test me and see, or do you want to come with me voluntarily and have at least some chance of surviving this?'

Bayly laughed as he finally emerged from the cabin. 'What Bartholomew will do to me if I go back to the mansion will surprise neither of us. I'm dead either way.'

'I'm his Second now,' Kulika argued. 'I can put in a good word.'

Bayly just shook his head. 'Face it, Kulika. I gambled it all to get me and Enzo out of here, and I lost.' Then his gaze shifted sideways to land on his boyfriend, frozen in Kulika's grip. 'He still didn't want to leave.'

Kulika looked between the two men, confused until Bayly explained further.

'We were supposed to trade the girl for Enzo's freedom from the covenant, but then you came along and spoiled that. Then we were supposed sail off into the sunset together and leave the girl behind on the pier for you to find this afternoon, hoping that Bartholomew would be too distracted with his plans to come after us, but Enzo still didn't want to go. Now we're both going to die because he can't stop dreaming of Bartholomew's glorious Silver future.'

'It's not a dream, Bayly,' Enzo said plaintively. 'It's *reality* and it's coming. Just a few more days, and you'll see.'

Bayly had the long-suffering expression of someone who'd been through this argument a hundred time before.

'We won't see,' he said, 'because we'll be dead.'

'Then go!' Enzo yelled. 'But I'm a part of it, and I'm staying.'

'And if I leave without you then he'll kill you just to take me off the board.'

'No, he won't,' Enzo insisted.

'Actually,' Kulika said, 'I think he probably will.'

'See?' Bayly said, but Enzo clearly wasn't listening. It was as though he'd plugged up his ears with all of Bartholomew's nonsense, and there must have been a lot of it in Enzo's head to get him to rob BioSilver in the first place. It wasn't a minor crime. Even Kulika would have thought twice about stealing from Solomon, and then she would probably have decided it wasn't worth it in the end. To get a young Silver like Enzo to agree to do something so reckless must have involved a serious degree of brainwashing.

But then Bartholomew was an expert at that.

'Academic now, anyway,' Kulika said. 'I've been ordered to bring you both in, so that's what's going to happen.'

'Dead or alive?' Bayly said.

'Preferably alive.'

'His preference or yours?'

'Both, I guess.'

'And mine,' said Enzo to Bayly. 'Let's make it alive, please.'

Bayly didn't seem inclined to agree, an inclination he proved when the boat's engine churned to life.

'Don't you dare, Bayly!' Kulika yelled.

She knocked Enzo out so he wouldn't go anywhere, then rushed towards the boat. She found Bayly in the cabin, downing bottles of blood from a cooler by the bed. It was the last resort of a man who knew he couldn't beat her in a fair fight, but even when he was fuelled up on blood, it took Kulika less than ten seconds to swipe a knife from the counter and stick it through his skull.

He'd recover, but he'd be out for at least twelve hours with a brain injury like that. Longer, if she didn't take the knife out. She left it where it was, turned off the boat's engine and took a good look around the cabin.

The space was kitted out with all kinds of mod-cons, which is only what Kulika would have expected from Bayly. He'd always been a crafty sort. There was a kitchen counter along one side, where she'd found the knife. It was equipped with all kinds of clever space-saving designs, like a fold-out breakfast bar and folding chairs that stacked away into the space beneath it. The whole thing looked bespoke, probably hand-crafted by Bayly himself. On the other side of the cabin was a bed, which looked for all the world like just a bed: a double mattress tucked against the wall on a raised divan. No drawers, no clever foldaway furniture, no storage, and that wasn't like Bayly at all.

Kulika lifted the entire mattress off the bed, meaning to take a look underneath, which is when she realised that it had been designed to lift in precisely that way. Gas struts kicked into action, raising the mattress off the divan on a platform of slats, like a drawbridge raising to reveal the moat beneath, or certainly something that smelled like a moat. It was a lead box, about a yard along each side, encrusted with sand and barnacles. Inside, Kulika could hear the faintest thud: a slow, erratic pulse.

This was the box that Bayly had kept buried in the Palisadoes for so many centuries, Kulika was certain. It smelled of salt and age and the kind of rank odours that attach to a place that's been used as a graveyard. All that, plus blood. A lot of blood. Old and curdled and rotten blood that had kept dead things alive beyond the point at which they should have long decayed.

Kulika looked around the room, her eyes skipping over Bayly's blood-soaked body, until she spotted a toolbox stowed under the edge of the counter. Inside, she found a couple of screwdrivers that she used to pry the edge off the box and lift the lid.

Almost immediately, she wished she hadn't. The stench that rose from within was like nothing Kulika had ever smelled before. It scorched the insides of her nostrils with ammonia and putrescence, making her eyes water until she had to dash the tears away to see inside the damned thing.

The first thing she saw was the woman. She was blood-stained and barely conscious, and so thin she was practically emaciated, but Kulika had no doubt that this was Dr Evita Khalyed. She'd changed, but not enough to stop Kulika from recognising her from her picture. Her eyes were closed, but she was alive, barely.

Then Kulika noticed the black vines that had wrapped their way around Evita's hips, shoulders and throat, tightening into her skin until they strangled her flesh in their grip. It was while Kulika was trying to work out how to extricate her from the off-puttingly moist tendrils around her throat that she noticed a round mass attached to Evita's neck. She leaned in to examine it more closely. There was something wrong with the shape, something familiar and yet twisted about its construction that set alarm bells clanging in the back of her head.

Then two white circles snapped into existence in the black morass. The part of the black shape closest to Evita's neck pulled away like a snail's foot writhing in the air for purchase, revealing the teeth that were sunk into Evita's skin.

'Shit!' Kulika yelled, dropping the screwdrivers as she jumped back in fright.

The figure that she'd initially mistaken for a growth of slimy black vines started unwrapping itself from around Evita's body, then it pulled itself slowly out of the box, bone by blackened bone. Its jaw gaped open to reveal a tongueless mouth. Parts of its skull were caved in and misshapen, to the degree that it surely wasn't capable of conscious thought. It couldn't walk. It couldn't stand, but it could drag itself over the lip of the box one barely-connected piece at a time, leading with teeth that snapped rapaciously in Kulika's direction.

She could put two and two together now: Bayly hadn't just buried Evita in the same place as he'd buried his old boyfriend over three hundred years ago. He'd buried her in the same bloody box.

By the time she'd got over the shock of that realisation, the skeletal oil slick was dragging itself towards Bayly's unconscious body, having honed in on the easier prey of the two of them. It took Kulika a moment to get Evita's body out of the box, long enough that when she returned to wrestle the Digs creature back into the box and seal it in, it had already taken a chunk out of Bayly's leg.

She figured that was the least he owed him.

'Shit,' Kulika panted to herself as she bent the edges of the lead box closed again and slammed the mattress back down on top of the divan. She heard movement behind her and swivelled, thinking maybe one of those horrible grasping hands had become detached and got left behind, but it was just Evita Khalyed, pushing herself weakly up from the floor. Kulika gave her a hand up on to the mattress, where she'd not only be more comfortable, but could also give Kulika some extra reassurance that the sticky skeletal bastard wasn't going to get back out again.

Jane, Kulika reminded herself. *She thinks her name is Jane.*

'Jane,' she said gently, 'I know you don't know me, but —'

'Evita,' she whispered.

Kulika froze. 'Excuse me?'

'My name's Evita,' she coughed weakly. 'Dr Evita Khalyed.'

'You remember?'

Evita tried to laugh, but ended up hunched over herself as she coughed and coughed. Kulika tried to offer her a drink of blood from one of the bottles in Bayly's cooler, but Evita just coughed it right back out again. The coughing fit was taking so long to subside that Kulika was considering cutting a hole in the woman's throat to pour the stuff straight in. The wound would heal quickly enough, but Evita wasn't going to heal at all if she couldn't get any new blood in her system. Finally, though, she stopped coughing enough to swallow.

'I've had some time to think in there,' she whispered after she'd emptied the bottle. 'Time to remember. I wondered why I knew so much pirate history, enough to have me cruising across the Caribbean on some stupid treasure hunt — But yes,' she said, with more strength in her voice. 'I remember who I am, now.'

Kulika smiled. 'Patience Quick is going to be thrilled to hear it.'

'You know Quick?'

'Yes.' Kulika didn't want to say too much. She couldn't imagine that Evita would be pleased to hear how much her best friend had suffered in her attempts to find her. 'She's back at the mansion.'

'What do you mean, she's… She's *Silver*?' Evita's tone of voice made it clear that this would not be a good thing.

Reluctantly, Kulika said, 'Yes.'

Evita's face clouded over. 'So while I've been stuck in this box, my best friend came looking for me and got herself mixed up in my mess. Is that about right?'

Kulika shrugged helplessly.

'I'm going to kill him,' Evita said.

'Bayly's part of the crew,' said Kulika. 'I don't blame you for being angry, but…'

'*Angry*? I just spent however long locked in a box with a blood-starved skeleton from the seventeenth century. I'm not angry, I'm fucking *livid*. But not with Bayly. That was my own fault for letting Brandon and Penny drag me into their stupid treasure hunt. No, it's Bartholomew who deserves to die,' she said, brushing the dried and crusted blood from her bare arms. 'He's the one who turned me into *this*.'

For a moment, Kulika thought she must have heard wrong. She was the only person Bartholomew had ever turned Silver. She was sure of this, and had been sure of it for three hundred years. He'd never cared enough about anyone else to turn them Silver, he'd told her himself.

At least until six months ago.

The implications were troubling, but if this meant what Kulika thought it meant, then it explained why Bayly had been under the impression that he'd be able to trade Evita's freedom for his and Enzo's. And if Bayly had been planning to make that deal, couldn't Kulika make a similar one?

Oh, yes. Evita Khalyed was going to be very useful indeed.

21

THERE WERE SEVEN zombies chained up along the garage wall, and they weren't like the one Quick had seen back in the cellar.

'Why are their eyes bleeding like that?' Penny asked, her face pale and horrified. 'And why are they moving so... weird?'

The zombie in the blood cellar had moved in an almost animalistic way, snarling and snapping and hunched like a hyena. These ones were different. Instead of lunging at Penny and Brandon and Quick, they were watching them through crying eyes that streaked bloody tears down their faces. All the while they swayed together in a constant, sinuous motion, like tree branches waving in the same breeze, as though they were all part of one entity rather than individual beings.

Whatever was up with these creatures, Quick knew in her gut that it wasn't right. It made her want to turn around, get back into the SUV and drive straight to the airport, consequences be damned. Unfortunately, with Brandon and Penny here, that wasn't an option.

'Let's find Bella,' Brandon said, keeping a careful eye on

the zombies as he stepped past them, following bloody footprints through the open doorway into the house.

But Bella wasn't in the house. She wasn't in the kitchen, or in the sitting room, or in the game room, or in any of the grandly-appointed bedroom suites. Eventually, Quick found her underneath the breakfast bar, but only because she literally tripped over her.

'What's all this dust?' she said, more to herself than to the others, who were still searching upstairs. The stuff was thick and almost sticky. It coated Quick's polished leather chauffeur shoes, dulling the patent shine to a matte grey. She toed through the pile, spreading it around to see if maybe it was an ant or termite nest that had erupted through the floor, or the remains of a fire that might have left a char mark beneath it, but instead she dislodged a small, shiny object that went skittering away over the tiles.

It was a locket on a silver chain. A familiar locket, the one that Quick had noticed Bella twisting around her neck the previous day. When she scooped it up from the floor and snapped it open, there was a smarmy photo of Enzo inside. That was the kicker.

'Oh, no,' Quick murmured.

'What?' Brandon yelled from upstairs.

'I think I found Bella.'

'What?' Penny said, rushing back into the kitchen with Brandon hot on her heels. 'Where?'

Quick pointed at her feet.

'I don't know what TV shows you've been watching,' Brandon said with a laugh. 'But real vampires don't turn to ash when they die.'

'This one did,' Quick insisted. She showed him the locket, dangling it from her fingers.

'But that's not… It doesn't work like that.'

'Did you find the vial of poison?' Quick asked.

Brandon and Penny went still.

'No,' Brandon said after a moment.

'Maybe that's how it works with the poison,' Quick said, pointing to a suspiciously vial-shaped piece of broken glass on the countertop. She'd missed it in the first search, because there was a lot of glass in the kitchen, mostly broken beer bottles. There was a lot of blood, too, some of it on the broken vial.

'Don't touch it,' Penny said.

'I wasn't going to.'

'Shit!' Brandon yelled, looking from the pile of ash to the broken vial to the zombies who were leering at them through the open door to the garage. 'What's the story, then? She got so pissed with Enzo that she killed herself?'

'Or she was trying to turn her first Silver and got depressed after failing seven times in a row?' Penny suggested. 'That would explain the zombies.'

'I don't think anything can explain *those* zombies,' said Quick.

'It's the fucking vial, isn't it?' Brandon said, letting off a stream of invective.

'She thought it was a cure,' Quick said, putting the pieces together. 'Maybe she was trying to cure the zombies with it, and instead she turned them into… whatever that is.'

'Maybe she was trying to cure herself,' Penny suggested quietly, then she turned away to wipe her eyes without Brandon noticing. Quick noticed, though.

'We'll need to take her back to the mansion, so the crew can consume her power,' said Brandon.

'I'm not eating *that*,' Penny wailed, pointing at the ash that had once been their friend.

'Then you can argue with Bartholomew about it, but

we're taking it. We need to clean the rest of this shit up, too. And be careful with that glass, newbie. Don't need you going up in smoke too.'

Quick got to work, but the ash, the broken vial and the blood and glass all over the kitchen floor weren't their only problems. There were drag marks leading from the dining area back into the garage, which Brandon followed to a body in the chest freezer.

'Oh, fuck me sideways,' Brandon yelled. 'Not another one.'

'Human,' Penny said. 'Dead. From the clothes and the gloves, he looks like the gardener.'

Which was when Quick abandoned her cleaning to take a closer look at the zombies.

'Maid service,' she said, looking at the logo on one woman's T-shirt. 'Security guard, window cleaner, HVAC technician, postal worker,' she said, listing off the other logos she could see. 'There's only two people here who aren't wearing uniforms for some kind of service. They probably all came to the house.'

'It's like Bella was sitting here and waiting for her food to just walk into her mouth,' Brandon said.

'Ugh,' Penny sneered. 'You don't have to put it like that.'

'Well, how would you put it?'

'I don't know. But not like *that*.'

Quick should have gone back to cleaning, but now that she was standing in front of the zombies again, she found she couldn't look away.

'What's wrong with them?' Penny asked.

'It looks like they're afraid of the light,' said Quick, watching how they avoided the light coming in from the high garage window. 'Maybe that's why their eyes are bleeding.'

'Yeah,' Penny said, taking a step closer so she could watch the zombies shy away. 'And it looks like they're scared of us, too.'

'Neither of those things are normal, are they?' Quick asked.

'Nope,' said Brandon. 'Nothing about this is normal.'

The three of them watched the zombies' undulations with a strange fascination. They didn't speak or howl or make any sound that even approached verbalisation, but each wave-like motion of their bodies was accompanied by the gentle clanking of chains and the continued *drip drip* of bloody tears from their chins. It was gruesome and hypnotic.

'Can we just put them out of their misery and get out of here, please?' Penny said after a while.

'Bartholomew'll want to study them,' said Brandon.

'Then he can study a dead one,' said Penny.

'Fine,' said Brandon. 'Then you stab them through the brain and I'll pile them in the back of the SUV.'

'Why can't you do the stabbing?'

'Why can't you?' Brandon argued.

'*Someone* has to do it,' said Penny.

Quick wasn't sure she agreed, but then she didn't get a vote.

'Then that someone's going to be you,' said Brandon to Penny.

'Fine!' Penny yelled.

Quick chose to absent herself during the stabbing, turning her attention instead to what remained of Bella. She found an old tea caddy in one of the kitchen cupboards, swept up the ashes with a dustpan and brush and poured the cremains into the tin.

But she was still close enough to hear the unpleasant crunch of metal on bone as the first zombie was put to rest.

Or, at least, *should have been* put to rest.

There were several more unpleasant noises, then Penny said, 'Why isn't he dying?' in a desperate, high-pitched voice.

Quick didn't mean to go and look. Truly, it was the last thing she wanted to do, but she couldn't *not* go and see for herself. Afterwards, she had a feeling she would never stop seeing the image of that broken creature, still trying to move as Penny broke one part of it after another. The injury to its head didn't make any difference at all. It didn't seem to need a brain to function.

'Fuck,' Penny said after a few more seconds' gruesome work. 'That's it. I'm done. He's not going down, and we can't put them all in the SUV like this. Call for the truck.'

'They'll dock our points,' Brandon pointed out.

'Fuck the points,' Penny replied. 'I don't want to be here anymore. Call the fucking truck.'

'Seconded,' Quick said quietly from the doorway.

Brandon called the fucking truck.

22

EVITA WAS QUIET on the drive back to the mansion, which wasn't surprising. She'd been blood-starved for months, locked in a lead box with the wraith that had once been Digs – who by all accounts hadn't been a very nice guy to begin with – and buried six feet under in the sand beneath the Palisadoes. In the circumstances, Kulika was amazed to find her capable of rational thought, but it was clear from the suspicious way she was watching Kulika that she was. Since Evita had just seen Kulika incapacitate both Bayly and Enzo, then throw their broken bodies in the back of the car, her suspicion wasn't much of a surprise.

'You're taking me back to him, aren't you?' Evita said eventually.

'For now,' Kulika admitted.

'For how long?'

'Until the weekend, maybe? By then, it'll all be over, one way or another.'

'It's happening *now*?'

Kulika glanced at Evita, wondering just how much she knew. Bartholomew's plan for the revelation must have been in play since the beginning of the year, because that's when he'd first begun gathering the Silver in numbers, and making more. In fact, thinking about the timelines, Evita might have been one of the very first Silver to be turned.

'He's in the final stages of his revelation timeline,' Kulika confirmed.

'And you're helping him?'

'I don't… Sort of.' Kulika didn't know what to say, so she just said, 'It's complicated.'

'There's a painting of you in his bedroom,' Evita said.

'Huh?' Kulika had been paying attention to the road, so it took her a moment to process the subject change. 'Whose bedroom?'

'Bartholomew's.'

'You've been in his bedroom?' Kulika asked incredulously. *No one* went in Bartholomew's bedroom. He was like a monk.

'I woke up there after I was turned,' Evita said. 'Long, irrelevant story. My concern is that you're close to him, and since he's the antichrist, that makes me reluctant to trust you.'

'I can understand that,' Kulika conceded.

'Then tell me: why should I?'

Kulika was quiet for a moment. Her first instinct was to do something incredibly ill-advised. She wanted Evita to trust her, but—

Oh, fuck it.

'Maybe I was close to Bartholomew once,' Kulika admitted. 'Maybe we're close again now, but he's not the person I care most about at the mansion.'

'No?'

'No. The person I care most about is Quick.'

Evita *humphed* dismissively. 'You've known Bartholomew hundreds of years. You can't have known

Quick longer than six months.'

'About six days, actually.'

Evita *humphed* again.

'You know about silvering?' Kulika asked.

'Yeah. Bayly and Enzo, right?'

'Not just them,' Kulika said, then she looked away from the road for a moment to reveal her silver to Evita.

The other woman went still.

Kulika looked back to the road. 'You might not be able to trust me with anything else,' she said quietly, 'but believe me when I say that you can trust me with Quick.'

'I see,' said Evita.

A minute passed in silence, after which Evita added, 'Then you'd better fill me in on everything that's happened to her since I got locked away in that box.'

<h1 style="text-align:center">23</h1>

THERE WAS PANDEMONIUM when Brandon and Penny arrived back at the mansion with a truckload of mutated zombies. It was the start of the evening pool party, so people were milling. When they heard something interesting was happening on the drive out front, they abandoned the pool and wandered around the side of the mansion in their bikinis, chasing excitement. Penny was right about one thing: they were bored.

Quick had driven the SUV back on her own, but no one was paying her any attention at all. Instead, they clustered around the back of the truck as Penny led six of the zombies out in chains and Brandon carried the seventh, who wasn't going anywhere under his own power.

'What the fuck?' someone said with revolted glee.

'The boss says to put them in the wine cellar,' said Monty, coming out of the mansion's front door. 'Through the kitchen. Come on.'

Quick wasn't going to get a better chance than this, but the distraction wouldn't last long. She had to move.

She walked casually back towards the block, passing dozens of people going in the opposite direction as they rushed to see what the commotion in the driveway was all about. That left the coast clear for her to saunter back into the wardrobe and retrieve her sweatpants from the previous day, then transfer the contents of their pockets into a loose sundress that she might reasonably choose to wear to a pool party. When she sauntered back out of the block again in her flip-flops, she was sure she looked the part, but she was also starting to get nervous.

People were already gathering poolside again, dissatisfied with the brief entertainment the new zombies had offered them. Quick had been hoping to do this next bit alone, but instead she had to pretend there was something wrong with one of her flip-flops to give her the cover she needed to bend down and empty the lighter fluid under the porch. In the end, that turned out to be a blessing – once she'd set her little fire, the broken shoe gave her an excuse to return to the block for a replacement.

No one chased her. No one raised the alarm. In fact, no one seemed to have noticed her at all. Finally, her status as newbie Silver pariah was coming in handy.

Back at the block, she ran straight to the hidden cupboard, pulling the false wall closed behind her as she lifted the hatch, with difficulty. She was stronger now, though. Strong enough, but she still couldn't see very well in the dark.

'Put the lights on, Xiaoyu,' she called softly. 'It's Quick.'

Nothing.

The cellar beneath her remained dark.

'Xiaoyu? Are you okay?'

For a moment, Quick thought maybe the humans had been moved, or – god forbid – killed, but she could hear people moving and breathing beneath her feet.

Breathing?

Maybe her senses were more attuned than she thought.

Because she was *Silver*, she reminded herself. She wasn't a prisoner in that hole anymore. She had authority that they didn't. Maybe Xiaoyu hadn't made it, but whatever was going on in the cellar, she could make the others tell her what had happened to Xiaoyu.

'I can hear you down there,' she said. 'Put the lights on. Now.'

The fluorescents blinked on and, not sure whether she was being brave or foolhardy, Quick jumped down to the dirt.

A brief survey of the space told her things had changed dramatically in the few days since she'd left. All the people were gathered down the far end, by the bathroom space, and there were about half as many as there had been before. Clearly, the Silver had been hungry.

She'd been hungry, Quick reminded herself. And this was the cost of her hunger.

But the appetites of the Silver weren't the only thing to blame for the blood bank's diminished size. In one corner, the corner nearest the hatch, there was a foul-smelling pile that Quick first mistook for rubbish bags. As she stepped closer, though, something at the edge of the pile shifted and groaned. Something with, Quick realised as she looked more closely, bleached-blonde hair and black roots.

'Xiaoyu?' Quick asked as she stepped closer, not wanting to believe the evidence of her own eyes.

The rubbish heap was a charnel pile of broken bodies and filth. Some of them were the newcomers who'd been broken when they'd been shovelled down through the hatch before the Casting, people who probably never recovered from their injuries. Others were just drained.

So many, in so few days.

And there, right at the edge, too exhausted to do much more than smile cockily at Quick, was Xiaoyu.

'She needs help!' Quick yelled at the others. 'Bring me some water.'

No one moved.

'I said, bring me some water.'

No one would meet her eye. Some even turned and started scuttling off towards the farthest corner of the cellar, or pulled themselves under their blankets like the cockroaches they were.

Xiaoyu wasn't like them. She'd guarded the hatch, and kept them safe from the zombies, and taken more than her fair share of feeds just to spare the others. She was worth more than this.

Maybe that was why Quick got so angry. Maybe she was just angry at herself.

'She looked after all of you, and you've just left her here to die,' Quick snarled. 'Well, fuck you all. You can rot down here for all I care. Come on, Xiaoyu.'

'We got sick,' one of the others said from the far side of the cellar. '*She* got sick. What were we supposed to do?'

It was a good question, but Quick didn't have an answer for it. She didn't even want to think about what the right answer might be, because she was worried that it was probably *exactly what you've done*. That would complicate things, because Quick knew very well she could probably only get one person out of this hellhole, and she wanted that person to be Xiaoyu.

Fuck complications.

She slung Xiaoyu over her shoulder and jumped up out through the hatch, slamming it shut behind her, then grabbed the bag of supplies she'd stashed in the wardrobe. If the Silver were expecting Xiaoyu to be dead any minute anyway, then surely they wouldn't miss her, which might actually give Quick the opportunity to get her off the property, once and for all.

For once, it looked like one of Quick's plans was actually working out. Behind the mansion, the eerie blue glow of the pool had been replaced with a merry orange glow coming from the porch. It was burning hard and strong, and despite a lot of activity in that area from the Silver who'd realised the mansion was on fire, it didn't look like they were having much luck putting it out.

Hopefully, it would burn the place to the ground.

Quick would come back to whatever was left. She'd have to come back to find Evita, and she was crew. The others wouldn't stop looking for her if she left, not ever. But she could get far enough away to give Xiaoyu a chance.

Quick carried her out of the block and through the trees towards the woods at the property line adjoining the road. Then Xiaoyu started coughing, and Quick had to let her rest and recover her breath so the noise didn't draw attention to their escape. Quick pulled a bottle of water out off the bag and fed it to Xiaoyu, followed by a juice box and some fruit. After that, she started to look almost human.

'What are you doing?' Xiaoyu murmured.

'First, I'm getting you away from this place,' Quick whispered, 'and then I'm putting you on a plane out of this fucking country for good.'

'No offence, Quick,' Xiaoyu groaned, 'but the only reason I have to live through this is to go back to my kids, and they're *in* this country.'

'*Kids*?'

'Yeah,' Xiaoyu said quietly. 'Kids.'

Turned out she had two of them, a boy and a girl, ten and twelve. They'd been staying with their dad while Xiaoyu had gone on holiday with her new boyfriend, but then she'd found out that the boyfriend wasn't that new after all, because he was over three hundred years old, and Silver.

'After me, the vampires chose more carefully. It's why they could never bring themselves to kill me, I guess, but they couldn't let me go, either. Not with all I know.'

'Well, they're letting you go now,' Quick said with conviction. 'You ready?'

'As I'll ever be.'

They nearly made it to the road. By that point, the fire had been quelled from flames to smoke to nothing at all. So much for Quick's plan. She could hear people moving through the woods, too, tracking her, so she opted to leave Xiaoyu for a moment to try to lead them away, but she must have got turned around at some point because she ended up bursting out of the trees onto the mansion's driveway, where a car was just pulling up.

Was that Kulika getting out of it?

Kulika.

Quick saw her circle the car until she came to the passenger door, which she opened so she could lift an unconscious figure out.

'Evita,' Quick said in disbelief, then something thudded into her from behind, pushing her face-first onto the ground. Dirt was forced up her nostrils and into her mouth, and her lungs burned with the weight on her back. She was about to throw it off and use some of the fighting techniques Kulika had shown her to get free, then there was a sharp pain in the side of her neck and spots strobed in front of her eyes.

She couldn't breathe. She didn't need to breathe, she reminded herself, but she couldn't *breathe*, and the pain in her neck didn't stop. She was hot and chilled and freezing and burning and then just numb.

Still, the pain went on and on and on.

24

KULIKA HAD TAKEN a diversion on the way back to the mansion to drop Evita's blood sample off with Dr Ross. She could have taken Evita directly into the lab so the doctor could draw a fresh sample, but Evita had fallen asleep on the drive and frankly Kulika didn't feel like she could spare the blood. They had the sample from Enzo in the cooler, and that was good enough.

Because of the diversion, it was already dark by the time they pulled up at the house, and the evening's festivities were in full swing. There was a foul odour in the air too, something burning and rotten that made Kulika worry about what she had missed in her absence.

Probably best she didn't know. She'd seen enough horrors today to last her a long while.

'There's a room for her in the house,' Monty said, hurrying out of the mansion as Kulika lifted Evita, still sleeping, from the passenger seat. 'The one next to yours.'

'Are you sure?' Kulika asked.

'Captain says,' was all the reply Monty would give.

'Bayly and Enzo are in the back,' Kulika said. 'They won't wake for a day or so, I guess.'

'I'll put them somewhere safe.'

'Where, exactly?'

'Somewhere safe,' was all Monty would say, but Kulika had Evita to look after, so she didn't have much choice but to take the kid at his word. He would only be doing what Bartholomew had ordered him to, and Kulika wasn't in a position to contradict that. All things considered, it seemed best to get Evita set up, then go find Bartholomew herself so she could hear it from the horse's mouth.

In the end, he found her, just as she was leaving Evita's new room.

'Is she well?' Bartholomew said, his voice soft in a way that made it unrecognisable.

'As well as can be expected,' Kulika said, closing the door gently behind her. 'She'll need a lot of blood when she wakes up.'

'She'll get it,' he promised.

'You're very solicitous,' Kulika commented.

That was a mistake. Bartholomew shut down instantly, his usual supercilious demeanour sliding back into place as though it had always been there.

'You've been keeping things from me, Kulika,' he said chidingly, guiding her along the corridor towards her own room. 'About the baron.'

'I'm your Second,' she replied diplomatically. 'You delegate to me. Surely you don't need to know all the details.'

'When they threaten my life and the lives of my crew?' he said, barely controlling the volume of his voice. She'd properly pissed him off now. 'I granted you autonomy when I excused you from drinking at the Convocation,' he said. 'Do you have no appreciation for that? The other Silver in the crew are bound to my blood, but it's been three hundred years since you tasted it. I've given you my trust, and your freedom with that trust. Do we need to revisit that arrangement?'

No.

Every cell in Kulika's body rebelled at the notion. She remembered how it had felt as he'd turned her Silver, forcing his blood down her throat. She remembered the feeding in the breakfast room and how she could taste his spit on the woman's throat.

She absolutely didn't want his blood inside her.

'I'm sorry,' she said, trying to hide her fear. 'It won't happen again.'

'No, it won't,' he said. 'But as luck would have it, I'm in a good mood. Bayly and Enzo are under control, our missing crew members are returned to us, and Cara Alton's body is on its way back to Oklahoma to pose a fascinating conundrum for the local ME's office. By Friday, the stage will be set for our grand introduction to humanity, and we will once again have the freedom we lost three hundred years ago. I'm about to become the king of all creation so, despite the fact that you chose not to inform me that Drake's agent brought a fatal serum into my territory that seems to have transformed a normal failed turning into a handful of unkillable zombies, I've decided to be lenient. Better still, I've left a gift in your rooms,' he added with an indulgent smile. 'Enjoy.' Then he walked away down the corridor whistling to himself, as though he hadn't a care in the world.

Kulika stood blinking for a moment, trying to make sense of Bartholomew's ever-changing moods. Then she heard a disquieting noise from the direction of her rooms, and she was too full of terror to do anything but run.

She flung open the door to find Quick tied to her bed frame by her wrists. Her mouth was gagged, her eyelids fluttering and her skin pale. She was moaning with pain.

'What happened?' Kulika asked, rushing to Quick's side to snap her bonds. They were formed from metal cable, thick and strong, but Quick should still have been able to break out of them, not least by breaking the bed frame.

Which is when Kulika saw the bite on Quick's neck, the bite that wasn't healing.

Bartholomew had drained her.

The *bastard*.

Kulika turned Quick's head so she could untie the fabric gag that cut into the sides of her mouth, then took Quick in her arms and wrapped the blankets from the bed around her body, desperately trying to warm her freezing skin.

'I set the house on fire,' Quick whispered, then she grinned a weak but mischievous grin that set off fireworks in Kulika's chest.

Christ, she was a live one.

But she wouldn't be much longer if Kulika didn't get some blood in her.

Kulika bundled Quick up and laid her gently down on the bed, saying, 'I'll be right back,' then she nipped back next door into Evita's room to fetch the last of the bottles from Bayly's cooler. It took Quick some time to sit up and drink them, with Kulika's help, but when she had, her colour was better, her wounds healed. Kulika could have used the bond to patch her up, but that would have raised questions Kulika would prefer not to answer right now.

It wouldn't be fair on Quick to tell her about the silvering. Not until she was ready.

Maybe never.

'You found Evita,' Quick said, sitting crosslegged in the middle of the bed while Kulika perched on the edge beside her.

'I did.'

'I saw you carrying her. She doesn't look well.'

'She's not. I think she'll get there, though.'

Physically, at least, Kulika thought to herself. Mentally? The woman was strong, but she'd been locked in a box with a monster for months, and Kulika was certain that worse had happened in that lead coffin than Evita had been willing to admit. It would take time to bounce back from that.

'Thank you,' Quick said. 'For bringing her back.' Then Quick reached out and took Kulika's hand in her own, pressing their joined hands together into the soft sheets that covered the bed.

Their eyes locked. It was suddenly impossible for Kulika to ignore that they were in her bedroom together, sitting on her bed, touching each other's skin, palms and fingertips. The room smelled of blood and dirt, but also of dew evaporating in the dawn, frosted autumn leaves crushed underfoot, and bluebell woods bursting with the spring. It amazed Kulika how being close to Quick transported her to another place, how the scent of her skin offered a calm sanctuary as a physical place, far away from South Carolina. Kulika could feel herself reaching for the dream of that escape like a rope in a storm, desperately, in the same way she wished she could reach for Quick now.

'Kulika…' Quick whispered.

Quick reached out to her, then. Her fingertips played tentatively over Kulika's bare shoulder and up the side of her neck until she was holding Kulika's cheek in her hand. It was impossible not to lean into that touch, so Kulika didn't even try to resist. Worse, she reached out to Quick and let herself do the very thing she'd spent the past days dreaming of: she gently brushed Quick's hair away from her face, then sank her fingers into the thick locks up to the knuckle, feeling the weight of them gathered in her palm against Quick's warm neck.

Quick closed her eyes and moaned.

'Kulika,' she whispered again, then she wrapped her hand around the back of Kulika's neck and pulled her closer until they were just a breath away.

Just one taste, Kulika thought.

Then there was a noise. It was a small noise, just a little *click*, like the sound of a latch raising. Kulika wouldn't have noticed had she been even a tiny bit further into the spiral down which Quick's scent was pulling her. But she did notice it, because it was coming from the connecting door that joined her rooms to Bartholomew's.

And Kulika realised she could never touch Quick again. Not like this, not here, where Bartholomew was always watching, listening, *seeing*. The bond between them might be unbreakable except by death, but the new relationship they were building was fragile and precious. Kulika didn't know what it was exactly, because she'd never experienced anything like it before, but she did know it couldn't be like every other short-lived tumble in the dunes that she'd indulged in under Bartholomew's eye.

It had to be different.

But it wouldn't be, would it? For as long as they were here, in this mansion, every moment they had together would be by Bartholomew's gift, at the times of his choosing, by some twisted condition, and within his control. But Kulika could never be anywhere else, either. She couldn't leave the mansion without Bartholomew's permission, not now that Quick was in his power.

She would have killed Bayly today if she'd had to, and Enzo too, just because Bartholomew had asked it of her. He would always be just behind them, watching. There was nothing she could do to stop him.

But she could stop *this*.

'I can't,' she said, pulling away from Quick.

Quick looked surprised for a moment, then hurt, then ashamed, in a rapid kaleidoscope of emotions that Kulika could track as it played out through her scent as well as her expressions. First sharp citrus in the dawn, then peaches bruised at harvest time, and finally those same peaches at the end of the season, forgotten in the leaf litter and made acrid with fermentation.

'We... I...' Kulika pushed herself from the bed. 'I need to check on Evita.'

Quick blinked, schooling her expression, then asked, 'Can I see her?'

Kulika couldn't see the harm. After all, Bartholomew had brought Quick up here, not Kulika. Why shouldn't she see her friend when she was only next door? Besides which, Kulika was feeling guilty enough about what had just happened that she would have done almost anything Quick asked.

Anyway, Bartholomew was watching. If he wanted to object, then let him.

'She's next door,' Kulika said, then she led Quick out of her room and into Evita's.

It was a smaller room than Kulika's, but not by much. This one was arranged as a twin room, with two double beds. It seemed an odd arrangement to Kulika, because it wasn't as though there were any Silver children on the property who might share a room together, but then the crew had grown a lot over the past six months. Maybe they were all sharing rooms now.

Quick rushed to Evita the moment she walked in, falling to her knees at the bedside to take her friend's hand.

'She's cold,' Quick said. 'And thin. And the wrong colour. She's just lying here like— Oh, shit.' Quick turned to Kulika with a look of horror on her face. 'Xiaoyu.'

'What about her?'

'I left her in the woods by the road,' Quick said, panicking now. 'I was trying to get her out of here when I got attacked, and I left her in the woods, but she's ill, Kulika. She's so ill.'

'I'll see what I can do,' Kulika said, turning back to the door. *That* was going to take some explaining to Bartholomew.

'Kulika?' Quick said.

'Yeah?'

'Evita's going to be okay, isn't she?'

Kulika shrugged. 'It'll take time.'

'What happened to her?'

Another thing Kulika had been hoping she wouldn't have to explain.

'She was taken by one of the older members of the crew,' Kulika admitted. 'A friend of mine, I'm afraid. Bayly.'

'Bayly,' Quick murmured, like she was trying to place the name. 'Why?'

'He was going to bargain Evita's life for Enzo's freedom from the covenant. He thought it was the only way to free him. He loves him.'

There was no excusing it, but…

I would have done it for you, Kulika thought.

'So I'm supposed to think that's *romantic*?' Quick said scathingly. 'That's not romantic. That's monstrous.'

'We're all monsters here,' Kulika laughed bitterly. 'Didn't you know?'

But Quick didn't have to be one.

She had the friend she'd come here looking for, and Kulika hoped that would be enough. It would have to be.

She left the two of them alone, and went off to find Xiaoyu.

25

KULIKA HAD ALREADY been sitting at Bartholomew's desk for twenty minutes when he walked into the library at midnight. That had given her time: time to find the old leather-bound covenant book, time to ink the quill, and time to write out a bargain she was ready to sign.

'I've got a new deal for you,' she said as Bartholomew looked at her with interest – and a little disapproval. After all, she was sitting in his chair. She didn't give it up, though. Instead, she turned the open book to face him and drove the quill's nib into her fingertip. 'Read it,' she said. 'I'm ready to sign when you are.'

Bartholomew looked at the book, and at Kulika, then he pulled up a chair on the other side of the desk and sat, pulling the book towards him.

'This is about our Patience, I presume,' he said.

'Yes,' Kulika replied, suppressing the urge to shift anxiously in her seat. She needed him to see that she was serious about this. 'And no. Not *our* Patience. Just Quick, being her own self, out in the world, belonging to neither of us.'

Bartholomew had been reading Kulika's handwritten

bargain, but now he looked up at her in surprise. 'You're giving up your claim on her?'

'If you will too,' Kulika said. 'And your claim on Evita, and one of the humans from the blood cellar. The one I've left in Evita's room.'

He laughed incredulously. 'Just one? Why not all of them? Why not ask me to throw the mansion and the crew into the bargain too? My dear girl, have you lost your mind?' He threw the book back onto the desk, where it landed with a thud that rattled the floorboards. 'If I let them go, what makes you think they won't go telling stories about what we're planning?'

'Does it matter?' Kulika asked. 'You're revealing Cara Alton's body tomorrow. You're revealing us all by the weekend. If anything, the stories they tell are only going to help your cause.'

He considered this for a moment.

'And in return for this generous surrender, what am I getting, exactly?' he asked.

'Me,' Kulika said. 'Forever.'

'Ah,' he smiled, 'but I already have that.'

'Willingly,' she clarified. 'Without argument, as whatever you want me to be. You won't have to bribe me, or blackmail me, or even explain yourself to me. I'll do whatever you want, without question, for the rest of my life, and I'll never try to leave or break that covenant. I swear it, on her life. Whatever you want. Just let her and her friends go.'

'*Whatever* I want?' he asked, his interest sharpening.

'Yes,' Kulika said hopelessly, because she knew there was no other way.

'A blood exchange?'

Kulika gritted her teeth. She'd known it would come down to this, and she knew what it would mean. She'd seen the effect Bartholomew's blood had on his crew. She wouldn't have believed it until the night of the Convocation, but she understood now that there was an extra something in his blood that kept his people close to him. Once they'd drunk enough of it, they didn't want to leave him. Maybe they couldn't.

Kulika didn't want to agree, but she had to. The whole point of this new bargain was to put Quick beyond Bartholomew's influence – and hers – before it was too late. Kulika didn't want Quick to become so bound up in his blood that, like Enzo, she could no longer contemplate being away from him and his crew.

She'd lived that hollow existence herself, several lifetimes ago now, and she wouldn't wish it on Quick for all the free will in the world.

Instead, she surrendered herself to him.

'Even that,' she said.

But still, Bartholomew didn't reach for the book.

'I've offered you everything,' he said. '*Everything*. And am I not delivering? Why give it all up when we're on the brink of victory? You could have everything you've ever wanted *and* our Patience as well.'

'Not like this,' Kulika said. 'Not *our* Patience.'

'Ah,' Bartholomew said quietly, leaning back in his chair. 'I see.'

'Do you?' Kulika asked.

She had to wonder about Evita. It was more than a little surprising that he'd conjured up sufficient feelings to turn her Silver. Back in December, he wouldn't have had the benefit of the BioSilver formula, so he must have had some genuine affection for Evita to make the turn stick. Kulika hadn't realised he had that in him anymore.

Did he feel protective of Evita in the same way that

Kulika was protective of Quick? Was that why he had sent Kulika to find her? And would that make him less willing to surrender her now?

'I understand the instinct to send her away,' Bartholomew said. 'I don't share it, but I understand it.'

'Are you saying you won't give Evita up?'

'No,' he laughed. 'No, I'll happily give her up.'

Kulika was a little surprised by his levity.

'Did you think she actually meant something to me?' he asked incredulously, leaning forward in his chair. 'She's *new*. She's practically still human,' he added derisively. 'Do you really imagine that someone so insignificant could ever mean *anything* to me?'

'Quick means something to me,' Kulika argued. 'She's new.'

'And I won't hold that against you, but really, Kulika.'

'I was new once.'

'And you were fearsome from the very moment you were remade. You didn't forget yourself and become like a true newborn, helpless and pitiful,' he spat disdainfully. 'You remembered it all.'

'And you it hold it against Evita that she didn't?' Kulika asked, trying to understand the expression on his face. On the surface, it was all disgust, but there had been something deeper in his eyes for a brief flash of a moment that made her wonder: did he actually *care*?

Maybe the problem was rather that Evita had remembered everything now, and hated Bartholomew for it. Kulika had told him as much. It had seemed only fair to warn him.

Bartholomew dipped his head, hiding his face. 'Give me the quill,' he said, waving his hand impatiently.

Kulika signed the page quickly before he could change his mind, then pushed the book and quill across the table to

Bartholomew. He pricked his own finger, blending his blood with Kulika's on the nib, and spread the mixture across the paper in his own looping signature. Then it was done, and there was no backing out.

For any of them.

PART THREE

QUICK AND THE DEAD

I

IN THE COLD stillness of the wine cellar beneath his mansion, Bartholomew Sometimes-Roberts stood looking at seven zombies that wouldn't die.

God knew he'd tried to help them along, as the three broken figures on the floor amply demonstrated. He'd dismembered, decapitated and disembowelled, but all he'd got for his troubles was a slightly shorter pile of zombie pieces, moving in that eerily hypnotic way of theirs, like waves across the sea, synchronous and undulating. They flinched away from him as he chained the ones that hadn't been reduced to puddles back up against the cellar wall, as though they recognised the threat he presented to them. They shouldn't be clever enough to react with fear, even after he'd cut a couple of them down, but they'd been flinching from the moment he'd walked into the room.

That wasn't just abnormal, it was fascinating.

There had always been the zombies. They went hand in hand with the Silver, the failure that resulted whenever someone tried to turn a new Silver and got it wrong. The zombies were the remnants, the dregs that remained once the potential Silver evaporated, or at least that was how

Bartholomew had always thought of them.

Waste products.

But these new creatures that Bella had somehow created with Dr Ross's serum? He wasn't sure what they were.

Across the cellar, someone moaned.

'Oh, good,' said Bartholomew. 'You're awake.'

Bayly looked at Bartholomew, then at his lover Enzo lying unconscious beside him, then at the zombies, and finally at the chains around his wrists.

'You drained me?' he asked.

'Didn't have to,' said Bartholomew. 'Your old friend Digs did that for you.'

Bayly raised an eyebrow stoically. 'Kulika told you about that?'

Bartholomew tutted, then surveyed Bayly disapprovingly. He leaned back against the stone plinth in the centre of the room. 'She didn't need to say a thing. What am I always telling you, Bayly? There's no point trying to hide from me. I see everything.'

Then he pushed the lid of the plinth, sending it crashing onto the brick floor. There was a moment of utter silence, followed by an exhalation that sounded like paper flapping in the wind. A black, twisted thing that might once have been a hand hooked itself over the edge of the open plinth – sarcophagus, more properly – and tightened its grip on the stone.

Bartholomew grinned. 'I thought the two of you might like some time to catch up,' he said. 'It's been so long.' Then he put his hands in his pockets and hummed to himself happily as he climbed back up the brick stairs to the kitchen, accompanied by a symphony of screams.

Several storeys above, in the suite next to Bartholomew's,

Kulika Yadav was flicking restlessly through her phone.

By now – the early hours of Wednesday morning – the discovery of Cara Alton's body was all over the news. She'd been found by a jogger, propped up against a tree in a suburban neighbourhood just fifty miles from her parents' house in Oklahoma. And how she'd been positioned…

If the jogger hadn't taken photos before the police arrived and sold them to some disreputable online "journalists", the world would never have known how she'd been positioned, but he was a scumbag, so he'd done both of those things.

Kulika had a suspicion that Bartholomew was somehow responsible for the scumbag. He'd always had a talent for bringing out people's baser impulses. But whether it was his fault or not, the whole world now knew that Cara Alton had been sitting with her legs crossed, shirtless to display the silver handprint on her stomach, with her short skirt bunched up around her hips to display the bite mark on her femoral artery. There had been no blood in her body, which had been so cold that when the jogger touched her – because of course the little pervert touched her – he'd left some of his own skin behind on hers.

Served him right.

But Kulika was worried.

The rumours were churning more quickly now than they had when Cara first disappeared: it was aliens in the beginning, then it was special effects, but already the media was starting to report the girl's death as a vampiric mystery. It was as though they *wanted* to believe there was something paranormal going on. At this rate, by the time the autopsy was finished no one would be able to deny it, and with the current level of public outcry, no one would be able to cover it up either. Then the stage would be set for Bartholomew's grand revelation. He had been right: it was a good plan.

Kulika wished like hell that she didn't have to be part of it, but she'd made a deal with the devil to keep the woman she loved safe. Soon, it would be time for her to pay up.

In the room next to Kulika's, Evita Khalyed woke before dawn to find her best friend kneeling at her bedside with her head pillowed on Evita's hand. She was fast asleep.

That was a shame. Evita didn't want to involve Quick in what she had to do next, and Quick had always been a light sleeper. Now that she was one of the Silver, with all the enhanced senses that came along with it, Evita had no doubt that Quick would wake up the moment she tried to move.

Bugger.

Then she noticed Xiaoyu, lately of the blood cellar, occupying the room's other bed. The human was on a drip, which was enough to give Evita pause. Since when did Bartholomew give enough of a shit about any of the humans on his property to bother nursing one back to health?

Strange indeed.

But there'd be time for questions later. First, Evita needed to get out of this bed, track down Bartholomew fucking Roberts, and nail him to the wall. Through the heart, for preference.

The crew would kill her, of course. She wasn't naïve enough to think that she could get away with murdering their captain without repercussions, if she managed to do it at all. That's why she needed to give Quick the slip first, so she could do it alone. Then she could free them both, even if she had to die to do it.

Later, though, when the time was right. If the past few weeks she'd spent trapped in a coffin with a blood-starved pirate had taught her nothing else, Evita Khalyed had at least proved one thing to herself: she was good at waiting.

* * *

On a property abutting the Cooper River, the Charleston Historical Society was preparing to unveil its greatest accomplishment to date. Funded generously by an anonymous private donor, and requiring an army of rare and specialised craftsmen to build, the replica of the fourth-rate frigate the *Royal Fortune* was truly a sight to behold.

Aloysius Truman, Society Chairman, was obsessed with it. He'd spent his long, dull life dreaming of pirate ships, and now he had one right in front of him. And not just any old pirate ship, but the flagship of the most successful pirate captain of all time, Bartholomew Roberts. The ship on which he'd *died*, no less. As Aloysius stood in the shipbuilding hangar, watching the painters stroke the last letters onto the prow of the incredible vessel, he could almost hear the clash of blades, smell the gunpowder, feel the sea spray on his bare forearms. Lord, what a rush.

He could almost see *her* too, the woman who haunted his dreams.

The original *Royal Fortune* had started out its life as a British Royal Navy frigate called *Onslow*, before being captured and repurposed by Roberts as his flagship. There had been women on board that ship, Aloysius knew. Those women had become captives of the crew, and they had been mistreated in ways that even the court transcripts had balked at reporting. Most were released. One, a blonde-haired waif, had disappeared without a trace. That disappearance had preoccupied Aloysius all his life, both mightily and thrillingly. Perhaps she'd dressed up as a man and joined the crew, or perhaps – more enticingly – Roberts had fallen in love with her and decided to break his own code to keep her close to him as he pirated his way from one side of the Atlantic to the other.

Perhaps.

Driven by every tantalising mention he'd uncovered in his amateur investigations – a blonde woman reported seizing a ship off the Ivory Coast, a fleeting reference in Captain Johnson's famous compendium of pirates, an eighteenth-century artist's sketch of a windswept woman on a ship's prow annotated with the letters "KUL" – Aloysius had diverted the society's attention increasingly towards the woman known to history only as *Kulika*.

That had become a source of resentment amongst the society's membership. It was bad enough that Aloysius had become chairman without proper academic credentials, but now they had to suffer his fanciful ideas as well? But they didn't have much choice. Suffice it to say that Aloysius's money was as old as the central Charleston Rainbow Row house in which he lived, and running the society was a surprisingly costly enterprise.

But really. Crossdressing women? Love affairs on the high seas? These were the artefacts of tacky films and bad novels. If Aloysius's money hadn't been keeping the society afloat for the past decade, that kind of bull crap would never have been tolerated.

Then he'd brought them this commission, and suddenly the society members had been willing to tolerate a lot more. They'd happily let Aloysius reconstruct an elaborate ladies' boudoir in the cabin next to the captain's to sate his fantasy, because it allowed each of them free rein for their own particular specialisms, and there were a lot of those amongst the society. Several years and several fortunes later, all forty cannon were now in working order. The glass for the windows at the stern of the ship – glazing the captain's cabin, state room and ward room – had all been hand blown in local workshops using traditional methods appropriate for the period. The history department head at the local university had gone wild with period furnishings and armaments, at astronomical expense. The donor hadn't batted an eyelid as the costs soared. In fact, he'd let all of them put their own stamp on the project, making just one stipulation of his own: the ship was to be called the *Primus's Fortune*.

Aloysius fully intended to use it to make his.

2

'GREETINGS!' BARTHOLOMEW CALLED into the pre-dawn air, addressing the hundreds of Silver who were gathered on the riverbanks at the edge of his property. 'And welcome to the Golden Age of my Primacy!'

The younger ones didn't get the reference to the Golden Age of piracy, but Kulika and the other Silver did. She wondered then if the reason Bartholomew had dragged them all down here in the dark had less to do with the dramatic silhouette he would shortly cast against the sunrise, and more to do with their proximity to the water. When the frigate rounded the turn in the river, sailing on the morning breeze, her suspicion was confirmed.

'What the…'

'Impressive, right?' said the man beside her, an older Silver Kulika didn't recognise. 'I helped draw up the plans. Replica of the *Royal Fortune*. I used to be a shipwright, you know,' he added with some pride.

'Hey, don't you know who that is?' the man next to the shipwright said to him, speaking in a horrified, hushed whisper as he shepherded his friend away.

Kulika didn't stop them. She was still picking her jaw up

off the floor. Good thing the river here was both wide and deep, because otherwise the frigate wouldn't have fit down the channel. It was enormous, but simultaneously smaller than Kulika remembered it being.

The sight of it made her sick.

'We're not all going to fit on that,' someone muttered from behind Kulika.

'That's not the point, dumbass,' someone else replied. 'We're not supposed to. It's a symbol. Don't you get it?'

A symbol. Well, they were right about that.

The Onslow.

The Royal Fortune.

Same ship, same shit: bloodshed, fire, death.

Of course the vessel sailing their way was a replica, because Kulika would have been able to smell the real ship from miles away. Its decks had been swabbed with gore, its hold filled with coffins full of treasure. It had been a ghost ship, inhabited by the living dead.

Bartholomew wanted to relive those glory days. Kulika just wanted to burn them from her memory, and from the memory of the world.

'I've gathered you all here for a momentous occasion,' Bartholomew continued, as the dawn breeze picked up long locks of his glossy brown hair and played with them. 'Today, not only are we celebrating the launch of the *Primus's Fortune*, but also the launch of the reign of the Silver!'

Cheers erupted from the riverbanks with an enthusiasm that Kulika couldn't share.

'We used to be gods on this earth,' Bartholomew continued, gesturing widely at the crowd. From the way they nodded along, it was clear these were words they'd heard before. 'We used to *rule*. But what are we now? Rats and cockroaches, forced into the shadows where they can't find us, feeding on scraps. Well, not anymore. By this evening, the details of Cara Alton's autopsy will hit the news, and tonight we are hosting the biggest party this mansion has ever seen. There will be journalists here to cover the unveiling of the *Primus's Fortune*, with live feeds around the world. Then we'll show them what we really are, and exactly how low they should bow.'

The ship came in to dock behind Bartholomew just as the dawn broke over the horizon, bathing him in an eerie red glow.

'Tonight, my crew,' he said, 'there will be blood.'

Apparently dawn wasn't too early – or too late – for a party at the mansion. The part of the crew that had sailed the ship downriver had all eagerly disembarked, heading for the pool. Someone was behind the bar before the cheering that followed Bartholomew's speech had even died down, and the crew were all either carrying on drinking from the night before or getting an early start on the day. It didn't seem to matter one way or another; everyone was joining in.

Everyone except Kulika, that was. She'd left the kids to it and taken a single bottle of beer down to the dock, where she could dangle her feet off the end and fish for gators. It was a beautiful morning, which made Kulika feel worse somehow. The sun glinted off the river in sheets of blinding light, its warmth soaked into the marshland, and the whole place smelled of green things breathing heavily in preparation for the heat the day would bring.

She had come here to be alone, but she didn't stay that way for long. She was only halfway down her beer when a confident tread on the creaking wood of the dock behind her heralded Bartholomew's approach.

'What do you think of her, then?' Bartholomew said,

gesturing at the ship that loomed over them both. 'Beautiful, isn't she?'

'She's a bad memory,' Kulika muttered.

'Oh, don't be like that.' He sat down next to her, pulling off his shoes so he could dangle his own feet in the water. 'She's a marvel. Some of the craftsmen had to relearn techniques from scratch. She's a feat of un-modern engineering.'

'She's too big for the dock. Too big for the river.'

'Then it's a good thing I'm not planning to keep her here long.' He leaned back on his hands, tilted his face to the sun, then gave Kulika an assessing look. 'You don't like her.'

'I just don't see the point of her,' Kulika argued. 'It's the twenty-first century, not the eighteenth. Why would anyone need a sailing frigate?'

'To make a promise,' Bartholomew said. He looked up at the shining new wood, smiling gently to himself.

Kulika couldn't remember the last time she'd seen Bartholomew look genuinely contented. Had she ever? But here he was, beaming at an inanimate bunch of wood and sails in the same way a parent might beam at their child.

'What kind of promise?' she asked him.

'Hmm?' When he turned to her, the vague smile was still warming his face.

'What promise?' she said.

'To the crew, of better things to come. You're not the only one who misses our pirating days.'

'I don't miss them at all.'

Bartholomew scoffed emphatically; they both knew that was a lie. Kulika might be resisting it as hard as she could, but she felt the pull of the sea just as strongly as she ever had. More, even, now that she was losing Quick. She wanted to leave the land behind her and run away to the waves. She wanted to be free again, but she knew the cost of that freedom too intimately to admit the depth of her desire.

Kulika could see the future in that moment, and she hated it as much as she yearned for it. Bartholomew would play on her ambivalence, as he always had, and before long she'd be up to her elbows in blood and treasure once more. That's what the *Primus's Fortune* represented to her: total relapse.

'None of the old crew are here anyway,' Kulika pointed out. 'Except Bayly, wherever Monty's put him.'

'Somewhere safe.'

'That's what he said,' Kulika replied sceptically.

'And the others are coming tonight, for the launch. You'll see your old crew again.'

'Most of them were human,' Kulika pointed out. 'They're all dead.'

'But not Wolfrie. Not Phinchas.'

Kulika's mouth dropped open. Hearing the familiar names in Bartholomew's voice made her ache with nostalgia.

'They're coming?' she whispered.

'They are.'

Kulika eyes were filling with tears. God, why was she welling up? She hadn't cried when she'd signed over her life to Bartholomew in return for Quick's. She wasn't crying about Quick now, even though she was about to say goodbye forever and her heart was breaking. It made no sense that she should respond to the news of Wolfrie and Phinchas's return with such emotion, but it had been so long. Maybe this was just the final drop of water that had overflowed the vessel where she held her pain.

She tried to hide her reaction from Bartholomew, knowing he'd use it against her – but what motivation would he have for that now? Why bother threatening her when she had already given herself entirely into his power? On the other hand, if he wanted nothing he couldn't already take from her, why would he trouble himself to offer her such a gift?

Phinchas and Wolfrie.

Besides Bayly, they were the only true friends she'd had in Bartholomew's crew, and the only reason she'd hesitated to leave. She loved them like siblings, but she'd spent the past hundred years trying to forget they'd ever existed, because of what they represented to her.

'If you're messing with me—'

'This is my promise to them,' he said, waving up at the ship. 'And they're my promise to you.'

'Of?'

'Crew. Real crew. I'm not completely unfeeling, Kulika. I know you need more than these new Silver, who look at you with more reverence and fear than kindness. They're just your army. Wolfrie and Phinchas can be your generals.'

'And Bayly?'

'Will serve his sentence. After that… we'll talk.'

There would be an after, though. That was more than Kulika had dared hope for.

Phinchas and Wolfrie.

Last she'd heard, they'd been causing havoc on the west coast in the entertainment industry. They could be sharks, those two, when they got together. It was the perfect playground for the pair of grifters, and one she hadn't thought they'd ever want to leave.

'What did you have to offer them to get them back here?' she asked.

'Not much,' he said, that contented smile returning to his face. 'Just you.'

'Me?'

'They missed you, Kulika. We all missed you. After you left… Well, I told you I would hold us together, and I will.

The new crew with the covenant, and the old crew with something stronger still.'

Kulika's blood ran cold. She looked at Bartholomew, waiting for the word she knew was coming: *blood*. She waited despite knowing, because that's what Bartholomew expected, but in the end he didn't deliver that word. Instead, he tilted his head, letting his hair tumble over his shoulder as he assessed her.

'Honestly, if I didn't know better,' he said, 'I'd think you were already regretting our deal.'

'No backing out,' Kulika said sharply. 'We made a bargain.'

'I haven't forgotten.' He reached out and took her hand in his, rubbing his thumb gently over the new covenant mark that nestled in her palm. 'Have you?'

'I'll keep my side,' she promised. 'If you keep yours.'

'Well, then.'

A heron came to land on the far side of the river, then strode through the shallows in search of morsels to snap up in its beak. Until the music started up, sending it flapping off into the sky once more.

Kulika turned to look over her shoulder at the pool. Someone had dragged a tower of speakers out from the block and was using them to blast thudding beats towards the party, but not all of the crew were joining in; some of them were getting ready for tonight's press conference. Silver were carrying lights and rigs and boxes in a never-ending procession from the driveway to the riverbanks. At this stage, Kulika couldn't work out exactly what they were building, but it looked like they were preparing for a performance and a half.

Kulika found her gaze dragged back towards the house, to the window next to her own. With any luck, Quick and her friends would still be asleep behind it, despite the noise. The blinds were drawn and dark.

'I'll send the kid to give them their marching orders,' Bartholomew said, following the direction of her gaze. 'Our Patience—'

Kulika scowled at the possessive pronoun, just as she was sure Bartholomew had planned her to. Even now, with all the assurances he had, he was still trying to get a rise out of her.

And succeeding.

'Just Patience, then,' he corrected himself, with a smile. 'She and her friends will be out of here this morning. You have my word.'

'So soon?'

'You wanted to draw it out? Kulika, our deal was clear.'

'I know that.'

'The kid's arranged a car to take them to the airport. It'll be here shortly.'

Kulika looked at him in disbelief for a moment, then pulled her feet out of the water, dried them haphazardly on the cuffs of her trousers and shoved them back into her boots.

There was a tinkling noise, and she looked over to see that Bartholomew was holding a set of keys out to her. A set of very shiny keys, with a distinctive high-end sports car logo on them that matched the emblem on Bartholomew's personal vehicle.

'I suggest you absent yourself,' he said. 'I'm planning to do the same.'

'And leave the crew here on their own, unsupervised?'

'They're not children.'

'No, they're worse: they're immature, untested Silver.'

'They'll manage. You don't need to be here to watch Patience leave.'

Which was the real problem, of course. He wanted Kulika out of the way, so there was no risk of her reneging on their agreement.

'But…' she said, grasping for closure. 'I thought if I just said goodbye, then at least—'

'She won't take it any easier,' Bartholomew said, pretending sympathy that Kulika was certain he didn't feel. 'And in case you've forgotten, you gave up your claim on her. She's leaving the mansion today, just as you wished. We have a blood bargain, Kulika. Do you expect me to honour my part of it, or…?' His eyes drifted upwards, to the window behind which Quick and her friends were sleeping.

'No,' Kulika said quickly. 'No, I'll…' She snatched the keys from his hand. 'I'll go and check on Dr Ross at the lab. She was going to work through the night on the formula.'

'Then you can send her on her way back to Oxford and say goodbye to Drake once and for all,' Bartholomew said pointedly as he got to his feet. 'I'm going to inspect my new ship, take her for a test float. I'll be back before long, and then we'll talk. We have much to talk about, you and me. Don't we?' He reached out and tugged gently at the strand of hair that was hanging over Kulika's eye, almost playfully. That was, she knew, a bad sign; the things that put Bartholomew in a playful mood were not most people's idea of fun. 'Say, midday?' he added. 'The library, I think.'

Kulika just nodded numbly. She couldn't refuse him.

Not now. Not ever again.

3

IT WAS MID-morning when Quick woke to find herself drooling on her best friend's hand.

'Oh god,' she said, wiping the moisture away with the bedsheet. 'I'm sorry. Are you okay? I didn't mean to get spit on you.'

'You snored, too,' Evita said. 'Loudly. As bloody usual.'

'I'm sorry.' Then Quick blinked as the implications of that last comment sank in. 'You remember me,' she said.

'Of course I remember you, Impatience.'

Quick laughed at the familiar nickname. It had been so long. 'I mean, you got your memory back. Kulika said you'd lost it when you turned Silver, and no one knew who you really were.'

'Right,' Evita agreed, but her expression flashed into anger, just for a moment, for reasons Quick didn't understand. 'I was Jane Doe for a while, but I had time enough to remember myself while I was locked in Bayly's treasure chest.'

'His *what*?' Quick said, horrified. 'Kulika told me he'd taken you, but she didn't say anything about—'

'Forget it.' Evita laughed. 'I'm just glad to see you.'

'God, yes. Me too.' Quick perched on the edge of the bed and pulled Evita gently into her arms, squeezing her as tightly as she felt was safe.

'I'm not made of glass,' Evita said. 'You can hug me properly.'

Quick did.

After six months of searching and finding nothing, and after a week stuck in this hellhole of a place battling vampires and zombies and potential emotional attachments she'd rather not dwell on right now, she had Evita in her arms. It felt good, but surreal, and a little scary given that they were both *still* stuck here in this hellhole of a place with vampires and zombies and all the rest. That might have been why Quick was crying, or maybe it was the relief of finding her best friend, but Evita couldn't judge her because she was crying too, even if she was trying to hide it.

Evita had never been very good at emotions, which was saying something, coming from Quick.

'You look better,' Quick said, holding Evita at arm's length while her friend pretended to have something in both eyes simultaneously.

'Allergies,' Evita sniffed. 'Terrible pollen in this place.'

'You don't get hay fever,' Quick said dismissively. 'Are you feeling better?'

'I'm fine,' Evita said, brushing Quick's solicitous hands away. 'I'm Silver. It's her we have to worry about.' Evita nodded towards the other bed, where Xiaoyu was just beginning to rouse.

Someone had hooked her up to a drip, which must have happened in the early hours because Quick had sat up awake most of the night and no one had come in. Xiaoyu tugged the cannula impatiently out of the back of her hand and sat up in bed. That felt miraculous enough, given the state Quick had found her in when she'd rescued her from the blood cellar, but that wasn't the only thing that had changed. Xiaoyu's eyes were brighter, her skin less pallid, her face less gaunt.

'You look better,' Quick said, looking her up and down.

'Couldn't have got much worse,' Xiaoyu commented.

She swung her legs off the side of the bed and got unsteadily to her feet. Quick managed to catch her before she fell, but only with the benefit of Silver speed.

'I'm fine,' Xiaoyu said, batting her away.

'No, you're not. You fell over. When I found you last night, you were practically dead.'

'Dehydrated,' Xiaoyu said dismissively, pushing Quick away. Quick let her, but the woman was wobbling.

'You're both fine, then?' Quick said irritably, glaring at the two of them.

'Yes,' they chorused, with equal irritation.

'You can't stand up straight,' Quick said, jabbing a finger in Xiaoyu's direction as she fell back onto her bed, 'and you're crying for the first time in maybe forever,' she added, jabbing a finger at Evita. 'You are neither of you *fine*.'

There was a knock at the door, and Monty poked his head around it. Monty, of all bloody people.

'You can leave now,' he said.

Quick sighed. 'Maybe Evita and I can go back to the dorm, but Xiaoyu can't go back to the cellar. Not like this.'

'You're not understanding me,' Monty said, slowly and loudly, as though she was hard of hearing. 'I mean you can *leave*. As in, go away. All three of you. You two are released from the covenant, officially.' He pointed at Quick and Evita. 'Your car will be here in an hour, for the airport, or wherever you want to go. If I were you, I wouldn't keep it waiting, or Bartholomew might change his mind.'

'But…'

Quick had so many questions that she didn't know where to start. Why was he letting them go now, after everything? Why them? And *how*?

But most importantly: what about Kulika?

'We can't just go,' Evita pointed out. 'We signed the covenant. We're crew. If we leave, the crew will feel it. It'll hurt them. It'll hurt *us*.'

'That's what these are for,' Monty said, pulling a couple of plastic-wrapped tubes from his pocket as he approached Evita's bed: vacutainers for collecting blood. 'Come on,' he said to Evita and Quick. 'Arms.'

Evita rolled up her sleeve and let Monty sloppily extract a vial full of blood from the vein in the crook of her elbow.

'You're not very good at this, are you?' Evita said as he pulled the needle back out.

'Did you want to do it?' he challenged.

'Yes, actually. Here.' She snatched the last vacutainer from Monty and waved Quick closer. 'Roll up your sleeve,' she said, then she applied pressure around the top of Quick's arm and gently slid the vacutainer's needle into Quick's vein.

'You've done this before,' Quick said, with a hint of accusation in her tone.

'A lot happened in the past six months,' Evita murmured. She expertly extracted the needle and sealed the vial, then passed it to Monty, saying, 'What now?'

'Now we'll do the same ritual we do when people die. The crew will forget you soon enough.'

'But what about us?' Evita asked. 'We'll still hurt for the crew, won't we? And we've got these stupid tattoos,' he said, showing him the black spot in the centre of her palm. 'How do we break the covenant without hurting ourselves?'

'Look, do you want to leave or not?' Monty said impatiently.

'Yes,' said Xiaoyu from the other bed. 'Definitely yes.'

'Well, then. Cut out the tattoos, if you want. The pain's your problem.'

Then he left, at speed, before Quick had screwed up the courage to ask about Kulika.

'Dick,' Evita commented.

But Xiaoyu was laughing. 'See?' she said. 'Ladies, it's our lucky day.'

Quick wasn't so sure, and from the look on Evita's face, it was obvious she had her own misgivings.

'I'm going to get cleaned up,' Xiaoyu said to the others, looking down at her filthy clothes. She was still wearing the dirty jeans and ripped top she'd had on when Quick had carried her out of the cellar the night before, and her skin was streaked with blood. Evita didn't look much better, though she was at least wearing clean grey sweats that covered up the worst of the grime.

'Like the kid said,' said Xiaoyu, 'let's get out of here before Bartholomew changes his mind.'

'I should wash too,' Evita said as the ensuite door closed behind Xiaoyu. 'Are we cutting these out, or…' Evita spread her fingers to show her covenant stamp.

Quick ran her fingers over her own, feeling the way the skin had healed right over it, without any texture at all, as though it had always been there. The skin would heal just as cleanly if they cut them out, she supposed, but she hadn't forgotten the pain from the initial stamping. It was going to hurt like a bastard.

Still, she really, desperately wanted it gone.

'I'll do yours, you do mine?' Evita suggested.

'What are best friends for?' Quick said darkly.

Quick tried to get through the whole thing without thinking, because if she thought too hard about it, she was going to chicken out. She fetched a knife from the kitchen, and alcohol for antiseptic. They went as fast as they could, cutting shallow and sure, but by the time they were done, the sheets of Evita's bed looked like a crime scene, even if the wounds had already healed beneath the blood.

Quick had been right. It had hurt like a bastard.

But she was *free*. They were both free.

'There's another bathroom along the corridor,' Evita said shakily. 'Do you mind if I...?'

Quick kept forgetting that Evita had lived in this place for months before she'd been been taken captive by Bayly. She knew the mansion much better than Quick did, and had clearly held a much higher rank than Quick had managed in her short tenure here if she'd been up on this floor before. Other than her brief visits with Kulika, Quick had never made it above the ground floor, and she'd certainly never had permission to explore.

'You go ahead,' Quick said, then she watched as Evita extracted herself from the bedsheets, alert to any sign that she might need help. She moved easily, and she looked strong, but she couldn't hide the dried blood covering her bare feet.

'Vee,' Quick said, with shock.

Evita followed her gaze to her gore-painted toes.

'It's fine,' Evita said dismissively. 'I'm healed. Anyway, don't you have stuff to fetch from the dorms? Goodbyes to say?'

Quick felt like her best friend was trying to get rid of her. After so many months apart, that stung a little, but with everything Evita had been through, she knew she had to tread carefully. Evita tended to get spikier when she was hurt, not softer. That wasn't uncommon for kids with their kinds of histories; your protective instincts kicked in and you coiled in on yourself, lashing out to push people away rather than opening up to pull them close. It was only natural, Quick knew, but still.

Six months.

'We've only got an hour,' Evita added pointedly. 'Less, now.'

'One goodbye, maybe,' Quick admitted, thinking longingly of Kulika's sea grey eyes.

'Then I'd go now. This might be your only chance.'

With that, Evita shoved her bloody toes into a pair of socks that had been left on the floor by the bed and padded out into the corridor, with every appearance of health.

Left alone in the room, Quick felt strangely deflated. She'd come here looking for Evita, and she'd found her. Not only that, but she'd found Xiaoyu as well. Now they were all leaving together – changed, certainly, but safe. That was a triumph in the circumstances.

So why did Quick feel so empty?

If she'd been a better person, the answer would have had something to do with all the humans who were still stuck down in the blood cellar, but that wasn't it. The real answer was this: the idea of leaving Kulika behind made her ache.

Quick returned to the dorms to clear out her bunk, passing all the other Silver in the middle of a colossal pool party. There was an electricity in the air that made Quick glad they were leaving now, a sense of anticipation that sharpened the miasma of hopelessness that generally hung around the mansion. The excited tension was palpable, pulling the atmosphere until it felt so tight it might shatter.

Bartholomew was about to press the big red button. Quick and her friends were getting out just in time. She should be grateful for that.

And yet.

Kulika wasn't at the house, or in the block, or anywhere else on the property. As far as Quick could tell, Bartholomew wasn't either.

'Did you find her?' Evita asked when Quick returned to the suite at the house with her packed handbag.

'No. Did you?'

'No, but I found that little shit Monty,' said Evita. 'He said they went out, Kulika to do this formula thing and Bartholomew to go do whatever he does with his free time. Setting things on fire or torturing animals, probably.'

'Without even saying goodbye?' Quick said. It came out as a whine.

'Probably to avoid it, definitely in Bartholomew's case,' Evita said bitterly. 'He knows that if I ever get my hands on him I'm going to fucking murder him.' She gathered up her own meagre possessions and said, 'Home, then.'

'Home,' Quick repeated.

The word felt unaccountably big.

Their cab was late.

Quick kept thinking it was fate, that Kulika would come rushing around the corner at any second to sweep her up in elaborate goodbyes and promises of being reunited in future, or maybe she'd even ask to come with them back to the UK. They were childish fantasies, she knew, but she wished them true anyway.

Of course Kulika hadn't come. Other people had, though: Penny, Brandon, and other Silver Evita knew from her days at the mansion whom Quick had never met. They didn't seem to come out of fondness, but more out of boredom, inebriation, and a vague fascination about whatever had happened to make Bartholomew release them from his covenant.

They were all gone now, though, back to their party. The cab was twenty minutes late and Quick was sitting under her parasol on the mansion's front steps with Evita, looking out onto the drive as they waited for it to arrive. They'd all had to pick new clothes out of the wardrobe at the block so they'd have something to wear that wasn't dirty and covered in holes. Quick had dug out a copper-coloured, long-sleeved cotton dress and Evita had found some jeans and a T-shirt that fitted her, which was easier at her size. Quick just had to take what she could get. They each had a small bag of items with them too, the scavenged remnants of what they'd brought to this place, and they were lucky to have that. Xiaoyu had nothing at all.

The only human in their party had been nervous all morning. She wanted to look as nice as she could for her return home. As they'd been sitting there in the sunshine waiting for their ride, she'd seen a speck of blood on her inherited jeans and rushed to the mansion's bathroom to rinse it off. She didn't want her kids to see it.

It seemed like whatever they did, blood would follow them. Unfortunately, Quick and Evita still needed it to survive, a fact Quick was trying her hardest to ignore. They were already painfully underfed. Quick had maybe one or two short bursts of speed left in her, but Evita had nothing in the tank at all. She'd used everything they'd given her just to heal her wounds.

'We might have to grab someone in the airport before we leave,' Evita murmured the moment Xiaoyu left for the bathroom. 'For the blood.'

Quick gave her a horrified look.

'I know, okay?' Evita continued. 'But if we touch down in the UK blood-starved like this, and if Bartholomew's already done his grand revelation, we might have to fight our way through on the other side. A pair of sunglasses isn't going to fool people for long once they know to look for the silver in our eyes, and when they see your parasol' – Evita flicked the handle – 'people are going to get suspicious.'

'And your solution is to attack someone at the airport? Don't you think that'll make people even more suspicious?'

'Not if we do it carefully. In the bathrooms, maybe, when no one else is around.'

Quick considered the offhand way Evita was talking and the fact that she already had a plan, and came to a conclusion she didn't much like.

'You've done this before,' Quick said.

Evita was quiet for so long that Quick began to regret the accusation in her words.

'I didn't mean to—'

'Do you know that one of the most effective ways for cults to brainwash their members is by limiting their food intake?' Evita interrupted. At first it sounded like a non sequitur, but then she continued: 'It makes people more suggestible. When you don't get enough food – or blood – then your brain starts weakening along with your body. Then, just when you're starting to feel that weakness, they start working you like they worked us back at the block. They get you to do manual labour, or to run laps or fight or whatever. Combine that with a starvation diet of high-carb food, and weird things start happening. You get periods of complete euphoria followed by crushing misery, apparently for no reason at all. You're so tired that you can't think straight, so you don't put two and two together. Maybe they pair you up with some hottie, someone who's all-in on whatever the cult's doctrine is, so you don't notice the craziness of it because the words are coming from a face you wouldn't mind waking up next to.'

Quick knew whose face that was for her, but it made her wonder about Evita.

'The outrageous starts to sound reasonable,' Evita continued. 'In that state, you do things you would never even have contemplated previously, awful things, so if you ever do surface for brief moments of lucidity, you want to dive right back into the depths of your delusion just so it can all make sense again. You're not a bad person, it's just that terrible things are necessary in the cult's reality, so you cling to that reality like a lifeline. You can't accept any challenge to it, because if you do then all your excuses will shatter along with the world that's been constructed around you, and suddenly you have to look yourself in the eye and admit the truth: not only are you not a good person, you're just someone else's pawn.'

Who'd convinced her to do terrible things, and what exactly had she done?

'What are you telling me?' Quick asked.

'I was here for months before you arrived,' Evita replied. 'You've barely been here a week. All I'm saying is: don't judge me for doing what I had to do to keep my head above water. And if I have to do it again, for both of us, then I will.'

Xiaoyu returned then, putting an end to the conversation before Quick could smooth things over. It made the atmosphere awkward, which wasn't helped by the fact that she felt more self-conscious around Xiaoyu now, particularly after what had happened with Brandon this morning. When Quick had told him they were taking Xiaoyu with them when they left, he'd said, *Little snack for the journey?*

Evita had punched him, right in the face. She had a right hook that would make Kulika proud.

Kulika.

Quick didn't need that intrusive echo in her already

muddled mind, so she pushed the thought away. In much the same way Kulika had pushed *her* away: mercilessly, and with determined finality.

It was time that Quick did the same, and turned her mind to the future instead.

'Do you think they'll let us have our old jobs back?' she asked Evita. She was over a week late coming back from her sabbatical at this point, but she had to believe the university would give her a little leeway on that, particularly since she would be returning with their star historian in tow.

'Do you think they'll willingly employ vampires once Bartholomew drags us all out into the open?' Evita asked bluntly.

'Probably not,' said Xiaoyu.

'I guess that's the end of our academic lives, then,' said Quick.

'I don't know,' said Evita. 'Bartholomew told me one of the Oxford colleges is mostly Silver.'

'Oh?'

'Solomon College.'

Quick thought hard, trying to remember if she'd ever met anyone who tutored there. It was part of the job when you were a university lecturer – circulate around the conferences, network with other professionals in your field, read their papers – so she recognised most of the colleges and universities in the UK, at least the ones that had a history faculty. But Solomon College wasn't ringing any bells.

'Yeah,' said Evita. 'I'd never heard of it either.'

The car finally arrived, and they all piled inside. No one came to wave them off. Quick stared out of the window as they circled the drive, her eyes fixed on the mansion's front door, imagining in vain that Kulika might be somewhere inside, that she might run out to stop the car before they left.

As they started down the long road to the highway, Quick turned in her seat to look out of the back window, her eyes scanning the house until it was swallowed up by the oaks and Spanish moss that hung over the drive.

'I'm sorry,' Evita murmured, taking her hand.

'She didn't come,' Quick whispered back.

'We're free, though,' Evita replied. 'Isn't that better?'

Quick forced a smile onto her face and squeezed Evita's hand, pretending that she agreed. Evita smiled back, apparently convinced.

If only Quick could convince herself as easily as she could convince her best friend.

4

KULIKA DROVE BARTHOLOMEW'S stupid little sports car too fast around the corners, willing it to roll. She'd like to see it dented. She'd like to smash it to pieces, scratch up the paint and shatter the headlights. She wouldn't be hurt, not in the long run, but Bartholomew would certainly be angry if she stained his cream leather seats with her blood. She'd like to see that, too.

I couldn't help it, she'd say. *Someone was driving on the wrong side of the road, coming the other way. I had to spin off the road to avoid hitting them.*

He couldn't punish her for that, could he?

It was a petty rebellion, but she'd get to watch a little piece of his soul getting crushed by the loss, and that would be worth her pain. For the pain he'd caused her, she'd suffer the same all over again if it would cause him even the tiniest discomfort.

But there were always more cars. He wouldn't have lent her this one if he cared much for it; it wasn't as though the thing was irreplaceable. Not like a person. Not like Quick.

She cut the speed. As rebellions went, it wouldn't just be petty, it would be pointless as well. Quick would be gone by

438

the time she returned to the mansion, and that was for the best. Bartholomew was right about that, for all that Kulika hated him for it. It was time she put Quick behind her and concentrated on the people she could still help: her crew, Jack bloody Valentine, and Baron Drake.

She drove carefully the rest of the way to the lab, watching her speed the whole time.

When Kulika walked in through the security doors, Dr Ross had her glasses in one hand and was rubbing her eyes with the other. At first, Kulika thought she must be tired – after all, she'd stayed up all night to work on the formula – but when the doctor took her hand away to look at Kulika, her eyes were wet with tears.

'It didn't work,' Dr Ross said.

Kulika stopped dead in the doorway. 'What didn't work?' she asked stupidly. She already knew, she just didn't want it to be true.

'Evita Khalyed's blood isn't close enough to Jahan Khalyed's. The formula doesn't behave the same way in her blood as it did in his. It's not bonding, it's just burning through it, like it does with all the other Silver.'

'Which means?'

'I can't replicate the toxin that's poisoning Jack,' Dr Ross said hopelessly. 'And if I can't replicate it, I can't make an antidote. Jack Valentine is going to die.'

Kulika sat down heavily onto the nearest chair. 'And Baron Drake along with her,' she said.

Dr Ross nodded, wiping her eyes again.

Once upon a time, Dr Ross had been almost as close to Jack Valentine as Baron Drake was now. She might pretend she was crying for the baron, but they both knew her tears were really for her former flame. Kulika felt like crying too.

It had all been for nothing.

She'd come to South Carolina in search of Evita Khalyed. She'd walked back into Bartholomew's mansion, a place she'd hoped never to see again, all so she could find Evita, so Dr Ross could make an antidote for Jack. Kulika had done *everything* right. She'd discovered what had happened to Evita, tracked her down – with no help from Job Bayly – rescued her, and secured a sample of her blood. She'd even negotiated a place for Dr Ross to do her work in Enzo's lab at BioSilver, and it had all come to nothing. All that effort on a gamble that hadn't paid off.

And now she was bound to Bartholomew again, more tightly than ever, with nothing to show for it but a love she would never see requited.

For a moment, the two of them were silent, then Dr Ross took a deep, shuddering breath and settled her glasses back on her nose.

'I need to call him,' she said. 'Maybe I can bring the blood samples back with me and fiddle with them in the lab a bit, maybe fudge a little, but it's a slim chance and... But maybe...' She was procrastinating, Kulika could tell. She didn't blame the doctor for that. She didn't like giving bad news to the baron either, and it couldn't get much worse than, *You and the woman you love are both going to die.*

'I'll call him,' said Kulika. 'He should... He'll want to hear it from me, and you need to get back to Oxford. He'll need you. Besides, things are happening here at the mansion, and I'm not sure I...' She trailed off.

'Kulika?' Dr Ross asked, but Kulika didn't know how to finish the sentence.

She was unsure of so much, but what she couldn't admit to Dr Ross was the one thing of which she was completely certain: Bartholomew was about to unleash hell on earth, and he was going to use Kulika to do it.

In the end, Kulika just said, 'You should go.'

Dr Ross was already packing up her things. 'You'll tell Baron Drake that I'll keep trying?'

'I will.'

The doctor unzipped an insulated carrying case that had space inside for six tubes. She stowed five in the padded holders, then looked at Kulika expectantly. 'Did you find my missing vial?'

In all the commotion of the past day, Kulika hadn't thought to call Dr Ross about the trouble with Bella, and the vial. She'd just left her to get on with her work.

'We did,' Kulika said quietly. 'But not until it was too late.'

'Oh, god.' The doctor sat back down again, face in her hands. She looked up at Kulika through her fingers and asked, 'Who died?'

'One of the newer Silver from Bartholomew's crew. No one else.' Kulika paused. 'At least, not exactly.'

Dr Ross dropped her hands, gave Kulika a blank look for a moment, then said, 'Explain.'

So Kulika told Dr Ross what Bartholomew had told her last night: about Bella's experiment with the zombies, and how instead of having one normal failed-turning zombie, they now had seven super zombies who were apparently indestructible.

'How is that possible?' Dr Ross asked when Kulika was finished.

'I don't know. Bartholomew's been testing them and... Well, I took his word for it.'

'I suppose it makes sense,' the doctor said thoughtfully. 'After all, when Jahan Khalyed took the serum, it made him insatiably hungry for Silver blood. If it's putting the same hunger in the zombies... The resilience, though. That's new.

But not entirely, maybe,' she murmured, talking to herself now. 'After all, the formula makes most Silver burn up to nothing, and when Dr Jay bit the Silver, his victims did exactly that, so maybe there's some inheritance of the formula that passes to the carrier in the same way that... Hmm.'

'Dr Ross?'

'I want to see them,' she said, getting to her feet and smoothing down her skirts. 'If this is a side effect of the formula, then I need to know about it. It might help with the antidote. If I took a sample of their blood—'

'I'll get you one. Just book yourself on a flight—'

'The Baron sent me in his plane. It's waiting for me at Charleston.'

'Then wait here, and I'll be back in an hour.'

The doctor gave Kulika a level look.

'You want to go back to the mansion, don't you?' Kulika asked hopelessly.

'Yes.'

'But you know how dangerous he is. I'm already stuck here. I don't want you to get stuck too. The baron needs you.'

'He needs *you*,' the doctor said.

'Then don't risk him losing both of us at once.'

'We're going to lose *him* if I can't get to the bottom of this antidote. Please, Kulika,' she said, looking pleadingly into her eyes. 'If there's a chance that I could learn something from them, I have to go, whatever the risk. You understand that, don't you?'

Kulika did, all too well. It was the reason she'd walked back into the mansion in the first place, even though she'd known in her heart of hearts that she would never freely walk out again.

'Have you got all the other vials?' Kulika said, eyeing the doctor's bench carefully.

'Yes,' Dr Ross said, stowing the padded bag inside her doctor's bag. 'And don't worry: I've got all the waste products in here too. I'm not leaving anything behind for BioSilver to find.'

'Good,' said Kulika. 'Then let's go.'

'Thank you,' the doctor started saying, but then Kulika's phone buzzed in her pocket, at the same time as the landline on Enzo's desk started chirping.

'Yeah?' Kulika said as she answered, surprised to see that the call was from Bayly's number. She wasn't sure what Bartholomew had done with her old crew-mate, but she was relieved to see the name pop up on her phone.

Except he wasn't the one making the call.

'They got out,' a panicked voice said on the other end of the line.

'What got… Penny? Is that you?'

'The zombies. The weird ones we took off Bella,' she said. 'They got out and…' Her voice was hushed and shrill at the same time, and in the background Kulika could hear screaming. A lot of screaming. Somewhere in the distance, a siren was blaring, then another, and another, and they couldn't be coming from the mansion because Kulika knew Bartholomew didn't have an alarm system, for fire or security or anything else.

'Where's Quick?' Kulika asked. 'Did she get to the airport all right?'

'They got a cab,' said Penny. 'They were already gone by the time we noticed the first zombie in the trees, then we saw the wine cellar was open, and…'

'But you caught the zombies, right?'

'One of them. The others…'

'You're Silver,' Kulika said impatiently. 'They're zombies. This isn't difficult. You can move a hundred times faster than them.'

'Not *all* of them,' Penny insisted. 'There's… They just… We're not supposed to go down there,' she trailed off hopelessly. 'And the things that got out, they're not *normal*.'

'Where's Bartholomew?'

'Still sailing. That's why we're calling you.'

Kulika locked eyes with Dr Ross for a moment. It was clear from the doctor's expression that she could hear everything that was happening on the other end of the line.

The doctor said, 'We're coming.'

When Kulika screeched Bartholomew's sports car to a halt on the driveway outside the mansion, Penny was already waiting.

'They were down in the wine cellar,' she said, leading the way to the kitchen at the back of the mansion. 'Monty told us to chain them up, and then the cap— the Primus came in and was… I don't know.'

'What were the sirens?' Kulika asked.

'They were in the block. There was a fire.'

'Another one?'

'It's fine. It's out now, and anyway: one disaster at a time, right? It's down here,' Penny said, crossing the kitchen to the wine cellar's door.

'I know,' Kulika replied.

Bartholomew had taken her down into the unnatural cold of that cellar to see Cara Alton's body. That was before he'd sent it off to be displayed for the creepy jogger who'd taken her photos. She wouldn't soon forget the atmosphere of the place, or the smell. It was worse now, though: thick and bloody and sweet to the point that it smelled rancid.

'I recognise that smell,' Dr Ross said, hesitating at the top of the brick stairs as Penny held the door open for them.

'Blood?' Kulika asked.

'Dead things,' the doctor said.

'How many were down here?' Kulika asked Penny.

'All of them. All seven.'

'How many got out?'

'At least two,' Penny said. 'We saw them running across the lawn.'

'You haven't gone down to check?' Kulika asked, angrily pointing at the cellar. 'Don't you think maybe that should have been the first thing you did?'

'We didn't think— That is, with what the Primus was keeping down there…'

'Where's everyone else?' Dr Ross asked.

'Over at the block, or out searching. Monty's organising them. But I don't think you understand,' Penny said, turning back to Kulika. 'There's something *else* down there.'

'What?'

But Penny just shook her head, looking like she was genuinely scared. That didn't add up. It was enough to hurry Kulika's steps down into the cellar, with Dr Ross hot on her heels.

There was blood. That was the first thing Kulika noticed; it would have been hard to miss. It started in a pool at the foot of the stairs, then spattered up the walls and the stone plinth in the centre of the room and ran in tacky streams along the walls. There was so much of it that it took Kulika a while to see what she was actually looking at.

'Christ alive,' the doctor muttered, standing on the bottom step beside Kulika as they both stared down into the pool beneath them.

It was moving.

When Kulika adjusted her perception with that in mind, she finally saw that the pool wasn't as shallow as it had first appeared. In fact it was nearly half a foot deep, filling the part of the uneven cellar floor that sloped down towards the base of the stairwell.

And there were… *things* in it.

'I count three skulls,' the doctor whispered.

'Zombies?' Kulika asked her.

'That would be my guess. If they were Silver, they would be healing, and if they were human—'

'They'd be dead.'

'Right.'

But whatever they were, they were definitely not dead, or at least not inanimate. Pieces of what had once been people bobbed and dipped in the puddle of gore, moving in a fluid way that seemed impossible for such dissected things.

'Do you want to take your blood samples from that?' Kulika asked, pointing towards the writhing pool, but then her attention was caught by a noise on the other side of the cellar. 'Wait here,' she said to the doctor, then she leapt up onto the plinth to get clear of the blood pooling on the floor.

Which would have been an excellent idea, had the plinth still been sealed. Unfortunately, the lid was now lying smashed on the floor, hidden from view from the doorway by the plinth itself. Instead of landing neatly out of the blood, Kulika stumbled into the open casket and ended up on her knees inside it. There was a dark, viscous fluid smeared around the inner walls. When Kulika got to her feet, it was all over her hands, too.

It smelled familiar.

'Are you all right?' the doctor asked.

Then Kulika heard the noise again: a gravelly rasp, like the scraping of nail on stone. She had to peer around the corner of the alcove where Cara Alton's body had been before she could identify its source.

'Bayly?' Kulika said.

Like the puddle at the bottom of the stairs, at first she couldn't put together the objects in the alcove and form them into a figure. Eventually she realised that this was because there were two figures in the alcove, both Enzo and Bayly, curled together and bloodied. Neither of them was moving.

'Shit,' she muttered, jumping down from the plinth to the alcove.

Bayly was in pieces, quite literally. There were chunks of flesh missing from his calves, his upper arms, his stomach, and parts of him had been entirely removed: a finger, a toe, a knee cap. Worse, he wasn't healing, because the only blood he had left was what had been smeared over his skin. Wrapped in Bayly's arms, Enzo had been drained too, but not mutilated. From the way Bayly was curled around him, it looked as though Bayly had used his own body to shield Enzo from harm.

The gesture made the part of Kulika that missed Quick ache.

'Doctor, get over here please,' she said. 'I need your help.'

There was a gentle *thud* as Dr Ross leapt over the puddle of zombies, then she was standing at Kulika's side, her fingers pressing gently against Bayly's wrist to feel for a pulse.

'God, is this what Bartholomew does to his prisoners? This is torture.'

'Maybe,' Kulika said, 'but I don't think this was Bartholomew.'

'He's shut down,' the doctor said as she released Bayly's wrist. 'We're going to need to get him into a blood bath.'

'And the other?'

The doctor felt Enzo's wrist, then declared, 'Not so bad, but we may as well put them in together. Assuming, that is…?'

'This one silvered for this one,' Kulika said, pointing between the two men. 'They're together.'

'Then they'll heal better if we keep them that way. Help me get them upstairs.'

Kulika held up her hands, showing the black goo to the doctor. 'I don't want to touch them with this,' she said.

'What *is* that?'

Now that she'd had a moment to think about it, and now that she'd seen the state of Bayly, Kulika had a pretty good idea. She recognised the strange sheen of it, and she could follow its trail to the outside corner of the cellar, where bricks had been pried up from the ground to form the entrance to a tunnel leading out.

Well, she supposed, they hadn't called him *Digs* for nothing. Bayly's ex had drunk enough Silver blood to put him back in action, and now he was loose.

5

QUICK WAS THOUGHTFUL and quiet on the drive as she watched the trees whipping by along the roadside.

First the cab was dropping her and Evita at the airport, then it would carry on into Charleston proper to take Xiaoyu home. It turned out that she was a local, despite her accent, the answer to yet another question Quick had never bothered to ask. Somehow, home addresses hadn't seemed like vital information when they'd been down in the blood cellar. Now, thinking of all the people they'd left behind there, and all the missing persons who'd disappeared into that mansion, Quick wondered if they should have been. She could have made lists. She might not have been able to save everyone, but she could at least have brought some answers back for the families who'd been searching for them.

It was too late now. Quick was leaving with nothing but a bruised heart and the guilt of having done so little when she'd had the chance.

The radio was on, full of reports about the discovery of Cara Alton's body and the strange silver marks on her skin. The passengers all exchanged a few looks at that, but they couldn't talk about it, not with the cab driver listening.

Instead, Xiaoyu and Evita chatted a little, getting to know each other. Quick didn't have much to say. She couldn't help but feel that she was making a mistake by leaving, abandoning all those people in the blood cellar to their fate, however shitty they'd been to Xiaoyu.

Quick was under no illusions about the fact that she'd sacrificed them all for the chance to get Evita and Xiaoyu out. That was something, though, wasn't it? Only…

Kulika.

'What I said about seductive hotties and cults,' Evita said quietly, reading Quick's mind as usual. 'I wasn't talking about you, you know. You might not understand Kulika's motives, but at least you can trust they were good ones.' Then she added lightly, 'You know she actually loves you.'

That shocked a laugh out of Quick. 'I don't know what gave you that idea.'

'She showed me her silver,' Evita said, fiddling with the strap of her bag. 'When she rescued me from that bastard box. I got all twitchy about her, and needed a reason to trust her, so she showed me her silver. It's all in the grey of her eyes.'

'I know,' Quick said, not following.

'So she's silvered for you,' Evita said, implying by her tone that she expected Quick to understand more from that statement than she in fact did.

Quick looked at her blankly. 'Okay,' she said. 'I'm still not following you.'

'Oh,' said Xiaoyu. 'Well, that explains a lot.' Then she leaned forward to look past Evita at Quick. 'You could have just told me,' she added. 'I wouldn't have told anyone.'

'Told anyone *what*?' Quick asked, looking between the two of them, bemused.

'Those silver marks that were on the back of your neck,'

Xiaoyu whispered. 'Kulika healed you, right? It was a handprint, like Cara Alton' – Xiaoyu mouthed the name – 'had on her stomach.'

'It was a—' Quick cut herself off, because suddenly she couldn't find the words.

The silver marks at her neck, from where Kulika bit her.

The silver at the roots of her hair, from where Kulika had held her as she'd saved her life.

The distant look in Kulika's eyes as she'd said goodbye last night, before Quick had even realised it *was* goodbye, a look that had burned into Quick's brain, and that she now recognised as barely-suppressed pain.

'It means she loves you,' Evita whispered. 'It's what gives her the power to heal you. Christ, Quick, are you telling me you didn't *know*?'

'No!' Quick yelled, loudly enough that the taxi pulled over in a scream of brakes.

'Hey,' said the driver solicitously, turning in her seat. 'You all right, there, baby girl? Damn near jumped out of my skin up here.'

'Sorry,' Quick said. 'I'm sorry, I didn't… Sorry. Just…'

'She's had a bit of a shock,' Evita explained.

Quick dropped her head between her knees. She couldn't breathe. She didn't actually *need* to breathe anymore, but it was a habit that was proving difficult for her body to break.

'Oh, god,' she said.

'Did she not tell you what it means?' Evita asked. 'It means—'

'Just give me a minute,' Quick said. Her brain felt like it had frozen.

'Do you want to go back?' Evita asked gently.

'Fuck, no,' said Xiaoyu. 'I'm not going back there. Not ever. Not if you paid me a million dollars.'

'Er,' Evita said uncertainly. 'You might want to drop that number a little. A lot, actually.'

'What's this, now?' the driver asked wonderingly. 'They making a zombie movie out here?'

Quick lifted her head and leaned over Evita into the centre of the back seat so she could see out of the windscreen. There were three figures walking down the centre of the road. Shambling, really. Quick recognised the one out in front.

Evita leaned forward. 'Is that—'

'That's one of the guys we brought back with Bella,' Quick said, her stomach dropping. 'The ones she turned zombie when she was out on her little frolic.'

'The ones who—'

'Don't die. And we've got two humans here. Back up,' Quick said urgently, but their driver hadn't grasped the urgency of the situation. 'Back up!' she yelled again, but by now it was too late: the zombies had already reached the car, and before Quick could even undo her seatbelt, Bella's zombie had smashed his fist through the driver's side window and was dragging their driver out by her throat. Quick grabbed her and tried to pull her back inside while she made a terrible noise somewhere between a scream and a gurgle, but the zombie pulled harder. Their driver was out on the road before either Evita or Xiaoyu had moved.

For a moment, there was no sound at all except the gentle purr of the engine as the car rolled forward, then their driver was back on her feet again, eyes bleeding and teeth bared, reaching back through the broken window towards Xiaoyu.

In the space of a second or less, their driver had turned into a zombie.

'Shit!' Quick yelled, then she scrambled over the centre console at Silver speed, slipping into the driver's seat. Their erstwhile driver reared back, giving Quick just enough time to slam her foot on the accelerator and jerk the car forward down the road.

'Christ,' Xiaoyu said from the back seat. 'What the fuck was that?'

'You saw that, right?' Quick asked incredulously.

'I saw a zombie bite a human and turn her into one of their own,' Xiaoyu said as the car sped along. 'But that's just science fiction. Real zombies don't do that.'

'They do now,' Evita said.

'Bella gave hers some kind of potion,' Quick said, taking the next turn fast enough that two of the car's wheels lifted off the road for a heart-thudding moment before slamming back down again. 'Maybe it didn't just make them indestructible. Maybe it made them infectious, too.'

'Shit,' said Xiaoyu. 'But if they infect any human they bite, and then that human infects any human *they* bite…'

'It's like the world's shittest game of dominoes,' said Quick.

'And they're all after me,' Xiaoyu said darkly.

It was a reasonable assumption: she was the only human left in the car.

Quick took another corner that sent the sunshine streaming in through the broken driver's side window, and before she'd even noticed the danger, her left arm was on fire.

'Shit!' she screamed, pulling her arm close against her body to try to extinguish the flames. Her foot slammed on the brake, but the pedal wasn't quite where she'd expected it to be, and she only succeeded in slowing the car briefly before her foot slid off. By that point, Evita had reached over the back of Quick's chair and thrown her jacket over the steering wheel, effectively quenching the fire.

'Shit,' Quick winced. The flames were gone, but the burning pain they'd left in their wake was enough to have Quick blinking back tears.

'Pull over,' Evita ordered. 'I'll drive.'

'No,' Quick insisted. 'I'm fine. Just…' She fumbled her feet around on the foot pedals until she found the accelerator, then they were off again. 'I'm fine.'

'I'm not,' Xiaoyu muttered. 'Holy shit.'

'I thought the zombies were locked up,' Evita said.

'So did I,' Quick replied, accidentally putting the car into park when she tried to change down for the next corner. She fumbled with the gearstick. 'Shit,' she said. 'I keep forgetting this is an automatic.'

'So pull over and let me drive,' Evita said again.

'I said I'm fine,' Quick bit out. 'Anyway, I can't get out of the car to change seats. I'll burn to death out there.'

'We don't have to get out of the car,' Evita argued.

'She said she's fine,' Xiaoyu said, with unexpected gentleness. That was enough to calm Quick down a little, then everything got easier.

Eventually, Quick got the car back into drive, but she still kept thumping an invisible clutch with her foot as they sped along, trying to change gears. She didn't have anywhere to put her left foot and she kept hitting the brake and the accelerator at the same time. She risked taking a split-second to peek into the footwell so she could work out where the pedals actually were, and in that split-second everything went wrong again.

'Quick!' Evita yelled from the back seat, then something hit the front of the car. Quick slammed on the brakes, but Xiaoyu was yelling, 'Drive! Drive!'

The windscreen cleared with a thump that sent something flying off to one side of the road. It was a body, Quick realised. She'd hit someone. Oh god, she'd hit someone.

Then she saw exactly what she'd hit, and she had to blink to make sure she wasn't seeing things.

'Drive!' Xiaoyu yelled again.

On the grass verge by the side of the road, a woman was getting to her feet. She wasn't alone, though. Melting out of the darkness between the tress, there were more of them. A *lot* more of them. There were people in every state of dress and undress, some of them scratched and muddy, all of them bloodstained, and some so badly injured that it made Quick squeamish even to look at them. She couldn't imagine how they were still walking on legs that looked twisted and broken, and with gashes across their torsos that spilled out things that really should have stayed tucked away inside. Their injuries were as varied as they were numerous, but they shared one common wound: every single one of them was crying bloody tears from red eyes.

They were crowding towards the car now, blocking the road right across its width. Quick worked the gearstick clumsily, and the car sped back the way they'd come, in reverse.

'Shit shit shit,' she muttered.

'Turn around!' Evita yelled.

'Don't turn around!' Xiaoyu yelled. 'They must have come from the mansion. We can't go back there!'

'Well we can't go through here either!' Evita yelled.

In the end, their argument was academic. Unseen by any of them, a large pick-up truck had barrelled around the bend behind them going twice the speed limit – doubtless trying to escape the zombies – and slammed right into the back of their car, pitching it off the side of the road and into the trees. The two vehicles rolled down the highway embankment together for twenty yards or so before finally coming to rest in a steaming, mangled pile of metal in a stream at the bottom of a scar they'd carved through the forest.

Up on the road, a hundred broken people turned in the direction of the crash. Following the vehicles, or seeing the smoke, or attracted by the noise, or maybe even scenting blood – who knows what goes on in a zombie's head? – they ran.

6

KULIKA HAD WASHED her hands thoroughly and was now helping the doctor to carry the unwieldy, curled-up bodies of Bayly and Enzo up the staircase to the bathroom on the first floor. She'd tried calling Bartholomew before they'd moved the pair, but she kept getting an error message. Wherever he'd taken the ship for his test sail, apparently it was out of network range.

'Why was Digs even in the cellar?' Kulika asked Penny irritably. 'I left him on Bayly's boat for a reason. He was locked up tight.'

'I don't know,' Penny replied.

'Did he get loose and follow us here, or did someone put him down there?'

'I don't know,' Penny said again.

'Well you must know *something*.' Kulika was quickly getting exasperated. Penny was the most senior Silver left at the mansion, they couldn't get hold of anyone else on their phones, and she knew absolutely nothing of use.

'Where are you holding the one zombie you caught?' Kulika asked, not expecting a helpful reply.

'In the back of the truck parked on the driveway,' Penny

said. 'We locked it in. We couldn't think of anywhere else to put it.'

'We're going to need blood,' the doctor said. 'A lot of blood. Do you have bottles?'

'No,' Penny said.

Dr Ross gave her a quizzical look.

'Bartholomew makes them all drink from the vein,' Kulika explained. 'No bottles or bags at the mansion.'

'What?' the doctor asked. 'Why?'

'It's a pirate thing,' Kulika said. 'A stupid pirate thing,' she added.

Kulika hated the blood cellar. She hated taking blood from people who didn't want to give it, and she hated that Bartholomew had made it so that the crew had no other choice. She'd do it, though. To save her crew, she would do anything that was necessary, but she could at least minimise the harm caused by the process.

She turned to Penny. 'Bleed some donors from the blood cellar. You're going to need a lot of them, because I only want you to take a little from each, and only from the ones who can spare it. Be careful, too; I'm going to be checking on them later to make sure you were.'

She was expecting Penny to snap to it, but the redhead was still trailing along behind them. They were on the landing now, shuffling along the corridor to the bathroom, and there wasn't enough space for Penny to walk alongside.

'What?' Kulika asked.

'It's just… When the Primus comes home and sees that Bayly and Enzo are out of the wine cellar—'

'Bartholomew can give whatever orders he wants when he's here. When he's not, I'm in charge. Is that understood?'

'Yes, okay.'

'Get the blood and get back here, and I want a report from

the search parties. Send someone to find them. And get Monty up here, too. We need to find Digs, and we need to do it now.'

Penny hurried off with another murmured, 'Yes, okay,' leaving Kulika and the doctor to manoeuvre Bayly and Enzo through the bathroom doorway and gently lower them into the clawfoot bathtub.

'They don't seem very organised,' Dr Ross commented.

'They're not.' Kulika sighed, pushing her hair back from her face. 'They can't look after themselves. I did try to warn Bartholomew. The problem is, they're all so young.'

'The problem is,' the doctor countered, 'what he's doing here is utter madness. It's dangerous, it's uncontrolled, and it's only going to get worse. Tell me you realise that.'

'I'm trying my best to manage it,' Kulika said helplessly. 'That's all I can do.'

'You could leave.'

'No,' Kulika said. 'Not without hurting Quick. At least she's safe now.'

'With what he has planned, I don't think any of us are *safe*,' the doctor muttered, then she turned her attention to the men lying in the bathtub. She sighed. 'Right. Let's get them as clean as we can before we soak them. Help me turn them?'

Thank god that the bath had a shower attachment, because without that there would have been no chance of rinsing the dirty blood from the bodies of the entwined men. As the filth washed away, the true extent of Bayly's injuries became clear. Just as he had done back on the boat at the marina, Digs had bitten chunks out of Bayly's flesh. Kulika could see the teeth marks.

'Tell me again about Digs,' Dr Ross asked as she leaned in closer to examine one of the bites.

'He was a pirate who got locked in a box for more than three hundred years,' said Kulika. 'That's about all I know.'

'Hmm.' The doctor muttered a sentence or two to herself, but Kulika couldn't make out the words. Then she said, 'This isn't the first time a Silver has been locked in a box for decades, centuries even. It's normal for them to come out thirsty, but they don't usually start eating chunks of other Silvers' flesh.'

'They do often lose their minds, though,' Kulika pointed out.

'True. Maybe that's all this is. I certainly *hope* that's all it is.'

'Why? What are you thinking?'

Dr Ross pursed her lips for a moment, as though she was considering whether or not to voice her suspicions at all.

Kulika raised her eyebrows.

'It's just a theory,' the doctor said. 'Not even a theory, just a thought, really. I don't want to set hares running if it's all in my head, but I think there is a possibility that he's been contaminated by the zombies in the wine cellar. Either way, we'd better find him, and quickly.'

'Contaminated how?' Penny said, returning to the room.

'Long story,' said Kulika.

'Contaminated *how*?' Penny insisted. 'I touched those zombies. We all did. Are we going to get contaminated too and turn into… that?'

'No, it's…' Dr Ross said. 'It's complicated.' The doctor looked down at the floor for a moment, arranging her thoughts before launching into the explanation. 'About twenty years ago – longer, even – there was a doctor who worked for Solomon's research department in Oxford, a man named Dr Jahan Khalyed. He was trying to develop a formula that would prevent the Silver from needing to drink human blood. A philanthropic endeavour. Laudable, I think you'll agree.'

'Stupid,' Kulika said. 'Because it went wrong.'

Dr Ross sighed and said, 'Yes, it went wrong. After a little self-experimentation, he started biting other Silver in a semi-conscious state that he couldn't control. Every time he bit another Silver, some part of the formula transferred to them through his saliva, and they just… burned up. In flames. The same way that the unadulterated formula kills most Silver. Eventually, we had to imprison Jahan, for his own safety and the safety of everyone else.'

'But?' Penny asked.

'But someone—'

'Jack Valentine,' Kulika supplied helpfully. Perhaps spitefully.

'Yes,' Dr Ross grudgingly agreed, 'Jack broke into his cell and stole some of Jahan's blood, intending to use it to kill the Primus, Solomon.'

'Would that have worked?' Penny asked, wide-eyed.

'Probably,' Dr Ross said. 'Yes. On its own, the formula Jahan created is only strong enough to kill younger or weaker Silver.'

'But it didn't kill Jahan?' Penny asked, confused.

'No. He had a kind of immunity to it. When combined with Jahan's blood, the formula… mutates, is the easiest way to explain it. Instead of burning through his body like it would with most other Silver, the formula bonded to Jahan's blood to become an incredibly potent poison. That's what Jack hoped to use to kill the Primus.'

'But this Jack didn't succeed, right?' Penny asked.

'No, of course not,' Kulika said. 'She's an idiot.'

'Yes,' Dr Ross agreed again. 'Sometimes she is. Jack managed to smash the vial of Jahan's infected blood, and accidentally infected herself with a tiny drop of the poison, which is now killing her slowly. I've been working on an antidote, but I can't make one without replicating the original poison, and I can't do that without Jahan's blood. But, due to a very unfortunate series of circumstances that I won't go into right now, there's none left. I came here to take a blood sample from Evita – Jahan's last living descendant – in the hopes that I might be able to combine it with the original formula Jahan took in order to recreate the poison and manufacture an antidote to it. Unsuccessfully, unfortunately.'

This was all old news to Kulika.

'Can we get back to the contamination theory, please?' she asked impatiently.

The doctor sucked her bottom lip anxiously for a moment, then said, 'The thing is, I have a concern.'

'Which is?' Kulika asked.

Dr Ross fiddled with the coffee stirrer that was still valiantly keeping her hair in place, then said, 'When Jahan turned into… whatever he turned into, he stopped craving human blood at all. That was his intention, of course, but there were unintended side effects. Instead of human blood, he started biting the Silver.'

'Like Digs bit Bayly,' Kulika said in a hollow voice, looking at Bayly's mutilated body in the bath tub.

'Precisely. This is my concern: *if* Evita's blood has indeed inherited the same traits that made Jahan immune to the formula, and *if* Digs drank enough of it while they were in that box together for it to affect his own immunity, and *if* he then drank enough blood from the zombies in the cellar – who had ingested the formula – that he has himself effectively ingested the formula, *then* it is possible that he has become the same kind of creature that Jahan once became.'

'You mean, someone who's immune to the formula?' Penny asked.

'I mean a zombie vampire who incinerates everyone he bites.'

Shit.

Kulika was silent for a moment, assessing all the weapons at her disposal in the mansion and finding them wanting against a mutated Silver who could kill them with a single bite.

'But we know that Evita's blood isn't the same as Jahan's was,' Kulika said. 'Your tests proved that. And Bayly didn't actually die when Digs bit him. Didn't you say the Silver that Jahan bit went up in smoke?'

'Yes, I did,' the doctor said. 'And those are about the only things that are giving me hope right now, but it's not black and white. With all these volatile substances combining and interacting, there's a possibility that Digs has become something else entirely.'

'I don't know,' Kulika said. 'It all sounds a little far-fetched to me. Seems more likely he just lost his marbles.'

'Well, I certainly hope you're right, because if that's true, then we can kill him with this,' the doctor said, patting the cool bag that held the vials of her formula. She was wearing it across her body, unwilling to let it out of her sight.

'And if we can't?' Penny asked.

'Then we box him, again,' said Kulika. 'This time for good. Where's the blood for Bayly?' Kulika demanded, only now noticing that Penny had arrived empty-handed. 'Where's Monty?'

'Still out searching,' said Penny. 'I've sent some of the newbies out looking, but we can't find him yet, or Brandon.'

'What about the older crew members?' Kulika asked. 'The

Silver who were here at the Convocation, and who were here this morning at the river? Why is the mansion suddenly empty?'

'They went with Bartholomew on the ship, or off site to prepare for tonight. And it gets worse.'

Kulika groaned. 'We've got three missing zombies and a bloodthirsty, centuries old, possibly cannibalistic Silver on the loose, plus half the crew is missing. How does that get worse?'

'The blood cellar's empty,' Penny whispered.

'What?' Kulika yelled. 'There were a hundred people down there!'

'More,' Penny admitted. 'We were busy setting things up for this evening, and then—'

'You mean you were busy partying.' Kulika gave Penny a stern look, and the woman crumpled.

'They must have got out while we were putting out the fire, then we found out the door to the wine cellar was open, and everything got busy,' Penny said desperately, her voice rising in pitch as she went on. 'And I tried to find the others, but I'm not the best tracker, which is why I'm still here, and honestly? I'm scared. I'm nervous about this evening, I feel sick ever since Bartholomew left the property this morning, like I can't even think straight, and now that the rest of the crew has gone off and left me here—'

'Okay,' said Dr Ross, gathering Penny's hands into her own. 'Okay, deep breaths.'

Penny was going to pieces. Less literally than Bayly, true, but she was going to be about as much use as he was right now.

'Can you handle this?' Kulika asked Dr Ross quietly.

She nodded back. 'Go find Digs and the others. We can't do much for these two without blood,' she added, glancing towards the bathtub. 'I've got a few of bottles of my own in my bag downstairs. Take what you need, and we'll use the rest to do what we can here.'

'All right.' Kulika was already heading for the stairs. 'And if you still want samples from those zombies,' she called back to the doctor, 'then get them now. I'm calling the baron, and you're going to the airport as soon as I get back.'

At least that would put Dr Ross out of harm's way, and give them a chance of salvaging an antidote from what had otherwise been a complete failure of a mission. Kulika tallied it up in her head as she ran to the car.

Antidote: nope.

Quick: gone.

Kulika: bound to Bartholomew.

Collateral damage: three indestructible zombies, one blood-starved vampire, and over a hundred formerly-captive humans on the loose together in the woods.

What a mess.

If only the newly-turned Silver that comprised the rest of her crew weren't so completely useless. Kulika sighed. If she wanted this done properly, she was going to have to do it her own damn self.

Kulika made the call on speaker as she drove, which would have been easier if her phone hadn't been sliding around on the passenger seat while she cornered hard on her frantic drive away from the mansion.

'Kulika,' he said on the second ring. 'Tell me you've got the antidote.'

'I haven't,' she yelled, hoping the baron would still hear her, despite the fact that her phone had slid down somewhere beside the centre console on the last turn. From his groan, she guessed he had.

'It gets worse,' she yelled. 'I'm sorry, but it didn't work. And things have gone a bit… wrong here. Look, I'm sending Dr Ross back to you, and quickly. She can tell you about it, but I'm…'

'You're what?' the baron's voice asked through the muffled speaker.

'I've been delayed.'

'Indefinitely?'

'Yes.'

He groaned again. 'I'm so sorry, Kulika. I didn't mean to do this to you. I didn't mean to lose you, as well as—'

The call cut out then, which was just as well. Kulika was too focused to manage a sentimental goodbye, and that's what Baron Drake would have wanted. It was better this way. A hundred years of service, abruptly ended. And when Jack didn't get her antidote and met her inevitable end, that would be nearly five hundred years of his life, abruptly ended with hers.

It didn't seem fair, but then life wasn't fair. Kulika had never been under any illusions that it was otherwise. All she could hope was that she could gather everyone back to the mansion in time to salvage something from this mess.

She'd already searched the woods surrounding the property and found them empty. There were trails marking the low branches of trees and trampled through the underbrush, but it was difficult to tell whether they'd been made by zombies or humans or Silver; the tracks were muddled, and there was so much activity, without any clear trail to follow. One thing had been clear, though: all the tracks headed away from the river, in the direction of the highway. Figuring that she'd catch up quicker by car than she would on foot with only the single bottle of blood she'd nabbed from the doctor's bag to speed her along, she'd hopped back into Bartholomew's sports car and hit the road.

She rolled all the windows down, letting the air pour through the car as she drove, and breathed. There were so many scents that it was difficult to discern what was going on, so she concentrated on scanning the sides of the road instead, looking for dropped items, footprints or other marks of passage to point the way. She hadn't been driving long when something caught her attention. If it hadn't been for the smell, Kulika might have driven straight past.

Fear.

But not only that. Underneath the sharp, animal scent of terror, there was another aroma: fruit ripening in the sunshine, crisp water bursting out of hillside springs, beds of moss covered in sheets of autumn leaves.

Quick.

But she should be at the airport by now. Hell, she should be in the air, flying back home with her best friend at her side, safe from everything that was happening in this godforsaken corner of South Carolina, and everything that was about to happen.

That scent, though. Kulika would never mistake it for another.

She careened across the road and braked Bartholomew's fancy car so sharply that she could smell burning. Then she threw herself from the driver's seat, leaving the door hanging open behind her, and pelted down the embankment, following the dark path that had been gouged out of it by the descent of two vehicles going far too fast.

The pick-up truck had come to rest first, its bumper wedged tightly between two trees. The driver's side door was open, the window smashed, and blood was smeared over the broken glass that littered the seat. The engine was still running, but from the way it was sputtering, it didn't sound like it would be for long.

The cab had tumbled further down the embankment, barrelling through the gaps between the trees, and sometimes pushing them over with the force of its passage. It must have rolled at some point, because it was now lying on its roof in the leaf litter, but it took Kulika a moment to notice that. The first thing she noticed wasn't the car at all, it was the ring of zombies surrounding it.

How was it possible that there were so many of them? She'd come out here looking for three, but there must have been fifty times that number surrounding the car. The crowd was stacked five people deep in places, which begged the question: what exactly had Bartholomew been doing with the zombies his crew had created over the past six months? Bayly had told her they'd fed them to the gators, but the plentiful evidence standing in front of Kulika right now suggested that had been a lie. All these extra zombies had to be from previous failed attempts to make Silver. Where else could they have come from?

They didn't seem like normal zombies, though. None of them was making any attempt to move forwards. Instead, they were holding vigil at a distance of about ten feet from the car, leaving a perfect circle of empty space around the crashed vehicle. The zombies' feet were still, but everything else about them was in constant motion. They moved as a group, knees gently flexing and shoulders swaying in uncanny unison to give the eerie impression of waves rippling through the collective.

Kulika didn't stop to admire the effect, she just pushed her way through the zombies gathered at the closest edge of the ring. They parted for her like the Red Sea.

'Quick?' she called desperately, kneeling down beside the car. This close, she could see the blood spattered across the paintwork. There was a lot of it, enough that she started to panic.

But then a small voice whispered, 'Kulika?' from inside the car.

Kulika ducked her head to find Quick crouching in the front of the car, with Evita and Xiaoyu huddled in the back.

'Are you okay?' Kulika asked, scanning them all for any sign of serious injury.

They looked a bit bashed up, but beyond the odd scrape they'd all escaped the crash remarkably unharmed. Quick and Evita must have protected the human between them, because otherwise there was no way she would have survived a wreck that bad, not without a miracle.

But if they were all okay, why were they still huddling in the car?

'They must have followed us down here,' Quick whispered. Her fearful eyes were scanning the zombies behind Kulika.

'Then just shove them out of the way,' Kulika said, bewildered. 'They're just zombies. They won't hurt you.'

'But the sunshine will,' Quick said. 'I can't find my parasol.'

'And they'll definitely hurt me,' said Xiaoyu.

Then Quick dropped the bomb.

'They're contagious,' she said. 'One drop of their blood, and we'll lose Xiaoyu.'

7

IN THE MOMENTS following the crash, Quick was disorientated.

When the car had first shot off the road, she'd acted on instinct. She'd unclipped her belt as they careened down the embankment, then she'd forced her way into the back seat at speed as she'd felt the car start to roll, using the last reserves of blood in her body to get to Xiaoyu fast. Evita had the same idea, because she'd already wrapped herself around Xiaoyu, the only one amongst them who was likely to suffer permanent injury from a car crash. With the car flipping like it was, there was no way to get her out.

'Hold on!' Evita yelled.

Quick clung onto Evita, using their bodies to form a cage around Xiaoyu, then there had been an almighty crash. Everything went still.

When Quick blinked her vision clear of blood and smoke, they were all upside down. Unlike the others, Quick wasn't wearing a seatbelt, so when she relaxed her grip on Evita, she fell headfirst into the roof of the car. From her newly-prone position, she could see what the others couldn't: a little way up the embankment, the pick-up truck had stopped between two trees. The driver's side door was smeared with blood, and the glass in it had shattered. At first she thought the driver might have been thrown out of the side window, but then the door popped open and a middle-aged man stumbled unsteadily out. He was propping himself up on the body of the pick-up as he walked towards the cab, one hand trailing along the top of the door.

What happened next took only a fraction of a second. The man's hand slid into a tiny smear of blood on the top of the car door and then, as Quick watched in horror, he changed. First, he froze. Next, his eyes became bloodshot and he started crying bloody tears, as though the blood vessels had swollen and broken and were now streaming their contents down his face. Then there was the way he moved. When he'd first got out of the car, he'd been walking in a jerky, stumbling shuffle that suggested he was compensating for an injury. Now, his movements became rhythmic and fluid and horribly familiar.

All from touching one tiny drop of blood.

'Shit,' Quick muttered.

'We need to get out of here,' said Evita, working at her seatbelt. 'The petrol tank could blow.' Her belt sprung free and she joined Quick on the inverted roof, though she made the descent with more grace than Quick had managed herself. Then she started on Xiaoyu's belt.

'Mind the blood, Xiaoyu,' Quick said, slowly processing what she'd just seen. 'Don't even touch it.'

'But there's blood everywhere,' Evita said, stopping in the middle of ripping through Xiaoyu's seatbelt.

'Then don't touch anything.'

She quickly explained what she'd just seen happen to the pick-up truck driver, who was now standing in the trees just a short distance from their upturned car.

Evita gave her an incredulous look.

'I'm serious,' Quick said.

Evita's jacket was still stuck painfully to the raw skin on Quick's burned arm, wrapped around it in a mess of blood and pus. There was nothing Quick could do about that now. She'd only make it worse if she tried to remove it, but she wasn't healing either. She'd used the last of her reserves making sure Xiaoyu was safe from the crash. Thank god she hadn't infected her with any spatter in the process.

'And don't touch me, either,' Quick said. 'I can't tell how much of this blood is mine and how much came in through the window with the zombies.'

'Fuck,' said Xiaoyu.

'I'll move into the front,' Quick said, shifting along the roof in that direction. 'Then you'll have more space.'

It was awkward and claustrophobic, but Quick managed to wriggle out of the way and Evita got Xiaoyu down from her seat without too much trouble.

But the moment Xiaoyu hit the ground, everything went wrong again.

'Uh-oh,' she said quietly, looking out of the window.

Quick and Evita lay down to follow her gaze and saw that the pick-up truck driver was no longer alone. From their vantage point, Quick could only see up to their knees, but she was counting an awful lot of them, in every direction.

'Shit,' Evita muttered. 'Are they going to reach in here like they did on the road?'

'I don't know,' said Quick. She looked at the zombies again, but they weren't showing any signs of movement, they were just holding their positions in a ring around the car. 'The ones Bella turned in the garage acted like they were scared of us,' she said, trying to puzzle through it.

'That's not normal for zombies,' Xiaoyu commented.

'No, but they're not normal zombies,' said Quick.

'So,' said Evita. 'Options are: go out there or stay in here. If we go out there, Xiaoyu maybe turns into a zombie.'

'And I definitely catch on fire,' said Quick.

'But if we stay in here and the gas tank blows...' said Xiaoyu.

'Then the two of you go,' said Quick. 'Test it out first, Vee, to make sure they'll leave you alone. Then, if you've got enough energy for it, maybe you can run Xiaoyu out of here.'

'And leave you behind?' said Evita.

'That's the most slapdash plan I have ever heard,' said Xiaoyu. 'You're going to get me killed.'

'You got a better one?' Quick asked.

That's when they heard the voice outside. At first, Quick thought it was in her head, because surely she couldn't have conjured the one person she wanted to see more than anyone else in the world right now, but then the voice came again.

'Quick?' Kulika called. 'Are you in there?'

The zombies parted, a pair of black boots came into view, followed by a gloriously familiar face, with blonde hair falling into serious grey eyes. For the first time all morning, Quick felt like she could breathe again.

'Kulika,' she whispered.

Then Quick explained about the zombie contagion, and Kulika's face paled.

'From just a drop?' she asked.

'It looked that way from here.'

'Well, your car's fucked,' Kulika said, surveying the crumpled bonnet of the upside-down vehicle disdainfully. 'We'll have to take mine, but we're going to do this very carefully. Give me a minute to test it out.'

The zombies were still gathered thickly around the car,

though they'd stepped back a little from the spot where Kulika crouched. As she stood, they reared back further, and as she walked towards them, they parted like curtains to let her pass. When she came back the other way, they did the same, all while sticking as close to the car as Kulika's proximity would allow. They wouldn't get closer than about ten feet to Kulika, but neither would they give up on the potential prey that Xiaoyu represented. They were biding their time, waiting for their moment.

Calculating.

'You're right,' Xiaoyu said. 'Those are not normal zombies.'

'We can't leave them out here,' said Kulika. 'We're going to have to corral them back to the mansion.'

'With one working vehicle?' said Quick incredulously. 'Unless you have a lorry up there on the road, or one you can call, they're never going to fit.'

'They don't need to,' said Kulika, turning to Xiaoyu with a smile that made Quick worry. Rightly, as it turned out.

'We've got bait,' Kulika added.

Xiaoyu laughed and said, 'You're joking,' but she stopped abruptly when Kulika's expression didn't change.

She was deadly serious.

On the first run to the car, Kulika carried Xiaoyu while Evita trailed along behind, just in case. The horde of zombies followed. When Kulika returned a minute or so later without incident or escort, Quick started to believe this might actually work.

'They okay?' she asked.

'They'll be fine,' Kulika replied. She opened the driver's side door, crouched beside the upturned car and passed Quick a blanket. 'The zombies are surrounding the car, but they're keeping their distance while Evita's there.'

'Good.'

Which meant all Quick had to do now was engineer a sun shade for herself with one arm. The burn on the other was so severe she wasn't sure she could raise it at all.

'You're bleeding,' Kulika said, her brow furrowing as she spotted the bloodstained jacket wrapped around Quick's arm.

'Broken window,' she explained. 'I was driving. I caught on fire. You know, the usual.' She laughed, but the sound had a manic edge that gave her away.

'Can you manage the pain until we get back to the mansion?' Kulika asked, surveying her with concern. 'I've only got Bartholomew's tiny sports car, so you're going to be crammed in close, and I can't promise it'll be comfortable.'

She could manage the pain, right? It was just shooting, burning, prickling agony. And anyway, pain wasn't the real problem.

'I'm worried I got some of the zombies' blood on me,' Quick said. 'I don't want to transfer it to Xiaoyu. Our driver got pulled out through the window, and she turned, then I was up front, and...'

'Well, could you walk?' Kulika asked. 'If you keep alongside the car with the blanket held over your head like a parasol—'

'I'm not sure I can hold it up,' Quick admitted. 'With my burned arm, I mean.'

She couldn't bring herself to say aloud the thing she wanted most in that moment, so she tried to communicate it silently instead. Her eyes locked with Kulika's. For a brief flash, Quick could see the silver threading through the grey of Kulika's irises. Surely that meant she knew what Quick was asking for?

But Kulika didn't offer it. Instead, she said, 'I've got a

bottle of blood in the car.'

'I don't want blood,' Quick whispered.

'I can't…' Kulika said, but her gaze flicked down to Quick's lips in a way that suggested she could be persuaded.

Kulika loved her, Quick reminded herself. That was what Evita had said. The proof of it was right there in her eyes, and that made Quick braver than she might have been otherwise. She reached one hand out, spreading her fingers over the padded ceiling of the car next to the spot where Kulika's own hand was resting. Then slowly, not wanting to scare her away, Quick moved her little finger until it was resting against Kulika's.

That tiny point of contact felt like an anchor. It pulled them together, clicking their bodies into place like magnets. With a sense of wonderful inevitability, Kulika was suddenly in the car beside her, her fingers sliding into Quick's hair, her lips just a breath away from Quick's own.

When the cool wave of Kulika's healing came this time, it came hard and fast, bursting across Quick's body from the spot where Kulika cradled the back of her head in her hand. So the silver mark would be hidden by her hair, Quick realised, but then there was no time for thinking. Kulika inhaled sharply, as though she was surfacing for air, and Quick found herself matching her breath without thinking. That was what undid her, finally. With that breath, Quick was surrounded by the fresh saltiness of Kulika's scent, like sunshine and sea air on bare skin, and she couldn't hold herself back any longer.

Thankfully, she didn't have to, because it was Kulika who closed the paper-thin gap between them. She kissed Quick hard and fiercely, as though she was searching for something she couldn't quite find. Quick was more than happy to let her keep looking a while, but she pulled away all too soon.

By that point, the two of them were sprawled across the upturned ceiling in the front half of the car, lying in blood and broken glass and all the detritus that used to be on the floor and in the side pockets of the car: pens, coins, receipts, wires. It was tangling in Quick's hair and poking into her back, but she couldn't bring herself to care because there was Kulika lying half on top of her, the tips of her platinum hair tickling Quick's cheek, and one of her legs resting between Quick's. If she just bent her knee a little, she'd pull up the hem of Quick's dress with it and then maybe—

'You're healed,' Kulika said.

Quick looked down at her arm, from which Evita's jacket had now slipped free. Kulika was right: the skin was unmarked underneath the dried blood that covered it. By the time Quick looked up again, Kulika had slipped away from Quick like a retreating tide, leaving only cold emptiness in her wake. She was fully out of the car now, standing in the disturbed dirt outside the door. It had happened in a blink. Had she really just used Silver speed in her desperation to get away from Quick?

'Come on,' Kulika said, without crouching down to meet Quick's eye. 'We should get back to the others. Throw the blanket over your head and let's go.'

She didn't bend down to help Quick out of the car; she didn't even wait for her to follow, she just turned and started walking back up the embankment, leaving Quick to follow on behind with her makeshift parasol, as though nothing had just happened between them.

As though Quick's world hadn't just been turned upside down, with a crash and a kiss.

The flotilla that trundled along the road towards the mansion would have been a strange sight to anyone who had passed it, but thankfully this corner of South Carolina remained quiet. The only vehicle on the road was Bartholomew's little silver sports car, crawling along at snail's pace, surrounded by a fat doughnut of zombies. The blood covering the car's hood spoke to the time it had taken Kulika to adjust to the zombies' speed, but they were perfectly in sync now. The creatures ran constantly in that fluid, sinuous motion of theirs, backwards or sideways or forwards, whichever orientation allowed them to keep their eyes on the car, and on Xiaoyu.

In the passenger side, Xiaoyu was crammed together with Evita in the awkward bucket seat. Quick jogged alongside the car on the driver's side next to Kulika's open window, holding the blanket over her head. Kulika was keeping her close as a precaution, she had said, so she could get to Quick immediately if there was an accident and she started burning again. Quick was working hard to make sure that didn't happen for Evita's and Xiaoyu's sakes, though personally she would have suffered any number of burns to be kissed like that again.

'Why are there so many of them?' Quick asked, looking around at the zombies. 'Have they just been hunting along the highway?'

'No,' said Xiaoyu quietly. 'I recognise some of them.'

'There was a breach at the blood cellar,' Kulika confirmed. 'They got out. They must have run into the ones who escaped from the wine cellar and…' She looked around at the zombies who were running alongside the car. 'This is what happened.'

Quick made an involuntary noise somewhere between a sob and a sigh, choking on the enormity of it. Looking around at the horde that followed them, she thought she recognised a face or two as well. They were close enough for her see where the whites of their eyes should have been, but with the gore that now dripped and smeared across their cheeks, and with the distortions their changed states brought to their expressions and mannerisms, it was hard to be certain that they were familiar. It wasn't Quick they were watching, either; they were all looking at Xiaoyu, who seemed certain enough for both of them. She had her face pressed against the passenger window, her fingers spread wide against the glass. She had known most of these people personally, Quick realised. She'd lived with them, and kept them safe, and done her best to put herself between them and whatever creatures came down the cellar hatch to prey on them. If seeing them like this was upsetting for Quick, she couldn't imagine what it was doing to Xiaoyu, particularly since she was now their target.

'We can't turn them back to how they were, can we?' Xiaoyu asked.

'No,' said Kulika. 'They're gone. And anyway, look at them: with injuries like that, most of them wouldn't make it even if you could.'

Unwillingly, Quick's eyes were drawn to the zombies that circled the car. She started cataloguing their injuries: broken limbs, gored throats, stomachs that gaped open in a way that should have been fatal, yet left them still walking. When she started looking for the wounds that should have cut the zombies down, she couldn't stop seeing them. After that, Quick pulled the blanket down lower and kept her eyes on the road, trying not to look at all.

They'd been running for a mile or two when she noticed that something was up with Kulika. She watched her for a while, trying to work out if it was something to do with their kiss, but then she saw that Kulika was peeking over and around the zombies, trying to get a look at the tree line beyond them as she drove.

'What are you looking for?' Quick asked her.

'Nothing,' Kulika replied, but there was something off in her voice. Although her tone was blasé, it didn't feel convincing.

That put Quick on edge, and had her looking in the same direction for the next mile or so, scanning the trees. Then Evita noticed too, and she started doing the same. When Xiaoyu finally pulled her eyes away from her former cellar-mates for long enough to see what the others were doing, she got spooked.

'What's going on?' she asked.

Kulika sighed. 'I was trying not to worry you all.'

'I think we're already worried,' Evita pointed out. 'I can feel the anxiety coming off Quick in waves.'

'And I can feel it coming off you,' Quick said to Kulika.

'Really?' Kulika replied, as though that surprised her.

'Yes,' Quick replied. 'Really.'

Although Kulika wasn't showing anything on her face, which was as impassive and controlled as ever, there was a nervous energy to her that Quick couldn't see as much as she could feel it. Now that she was looking for the tell that had tipped her off, Quick couldn't pinpoint it, but nonetheless she knew in her gut that Kulika was worried.

'I still don't want to worry you all,' Kulika said.

'Tell us anyway,' Xiaoyu insisted.

Kulika hesitated for a moment, looking first around the ring of zombies that was keeping pace with the car, then from Quick to Xiaoyu and, finally, to Evita.

She said, 'The zombies aren't the only thing that escaped from the wine cellar.'

8

KULIKA'S STOMACH TURNED every time she remembered the look on Evita's face as she'd told them about Digs. She knew how traumatising her weeks spent alone in that box with him must have been. She'd been hoping she wouldn't have to say anything, but then Quick had noticed her looking, and she'd had to confess.

Kulika still couldn't understand how Quick had picked up on her anxiety. It wasn't as though Kulika went around broadcasting her emotions. She was a security expert with over three hundred years' experience and the kind of knowledge you couldn't get from training. When she was out in the field, she controlled her expressions, she controlled her reactions, and she controlled her respiration – such as it was – so there was nothing that should have tipped Quick off. Somehow, she'd just known.

Christ, she was dangerous. Kulika shouldn't have kissed her. And that look Quick was giving her now, as they drove the last excruciating half-mile up the road to the mansion? Kulika couldn't tell what that look meant.

In fact, she couldn't tell what Quick was feeling at all, which was strange. After a moment's confusion, Kulika realised she was missing something that had become so familiar she'd barely noticed it until it was gone: usually, she could read Quick's mood through the tone of her scent. Now, though, she was getting nothing. She could smell the complex mixed-seasons scent that was Quick's personal perfume, wafting through the car's open window, but it was no longer kaleidoscoping in the way that had become so familiar and intoxicating. It wasn't ebbing and flowing in the way it had done previously, which suggested there was something seriously wrong with Quick. Or maybe Quick's scent was behaving exactly as it always had, but Kulika could no longer perceive it.

She wasn't sure which of those possibilities was more terrifying.

Quick's scent wasn't the only thing about her that had gone awry, though. The red in her hair was somehow less bright, her perfume was generally less strong, and Kulika couldn't feel the air sizzling between them the way it had just last night, before she'd said her goodbyes. Maybe that was only because the others were in the car beside her, but surely their presence shouldn't be enough to stop the electricity jumping between Quick and Kulika as they crept along the road, mere feet away from each other? Being in company had never stopped that spark before. Besides, there had been the same strange absence in their kiss in the crashed cab, even though every look from Quick still had the same effect on Kulika as sunlight did on Quick's skin, starting rampant fires all over her body that she couldn't seem to quench.

Which left Kulika with one explanation: there was something wrong with Quick that her healing kiss hadn't been able to fix.

Kulika *really* shouldn't have kissed her. She'd known that

if she even touched her, Bartholomew's nose was sensitive enough that he would smell her scent on Kulika's skin the moment they got back to the mansion. Even the distance between them now was probably too close; tantalisingly, enticingly close. Quick was no longer hers, she reminded herself. She'd given up her claim, just as Bartholomew had given up his.

He'd make Kulika pay for crossing that line. She could only hope he wouldn't take her transgressions out on Quick. All she could do now was keep her distance, and try not to make the situation any worse.

Monty and a gang of the others were waiting in the driveway when they pulled up, gawping at the entourage she'd brought along with her.

Quick had moved to the other side of the car, wanting to be closer to Evita. That meant the ring of zombies bowed out wider on the passenger side of the car as they tried to avoid getting too close to Quick, so Kulika pulled up with the driver's side facing Monty and the other new Silver, keeping a fifteen feet gap between them and the outer edge of the ring; she didn't want to pincer the zombies' comfort zone and force them any closer to Xiaoyu.

'Round them up!' Kulika yelled at the crew. 'Come in slowly and corral them away from the car.'

'And be careful with them,' Quick added from the other side of the car. 'They're contagious.'

'What do you mean, *contagious*?' someone asked. With the ring of zombies standing between Kulika and the Silver, she wasn't sure who had spoken. Not that she would have recognised them anyway; she barely knew this crew she was supposed to be leading.

'I mean if any of them bites a human,' Quick said, 'they'll

turn into a zombie.'

'Bullshit,' someone muttered. He was hiding in the crowd, but Kulika recognised the voice.

She slammed the driver's side door and stepped away from the car. The zombies parted theatrically to either side of her as she approached the gang of new Silver, giving her the kind of entrance that would have made Bartholomew proud.

'Got something to say, Monty?' Kulika said, getting up close to him, steely-voiced. 'Maybe you'd like to explain to me how all this happened on your watch in the first place?'

'*My* watch? I just look after the block.'

Kulika sighed loudly. 'And where exactly is the blood cellar?'

'Well…' Monty's initial reply was automatic, as though he couldn't help but argue. He couldn't follow it up, though. He, like the rest of the Silver gathered in front of her, had clearly been drinking.

Alcohol didn't usually have much of an effect on the Silver, but these ones were young and stupid, and had probably drunk far too much. No wonder they hadn't answered their phones when Penny called. No wonder they hadn't managed to find the zombies, either. Kulika was surprised they'd managed to find their own feet.

'Has anyone bothered to check the blood cellar?' Kulika asked. 'How did the humans get out in the first place? Is it secure enough to hold the zombies?'

'Yes,' Monty said. 'There's nothing wrong with it, it's just that the hatch was left open.'

Kulika had seen enough of that hatch to know it would be impossible to open it from the inside. That could only mean one thing: someone had opened it to let the humans out.

Kulika looked over the zombie horde to where Quick stood beside the car. She was holding the blanket too low over her face for Kulika to see her eyes. Maybe that was just a matter of perspective, since Kulika was no longer looking up at Quick from inside the car, or maybe Quick was hiding deliberately. Either way, Kulika had her suspicions about Quick's involvement in the escape. She hadn't made much of a secret of her desire to see the humans of the blood cellar liberated.

Hadn't Penny said there'd been a fire just before the escape? And hadn't Quick been caught just the night before, using a fire under the mansion's porch as a diversion so she could set the blood cellar free?

'Put them in the cellar,' Kulika said to Monty. 'And count them. If there's anyone missing, I need to know about it immediately. Assume the whole blood cellar turned, plus the zombies that were supposed to be locked up in the wine cellar. And there were two drivers they met on the road. I assume you know how many people were in the blood cellar to begin with?'

'Yes,' Monty replied, but he sounded worryingly uncertain.

'Then work it out,' she snapped. 'And we need people out on the highway looking for wrecks we might have missed. Where's Penny?'

'Here,' said a voice from the back of the crowd.

When Penny had pushed through the Silver to the front, Kulika grabbed her and pulled her alongside, so she was facing the others. 'Penny's heading up communications from here. You need to stay in touch with each other. If she calls you, you answer. Got it? I'm not having a repeat of this morning.'

'We've got to go silent when we're searching,' Monty argued.

'Then you make sure you're checking your messages

regularly. Now get these zombies safely away.'

'What about them?' Monty asked, nodding his head at the car.

Quick and Evita were both outside now, guarding the passenger-side door from the zombie ring. Quick looked over at Monty from under her blanket and sneered, clearly unhappy to be returned to his company. Then she looked at Kulika. There was a question in her eyes, maybe even an offer.

But the answer had to be no. Quick couldn't stay here. None of them could stay. Kulika had made her bargain, and there was no backing out of it.

She had to let Quick go, again.

'Put them in the library,' Kulika said. 'As soon as all the zombies are accounted for, they're leaving. And they're not leaving alone.'

Dr Ross was sitting on a chair next to the bed in what had once been Bayly's room. The single was now full to bursting as Enzo lay there wrapped in Bayly's arms. They'd changed position slightly, so they were no longer as tightly coiled together as they had been in the bath, and what Kulika could see of Bayly's skin above the sheets looked to be in much better condition than it had been when she'd left. His finger had grown back, too.

'How are they?' Kulika asked.

'Getting there,' said Dr Ross, leaving the bedside to talk with Kulika out in the corridor. 'But we need more blood than I have.'

'I've still got this,' Kulika said, pulling the bottle out of her pocket. 'But I don't have any more to offer you.'

'It might not be enough,' the doctor said, taking the bottle sceptically, 'but I'll do what I can. You didn't find the humans?'

'No, we did.'

'Then where are they?'

'Back in the blood cellar.'

Dr Ross shook her head and said, 'I don't like using unwilling donors any more than you do, but in the circumstances—'

'The zombies are infectious,' Kulika said, then she explained what had happened out on the road. 'One bite, or one drop of blood, and they turn humans into creatures just like them.'

The doctor's eyes went wide.

'They all turned?' Dr Ross whispered.

'Yes. Quick saw it happen from just a tiny smear of blood on a car window. It was instant.'

'Oh my god,' the doctor muttered, leaning back against the corridor wall. 'The blood is contaminated,' she muttered. 'The woods are contaminated. This house is contaminated.'

Kulika thought about the pool of blood in the wine cellar, the blood on Bayly and Enzo's bodies, and all the blood on their clothes and shoes that they'd trailed up the stairs as they'd carried the two men to the bathroom.

'It'll be an epidemic,' Dr Ross whispered. 'Are there any other humans in this house?'

'There were human crew members when I first arrived, but I think they're gone now.'

'Good. That's good.'

Then a terrible thought occurred to Kulika: 'But the whole world is coming here this evening to watch Bartholomew launch his new ship.'

The launch party took a while to explain, as did the ship, but when Kulika had finished, the doctor looked haunted.

'You have to stop it,' she said. 'It'll be a bloodbath.'

'Bartholomew's never going to let the press into the house,' Kulika said. 'They'll all be down by the river.'

'And what if one of the escaped zombies went out that way before going into the woods? What if there's a drop of blood on the drive, or on the grass, or it gets on the bottom of someone's tyre or shoe, and they spread it even further? If it's as infectious as you say it is, then you can't take that risk, at least not until you've let me take a look at it under a microscope.'

Kulika groaned. This wasn't the news she wanted. She wanted to send the doctor home, and Quick along with her, as quickly as possible.

But after seeing what had happened out on the road this morning…

'Did you get your samples from the zombies downstairs?' Kulika asked.

The doctor patted her bag and said, 'I've got everything I need.'

'Then Bartholomew keeps the basics in his library. Everything's antique and outdated, but I've definitely seen a microscope on the shelves.'

'That'll do for now. Let me get this last bottle of blood into Bayly,' she said, hefting it in her hand, 'and then we'll see.'

'Please work fast.' Kulika took a deep breath and added, 'Because I need you to do me another favour too.'

The doctor looked at her quizzically.

'I need you to take Quick and her friend back to the UK with you.'

If anything, the confusion on Dr Ross's face intensified. 'I don't understand,' she said. 'I thought you love—'

'Which is why,' Kulika interrupted. 'I need you to keep her safe, please. And maybe just… keep an eye on her for me, okay?'

'What? Why?'

'I'm worried that there might be something wrong,' Kulika confided.

'With Quick?'

'She just seems different.'

The doctor's interest sharpened. 'Different how? Is it something to do with the zombies?'

'I don't know.' That was the fear Kulika was too scared to articulate. 'Her colours aren't as bright, and nor is her scent. And before you say anything, I know that makes no sense, but I'm telling you there's something off. I healed her earlier and it... I don't know. It didn't feel the same. With her sun sensitivity... I'm worried. You might want to take a look at her blood, while you're at it.'

Dr Ross looked at Kulika for a moment, assessing her. She said, 'Let me see your silver.'

'Excuse me?'

Amongst the Silver, a demand like that was not so much abrupt as it was downright rude.

'I said, let me see your silver,' the doctor repeated unrepentantly, leaning in close to Kulika's face. 'Something's off with you, so show me.'

'Nothing's *off* with—'

'Kulika,' Dr Ross said sternly.

'Oh, fine.'

Kulika relaxed the unconscious control she was exerting on her eyes, letting the silver flood back into the whites, and on into the irises. That extra reach – the silver in the grey of her eyes – was the mark of her bond to Quick.

Except it didn't feel right.

When she'd released control like this previously, she'd felt a gentle thud of satisfaction as the silver circled around her pupils, completing its course with a finality that settled reassuringly in her chest. This time, that didn't happen. She felt the silver reach, but she didn't feel it land. Something was off.

'What's happening?' Kulika asked.

'I can't... It's...'

The doctor leaned even closer, then reached out and pulled up one of Kulika's eyelids.

'Is it bad?' Kulika asked.

'I don't know what it is,' Dr Ross said, finally releasing Kulika and leaning thoughtfully back against the wall. 'I've never seen it before. It looks as though the silver is sort of... stuttering.'

'Stuttering?'

'Like it's being blocked, and only partially penetrating into your iris. It's not as though I've made an extensive study of this, you understand, because of course the sample pool is very small, and even if it wasn't, how could you experiment ethically? Of course, the Silver can heal from physical injury without too much inconvenience, but psychological injury? My days of manipulating the emotions of my subjects for the purposes of science are behind me, I can tell you that much for free.' The doctor laughed bitterly.

'Okay,' Kulika said uncertainly, not following.

'My point is,' the doctor said, re-boarding her train of thought, 'from a very cursory examination – *very* cursory – it looks as though the silvering is starting to reverse itself, which is, of course, impossible.'

'Reverse itself?'

'Exactly. And if the silver in your eyes is disappearing, that would mean—'

'The bond is disappearing too,' Kulika finished.

'Which is, again, impossible,' the doctor added.

But it would explain so much. The way Quick's touch suddenly left her cold, the distance she felt growing between them, the fact that Kulika could no longer discern Quick's mood from her scent. In fact, everything about Quick felt dulled to Kulika. The brightness of her hair, the variations in her scent, the electricity of her touch.

Oh, god.

The silvering was reversing.

'But why?' Kulika asked desperately.

'I don't know. Something must have changed.'

'Well, how do I stop it?'

'I don't know,' the doctor repeated hopelessly.

With a growl of frustration, Kulika turned and paced towards the stairs, leaning against the banisters as she looked down to the ground floor below. That was where it had all started, down in the hall on the night of the Casting. Was this how it was going to end, her silvering dissolving into nothing with a quiet sigh?

'Can I ask you something?' Dr Ross said after a moment.

'What?'

'Do you actually want to stop it?' she asked tentatively.

Kulika turned to face her. 'Of course I do. Quick's the only good thing in my life.'

'But she's not going to be in your life anymore. She's leaving again, and she's not coming back. Wouldn't it be easier if you could let the bond go with her?'

Maybe that was what had changed: Quick had left, and the bond was stretching thin with her absence. If she left for good, maybe it would stretch so thin that it became nothing at all. Would that be better than this pain in Kulika's chest, making her want to fold in on herself every time she remembered that Quick would never touch her again?

'Maybe,' Kulika agreed. 'If I had the choice, but it's not in my control, is it? Will you just look at her blood for me? Please?'

'All right,' the doctor agreed.

'Then the library's this way.'

Kulika started down the stairs, the doctor and her bag close on her heels.

'I don't suppose you found Digs?' Dr Ross asked.

'Not yet,' said Kulika. 'That's the next emergency on my list. Maybe ask me again in an hour.'

She led the doctor to the library, made brief introductions to Quick, Evita and Xiaoyu, then strode off outside to find Monty. She didn't want to hang around; she couldn't stand to look at the hope and expectation in Quick's eyes when she knew she was about to wipe it out. It was easier to deal with the task at hand, so that's exactly what she did.

She tracked Monty down to the block. He was hanging around the glass doors that led into the common room at the front of the building, watching the trees as though he was expecting someone to emerge from them any moment. When he saw Kulika coming, he stood up a little straighter.

'You got them all?' she asked him.

'I guess,' Monty said dismissively.

'No, not "I guess",' Kulika snapped back irritably. 'Do you understand what would happen if we left one of those things to wander around out there? So let's try again, shall we? Did you bother to count and make sure we've collected every single one of the incredibly contagious zombies you just allowed to be created?'

'Yes,' he said shamefacedly.

'The seven original from the wine cellar?' Kulika asked, still not trusting Monty's confirmation. 'And however many humans used to be in the blood cellar, and the driver—'

'I did a full count,' he said, finally acting like he was

taking things seriously. 'I promise you, we've got them all. I'm sure.'

'Sure enough to swear it to Bartholomew?'

'By blood, if necessary.'

Which was just as well, because Kulika did not have time for this. She needed to check the zombies were secure, create a safe space for the press conference this evening, and find Digs, and she needed to do all of those things immediately.

'Where the hell is Bartholomew?'

'The Primus?' Monty asked, with an edge of disapproval in his tone.

So much for taking things seriously.

'Don't test my patience, kid.'

'He's still on the boat.'

'The *ship*,' Kulika corrected him. 'He was supposed to be back hours ago.'

As if on cue, Kulika saw the *Primus's Fortune* hove into view on the other side of the lawn, travelling upriver by virtue of a gentle breeze and a hell of a lot of manpower. A few of the crew who'd left with Bartholomew were down on the bank, heaving the ship along with the assistance of ropes and superhuman strength. Kulika dreaded to think how much blood they would have consumed to haul it against the current like that, for god knows how far. It was a lot of veins to open for the sake of a rich immortal's vanity project. Given the current drought, it might be the last they saw for some time.

'Sort your people out into search parties,' Kulika ordered Monty. 'Use runners for messages if you have to, but get them on a grid and be methodical. And keep half of them here to prepare for tonight. It's only a few hours until people are going to start arriving. We're running out of time. When I come back, I want to see this whole crew sober and organised.'

'Yes, Secundus,' he said.

Kulika couldn't tell if he was being mocking or obedient, but she also didn't care as long as he got the job done. Right now, she needed to speak to Bartholomew.

9

OF ALL THE people Kulika could have handed them off to, Quick thought Monty might have been the worst. He'd glared at Evita – who'd glared right back – grimaced at Xiaoyu, then looked at Quick as though she were a terrible disappointment.

'Stay here,' he'd told them as he'd bundled them into the library. 'And no snooping around.' Then he'd left and shut the door behind him. Quick heard the lock tumble.

She threw down the blanket, relieved to be rid of it, and looked at her two bedraggled friends.

'Idiot,' Evita muttered. 'He does know that I can bust right through that door, doesn't he?'

She slumped down into one of the library's armchairs and Xiaoyu took the other, leaving Quick with the chair behind the desk.

'I've decided I don't like being bait,' Xiaoyu said. Her voice was a monotone, her gaze hollow and haunted. After that long, torturous drive in the sun, she looked ten times worse than she had when she'd woken up that morning. 'I suppose I deserve it, though.'

'You don't deserve any of this,' Quick said.

'I was supposed to protect them.' Xiaoyu's face crumpled. If she hadn't been so dehydrated, she would have been crying. 'They were my responsibility,' she said, biting the words out through her grief. 'Them and so many others. It's my fault they're gone.'

'Hey, no.' Quick hurried back around the desk and perched awkwardly on the armchair, trying to take Xiaoyu into her arms. The other woman didn't want to be comforted, though. Her body was stiff and tense, shuddering with all the emotion she was trying to contain. 'This is not your fault.'

'I think I need to tell you both something,' said Evita. She was looking down into her lap and worrying at her cuticles; a nervous habit she'd had for as long as Quick had known her.

'About what?' Quick asked.

'Please don't hate me, okay?'

Quick scoffed. 'We're not going to hate—'

'Just hear me out.'

Then Quick registered the guilty look on Evita's face and realised she'd just made a promise she might not be able to keep. 'What did you do?'

'Before we left the mansion this morning,' Evita said, 'I did something potentially stupid.'

'Okay…'

'I was looking for Bartholomew,' she explained, talking faster now, like a penitent child, 'and I heard someone saying he'd been down in the wine cellar visiting Bayly.'

Quick groaned. 'You didn't. Please, Evita, tell me you didn't.'

'Seriously, hear me out. I just went down there looking for him, that's all. Can you blame me? Bayly and Bartholomew in one place… You think I wasn't going to speak my mind?'

'No,' Quick said on a sigh. No one had ever accused Evita of being a shrinking violet.

'But then I saw… something, and I ran, okay? I just ran. I think I left the door open.'

'Vee…'

'You don't understand.'

'What I don't understand is why you had to go looking for Bartholomew. We were nearly out of here.'

'I had to,' Evita said. 'Don't make me explain it. It was just something I had to do.'

'Well, you've certainly done it now,' said Quick.

If that sounded harsh, merciless even, then perhaps it was, but Evita had form for doing stupid things for stupid reasons.

Quick could be impulsive and impatient, yes, but Evita took it to another level. Like that time when they were undergraduates, and Evita had dosed herself with some kind of pill – to this day, Evita couldn't tell Quick what it had been, she'd just accepted the offer of a high from a vague acquaintance – started seeing colours, and hatched a brilliant plan to steal a keg from behind the student bar at five in the morning. Quick had intervened in time to save the keg from being accidentally rolled into the river, but not in time to stop them being caught by campus security. It was all on tape, of course. It was a minor miracle they hadn't both been kicked out, there and then, but Quick had spun a sob story and got them off with a harsh reprimand.

She'd thought those days were over, but apparently she'd been wrong. Now Evita hadn't just risked getting them both saddled with a criminal record, she'd started a zombie outbreak.

'Please don't give me that look,' Evita said. 'I didn't mean to let them out, if I in fact did, which I maintain is debatable. It was an accident.'

'It was careless.'

'And you're perfect all the time, are you?'

'No, of course not! But I didn't start a fucking zombie apocalypse, either.'

'It's been averted, all right?'

'After people died, Vee. Our driver. The guy in the truck. All those people in the blood cellar. All dead.'

'I know,' Evita said, chastened. 'And I feel terrible, but I didn't know they were contagious. I thought they were just regular zombies, except for the fact that they don't die.'

'It wasn't you,' Xiaoyu said quietly. 'It was me.'

'What?' asked Quick. Xiaoyu had been quiet for so long that Quick had started to forget she was there at all.

'It was me who killed all those people,' Xiaoyu said again. 'It's my fault they're dead. I was the one who started the fire and opened the blood cellar.'

'What?' said Quick. 'No, Xiaoyu, that was me. Last night. I started the fire at the back of the mansion then got you out of the blood cellar.'

'Which is where I got the idea, but no,' she insisted, her voice a haunting monotone. 'When you were both sitting on the doorstep this morning, and all the other vampires were busy partying, I went back to the block, opened the blood cellar hatch – fairly simple with the right leverage – then set a fire on the other side of the building as a distraction while everyone got out. I didn't know there were zombies in the woods, or that they were contagious, but when I say this is my fault, I mean it. It's my fault they got turned into… whatever they are.'

'You were just trying to help,' Evita said.

'And I still got them all killed,' Xiaoyu replied.

'I should have done the same,' said Quick. 'You weren't to know that—'

'Stop,' Xiaoyu said. 'Just… stop. I know what I did. Let me make peace with it.' Then she turned away, staring out of the window and into her own thoughts.

She was clearly done talking.

Quick closed her mouth around the placations she was about to spout. There was no point; Xiaoyu had sunk so far down into her misery that there would be no pulling her out of it. She'd have to swim through it on her own.

When Quick turned away from Xiaoyu, she found Evita glaring at her. She would have asked what the problem was, but then the key turned in the lock to the library door, interrupting whatever pseudo-sibling bust-up they were about to have.

In the second before the door swung open, Quick could smell the sea, only Kulika's scent was *better* than the sea. It was fresh and light and charged with sunshine and hope. Just one breath of it was enough to set Quick's heart racing before Kulika had even stepped into the room. She was open-mouthed and expectant, rising from her perch on the edge of Xiaoyu's chair as her hopes rose with her.

Only to be dashed the moment Kulika walked inside.

'Dr Ross,' she said, avoiding Quick's eyes. 'These are Patience Quick, Evita Khalyed and Xiaoyu…' She paused, apparently waiting for Xiaoyu to fill in the blank with her surname, but Xiaoyu just carried on staring out of the window. 'Xiaoyu,' she finished. 'Microscope's somewhere on the shelf up top. Help yourself.'

Then she left, closing the door behind her without speaking a single word to Quick.

Kulika had kissed her, just this morning. She'd held her in her arms, and healed her burns, and made her feel like she wasn't the only one whose skin was on fire.

But now: nothing.

Nothing at all.

'Nice to meet you all,' said Dr Ross with a smile. She was

a short, round woman with a cheerful face and a strong Scottish accent. Her hair was messy and her lab coat was stained, but she had an air of openness and competence that Quick found instantly appealing. 'I've just got a few tests to run, then we'll be on our way to the airport. Ms Quick, I'll be needing a sample of your blood, if you don't mind obliging me.'

'Why?'

'Just a control sample,' the doctor said, then she dragged the desk chair up against the nearest wall and started poking around on the top shelf of the bookcase. 'Take this, would you?' she asked Quick, handing down an ancient-looking microscope and a couple of boxes. 'On the desk, please.'

Once she'd poked around on the shelf to her satisfaction and found nothing else she wanted, Dr Ross hopped down to the ground and carried the chair back around the table, then she opened the bag she'd brought with her and started pulling things out.

'I need a clear workspace, please,' she said as she set up the microscope and started peering down it, examining slide after slide. 'If all of you could stay on that side of the room, it'd probably be for the best. These are dangerous chemicals. Especially for you, Ms Xiaoyu.'

Xiaoyu ignored her entirely, still staring out of the window. Quick looked over at Evita, wondering what her reaction was to the whirlwind of Dr Ross, but Evita turned away and looked out of the window with Xiaoyu.

Sulking.

Quick wasn't the only one who noticed.

'What's up with you lot?' Dr Ross asked, looking up from her slides.

'Nothing,' Quick replied.

'Just tell her,' Evita muttered from her armchair.

'Fine.' Quick sighed. 'Xiaoyu's the one who let the people out of the blood cellar, and Evita's the one who left the wine cellar open.'

'By accident,' Evita hissed at Quick.

'By accident,' Quick agreed. 'But yeah. She let the zombies out.'

'No, she didn't,' Dr Ross said, putting her eye back to the microscope.

Quick was nonplussed for a moment, then she insisted, 'Yes, she did.'

'I really did,' Evita added.

'Maybe you left the door open,' said Dr Ross, looking up at Evita, 'but you didn't let the zombies out. They'd already got themselves free on their own. They tunnelled out through the floor, following Digs.'

The sigh of relief Evita let out was so large it must have been filling her whole chest. 'Did you find him?' she asked.

'Oh, I'm not looking. I'm the doctor, not the search party. I'll see him right when he's found, but until then I've got other things to bother about. Now,' she said to Quick, 'about that blood sample?'

10

'PHINCHAS!' KULIKA YELLED, striding to the dock where he was standing beside the *Primus's Fortune*. 'Wolfrie!'

The two men grabbed her around the back of the neck and pulled her close, the three of them pressing their foreheads together to seal their reunion. For the first time in more than a hundred years, Kulika was breathing the same air as them, inhaling the smoky fireside scent of Wolfrie and the sawdust scent of Phinchas. Together, the two of them smelled like camping on the beach and falling asleep in a tumbled heap of rum and stolen silks.

They were here.

They were *really* here.

They were deceitful, violent bastards, but they were *crew*, and she could trust them to get the job done. Their mere presence settled the anxiety roiling in Kulika's stomach.

Phinchas was a tall, lanky man with brown skin and watchful eyes. Wolfrie was the polar opposite: shorter, bearded, barrel-chested and gruff. Neither of them was the kind of person who would come across to a stranger as warm, but then Kulika herself was not warm either.

Bartholomew's crew had always been known for their spikes rather than their softness.

'When did you arrive?' she asked, pulling back to assess them both. Perhaps unsurprisingly, they looked exactly the same as they had the day she'd left. The clothes had changed – jeans and T-shirts now instead of breeches and shirts – but otherwise they were the same old Phinchas and Wolfrie.

'Just now,' Wolfrie said. 'Came up on the new *Fortune*.'

'You mean the *Primus's Fortune*,' Phinchas corrected him. Wolfrie scoffed.

'Insubordination, Wolfs,' Phinchas chided. 'And in front of the Secundus, no less. Would you have me beat him, sir?' he added to Kulika.

'Just tone it down in front of Bartholomew, will you?' Kulika asked quietly. 'He doesn't have much of a sense of humour these days.'

'Did he ever?' Wolfrie asked with a laugh.

'I'm serious,' Kulika said. 'Right now, I don't have much of one, either.'

She explained about the zombies, about the wine cellar, about Digs, Bayly and the hole in the wine cellar floor.

'That wily bastard,' Wolfrie said.

'He's not Digs anymore,' Kulika warned him. 'Not like you might remember him.'

'You never knew him in the first place,' Phinchas pointed out.

'No,' Kulika agreed, 'but I'm guessing he used to be more than a mouth and a set of teeth. Just watch yourselves, okay? You'll want to check in with the kid, Monty. The one in the green T-shirt.' Kulika pointed off towards the block, where Monty was organising the younger crew members into groups out on the lawn. 'Work out where he's searched, and where he hasn't. I've told him to organise the others, but make sure he actually does, okay?'

'Unreliable?' Wolfrie asked.

'Inexperienced,' Kulika said. 'And can you get some of the better noses searching around this area?' she asked, indicating the space on the riverbank where a stage was in the process of being constructed. 'The driveway, too. We need to know if any of the zombies came out this way, and if they did, every trace of them needs to be cleaned away by eight thirty. Ceremony starts at nine.'

'You got it,' Phinchas said. 'We'll pull some of the crew off the ship to help.'

'What do you think of her, then?' Wolfrie asked, patting the bow of the *Primus's Fortune* affectionately.

'She's a replica of the ship Bartholomew died on,' Kulika muttered. 'It's… creepy.'

'Pretended to die on,' Phinchas corrected her.

But it hadn't felt pretend to her. Bartholomew had made her promise, as he'd prepared for the final sea battle with the *Swallow*, that she'd find his body and throw it overboard before the British could capture it. He would heal, he'd told her. It was the only way for him to get them off his back, he'd told her. She'd known all of that, of course, but there was a strange madness to knowing something to be true while seeing evidence with your own eyes that directly contradicted that truth.

Bartholomew *had* been dead that day. His body had fallen on the main deck, close to the cabin door, his throat so riddled with grapeshot that his head was barely attached to his shoulders anymore. And the blood.

So much blood. Bartholomew's blood, that she shared.

It had felt sacred to her, back then. In those early days, he had been Kulika's god. To take his broken body in her arms and throw it over the side of the ship for the sharks that circled in the Gulf of Guinea…

He'd found her in new Port Royal, a week later, alive and well and exactly as he had always been. Kulika had never been able to erase that image from her mind, though: the lolling head, the shredded flesh, the disrespectful *smack* as his body had flopped onto the water below the ship. She remembered it as clearly as she remembered his second false death, a hundred years later, at her own hand: surprise on his face, the power she'd felt as his heart beat between her fingertips, the visceral force it took to break open his ribs with her bare hands.

With that much behind them, how could there be a future for Kulika on Bartholomew's crew?

'Hmm,' Wolfrie murmured, dragging her back to the present.

He and Phinchas had concerningly contemplative looks on their faces.

'What's wrong?' Kulika asked. 'Why are you both looking at me like that?'

Phinchas and Wolfrie looked at each other, then Wolfrie said, 'We heard you silvered.' He was looking at her eyes, as though he would be able to spot the silver she was masking just by squinting really hard.

'I don't want to talk about it,' Kulika said, striding towards the rope ladder that stretched from the deck of the *Primus's Fortune* to the dock below.

'It's nothing to be ashamed about,' Phinchas pointed out.

'Well,' Wolfrie said, 'it might be considered a weakness. I heard the girl is new.'

'I heard the captain was jealous,' Phinchas added.

'I heard he turned a girl himself,' said Wolfrie.

'I heard that, too.'

'I heard the captain *fancied* the girl he turned,' Wolfrie

added. 'The new one, I mean. Obviously, he's not pining after his Secundus, here.'

They both laughed, and Kulika's patience began to wear thin. She turned with her foot on the bottom rung of the ladder. 'And who exactly is telling you all this when you only just arrived?'

Wolfrie shrugged. 'People tell us things,' he said.

'We're likeable guys,' Phinchas added.

'You're manipulative bastards, is what you are,' said Kulika.

Wolfrie shook his head. 'All I'm saying is: has anyone seen Bartholomew's silver lately?'

Kulika thought back over the past week, but no, Bartholomew had never flashed his silver at her. That didn't mean anything, though. It wasn't something the Silver generally did, because it was more than just a gesture. When you revealed your silver to someone, you were inviting them in, or offering a threat. You didn't do it lightly. Unless, of course, like Quick and the other newbies, you were too young to hide it at all.

'I'm not sure he's capable of love,' Kulika said uncertainly.

'Maybe not what you'd call love, but...' Wolfrie shrugged. 'I heard the captain kissed her. That kid you pointed out, Monty? Saw it all, I heard.'

'No,' Phinchas said incredulously.

'Yes,' Wolfrie insisted.

The worst thing was, Kulika believed it. It occurred to her that she'd never spoken to Monty while she'd been conducting her first interviews with the crew into Evita's whereabouts. Monty had brought all the other new Silver to her, but he'd never volunteered any information himself, even though she knew he'd been here from the very beginning, like Evita. He was probably the only other person in the world who knew what had happened between Bartholomew and Evita, and he had kept his mouth firmly shut.

With Kulika, at least.

'I'm serious,' Wolfrie went on. 'Think about it: the captain turned her Silver, and he hasn't done that ever, for anyone.'

'Except Kulika,' Phinchas interjected.

'Right,' Wolfrie agreed, 'but she was a special case. This Evita… Well, imagine the possibilities. If he really has silvered for her, then we could take him out, once and for all.'

'By killing Evita?' Kulika said, horrified.

Wolfrie shrugged again. 'Small sacrifices.'

Small sacrifices.

That had become their motto at the mansion in the old days. Giving up piracy to hide their true nature? *Small sacrifices.* Putting one crew member down to keep peace amongst the others? *Small sacrifices.* Abandoning your crew to Bartholomew's whims because you couldn't hold yourself together a moment longer? Well, maybe that sacrifice hadn't been quite so small. It wouldn't have felt that way to Phinchas and Wolfrie when she'd left, Kulika was certain.

But the way they were talking now…

'Bartholomew is your Primus,' said Kulika forcefully. The rest of her patience had evaporated, along with her good mood. 'It doesn't matter whether he's silvered or not, or who he's silvered for, because that information is never going to cross your lips again. I mean, Christ, Wolfrie. Did you come back here just to start a mutiny?'

'No,' he said, blinking in surprise. 'We came back for you.'

'But you're sworn to him,' she pointed out.

'No,' said Phinchas. 'We're not. Not anymore. We bought our way out years ago. When Wolfrie says we came back for you, he means it. We came back for *you*. To get you out.'

Kulika shook her head, unwilling even to admit that idea into her mind. She couldn't leave. She could never leave. She'd bought Quick's freedom with her own, and the consequences of breaking that deal were too terrible to contemplate.

'You may not be sworn to Bartholomew,' she said hopelessly. 'But I am. We have a covenant,' she added, showing them the black spot on her palm.

They hadn't known. She could tell that easily enough from the way their faces fell.

'If you really came back for me,' she said, 'then I need you to do what I've asked you to do. So are you going to fall in line with me, and with the Primus, or am I going to have to find someone else who will?'

'Nope,' Wolfrie said, holding his hands up in surrender.

'We're already gone!' Phinchas called.

And they were indeed gone, disappearing into the trees at speed, searching for Digs: the man they'd called their crewmate before Kulika had even been born. Perhaps they should have had more loyalty to him than they did to Kulika, but reversals in favour were common fare for pirates. No one's word or friendship meant much for long, not without the enforcement of blood or threat.

She could only hope that Wolfrie and Phinchas's loyalty would last for long enough to get them all out of this mess.

II

QUICK AND EVITA were bored in the library while Dr Ross carried on her work in the kitchen – better light, she said – so they were indulging in their default activity: bickering. Xiaoyu had fallen asleep in her armchair, so at least they had some privacy.

'You're pining,' Evita said. 'It's revolting.'

'She didn't even look at me.'

'Because she's busy. Would you rather she dealt with the zombies or soothed your ego?'

'It's not ego! You said she was in love with me.'

'Right, so why are you being so pathetic about this? *She* loves *you*, not the other way around.'

'And how do you know I don't love her? Maybe I do.'

'Because you're not the one with silver in your irises, are you? Did you not listen to a word I told you in the car?'

'Well, I'm sorry I neglected to retain every detail of a conversation we had just moments before we were attacked by zombies. Clearly that's a sign of some great moral failing on my part.'

'No, the moral failing is that you actually want a vampire to have feelings for you.'

'So you're only dating humans from now on, are you? How do you expect that to work out for you, now that we're both vampires?'

'Better than your relationship with Kulika is, clearly.'

On and on it went, relentlessly. It sounded almost like normal banter, but it had too much edge for their usual back and forth, particularly when it should have been tempered by their recent reunion. They were both raw, and suffering, and they were rubbing up against each other's sharp edges. Quick could just accept that as part of the process of resettling their friendship, and maybe she should, but she couldn't let it lie. She wasn't destined to live up to her first name.

'Why are you sniping at me?' Quick asked abruptly. 'What did I do?'

Evita crossed her arms and pouted. For a moment, Quick thought she wasn't going to spill the beans, but then she uncrossed her arms and turned back with a fierce look on her face that Quick recognised. It meant she should run for cover.

'You're so ready to forgive Xiaoyu,' Evita said, 'but you come down on me for a mistake that it turns out I didn't even make?'

'Because Xiaoyu was trying to do something good. She was trying to save people. You were just chasing Bartholomew around the mansion like some kind of avenging angel! And now Digs is loose, and god knows what he'll do.'

'I do,' Evita said quietly.

'Do what?'

'I *know*. I spent weeks locked away in a box,' Evita said quietly, 'with him.'

Quick could feel her cheeks cooling as the colour drained

from them. She hadn't known.

'With *Digs*?' she said.

'With Digs,' Evita confirmed. 'I haven't forgotten how dangerous he is. I lived it every hour of every day for weeks and weeks.'

'Vee,' Quick said in horror. 'Why didn't you tell me?'

'What did you expect me to say? You want me to relive it for you, in every gory detail?'

'No! Of course not. But I didn't know.'

She also hadn't asked, though. She'd got the impression that Evita hadn't wanted to talk about her time in the box, so she'd left it alone. She was now realising belatedly that this was a story she should have asked for herself, rather than waiting for Evita to volunteer it. In her defence, it had been a hell of a day, but her neglect made her feel like a crappy friend, as did the bickering.

She slumped into the desk chair Dr Ross had recently vacated, all the fight going out of her. The moment she stopped resisting, Evita did too, relaxing back into her armchair with an exhausted sigh. They were both stretched so thin that it had been inevitable that they would break, sooner or later, but it was time Quick stopped making things worse for her friend.

'I'm sorry,' she said.

'Yeah.' Evita's reply was neither an acceptance nor a rejection. It was evasive instead, which hurt Quick more. She and Evita had never kept things from one another. Not before the mansion.

'I didn't think about what it must have been like for you,' Quick said. 'I'm sorry, Vee. I'm really sorry. Did you want to talk about it, or…'

Evita chewed on her bottom lip, avoiding eye contact. At first, Quick thought Evita was just going to ignore her, but then she said, 'You know the first thing I saw when I opened the door to that wine cellar?'

'Tell me,' Quick said, dragging the chair over so she could sit beside Evita's armchair.

'I saw this stuff smeared on the brickwork, thick and black like tar. But I'd seen it before. I'd spent weeks with it sticking against my bare skin, so I knew what it was and what it smelled like, and I ran. I was too scared to do anything else.' Evita's eyes were so wide that Quick could see white all the way around her irises, and her lips were trembling as she spoke. 'Maybe Digs didn't get out that way, but he could've done. I was too scared to stop. I didn't think about the door being open or what else might have been down in the cellar with him, I just saw that smear of black shit and I ran.'

Evita curled in on herself as she pulled her knees towards her chin.

'But you're right,' she said quietly. 'I shouldn't have gone looking for Bartholomew in the first place.'

Well, now Quick felt wretched. What was she supposed to say to that? The trauma Quick had gone through herself in the blood cellar, and at the Casting, and at the block… All that was nothing compared with the weeks Evita had spent locked in a box with a monster.

And the months before that? In truth, Quick had no clue what her friend's life had been like at the mansion before Bayly had cut it short by literally burying her alive.

Quick shuddered.

'No,' she said quietly. 'I'm sorry. I know Bartholomew deserves to suffer for what he's done—'

'Do you actually *know* what he's done?' Evita asked, her expression sharpening.

Quick laughed bitterly. 'Where do you want me to start?

He's responsible for all of this, isn't he?' She gestured around the library, but she was really encompassing herself, Evita, Xiaoyu, the whole property, and every broken person in it.

'Yes,' Evita agreed, but then she added, 'and no. None of this was here in the beginning, you know. It was just me, and Monty, and… *him*.'

'Just the three of you?' Quick asked.

Evita nodded, just a little, then looked down at her hands as though she had nothing more to say. If she'd wanted to leave it there, Quick would have accepted that, but it didn't feel like she was done talking.

'What happened to bring you here, Vee?' Quick asked, more softly now. 'Last thing I heard you were going to do your talk for the Charleston Pirate Association, and then you were gone.'

Evita took a deep breath, then let it out again slowly. After that, it all came tumbling out.

'Bartholomew came to the talk,' Evita said, sounding as tired as Quick felt. 'We spoke for a bit. He was rude and condescending… Well, you've met him. Afterwards, I went to that seafood place Richard Lewis is always banging on about. You know, the one with the fit barman?'

'Oh god,' said Quick, remembering her own path to this place. 'The one where Monty works.'

'You found it too, then?' Evita laughed darkly. 'I thought that might be how you ended up here. We always did have the same terrible taste in men.'

'That little shit really has no business being that good looking.'

'Funny how it wears off when you get to know him.'

'And how fast,' Quick agreed.

'He wasn't the one who brought me here, though,' said

Evita.

'No?'

'No. That was Bartholomew.'

Quick's stomach sank. If she thought she'd got herself in over her head in her association with Kulika, she couldn't imagine what it must have felt like to find yourself the target of Bartholomew's attention.

'He came to the bar,' Evita said. 'I kept telling him to leave me alone, but he wouldn't take no for an answer and… Fuck. Look, I thought he was hot, so maybe I wasn't *really* telling him to leave me alone. Maybe I just wanted to see how hard he was willing to fight for me. It sounds so stupid now, but when he looked at me in that predatory way that made every instinct in my body twang and tell me to run away, it twanged other things too. Hard.'

'Oh, Vee.'

'I'm not proud of it, all right? But I wasn't intending to act on it either. I swear, I was on the verge of turning and walking away, but then he told me all my theories about pirates reinventing themselves were correct. He said he could prove it. He told me he could show me the Articles of Agreement of Bartolomeu Português and his fellow buccaneers, the holy grail of pirate history. And then he actually did it.'

'They were real?' Quick breathed.

'Oh, they're real,' Evita said. 'And he should know; he bloody wrote them. They're probably in this room somewhere,' she added, looking around at the shelves of books and glass-fronted cases. 'Along with god knows how many other relics that could prove my theories. For all that it matters now.'

'But… Bartolomeu Português?' Quick asked. She didn't know much about Evita's field of study, but she knew enough to know the name of the buccaneer who'd founded the pirate code.

'Bartolomeu Português, Bartolemé de las Casas, Bartholomew Sharp, Bartholomew Roberts,' Evita said. 'He was all of them, and probably more besides.'

'Then you were right,' Quick said, feeling a little overawed. 'The old buccaneers really were reinventing themselves under new names.'

'I was right, and now I can't tell a soul about it. Can you imagine how I'd explain it?'

'Pretty easily after Bartholomew's revelation this evening. You can go back to the university in triumph.'

'Ha,' Evita said without humour. 'Some triumph.'

Kulika had filled them in on the launch party as they'd driven back to the mansion earlier. Quick has assumed they'd be gone again in time to miss it, but the afternoon was already rolling into evening, and here they still were.

'You know we're never leaving this place, right?' Evita said quietly. 'Bartholomew doesn't just let people go.'

'But he did let us go,' Quick argued. 'We just had a little setback. We'll be on our way soon enough. You'll see.' She tried to sound convincing for Evita, despite her own concerns.

'If the doctor isn't back in an hour, I want you to promise me we'll just take a car and go,' Evita said quietly.

'But she's got her own plane,' Quick pointed out. 'She can take us straight back to the UK.'

'If Bartholomew doesn't stop her first. Please, Quick, don't give him time to reconsider. He only wanted me gone because I remembered what he did.'

'What *did* he do?'

Evita paused for a moment, shifting in her chair. 'I told you I was at the bar with Bartholomew and Monty,' she said.

'Yes?'

'I woke up in his bed.'

'Monty's?' Quick asked, knowing that wasn't the *he* Evita meant, but hoping to hell that it might be, because the alternative was too terrifying to contemplate.

Evita tutted irritably. 'You know Monty never turned anyone before the girl last week.'

'Angelina,' Quick supplied.

'Whatever. My point is: no, Monty didn't turn me.'

'But you're saying that Bar—' Quick interrupted herself to lower her voice, just in case. 'You're saying *Bartholomew* did?'

'He bit me,' Evita confirmed.

'But Kulika said she was the only person he'd ever turned.'

'Well, maybe she was, until me. Or maybe he's been turning people for years and just never told her. I don't know, but what I can tell you is the last thing I remember before I woke up in his bed was his teeth in my neck. Of course, I didn't remember that at the time. When I woke up, it was like my whole life had been washed away by his blood. I remember it now, though.' The anger burned in her eyes. 'I remember it *all*.'

Quick couldn't parse her friend's emotions. She was angry, yes, but there was more to it than that. There was pain in her eyes, but grief too, and something else that Quick couldn't believe.

'What aren't you telling me?' she asked.

Evita fiddled with her cuticles, pushing them back and picking at the edges, avoiding the question. Finally, she stilled.

'He didn't just bite me,' she said, looking away from Quick as she whispered the words. 'He kissed me first. And

I...'

Quick's mouth had dropped open, but she closed it again to ask, 'You what?'

Evita swallowed. 'I wanted him to.' She turned to Quick with a pleading look in her eyes. 'I kissed him back.'

I2

KULIKA BURST INTO the cabin of the *Primus's Fortune* without knocking.

Along the back wall, where late afternoon light streamed through the windows set into the ship's stern, there was a desk and matching chair. The desk looked a lot like the one that Bartholomew had in the library back at the mansion, the desk that had once resided in the cabin of his flagship. In fact, it was so alike that Kulika had to stop to confirm to herself that they were not one and the same – but no, this piece of furniture was new, unmarred by the blade marks, candle burns and bloodstains that scarred the original.

It was the same story with all the furniture in the cabin: a map table she recognised from the parlour, chairs that strongly resembled the ones in the mansion's breakfast room, and a bed in one corner of the cabin that was the spitting image of the one that Bartholomew slept in today. It was more than that, though: these weren't just reproductions of Bartholomew's things, they were reproductions of the things he'd had back on the *Royal Fortune* three hundred years ago. Walking into the cabin was like stepping back in time, and it chilled Kulika to her bones.

Mostly.

Almost every part of her wanted to close her eyes and block out the memory of the terrible things they'd done in this room, but the part that was speaking the loudest wanted to revel in the rebirth of the venue of her crimes. She had been powerful in this place once, or in a place that looked a lot like it. Returning here sent the same power rushing through her again. It was a warm welcome from the side of her she had tried to forget, but that had not forgotten her.

Bartholomew should have been used to to Kulika's abrupt entrances by now, but apparently he hadn't been expecting her, because she caught him leaning against the bed frame, staring at a playing card that had Evita Khalyed's face on it.

'Regretting our bargain?' Kulika asked.

'Of course not,' Bartholomew replied, slipping the card into the back pocket of his jeans. 'Sending that woman away was the best thing I could have done, for all of us.'

'Right,' Kulika murmured, pointlessly delaying the inevitable. 'About that…'

'If you're about to tell me that—' Bartholomew stilled mid-sentence, his expression frozen on his face while a single nostril twitched.

Shit.

'We had a blood bargain,' he snapped, his lip curling upwards to show his teeth. 'Given its terms, perhaps you'd like to explain to me why you reek of Patience Quick?'

He pushed off from the bed frame and strode across the cabin towards her, grabbing her by the neck and pinning her against the opposite wall. If he wanted an answer from her, Kulika wasn't sure how he expected her to give him one while he was crushing her larynx.

'I can smell her on your skin,' he whispered, leaning in. 'Her odour has sunk into you like rot sinks into meat. I can smell her on your fingers.' He ran his nose along her cheek and sniffed. 'I can smell her on your lips,' he growled. 'I can smell her on your breath.'

'I had to heal her,' Kulika gasped, scrabbling at his hand with both of hers, trying to pry it away from her neck. 'The zombies infected the humans from the blood cellar. They attacked Quick's car. I had to bring them all back here to lure the zombies back. Quick got burned.'

'Badly enough to threaten her life?' Bartholomew asked, his grip as tight as ever. 'Badly enough to threaten *your* life?'

He saw the answer in her eyes. As his grip squeezed tighter, she didn't have the breath to speak it.

'You gave me your word that you wouldn't touch her again,' he said. 'You broke it.'

He dropped Kulika to the ground, then turned his back on her and started walking away.

'And you broke your word,' Kulika croaked from the floor, rubbing her throat. 'You gave me your word that they'd be out of here this morning.'

'And they were!' Bartholomew yelled back, uncontrolled in a way Kulika had rarely seen him. 'I promised you they'd be off the property, and they were. If you hadn't brought them back—'

'You would have preferred I left them in a ditch to get torn to pieces by whatever the hell these new zombies are?'

'Them, or their pet human?' Bartholomew countered scathingly. 'Even these new zombies can't kill the Silver.'

'But Digs could. Did you know that he got loose, and that he ate half of Bayly on his way out? Dr Ross thinks he's been contaminated by the zombies you locked up in the wine cellar with him. He's not interested in human blood anymore. He wants *ours*.'

Bartholomew practically growled in frustration. 'We wouldn't even be in this mess if you hadn't insisted on bringing Drake's little doctor here with her Silver-killing, zombie-horde-making formula.'

'And I wouldn't have needed to do that if you hadn't turned Evita Khalyed Silver.'

'And you think I don't regret that every single day?' he yelled. 'I don't need you to tell me that was a mistake because believe me, I fucking know.'

Shoulders heaving with his ragged breath, Bartholomew put his hands on the desk with his back to Kulika and hung his head. She pushed herself up to her feet, keeping her back against the wall and her eyes on him. She hadn't seen him this angry since the night she'd left him the first time. It made him unpredictable, so Kulika paid attention.

'I would see you rid of this bond,' he muttered finally.

Kulika laughed bitterly. 'It's the only reason I signed your covenant. Without it, you wouldn't have me at all.'

'But I don't have you now, do I?' he asked. 'Your head is somewhere else, at the beck and call of a Silver so new she can barely use her powers, performing petty healings when you should be walking into glory at my side.'

'You have my contract in blood,' she said, taking a tentative step forward.

'And you still broke it.'

'Not intentionally. She's not staying, Bartholomew. None of them are staying. I'm packing them off with Dr Ross and sending them to the airport, just as soon as the doctor's had a look at the blood of the new zombies.'

Bartholomew really did growl this time.

'We need her expertise,' Kulika argued. 'With Enzo… indisposed' – another growl – 'she's the only person in South Carolina who can tell us what we're dealing with. We need to know what threat the zombies present, and how we can get rid of them safely. I've already gathered them all up. Now we just need to clear the premises for tonight's launch party.'

The set of Bartholomew's shoulders softened, and she knew she had him. There was a smile in his voice when he said, 'I heard you went fishing for zombies with the pet human.'

'Oh?'

'The kid called.'

And hadn't said a word to her about it, the little creep. Kulika would have to deal with him, sooner or later. She supposed she should be grateful he hadn't blabbed to Bartholomew about Quick and Evita from the start, for all the good that delay had done her.

'I also heard what you did to my car,' Bartholomew added.

'Honestly,' she said, 'the zombie came out of nowhere.'

'Hmm,' he grunted, which made it clear just how irritated he was. She had to turn away to hide the petty grin on her face, which is when she noticed the room's focal point.

'Why is there a painting of me on the wall?' she asked, horrified to see her features rendered in oil and hung in a massive gold frame above the bed in the captain's cabin. The pose was dramatic: one of her feet rested on the prow of the ship while she balanced on the rail with the other, her long hair blowing back in the wind as she faced into a thunderstorm. The artist had made her look like some kind of Valkyrie, rather than the bloodthirsty demon she had truly been three centuries previously.

'It's a reproduction,' Bartholomew said dismissively. He stepped to her side to admire it with her, though for Kulika "admire" was definitely the wrong word.

'A reproduction of *what*?'

'Of the painting that hangs in the mansion.'

Then she remembered what Evita had told her when Kulika had first rescued her from the coffin on Bayly's boat: *There's a painting of you in his bedroom.*

'Why do you have a painting of me in your bedroom?'

'Because you belong at my side,' he murmured. 'I knew you would leave me. I planned against that eventuality, but weapons as sharp as you only become blunted when you keep them sheathed. You needed to use your claws. Of course, I would have preferred you hadn't used them to rip out my heart and run away with that bastard Drake, but... Still. I wanted a way to keep you close to me until you returned.'

'You were so sure I would?'

'You are the only person in the world on whom I can rely.' He turned to face her so they were chest to chest instead of shoulder to shoulder, and too close. 'I have always been sure of you.'

'And Evita?'

He flinched. He tried to control his reaction, but his eyes tightened a fraction, his head jerked back the tiniest distance, and irritation hitched up the side of his lip before he could tamp it down.

'The girl should be long gone,' he said.

'But it bothers you that she isn't?'

He shrugged, pretending nonchalance. Kulika wished she could do the same. She shouldn't care what Bartholomew felt for Evita. It shouldn't matter that he had turned her Silver, or that Kulika was no longer the only one who carried his blood. She couldn't understand the crushing sensation she was feeling in her chest, but she couldn't deny it either.

She was riling at the competition.

'What is she to you, Bartholomew? Really?'

'What are either of them, to us?' he whispered, reaching out to cup Kulika's face in his hand. 'New and soft, without any understanding of the lives we live now and have lived before. You and me, Kulika? We're sharp, like blades whetted against each other. No one can ever be to me what you are, nor be to you what I am. Without you, this endeavour has no meaning. I can't be Primus without you at my side.'

Without thought, Kulika felt herself leaning in to his touch, rubbing her cheek along his palm as a cat might rub at the ankles of its owner. The gesture was entirely involuntary. It brought with it a shudder of pleasure she hadn't been looking for, and had never expected to find at Bartholomew's hand. Here was the electricity she'd been searching for in Quick's touch, but had failed to find. Here was the thudding *rightness* she had missed. It was backwards, and beyond her comprehension, but it was undeniable. With Bartholomew's skin pressed against hers, she felt a connection.

She belonged with him. She belonged *to* him.

He'd been right, all those days ago: without him, she was an empty thing.

'What do we do now?' she asked quietly.

'We send them away, as though this morning never happened, and we send Drake's spying doctor away with them.'

'But the zombies—'

'You've contained them, and we can get more humans.' He laughed. 'They'll come to us. This evening, everything will come good. You'll see.'

'But Digs—'

'Is a minor inconvenience,' he said, stroking her cheek

and soothing her soul at the same time. 'You'll find him. Relax. You've done well, my Secundus.' He brushed the hair back from her face, letting his fingers rasp gently along the shaved portion of her head.

The sensation tugged at a memory of someone else, but Kulika couldn't recall why. Then a flash of scent surfaced in her mind – blackberries, frost, earth – and the name rose to her lips without conscious thought.

'Quick,' she breathed.

Bartholomew's face darkened for a moment, then he smiled and said, 'Come, sit.'

Bartholomew led Kulika to a chair, then circled the desk to sit behind it, opening the desk drawer. The runners rumbled ominously with the weight of its contents. When he pulled out the book, it fell open immediately to a page coated with dense writing in Kulika's hand – and blood. She wondered about that. How many hours out of the past twelve had he spent poring over those words, creasing the spine, revelling in his final possession of her?

The thought should have made her angry, but instead she felt a whisper of satisfaction at being so desired. It thrummed in her veins and thudded to the slow rhythm of her heart. He wanted her to belong to him, and that made her worthy of possessing. If she was not possessed by him, she was worth nothing at all.

'Shall we do this again?' he asked softly. Then he pulled the metal-tipped quill from between the pages of the book and offered it to Kulika by the feather end.

'What do you want me to write?' she asked, confused.

'Nothing,' Bartholomew replied. 'I don't want you to write anything. It's all here already,' he added, running his palm across the page. As he did so, tiny particles of blood released their scent into the air: copper and decay,

Bartholomew and Kulika, wound together like a braid and bound with ocean spray.

Bartholomew didn't explain any further. Instead, he took a second quill from the top drawer of the desk and used it to slice a bloody line down the centre of his palm.

The sight of it shouldn't have made Kulika thrill the way she did. The sensation was so foreign that she didn't even acknowledge it at first, but then her mouth began to water as the scent of Bartholomew's blood reached her nose, and she could no longer hide her hunger.

The scent was like nothing else. It wasn't salt, or sugar, or copper, or spice. Instead, his blood smelled somehow of life itself. It was everything.

Last night, it hadn't called to her like this. Last night, they had exchanged blood by pressing their bleeding palms together, but now it didn't feel like that would be enough. Kulika wanted more than just the passive flow of blood from one vein to another. She wanted to take it and fill herself with it. She wanted to bite it out of him, and taste him on her tongue.

Her gaze drifted from his cut palm to the vein at his neck, drawn there without her consciously willing it.

Bartholomew followed her gaze.

'Oh,' he said, a soft smile twitching at his lips. 'So that's how you want to do this?'

He stood from his chair and tossed it out of the way, paying it no mind as it clattered to the floor, then circled the desk towards Kulika.

'Take it,' he said, offering her his palm.

She didn't hesitate. She was salivating, her thirsty tongue already reaching out to lap at his hand as she grasped it to her mouth. She closed her eyes and groaned, then he groaned, and for a moment she forgot who he was supposed to be to her. All she knew was his blood, and how much she thirsted for it. Then the wound healed itself – he had always been a fast healer – and Kulika was left with nothing but a dry mouth and a hunger she couldn't sate.

She moaned her frustration, gripping his hand more tightly as the well ran dry.

'You want it,' Bartholomew said, closing his hand around hers to pull her to her feet. 'So take it.'

As she rose, she opened her eyes to see what he was offering. There was the copper token he wore at his throat, pulled to one side. There was his long, dark hair, cascading over one shoulder as he inclined his head. There was his henley, tugged open with one hand to bare his neck.

He was *baring* his *neck*.

Bartholomew Roberts didn't bare his neck for anyone. He'd certainly never done it for Kulika in all the long years of their acquaintance. The offer was shocking enough that she could do little more than stare.

'You don't need your meat cut for you,' he whispered into her ear. 'You have teeth.'

That was all the invitation she needed. Before the thought even reached her brain, she was biting into his neck and moaning again, this time with the pleasure of her conquest.

'My feral little pirate,' he groaned. Kulika felt the vibration through her teeth. 'Whatever am I going to do with you?'

Anything, Kulika wanted to say, but her mouth was full of his blood and she couldn't spare the time to speak. She wanted to consume him, to take little pieces of him inside her and let them breed in her bones until she was filled with nothing but him. When his teeth pierced her neck, sending his saliva deep into skin and muscle and vein, she thrilled to it. What had felt like violation only days before now felt like catharsis.

She needed this. She needed him to rinse away every trace of the person who had been in her arms before and replace them with himself. She wanted to forget, and she could forget three hundred years if she gave herself over to him. It could be the Golden Age again. He could be nothing but a pirate king and she could be nothing but his weapon, wielded and directed by his hand. She would surrender to him if it meant that she'd no longer have to feel the pain of all the love she would never have.

He wanted her, and that would be enough.

When he finally drew his teeth from her neck, Kulika forced herself to do the same. The dissatisfied noise she made when doing so was not intentional.

'I always knew you would come back to me,' he whispered, cupping her face in his palm. 'My Kulika.'

There was a quiet gasp from the other side of the room. Kulika turned quickly, attuning her hearing to pick out the nearest heartbeats, and beyond Bartholomew's she found another, human. It belonged to a pair of eyes that was peeking out from underneath the bed.

'You've got a stowaway,' she said, hastily wiping the blood from her mouth with the back of her hand.

'Oh, yes,' Bartholomew said. 'I'd forgotten about him.'

'Who is he?'

'Just a human from the historical society who thought I hadn't noticed him creeping onto my ship when we stopped at the harbour. He can wait.'

Bartholomew took Kulika's hand in his and licked the blood from it, watching her eyes for her reaction every step of the way.

She didn't pull back. She should have done, because not only did they have an audience, but they were fast nudging up against a line that the two of them were not meant to cross. Despite that, she found herself enjoying the feeling of his mouth on her skin. It was an abrupt change, but perhaps – like the reversal of her silvering – it was one she was meant to embrace.

There was a scuttling sound from the other side of the room.

'Impatient, Aloysius,' Bartholomew said with irritation, then he dropped Kulika's hand and raced at Silver speed to the other side of the room. He caught the human before he'd managed to get out from under the bed, then he pinned him down onto the mattress with a foot resting across his neck.

'You're Kulika,' the human said reverently, his gaze flicking in disbelief between the painting on the wall above his head and the real deal standing in front of him. 'And you're… you're…'

'You know my name,' Bartholomew said. 'We've been working on this ship for long enough.'

'But you're *the* Bartholomew Roberts. You're over three hundred years old.'

'Five hundred, actually, but who's counting?'

'And you,' the man breathed, his eyes lighting up as he looked at Kulika once more. 'You are the living embodiment of all I ever dreamed.'

Kulika didn't like the sound of that.

'Steady on,' she said.

'I told them,' Aloysius said triumphantly. 'I found the sketches from that very portrait, and I read the stories about the capture of the *Onslow*, and I *told* them that you fell in love with her and dressed her up as a pirate so you could take her to sea with you.'

'Excuse me?' Kulika said. She'd been following him for the first part of his speech, but then it had taken a sharp left turn into the land of what-the-fuckery.

'Dressed her up?' said Bartholomew. 'I assure you, Aloysius, she was not *dressing up*.'

'And he isn't in love with me,' Kulika said.

The human laughed. 'I've been in the room this whole time,' he said. 'He was *licking* you.'

Shudders raced down Kulika's spine, but she couldn't tell whether she was creeped out or… something else. Bartholomew had always had that uncanny edge to him, the hunger in his eyes that made you ride the boundary between fear and attraction, but Kulika couldn't remember ever having come so close to tipping over it before. Worse, she couldn't bring herself to care that she almost had.

'Shall I get rid of him?' she asked Bartholomew.

Bartholomew laughed. 'Still thirsty, my little pirate?'

'Still security-conscious,' she countered, 'in light of this evening.'

'Oh, I don't think Aloysius will be any threat to our event,' Bartholomew replied, eyeing the grey-haired human with consideration. 'In fact, now that our blood cellar has run dry, I think he might be exactly what we need to prove our point,' he added, then he touched the tip of his tongue to one of his canine teeth.

Kulika heard Aloysius's gulp.

Bartholomew just grinned and grinned.

IN THE MANSION'S library, Quick was growing itchy. Part of this could be ascribed to her general impatience, but most of her restlessness had been building as Evita had sat hollow-eyed, telling her story after story of the deaths and deviancies she'd experienced during her time at the block. Now that she'd started talking about it, she didn't seem able to stop, the horrors pouring through her teeth in bitten whispers and gasps. After hearing all that, Quick could finally appreciate how much worse it was for Evita to be back here than it was for Quick herself.

'I'm calling a cab,' she said, pulling the doctor's phone out of her bag. Evita was right: they shouldn't be here, and they needed to go.

'Without the doctor?'

'Like you said, she's got her own plane. She can leave in her own time.'

Quick held the phone up, getting no reception at all, then looked around the library for a landline, in vain.

'Shit,' she said. 'Look, you get your stuff together. I'm going to go outside to get a signal.'

'Not on your own,' Evita said, standing from her chair.

'With Digs on the loose—'

'Well, we can't leave Xiaoyu here, can we?' Quick replied, gesturing at their sleeping friend. 'Just… I'll be right back, okay? Just be ready.'

Evita gave Quick a warning look that told her she'd bloody well better be right back, then Quick slipped out of the door – Dr Ross had left it unlocked, bless her – and into the halls beyond.

It was quiet.

Quick's every step creaked and clacked on the floorboards in a way that made her certain someone was going to come running to lock her back in the library where she belonged, but they didn't. In fact, she made it all the way to the porch before she saw another soul at all.

Then she saw *her*.

Kulika was striding along the side of the pool with her head down, barrelling towards the porch door like a woman on a mission. It reminded Quick of the first night they'd met, when she'd watched Kulika striding towards a conversation with Bartholomew like she was striding into battle. God, she was incredible.

Then she looked up and saw Quick, and paused mid-step.

Quick wanted to imagine that Kulika had frozen for the same reason she herself had: because the sight of the other woman made it difficult to catch a breath. When Quick met Kulika's eyes, she didn't just see flint-grey threaded with silver, she saw a world of possibilities that spread out in front of her like the wide horizon over the open sea.

But Kulika's eyes were turning stormy now, her silver hidden once more. She looked angry.

'You were supposed to wait in the library,' she said, brushing past Quick without looking her in the eye.

'I was trying to get reception to call a cab,' said Quick,

following Kulika inside the mansion. 'What happened to your neck?' she added, her eyes drawn to the wound at Kulika's throat. It was healing – nearly healed, in fact – but she could see broken skin and indentations in her flesh. 'Is that... did someone bite you?'

'No,' Kulika said, running her hand over the wound. By the time she removed it, there was nothing there at all.

'Was it Digs? The thing that was in the box with Vee?' Quick asked. 'Did you find it?'

'*Him*,' Kulika corrected her. 'And no.'

A terrible feeling began to churn in the pit of Quick's stomach. She remembered the night that Kulika had turned her Silver, and all that had entailed. She remembered the unexpected ecstasy of Kulika's bite and the way it had blazed through her body in an unstoppable wave. The feeling surging through her now was an entirely different kind of fire.

'Someone bit you, though, didn't they?' she said angrily, following close on Kulika's heels. She had no right to be jealous, but she couldn't help it. Kulika had healed her – kissed her – just hours before, and now she had someone else's teeth marks in her neck.

Kulika abruptly turned around, and Quick nearly barrelled straight into her. They were close, so close, for a tantalising moment, then Kulika stepped back, putting space between them that Quick wished she could obliterate.

'I'm sorry,' Kulika said, her voice cold and distant. 'For what happened back at the car... I shouldn't have done that. You should leave, now.'

'I'm not leaving until you give me an answer.'

It was the wrong thing to say. Quick knew that the moment the words had come out of her mouth, but she couldn't call them back. They were out there now, casting more storm clouds through the grey of Kulika's eyes.

'I don't owe you that,' she said, her voice terrifyingly calm. 'I don't owe you anything.'

'I know,' Quick said desperately. 'I know that, and I know I don't have any right to ask for an explanation, but I need one. Look, Vee told me you've silvered for me, because otherwise you wouldn't be able to heal me, and that it means you must have feelings…'

Kulika looked away, biting her lip irritably. She clearly didn't want to have this conversation, but Quick wouldn't be able to live with herself if she didn't ask.

'Please,' she said. 'I just want to know what all this means.'

'It doesn't matter what it means,' Kulika said. 'You need to go, and I need to stay.'

There was lead in Kulika's words.

'You could come with me,' Quick said. 'You don't want to be here any more than I do, do you? We could run together.'

'From Bartholomew?' Kulika laughed incredulously, as though it were inconceivable.

'From everything,' Quick insisted. 'From Bartholomew, from this plan of his, from his country. Why not? We could just be us, somewhere else.'

Kulika didn't show any outward reaction that Quick could see, but all the same she could feel Kulika's wanting. It was hot and tight, filling the space between them with an intensity that Quick didn't understand, and was afraid to ask about.

'And what if I don't want to run from him?' Kulika asked.

It wasn't until then that Quick realised how badly she'd misread the situation. She went cold, then hot, then itchy with embarrassment.

'You're barely a week old,' Kulika said. 'Bartholomew

has lived for half a millennium. He made me to be his equal in ways that you could never be mine. What makes you think that I would *ever* give him up for you?'

There should have been words spoken, then. Quick should have been able to find them, on the tip of her tongue, in her pockets, or pulled up from the earth through the soles of her feet. There were none, though. Her heart was empty, her hands were empty, her mouth was empty.

There were no words. She just stood there and hurt.

'Go home, Quick,' Kulika said as she turned and walked on to the library without a backward glance. 'There's nothing for you here.'

For a moment, Quick couldn't move. Her temperature was all wrong, and she could feel her pulse in her tongue. Was she going to be sick? She felt like she was going to be sick. Actually, she felt like she'd just been punched in the stomach by an articulated truck. She wanted to curl up in a ball and cradle herself until it stopped hurting, but something told her that wouldn't help, not here. Instead, she stared at the floor until she got her breath under control, wiped away the tears she hadn't noticed she was shedding, and shakily followed Kulika back to the library.

Where she found Xiaoyu still asleep in her chair, but Evita nowhere to be seen. Quick was certain that the windows had all been closed when she'd left the room a few minutes ago, but now the one behind the desk was open.

No, not open, missing entirely. There was glass on the floor. Glass, together with smears of a sticky black substance, somewhere between treacle and tar.

'No,' Quick murmured, racing to the window. There was blood on the couple of shards of glass that still held in the frame, but nothing beyond except a few trampled plants in the flowerbed outside. 'No!' she yelled out of the window.

'Evita!'

Not again.

She couldn't lose her best friend again. They'd barely begun patching up the rifts that had been punched through their relationship by the trauma they'd each suffered in this hellish place. It couldn't end here, with two broken girls, who'd become broken women, fracturing apart at the hands of an irrevocably broken man.

'Don't touch the blood,' Kulika said, all business. 'Get over there,' she ordered, 'next to the human.'

'You mean Xiaoyu,' Quick corrected her, not quite believing the change that had come over Kulika since this morning.

'Just go,' Kulika snapped.

Quick was used to seeing warmth in Kulika's eyes, sometimes humour, and even a painful edge of longing that Quick was all too familiar with herself. She still felt that longing when she looked at Kulika, but it was no longer reflected back at her.

Now, there was nothing in Kulika's eyes at all.

'You want me to go?' Quick asked. 'Fine. I will.'

Then she grabbed her blanket, leapt through the window, and ran. At superhuman speed, frantically burning through the last of the energy in her exhausted body. Now that Quick had finally begun to understand the pain Evita had suffered at Digs's hands, there was no way she was going to leave her to suffer again alone. She could see a faint trail of blood and black ichor, and she followed it haphazardly across the lawn towards the river.

Haphazardly, because it was possible that she'd slightly miscalculated the protection she'd get from the tattered old blanket she was holding above her head. There were new rips in it that she was sure hadn't been there earlier. When she'd been walking down the road under it this morning, she'd had a little protection from the trees, too, and the sun had been overhead. Now, the dying light shone sideways across the open lawn from the horizon, cutting right under her cover and slicing into her face like a hot blade.

She could hold the blanket low enough to protect her skin, or she could hold it high enough that she could see where she was running to, but she couldn't do both, however hard she tried.

'Quick!' Kulika yelled, already close behind. 'Stop!'

Her arms were burning. Her face was burning. There was a noise like a kettle boiling and Quick realised that she was screaming through her gritted teeth as she ran, but she kept following the spotty black trail nonetheless. She followed it all the way across the lawn, through the trees, down to the river, where it split in five directions, each apparently as fresh as the other. One went right down to the water, another past a dock where an incongruously large ship was moored, a third back through the trees at a slightly different angle, the fourth across the lawn to the block, and the final one along the riverbank. Dozens of Silver were moving at speed in that area, putting the finishing touches to a bank of seating and a little stage in front of the dock.

Quick had no idea which direction was the right one to follow.

'Fuck!' she yelled.

The Silver working on the stage turned to stare.

'Did you see anyone come this way?' she called over to them.

'Besides a woman literally on fire?' Angelina called back.

Quick shifted the blanket, wrapping it around her forearm to quench the flames that were starting to crackle along her skin, but in the process she managed to dislodge the whole thing, and now her face was burning too. It wouldn't be long before her eyes melted shut—

The pain.

God, she'd forgotten it could get so bad.

Then something hit her in the side and tackled her to the ground, rolling her onto the dock and into the shade of the ship.

'You have to stop,' Kulika said desperately, looming over her, holding her shoulders down against the cool wood of the dock, as though she thought Quick was intending to go right out into the sun again. 'Please. I'm sorry I was… Just stop.'

'They came this way,' Quick said, struggling gingerly up onto her elbows. 'They came this far, at least, but then the trail goes off in all different directions—'

'I know, and we'll follow it. But you have to go back inside.'

'I can't just leave her,' Quick said, salt tears scalding their way through the raw skin on her cheeks. 'Not again.'

'And you won't have to. Look,' Kulika said, pointing to the trees in the west, 'the sun's already setting. In fifteen minutes, it'll be dark, and if my team haven't already found her by then, we'll go out searching together. But you can't do it like this.'

'I have to—'

'Quick,' Kulika whispered. 'For the next quarter of an hour, please, just let me handle it.'

There was more softness in Kulika's eyes as she spoke than Quick had seen all afternoon. Quick was no longer certain if that meant something, or nothing at all, but she couldn't argue with the sense of Kulika's words.

Quick was no use to Evita like this.

'All right,' she agreed hopelessly. 'I'll wait.'

Kulika's gaze softened further, so much that Quick

wondered if she was about to take back everything she'd said in the house. All Quick could see was silver-grey eyes and a face she wanted to wake up next to every day for the rest of her life, but what was Kulika looking at? Quick wished she knew. The silver in her eyes should mean that Kulika loved her, but with everything that she'd said earlier today…

Quick just wished she could trust her.

There was a sound like a fist slamming into a wall, loud and startling, and the dock shook beneath Quick's back. Kulika abruptly pulled away. Bartholomew had jumped from the ship, and now he was standing behind Kulika, looking down at them both with an expression of angry disapproval.

Kulika didn't turn to face him immediately. Instead, she closed her eyes for a moment, then hissed at Quick, 'Sit in the shade. Don't say a word.' After that, she stood and turned her back to Quick, putting herself between Quick and Bartholomew.

'Primus,' she said.

'Kulika,' he replied. 'You told me you were sending her away.'

'And I am, as soon as possible, but Digs has taken Evita.'

For a moment, Quick thought Bartholomew looked almost concerned. His brow pinched, just for a fraction of a second, one that Quick probably wouldn't have noticed before she'd turned Silver, but all traces of that concern were immediately replaced with rage.

'Then find him, find her and deal with it!' he yelled. 'Have you forgotten that the press are arriving within the hour?'

'No, Primus,' Kulika replied. 'I'll see it done. I just need to heal Quick's wounds, then—'

'Oh, no,' he interrupted. 'I don't think so. I think she

needs to feel the consequences of her actions for once. Don't you?'

Quick looked down at the raw red of her arms, felt the burning in her cheeks, and began to regret her choices.

'She goes back to the mansion,' Bartholomew said. 'You go out on your hunt. And kill him, this time, will you?'

'Kill him?' Kulika asked.

'Yes,' Bartholomew confirmed. 'Kill him. Dead. I've got everything I wanted from him.'

Then Bartholomew returned to the ship, leaving Quick to wonder what, exactly, he had wanted from the monster that Digs had become.

'Back here again?' Xiaoyu asked Quick when Kulika deposited her back in the library.

'Back here again,' Quick agreed, defeated. 'You know what happened?'

'I can guess,' Xiaoyu said. 'It's not good, is it?'

'Digs took Evita,' Kulika said, then she took a key out of her pocket and used it to unlock a high cupboard on the wall behind the library door. It swung open to reveal a handful of old guns that looked like they belonged in a museum. Kulika stuck two fingers in her mouth and whistled out of the library door, so loudly and at such a pitch that Quick had to cover her ears.

'What are you going to do?' Quick asked Kulika, but she didn't get an answer before a couple of strangers joined them in the library.

'What the hell were you doing?' Kulika was yelling at the two men. 'How did he come back to the property and get into the mansion – into the *library* – when you were supposed to be tracking him?'

The tall, skinny one said, 'We did track him. We tracked

him round and round in circles. He's crossing over his trail, trying to throw us off, so we can't work out where it starts or finishes. Whatever he's turned into, his brain's still working just fine.'

'And his teeth are, too,' the other man said. He was the polar opposite of the first, short and round and covered in hair. 'We found two dead Silver in the woods.'

'Not Evita?' Quick said desperately, snapping the men's attention to the corner of the room where she and Xiaoyu were standing.

'Two young men,' the hairy one clarified, and Quick nearly collapsed with relief.

Meanwhile, the tall man had frozen, staring off over Quick's shoulder.

'Xiaoyu,' he breathed.

Quick looked at him, then at Xiaoyu, then back again. Xiaoyu did not look pleased.

'Um, Xiaoyu?' she asked.

'Quick,' she said stonily, 'meet Phinchas. The lying shit who abandoned me here six months ago.'

Excellent, Quick thought. *More drama. Perfect timing.*

'I can't believe you're still here,' he whispered to her.

'Why?' Xiaoyu replied defiantly. 'Did you expect me to be dead by now, drained dry in that fucking blood cellar?'

'The… What?'

'Oh, come on. Don't even try to pretend that you didn't know what was happening when you dumped me here with *him*.'

'Who, Bartholomew?' Phinchas said, wide-eyed and innocent-looking. 'He said he'd look after you.'

But Xiaoyu wasn't buying his act. 'Go fuck yourself.'

'Later,' Kulika said, fiddling with the guns she'd retrieved from Bartholomew's safe. They were old, and rusty, and

Quick was certain they weren't going to be enough to take down Digs. 'Phinchas. Wolfrie. You said you couldn't find Digs because you couldn't work out where the trail started? Well, you have his starting point now, so go. It stops down at the dock, then splits five ways. Follow them all. I'll be coming after you in ten minutes.'

'Yes, Secundus,' Wolfrie said with a lazy salute, then they went, with Phinchas looking mournfully behind him the whole way.

'I'm going to find the doctor. Xiaoyu,' Kulika said, 'look after Quick.'

Quick was confused by that for a moment, until she turned to see Xiaoyu rolling up her sleeve to bare her wrist.

'Hey, no,' Quick said, backing away. 'I'm not taking her blood. She's still an invalid.'

Kulika made a *tsk* noise and said, 'One sip won't kill her, but it will heal you. If you want to come looking for Evita, you'll drink.'

'You told Bartholomew I'd stay at the mansion.'

'I know what I told him,' Kulika said irritably, then she left the room, leaving Quick and Xiaoyu alone.

'Let me,' Xiaoyu insisted. 'It's the only way I can be useful.'

So Quick let her. It was fast – just a tiny puncture to her vein with the point of the knife that served as Bartholomew's letter opener – but effective. The puncture had practically closed by the time Quick had drunk her mouthful, along with the burns on Quick's exposed skin.

'Thank you,' Quick said.

'Don't thank me,' Xiaoyu said bitterly. She had been crying. There were no tears on her face, or on her sleeves, but Quick could see their ghosts in the redness that still coloured her eyes. 'I'm sorry,' Xiaoyu said, looking out of the broken window towards the river. 'I shouldn't have fallen asleep.'

'It's not your fault,' Quick replied, her voice as hollow as she felt. 'I shouldn't have left the room. I was trying to get phone reception to call us a cab and finally get us out of here, and then—'

'I didn't even wake up,' Xiaoyu said, shaking her head. Then she stopped, frozen, looking out of the window. 'Is that a ship at the bottom of the garden?'

'Yes,' Quick said, tossing the phone back into the doctor's bag before joining Xiaoyu at the window. 'A frigate, I think. Pirate ship.'

'You know a lot about it?'

'Evita does,' Quick said quietly.

Evita would love that ship, Quick thought. She'd had ship diagrams taped all around her office back at the university. She'd always been talking about how pirates would capture navy vessels, then convert them with more cannon, and bigger cabins to accommodate the whole crew, not just the officers. No elitism on a pirate ship, she'd said. Pure democracy.

Well, that hadn't been Quick's experience of being on Bartholomew's crew. That hadn't been her experience *at all*.

'We'll get her back,' Quick said.

'We'll get her back,' Xiaoyu repeated, taking Quick's hand in her own. 'Then we'll get in that car, and we'll drive to the airport, and you'll fly away. I'll get back to my kids, and everything will be okay.'

'Do you really think that?' Quick asked.

'No,' Xiaoyu admitted. 'But isn't it nice to pretend?'

14

KULIKA FELT LIKE weeping. She didn't actually weep –
she was holding vicelike control over her emotions, crushing
them down at the slightest hint of rebellion – but she felt like
doing it all the same.

The *burning*. She could still smell it, coating the insides of
her nostrils. The raw wounds on Quick's cheeks and arms
had not been as bad as the first time she'd burned, so Kulika
was reassured that her tolerance to the sun was slowly
increasing, but she was worried by how slowly the wounds
were healing. There just wasn't enough human blood left in
this place, and if Bartholomew wasn't going to let her heal
Quick…

Kulika was far from squeamish, but every time she
remembered Quick's face contorted in pain, she winced. She
should have known that she was going to run. Even a
passing acquaintance with the woman would have been
enough to teach her that Quick wasn't the type to sit around
and wait, and Kulika and Quick were certainly more than
acquaintances.

She'd nearly kissed her, back on the dock. In front of
Bartholomew, no less. She couldn't let herself get that close

544

again. She was Bartholomew's, she reminded herself. She had sold herself to him to buy Quick's freedom, and she wasn't going to void the deal she'd worked so hard to broker.

Quick *would* be free.

Until then, Kulika just had to avoid looking her in the eye. If she did, she was going to break and try to take back everything she'd said out in the corridor earlier. Even if that was an option, now would not be the time. Quick didn't need Kulika to be emotional right now. She needed a fighter and a tracker, someone who could find her friend and bring her back unharmed. That was who Kulika would be, even if the teasing scent of Quick's skin was begging her to be someone else.

It didn't take long to find Dr Ross. She'd set up in the kitchen on the other side of the mansion, glass slides littering the countertops as she squinted at one after another through the ancient microscope.

'You left them alone,' Kulika accused, unexpected rage bubbling up inside her. It took her a moment to work out why she was feeling so angry, then she realised: *it could have been Quick.*

'You've got blood on your collar,' the doctor said, looking at Kulika with a mixture of concern and disapproval. 'And you smell like him. Bartholomew.'

'The Primus, you mean.'

'No,' Dr Ross said calmly. 'That's not what I meant at all.' Then she looked Kulika dead in the eye and said, 'Show me your silver.'

'No,' Kulika replied. Then she added, 'Come with me,' and started walking back towards the library.

'Kulika.' The admonishment in Dr Ross's voice was enough to irritate Kulika into turning around.

'I don't answer to you, doctor,' she snapped. 'We don't

even answer to the same master anymore, but right now we need to work together, because Digs has taken Evita.'

The emotions flitted across Dr Ross's face in quick succession: fear, pain, concern. But she didn't move.

'Are you coming?' Kulika demanded.

'Not until you show me your silver.' Dr Ross's jaw was set, her eyes glinting with determination. It was clear she wouldn't easily be put off.

'Fine,' Kulika muttered angrily. 'If that's what it takes.' She relaxed her control and let her silver flood back into her eyes. The sensation was diminished, again. There was a twitching, stuttering feeling in Kulika's eyes, but no feeling of satisfaction followed. It was underwhelming.

Dr Ross examined her eyes, going up on her tiptoes to lean over the counter, then she leaned back and gave Kulika a level look. 'I checked Quick's blood, like you asked. There's nothing wrong with her, though, is there?' she said. 'It's you, or something *he's* doing to you.'

'That's ridiculous,' Kulika said.

'Are you drinking from him?' the doctor challenged her. 'Is that what this is?'

'Why would you ask that?'

Dr Ross raised her eyebrows at Kulika, looked pointedly at the blood on her collar, then back to her eyes.

'His blood shouldn't be able to do that,' the doctor said.

'Yeah, well.' Kulika thought about the control Bartholomew had over the crew, the blood rituals they underwent, and the way it hurt his people to be apart from him. 'His blood shouldn't be able to do a lot of things that it does.'

'Hmm. Do you know who turned him Silver?'

'No,' said Kulika. 'We're wasting time. We need to be going after Evita.'

'And – like you – Evita was turned by Bartholomew. She carries his blood. Digs has drunk from her. There's an addictive quality to Bartholomew's blood, isn't there?' the doctor probed, coming around the counter. She had to look a long way up to look Kulika in the eye, but once she had Kulika trapped under her scrutiny, there was no escaping it. 'It keeps you close,' she said. 'It calls you to him, and that's a little out of the ordinary, isn't it? That's why I'm asking: who turned him Silver?'

Kulika shrugged, pretending she hadn't just been bullied into submission by a tiny Scottish doctor, and said, 'All I know is it happened in the early sixteenth century, on Hispaniola. He doesn't talk about the rest.' People didn't, generally. It was personal.

Dr Ross was murmuring to herself again in that irritating way she had that meant she was working something out in her head, but she wasn't going to fill Kulika in.

'What?'

'Nothing.'

'Doctor,' Kulika said in an admonitory tone. 'Tell me.'

Dr Ross looked Kulika in the eye. 'I only know one bloodline with that kind of power.'

'Just spit it out,' Kulika said irritably.

'Fine,' the doctor replied, with equal irritation. 'I think Bartholomew's bloodline is descended from the Primus – the *real* Primus. Solomon.'

That shut Kulika up.

'With Bartholomew's blood being as powerful as it is,' Dr Ross went on, 'it's the only explanation that makes sense. The timeline works too.'

Kulika looked at her, silently requesting an explanation. It couldn't be true, could it?

'The last Silver that was sired by Solomon,' Dr Ross said,

'the only one I know of, anyway – died in the sixteenth century, in what they called the New World.'

'But that would mean that I…'

'You share blood with the two most powerful Primi in the world. In any world, old or new. Your bloodline is *the* bloodline, and Solomon is your great-grandsire, and Evita's. Since Digs has been drinking from Evita—'

'He now has that blood in his veins too,' Kulika finished.

'Maybe. The properties of a bloodline shouldn't transfer like that, not if the Silver isn't made with them, but then Digs isn't a normal Silver.'

'Shit.'

Kulika ran her fingers through her hair, wondering how they were going to kill Digs if they couldn't use the doctor's formula. Taking the Silver out was no easy matter. The young ones were vulnerable, sure, but once their ages got into the centuries, they were practically indestructible. She supposed they could take him apart, piece by piece, and let the tide take him, but she'd heard of ancient Silver coming back from worse.

She could understand now why Bayly had just locked him away in a box.

'If you keep letting him do this,' Dr Ross said, 'I think he's going to break the bond.'

'What?' Kulika said, not following her train of thought.

'If you keep drinking Bartholomew's blood,' Dr Ross clarified. 'It's going to destroy your bond to Quick. In more ways than one.'

'Which you said would be a good thing, so why are you giving me a hard time about it?' Kulika said.

'I said it would be *easier*, assuming you took the time to think about it and decide whether or not it was what you wanted. I didn't say you should fall into it just because he wants you to. I didn't say it would be *good*.'

'What wouldn't be good?' Quick asked.

Kulika turned around to see her standing with Xiaoyu in the doorway, looking decidedly impatient.

'It wouldn't be good if you hung around much longer,' Kulika said, improvising desperately.

'Yes,' Quick said sharply. 'You've made your thoughts on that perfectly clear. And once we find Evita, you'll never have to see me again.'

Kulika couldn't stand the pain in Quick's eyes. God, how she wanted to take the words back, but she couldn't. She *shouldn't*.

It wasn't too late to get Quick to safety. If she could just get Evita back from Digs, and get them all bundled back on their way to the airport, then everything would be fine. She should have done it hours ago, but then there had been the zombies, and Bartholomew, and now Evita. Still, it was done, and it was done the best way she'd known how at the time. All of it, even the terrible things she'd said. The easiest way to get Quick gone was to push her away, so Kulika had pushed.

It had been necessary.

'You've got the vials?' Kulika asked Dr Ross.

'In the cool bag,' she replied, pointing to where it sat on the counter. 'Remember what I said about Digs's blood.'

'I remember,' Kulika said.

If the doctor's theory was right, then her formula would be completely useless against Digs, but the only way they could know for sure was by testing it, so that's exactly what Kulika intended to do.

'Are Bayly and Enzo still out?' Kulika asked the doctor.

'Yes. They're sleeping upstairs.'

'Under guard?'

'Penny's with them.'

'Hmm.'

That didn't seem like enough. Kulika would send a real guard up there, maybe a couple, with radios. She wouldn't put it past Digs to come back for Bayly if things went wrong with Evita.

'Sun's setting,' Quick reminded her.

'All right,' Kulika replied, leaning over the counter to grab the four remaining full vials from Dr Ross's cool bag. 'Then we're going to need these.'

15

QUICK AND DR Ross followed Kulika through the house to a cupboard by the porch doors, which turned out to be another gun safe. She pulled out four long-barrelled guns from the cabinet and started racking the vials into each of them.

'You know how to use one of these?' she asked Quick.

Quick had never touched a gun in her life, but she said, 'Yes,' anyway, because if everyone else was going to have one, then she wanted one too.

Kulika was not fooled. She gave Quick an unimpressed look – one that had become painfully familiar over the past few hours – opened one of the guns up again and passed the vial inside it to Quick. She didn't let go immediately, though.

'If this breaks,' Kulika said, 'and if it gets into your body, then you're going to burn up. And I'm not just talking about sunburn, I'm talking spontaneous combustion. I won't be able to get to you fast enough to stop it, so please, don't break it.'

'Don't scare the girl,' Dr Ross said, then she turned to Quick and added, 'For what it's worth, I'm fairly certain that your bloodline's immune to it anyway, so I don't think it'll cause you any harm. You, or Kulika, or Evita, for that matter.'

'I'm not relying on that,' Kulika said, with a warning in her voice. 'You haven't tested it.'

'I haven't had time,' the doctor replied. 'You've had me testing *a lot of things,*' she added significantly.

'But it *will* kill Digs?' Quick asked.

'That's the plan,' Kulika said.

Quick did not find her evasive turn of phrase reassuring.

'Here,' said Dr Ross, fumbling in her cool bag for a moment before pulling out a tube with a capped syringe on one end. 'This is easier to use.' She took the vial from Quick's hand and fitted it into the back of the syringe apparatus. 'When you're ready to use it, you just press the end of the vial into the syringe until it clicks, like a cartridge in a fountain pen. Once the vial is loaded, you uncap the needle, stick it into your target, and it'll discharge the formula. Okay?'

Dr Ross handed the syringe to Quick, who took it carefully and stashed it in the pocket of her dress. Not the most practical clothing for hunting vampires, she was prepared to admit, but she hadn't got anything else. It would have to do.

Kulika strapped a radio to her belt, handed one to the doctor, then whistled out of the porch door, and within seconds Phinchas and Wolfrie were standing in front of them.

'Report,' she said.

'He's still doubling back on himself, overrunning old trails,' said Wolfrie. 'Seems to me like he planned it that way, sending off tracks in dozens of directions before he snatched the girl, so we wouldn't know which one to follow when he did.'

'Fuck,' said Kulika. 'You've got people running them down, though?'

'Yup,' said Phinchas. 'Got a pair of the new Silver running each spur to its end, but he's covered a lot of ground. I think we need to search the property again, make sure he hasn't just found a place to hole up here and watch us spin. I want to start at the dock.'

'Then let's do it. You ready?' Kulika asked Quick.

'Ready,' she said, though the bubbling feeling in her stomach said otherwise. She felt sick with anxiety, and exhaustion, and fear. If they didn't get Evita back, if it was too late—

'Hey,' Kulika whispered, taking her hand for a moment. 'We'll find her. I promise you. Now, are you ready?'

How was it that, after all the times Kulika had pushed her away, Quick still felt so settled by her touch? Those points of connection – finger to palm, fingertip to wrist, thumb to thumb – seemed to ground her to the earth in ways she couldn't explain. She still wanted Kulika, much though she might wish she could stop, but there was so much more than that to Quick's feelings. When she was this close to her, breathing her scent and hearing the slow pulse beneath her skin, it was as though Quick's body slowed to keep time with Kulika's.

Joyful synchronicity. Quick had never known anything like it. Together, they just clicked.

Quick took a deep breath and said, 'I'm ready.'

This time, she meant it.

Quick didn't like the mansion at night. It reminded her of when she'd first arrived in this inescapable place, with the pool lights reflecting off the Spanish moss with an eerie blue glow. She should have taken that as the ill omen it was and got herself right back out of here, but then she wouldn't have found Evita, even if she had lost her again now. She wouldn't have found Kulika either, even if she was about to lose her, too.

Kulika and her two generals didn't go slow on Quick's account. It had been days since she'd used her Silver speed for any prolonged stretch of time, and the mouthful of blood she'd had from Xiaoyu wouldn't keep her running like this for long. But for as long as she had it, she'd use it to find Evita.

They started at the ship. The Silver from the block were putting the finishing touches on the stage and seating as they sped past following what Phinchas said was the newest of the trails, back into the trees at an angle to the direction from which they'd come. The route took them downriver, into parts of the property on the far side of the mansion, where Quick had never been before. They ran into Brandon and Monty there.

'The trail splits into three different directions just up here,' Brandon said.

'We've run these two,' Monty said, pointing to the two trails closest to the mansion.

'We'll take the third,' Kulika said. 'Go mark the ones you've already run on the map, then get everyone picking up the other trails from the riverbank. Set up there. We'll follow this one and loop back. Keep your radios on.'

'Yes, Secundus,' said Monty, then he left with Brandon, but not before giving Quick a dirty look.

Quick, Phinchas, Wolfrie and Kulika ran on, and on, in looping circles through the trees, following trails Quick could barely scent, until she felt a pull in her chest that stopped her dead.

'What?' Kulika said, halting the others when she realised

Quick was no longer following the pack.

'There's something…' said Quick, but it was such a strange feeling that she didn't know how to put it into words. It was a tugging in the pit of her stomach, like falling in love, or stepping on a stair that wasn't there. It was a horrifying mixture of attraction and repulsion. She didn't know whether she truly wanted to find its source, or if all she wanted was to reassure herself that there was nothing there at all, in the same way she'd felt a compulsion to check for monsters under the bed as a child.

Either way, it drew her irresistibly closer, though at the same time she couldn't work out where it was coming from. From the intensity of the sensation, she should be right on top of it. It was dark in the woods at night, but she had senses that were more than capable of dealing with that. If there was anything here, she should be seeing it.

'I think I can feel her,' Quick whispered.

'Maybe it's the blood,' Kulika suggested.

'What?'

'Bartholomew shared his blood with Evita when he turned her Silver. I shared it with you when I turned you. There's something about his blood: it calls to us.'

'Does that mean you can feel it, too?'

For a moment, Kulika stood still, then her gaze panned upwards into the canopy above Quick's head.

Shit.

It was coming from the trees.

Phinchas and Wolfrie leapt up into the branches, but it was too late, because Digs was already coming down. He landed on the ground in front of Quick, crouching like a tiger, gripping Evita's waist in one sinewy, distorted, gore-rimmed arm. She wasn't moving, and even at a moment's glance Quick could see that she was riddled with bite marks. Her head lolled at a terrifying angle; all Quick could see at the spot where her neck joined her shoulder was blood and black filth. If she hadn't been groaning, Quick would have thought she was dead.

The Digs creature hissed, then relinquished its grip on Evita to lunge at Quick. It took her to the ground, digging skeletal digits into her shoulders so hard that they broke the skin. She screamed and tried to push him off, but his open jaws were dripping horror onto her face, rotten liquid that smelled like old blood and dead things. It burned her skin, blistering her like the sun did. She thought for sure that his teeth would be in her neck next, but then Kulika was there, ripping Digs from her body and his fingers from her flesh.

They wrestled for a moment, then the Digs creature leapt back into the treetops, empty-handed this time.

'After him!' Kulika yelled at Wolfrie.

He jumped into the branches after Digs and disappeared into the night. Quick rushed to Evita's side, gathering her into her arms.

'She's alive,' Kulika said to Quick. 'Get her out of here.'

'She can't walk!' Quick looked down at her barely-conscious friend, horrified at the new bites and scratches punched through her clothes and into her flesh. 'She's barely even awake!'

God, there were so many bites. Not just indentations, but pieces of missing flesh.

'Then carry her,' said Kulika. 'Phinchas?'

'I've got her,' he said, scooping Evita gently up into his arms.

'Get her healed,' Kulika said.

'How?' asked Quick desperately. 'The blood cellar's full of nothing but zombies. There's just Xiaoyu, and she can't spare enough blood to heal this much damage.'

'Take her to the ship,' Kulika said after a moment's pause. 'Bartholomew has a human there with him. She can drink from him. Phinchas, make sure they're safe, then come right back here afterwards, okay?'

'You want us to stay on that ship with Bartholomew?' Quick said, horrified.

'No,' Kulika said, already heading off in the direction Wolfrie had gone. 'I want you to get out of here. Digs is our problem. All this is our problem. Get Evita healed, then go straight to the house, collect Xiaoyu and Dr Ross, go to the airport, and fly home.'

'I can't just leave—'

'Go home, Quick.'

'Kulika...'

But she had already followed Wolfrie into the trees. Kulika was gone. Quick looked after her hopelessly. That was to be their final goodbye, then.

'Come on,' Phinchas said quietly. 'Let's get her to the ship, fast.'

Quick turned her back on the spot where Kulika had disappeared, and walked out of the trees with Phinchas carrying Evita at her side.

Go home.

She could try. Maybe this time, she'd be lucky, and she'd finally succeed.

When they arrived at the riverbank, it was buzzing with activity. The stage was fully-constructed now, black-skirted and sombre against the river's surface, which glittered in the moonlight behind it. The stadium-style seating opposite, four rows tall and running the length of the stage, looked large enough to accommodate hundreds of people, and it was plush. No raw wood for this audience; the benches had been upholstered and padded, seat and back, bringing the impression of class and comfort to what had just been bare bleachers earlier in the night. There were even tables built into the structure at regular intervals. The Silver from the block were ornamenting them with flowers and tea lights, and draping them with blood-red satin.

Finishing touches.

Other Silver were running between the driveway on the far side of the lawn and the stage at the riverside, laying a red-carpeted path between the two that was lit with torches. It was a spectacle, luring people towards Bartholomew's stage, which was clearly the main event. As glorious as the ship looked, glinting enticingly in its berth, it was merely the backdrop to the podium that stood centre-stage. Quick could imagine how it would look when Bartholomew was standing there, making his revelations.

But that was not why she was here.

'Can you jump?' she asked Phinchas as they ran down onto the dock, pushing through the bustling crowds of Silver at work.

'To the ship?' he asked. 'Of course. Why? Can't you?'

'Just go,' Quick replied irritably. 'I'll catch up.'

She started hauling herself up the rope ladder. By the time she arrived at the top, Phinchas had laid Evita on the moonlit deck. There were a few Silver up here, polishing the wood and carrying boxes around, but she paid no attention to them. Evita still wasn't moving.

'I don't like the look of those bites,' Quick said, hurrying over to join Phinchas and Evita. They were seeping blood and black goo. 'And I don't want to keep moving her around. Can you radio Dr Ross and ask her to come to us?'

After a brief conversation over the radio, Dr Ross appeared, carrying Xiaoyu, and the two of them started assessing Evita's injuries.

'Multiple lacerations,' Xiaoyu said, twisting Evita back and forth gently. Her head lolled on her neck, which was so gruesomely mangled that Quick couldn't bear to look at it. 'She's losing what little blood she has left.'

'We're going to need a serious amount to heal her,' said Dr Ross, 'and I've already used everything I had on Bayly and Enzo.'

'I know where we can get more,' Quick said.

'Hey,' said one of the guys from the block. 'You're letting her bleed all over the deck. We just got that cleaned.'

'Then clean it again,' Quick said as she stood and crossed the deck towards him. 'Where's Bartholomew?'

'The Primus?' the guy said uncertainly.

'Do you know another Bartholomew?'

'He's in his cabin,' the guy said, pointing the way, 'but he's preparing his speech for tonight. He said he doesn't want to be disturbed. Hey! You can't go in there!'

The guy tried to stop Quick, but she was a desperate woman on a mission. She batted him aside easily and slammed her way into the cabin.

Bartholomew was sitting at a desk on the far side of the room, writing notes with a fountain pen on a few loose leaves of expensive-looking paper. When Quick barged in, he looked up, his irritated expression morphing instantly into one of undisguised interest.

He looked hungry.

'Patience,' he said with a grin. 'What brings you back to me?'

'Kulika said you had a human here. We need him.'

'Why?'

'For his blood.'

'Clearly, but again, I ask you: why?'

'We found Vee,' Quick explained. 'But Digs drank from her, a lot. She's lost almost all her blood. She's covered in bites, and she's not conscious.'

Was Quick just imagining the concern that flashed across Bartholomew's expression? She was watching for it this time, in a way she hadn't been when she'd seen him almost flinch on the dock earlier, when Kulika had told him that Digs had taken Evita. He masked it quickly with nonchalance, but that little flicker of emotion was enough to make Quick hope that he might actually help.

That hope was crushed the moment Bartholomew opened his mouth.

'Is she going to die?' he said. 'Hardly. She survived weeks in a box with Digs while he continually drank her blood, so it seems unlikely to me that he's done enough damage to her in, what? A half hour? For her to be in any real danger. So explain to me, Patience, if you please: why should I squander the blood of the last viable human on the property to heal her?'

'You turned her Silver,' Quick said incredulously. 'You must have cared about her at least a little to do that. That's what turning someone Silver means, right? All I'm asking you to do is help her.'

'And if I do that,' Bartholomew said. 'What then?'

She hesitated, not immediately understanding what he was getting at, then he slid open the drawer of his desk and pulled out a book. It wasn't the same one that Quick had signed on the night of the Casting, but it was similar enough that she could guess what it was for.

'Are you seriously bargaining with me right now?' she asked.

Bartholomew didn't reply, he just pushed the book across the deck, then sat back in his chair and stared up at her, resting his elbows on the chair's arms and his steepled fingers on his bottom lip.

What were her options, realistically? Quick couldn't put Evita on a plane in the state she was in. She was scared even to move her with her throat all torn up like it was, and she was certain the doctor would object if she tried.

'What's your offer?' she asked, eyeing the book hesitantly.

'I have plans for Aloysius,' Bartholomew said. 'Do you know that he has an encyclopaedic knowledge of my entire life as a pirate, and Kulika's too?'

'So he's a fan?' Quick asked, making clear by her tone just how ridiculous she thought it was that anyone would be a fan of Bartholomew.

'He's an archivist,' Bartholomew replied reproachfully. 'He's wealthy. He's influential. And he's exactly the kind of sponsor and ambassador I can use, so I really will only use his blood as a last resort. Isn't that right, Aloysius?'

Bartholomew looked off to one side, and Quick followed his gaze to a four-poster bed tucked into a recess to her right. There was a middle-aged man sitting on the floor on its far side, tied to one of the bedposts. He was in no position to answer Bartholomew's question, because he was gagged.

'But of course,' Bartholomew continued, 'he is, above all, a storyteller. A bit of a fantasist, true, but such men can be useful. I'm loathe to share him.'

'I'm sorry,' Quick said to Aloysius, 'I don't know you, and I'm sure you're a very nice man, but taking a cup of your blood won't hurt you, and it'll heal my best friend. I've got a doctor up on deck, two actually, and they can—'

Quick stopped talking mid-sentence, her mouth falling open. She'd just noticed the enormous portrait hanging over the bed.

'Is that Kulika?' she asked.

'Of course,' Bartholomew replied. He got to his feet and walked around the desk so he could see it better himself. Unfortunately, that put him closer to Quick than she would have liked, leaving just a couple of feet between them. 'It's a few centuries old now,' he went on, 'but a good likeness, don't you think?'

It was, admittedly, a good likeness. Kulika looked like the warrior she was, facing down a storm with steely-eyed determination. It was an expression that Quick recognised, and she hated to see it hanging over Bartholomew's bed. The jealousy churned in her stomach, and she wasn't doing a very good job of hiding it.

'She was mine first, you know,' he reminded her. 'And you don't love her, anyway. Anyone could see that plainly enough.' He snatched her face into his hands, too abruptly for Quick to react, then ran a fingertip down her temple and along her jawline. Staring at her the whole time, his grip tightening with every second, he traced the same fingertip up her cheek until it rested just below her eye, close enough to tickle her lower lashes. 'There's nothing in your irises except green. Besides, she signed you away, you know.'

He dropped Quick's face as though it disgusted him, then turned back to the desk. Opening the book, he flicked through the pages until he came to a page that was dense with red ink.

No, not ink. Blood.

Kulika's blood, sea fresh and thick with salt.

'But still,' he said, 'she can't seem to let you go.'

Quick leaned in closer, trying to see what was written on the page, but Kulika's handwriting was dense and choppy. She picked out just a few names and phrases: *a new covenant, Patience Quick, Evita Khalyed, release your claim.*

'And it seems to me,' he continued, 'that you're not entirely ready to leave her either. Are you?'

'All I'm asking for is a little blood,' Quick said. 'I didn't come here to talk about my feelings.'

'Very well,' Bartholomew replied, amused in a way that unsettled her. 'I will give you a little blood, then. But not Aloysius's blood. You'd need half of what's in his body if Digs really has drunk as much as you say, and I won't risk him on that. No. Instead, I'll give you a small measure of my own blood, which I assure you is far more potent than that of any human.'

He made it sound like an upgrade, but there had to be a catch. There was always a catch.

'In return for what?' Quick asked suspiciously.

Bartholomew pushed the book towards her again, opening it to a blank page.

'A cupful of my blood, along with all the healing properties it possesses, in return for your name in my book.'

Quick froze.

'Your friends leave tonight,' he added. 'You stay.'

'I'm not signing your covenant again,' Quick said, horrified. 'I only cut the damned thing out of my skin this morning.'

'Then you shouldn't have come back here, should you?' he said plainly. 'Now, if you don't mind, I have a press conference that's starting shortly, so what is it to be? It's your signature for your friend's health and freedom. Do we have a bargain?'

It was a terrible deal. One cup of blood in exchange for Quick's freedom? But if she didn't make that deal, they'd all be stuck here beyond Bartholomew's grand revelation, and after that Quick was certain there would be no escape, ever again. Evita needed help if she was going to catch a plane out of here tonight, and Quick was determined to make that happen.

She owed it to her friend.

'Pass me the bloody quill,' she said, before she had a chance to second-guess the decision she knew she had to make.

Bartholomew pulled the covenant stamp out of his desk drawer and gave her a smile of such satisfaction that Quick had to restrain herself from ruining their deal by slapping it right off his face.

'As I'm sure you remember,' he said cheerfully, 'this is going to hurt.'

16

IN THE WOODS on the far side of the mansion, Digs was leading Kulika and her generals around and around in circles. At first, he'd been easy to follow. Wolfrie had been right behind him when they'd found Evita, matching him jump for jump as he leapt between the branches, but by the time Kulika had caught up, Digs was already beginning to slip the net. It wasn't long before he was out of sight entirely. They were stuck looking for subtler signs then, picking out broken twigs and smears of black gore, but it was impossible to tell if those marks had been left two minutes or two hours before. They fell behind.

'Left, in the trees,' Phinchas murmured from somewhere behind Kulika. He'd always had a keen nose, and he'd crewed with Digs before Kulika had even been born, so she trusted him to pick out Digs's scent better than most, even if it had now become corrupted by time and god knows what else. If Phinchas had been the one who'd stayed behind with her instead of Wolfrie, maybe they wouldn't have lost Digs by the time he joined them again.

But there was nothing Kulika could do about that decision now. At least she knew Quick was safe.

565

They tracked Digs like this, following him through the woods slower than Kulika would have liked. He was moving at Silver speed, jumping from one tree to another, but tracking took longer. The more they tracked, the more they lagged behind, until they looped back to the mansion where the trail dead-ended at the tunnel Digs had dug out of the wine cellar.

'Fuck,' Kulika said. 'Did he go in?'

Phinchas crawled his way through the tunnel and popped back out again a few minutes later. 'Locked up tight,' he said. 'The guards in the house didn't see or hear anyone, and they would've done. They were close.'

'Then we must have lost his trail when it crossed another. He hasn't been back here since he got out this morning.'

'Orders?' Wolfrie asked. He got terse when he got irritated, and now that Digs had slipped through their fingers, they were all feeling pretty fucking irritated.

'Back into the woods,' Kulika said, already speeding in that direction herself.

It didn't take long to find the point where they'd gone wrong; fresher black marks stained the trees on the trail they hadn't taken, but those marks had been hidden by dense foliage. Now, approaching from the other direction, they were clear as day.

'This way,' Kulika said.

The others followed, but before long they hit another fork in the scent trail. Kulika stopped and listened, trying to pick out his heartbeat somewhere in the woods, but it was no use. If a normal Silver's heartbeat was slow, then Digs's moved at a glacial pace. Maybe it was something to do with his enforced stasis in that box. He'd been trapped in there for three hundred years before Evita was thrown in there with him, and who knew what transformations his body had gone through during that time? When Evita's blood woke him up – not just any blood, but blood that had inherited power from Bartholomew, and probably from Solomon as well, if Dr Ross was to be believed – it had turned him into a creature unlike anything the world had ever seen before.

Kulika could buy that part of Dr Ross's theory. But the idea that zombie blood had contaminated him with her formula? She wasn't so sure that the drug was responsible for Digs's hunger for Silver flesh. He'd bitten a chunk out of Bayly's leg on the boat at the marina, and he hadn't even come into contact with the zombies by then. Kulika was inclined to believe that Digs had been a monster long before he'd come out of that box.

Which would be convenient, because it would mean the vial loaded into her gun was plenty powerful enough to kill him. If only she could bloody find him.

There was a noise from the direction of the river. This far into the woods, it wasn't more than a faint echo at the edge of Kulika's hearing, a nearly-not-there sound that had her questioning her own senses. But she had heard *something*.

It had sounded worryingly like an interrupted scream.

'Penny,' she said quietly into her radio. 'All quiet with you?'

The radio buzzed, and Penny said, 'All quiet at the house.'

Which was what Kulika had hoped to hear, and yet it worried her.

'Phinchas,' Kulika said as a horrible feeling pooled in her stomach. 'You got Quick and Evita to safety, right?'

'Right,' he said. 'I left them on the ship, like you said.'

'You didn't take them back to the house?' she asked, panicking now. 'You didn't put them in a cab?'

Phinchas looked confused. 'You said to come right back here.'

'I meant *after* you'd— Never mind.'

Kulika spoke into the radio again. 'Do you have Evita and Quick with you?' she asked. 'Did they come to the house?'

'No.'

'They're not with you?' she pressed.

'No,' Penny replied. 'Should they be?'

The horrible feeling in Kulika's stomach became a stone. It weighed so heavily that it threatened to drop her to her knees. Digs couldn't have looped back around again, could he? They'd been following his trail the whole way, so unless he'd somehow got behind them and circled back—

'Shit!' Kulika yelled.

'What?' Wolfrie asked.

She'd made a serious fucking miscalculation.

'Back to the ship!' Kulika called to him and Phinchas, already speeding in that direction herself. 'Right now!'

There had been precious little blood in Evita's veins when they'd found her. She'd been emptied out like a juice box, sucked almost dry. If Digs had gone after her because of her addictive blood – the same blood that ran in Kulika's veins – then he would have no further use for her. But there were two other people on the property with that bloodline, one of them being the person that Kulika herself had turned, the other being the person who had turned her.

And they were both on that ship.

Down by the dock where the *Primus's Fortune* rested, the Silver of the block were standing to attention, eerily still and dressed in their finery as they awaited their guests. It wouldn't be long now. Kulika could hear cars in the driveway back at the house, and wisps of voices were drifting along the red carpet on the breeze towards the moonlit stage. It was very grand, and very beautifully presented, but it held no interest for Kulika. Her eyes were fixed instead on the ship, scouring every varnished surface for a trace of Digs's passage.

Monty was waiting by the rope ladder.

'Hey!' Kulika said to him. 'What happened to the search? You were supposed to be coordinating from here.'

'I got new orders,' he said with a shrug. 'The press are arriving for the party.'

'And what do you think will happen if Digs wanders right into the middle of it?'

'I'm not a complete idiot,' he replied, which was exactly what Kulika was thinking he was. 'I set up a perimeter around the area. He's not getting through.'

'Then what was that scream I heard a minute ago?' Kulika asked.

Monty shrugged and said, 'I don't pry into the Primus's business.' His eyes drifted towards the ship behind him.

That sounded horribly ominous. Kulika could smell Quick's scent, and it was definitely coming from the ship, but it wasn't *right*. The problem wasn't just that Kulika could no longer detect Quick's mood from her changing scent, it was that the core scent itself had almost... soured.

'Where are Quick and Evita?' Kulika asked, dread filling her stomach.

'Last I saw, Dr Ross was carrying Evita along the deck. I guess she got hurt? They were heading for one of the rooms at the back of the ship,' said Monty.

'The "back"?' Kulika asked. The kid had clearly never served on a ship in his life.

'You know,' he said. 'The rooms under the bridge thing down behind where the steering wheel is, with all the windows.'

The sterncastle.

Kulika didn't bother to climb aboard. Instead, she ran straight along the dock to the stern of the ship, where a balcony protruded out over the water from the captain's cabin. Phinchas and Wolfrie ran with her. Once they were there, they could jump straight up to the balcony and get inside the—

There were smears of black gore on the balcony railing. The windows underneath it were smashed and bloody.

'Wolfrie,' Kulika breathed.

'I see it,' he said, then he was leaping from the dock, hanging off the edge of the balcony by his fingertips, and swinging through the already-smashed windows into the infirmary beyond. Kulika and Phinchas landed beside him in the small room, one after the other, packed in like sardines. It was otherwise empty, but it was clear that it hadn't been that way for long. There was blood on the floor, and blood on the door, and it all smelled like Quick.

Kulika's stomach lurched.

Everything here smelled like Quick, so strongly that Kulika couldn't get a bead on where the woman herself might be. The ship was noisy, and unfamiliar despite its familiarity, so she couldn't work out which creaks were footsteps and which were just the normal sounds the ship made as she settled against the dock. She was panicking.

'Look,' said Phinchas, pointing at a trail of wet black marks, dragged across the cabin floor and out of the door.

'He came through the water,' Kulika said.

'Clever,' Wolfrie commented.

Clever enough to worry Kulika more. The trio followed the tracks into the officers' mess and through it, then down into the cargo hold in the bowels of the ship. That's where they finally found their quarry.

Bayly and Enzo were there, unconscious and bloody

against the galley bulkhead. Digs must have brought them here, which explained why she and her generals had followed his trail back to the house: he'd gone back for another bite of his last meal. Dr Ross was lying on the floor beside them, bleeding profusely from a filthy-looking wound that went right through her shoulder and out the other side. Behind her, Evita was standing – conscious, but unsteady – in front of Xiaoyu.

Then there was Digs. He wasn't paying attention to any of the others, because he already had what he wanted in his rotting, skeletal fingers. Quick was pinned up against the hull, her face hidden behind a messy curtain of hair as she twisted and kicked in Digs's grip. Digs's dark mouth salivated in viscous, black drips as he leaned in, his teeth inching ever closer to Quick's neck as she tried in vain to break free. It wasn't a fair fight. Quick had barely drunk enough blood over the past week to replenish her strength, whereas Digs had a belly full of the most powerful bloodline in the world.

He was winning.

Kulika didn't stop to think, she just waded in. Her hands were around Digs's throat, closing over the slimy tendons of his neck and sinking far deeper into his flesh than should have been possible. Under the disintegrating scraps of his clothes and whatever rotting shreds of skin he'd retained, Digs was a construct of bone, bare muscle and raw nerves.

'Get them out of here!' Kulika yelled to Phinchas and Wolfrie.

'You sure you don't want us to—' Phinchas started.

'Just do it! Get them up top!'

Kulika hooked one arm around Digs's neck, then climbed onto his back and reached out to unhook his fingertips one by one from the spots where they had embedded themselves bloodily into Quick's shoulders, reopening the wounds he'd made earlier this evening. He threw Kulika off within a few seconds, but by that time Quick was free too, falling down the inside wall of the ship's hull to crumple into a pile on the floor. When Kulika glanced to the side, the other injured Silver and Xiaoyu had all disappeared, along with Phinchas and Wolfrie.

Now she had space to make some mess.

But fighting Digs this time wasn't like it had been back on Bayly's boat. Then, he'd been blood-starved and weakened by three hundred years in a box, so wrestling him back into it had been a piece of cake. Now, full of stolen blood and hungry for more, he moved less like a wraith and more like a demon; with purpose.

Kulika realised then that the problem with sending her generals away with the wounded was that it meant the people left in the room were exactly the ones Digs wanted: the ones with Bartholomew's blood. But it was too late to regret her choices now. Digs was already hurling himself across the cargo hold towards her, a snarling morass of dripping black claws and sharp teeth. He thudded into her with the speed of a cannonball and took her to the deck just as hard, slamming her against the planks so forcefully that they splintered underneath her shoulders, along with a couple of her ribs. She grunted and pushed back, managing to flip him over so she had the upper hand.

Then Quick groaned.

Kulika shouldn't have looked. She was in the middle of a fight with a supercharged and cannibalistic Silver. She should have given him her full attention, but she couldn't resist the urge to look and see if Quick was all right. In the split second it took for Kulika to ascertain that no, Quick was not all right – in fact she was bleeding out against the bulkhead – Digs was on her again. This time, he didn't just flip Kulika, he hauled her to her feet and spun her around, then pinned her against the hull with one hand to her sternum. With the other, he reached down and grabbed Quick, then pinned her to the hull next to Kulika, lining them up on a level with his jaws.

Kulika was left staring into the wrecked remains of Digs's face.

His skull wasn't as misshapen as it had been, nor was the rest of his body. He'd already amply demonstrated that he could move as fast as the rest of the Silver, and he was stronger than Kulika had expected, even if his gait was strange and his limbs were deformed.

But his face. Up to this point, Kulika hadn't looked at it closely. Now, she could see that his blank white eyes were in the process of healing, but they were growing back wrong. Eyeballs that should have been uniformly round were sitting twisted and bulbous in their sockets. His mouth wasn't much better formed, with a half-healed tongue that lolled inside a mouth whose innards were always visible through his cheeks, only half-covered by skin and tendon.

For a moment, Kulika was too horrified to do anything. She wasn't sure how long she might have stared into Digs's shredded maw if she'd been on her own in his grip, but Quick was there beside her, and she wasn't down just yet. She was fumbling for her pocket, the one where she'd stashed the syringe full of the doctor's formula. Kulika's gun containing her dose of the same had been batted aside with Digs's first attack, but it would be useless at this close range anyway. Quick's syringe was precisely the weapon they needed. The problem was that Quick seemed to be having trouble gripping it, as though her hand wasn't working quite right. If Kulika could just inch her hand along the hull and…

Kulika's fingers brushed the syringe. It was at the very edge of her reach. She scissored it between her fingers, then teased it out of Quick's pocket as quickly and gently as she could, flicking it up into her fist. But in the instant before she could inject the syringe's contents into the remains of Digs's stomach, he spotted the movement with his roaming eyes and stabbed a sharp fingernail into Kulika's arm. Her fist unravelled, unintentionally, and the syringe clattered to the ground, unused.

That wouldn't have been the end of it, Kulika told herself. She would have got her and Quick out of the situation one way or another, but she never had a chance to find out exactly how she was going to do that, because at that moment Bartholomew breezed down the stairs from the upper decks and came up behind Digs. Kulika could have saved them both, she was almost certain, but it was Bartholomew who *actually* did. He reached out and grabbed Digs's head in one hand, then twisted it sharply until it snapped with a sickening crunch.

Digs dropped both Kulika and Quick, and while he was writhing on the floor trying to put himself back together, Kulika snatched up her gun from where it had fallen. She shot Digs in the stomach, where his broken body was thickest, and Dr Ross's formula did its job.

Thank god.

It started in his stomach, where the dart containing the vial had embedded itself, a spreading glow of red. At first, it looked like blood pooling around the wound, but then the colour intensified through red to orange to yellow to white as it filtered out through Digs's body. The surface of his mutilated muscles hardened over it like porcelain, forming a baked black crust where his skin should have been. That skin cracked open, creating a multitude of fault lines that pulled apart to reveal white-hot emptiness inside his trunk and limbs, then there was nothing except a pile of ash and a charred circle on the planks to mark the spot where his body had burned.

It was over in just a couple of seconds, but the flashing glare was burned into the backs of Kulika's eyes for far longer.

Digs hadn't been a creature like Jahan Khalyed, then. He hadn't been contaminated by the zombie blood, and however much of Evita's blood he had in his body, it hadn't been enough to protect him from the formula in the doctor's vials.

Kulika rushed to Quick's side. Bartholomew watched her go.

'You killed him?' Quick asked Kulika in a broken whisper. 'He's properly dead?'

'Yes,' Kulika promised.

'You're welcome,' Bartholomew interjected, with a smile in his tone.

Kulika looked over her shoulder as she cradled Quick in her arms and asked, 'Are you expecting my thanks? You should never have brought him here in the first place.'

'I had a use for him,' Bartholomew replied nonchalantly.

'*Had*?'

'As I told you,' Bartholomew said as he flicked Dig's black ichor from his fingers, 'I've got everything I wanted from him.'

'And what exactly did you want?' Kulika asked.

But Bartholomew didn't answer the question, he just smiled and said, 'It's good to have the crew back together, isn't it? And now that Digs is dealt with, I have a revolution to incite.' He looked disdainfully at his blackened fingertips and the drips staining his sleeves. 'After I've changed.'

Then he stalked back up the steps as though nothing had

happened.

Kulika put him out of her mind and turned her attention to Quick, whose blood was pooling on the boards of the cargo hold. Kulika was kneeling in it, feeling it sink into the material that covered her shins. Quick was still bleeding, albeit slowly. She wasn't healing, either. When Kulika pulled Quick across her thighs and tried to get a better look at the wounds Digs had punched through her chest with his fingers, her faint moan of pain was quiet enough to worry Kulika more.

Well, Bartholomew hadn't told her she *couldn't* heal Quick, had he? He'd known she was injured, and he'd left her here alone with Kulika. What did he think she was going to do, with no blood available?

Tacit permission, Kulika thought. Or as close as made no difference.

Kulika pushed her fingertips into Quick's hair, curving her hand around the nape of her neck until she could feel the thick gathering of Quick's locks between her fingers. The weight of it in her grip settled the anxiety twitching through her muscles as she sent her healing strength through her palm and into Quick's skin, pushing it out through her body until the wounds at Quick's shoulders began to seal themselves shut.

It felt like coming home.

If Kulika could have kissed Quick then, she would have done, but it would only have made what was to come more painful, so she held herself back. With difficulty.

'All right?' Kulika asked as Quick pushed herself first to her elbows, then up to sitting, and finally to her feet.

For a moment, Kulika just sat on the floor and let herself bask in Quick's presence. Standing over Kulika like that, bloodstained and ready for a fight, with her flame-red hair spreading over her shoulders like a cloak of fire, she was glorious.

One last moment, Kulika told herself. Then she'd give her up for good.

'I'm fine, thanks. Are you all right?' Quick asked, giving Kulika a strange look. It snapped Kulika into action, and to her feet.

'I'm fine. We've got,' Kulika checked the time on her phone, 'less than fifteen minutes before the event starts, and the press are already here. Let's get up on deck and find the others.'

17

QUICK FOUND HER friends in the middle of the ship, by the biggest mast, arguing. Xiaoyu and Evita were trying to get back downstairs while Wolfrie and Phinchas held them back. Dr Ross was lying on the floor, bleeding profusely from her shoulder while she tried to tend to Bayly and Enzo, both of whom were still unconscious.

'You've got to let me back down there!' Evita was yelling. 'She needs me.'

'You can barely stand up straight,' Wolfrie pointed out.

'Maybe she can't,' Xiaoyu said, 'but *I'm* fine. I can go help.'

'No, you bloody can't,' Phinchas said with horror in his voice. 'You're human. It's not safe.'

Then Evita's gaze landed on Quick, coming up from below deck, and her face sagged with relief.

'Oh, god,' she said, pushing past Wolfrie to pull Quick into her arms. 'You're okay? You're not hurt?'

'I'm fine,' Quick said.

'Digs?'

'Dead,' said Kulika.

Quick couldn't stop her gaze from sliding sideways

towards Kulika, wondering whether her body was still rushing with desire the way Quick's was. If so, she was hiding it well. But there was a slight flush to her cheeks, a sparkle in her eyes, and an edge to the ocean salt of her scent that was driving Quick to distraction. Taken together, those three things gave her pause for thought.

Then Kulika said, 'You all need to leave, right now.' She was looking at Quick as she spoke, then she turned to Wolfrie and Phinchas and said, 'Get Bayly and Enzo down to the infirmary, then come right back here. Doctor: hang on, and I'll find you some blood.'

Then Kulika disappeared below decks with her generals, each of whom was carrying an unconscious Silver.

Quick felt empty as she watched them go. Kulika wanted her to leave with the others, but she couldn't. She was bound to Bartholomew as much as Kulika was now, and she was stuck here in exactly the same way. Whatever events Bartholomew was about to set in motion with his speech, she was in it for the long haul.

Kulika was not going to be pleased when she found out.

'Whatever reason you think she has for sending you away, she's not doing it because she doesn't want you,' Evita said quietly, misreading the cause of Quick's concern. 'She loves you. That's the end of that. That's what silvering means, and it's forever.'

'Usually,' Dr Ross muttered, barely loud enough for Quick to hear. Maybe Quick wasn't supposed to hear at all, but she did.

'What does that mean?' she asked.

'Sorry?' the doctor said, turning towards Quick. She'd been looking at her wound, apparently engrossed in her own thoughts and her own pain. Maybe her comment had nothing to do with Kulika.

'You said *usually*,' Quick said. 'Usually what?'

'Usually…' the doctor started, but she didn't seem to know how to finish the sentence. 'Oh, fuck it. Look, something's wrong with Kulika. I don't know exactly how, and I didn't even know it was possible, but the silvering is reversing.'

'Excuse me?' Quick whispered.

'In the circumstances, it's probably a good thing,' Dr Ross said gently. 'You're leaving, and with everything that's happening, you'd be better off if the bond was gone. You don't actually *want* her life to be tied to yours, do you?'

'My life to—' Quick spluttered. 'What are you talking about?'

'If you die, she dies,' the doctor replied.

'You didn't know that either?' Xiaoyu said.

'You *did*?' Quick asked.

'Well, yeah.'

'Assume I know nothing,' Quick said, sitting on the deck beside the doctor. 'Then tell me everything I need to know about what happens when someone silvers.'

She'd barely had a chance to digest the facts she'd been missing before Kulika returned, tossing a plastic drinks bottle filled with blood to Dr Ross.

'Where did you get that from?' Quick asked.

'Same place you did,' Kulika replied. 'Bartholomew's human historian. Aloysius.'

Quick felt like she was going to be sick.

'What?' Kulika asked her.

Quick just shook her head. She'd have to tell the truth eventually, probably very soon indeed, but for now the nausea was so thick in Quick's throat that she wouldn't have been able to get the words out, even if she'd wanted to.

Bartholomew had tricked her. Of course he had. He could

have given her Aloysius's blood for Evita, but he'd spun a sob story and made her trade her freedom for his own blood instead. She felt like a complete fool. It seemed so obvious now, in retrospect, that she couldn't bear to admit how easily she'd been conned.

'Okay,' Kulika said once Dr Ross had drunk the blood and healed her injury. 'Now you need to go.'

'We haven't had time to call a cab, and with the blood—' said Dr Ross, looking hopelessly at the stains on her clothes.

'Grab a clean shirt from the house, then take one of the cars,' said Kulika. 'Leave it at the airport. Get straight into your private plane and fly out of here. Just go, now, before it's too late.'

She was looking straight at Quick as she spoke, but Quick couldn't leave. Evita and Xiaoyu, though? They were free.

'She's right,' Quick said, moving to stand alongside Kulika. 'You should go.'

'Impatience,' Evita said, looking between Quick and Kulika. 'What are you doing?'

'I'm staying,' she replied.

'No, you're not,' said Kulika. 'You can't be here when Bartholomew makes his announcement. All hell's going to break loose. You'll be right in the middle of it. You'll be stuck like the rest of us.'

'I'm still staying,' Quick replied.

Kulika's face was a picture of pained incomprehension.

'No,' said Kulika, anxious now, 'you're not. You're going to run to the utility room, take the first set of car keys you find on the rack, then drive out of here as fast as you can without looking back. You're going, Quick. Right now.'

Quick didn't reply. She didn't know how to say the words. Instead, she just held out her hand, slowly unfurling her fingers to reveal the ugly black mark that scarred her palm.

Again.

'No,' Kulika whispered.

'Evita needed blood,' Quick said.

'What did you do?' Evita asked, her shaky voice full of disbelief.

'You needed blood,' Quick repeated. 'Bartholomew said… Well, it doesn't matter. I got the blood, but he made me sign his book.'

'No!' Evita yelled, tears already starting down her cheeks. She was so upset that she was angry, and it tied Quick's stomach in knots. 'I would have been fine! We could have found more blood. You didn't need to trade for it with Bartholomew! It wasn't worth your freedom. If I'd known —'

'I thought it was the only way to get you home,' Quick said calmly. 'And that's exactly what I'm doing now. If you get on that plane safely tonight, it'll all have been worthwhile.'

'No,' Evita said.

'Yes. It was the right decision at the time. I don't regret it.' Quick crouched down beside her friend and pulled her into her arms, kissed each of her cheeks, then held her tightly for a moment before pushing her away. 'Now go on. Make it mean something,' she begged. 'Please. *Please.*'

Evita just shook her head, crying with her teeth clenched.

'Here,' Quick said. She took the syringe she'd collected from the cargo deck out of her pocket and passed it to Dr Ross, but the doctor curled Quick's fingers back around the vial.

'Keep it,' she said quietly. 'You might still need it.'

Her gaze landed somewhere over Quick's shoulder.

'If you'll excuse me, ladies,' Bartholomew said, worming his way through their group to reach the rope ladder that led down to the dock. It was a pointless interruption; he didn't need to use the ladder. He was more than strong enough to jump the short distance from anywhere along the edge of the ship. He just wanted to rub his triumph in their faces.

Kulika had been standing off to one side up until now, arms crossed and attention fixed on the floor, but now she snapped up straight, her eyes narrowing on Bartholomew.

'We had a bargain,' she said to him, biting out the words.

'And I made another that superseded it,' Bartholomew shrugged, with infuriating calmness. 'I thought you might be pleased, even. After all,' he grinned, 'now you match.' Then he took a long step off the side of the ship and disappeared from view.

'Get them gone, Phinchas,' Kulika said when he and Wolfrie returned, her voice hollow. There was cold rage in her tone.

Quick finished her goodbyes with a briskness that tore at her, hugging Evita while she wept until all the others had already left, and she could delay their parting no longer. Evita followed them down the rope ladder without saying a single coherent word.

Up on the deck, Kulika stood beside Quick and watched as the group moved quickly along the red carpet to the mansion. A few minutes later, an SUV pulled away from the drive in the distance, and then they were gone. Quick had thought they might talk then, but instead Kulika turned and jumped down to the dock without a backward glance, following Bartholomew to the stage. Wolfrie went after her, leaving Quick alone on the *Primus's Fortune*.

Evita was gone. Xiaoyu was gone. The bond between her and Kulika would apparently soon be gone too, but Quick was stuck here forever, come what may.

Alone.

18

'GOOD EVENING, AND welcome,' Bartholomew said from the podium.

Kulika stood behind him on the stage and glared at his back.

Most of the well-dressed crowd had already taken their seats, but those who hadn't now hurried to grab their glasses and find a good vantage point from which to take their pictures. When Bartholomew had told Kulika that he was holding a press conference, this was not what she had expected. She'd imagined there would be cameras and reporters with microphones, poised and ready to ask difficult questions, but of course that was not the crowd he had assembled. Instead, his audience was filled with influencers and internet celebrities, people who'd brought just their phones and their beautiful selves to disseminate the information they were going to learn this evening.

It was a good strategy. Bartholomew had always been skilled at playing his cards to his best advantage. Just look at how he'd played her: he'd got Kulika to sign his covenant by agreeing to break his covenant with Quick, then he'd fed Kulika his blood to reverse her silvering, so he could have her all to himself. But that wasn't enough for him, was it? Nothing was ever enough for Bartholomew. No, he had to have Quick as well, just in case, so he'd found a way to talk her into signing his covenant again. He was as greedy and vicious as the alligators that lived in the river bordering his property. He'd snapped her up in his jaws, then he'd stored her in his larder, playing with her occasionally, until he had need of her.

Tonight, finally, it was time.

With the new Silver slotted in amongst the guests to host and seduce them – Silver who were just as shiny and camera-ready as their guests – the evening felt more like an exclusive cocktail party than a declaration of war. Which was what it actually was.

'Thank you all for coming,' Bartholomew said, holding his hands up as he waited for everyone to settle and take their seats.

He had dressed the part. Gone were the bloodstained jeans and henley from their battle with Digs. Instead, he was now wearing a plain black suit and white shirt, a simple outfit that was understated, yet so well fitted that it gave Bartholomew a subtle aura of power.

Maybe that was just his blood talking.

Kulika's own blood was thundering in her ears. If she could have killed Bartholomew for what he'd done to Quick then she would have done, but every time she thought about making a move, she got this stabbing pain above her eye that didn't subside until she thought about something else. It wasn't part of any Silver lore she'd ever heard of, but it felt as though his blood had poisoned her thoughts themselves. Her own body was conspiring against her, for his benefit, and all the while Quick felt further and further away.

Kulika still felt the tug in her chest that pulled her towards

Quick's spot up on the ship's deck behind her, but the tug was getting weaker. Healing her earlier had been harder than Kulika wanted to admit, harder than it ever had been before. It was as though a barrier had been erected between the two of them, so Kulika could only experience Quick through smoked glass: her scent dulled, her emotions indiscernible, her light muted. She was slipping through Kulika's fingers, and Kulika was just standing back and letting it happen.

Because of him.

As Bartholomew smiled at his audience – who were all smiling back, already suckered in – a few stragglers approached from the driveway, following the torches along the red carpet. Kulika hadn't heard any late cars pulling up, but perhaps the stragglers had stopped at the mansion to use the bathroom before joining the party. They were all dressed appropriately, so they didn't strike her as strange at the time, which was how they got almost halfway to the stage before she realised that something was wrong.

Their movement was odd, that was the first thing she noticed. They swayed and rocked as they walked, but in unison, as though they were dancing to a song only they could hear. Then Kulika thought to look at their eyes, and she saw the bloody tears just beginning to form in the corners of their eyes.

'Shit,' she murmured. Then she yelled for Wolfrie to back her up, and she ran.

There were only five of them, enough for Kulika and Wolfrie to handle on their own, but by that point the audience had turned and seen exactly what was slavering in their direction. For the moment, they were just confused, thinking perhaps it was some kind of stunt, but if Kulika didn't contain the zombies quickly, then the mood would turn.

'Monty!' she yelled.

The kid had been standing at the back of the stage with Kulika and the other favoured Silver, but he arrived immediately. Across the space that separated them, Bartholomew gave Kulika a look that told her she'd better sort this out, right now.

'Back to the cellar,' Kulika ordered.

Monty waved Brandon and Penny over from the stage to join them, then the five of them escorted one zombie each to the block. Now the creatures were under control, with startling ease, Kulika was finally getting a good look at them, and she didn't like what she was seeing. They were dressed in black tie, they were clean and well-presented, and they certainly didn't look like they'd spent the day rambling around mindlessly in the woods.

'They didn't escape from the cellar, did they?' Kulika asked.

'I doubt it,' Monty replied. 'I've got people guarding the block.'

This proved to be true when they dragged the zombies across the lawn and into the building, where they found a Silver standing in the corridor right outside the hidden door that led to the cellar hatch. It was sealed tight.

'Then where did they come from?' Kulika asked as the new zombies were manhandled into the cellar with the rest. 'I thought you said you got them all.'

'We did!' Monty replied, indignantly. 'But there was blood in the wine cellar, and on the grass, probably in the woods too, which we tried to clean up but, you know...'

'We *did* clean it up,' Wolfrie replied. 'There's no blood left on this property.'

'Then on the road,' Monty replied. 'There must have been a lot of blood out there. You said there was a car crash and that some driver got turned zombie, so there must have been —'

'Two drivers,' Kulika said, her stomach falling. 'Two drivers, Monty. One from Quick's cab and one from the pick-up truck that hit it.'

For a moment, no one said anything, and all they could hear was the gentle shuffling of the zombies in the cellar below them.

Then Monty said, 'Oh.'

'Fucking hell,' Kulika muttered. Her voice was low and tight with barely-controlled rage. 'Everyone back outside. Now.'

That's when the screaming started.

From her perch on the deck of the *Primus's Fortune*, Quick had a good enough view to know exactly what kind of creatures had just been bundled into the block by Kulika and her helpers. She was also perfectly-placed to see Evita and Xiaoyu's SUV barrelling back down the drive the same way it had left, before careening right past the pool and over the lawn, then finally screeching to a stop behind the tiered seating that now held Bartholomew's audience. By the time Dr Ross, Evita and Xiaoyu tumbled out of it, Quick had already reached the dock.

She heard Bartholomew calling, 'If you'll please remain in your seats, ladies and gentlemen…' before another zombie rounded the corner from the mansion, following the trail the SUV had left from the drive to the riverside. There were ten others behind it, then fifty, then a hundred, all of them running, then Quick lost count as she rushed to the SUV.

'Ladies and gentlemen…' Bartholomew was calling, but it was no use. His audience had seen the zombies too. They might have hesitated in their seats as the first batch was escorted away, but they were not going to sit and wait for who knew how many hundreds of zombies to engulf them.

They screamed. They ran, tripping over heels and hems. They generally got in the way as Quick tried to reach her friends, but they had no real direction, and Quick knew exactly where she was going.

'What are you doing here?' Quick asked, horrified to see Xiaoyu once again in harm's way.

'Did you really think we'd get out?' Evita laughed bitterly.

Then there was no more time for talking, because the zombies had arrived, and they weren't keeping their distance from the Silver anymore, not like they had that morning. There was no ten-foot radius, no safe zone. They were coming straight for Xiaoyu, pushing Silver out of the way to get to her, with no consideration for their strength. Whether the formula had mutated, or things had changed now it was dark, or the zombies had simply got hungrier and more daring as their meals became scarcer, the Silver were clearly no longer a source of fear for them.

Quick and the others were going to have to fight tooth and nail to get Xiaoyu out of here alive.

When Kulika and the others stepped out of the block, it was already too late. There were zombies all over the lawn.

Tyre-treads were gouged either side of the red carpet, following a trail of lanterns knocked over and smouldering gently in the dry grass, leading to an SUV parked behind the seating area.

No.

But there they were, clustered behind the SUV: Evita, Dr Ross and Xiaoyu, with Quick at their side, desperately trying to fend off the zombies that were already beginning to surround them.

'Protect the humans!' Kulika barked to the others. 'Get them on the ship and keep the zombies off it.'

'You don't want to put them in the cellar?' Monty asked.

Kulika gave him an incredulous look and said, 'No.'

There were thousands of zombies on the property already, streaming from the road and the woods in an endless deluge. Even if they could get them all in the cellar and protect the humans at the same time, they would never fit. It would be a futile effort. The only possible solution was to get the humans somewhere safe, and worry about the zombies later.

'You have your orders!' Kulika barked, then she rushed to the SUV, and to Quick.

'Protect Xiaoyu!' Quick yelled the moment Kulika joined them.

'We need to move her somewhere safe,' Kulika said. 'Dr Ross, can you get her on the ship? We'll clear your path.'

The doctor nodded, then Xiaoyu climbed onto her back. It looked a little comical because of Dr Ross's height, like an adult trying to ride a Shetland pony, but the doctor was plenty strong enough to carry one human. While she ran towards the dock with Evita clearing the way, Quick and Kulika fell into position behind the piggybacking pair, moving back to back as they fended off zombies from either side. Kulika should have been concentrating on protecting their precious human cargo, but instead she couldn't stop thrilling at the pressure of Quick's back against her own. There was the push of an elbow against her waist as Quick neatly tossed a zombie away, the brush of a shoulder as she turned to face a new challenger, and the press of hip and flesh as they leaned back against each other for support. It reminded Kulika of the time they'd spent sparring on the training ground – a time that seemed so long ago now that it might have happened in another lifetime – and she warmed at the memory, whilst simultaneously feeling that something was terribly wrong. That smoked glass still spread between them, even when there was nothing between them at all. It was a relief in more ways than one when they reached the ship, and Dr Ross leapt up to the deck safely with Xiaoyu in her arms.

'Go with them,' Kulika said to Quick and Evita.

'But we can help here,' Quick argued.

'You can help by keeping the ship safe for the humans I'm about to send your way. Get up there and guard it, okay?'

'Okay,' Quick said.

Quick reached out, and for a moment Kulika thought she was going to take her hand, or cup her face, or touch her in some other exquisitely tantalising way, but then Quick snatched her hand back, turned without word and started climbing the rope ladder, with Evita close behind. Kulika didn't have time to obsess over what might have happened in that moment, because on the riverbanks, everything was going tits up.

The Silver were everywhere now, trying to form a line behind the tiered seating under the direction of one of the older crew so they could push the zombies back towards the road with brute force. The problem was that there might have been a hundred or so Silver on the property who were each hundreds of times stronger than the zombies, but they were seriously outnumbered. They only had one set of hands each, so when the zombies got backed up behind the barricade of bodies and started climbing over each other to breach the line and reach the humans beyond, there was no one left to catch them. They had a clear field ahead of them, and just a few Silver to pick them off. When the wave of zombies broke over the Silver barricade en masse, there was no holding it back.

On the stage, Bartholomew stood still beside his lectern. He was watching the humans running and screaming, watching the zombies chasing them, watching and watching and doing nothing at all.

'Bartholomew!' Kulika yelled at him.

He turned towards her, then shrugged and called, 'Just let them have the humans. Clear up afterwards, when they've calmed down. It'll be easier that way.'

Which was true, but it was an idea that never would have occurred to Kulika. Let all these people die, for nothing? That was the difference between her and Bartholomew.

But not all the crew were of her mind. The older ones were already gathering beside Bartholomew on the stage, standing in eerie stillness as they watched the carnage churn around them.

Bartholomew shouted, 'Call me when it's over, and we'll start again,' then he walked off towards the mansion with a crowd of nonchalant Silver following on behind.

Kulika gaped after him.

He seriously thought they'd be able to salvage something from this mess? That they could just gather up thousands and thousands of unkillable zombies and, what? Stash them in every waterlogged cellar in the Low Country? He'd had crazier ideas, Kulika supposed, but she didn't have much faith in their ability to turn the tide.

Meanwhile, the audience was dispersing in all directions. A few had locked themselves inside the SUV, but the zombies had already managed to shatter one window, and it wouldn't be long before they were inside. Some ran behind the stage and along the dock, which was where Kulika wanted them to go, but others ran along the river in both directions, where zombies leapt from the rushes and the darkness under the trees to drag them into the water.

'Fuck,' Kulika muttered to herself. 'This isn't good.'

Wolfrie raced past carrying two humans under each arm. As he passed Kulika, he said, 'Things are getting out of control.'

Which was an understatement.

'Get on the ship!' she yelled, herding whatever part of the audience remained towards the *Primus's Fortune*. 'Cast off!' she called to Wolfrie.

'Aye, aye!' he yelled back.

Kulika gathered the last few humans in her own arms and carried them up to the deck, then helped the remainder who were still climbing the rope ladder to reach safety before pulling the ladder up onto the deck so the zombies couldn't follow.

There had been over a hundred humans in the audience. They were sailing away with maybe thirty.

'Anyone Silver who's coming with us,' Kulika yelled from the bowsprit, leaning out over the water, 'you'd better get on board now!'

From where Kulika was standing, it seemed overwhelmingly unlikely that Bartholomew was going to get the calm zombie clean-up he'd been banking on. She couldn't see a single human left in the mass of bodies moving on the riverbanks now, but the zombies weren't giving up. They were chasing in either direction along the river, looking for new prey, and some of them were even going after the remaining Silver, those who hadn't followed Bartholomew back to the mansion. The last few crew members who leapt onto the ship as they pulled away from the dock had scratches gouged onto their faces and bite marks on their arms.

Kulika was fairly certain there would be no starting again from this, for any of them.

The lawn was on fire. It was already catching in the dry Spanish moss, chasing up into the tree branches and blowing onto the block. In the distance, Kulika could see the porch of the mansion smouldering. The whole place was going to go up in flames.

Just like she'd always wanted.

With any luck, there'd be no mansion left to come back to, and Kulika could just sail off into the sunset. The thought gave her a frisson of glee.

If Bartholomew was angry about her scratching up his car, just imagine how angry he'd be when he realised she'd taken his ship.

<h1 style="text-align:center">19</h1>

THE *PRIMUS'S FORTUNE* cruised down the Cooper River, picking up stragglers as it went. A few of the left-behind Silver were following it now as the zombies chased them along the waterside, then diving into the water before hauling themselves up onto the deck. The moment they hit the boards, they came face to face with Kulika and Wolfrie, who were shouting orders Quick didn't understand.

They used to be pirates, Kulika had told her. Well, she was seeing the evidence of that now.

But the Silver weren't the only figures in the water; the zombies were following them in. They didn't seem to have the strength to pull themselves up the sides of the ship, or maybe they just hadn't yet worked out how, but Silver were patrolling the sides of the boat all the same.

'Where are we going?' Quick asked Kulika.

'Out into the harbour,' she replied, 'for now.'

Then one of the ropes got tangled in a way that made Kulika frown, and she rushed off to fix it, leaving Quick with the distinct feeling that they didn't have much of a plan at all. Quick was no use up here, though. All she was doing was getting in the way, so she went below decks to the space where cannon and hammocks crowded in the centre of the ship. The others were waiting there, peering out of the cannon ports with worried faces.

'They're in the water,' Evita said as Quick hopped up into the hammock across from hers.

'I know,' Quick replied.

'Not just in the water,' said Dr Ross.

She was looking at the screen of her phone, but she turned it then to show Quick a news broadcast. It cut from CCTV footage of downtown Charleston, to the waterfront, and then to the airport. All of the shots were filled with zombies.

Quick took the phone from the doctor's hand and watched in horror as images and text scrolled across the screen, before it abruptly went black.

'Battery's dead,' Quick said, handing it back.

'I don't think so,' Dr Ross said, fiddling with it for a moment before bringing up a lock screen. 'We've lost signal. Maybe we're too far away from a tower out here.'

'But we're still on the river.'

Dr Ross just shrugged and put the phone back in her pocket.

'Just one stowaway, one smear of blood on a plane flying out of here,' said Evita, 'and the whole world is fucked.'

'We know,' said Xiaoyu. 'You don't have to say it.' She was sitting in a hammock on the other side of the ship, swinging gently as she looked out of the cannon port.

When Quick saw Evita glance in that direction, she murmured, 'Her kids live in Charleston, remember?'

Evita looked at Quick with wide eyes, then at Dr Ross, who was nodding sadly.

'You couldn't get through, I guess?' Quick asked. 'Is that why you came back?'

'Road was blocked with zombies,' Xiaoyu said, still

looking out of the window. 'We had no choice.'

'Not that I would have been able to leave anyway,' Evita said bleakly. 'The minute we got more than a mile down the road, I felt like my head was about to explode. We were just turning around when we saw the zombies.'

'We had to turn back,' Dr Ross said quietly. 'I think it was the blood.'

'The blood?' Quick said, confused for a moment before she realised what Dr Ross meant. 'Bartholomew's blood made Evita's head hurt?'

'I think so,' Dr Ross said quietly. 'When she got too far away from him. He knows what his blood can do better than any of us, and he wanted Evita to drink it, to keep her close, I think.'

The conniving bastard. That's why he'd bargained with Quick for his own blood instead of Aloysius's. He'd wanted Evita to come back to him.

'And worse,' Dr Ross went on. 'I think he probably made sure that Digs would get loose in the first place. He sent him after Evita, to keep her at the mansion. To keep you both there.'

'I suppose we'd better hope the zombies keep Bartholomew busy for a while, then,' Quick commented.

'Why?' Evita asked.

'Because otherwise, he might decide he wants us back.'

Up on deck, Kulika was taking stock of her new crew. They'd stowed the humans in the cargo hold for now, as far away from danger as they could get. Kulika had been careful not to mention what exactly had caused the scorch mark on the floor. There were twenty-odd Silver up on deck – including Monty, Brandon and Penny – but only a few of them knew what they were doing on a ship like this, and that wasn't even half the number she'd need to teach the others what they needed to know. She could do with having Phinchas here to help, but he hadn't come up on deck yet. Still, they were muddling along for the moment. All they had to do was let the current take them as far as the harbour. After that, they could…

Well, Kulika didn't know what they were going to do then. She was bound to Bartholomew, like the rest of the crew, but if the mansion had just gone up in smoke, what was she supposed to do now? She'd call Bartholomew if she could, but her phone wasn't working, and nor was anyone else's. He didn't have a radio – hated using them – so she couldn't contact him that way, and besides, their range wasn't long enough to reach him from here. Short of battling her way through a horde of Silver-chomping zombies to go and ask him in person, Kulika didn't have any way to find out what his orders were, so she was stuck following his last one: wait for the zombies to go away.

That wasn't going to happen anytime soon.

It was hard not to consider her options. She had his ship. She had his covenant book, in the desk in his cabin. Most importantly, she had Quick and her friends, and they were safe. If she sailed away right now, what was Bartholomew going to do about it?

It was a risk, though, because with Bartholomew, who knew? Which meant it wasn't a decision she could make on her own.

'Mind the deck, Wolfs,' she said. 'I've got some thinking to do.' Then she headed down to the gun deck to speak to Quick and her friends.

They were lounging around in the hammocks, looking mournfully out of the gun ports. Kulika counted them up and found one missing.

'Where's Phinchas?' she asked.

'He said he'd be back,' said Evita. 'Then he ran off into the horde. Told us to drive back here and not to wait for him.'

'He ran into the zombies?' Kulika asked, horrified. She'd just assumed that Phinchas had come aboard with the others. In the chaos of their launch, she hadn't noticed that he wasn't there. 'When? Why?'

'On the road, about a mile out from the mansion.' Evita shrugged. 'He didn't say why. We thought maybe he had orders.'

'Not from me,' Kulika said.

On the other side of the gun deck, Xiaoyu was biting her lip and looking out at the river. With that many zombies in the water, Kulika thought she was right to be worried, but it turned out that wasn't the source of her misery.

'It's my fault,' Xiaoyu muttered. 'All of it. If I hadn't opened the blood cellar—'

'*You* opened the blood cellar?' Kulika asked, looking at Quick.

'You thought it was me?' Quick asked.

'Well, yeah. You have to admit, it fits your M.O.'

'Which I copied,' said Xiaoyu mournfully.

'You were trying to save them,' said Quick.

'But instead I doomed them all, and now Phinchas is gone…' Xiaoyu trailed off as her gaze wandered back out of the gunport.

'And I'm down one more sailor,' Kulika said to herself.

Which made the plan she had been contemplating far more intimidating. Following the current down the Cooper was one thing, but crossing the Atlantic in a Golden Age-era pirate ship? For a journey like that, you wanted safe hands on deck.

Without Phinchas, it would be harder to convince Wolfrie, too. But maybe not impossible.

'What if we left?' Kulika asked.

'Left?' asked Quick.

'Just went,' said Kulika. 'What if we just sailed this ship away, left Bartholomew behind us, and never came back.'

'Is that even possible?' said Dr Ross. 'Won't it hurt you? Physically, I mean?'

'And won't the rest of the crew come after us to enforce Bartholomew's covenant?' Xiaoyu asked.

'Half of them are on this ship already,' Quick pointed out.

'Less than a quarter,' Kulika corrected her. 'But I think the others are going to be busy for a while cleaning up the mess the zombies are making back at the mansion. Maybe for a *long* while.'

'Bartholomew got his supernatural revelation,' Dr Ross commented wryly. 'Just not the one he was planning.'

'Exactly,' said Kulika. 'I don't think we're going to get a better opportunity to run. We could try, if you want.' She was asking them all, but she was looking at Quick. Her reply was the only one that really mattered.

'Do *you* want?' Quick asked.

In truth, Kulika wasn't sure. Everything she felt for Quick, everything she'd ever felt for Bartholomew, it was all mixed up in a pot of emotions she was struggling to sift. But that was what Bartholomew and his blood did to you, wasn't it? The best Kulika could do was cling to the certainty she'd had when she came back to South Carolina in the first place: she'd never wanted to return to Bartholomew, or to his mansion, and she'd only signed his covenant under duress, for Quick's sake. There had been a reason for that, whatever she was feeling now.

'So your head isn't hurting?' Evita asked her.

'No,' Kulika replied, with some surprise.

'Mine neither,' Evita replied, but she didn't look happy about it. 'We must be miles from the mansion by now. Our heads should be hurting.'

'Maybe Bartholomew died in the fire,' Wolfrie said, coming to join them below decks.

'Who's at the helm?' Kulika asked.

'Don't worry,' Wolfrie said, slumping into a nearby hammock. 'Bellamy's got it.'

Of all the crew from the old days, Bellamy was the one Kulika would have trusted least with the helm, but given the choice between him and Monty or his friends, she couldn't deny that Bellamy was the best option.

'You're thinking of sailing away, then?' Wolfrie asked. His hearing was sharp enough that he'd probably picked up their conversation from up on deck and decided to join them.

'Thinking about it, if we can get clear of Bartholomew.'

'I still think we should have killed him,' Wolfrie said.

Kulika glanced at Evita, remembering Wolfrie's plan. 'It wouldn't have worked.'

'It would have been better, though.'

'I don't know about that,' said Evita.

'You've changed your tune since this morning,' Quick pointed out. 'You kept telling me how dangerous he was, how he's killed so many people, how he deserves to die.'

'Well, a lot's happened since this morning,' Evita replied, a little too defensively.

'Then what do you think we should have done?' Quick asked.

'It's not just the fact that he kills people,' Xiaoyu interrupted. 'You know that, right? The point is that he *controls* people. The doc was just talking about this,' she added.

'I was,' Dr Ross murmured, glancing at the covenant mark that stained Quick's palm. 'But it's academic now. There's no way to kill Bartholomew.'

'Right,' Kulika agreed. 'The only thing that might actually have killed him is the doctor's formula.'

'Not if he's from the Primus's – Solomon's, I mean – bloodline,' said Dr Ross. 'And I suspect he is. The formula wouldn't work on him. The only thing that would be strong enough to kill him would be the formula combined with Dr Jahan Khalyed's blood, which we don't have. I had hoped that Evita's blood would be a substitute, but…' Dr Ross smiled ruefully.

Kulika wondered if, like her, she was thinking about the baron and his impending death, which they had both been banking on Evita's blood to prevent. He had no hope now.

'Ancient history,' Dr Ross explained to the others. 'I tested a sample of Evita's blood that Bayly gave us. It wasn't a match to Jahan's. End of story. No point worrying about it now.'

'What are you talking about?' Evita said, confused. 'Bayly never took a sample of my blood.'

'While you were out of it, in the box,' Kulika explained.

'I was *never* out of it,' Evita insisted. 'I might have been weak and practically dead from blood loss, but I was conscious the entire time. I remember every single second of being stuck in that box. Believe me, I would have remembered if it had been opened, even for a second.'

'Then whose blood did I test?' Dr Ross asked, locking eyes with Kulika.

A long-dead hope started back to life in Kulika's chest. If they'd tested the wrong blood, then there was still a possibility that Evita's blood carried the same traits as Jahan's, and if it did…

They could save Baron Drake.

But Bayly. He'd *lied* to her. After all they'd been through together, after all she'd risked to wriggle him out of the covenant breach *he'd* created...

If he wasn't half-dead already, Kulika would have killed him herself.

'Whatever,' Evita said dismissively. 'It's done. We left Bartholomew behind. My blood doesn't matter now.'

Dr Ross glanced at Kulika as they shared the same silent thought: *it matters to Jack and the baron.*

'Yet somehow you're unhappy about leaving,' Quick was saying.

'Because it should hurt,' Evita said softly, 'like it did when we tried to leave the mansion this evening. But it doesn't hurt. Not at all.'

'Well, hopefully the zombies have killed him,' said Wolfrie.

'Unlikely,' Kulika replied.

'Dead or alive, they're welcome to him,' said Wolfrie. 'If you want to feel bad about anyone, then feel bad about Digs.'

'I will not,' said Kulika.

'Nor me,' said Evita pointedly.

'He was trying to kill us,' Kulika pointed out.

'But did he really deserve to die?' said Wolfrie. 'Bayly's the one who put him in that box. Who knows what that does to a mind. That much isolation...'

'Then all we did was put him out of his misery, right?' Kulika asked.

'But—'

'Wolfrie,' Kulika said. 'I know the two of you were close, but he deserved what he got. He even deserved being put in the damn box in the first place. You know that as well as I do.'

'Why?' asked Quick. 'What did he do?'

Wolfrie shrugged his rounded shoulders, then sighed and said, 'He was already old when Bayly locked him away over three hundred years ago. There isn't a person on this earth upwards of a hundred years old who hasn't done something they deserved to die for, me included.'

'And me,' Kulika said quietly. 'The longer you live, the more time you have to make an unforgivable choice.'

God knew she'd made enough of those.

'So let's hope this isn't one of them,' Wolfrie said.

'We're decided, then?' Dr Ross asked. 'We sail away?'

'We do it by the code,' Kulika corrected her. 'We take a vote, and if the crew's decided – the *new* crew – then we sail away, up along the coast if we can find a port that's safe, or all the way back to Britain if we have to. Agreed?'

'Agreed,' the others chorused.

Kulika looked at Dr Ross, who nodded back. If Evita's blood could do what they needed it to do, then they would get the cure to the baron as fast as they could, by hell or high water.

The vote didn't take long. Kulika and Wolfrie gathered everyone on deck, Silver and human, and asked for a show of hands from those who wanted to return to the mansion, to Bartholomew. The only taker was Monty.

Kulika let Quick push him off the side of the ship into the river, then told him to walk back on his own. Quick's evil grin as he splashed into the water was an image Kulika would cherish for the rest of her days.

20

UP AT THE front of the ship, with the midnight breeze pulling the hair back from her face, Quick was trying to forget everything that had happened today, if only for a moment.

Unfortunately, her mind didn't want to cooperate. It didn't help that the zombies were still following them through the water, grabbing onto the ship at the waterline and riding with it for a short distance before the current pulled them spinning away. Another would take the place of each that spun off almost immediately, so it seemed from above as though the ship was being carried down the river on the shoulders of a thousand night-shrouded wraiths.

This was not how Quick had thought her day would end. This morning, she'd been hopeful that they'd get out of the mansion and away from the crew for good. But then there had been Digs, and Evita's injuries, and from then on it had been a non-stop ride. She was finding, though, that she could tolerate the crew better without Monty and Bartholomew in it.

'Regrets?' Penny asked, coming to join her at what Quick was seventy-percent certain was the prow, though she wasn't brave enough to use the word. She had learned fast that Kulika and her pirates were twitchy about terminology.

'About a hundred of them,' Quick said.

'Anything you can do about them now?'

'Nope,' Quick replied.

'Then I wouldn't worry if I were you,' Penny said lightly, but it seemed like she was talking to herself more than she was talking to Quick.

They stood side by side for a few minutes in silence, watching the water and listening to the shouts in the rigging above and behind them. Kulika's voice rang out the clearest, strong and commanding as she managed the crew. That was Quick's only actionable regret, she realised: Kulika.

'Has anyone checked on Aloysius?' Quick asked.

'Who?' said Penny.

'The historian guy,' she explained. 'The one Bartholomew was keeping tied up in his cabin.'

Penny just gave her a blank look, so she said, 'Never mind. I'll go,' and went to check on the man herself.

Quick made her way down to the deck by the light of the ship's lanterns, watching her feet so she didn't trip over anything. The layout was so unfamiliar and the rocking motion so unbalancing that she often found herself bumping into railings and grasping for ropes that weren't there. Compared with the agile Silver in the rigging, she felt like a clumsy ox. Perhaps that grace would come with time, as she learned to control her powers and listen to her senses. She was a natural fighter, it seemed, but not a natural sailor.

So intent was she on her feet that she didn't notice she had company until she reached the doors leading into the captain's cabin. Kulika moved so silently that it was only her scent that tipped Quick off.

'Could we talk?' Kulika asked. Her gaze was shifting, her

focus moving from Quick's hair, to over her shoulder, to away into the darkness of the night. She wouldn't look Quick in the eye.

That didn't feel like a good sign.

'Sure,' Quick said, trying to calm the anxiety building in her stomach.

Dr Ross had told her the silvering was reversing. Was that what Kulika was about to confess to her? That she didn't love her anymore, and that this thing between them was over before it had even begun? Because Quick wasn't sure she'd be able to bear that. It was far from over for her. She could feel the electricity between them in the anticipatory tingle of her fingertips as they ached to reach out and grasp the bare skin of Kulika's shoulders. Her yearning was there in the dryness that suddenly invaded her mouth, making the urge to lick her lips irresistible. And surely that yearning was reflected back to her in the way Kulika's gaze followed her tongue as she licked?

But Quick couldn't see the silver that Kulika was hiding in her eyes, so she had no way of knowing. She'd have to do this the hard way, and ask.

'I was just going to check on Aloysius,' Quick said. 'That is, unless you've already—'

'No,' Kulika replied. 'I'd forgotten about him, honestly.'

'Maybe we could go together?' Quick asked, holding the door open.

Kulika took a deep breath, as though she were preparing herself for a distasteful task, then stepped through the door and into what had until recently been Bartholomew's cabin. Like a pirate to the gallows, Quick followed reluctantly behind.

To Kulika, Bartholomew's cabin felt like a museum without

him in it. It was so familiar from their years at sea together that while he had inhabited this replica, she'd felt as though no time had passed since the Golden Age. Now, void of the character that held these antique pieces together, she could finally see it for what it was: a relic of a bygone era. There might as well have been cobwebs hanging from the ceiling.

'He's not here,' Quick said.

For a moment, the threads got crossed in Kulika's mind and she thought Quick was talking about Bartholomew, then she saw the discarded ropes tossed by the foot of the bed and remembered they were supposed to be looking for Aloysius. That wasn't why Kulika had followed Quick here, though.

'I thought maybe we should talk,' Kulika said. She had to do this fast, because if she put it off then it was just going to keep building and building like an avalanche until she couldn't hold it back anymore, and then it would all come out wrong.

'Okay,' Quick said, turning to face her. 'About the silvering?'

Kulika froze.

'Dr Ross said it was reversing,' Quick added.

Of course she did. Kulika should have guessed that the doctor would stick her oar in. Maybe that was a good thing. If Quick already knew what was happening, Kulika could just nod and leave. It would be easier that way.

'Then you know,' she said, heading for the door. 'That was all I wanted to talk about, really.'

'Hey, wait,' said Quick, rushing after her. 'We haven't actually *talked* at all, though. You've just confirmed what I already knew.'

'So we're done,' Kulika said, puzzled. 'Aren't we?'

'*Are* we?' Quick asked, stepping forward until she was close enough for Kulika to reach out and touch.

She didn't, though. She couldn't let herself do that. It wasn't fair, not now that all of this was going away. Maybe it had never been fair, given the circumstances of Quick's turning, and all the liberties that Kulika had taken since. With her position, she should never have touched Quick in the first place. Looking back now, all she could hear was Bartholomew's voice in her head, a guilty reminder of everything she never should have done.

We don't ask, we take.

Well, Kulika had taken. Now she could only apologise for it.

'I'm sorry,' Kulika said. 'For everything.'

'I don't want your apologies,' Quick said irritably. 'I want the truth. I want to know how you *feel*. You're acting as though this thing between us is over, but it doesn't feel over, not to me.'

'Doesn't it?' Kulika asked, because to her it felt as though Quick was still slipping through her fingers like sand through an hourglass.

'If you tell me I've had all I'm ever going to get of you, then fine,' Quick said, 'I'll take it on the chin and walk away, but that's not what I want. If it's not what you want either, then maybe we can find a way to reverse the reversing, but right now I have no idea how you feel about any of this.' Quick took one step closer until she was looking right up into Kulika's eyes. 'You said you wanted to talk, so talk to me. Please.'

Kulika broke, like a wave against the rocks.

'I love you,' she whispered, suddenly holding back tears that seemed to have sprung from nowhere. 'I do, or I did. But—'

Then the pain ripped through her, starting at her stomach and tearing out through her veins so it felt like her body was trying to turn itself inside out. She doubled over, breathing through her screams. When the pain subsided enough for her to be conscious of her surroundings again, she found herself kneeling on the floor in Quick's arms, holding her head and wincing.

'What was that?' Quick asked, fear written all over her face.

'The blood and the bond,' Kulika gasped, still getting her breath back.

'Blood?'

'I drank Bartholomew's blood when I made my bargain with him,' Kulika admitted. 'And again today. The doc says it's messing with the bond.'

'Which bargain?' Quick asked.

'In the book in his desk drawer,' Kulika said. 'Get it.' Then she slumped back against the bulkhead as Quick crossed the cabin to the stern.

Once Quick had taken the covenant book from the drawer, she brought it back to sit beside Kulika on the floor.

'Me, and Evita, and Xiaoyu,' Quick murmured as she found the right page and read.

'Good deal, right?' Kulika replied with a wry laugh, but she was distracted by the scent of Quick's blood spilling from the book. She turned the page in Quick's unresisting hands to find Quick's own bargain spelled out in blood on the next spread: her covenant in return for Bartholomew's blood to heal to Evita.

'Not such a good deal,' Quick said bitterly.

'We're leaving him behind us,' Kulika said, then she snatched the book from Quick's hands and tossed it across the room. 'We'll burn it.'

'And these?' Quick took Kulika's tattooed hand in her own, laying them both across her lap palm up, so the matching brands looked like a pair of dark eyes holding the two of them in their gaze.

'We'll burn them, too,' Kulika whispered, then she covered Quick's tattoo with her own, clasping them together as she clasped Quick's hand.

But Kulika knew she couldn't burn Bartholomew's blood out of her veins as easily as she could burn his mark off her skin. The pain wasn't going away, it was just coming in smaller waves. It swirled between the two of them, threatening to drag Kulika into its undertow.

'I don't know if I'll ever be able to get free of him,' Kulika said softly. 'However far we sail, whatever the world becomes. He's part of me.'

'And me,' Quick replied, squeezing Kulika's hand. 'His blood is in me too, even if it's only a drop.'

'His voice is in my head.'

'For now. You don't have to listen to it if you don't want to.'

Was that true, Kulika wondered? Was Quick a choice she'd ever be allowed to make on her own, without him watching over her shoulder and whispering in her ear?

Then she turned to look at Quick and saw exactly how much Bartholomew had stolen from her.

'Your eyes,' she said.

'Hmm?' Quick asked. She was looking at Kulika in a thoughtful way that made Kulika want to rip all her clothes off, but her eyes…

'Your eyes are silver,' Kulika said in a hollow voice.

'What?'

Quick pushed away from the bulkhead and up to her feet, then found a hand mirror on Bartholomew's bedside table and looked at her eyes. Kulika knew what she'd be seeing: the silver that traced the blood vessels in her eyes had now extended into the rich green of her irises, radiating towards her pupils so they looked like they were surrounded by emerald feathers, highlighted in platinum.

'But that's not possible,' Quick said, turning to Kulika in shock. 'Dr Ross told me how it works: when you silver for someone who's already silvered for you, the silver turns gold, in your eyes and in the eyes of the person you love. Bound in silver, sealed in gold. That's what the doctor said. Requited love is supposed to be golden, not silver.'

'Maybe it's not me you've silvered for,' Kulika said bleakly as the horror of that possibility ran through her like a chill.

'Don't be ridiculous,' Quick said dismissively. She looked at Kulika for a moment, then crouched down next to her on the floor and said, 'Show me your silver.'

'I love *you*,' Kulika insisted.

Which set off another wave of excruciating pain that she had to ride until it was over. When she blinked back to awareness this time, she was lying on the floor with Quick leaning over her. Apparently she'd lost control of her silver during that episode, because the first thing Quick said was, 'It's gone.' She looked as though she was going to cry. 'The silver isn't in your irises anymore, just the whites of your eyes.'

Quick grabbed the mirror again and passed it to Kulika so she could see for herself, but Kulika pushed it away. She believed Quick. She didn't want to see it for herself. She didn't need to; she could feel the emptiness in her chest that had been left behind by Bartholomew's vindictive jealousy.

'I should have killed him,' she said, but the words had no force. Apparently, with this much of Bartholomew's blood in her, she couldn't even hate him properly.

She looked at Quick hopelessly, tracing the shimmer of

silver in her irises with her gaze. How unfair. It was the promise of a perfect ending that might have been fulfilled, if only Bartholomew hadn't got in the way. It had been so nearly within her grasp.

How terribly fucking unfair.

'This doesn't mean it has to be the end, does it?' Quick asked.

'I don't know,' Kulika replied.

She didn't know what it meant. She didn't know what any of it meant, because she'd never seen this happen before. Never even heard of it happening before. It shouldn't be possible to reverse a bond. It shouldn't be possible for one Silver to impose their will on another just by infecting them with their blood. It shouldn't be possible for a bond like Kulika and Quick's to be broken.

And yet.

'Kulika?' Wolfrie called from the deck.

'Yeah?' Kulika called back. She was too deflated to move.

'Can you come out here?'

'Why?' she groaned, not relishing the prospect of returning to teach Seafaring 101.

But then Wolfrie called back with, 'I think we've found the historian.'

21

KULIKA FOLLOWED WOLFRIE down to the bottom deck of the ship with Quick trailing along behind. Part of her wished that Quick had stayed up top in the captain's cabin. After everything that had just happened, she didn't know how to look Quick in the eye and not see self-reproach written in the silver threading through her irises.

Kulika should never have bargained with Bartholomew. She knew him well enough to know that he would turn every deal to his own overwhelming profit, even when it was Kulika setting the terms. Now, she couldn't help but wonder if he'd known exactly what his blood would do to her. He'd experimented with it in every other way, she was sure, but using it to break a Silver bond? It felt calculated and cruel enough to be deliberate, but silvering was so rare that she couldn't imagine he'd ever had the opportunity to test it before.

It was too late to ask him now.

They found Aloysius bundled up in a chest in the gun magazine room, behind the galley.

'Is he alive?' Quick asked.

'Yes,' said Kulika. She could hear his pulse, strong and

regular. 'Drugged, probably. Let's get him out. Can you get Dr Ross, please?'

Kulika hadn't addressed this request to either of them in particular, but it was Quick who said, 'I'll go.'

When she returned with the doctor, Kulika and Wolfrie had Aloysius laid out on the floor. There was a conspicuous needle mark in his arm.

'Dr Ross,' Kulika said.

'It's probably time you all started calling me Tabitha,' she replied with a grim smile.

'Tabitha, then. Can you do anything for him?'

'Maybe,' she said, examining the needle mark in his arm. 'If the infirmary is stocked with any supplies from this century.'

'It's one level up, at the stern,' said Kulika. 'The cabin with the broken window. You can't miss it.'

'Broken window?' the doctor said uncertainly.

'It's how Digs got in,' Wolfrie explained.

'I guess we'd better patch it up before we head out into the Atlantic,' Kulika said, wondering how many other things they'd have to patch up on the journey.

This ship had never been designed to go to sea, and most of the people who'd built it had never made a ship like this before in their lives. Maybe they'd be better off stopping at the harbour for a more modern vessel, but that would delay them, and Kulika didn't want to delay even for a moment. Delay meant more exposure, more vicious zombies to fight through, and more chance that Bartholomew would come after them.

Kulika and Wolfrie knew what they were doing, and that would have to be enough. They could manage the risk, just until they reached the next port up the coast.

'I'll find some tools and meet you in the infirmary,'

Wolfrie said to the doctor.

'I'll help you get him upstairs,' Quick offered.

'Then I'll go and make sure we're sailing in the right direction,' said Kulika.

She hadn't even reached the main deck before Wolfrie called her name again.

'Kulika?'

'Yeah?'

'Can you come here, please?'

It was the "please" that told her something was wrong. Pirates didn't have much time for politeness. If you hesitated on board, whether in battle or when navigating in a storm, people died and ships sank. You didn't ask nicely when a job needed doing, you just demanded what was required and left courtesy to those who could afford it. A habit like that crept into your everyday way of speaking, and your way of doing, until it became an unshakeable characteristic.

Pirates didn't say please.

That's why, when she heard that word, Kulika ran to the infirmary. She found Wolfrie, Quick and Dr Ross staring at the patient's bunk. It wasn't occupied by Bayly or Enzo, who seemed to be missing, or by Aloysius, who'd been abandoned on the floor at their feet, but rather by Evita – and Bartholomew, who was sitting calmly on the bed next to her, wiping blood from his face with a wet cloth. There was blood all over him, the majority of which was flowing from scrapes on his shoulders, perhaps caused as he'd climbed in through the broken window. His arms were pockmarked with bite marks that had left bloody rosettes over his white shirt. There was a gaping wound over his heart that looked like it had been dug out with nails and teeth, and there were a couple of bites on his face, too, ripped through his cheeks so he bore more than a passing resemblance to the creature they had once called Digs. If this was how he looked *after* he'd healed, Kulika didn't want to imagine how bad the wounds had been when they'd first been inflicted.

'My Second,' he said to her.

It was a statement of possession, and it shivered through Kulika in the worst possible way.

You're an empty thing without me.

She was an emptier thing with him. She hadn't realised until this moment just how free she'd felt when she thought he'd no longer had any claim on her.

But the lack of pain she'd felt at their separation made sense now. She hadn't hurt when she'd left the mansion, despite the amount of Bartholomew's blood she'd drunk, because he hadn't been *at* the mansion. He'd been right here all along, stowed away on the *Primus's Fortune* with the other stragglers. If Kulika hadn't been so distracted by her attempts to command a frigate for the first time in three centuries, and her attempts to salvage her relationship with Quick, she might have noticed his scent on board. Now that it was in her nostrils, it was stuck in there like the cloying odour of mould, impossible to ignore.

And impossible to cure.

He was in her head, and in her veins, and she couldn't raise a hand against him, however hard she tried. She was powerless against Bartholomew Roberts.

Just as he'd always wanted her to be.

Quick had never cared that she couldn't hide her silver, not until the moment that Bartholomew's gaze landed on her. The way he smiled when he saw her newly-silvered eyes made her stomach turn.

'Show me your silver,' he said to Kulika.

Without a word, and apparently helpless to resist, Kulika

did exactly as he asked.

Bartholomew's smile twitched a fraction wider.

'Here we all are, then,' he said, curling one hand around Evita's waist while he tucked her hair over her shoulder with the other, baring her neck. The gesture felt like a threat, one that gave Quick pause. Meanwhile, Evita just sat placidly, appearing perfectly content to let herself be held and stroked by the man who, only this morning, she'd been champing at the bit to murder.

There was only one explanation Quick could come up with: Bartholomew's blood. Maybe Dr Ross was right. Maybe there was something in that. He hadn't just wanted Quick to sign the covenant, he'd wanted his blood inside Evita, so he could control her like he was doing now. Like he was probably controlling Kulika, too.

'You've already charted our journey?' Bartholomew said to Kulika.

'I've started, Primus,' she replied, as though she'd expected him to be joining them all along.

For a moment, Quick wondered if that was the truth of the situation, but she wasn't imagining the way Kulika was clenching her jaw and fisting her hands. She could feel her tension, too, like someone was strumming at the tether that connected her to Kulika through her new bond.

'Then perhaps we should reconvene in my cabin, to consult the maps,' Bartholomew suggested. 'I assume it's back to Britain?'

'Unless we can find safe harbour along the coast,' Kulika said, the words apparently falling uncontrollably from her mouth.

'Kulika,' Wolfrie said, looking at her in shock. 'You're not really going to just step aside and go along with—'

'There's no safe harbour in North America,' Bartholomew

said bluntly, ignoring Wolfrie entirely. 'The zombies are spreading too fast.'

'And just how much of that did you design?' Dr Ross asked. She was crouched anxiously on the floor beside Aloysius, who was finally starting to come around. 'Kulika said you had hours in that wine cellar with Digs and the zombies. You had plenty of time to study them.'

Bartholomew shrugged the shoulder that wasn't pressed up against Evita. 'I found that Digs liked the taste of my blood.'

'You knew he'd come after us,' Quick breathed.

'I had expected he would do it sooner, before you left the property at all. The zombies were a collateral effect that, I admit, I could have done without. I chained them to the wall, but...' He sighed. 'I'd owned that mansion for three hundred years, you know,' he added mournfully. 'By the end of the night, it'll be ash.'

'Do you really expect us to feel bad for you?' Quick sneered.

'Why should you?' he asked jovially. 'I have everything I want right here: my crew, my ship, my Second.'

He turned to Evita, pushing her hair behind her ear.

Quick could imagine what he wanted from her best friend, and she didn't like it at all. Something flared in Evita's eyes then, and Quick wondered if perhaps she wasn't as subjugated as she appeared. In the next second, Evita had snatched Bartholomew's hand away from her face and swung a punch at him, which he caught in his palm with infuriating ease.

With that, the spell broke. Up until now, Bartholomew had been able to pretend that everything was as he wanted it, but now even he couldn't deny that the cracks were beginning to show.

'I thought I'd found something in you, something that I'd never even thought to look for,' Bartholomew said to Evita, his top lip twisting into a grimace as he held her fists in his hands.

'Do you love her?' Wolfrie asked abruptly. He was weighing the box of tools he held in his hand like he meant to do something with them. Quick didn't like the way his gaze was fixing on Evita.

'Is that what you think?' Bartholomew asked him, with a harsh bark of laughter. 'You think I've silvered for a whelp, like my Second has? Well, I'm afraid I have to disappoint you. I won't be that easy to kill.'

The whites of Bartholomew's eyes flashed silver for a moment, but there was nothing in his irises except stormy grey. Wolfrie deflated, looking hopelessly at Kulika, who was doing nothing at all.

In the meantime, Bartholomew had turned back to Evita. 'I thought I'd found a *connection*,' he said angrily to her.

'You had,' Evita shot back with equal vitriol. 'That's the really sad thing, you know? I could have loved you. Maybe you could even have loved me, but you never gave us a chance to find out.'

Bartholomew laughed. 'You forgot me,' he said. His tone was disdainful, but Quick didn't think she was imagining the pain she heard in it too.

'When I lost my memory, I didn't choose to forget you,' Evita replied. 'That wasn't in my control. You did, though. You're the one who chose to forget me. To forget *us*.'

Bartholomew's expression switched from anger to pain, and back again. The cracks broke wide open, irreparable and unfathomable. He hurled Evita to the floor and stood from the bunk in a blood-soaked rage, towering over her as he yelled, 'I *made* you! I made all of you,' he added, looking first at Kulika, then at Quick, before turning back to Evita.

It was true: Kulika and Evita had both been turned by Bartholomew himself. Quick had been turned by Kulika. All three of them shared his blood, and the yoke that went along with it. He controlled them all.

'A little respect wouldn't go amiss,' he was saying to Evita. 'Have you forgotten who I am? I am your Primus, and the captain of this ship.' He looked at Dr Ross and Aloysius, then at Wolfrie, saying, 'If you're on this ship, then you're part of my crew, and my crew will enforce my word. If you prefer to leave, then the zombies are welcome to you.'

'Your crew are all back at the mansion,' Wolfrie pointed out. 'What you have here is a handful of deserters and a hold full of frightened humans, none of whom belong to you.'

'Don't they?' Bartholomew asked, pacing closer. 'My Second controls this ship, does she not?'

Wolfrie tipped his head in evasive acknowledgement.

'Then she does so on my behalf. Isn't that right, Kulika?'

Kulika said, 'I…'

But that was all she said.

Quick wanted her to argue. She'd *seen* Kulika argue with Bartholomew, in bright blazes of emotion, but now she was subdued, weighed down by the poison of his blood in her veins. Evita was the same: she might have mustered up enough strength to swing at Bartholomew once, but she wasn't trying to repeat it now. Instead, she just lay on the floor, staring up at him with a look of painful frustration that Quick couldn't bear. The two most powerful women in her life, the two women she loved, reduced to this.

'You understand, don't you, Dr Ross?' Bartholomew asked the doctor. 'You know what would happen if you left this ship right now.'

'The zombies are infecting every human in North

America,' she replied softly. 'When they do, there'll be nothing left for us to drink.'

'Exactly. I control the blood supply on this ship, and with it I control the rest of you. It's me, or a long, painful death.'

'One and the same,' Quick spat.

Unlike them, she had never been under his spell. She might share Bartholomew's blood, but she'd been turned by Kulika, at one remove from him. Her bloodline was diluted, and she'd drunk a lot less of his blood recently than the other two had.

'Do you really want to test me, Patience?' Bartholomew asked, almost playfully. 'You're not the only one who signed my covenant.'

He grabbed Kulika's hand, then drove his fingernail into the black spot in the centre of her palm and twisted it. She didn't scream, but her lips went white. Her pain was so palpable that Quick was sure she felt it in the mark on her own scarred palm.

'With your silvering, I have you as surely as I have her,' Bartholomew whispered, then he tossed Kulika's hand away and said, 'Now set course for—'

Quick didn't recall moving. All she recalled was a simple chain of thoughts: She was strong. She was fast. If the two people she loved most in the world weren't able to save themselves, then she would do it for them.

Her hand slipped into her pocket and brought up the vial-filled syringe, flipped off the cap, then plunged it into the messy open wound that had been gouged over Bartholomew's heart.

He looked down first in surprise, then in irritation.

'My blood is not so weak as all that,' he said, laughing as he plucked the vial easily from Quick's fingers and tossed it away.

Dr Ross had been right, then: Bartholomew's veins really did flow with the blood of Primus Solomon. If they didn't, he'd be dead right now. Instead, he was pinning Quick to the infirmary wall by her throat, leaving her feet to kick uselessly in the air.

'Foolish, Patience,' he said. 'Have you not realised that you're useless to me now that my Second's silvering has reversed? I can kill you with no consequences to her at all. Maybe she'll mourn you, for a day or two,' he said, leaning in closer so Quick could feel his breath on her cheek and smell the rancid putrescence of his open wounds. 'But I doubt it.'

Quick struggled and kicked, but Bartholomew was too strong for her. She looked at Kulika over his shoulder, searching desperately for help, but Kulika wouldn't meet her gaze. Instead, her eyes were fixed on the floor as Bartholomew's mouth lowered towards Quick's neck.

Kulika wasn't going to do a thing about this, Quick realised. After fighting to protect Quick from Digs, and even after the declaration of love she'd made in the captain's cabin mere minutes before, Kulika was just going to stand there and do nothing while Bartholomew tore Quick's throat out. Bartholomew controlled Kulika, and Evita, and Quick along with them.

Quick was going to die waiting to be saved by a woman who was no more capable of saving her from Bartholomew than she was of saving herself.

They'd never stood a chance.

Or so Quick had thought, but when she looked again, Kulika was no longer on the other side of the infirmary. Instead, she was standing right next to Quick, with Evita's wrist held tightly in her hand. In the blink of an eye, she took a knife from her pocket and used it to slice open Evita's palm, then slammed it onto the ugly gash where Quick had plunged the vial into Bartholomew's chest.

Bartholomew looked at Kulika, then down at Evita's hand as she withdrew it hastily, then back at Kulika.

'What's that supposed to achieve?' he asked derisively.

'An end to this,' Kulika whispered. 'I'm sorry, Bartholomew. I really am.'

'Sorry?' he laughed. 'For what, exactly?'

Then something changed.

Bartholomew looked down at his seeping chest in horror. 'What is this, Kulika?' he asked. 'Mutiny? Again?'

'I may have your blood,' Kulika said to him softly. 'But Quick still has my heart.'

Bartholomew threw Quick aside, slamming her head against the wall and crumpling her into a heap on the floor. It wasn't until she gathered her wits back together and looked up at him, blinking, that she realised what Kulika had done. Against all the odds, Evita had inherited Jahan Khalyed's immunity to the formula. By adding Evita's blood to the concoction that Quick had already injected into his chest, Kulika had created a poison that even Bartholomew couldn't overcome.

He was stepping back towards the bed now, throwing a wild punch at Kulika as he went, but she ducked it easily. He stumbled to his knees, following the force of his swing to the ground.

Quick could feel the heat, then. Bartholomew stared down in disbelief at the spot on his chest where the syringe and Evita's palm had found their mark, watching as the blood within the wound began to glow. Soon, the glow was visible through the surrounding skin, blending from red to orange to yellow to white hot as it burned the clothes from his body. Dark cracks blossomed out from it like black rot through infected veins, spreading down his arms and up his neck until they crossed his chin to reach for his lips.

He looked up. His gaze found Evita's.

'I knew you'd be the death of me,' he whispered with a smile.

Then the flames took him. All that was left when it was over was the copper token he'd worn at his neck, tinkling onto the charred surface of the deck.

22

AS THE SHIP sailed past White Point Gardens in the early hours of the morning, a small motorised dinghy pushed off from the tip of the Battery in Charleston Harbour and started heading in their direction. There were four people on board: two adults, and two children. Xiaoyu's children, as it turned out, plus her former husband, and Phinchas.

'Found them in the attic,' Phinchas said as he passed the children up the rope ladder and into their mother's arms.

They all cried for a while after that. Kulika and the others left them to it, giving over the navigation room so they could have a space to be together as a family, after so long apart.

Phinchas went with them. Kulika wondered about that, until she saw Xiaoyu reach out and take his hand behind her back, where the rest of her family couldn't see it.

Maybe they would get their happy ending after all.

Kulika wasn't so sure about her own. It had been mere minutes since Bartholomew had been reduced to ash in the infirmary, and she was still shedding the influence of his blood like a snake shedding its skin. It was coming off messily, in dirty pieces that got stuck in her teeth, leaving too many parts of her raw and exposed.

He had been everything to her. He was nothing now, except another notch on her conscience that she would never quite shake.

She'd come up to the sterncastle for the air, though there was plenty of that on the ship. Perhaps what she'd really wanted was somewhere she could stand and see everything she was leaving behind her, to convince herself it was real. There was Charleston, disappearing into the night. There were the fires lighting the horizon, from the mansion and any number of other properties that had been set alight in the panic induced by the zombies. If Kulika looked down at the wake of the *Primus's Fortune* as it set out for the Atlantic, she could still see them bobbing in the water behind them. That didn't seem like a good omen.

Kulika didn't get to enjoy her solitude for long, which was just as well.

'Ms Yadav,' the man said, with all the grace of a proper Southern gentleman. 'I know we've already met, but we've not yet been properly introduced. Allow me to do the honours: Aloysius Truman, Chairman of the Charleston Historical Society, amateur historian, and your humble servant.' He bowed.

The man actually *bowed*.

'I was intending to write a history of Bartholomew Roberts,' he said, 'but perhaps, since his – *ahem* – unfortunate demise, I might write yours instead?'

Kulika looked down again at the zombies in their wake.

'Knock yourself out,' she replied. 'But if that's really what you want to do, then I suggest you do it fast.'

'I have some questions,' he said, pulling a notepad from his pocket with a gleam in his eye. 'If you could just—'

Evita came to join them then, giving Kulika a convenient excuse.

'Later, Aloysius,' she said.

The man bowed again, then left Kulika and Evita alone, but not before giving her the distinct impression that he would be back. Apparently, she had a fan now, and he would be sticking around.

'Thank you,' Evita said. 'For… you know.'

Kulika said nothing. She didn't want credit for any of it. She'd killed her sire and her captain. Where she came from, they had punishments enough to fit a crime like that.

ARTICLE VI. No boy or woman to be allowed amongst them.

ARTICLE VIII. None shall strike another on board the ship.

ARTICLE VII. He that shall desert the ship or his quarters in time of battle shall be punished by death or marooning.

But now the Articles of Bartholomew Roberts were just ash in the galley stove, along with his covenant book and all the blood trapped between its pages.

'Do you feel it too?' Evita asked her.

'Feel what?'

'Nothing.' Evita smiled, looking out over the dark water. 'No pain in your veins, no clamp on your tongue, no voice in your head except yours.'

'Yes.' Kulika smiled back. 'I feel it.'

Had Kulika ever truly *felt* a night breeze in the past three centuries, one that hadn't been muted by the armour she wore? The wind skittered across her skin with a chill that shocked and thrilled her, teasing her hair from her forehead like it wanted to play.

'Evita,' Dr Ross said, climbing the steps from the quarterdeck.

'Yes?' Evita replied, her eyes still fixed on the distant water.

'I want to test your blood,' the doctor said. 'Properly this time.'

'Is that really necessary?' Kulika asked, leaning back against the gunwale to face Dr Ross. 'Don't we have our answer?'

'Yes,' Dr Ross conceded, 'but I want to have Baron Drake's antidote ready by the time we get back home. It'll take a while, particularly with the limited resources on board, so I want to start right now.'

'But you think you'll be able to do it?' Kulika asked, pushing herself up straight.

'Yes,' the doctor replied with a hopeful smile. 'Now I just need you to get us back to him in time.'

'We're already too late, aren't we?' Kulika pointed out sadly, remembering the baron's desperation in their last phone calls.

'We don't know that. Give him and Jack some credit. They're more creative than you might think.'

'Let's hope so,' Kulika said, with not much hope at all.

Dr Ross remained buoyant, though. When Quick came to complete their quartet, the little doctor smiled widely and pulled her into her arms.

'I knew you could do it,' she said.

Quick smiled at Dr Ross, then came to stand next to Kulika at the railing. When she raised her eyes to Kulika's, they were glinting with gold.

Gold.

'Have you seen your—' Kulika began, breathlessly.

'I know,' Quick said with a smile. 'Will you show me yours?'

Kulika did, relaxing the control she held over the silver in her eyes as she stared at the gold in Quick's. But she could feel immediately that her own were no longer silver at all.

Where the silver had always shot back into her eyes with a pinch, the gold moved in a sluggish caress, coaxing Kulika to a joyful crescendo as she felt the colour circle her pupils in triumph.

There was no fogged glass between them now. Though Quick's colour had seemed dull only hours before, her hair was now a riot of sunset and sunrise, and her scent...

Frost-chilled pine trees in thick winter forests; sunshine breaking late over crocus-filled verges; summer heat baking yellow climbing roses; plums ripening beyond the constraints of their skins and spilling golden drops of sugar down their sides.

Quick's scent was all of these things at once, and none of them, her perfume kaleidoscoping through all the seasons, and rising joyfully as Kulika took her face in her hands. She pressed a kiss to Quick's lips, tentatively at first, but then Quick flicked her tongue and it was all that Kulika could do to stop herself from laying her down right there on the deck in front of their audience. Kulika kissed her like she meant it then, with intent and emotion, trying to convey with her actions the simple things that she found hard to put into words.

She loved Quick.

Quick loved her.

However many zombies were in the water, nothing could be wrong with the world as long as those two things remained true. And now that Bartholomew was gone, they would remain true, forever.

An hour before dawn, Bayly and Enzo woke up. The others were sitting on the main deck, drinking and planning, when they slunk upstairs from the officers' mess where Bartholomew had left them.

Quick was horrified.

'Wait! Hey, we're not letting him just run around on deck, are we?' she asked when she saw Bayly.

'Why not?' Kulika replied.

'Yeah,' said Wolfrie.

'Why not?' Phinchas finished.

'Because he's responsible for all this,' Quick said. She looked around at each of their confused faces in turn and didn't believe what she was seeing. 'He caused a zombie apocalypse! If he hadn't put Evita and Digs in that box together, then none of this would have happened.'

'But he's crew,' Wolfrie said simply.

'Plus,' said Penny, 'it was technically Bella who stole the formula from the lab and made the first super-zombie.'

'Though to be fair, she wouldn't have got her hands on that formula if Dr Ross had been paying attention,' said Brandon.

'Excuse *me*,' the doctor piped up. 'If you'd *all* been managing yourselves a little better, I wouldn't have had to. Besides, neither Kulika nor I would have come here in the first place if it wasn't for Baron Drake.'

'Who wouldn't have sent us if Jack Valentine hadn't gone and poisoned herself,' Kulika added.

'By accident,' said Dr Ross.

'But really, all of this was Bartholomew's fault,' Phinchas pointed out.

'He's dead, by the way,' Kulika added to Bayly, whose only reply was, 'Good.'

'Look,' said Quick, 'all of those things might be true, but he put my best friend in a box with a monster. I don't trust him.'

'Stand down, Impatience,' Evita said with a sigh. She was busy cleaning a knife as she prepared to excise the black mark from Quick's hand, again. 'Let the bastard be. He was a prisoner here as much as the rest of us were.'

'Seriously?' Quick looked across the deck to where Bayly was now lounging against the rigging with Enzo at his feet, as though he hadn't a care in the world. She turned back to Evita and asked, 'You're fine with this?'

'I'm fine.' Evita ran the knife blade through the flame of the lantern that hung beside her. 'It wasn't Bayly I was angry with.'

'But he put you in a box with a blood-starved vampire. He buried you and left you, for weeks. If Kulika hadn't come along and found you when she did, god knows how long you would've been stuck in—'

Evita whirled and let the knife fly, sending it right into Bayly's eye. Apparently she'd learned some new skills during her time at the mansion. Bayly sagged in the ropes, then fell face-first onto the deck.

'Hey!' Enzo yelled.

'He'll live,' Evita yelled back. 'Okay, now I'm fine,' she added as she turned back to Quick. 'I can't promise I'm not going to do that again from time to time, but I'm fine.'

Quick looked at Bayly's prostrate body, then squinted sceptically at Evita.

'Truly,' Evita said. 'I got it out of my system. I got *him* out of my system, and his blood with it.'

'Out of *all* of our systems,' Quick added. 'You sort of saved the day.'

'You and Kulika did, you mean. And let's not get carried away. We're still in the middle of a zombie apocalypse. Speaking of which, what happens if the zombies are in Britain by the time we arrive? If they really did contaminate the planes—'

'Then we'll deal with it then,' said Kulika calmly. 'For

now, it's just us and the sea.'

Phinchas smiled and said, 'The way you always liked it, Captain.'

Kulika smiled back at him.

Quick was coming to learn that, on the water, *now* was all that mattered. Now, she had her best friend back, and if they both tried very hard, they could pretend she'd never been gone in the first place. Now, Bartholomew Roberts was nothing but a pirate who'd received less attention than the scale of his fleet warranted, just as he always had been. Now, Quick and Kulika had each other, as they always should have done. The in-between didn't matter, and neither did what was still to come.

On the water, they could live for now, and deal with tomorrow later.

Kulika finished plotting their course just before dawn. She took her place on the quarterdeck when she was done, and Quick came with her. Quick had come with her everywhere since the moment their bond had sealed into gold, and Kulika wasn't complaining about it. If she had her way, they'd never be parted again.

'Where to, Captain?' Wolfrie asked, his arm resting on the wheel.

'Into the sunrise,' she said, smiling at Quick.

Home.

'I'd better get below decks,' Quick laughed.

'Or you could stay here with me,' Kulika suggested, running her fingers into Quick's hair, then using that point of contact to send the healing power of their bond through Quick's body.

'You mean—'

'I think so,' Kulika said. 'As long as you keep contact

with me, I can heal you before you even start to burn.'

'So we can watch the sunrise together?'

'Every morning, if you like.'

The sun broke over the horizon then, and Kulika settled her hand at the nape of Quick's neck, playing with the soft strands of hair there as they watched the dawning of their new world. Quick snuggled into her side, resting her cheek on Kulika's chest in the indentation below her shoulder that seemed to have been made to accommodate Quick, and no one else.

'Beautiful,' Quick murmured as she watched the sun rise.

'By the time we get home, you should be immune to it,' Kulika replied.

'How long will it take to get back to Britain?'

'Four weeks, if we're lucky. Eight if we're not.'

'That long?'

'This is a proper ship,' Kulika said, stroking the wood of the railing fondly. 'She doesn't have engines, or oars, or propellers. She rides the waves at the whims of the wind.'

Quick smiled, squinting a little as she turned towards the new sun. 'You get poetic about the sea.'

'I could get poetic about something else if you prefer,' Kulika offered in a whisper, stroking her fingers through Quick's flame-red hair. Then she leaned in and kissed her neck, savouring the frost and hedgerow flavour of her skin. Quick's scent kaleidoscoped as Kulika did so, singing through sharp citrus to winter spice, then ripening into something more enticing still. 'I can be very poetic, with my lips,' Kulika murmured against Quick's skin.

'Yes, please,' Quick breathed.

Well, why not? They'd seen enough of the sunrise for one morning, and they were pirates, weren't they? It was past time they started acting like it. For once in her life, Kulika had permission to take the things she wanted, and she wasn't going to let the opportunity go to waste.

Thrilling at every untethered step, Kulika took Quick down to the berth where they kept the rum, and showed her just how poetical – and piratical – she could be.

Part Four

QuickSilver Short Stories

A Shanty in the Key of F You

HUGO HAD AN affinity for crows.

The birds were ubiquitous in the crowded thoroughfares of the Republic of Pirates, so it was just as well that he was fond of them. How could he not be, when so much of their character reminded him of himself? Like him, they swaggered like thugs, they stuffed their beaks full of any old shit, and they were often associated with murder: both by their collective noun, and by their habit of picking the eyes out of the gibbeted corpses that hung caged in the bay.

But those weren't the only things the crows and Hugo had in common. There was this, too: the crows were mimics. They listened to a tune or a noise once or twice, then sang it back in reflected perfection, passing themselves off as a seagull, or a cocking flintlock, or even a human voice, whatever served their purposes best at the time. Although their musical genius was wrapped in an unappealing package, it was genius nonetheless.

That same proficiency was the only card Hugo had left to play in this town and, god willing, today it was going to save his life.

Or not. Who knew? His story was a song that had yet to be sung.

'Hugo! Get your arse in here, now!'

The yell came from inside the tavern. He was out back, grabbing another barrel of the miscellaneous fermented liquid that passed for ale in these parts, but he could already hear the chaos that had ensued in his absence: glass smashing, furniture breaking, and everyone screaming bloody murder. Hugo had been a lackey at Mungo's for months now, doing everything from barrel-rolling to gun-running in Nassau's grubbiest bar, but his real job was to be conspicuous. With him in the room, only the stupidest and most inebriated of the bar's patrons would dare to start trouble. When they did, Hugo ended it quickly.

When he wasn't there? Well, the picaroons were pirates. Shit kicked off.

The first thing he saw when he pushed his way back inside was the fire, which wasn't a good sign in a tinderbox like the Republic. At this time of year, it was hot and dry and a little spark went a long way, as evidenced by the flames that were already licking their way up the back of the bar to the top shelf, where Mungo stored the only decent liquor he sold.

Oh, hell no.

'Fuck!' Mungo yelled. Some scurvy-looking bastard that Hugo didn't recognise had the boss pinned to the bar with a forearm across this throat. 'Save the rum!'

'No need,' a man said.

He was tall and lithe, fair-skinned and dark-haired, with a charcoal-coloured shirt and a rakish tip to his hat. He unfurled his purple-lined cloak with a flourish and threw it across the flames, tamping them down to nothing but a wisp of smoke. Then he slipped behind the bar, pulled Mungo's best rum from the top shelf, popped out the cork with his thumb and swigged from it, fixing his shark-black eyes on the brawling drinkers as he did so.

By that point, the fighting was so out of hand that even Hugo couldn't stop it without getting his fists bloody, so he waded in and did his damned job. The first few troublemakers were easy enough to dispose of – regulars who hung around waiting for an opportunity to prove themselves, and failed thrice weekly – but there were hardier folk in the mix too. Those took a little more beating. One was felled with a stool to the groin, another by a dish to the voice box, the third by a lit candle to the eye. In a place like Mungo's, it wasn't hard to find a makeshift weapon in the unlikely event that you had brought none of your own. Hugo worked his way through what came to hand, toppling disgruntled punters one by one until just the man strangling the boss remained. Maybe he should have dealt with the blackguard sooner, but Mungo was running behind on his wages, so Hugo had an axe of his own to grind. When he finally came to the rescue, it took only a second or two to kick the attacker to the ground and stamp him into compliance.

All the while, the man behind the bar just stood and watched, and drank his rum.

Hugo could imagine what he was thinking.

Brute.

That's what the denizens of the Republic of Pirates saw when they looked at Hugo's tall, bulky, muscular frame: a bully. An ox. They didn't see the repressed music in his soul, or the sores of venereal disease hidden under his clothes. Both were eating him alive all the same.

But hopefully not for much longer.

'I heard you were looking for me, musician,' the man said, draining the rest of Mungo's rum.

He spoke too well for the person Hugo had been expecting. This man was no deckhand or lackey. Hugo blinked away the blood and smoke residue, looking more closely at the quality of the man's clothes, the confidence of his swagger and the bottomless depths of his eyes; so dark that they appeared to be all pupil, no iris.

'You're...' Hugo murmured.

Captain Drake.

Drake was a living – undying – legend. Not only did he enjoy the unnaturally-long lifespan that graced several of the Republic's most infamous buccaneers, he also had a reputation for sharing the secret of his long life with others who were in need.

And who were prepared to offer him their indentured service in return, of course. He was a pirate, not a philanthropist.

Finding Drake standing in front of him now was the culmination of Hugo's hard work over the past few years, making a name for being a stalwart crew member and bruiser, even if he would rather have been known for his musical talent. The best Hugo had hoped for was that he might receive a messenger from Drake, at best. He had not been prepared for a visit from the man himself.

'You're looking for me?' Hugo asked hesitantly.

'You are Hugo, yes?' Drake replied. 'You play the tin whistle?'

'Yes.' Hugo's heart beat a little faster. Maybe, finally, someone wanted him for the music and not the fists. 'And you're...'

'Willem Drake,' the man said. Then he smiled a little and added, 'They call me "Kill 'em", I believe. At your service. Or rather, should I say, you are at mine?'

Hugo should have said *oh god yes please* or something to that effect, but he found that he didn't have the words.

'Come with me,' Drake said with an indulgent smile,

wrapping an arm around Hugo's back – he couldn't reach all the way around Hugo's shoulders – and leading him towards the door.

'Where are we going?' Hugo asked.

'To the pub,' Drake said.

'We're already in a pub.'

'Yes, but we're going to *my* pub. You want to see it, don't you?'

The famous Silver Pieces o'Eight? Hugo truly did.

He looked over his shoulder at his erstwhile boss, who was still coughing on the ground. He didn't feel guilty about that, because god knew well enough that Mungo deserved the same again three-score times over, but Mungo's had been a home, of sorts, for a time.

That time was over now.

He let himself be led away. To adventure, and to life eternal.

The Silver Pieces o'Eight was less a pub and more a private club. Most captains in the Republic couldn't even get in the door, and those that could were just *different* from those that couldn't. The distinction wasn't one of wealth, or style, or class, but somehow transcended every other indicator that segregated life outside the Republic of Pirates to make a novel elite of its own. The elite of the Silver – as people called the place, for short – had something indefinably inhuman about them.

They moved with more strength and speed. They had sharper reflexes and keener senses. And, most importantly of all, they never aged, they never got sick, and they never died.

As evidenced by the man currently striding along beside Hugo, getting him a free pass into the Silver.

He might have introduced himself as Willem Drake, but

that wasn't the man's true name. After months of poking his nose where it wasn't wanted, Hugo had learned that – contrary to popular belief – Francis Drake had not died of dysentery following his failed assault on Panama in 1596. Instead, he'd started a trend for reinvention that all the other buccaneer captains had followed over the next century, becoming first Henry Drake, then Richard Drake, and finally Willem Drake, at least for the time being.

The dysentery hadn't been his idea, of course. That little detail had come courtesy of rival captain Bartholomew Sharp, as he most recently had been. Bartholomew himself had apparently died in debtors' prison – an end barely less ignominious than Drake's own – but that hadn't stuck, either. If Hugo had learned anything during his time eavesdropping in Nassau, it was that pirates like Drake and Bartholomew didn't stay dead for long.

He'd come to the Silver to find out how.

Now, seeing the place filled to the brim with the most imposing pirates that roamed the Spanish Main, he was questioning the wisdom of his choices. The room wasn't any bigger the other dark and pokey taverns scattered throughout the ramshackle spread of Nassau. If anything, it was darker and pokier, but it felt richer, as though the few pirates who chose to make it their haunt were all successful enough to be generous with their payment. They sat in velvet armchairs and lounged on silk chaises longues, their bored gazes casting dismissively over the congregation of entertainers that was gathering at the back of the pub, as though they knew in advance that nothing here was capable of offering them any joy.

Jaded, Hugo thought.

He had an idea that he could do something about that.

'Sit,' Drake said, pointing at a stool against the back wall, then he retreated to the comfort of a cushioned throne amongst his peers.

There were a dozen other stools lined up beside Hugo's, all occupied by musicians of various stripes, judging by the colourful array of instruments they bore. He recognised a few of the players, the cream of the crop that Nassau had to offer. They looked at him askance, clearly struggling to imagine what business a tavern guard dog like him had in their company.

Musicians were valuable on board ship, and this group were behaving with a snobbery that reflected that value. Not only did they provide a much-needed escape from the drudgery of seafaring, they also helped the crew keep in time while rowing and hauling lines. Musicians could be assured of a warm welcome on any ship, but Hugo had too often found his captains impatient of his desire to waste his strength in music, even before they heard him play. He had muscles, and they expected him to use them.

But tonight was the Silver's musician draft, invitation only, and Hugo had been walked through the door by Drake himself. If that wasn't an invitation, he didn't know what was.

The captains sat arrayed before them, each with a coloured handkerchief close by. That was how they would indicate their bids for the evening's performers: a single flourish of the 'kerchief to indicate an interest in acquiring the performer as a crew member, a 'kerchief thrown to indicate a firm offer. There were all the colours of the rainbow in the room, each chosen to match the colour of the captains' ships' sails: red for Drake, cream for Constantine, black for Bartholomew, blue for Carmen, then four more colours for captains Hugo didn't know by name. Drake sat in the centre, almost-undisputed king of all he surveyed, with

Carmen and Constantine to either side of him. Bartholomew was the outlier, sitting at the back of the gathering, wreathed in shadows. His sea-grey eyes watched the other captains more than they watched the performers who were now plodding through their repertoires with varying levels of aplomb.

Some of the musical choices were… questionable at best. You didn't want to be a fiddler on board ship, however traditional it might be, because the damp played merry hell with the cow gut. You didn't want to be a concertina-player either, because once salt got into the leather the thing would start farting air out in all directions until you could replace the valves, not to mention the inconvenience of carting it around with you in the middle of a boarding action while bullets and sabres flew. Hugo himself favoured the tin whistle. It wasn't a showy instrument. Simple and pure, it presented him with no particular environment-related issues, and it tucked neatly away into the inner pocket of his tattered waistcoat when not in use. He pulled it out now as he walked to the cleared area in the centre of the room to take his turn, then paused with his eyes closed for a moment to let the anticipated jeers wash over him.

Oh, look, the brute thinks he can carry a tune.

He'd be better off carrying lumber.

Who let the ox have a pipe?

It seems like a toothpick in his fat hand, doesn't it?

He could have taken the time to wash the blood off before he came in here to dirty our floor.

Then silence. When he opened his eyes, several people around the room had blades pressed to their throats.

Captain Drake nodded at him and said, 'Play.'

Hugo nodded back, lifted the whistle to his lips, then stepped out of the pub and into the space between here and there, where the notes cascaded like waterfalls in symphony and soared to the sky on gossamer wings. At some point, he must have closed his eyes again, because when he opened them there were eight coloured 'kerchiefs piled at his feet like seaweed cast up the beach by the tide.

'Well,' said Drake with a hungry smile. 'It seems you may have your choice.'

Hugo looked again at the drift of 'kerchiefs on the floor.

'Choose wisely, friend,' called a voice from the edge of the room, so far away that Hugo was left wondering how his black token had reached the pile at all.

But really, it was no choice at all.

Red 'kerchief. Red sails.

A few of the Nassau captains dyed their sails with preservatives that gave them a red hue, so the colour wasn't entirely uncommon, but those hues were usually more ochre than crimson. None of those ships looked like an army had just bled out on their rigging, except the vessel captained by Willem Drake. Maybe that was why people had nicknamed him "Kill 'em", or maybe the moniker had a darker origin. If so, Hugo wasn't interested in hearing it. Drake ran the only ship in the Caribbean that he was sure could give him what he wanted, so he was determined to take a place on its crew.

Whatever the cost.

He bent to retrieve the red 'kerchief from the floor, then took a knee in front of the pirate throne to return it to his new master: Captain Kill 'em Sir Willem Richard Henry Francis Drake.

The rest of that night was a blur. Hugo remembered retrieving his meagre belongings from Mungo's – a hat, a coat, a spare blade – then it was back to the Silver Pieces o'Eight to celebrate. A few of the other musicians were there too, selected by different captains for their crews, and merriment abounded. With so much grog on deck, lips were loosened. Hugo had struggled to learn much pertaining to the reincarnation of his new pirate captain before that night, leaving him with little but whispers and rumours to go on, but now the tales flowed as freely as the rum.

Vampires, someone vouchsafed to him, though the exact identity of the vouchsafer was hazy. *A blood exchange, a little bite, and eternal life is yours.*

Better than a slow death from syphilis, Hugo had replied.

He remembered a smile, the confidential comfort of the shadows, and a hell of a lot of booze. The next thing he knew, he was blinking awake on the deck of a rocking ship to find himself staring bleary-eyed into the face of an immortal and infamous pirate of the Caribbean.

Problem was, it was the wrong fucking one.

Arse.

He'd been press-ganged.

'Welcome aboard the *Fortune*,' Bartholomew cackled. 'Like your rum, don't you, boy?'

Hugo groaned and tried to sit up, holding his head. He blinked into the cloudless sky above to see a score of faces silhouetted against the sun. People crowded close, legs surrounding him like bars in a jail cell, blocking his exit. As if there was anywhere for him to go. Even with his view impeded as it was, he could still see through the legs to the open ocean beyond.

So much for his deal with Drake.

'I'm sworn to another crew,' Hugo murmured groggily. 'Isn't kidnapping members of other ships against the Code?'

'The code of the Republic of Pirates? Perhaps,' Bartholomew said. 'The code of the Silver? Well, that's a different matter entirely.'

'The Silver?' Hugo asked, even more at sea than he had been a moment ago. 'The pub has its own code?'

'The vampires who populate it do. That's what you wanted, wasn't it?' Bartholomew crouched down beside Hugo, tilting his head as he contemplated him, as a vulture might contemplate a piece of carrion. 'Eternal life. A cure for the disease that's killing you, though no doubt a death by venereal disease is only fair punishment for the carnality of your sins.'

Hugo would have laughed at that if he hadn't worried that the force of it would unseat the liquor he was still somehow retaining in his poisoned stomach. What did Bartholomew care for sin? His sails might be black instead of red, but they doubtless hid just as many bloodstains as Drake's proudly displayed.

'I'll tell you what,' Bartholomew said, leaning low as he flourished a piece of parchment. 'You sign *these* Articles, and I'll think about giving you what you want.'

'*Think* about it?' Hugo repeated. 'That doesn't sound like much of a deal.'

'Maybe not, but I guarantee you that I *won't* think about it if you don't. Given that you're stuck in the middle of the Spanish Main on my ship, surrounded by my crew, I'd say that's about the best deal you're going to get.'

'I'd say a deal with the devil is no deal at all,' Hugo snapped back, earning himself a cuff around the ears that was so hard he started vomiting last night's rum after all. It pooled on the deck with the blood that dripped from his split lip.

'You'll come around,' Bartholomew said, delicately stepping out of range.

Shame. Hugo would have enjoyed dirtying his shoes.

'This is Wolfrie,' Bartholomew said, indicating a short,

barrel-chested man whose white face was so covered in hair that for a moment Hugo mistook him for a bear. 'And this is Phinchas.' The second man was dark-skinned, tall and lanky, like a greyhound walking on its hind feet. Neither of them wore expressions that filled Hugo with confidence. 'You're learning the ropes with them, so pay attention and maybe they won't throw you overboard.' Then Bartholomew held his hand down to Hugo and said, 'Whistle.'

Hugo was momentarily confused. 'You want me to play?'

'No,' Bartholomew said impatiently, 'I *don't* want you to play. Musicians get privileges on this crew, but you're not *on* the crew, are you? Not until you sign the Articles.'

Then he reached into Hugo's waistcoat pocket and snatched out the tin whistle before Hugo could object.

'If you'd ever like to see it again,' Bartholomew said, disappearing it into his coat, 'then I suggest you get to work.'

Life on board ship was painful and boring.

Hugo had known this, of course. This was hardly his first foray into piracy, and he'd never been one to flinch at hard work, but the crew of the *Fortune* were unlike any crew he'd served with before. When they slept – *if* they slept – they did so with a peace that was so still it was eerie. When they argued, each seemingly-innocuous exchange reordered their hierarchy in ways Hugo couldn't understand, and had no interest in learning. When they took a prize, they didn't look for treasure, they looked for blood.

Perhaps those raids might have been considered exciting to someone with more gruesome tastes than Hugo, but it was hard for him to be sure, since he spent each one locked up safely in the aft cabin with the rest of the human crew – just seven besides himself, less than half of the crew's full complement. Unlike his fellow humans, he never knew where the ship was, where they were sailing to, or why. That information was not entrusted to him, because although he was used by the crew, he was not part of it.

Every day, he was made to feel the inadequacy of his existence, not just by the sores that still ate at his flesh, but by the dismissal with which he was treated by the inhuman members of their company. On other ships, his status as even an occasional musician had earned him at least some respect, not to mention the fear he earned with his strength. Here, those things meant less than nothing. On a ship populated by vampires, he was suddenly weaker than half the crew. He was beneath them, but worse: he hadn't signed his mark in blood to Bartholomew's Articles, so they didn't trust him, either. The beatings came fast, seemingly without incitement, and so forcefully that even he was not strong enough to fend them off.

But Hugo, who'd always been possessed of more rebellious spirit than common sense advised, did not go quietly into his servitude. He might not have had his instrument anymore, but he still had his voice, and it was beautiful. Not choirboy beautiful, high and keening, but low and resonant, like the mourning call of the sea itself. If he was to be allowed no other weapons – they had taken his knives – then he would sing his protest instead.

Hugo soon learned that Bartholomew did not tolerate insubordination.

'I'd set my heart on sails of red,' he sang as he hauled buckets of saltwater up the side of the ship, 'but got stolen away by the black instead—'

His song was stopped by a rag pushed forcibly down his throat by Wolfrie, who had been standing at the other end of the ship just moments ago, but had somehow crossed its length in less than a second to mete out Bartholomew's punishment. The man himself stood at the wheel on the quarterdeck, watching the interaction with such an expression on his face that Hugo – blinking away the tears as he choked on the rag – could not quite tell whether he had ordered the punishment or not.

Days later, he risked a second song.

It started innocuously enough, the ballad of a man who went to sea seeking his fortune. Then came the climactic couplet of the second verse.

'I wanted to sign to a ship o' the line,' he intoned as he swabbed the floors, shaking the deck with the timbre of his voice, 'but blood-sucking Bart's no captain of mine—'

Phinchas was the author of the interruption this time, with a punch to Hugo's stomach that landed with such force it had him spitting up blood for a week. For days he assumed he'd suffered some internal injury that would slowly bleed him to death, but he wasn't so lucky. Every dawn he woke up alive in the bowels of the ship, bathed in the fetid odour of twenty other damp and unwashed men. Every dawn he returned to his work on the deck, anticipating the beatings that followed as surely as the sunrise, knowing the wounds he suffered would have no chance to heal before more were layered on top of them.

Still, he couldn't resist the urge to sing his defiance.

'Of all the vampires that hunt on the sea, my choice would be anyone else but thee—'

That one earned him a broken finger from Bartholomew himself. A minor hurt, in the scheme of things, until it turned gangrenous.

'Sign the Articles,' Bartholomew had told him when, three days later, the thing began to reek. 'Maybe then I'll give you what you want.'

Hugo hadn't understood at the time. His lackeys explained later.

'Vampires are able to heal themselves,' said Wolfrie.

'But if you lose that finger as a human,' Phinchas said, wrinkling his nose at the stench, 'then it'll stay lost.'

It was Hugo's left index finger. Not the most important of digits, but without it his ability to play the music he loved would be irreparably altered. For a musician trapped in a fighter's frame, it was exactly what he had always feared: that his body would become a cage for his soul. What was worse, then? To lose his finger, and with it part of his ability, or mortgage his entire life to a captain who would likely never grant him the eternal cure he craved?

Hugo chose to lose the finger. Eventually, it had to be amputated by the ship's cook. Given how dirty the knife had been, Hugo had more than a fleeting concern that he might end up losing the whole hand. That wasn't his only concern, though.

'One more song like that,' Bartholomew had whispered as he'd bent Hugo's finger until it snapped, 'and I'll cut that silver tongue right out of your mouth.'

Hugo sang no more.

Until, one day, a crow came to land on the railing of the quarterdeck, beside the spot where Hugo sat fixing a hole in the ship's fishing net. They couldn't be so very far from land, he reasoned, if the bird would fly out to join him here.

He passed a crumb of biscuit to the creature, watching as it pecked the dry fare from the railing with little enthusiasm.

'You'd prefer something bloodier, I suppose,' Hugo murmured.

The crow bobbed up and down in apparent agreement before kicking the remains of the biscuit to the deck in disgust.

'You'd fit in well here,' Hugo commented.

'You don't, though,' said Wolfrie.

The man had snuck up without Hugo noticing, which was surprising since he usually moved with such firm steps, regardless of the inhuman grace he possessed. Wolfrie was the kind of person who liked people to hear him coming, so they could tremble at the sound. With the sun setting brightly on the other side of the ship behind Wolfrie, Hugo had to squint up at him. That was why, at first, his tread was the only thing about him that seemed amiss.

'Drink this,' Wolfrie said quietly, handing Hugo a vial.

At which point it became apparent that this wasn't Wolfrie. He had the same barrel-like build, was roughly the same height, and bore the same hair-covered visage, but as Hugo looked closer he realised he couldn't be sure that the figure was even a *he* at all. The beard was fake, the barrel chest padded and the bare feet altogether too devoid of hair to belong to Wolfrie himself.

Hugo pushed the vial back into the imposter's hand. He wouldn't have drunk a mystery substance given to him by a genuine member of Bartholomew's crew, and he certainly wasn't going to drink one handed to him by a complete stranger.

'From Drake,' the imposter insisted, wrapping Hugo's fingers around the vial. 'Drink it. A gift, from him to you. He said to tell you that if you still want to join his crew, he'll give you an eternity in exchange.'

'What?' Hugo blinked. 'Why?'

'Not sure if you noticed,' the imposter said quietly. 'But he and your captain don't like each other much. Drink the blood.'

'The *blood*?'

But Not-Wolfrie had already backed up to the railing, slipped over the side of the ship and disappeared overboard with a gentle splash. That's when Hugo noticed the sails silhouetted against the setting sun, little more than dots on the horizon, so far away that the lookout in the crow's nest had not yet started screeching the alarm.

He held the vial up to the sun's dying light, tilting it this way and that to see the liquid inside. The glass was so thick and poorly-made that it was practically obscure, but not so dull as to mask the darkness of its contents.

A blood exchange, a little bite, and eternal life is yours.

Hugo popped the cork and gulped it down. The liquid was sickly and metallic, but not much worse than the slop he was forced to subsist on as part of the *Fortune*'s crew. After that, he only had a fraction of a second to act, and he was going to make it count.

'*Come all you seamen bold of heart,*' Hugo sang, standing as he threw the net aside and raised his voice into the rigging, '*all you that make frigates your homes…*'

Bartholomew's head snapped in Hugo's direction, to the east, just as Hugo had hoped it would.

'Hugo…' the captain called in a warning tone.

But Hugo wasn't so foolish as to sing of rebellion now. Instead, he held up one finger to the captain, asking for a moment's patience as he continued, '*Let's raise a glass for Captain Bart, far on the sea he roams.*

He is the boldest pirate that ever you did hear.

There's not been such a robber found for above this hundred year.'

The toadying was shameless and transparent, but in the rumbling bass notes of Hugo's voice, the lyrics felt reverent and true. He had little power with words when he spoke, but when Hugo sang he could turn preachers pirate and pirates preacher.

It helped that they'd been at sea for weeks now with little entertainment other than the murder and mayhem in which the inhuman crew revelled. Given everything Hugo had seen, they likely thought he'd had the insubordination beaten out of him. Surrounded by vampires who could end his life in a second, a little flattery was just common sense. Not only did the crew not find it suspicious, Bartholomew even seemed to find it *proper.* He smiled down on Hugo from the forecastle, fat with satisfaction.

So Hugo drew it out. He took some indulgences with the tune, stretching single syllables into cascading runs that settled in the base of his stomach like a dirge before cresting into notes so high and clear they sounded like siren song. By the time he reached the final verse, the entire crew had gathered around him on the quarterdeck, quiet settling over his audience like the air over a becalmed sea.

'And then the Royal flagship, she fired and fired in vain,
Till six and thirty of her men all on the deck were slain;
Go home, go home, says Captain Bart and tell your king for me,
If he reigns king on all the land, Bart will reign king on sea.'

As the last note rang out across the company, the cheers poured back, and Hugo smiled into the sunset. He was going to enjoy what happened next.

'Sails!' the lookout yelled from the crow's nest. He had been just as distracted as the rest of the crew, and had only just noticed the flotilla of ships that was bearing down on them. 'Sails to the west!'

Bartholomew growled and shot a look at Hugo that promised trouble later, then demanded of the lookout, 'What colour?'

'Red!' the lookout called down.

'What *colour* red?'

The lookout hesitated for a moment, by which time Bartholomew had become impatient and scrambled up the rigging himself, faster than should have been possible. He would only be able to confirm what Hugo could already see clearly for himself: they were a red so deep that it could only have been intended to imitate blood, or perhaps been created from the real thing.

And they were very, very close.

The crew tried to turn the *Fortune*, but it was no use. They had been making a leisurely pace during Hugo's song, and now it was too late to run.

'You took something that rightfully belongs to me!' Drake yelled from the prow of his ship, his voice carrying across the scant stretch of water that now separated them.

'We're pirates!' Bartholomew yelled back. 'What did you expect?'

'A little professional courtesy?' Drake suggested.

'For *you*? I suppose you want to parley.'

'No,' Drake yelled back. 'I just want my musician.'

'Then come and take him!' Bartholomew replied.

Which was rash, considering that the two ships were now within striking distance of each other.

The first cannon shot tore through the *Fortune*'s mizzenmast, ripping it up from its roots and toppling it over until it loomed precariously above Hugo's head, which was as far as the ropes that held it would allow. For now. It creaked and groaned, suspended halfway on its journey to the quarterdeck. It was clear that the stays wouldn't be able to slow its descent for long. When they inevitably gave out, it was poised to crash straight through the spot where Hugo was crouching.

Hugo leapt down to the main deck just in time, but by that point the splintering quarterdeck wasn't the only thing he had to worry about. Drake's ship was close enough that his crew was already boarding the *Fortune*, and they'd skipped straight from cannon fire to guns, blades and hand-to-hand combat. Hugo didn't have so much as a blade of his own, but he snatched a sabre from a fallen crewmate so he could at least defend himself. The problem was, he wasn't entirely certain whom he should be defending himself *from*.

For a moment, he cast around, trying to take stock, but everyone was moving so quickly that he could barely even see them, let alone work out which way the fight was going. Then someone blew a horn – an instrument that did not belong to the *Fortune* – and the battle stilled around him as the crew sought the source of the sound.

It was coming from the mainmast, barely ten paces from the spot where Hugo stood. Drake's crew were holding Bartholomew back against the spar, one wrangling each limb. They must have been as inhuman as Bartholomew was himself, or else they wouldn't have been able to restrain him.

'I'll be taking my musician now,' Drake said, calling down from the forecastle deck.

Hugo saw something familiar glinting inside Bartholomew's coat and saw his chance to change his fate. Before he could think too hard about it, he took those ten paces forward and pulled his tin whistle from Bartholomew's pocket.

'And I'll be taking this,' he said.

Bartholomew laughed, surprised for a moment, then angry as he realised that he had been deceived by Hugo's song. 'You can't even play it,' he hissed mockingly, his voice low enough that only Hugo and the pirates holding Bartholomew could hear. 'With that missing finger, what use are you as a piper?'

Hugo stared at the fury roiling in Bartholomew's ocean-grey eyes, and felt only emptiness in return. Bartholomew was right: the whistle felt foreign in his hand, now. He could retrain himself to play without the missing finger, perhaps, but when would he be afforded the time for such an endeavour?

The hopelessness of it all threatened to overwhelm him.

Then Drake pulled out his pistol and shot Bartholomew in the head. For a moment, no one moved, then in the next moment, *everyone* was moving. While Drake's crew had been holding Bartholomew captive, they'd been holding the rest of his crew captive too, but now that Bartholomew was down, his crew was eager to retaliate in kind. Hugo was surrounded by gunfire and screaming, some of the latter of which was his own. The whole fight moved at such a pace that he couldn't follow it, with brawls rolling from one deck to another in less time than it took him to blink. Barrels were exploding, cannon were somehow firing again, and wood was splintering all around him as he ran for cover. All he could do was stick his back to the wall of the forecastle with the other humans and hope he didn't get in the way. He thought he'd been doing a pretty good job of that until someone grabbed him by the shoulders and pulled him quickly and forcefully through the forecastle door and into the crew living quarters beyond.

At first, he fought, then he saw who was doing the pulling.

'Tell me you drank it,' Drake demanded. 'The vial.'

Hugo's head was spinning, but he managed to nod.

'Good enough,' Drake said, then he lunged at Hugo.

After that, there was only pain. It felt like the bite lasted forever, but Hugo couldn't be sure how long the transformation took exactly, because pain turned into cold turned into darkness, then into nothing at all.

When Hugo came to, he was lying in a hammock in an unfamiliar cabin. Night had fallen outside, and it was a quiet one. He could hear people talking out on the deck, but in the hushed tones that you only got in the predawn hours of the middle watch. Wherever he was, the fight was clearly over for him.

Hugo got to his feet more easily than he had in months, without pain or strain, and pushed his way through what turned out to be the forecastle door of an unfamiliar ship. He was on the main deck. Even in the low light, he recognised the blood-red sails.

'Ah,' Drake said quietly from his place by the wheel. 'Our slumberer awakens.'

Somehow, despite the noise of the ship and the wind and the waves, Hugo could hear every word perfectly. That seemed strange, until he remembered. He remembered the vial of blood, and Drake's teeth puncturing his skin, and felt for the bite mark he knew should be marring his neck. But there was nothing, just a bloodstain on his shirt that frankly might have come from anywhere.

Abruptly, he turned his back on the captain and opened his trousers, looking by lantern light for the evidence of the disease that had been killing him for more years than he could count.

Nothing.

No sores. No bleeding. Just clear skin and more strength in his limbs than he had felt since he was a lad.

Behind him, Drake was laughing softly, but not unkindly. Hugo turned back to him with a sheepish grin.

'Come,' Drake said. 'Join us.'

That was when Hugo noticed the person he'd been

thinking of as Not-Wolfrie standing beside the stays that were anchored to the quarterdeck, the padding gone from their chest and the beard mostly-gone, with just a few spots of glue and hair to demonstrate where it had been. They remained too androgynous for Hugo to make a guess at their gender.

''Lo,' they said, nodding at Hugo as they tugged at the ropes, checking that everything was secure.

The crow was there too, watching from the rigging as though it belonged there. At first, Hugo assumed it had followed him from the *Fortune*. When it hopped up onto Not-Wolfrie's shoulder and they petted it affectionately, Hugo was a little disappointed. It had not been there for him, after all.

'Bartholomew's dead?' he asked Drake.

'I doubt that,' Drake replied. 'But as you didn't sign his Articles— You didn't, did you?'

'No,' said Hugo.

'Then you're free to crew whichever ship you should choose. May I introduce you to the *Pelican*?'

Hugo thought on the name. 'Because she carries us all in her beak?'

'Because she feeds her brood with her own blood, or so they say.' Drake grinned a sly grin. 'You know the story? Never having observed that behaviour for myself, I cannot vouch for its accuracy, but I do enjoy the analogy.'

The man captained a ship with blood-red sails. It should have come as no surprise that his tastes veered towards the macabre, but it unsettled Hugo nonetheless. He was not yet sure that he had found the safe harbour for which he had prayed.

'So,' said Not-Wolfrie. 'Are you staying?'

'Do I have a choice?' Hugo asked.

'Certainly,' Drake said. 'I have done my part, admittedly in more straitened circumstances than I might have chosen. It remains for you to decide whether you will accept your part of our bargain.'

'As part of your brood?' Hugo asked, a slip he could only blame on the blood loss.

'As part of my *crew*,' Drake corrected him.

Hugo shrugged with resignation. 'I accepted that part back in the Silver Pieces o'Eight.'

'It's not so bad,' Not-Wolfrie said, pulling a small pan flute from their own pocket and waggling it at him. 'Musicians get Sundays off.'

Musicians.

Until he heard that acknowledgement, Hugo hadn't dared to believe that this crew might truly want him for his music rather than for his brawn. Perhaps Drake was just as unscrupulous and bloodthirsty as his reputation suggested, but he had kept his word. He'd given Hugo exactly what he'd promised, and if Hugo could finally be appreciated for his musical talent on top of that, did any of the rest of it matter? Was this not what he had always wanted?

'Yes,' Hugo said quickly. 'Oh god, yes, please.'

'Excellent!' Drake said. 'Then I must tender my apologies for the delay in coming to your rescue. But still, no harm done.'

'No, I…' Hugo looked down at the stump where his finger had once been, before hastily hiding it behind his other hand and agreeing, 'No harm done.'

What was he going to do, complain that the man who'd just given him eternal life hadn't come quickly enough? He wasn't so ungrateful, nor so stupid.

'Well, then.' Drake leaned on the wheel, the picture of satisfied control. 'On to Nassau!'

It was a dismissal. Hugo hesitated, wondering what he should be doing, but his tired feet were already walking him back to his hammock. Someone fell in step beside him, then gently reached out to pull his hands away from each other.

'Ah,' said Not-Wolfrie quietly, spotting the missing digit.

Hugo shrugged, trying to pretend it didn't hurt him to have his instrument back in his pocket, but not the fingers to play it with.

'Oh, well,' Not-Wolfrie said lightly. 'Lucky for you, you only need six fingers to play your whistle. Just learn to use a different one instead of the one you lost.'

Hugo smiled ruefully. 'I'd need to practice for months and months...'

'Good thing you've probably got centuries then, eh?' Not-Wolfrie smiled. 'Don't worry, musician. You'll play again. Until then, you can sing. We all know that you can; we heard you do it. I, for one, would like to hear you do it again.' Then they patted him on the shoulder and leapt up and away into the rigging.

As Hugo watched, the crow flew up beside its master and into the night, circling around the *Pelican* like it was marking out its territory.

Hugo's soul flew with it.

Lyrics for Hugo's "Captain Bart" song adapted from the seventeenth-century English folk song "Ward the Pirate".

Dolce Evita

DR EVITA KHALYED was sweating.

She'd realised her wardrobe was wrong the minute she'd stepped off the plane at Charleston airport. To an English girl from Newcastle, December in South Carolina was unseasonably warm. She should have checked the weather before coming, but between the last-minute flights and the rush to rewrite her presentation for the grandees of the Charleston Pirate Association, she hadn't had the chance.

So here she was, sweating in the winter sunshine.

The problem was, this wasn't Evita's gig. She wouldn't even be here right now if the top historian in her department hadn't gone and broken his leg in a skiing accident. Not that she wasn't grateful for the opportunity, because Lewis'd had the Pirate Association bagsied for years now. And not that she wasn't sympathetic to Lewis's plight, though honestly he was a dickhead who used his connections to bogart all the best speaking engagements. But still, it would have been better if she'd had time to prepare for it, and if she'd been dressed for the weather.

Now, standing in White Point Gardens at the pirate memorial after it was all over, she had ample opportunity to regret wearing her wool trouser suit. The blue was a beautiful complement to her mid-brown skin, but Christ, was it warm. She'd heard the festival would be outside and just assumed… Well, too late to do anything about it now. She'd given her lecture pink-cheeked and damp-underarmed, and they had the video to prove it.

Had her talk even been any good? She had no idea. It was a blur. Between the stress and the jet lag, she'd been so flustered that she could barely remember delivering it.

'An interesting perspective,' one of the grandees was saying as a bead of sweat slid down Evita's spine. 'I enjoyed your conjecture about the old buccaneers faking their deaths and reinventing themselves as new pirates.'

'Thank you, Professor,' Evita replied, trying and failing to remember the man's surname. Her mind was elsewhere. What she really wanted was an ice cold beer from the seafood place on Market Street, the one Lewis was always banging on about, but she had at least half an hour of schmoozing ahead of her before it would be even remotely acceptable to slip away.

'It's all bullshit, of course,' the professor continued blithely. 'I mean, there's no evidence.'

Evita hadn't really been paying attention, so the offhand comment took her by surprise. 'Excuse me?'

'Evidence. There isn't any, is there?'

'Well, as I mentioned in my presentation, Professor,' she said, with weaponised civility, 'there are a number of personal possessions from that period – rings, bibles – that indicate that names were changed, and then of course there's the passage in Exquemelin—'

'Oh, Exquemelin. You can read whatever you want into Exquemelin.'

'But if you review some of the items recovered from the site of Port Royal—'

'I've *been* to the lost city of Port Royal, ma'am. I was involved in the initial dives to establish the dig site there. Have *you* ever been to Port Royal, hmm?'

Of course Evita hadn't. She'd only managed to fund her trip here today by taking a paltry grant from the university and the most inconvenient flights available.

She was tempted to walk away right then, but she'd have to play nice if she ever wanted to get funded for another trip back here, so she took a deep breath and prepared to defend herself politely against this pompous prick.

'Well, no,' she said. 'But—'

'I've been to old Port Royal,' said a voice from over Evita's shoulder. 'I find your theories fascinating. I'd love to discuss them further.'

She turned to see a tall white guy with long, dark hair, tanned skin and pale eyes standing behind her. He was dressed more casually than the other attendees, in dark jeans and a loose henley with a collar that dipped just low enough to display a copper coin secured around his neck with a leather cord. For all his casual appearance, his bearing was serious. His face was angular and cold, and his expression did not suggest that his personality would be any different. Without meaning to, Evita found herself taking a step away from him.

'Mr Roberts,' the professor said, taken aback.

'Professor Anders Lee.'

'What are you doing here?'

'Listening to the talks. What are you doing here? Other than insulting the speakers, I mean.'

The professor said, 'Well!' He glared briefly at Evita, glared less briefly at Roberts, then turned on his heel and made his way through the crowd, doubtless in search of someone else to harangue.

'That's an interesting accent you have,' Evita observed, turning back to Roberts. She usually had a good ear for accents, but this one was impossible to place, veering from Spain to Wales and back again via Italy and Cornwall.

'So do you,' he replied. 'Geordie?'

'Yes. Not that interesting,' she said. 'But yours—'

'I've travelled,' he said simply. That, apparently, was all he was willing to say on the subject.

After a few seconds of silence, Evita said, 'You mentioned that you were interested in my theories?'

'Actually, I said I find them fascinating. And I do. They're wrong, of course,' he added, not unkindly. 'Fascinating, though.'

Evita gaped. She was too hot, she was seriously bothered and she didn't have the energy for yet another tedious stranger telling her that her life's work was *wrong*. 'But you said—'

'Oh, I'd never admit that Anders Lee was right. The man's an asshole.'

'But you've been to Port Royal. You've seen the carvings.'

'There was plenty in Port Royal that didn't make it out again. What you have are fragments. They don't prove anything.'

'They prove that the buccaneers changed their names.'

'Or that the items in question simply changed hands.'

'But only the *surnames* changed. Are you seriously suggesting that there was some strange convention that meant buccaneers only passed on their possessions to people who shared their first name? How likely is that?'

'Likelier than you'd think when so many people had the same forenames. The English weren't very creative back then, you know. It was all George and James and Charles and—'

'Phinchas? Kulika? *Wolfrie*? Because none of those sounds particularly common to me. Not to mention the number of Bartholomews of various spellings—'

'Very common name,' Roberts said with a dismissive shake of his head. 'My name, in fact. Old-fashioned now, but very fashionable back then. Biblical names were. Everyone had them in the—'

Evita laughed in scornful disbelief. 'You don't really expect me to—'

'I know a Wolfrie, actually. *And* a Kulika. Really, they're not—'

'Now you're just having me on, because there's *no way* —'

'And anyway, it's just a few little carvings, and you can't even make out most of the—'

'But Exquemelin—'

'Oh, *fuck* Exquemelin,' Roberts said expressively, and loudly enough that people nearby were now turning to watch their argument. 'He was a bastard.'

'He was a *buccaneer*,' Evita hissed, trying to quiet him down.

'And we were *all* bastards,' Roberts replied with heedless volume.

For a moment, Evita doubted her ears. With the long hair and the cruel features, it was true that the man looked a little buccaneer-ish, but…

'*We?*' she repeated.

Roberts's hesitation was slight, brief enough that Evita almost didn't notice it, then he laughed. 'I play one sometimes,' he said lightly. 'On the pirate tours, you know. For fun.'

The timbre of his laughter sent pleasant shivers across

Evita's sweating skin, though she couldn't pinpoint why. The man was brash and infuriating and far from charming, after all. Then he looked her up and down in a way that made the shivers multiply.

'Come on,' he said abruptly. 'Let's get out of here. I'll buy you some popcorn shrimp and hush puppies, and we can eat them while I explain to you all the many ways in which you're wrong.'

The fucking balls on the man. Were all Americans this way, she wondered, or was it just the academics who were so very punchable?

'As appealing as that sounds,' Evita replied briskly, 'I am working, and I need to circulate. Goodbye, Mr Roberts.'

'Bartholomew,' he said.

'You're right,' she replied. 'It is *extremely* old-fashioned. It suits you.' Then she turned and weaved away through the crowd of pirate enthusiasts, trying to pretend that the sweat between her thighs wasn't chafing them as they rubbed together.

Fucking hot Charleston winters. Fucking academics. Fucking Americans. Fucking *men*.

Santo Domingo, Hispaniola – 1514

Bartolemé de las Casas, Catholic priest of the lay clergy, sat at his writing desk and spun a copper coin through his fingers so it caught the light. He looked at the coin, then out of the window over the land his slaves were working on his behalf. *His* land, he supposed, though he had done little enough to earn it, as little as he had done to earn the service of those men.

He sighed. He'd been plagued by thoughts like these recently.

The problem was Ecclesiasticus 34:21.

As he contemplated the verse, he observed the copper coin between his fingers. It had been a talisman of sorts these past twelve years, a trinket he'd found buried in the soil outside the house he now occupied. Such a simple thing. An innocent piece of metal, he'd thought, until one of the other settlers had explained its purpose to him, and he'd finally learned the truth of Christopher Columbus's grand system.

Then he'd read that bible verse, and now he couldn't reconcile the two.

Bartolemé had met Columbus a few times back in Spain – Bartolemé's father had sailed with the great explorer on his second voyage to the Indies – and he'd heard stories of the enslavement of the Arawak. He'd been young, then. Hispaniola and its people had seemed a world away. At the time, Columbus's tales of conquest had sounded grand and exciting. His schemes to subjugate the godless natives had seemed both necessary and ingenious. Only now that he was here…

Seeing the people who lived on and farmed the fertile soil outside his window, it was hard to believe that barely twenty years had elapsed since Columbus first landed on Hispaniola's shores. Before he'd arrived, the Arawak people had been the island's sole inhabitants. Now, by the equal operation of disease and violence, they were all but gone.

And there was that Bible verse, still.

Columbus had liked to draw his lines simply and clearly, especially when it came to gold, and the copper tokens certainly did that. Convinced that Hispaniola was riddled with gold, Columbus had established a quota for each Arawak native. Either they brought him the requisite amount of gold and were rewarded with one of these copper tokens to wear around their neck, or their hands were cut off as punishment. Either way, their success or failure was evident to all. The problem was, whatever Columbus believed, there simply wasn't very much gold on the island. In less than two years, the system had collapsed and the remaining Arawak who were capable of labour were worked to death on Hispaniola's sugar plantations, leaving behind mounds of pointless copper tokens and barely any Arawak at all.

That was the history of the copper coin Bartolemé now held in his fingers; such a small thing to bear the weight of so many souls.

Bartolemé could not imagine that this was what Pope Alexander VI had intended when he told the Spanish to induce the natives of the islands of the Caribbean to receive the Catholic religion. How were they to receive it in their untended, unmarked, unhallowed graves? His countrymen seemed to think they could use the natives however they wished because they were not Catholic, and therefore not godly, but Bartolemé was beginning to think that it was the Spanish who were ungodly, so anaesthetised by their own greed and ambition that they had ceased to be human in any meaningful sense of the word.

With Ecclesiasticus 34:21 open in front of him, how could he think otherwise?

The bread of the needy is their life: he that defraudeth him thereof is a man of blood. He that taketh away his neighbour's living slayeth him, and he that defraudeth the labourer of his hire is a bloodshedder.

The more he read those words, and the more he spun the copper token between his fingers, the more Bartolemé could no longer deny that what had been done to the Arawak was against God's law. It hadn't stopped the Spanish. They'd just brought in slaves captured elsewhere in the Caribbean, or shipped in from afar, and those were the hands that now worked Bartolemé's land.

It was past time that he gave them all up, and past time he did something more besides. Sitting at his desk by the window in the Caribbean heat, he vowed that he'd devote his life to righting this wrong. He'd bear witness to this sacrilege, then go back to Spain and tell his people exactly what atrocities were being perpetrated in the Indies in their names. He'd school himself in the art of debate until he could be a voice for the natives against the rapacious avarice of the Spanish.

All this he vowed, and all this he would indeed achieve, but not without a significant hiccup along the way. Within the next year, shortly before his return to Spain, Bartolemé would learn that syphilis and smallpox weren't the only plagues that European settlers had brought with them to the New World. The one he contracted wouldn't end his life, but it would force him to end his own and remake himself in a new image, over and over again, for the next five hundred years.

By that evening, things were looking up for Evita. She had three days to burn until her flight back home, she'd finally tracked down Lewis's fabled seafood place – complete with a barman who was fitter than he had any right to be – and, despite the litany of things that had gone wrong on this work trip from hell, she was finally starting to enjoy herself. *Really* enjoy herself.

Until.

'Good evening.'

Evita turned, saw Roberts standing beside her at the bar, and felt her top lip curl back. 'Oh,' she said. 'It's you.'

'*You*?' he asked, as though he was actually surprised that she was being unfriendly.

The *nerve*.

'Yes, *you*. The arrogant wanker who thinks he knows everything about pirates and, worse, pretends he *isn't* an arrogant wanker who thinks he knows everything about pirates.'

'Not everything. But I do actually know quite a lot about pirates.'

'I looked you up, you know,' she said between sips of ice-cold beer. 'You're not from the museum, or the university, or the historical society.'

'So? The same, please,' he said to the barman, pointing at Evita's beer. 'And one for the lady, too.'

Evita resented this for three very good reasons: firstly, he was talking to *her* sexy barman, and said sexy barman was snapping to attention, which wound her up. Secondly, it was more than a little presumptuous of Roberts to order a drink for her without even asking. Thirdly and most importantly, if he was ordering a drink for himself, that must mean he was intending to stay, and Evita was absolutely not up for that.

Evita glared at him for a moment, then dismissed him with a light, 'Just piss off, will you?'

'No, I want to know what you mean,' he insisted, taking possession of both beers without paying. He must be running a tab. 'Are you saying that because I don't have a doctorate, I can't know anything about pirates?'

'No, I'm saying that my doctorate trumps your bullshit,' Evita said, then she took her beer – pointedly leaving behind the one Roberts had purchased for her – and headed up to the roof terrace. The barman had disappeared up there and she intended to follow. She'd been getting great vibes from him all night, and she wasn't going to let this blowhard spoil that.

But when she got upstairs, she found the first floor dining room full, the small dining terrace empty, and no barman in sight. Until Roberts followed her up the stairs, at which point the barman reappeared as if by magic, and ushered him out to the single table set at the far corner of the roof terrace.

'Sir,' the barman said. 'Your table.'

Roberts didn't thank the barman, because men like that never do; he just turned to Evita and said, 'Shall we?'

'Shall we *what*?'

'I promised you popcorn shrimp and hush puppies, didn't I?'

'And I declined.'

'Because you were working. You're not working now, are you?'

'Aren't I? Because let me tell you, you are *extremely* hard work.' Evita downed the rest of her beer, clunked the empty glass down on a passing server's tray and said, 'Now that you've ruined my evening, I guess I'll go back to the hotel.'

'Just to prove a point? Come on, have some shrimp. The crab dip's great.'

'I'm sure it is, in other company.'

'We don't have to talk about pirates.'

'I'm not interested in talking about anything else.'

'Pirates it is, then.'

'*Either*. I mean *anything else either*. I'm not interested in talking about *anything* with you.'

'Would you prefer to argue?'

Evita turned with a sigh and started to walk back downstairs.

'You seem to enjoy it, is all,' he called after her. 'The cut and thrust of intellectual debate. Am I wrong?'

She stopped halfway down the stairs. 'I love intellectual debate. Academia thrives on it. I'm entirely in favour, but that's not what this is.'

'What is it, then?' he asked, following her.

'At this stage, it's harassment. Fuck off.'

She fully intended to turn and walk away, but that's when he said, 'What if I told you I had real proof?'

She stopped. 'What?'

'Not crossed out names on an old pocket watch, or some veiled reference in that asshole Exquemelin's self-aggrandising buccaneer diary. What if I could give you real, concrete evidence that your theory is right, and that the buccaneers really did reinvent themselves as pirates. Would you have dinner with me then?'

She should have said no. He'd already told her he thought she was wrong, and yet suddenly he had exactly the evidence she needed to prove her theory? It was an obvious ploy. He was trying too hard, telling her everything she wanted to hear, but there was also something about him that felt earnest. She didn't want to trust it, but despite her misgivings, she found herself walking slowly back up the stairs.

'Show me,' she said.

'Afterwards,' he insisted.

Red flags. Big red flags. Big red flags flying all the way from here back home to Newcastle.

'At least tell me what it is,' she said.

'Treasure,' he replied.

The word was a clarion call to her soul. She hadn't studied pirates her whole life just because she'd read *Treasure Island* as a kid and dreamed of digging up chests spilling over with gold on palm-tree-laden desert islands, but she hadn't *not* studied them for that reason either. Treasure was… Well, treasure.

Then Roberts said the magic words: 'I have the first Articles from the founding members of the pirate code, the original seventeenth century document, and a whole heap of others besides. You can see the names. You can see the dates.

You can prove your theory.'

Treasure.

And Evita was a goner.

Off the coast of Campeche, Mexico – 1669

Bartolomeu Português had been celibate his entire life. Not just for this buccaneering life, but for the one before that, and the one before that, right back to his very first clerical incarnation.

It was a fact that did not overly concern him. You might think that his celibacy would have made sex seem irresistibly taboo, but instead Bartolomeu simply no longer understood the point of it. Perhaps it was a matter of habit. Perhaps it was a switch in his head that, since it had not been triggered at the right time, was now rusted shut. Either way, released from the bonds of his vows – as he now considered himself to be, since those vows could surely not have been expected to survive his own death and rebirth – he had no interest in exploring the realms of carnal sin.

Other sins, though? With those, he filled his boots.

He pillaged, he ransomed, he plundered, he set fire to entire fleets of Spanish treasure ships and never thought twice about the morality of any of it. If the past century had taught him anything, it was that God was blind to the plight of the New World. His eyes could not see past its turquoise waters and white sands to the sin that stained its bones. Which begged the question: if God did not witness sin, was it even a sin at all?

These thoughts preoccupied Bartolomeu as he slipped out of his bonds, strapped a couple of empty earthenware pots to his body for buoyancy, then threw himself off the treasure ship and into the sea, abandoning his crew to the Spanish brig in which they'd been imprisoned.

Perhaps he'd been ambitious with that last prize, but there had been so much gold in its coffers, and such sin to be had. Avarice, to be sure, and covetousness. Pride, perhaps. Wrath, yes, later, for the shots that never landed true, and for the hours they'd wasted while his crew busied themselves in the skirts of the women on the coast. Without that delay, he would have had the gold and the Spanish would never have taken them captive in the first place. As it was, he was here in the cold, dark water while his crew sat in their cell, as yet unaware of his flight.

He would return for them, he vowed silently, even if they were a bunch of lust-driven bastards. Bartolomeu might be a sinner himself, but he lived by the code he had established with the other buccaneers, and he would stick to it.

Every man gets his share. Any man who tries to abscond with what is due to the others will be marooned with one flask and a pistol with one shot. Every man injured on board ship will be compensated for any resulting infirmity. Any man bringing a woman aboard – and this was the important one, as far as Bartolomeu was concerned – *will suffer death at the hands of the quartermaster.* Harsh, perhaps, but once you'd seen the ruin wrought aboard a buccaneer's ship by the presence of a woman – ruin to herself and the crew alike – you learned intolerance quickly.

Women, Bartolomeu thought as he bobbed towards the dark hull of his beleaguered ship. *They're nothing but trouble.*

Evita waited at the table on the restaurant's roof terrace as the place slowly emptied and the lights below her on Market Street started winking out. Soon, the street was mostly dark.

She ordered another beer. She drank it. She ordered another. She cast anxious glances at the barman as the staff tidied the tables up for the night, but the previously flirtatious hottie – now notably cooled – assured her that he was happy to keep the place open for Mr Roberts. Beyond that, he left her to her own devices.

It was strange, that. She wasn't sure she liked it. In fact, she was starting to feel like this might all have been a terrible idea, but then the whisper in her head reminded her what she was waiting for – *treasure* – and she was glued to her seat once more.

When she heard the footsteps behind her, it had grown so quiet that the noise made her jump. She whirled in her seat.

Roberts.

'Oh,' she said. 'It's you.'

'And it's you, *Dolce Evita*.' He smiled.

She glared at him. 'Are you trying to be funny?'

'I think it suits you,' he replied.

'Unlike these hush puppies,' she said, gesturing to the second batch the barman had brought while she waited, 'I'm not soft or sweet, Mr Roberts.'

'I had noticed,' he said. 'And it's Bartholomew.'

Evita rolled her eyes. 'Sure, whatever.' His insistence on using that name was pretentious, and pathetic, but she didn't have the energy to argue about irrelevancies. She had to save it all to argue about the things that mattered, for example…

'Did you bring the documents?' she asked. 'You were gone ages.'

'The traffic was bad.'

'But you've got them?'

'Of course.'

Evita's fingers itched as the man took his time settling back down at the table, pulling a messenger bag from his shoulder. Her hands were feeling grabby. If what he said was true – which was unlikely – but if he really did have the proof she'd spent her academic career chasing…

'They're in there?' she asked, nodding at the bag he'd rested on the tabletop.

'Impatient, aren't you?'

'Infuriating, aren't *you*? Come on. Show me.'

'In a minute. I want a clean surface.' He waved the barman over, and the man not only cleared and cleaned the table, he also magicked a tablecloth from somewhere and spread it out smoothly. Once that was done, and once the barman had disappeared again, Roberts finally produced his treasure from the bag.

'This,' he said, brandishing the weathered and plastic-enclosed paper, 'is the Articles of Agreement of Bartolomeu Português and his fellow buccaneers.'

Evita stood from her seat and leaned over the table to get a closer look as he reverently laid the paper down. It was old, that much was obvious, or it had at least been made to appear old. There wasn't much to it, either: just a single sheet, weathered and torn, in browned ink on yellowed parchment. In her imagination, the writing would have been perfect, and the page would have been pristine, but this was a document forged on stained bar tables and carried across rough seas. The thing was a mess. Evita wasn't sure whether that made it seem more authentic or less.

'But it's not real, is it?' she said, trying to ignore the evidence of her own discernment.

'Isn't it?' Roberts asked with a twinkle in his eye.

'It can't be.'

'Did you see the signatures?'

She could hardly have missed them. They were right there, all the names she knew from Exquemelin and Dampier, Ringrose and Johnson. There was Português, and Sawkins, and Sharp, and Morgan. *Captain Henry Morgan.*

There were their names at the bottom of the pirate code, the mark of each signatory, the dates they'd signed. And, just as Roberts had said, there were the surnames crossed out and replaced by others, but in the same handwriting.

If this really was real – but how could it be? But if it *was*…

Then Evita noticed a detail that disproved the whole thing, once and for all. A surge of grief filled her throat, replaced by the inevitable disappointment for which she'd been preparing herself all evening. She sighed.

Of course it was fake.

'Look at the dates,' she said.

'I see them.'

'Well, that's the refutation right there. Some of these go on for hundreds of years. Take your namesake, for example. If we're sticking to my theory, then he apparently signs the Articles in 1660, then changes his surname from Português to Sharp in 1675, then to Roberts in 1719. Which would have put Bartholomew Roberts in his mid-seventies at the height of his pirating career, but we know he was a young man then, so unless there's something supernatural going on…'

The modern-day Roberts laughed. 'You can't seriously be suggesting that he was some immortal creature that just kept reincarnating and reincarnating like—'

'Did I say that? Did I say anything to even *imply* that—'

'—some real-life Dread Pirate Roberts—'

'I'm saying it's an inspiration, isn't it? Maybe it was just the name that passed on. The idea had to come from somewhere, and Black Bart was actually—'

'The real Dread Pirate Roberts? The *Princess Bride* is *fiction*, you know, not some—'

'And if you ever let me finish a sentence, maybe I could

—'

'Let *you* finish a—'

'Yes, let *me* finish, you infuriating, irritating, *arrogant*—'

And then he kissed her.

It seemed to surprise him as much as it surprised her.

Aboard ship between Arica and Iquique – 1680

Bartholomew Sharp had always been in control of himself and his crew. As such, he was not accustomed to mutiny. During his long career he'd never suffered it, but these men were new. They didn't yet understand what he was about.

They would learn, soon enough.

'It's just the winds, you know,' the new Commander Watling said to him. 'After weeks of storms so bad that we could neither sail nor drop anchor, and all the trouble we had with the scurvy last year, they just want someone to blame. They've chosen you. It might not be fair, but—'

'I told you we just needed to wait a few more days for the winds to change. Was I not right?'

'They don't doubt your skill at navigation, Sharp, but it's too late now. They've all signed new Articles with me, and if you'd only do the same, we can put this mess behind us and move on. So, what do you say?'

Sharp said nothing, but he signed. They were *his* Articles, after all, just with the commander's name changed from his to Watling's. As though that man would have the wits to draw up a document so concise. Did he even understand their history, their importance, or the legacy Sharp had created when he agreed them with the other buccaneer captains two decades ago? Of course he didn't.

But no matter. Sharp was a patient man, and Watling was a short-sighted coward. Sharp could bide his time and work quietly at his charts while he waited for the man to fuck up.

Predictably, it didn't take long.

The crew had taken an old mestizo man captive on the island of Iquique, hoping he'd be able to describe the lay of the land at Arica, which they were planning to raid in a few days' time. This didn't sit well with Sharp. He might no longer be a man of God, but he was still inclined to believe that the land of the New World belonged to the natives by divine right, and he didn't much like taking them aboard ship by force. He'd prefer to work with them than against them, but since his voice carried no more weight than the rest of the crew's did at this point, he held his peace.

And the old man had good information. He told them the Spanish had increased their fortifications at Arica significantly, and warned the buccaneers that they'd be facing serious opposition if they pursued their campaign against the city. But the information he imparted was not to the crew's liking, so they decided he must be lying. They resolved to shoot the messenger, literally, and then Sharp could no longer hold his tongue.

He stroked the copper token that he wore around his neck as he argued for the old man's life.

The crew voted against him once more.

The shot rang out.

Seething with cold rage, Sharp took a scoop of water from the barrel on deck where the crew was holding its convocation, waited until he had their attention, then washed his hands with it.

'Gentlemen,' he said, 'I am clear of the blood of this old man, and I will warrant you a hot day for this piece of cruelty, whenever we come to fight at Arica.'

So he vowed, and so it proved to be.

Huge numbers of the crew died. Both quartermasters died. And, somewhere supposedly-safe at the back of the fray, the cowardly Commander Watling died. If the circumstances of that last death were somewhat strange, none of the crew stopped to question them amongst the fire and fury of the fight.

Trapped by their own folly in Arica, they begged Sharp to take command again. Reluctantly, but graciously, he agreed, and led them out of the hell Watling had led them into.

When they returned to their ship, Sharp amended the Articles with specific punishments for rebellion, then had the crew sign them again. He heard no more talk of mutiny after that.

Roberts hadn't meant to kiss Evita. Really, he hadn't.

The plan had been very simple: talk to the woman, dispel her irritatingly-close-to-the-truth-theories, make sure she was so disillusioned that she'd never write anything so dangerously accurate again, then send her back home to England with no knowledge of his true nature and only a vague memory of an annoying American man whose arguments she couldn't refute.

Unfortunately, Dr Evita Khalyed was not who he'd expected her to be. He knew that idiot Lewis, the one who turned up at the Charleston Pirate Association's annual convention every year with his anachronistic outfits and his tired old theses, and he'd expected Khalyed to be more of the same: a lackey he could bend to his will. Instead, she was sharp, and self-assured, and argumentative, and devastatingly unaffected by him. In his world, people did what he told them to do, because they knew that bad shit would follow if they didn't. But Evita…

She unravelled him.

Dolce Evita.

Never had he met a person powered by such

determination. It was a quality he'd always admired. None of the Bartholomews had ever been much for romance, but after half a millennium of apathy, it was her determination that had broken him.

He should have seen it coming. After all, this wasn't the first time he'd allowed his admiration to compromise his judgement. He had form. But Evita… She was something else.

'Before this goes any further,' she said, pulling out of the kiss, 'there are some things I should probably know.'

'Like?' he asked breathlessly, because God knows now he'd started sinning, he didn't want to stop.

'Your name would be a good start,' she replied.

'You know my name,' he said, kissing his way down her neck.

'Your *real* name, I mean.'

'That's what it is.'

She pushed him away, looked him dead in the eye and said, 'You're telling me that your name is actually Bartholomew Roberts.'

'Yes.'

'That's your stage name, you mean. For when you're terrifying the tourists.'

'No, in real life.'

'I don't believe you.'

He shouldn't tell her. He shouldn't even have told her as much as he had, but he was seized with a reckless impulse that all his centuries of practised control couldn't restrain. He wanted her to know who he was. For once, he wanted someone to remember *everyone* that he was.

'Bartolomeu Português. Bartholomew Sharp. Bartholomew Roberts, Barti Ddu,' he said. 'Black Bart, and others besides. They are all the same, they are all me, and I am all of them.'

Evita laughed, but when he didn't join in, she stopped.

'Where did you think I got this?' he asked, gesturing at the plastic-wrapped Articles on the table. 'I wrote it.'

'You mean it's a forgery,' she said flatly.

'I mean it is genuine.'

She looked at him for a long moment, then took a step away from him and said, 'I think I should go.'

He caught her hand and said, 'Wait.'

She said, 'Let go.'

He said, '*Wait*.'

She said, '*Let. Go.*'

He should have done as she asked, but instead he held on to her and said, 'I can prove it.'

'I don't believe you,' she said. He could tell from the determined set of her jaw that she was going to fight her way free if she had to, but he couldn't give her up. Every fibre of his being was screaming at him to draw her into his arms, so he let his baser instincts win.

He didn't mean to bite her. Really, he didn't.

But what he meant to do was irrelevant. If Roberts had learned anything in his long life, it was that intentions are as worthless as prayers. Results are what matters.

Off Cape Lopez, Gabon – 1722

Below decks on the *Royal Fortune*, Bartholomew Roberts was preparing to die. He had the crimson damask waistcoat on already, and the matching breeches, and a red feather in his hat, but as he regarded himself in the glass, he couldn't help but feel that the outfit was missing… something.

Then his eye fell upon the diamond-encrusted cross pendant they'd taken from that Portuguese ship off the coast of Brazil. It was gaudy, sacrilegious in its extravagance, and bought with blood. He still wore the copper token at his throat beneath his shirt, but the Spanish had long ago forgotten its meaning. It couldn't be his talisman in this moment, but for what he was about to do, the glittering cross was perfect.

He sighed. *Here we go again*, he thought. Such a shame. He'd just been getting started, with his fleet of pirate ships and his campaign against Barbados and Martinique and all those British bastards, and if it hadn't been for that bloody woman…

If only they had never captured the *Onslow*. God, how he hated having women aboard. But when you were in the middle of the ocean and the options were either taking the passengers prisoner or drowning them, he'd rather set a guard to keep them chaste until he could put them ashore than have their souls on his conscience for the rest of eternity. Unlike the men he faced in battle, they hadn't asked for a fight.

Not all of them, anyway. Just Kulika: that little one, the tall, blonde waif of a thing who'd already managed to disguise herself as a man by the time they'd breached the cabin. As if that could fool Bartholomew. Hadn't she realised that he was the immortal pirate Roberts, preternaturally perceptive and supernaturally strong?

But then he'd seen the expression on her face, and he'd known there was no point in arguing. Pure determination, it had been, so he'd pretended he hadn't noticed the disguise. He'd broken his own code to let her sign the Articles and join his crew, and then that blood-soaked day at Whydah had followed, and now he was about to die.

Again.

It was hard not to connect the dots and follow them back to her.

He should never have allowed her on the crew. He certainly never should have bitten her and turned her into the same thing he was, but there had been that determined glint in her eye, and the way she looked at him with almost grudging respect…

Not anymore, though. That was the way she *had* looked at him, before Whydah.

He suppressed a shudder at the memory. He had never in his life failed so spectacularly as he had with the *Porcupine*. It had been weeks ago, a month at least, but he could still hear the screams as the fire reached the captives chained below decks. If only he could forget them.

But there would be no escape for him.

When his crew asked him what he coveted most, he'd always replied, *A merry life and a short one*. He would pretend that he'd got it. After this day's work, they would believe that he'd gone to his rest happily at the ripe old age of forty. Would that it could be true. Instead, at nearly two hundred years in excess of that age, he would continue to drag his carcass around the Caribbean, forsaken by God and beyond the reach of his mercy. He knew all too well that the Lord cared little for the man of blood he had become, and perhaps had always been.

No matter. It was far too late to repent now.

He fastened the diamond cross around his neck, slung a couple of pairs of pistols over his shoulders and took up his sword. The British were coming in the *Swallow* and he was going to meet them head on. He vowed that he would make this death one they would never forget.

Roberts did not have many regrets. The ones he still held were significant – Hispaniola, the *Porcupine*, Kulika – but he could count them on the fingers of one hand. In the seconds after Evita opened her eyes, he dared to believe that tonight's events would not be added to the roster.

The change had worked. He could see the silver filaments in the whites of her eyes, the mark that signified her transformation. He hadn't been entirely sure it *would* work. He hadn't turned anyone since the *Onslow*, and he hadn't been sure he remembered how to do it, but when it came to the moment it had been as easy as a thought.

What followed had been trickier. He'd had to carry her from the roof terrace to the car without anyone seeing, then get the kid to drive them both back to the mansion, pretending that Evita was just one of his usual victims. A tourist, no family in the country, an easy target to disappear. He'd taken her to his bedroom, because that's where they always went, then told the kid to piss off while he laid her out on the bed.

Then he'd waited. All the Bartholomews had been good at that.

It had all been worth it, though.

Evita looked up at him from the bed, her hair spread on the pillows. He saw the silver in her eyes, and there was that determined glint too, curious and irresistible.

'Oh,' she said.

'It's me,' he said with a gentle smile, leaning forward in his chair so she could see him better.

'It's you,' she replied. All the anger she'd shown him in her last conscious moments had disappeared during her transformation. Now she was just looking at him with curiosity. 'Who *are* you?'

He'd expected this. He'd known he'd have to explain what he was – what they both were – sooner or later. He should have had his script prepared.

But while he scrambled to find the words, she said, 'The

last thing I remember is… Oh, shit.' She looked down at her hands, then around at the room, before her gaze settled back on Roberts's face. When she spoke again, her voice was anxious. 'I don't remember. Am I in hospital? What happened? Did I hit my head or something?'

Roberts could feel the smile melting off his face.

'Seriously,' she said, sitting up in the bed and backing up against the headboard. 'Where am I, who are you, and what's going on? Why can't I remember?'

'I don't know,' he murmured. This wasn't normal. He might not have done a lot of turnings, but he was sure this wasn't normal.

'Do you know your name?' he whispered.

'I don't… What's going on?' she said, panicking now. 'Who are you? You don't look like a doctor. No, get away from me!' she yelled as Roberts approached, backing off the far side of the bed so that it formed a barrier between them.

She might have forgotten his assault, but along with it she'd forgotten their kiss, their arguments, their spark. Just when he thought he'd finally found someone interesting, she'd forgotten him, determinedly, along with everything else.

Roberts let himself out of the room and called for the kid. Let him tell her what they all were, and who he thought Roberts was.

'Well,' the kid said, 'objective achieved, then.'

'She's not dead,' Roberts said. 'She's turned. And she's lost her memory. Entirely, apparently.'

'Oh.' The kid thought for a moment, then said, 'Objective still achieved then, I guess.'

'What?' Roberts barked.

'I'm just saying, if she can't remember anything, then it's not like she's going to be publishing any more theories about pirates renaming themselves, or our never-ending lives, you know? So we're safe. Under the radar, as usual. Suspicion has been deflected. Objective achieved, like I said. Good work, sir.'

Roberts sneered at the kid and walked away.

He wasn't wrong, though.

As Roberts walked through the echoing halls of his home, he turned the copper token between his thumb and forefinger. Perhaps this was for the best, all things considered, even if it hurt. What could he have been to her even if she had remembered? A man who'd forced immortal life on her without asking. A man who, now that he considered things from her perspective, had probably scared her more than he'd attracted her. And, above all, a man whose worst misdeeds over the past half-millennium would be immediately apparent to an historian so well-versed in the golden age of piracy.

Hispaniola, the Porcupine, Kulika.

Evita could not remember him without also remembering all the things he had done. *This is for the best*, he told himself.

Even if—

He squeezed the copper token in his fist, bending the metal into the shape of his grip.

No.

Just let him be forgotten, as thoroughly as he would surely forget her. And he *would* forget her, even if it took another five hundred years.

This he vowed.

EX MARKS THE SPOT

WHITE POINT, CHARLES Town, November 1718

At the southernmost tip of the city of Charles Town, where the Ashley and Cooper rivers meet, they built a gallows. It was little more than a frame from which to hang the ropes, with only a cart beneath as a makeshift platform. The prisoners walked the short distance from their cell to the place of their imminent demise, paraded outside the city's southern wall so that everyone could see it was true: the pirates were caught, the city was safe, and the pirate blockade under which the city had suffered back in May would not be repeated.

Job Bayly, his hands held before him as he shuffled along in his chains, was glad that it was over.

His had been a funny sort of a life. He'd left England under duress, press-ganged into the navy. They'd had to force them back then, because not even a desperate fool would sign up willingly when they knew that a third of them would die before they could return home. Between injuries and the 'seasoning' new recruits would have to suffer as they fought the diseases endemic to the tropics, survival rates were low. Despite his present circumstances, Bayly counted himself one of the lucky ones. He'd fallen sick just before his naval frigate was due to leave Jamaica, so they'd abandoned him to recuperate on shore. Or not. The navy didn't care either way, as long as he wasn't on board to infect anyone else.

He'd recovered from that infection. The one he couldn't shake, would never shake in fact, was the one he'd picked up while he was hanging around the Caribbean, crewing with wreckers as he avoided being pressed into service on yet another British warship. That infection would reshape his entire life. This whole business in Charles Town was nothing but a regrettable interlude, the anticlimactic end to his own personal golden age of piracy.

The militia directed Bayly and his crewmates towards the gallows. They might have protested, but what would be the point? They were broke and broken, and the few who weren't exhausted into compliance were too proud to brawl. Bayly himself was resigned. He didn't object when they shoved him and his fellows up onto the cart, nor when they put the ropes around their necks, not even when they pushed him from the boards so the noose snapped tight around his neck. He especially didn't object when they cut him down before he was dead and threw him on the sand next to the other bodies. At that point, he was very quiet indeed.

They were buried in the marshy ground below the tide line, though 'buried' was hardly the word. Admiralty law required that pirates should only be afforded shallow graves, but it's not easy to dig a hole in a swamp, and the militia had barely tried. Instead, Bayly lay cheek-to-calf-to-chest with his former friends in the brackish water and tried to stay still until the business was done.

It might have ended there in the corpse-filled marshland off White Point. Perhaps it would have done, or even should have done, were it not for the man they called Digs.

* * *

Some three centuries later, at the southernmost tip of the city of Charleston, where the Ashley and Cooper rivers meet, there's a park called White Point Garden. It has dirt paths, shady trees, ornate benches, and numerous monuments, including various antique cannon, and statues commemorating both the Civil and Revolutionary Wars. It's all very interesting and historic, but not half as interesting and historic as the *other* monument in White Point Garden, the one about the pirates.

On a bright afternoon, three young people stand together and admire the stone through their sunglasses. The tallest, a man named Brandon, looks a little like a pirate himself. With an anchor beard, dark eyelashes, and long chestnut hair tied back with a piece of string, he wouldn't be out of place on the deck of a sloop. The pink flip-flops and fluorescent vest might raise some eyebrows, but his striking features and swashbuckling locks are just begging for a tricorne hat. He pushes his hair out of his face, frowning in concentration as he reads the inscription on the monument. The woman next to him, a pale redhead called Penny, crowds in close to do the same.

'Twenty-nine of Stede Bonnet's men were hanged too?' Penny asks.

'And our housemate is on the list,' Brandon says.

'Or just someone with the same name as him,' says their companion, a brown-skinned brunette who wears no makeup except bright red lipstick. No one back at the mansion knows her real name, and she forgot it herself during the trauma of her turning, so they call her Jane Doe. She thinks it's a boring name for a corpse.

Like Brandon and Penny, Jane's new to South Carolina and to life as a vampire. It isn't something she chose for herself – she remembers that much – but accidents happen, or so they keep saying. Judging by the number of new vampires that now inhabit the mansion, the tourists in this part of America are becoming rather accident prone. It's a big property, but it's filling up fast, and soon they're going to have to extend out or start sharing rooms. Communal living with a bunch of bloodsuckers is not Jane's idea of domestic bliss, but she has nowhere else to go and isn't sure she'd be allowed to leave even if she did. So, for the moment, she's trying to view this experience an extended holiday as she tries to adapt. Since that approach has landed her with Brandon and Penny, she wouldn't say it's going well.

'How likely is it that someone else would have the same weird name *and* the same weird spelling?' Brandon says, pulling a rolled-up paperback from the pocket of his jeans. He flicks to the page and points at a name. 'Right here, look. I'm telling you, it's him. Job Bayly was one of the crew. They hanged him here and buried him in the marsh beyond the low-water mark, just like they did with the rest of the pirates, so their bodies would be disturbed by the ebb and flow of the tides, and they could never rest, not even in death.'

Penny raises her freckled brows, her eyes widening with delighted horror. 'That's awful!'

'I suppose,' Brandon replies, 'but pirates were kind of awful too. They call Bonnet the gentleman pirate, but if you heard the things he did to his crew when he thought he was losing control of—'

'Is this going to take much longer?' says Jane. She stands apart, looking at her watch and fidgeting while the others read. For reasons she can't explain, she's desperate to get away from this place. Despite the sunshine, the birdsong and the shushing of the surf, it's creepy.

'Seriously, Jane,' says Penny. 'It's like you don't even want to find the treasure.'

'I keep telling you: there is no treasure,' Jane replies.

'Of *course* there's treasure.'

'Firstly: pirates aren't real.'

'Says one vampire to the other,' Brandon interjects.

'I think you'll find,' says Penny, 'that pirates are a matter of historical fact.'

'Yes, obviously,' says Jane. 'But they didn't exist in the way that we think of them. It wasn't all buried treasure and walking the plank and shivering the timbers. Pirate ships were disease-ridden and dangerous, and everyone who lived on them drank heavily not because they were fun-loving, but because they wanted a way to forget about their poverty, their fear and their syphilis.'

'Spoilsport,' says Penny.

'Which brings me to my next point,' Jane continues, as though she hasn't been interrupted. 'Pirates signed articles when joining a ship. They had to split their winnings amongst the crew, who'd then go off and spend it immediately on rum and sex. So what are they going to bury? And even if the whole crew *did* decide to stash their gold somewhere for safekeeping, why would they just dig a hole on some random island and leave it there unguarded? And even if, for the sake of argument, they were stupid enough to do that, why would it still be there hundreds of years later, with coastal erosion and hurricanes and all the other stupid treasure hunters trawling the Caribbean with their metal detectors trying to dig it up? It makes *no sense.*'

'Hmm,' says Brandon.

'What?' says Jane. 'Why are you looking at me funny?'

'No, nothing,' Brandon says. 'It's just that for someone who thinks pirates are stupid, you sure know a lot about them.'

Jane sighs. 'Can we just go home?'

'Go watch the dolphins in the harbour,' Penny suggests.

'Or ride one of the cannon,' says Brandon.

'You're ridiculous,' says Jane.

'When are we going to talk to Bayly?' asks Penny.

Brandon looks at her over his sunglasses. 'We're not.'

'We're not?'

'No, we're not going to tell the vampire pirate that we're looking for his buried treasure. That sounds like a bad idea.'

'Oh,' says Penny. 'Yes. That does sound like a bad idea.'

'So we should probably get out of here before anyone sees us,' Jane suggests.

'Just five more minutes,' says Brandon. 'And then I'll buy you some pecan pralines for the drive back.'

'All right,' Jane sighs, willing to suffer almost any delay in return for sugary treats.

It's too late, anyway. The trio may not have noticed him, but Job Bayly – standing at the harbour wall with a fishing rod beside him – has certainly noticed them.

He is not pleased.

Point Pedro Cays, Caribbean Sea, August 1691

Bayly stood on the deck of the *Diligence* and stared into the clear azure sea. With the sun beating down on the back of his neck and the breeze so soft they were practically in the doldrums, it was hard to imagine it was possible for anything to be wrecked in these waters, let alone three Spanish treasure ships. Nonetheless, he could see the evidence of it before his own eyes, and over the past few days he had held it in his own hands. From his vantage on the deck, he could make out the shadows of the bows resting on the reef and, he swore, he could even see the glinting of silver within.

'With haste, Bayly,' said the man to his right, words that made Bayly shiver with recollection. He knew the man only as Digs, a drinking companion who'd been enticed from his barstool by the same offer that brought Bayly to this sloop: an equitable share of the salvage. If they had a lucky dive, then they might find a fortune, and on a ship crewed by only thirty men, that meant they'd get a thirtieth of a fortune apiece. For that kind of compensation, even Digs could be persuaded to forego the sharp rum and soft companionship of Port Royal's many disreputable drinking establishments.

It helped, of course, that he was there with Bayly.

With haste, Bayly, Digs had said, knowing full well the effect the words would have on Bayly. He'd whispered them only the night before, and the night before that, so frequently in fact that his impatience had become a private joke between them, to the extent that it was possible to have any privacy at all on a sloop as small as the *Diligence*. There was only one aspect of Bayly's and Digs's relationship of which they were sure the crew were ignorant, a fact that would stretch the credulity of even the most superstitious sailor.

It had happened on the first day they'd spent diving in the warm seas surrounding Point Pedro Cays.

The wrecks were deeper than the clear water made them appear, deep enough that on that first day, more than one diver rose to the surface with water and blood pouring from their mouths, nostrils and ears. The *Diligence* was not the only ship sent a-wrecking from Jamaica, and they'd been close enough to see the blood when a diver on a neighbouring ship had haemorrhaged, then dropped dead on the deck. Between that, the manta rays and the sharks, diving for treasure was dangerous work. Still, the lure of the rewards that awaited them on the seabed was enough to allay Bayly's fears. Digs, on the other hand, seemed to have no fears at all.

'See you on the bottom,' he'd said to Bayly before diving in. With a laugh, Bayly had put an oil-soaked sponge in his mouth – a trick that would allow him another lungful of air, and thus more time in the wreck – and followed Digs to the seabed.

The first three, five, ten dives had passed without event. It was only on the twelfth or thirteenth dive that Bayly had seen it: the first glimmer of treasure. Pieces of eight twinkled in the deepest reaches of a pile of wreckage and, as Bayly blinked his eyes under the water in a futile attempt to clear his sight of the sand he had stirred up with his movement, he thought he saw something else besides, something rounded and so yellow in hue that he couldn't control his hunger for it. First, he tried moving away some of the wreckage to allow him access. Next, he tried prying it apart with a bar he took from the pile. Finally, worried that he wouldn't be able to locate the spot again if he left it now, he sucked the last of the air from the sponge and reached his arm into the pile up to his shoulder, feeling desperately for the smooth kiss of metal.

Instead, he felt only a sharp bite, followed by a numbing sting that spread quickly through his fingers. As he withdrew his hand, he saw the flicker of a tail within the pile.

A sea snake, he thought as he watched the sponge, useless now, rising away from him to be carried off by the current. He must have opened his mouth. Now that he thought of it, he could feel the water pushing its way in. He couldn't seem to fight it, though. He wasn't sure there would be much point; it was death by drowning or death by venom. Perhaps it would be both.

Gently resigned to his fate, Bayly was surprised to find Digs floating in the water in front of him, shaking his shoulders. *Digs never uses an oiled sponge*, Bayly thought. And yet Digs was always the first of them to dive in, and the last to surface. That was strange, wasn't it?

After a moment, Digs pressed his lips to Bayly's.

No, he tried to tell Digs. *Another breath won't save me.* But then he realised that Digs wasn't trying to give him a lungful of air. He was kissing him, forcing Bayly's mouth open with such violence that he tasted blood. Then Digs pulled Bayly into his arms, there was a sharp snap at his throat, and for a moment Bayly thought the bloody sea snake had him again.

But it was Digs. Digs was biting him.

The water turned red and Bayly blacked out, finally giving in to the water, or the poison, or so he thought. In fact, he had given in to something else entirely.

Port Royal's shipping accounts recorded an impressive salvage of one hundred and twenty pieces of eight on that first trip alone, one of many that the crew of the *Diligence* would make to Point Pedro Cays in those few months. The crown took a tenth of the salvage they declared, but not a shilling of the treasure that they smuggled past the port captain, treasure that included large quantities of silver plate, more pieces of eight, and a pair of golden rings.

These days, Job Bayly looks nothing like a pirate.

He's earned his clean-cut image, playing the part of a proper seafaring gentleman, which was a challenge for a lad born and raised in the east end of London. His life is neat and tidy, just the way he likes things, and his secrets are known only to the sea. At least they were, until… those bloody kids.

For as long as he's been in these parts, there have been rumours about Stede Bonnet and his crew, notorious for their betrayal by Blackbeard before they could retire from piracy and seek the King's pardon. But perhaps, the rumours go, the pirates had set a little something aside for their retirement, and perhaps it was still out there somewhere, waiting to be found.

Bayly is the last person alive who *knows* those rumours aren't true. The problem is that they're not entirely one hundred percent false either, and the last thing he needs is a bunch of treasure-hunting young vampires rootling around in his past. Unfortunately, it's difficult to avoid them when they're all living under the same roof. Safety in numbers, the boss says. Bayly is inclined to belief that the opposite is true.

Maybe it was arrogant to think that he could return anonymously to this city, where pirates are legends and his real name is known. It was only a matter of time before someone figured it out, but honestly he didn't think the sunglasses brigade would be the ones to do it. Their grubby, sugary fingers have been in his room, all over his kit bag, under his mattress and, worst of all, in the secret compartment at the bottom of his travel trunk where he keeps his documents, the ones that list his full name. Perhaps he could have passed himself off as a distant descendant of the Job Bayly who sailed with Stede Bonnet, but the name is uncommon enough to be suspicious.

That's why Bayly is sitting underneath an oak tree in the back yard, watching through the Spanish moss as Brandon, Penny and Jane emerge onto the porch. It's just one attractive feature of the generally attractive building, which is showing its age in the best way possible. Most of the older mansions were swallowed up by the city over time as it expanded, but this one still stands apart in its own substantial grounds, which puts Bayly some distance away from the porch. Despite that, he can hear their conversation as clear as a bell.

Their carelessness irks him. Even within the boundaries of the mansion, they should hide their secrets better. Particularly when their secrets rightly belong to him.

'Look what I found,' Brandon says, spreading some papers across the porch table. 'Ship manifests. Harbour records. *Diaries*. There has to be something here to point us in the right direction.'

Penny peers at them closely while Jane pretends disinterest, glancing casually at the writing over Penny's shoulder. Penny and Brandon are too distracted to notice the direction of her gaze.

'This is boring,' Jane says as she surreptitiously scans the text.

She's a tricky one, Bayly thinks.

After a couple of minutes, she freezes. The only thing that gives away her excitement is the tiniest momentary twitch of an eyebrow, an involuntary gesture that she has under control within a split second.

'Can't we go out?' Jane says, trying to distract the others from whatever it is she's found. 'When was the last time we went to, like, a bar?'

That catches Brandon's attention, and anything that hooks Brandon will hook Penny too.

'These'll still be here tomorrow, I guess,' he says.

'Just give me half an hour to get ready,' says Penny, already rushing off inside.

'Forty-five minutes,' Brandon calls after her. Then he strokes his beard and pulls a lock of his hair in front of his eyes, frowning at what he sees. 'Make it an hour,' he amends, then he follows Penny inside.

When the other two have gone, Jane sits at the table and starts leafing through the pages, her brow creased in concentration. She pulls one page out of the stack, then another, then another, and all the while her lips are shaping a single word over and over. With a sinking feeling in his stomach, Bayly realises she must have recognised the name from his papers.

Diligence.

Port Royal, Jamaica, December 1691

Two men sat in the corner of the room, hands linked under the table. A large leather bag rested on the floor between them, cradled by their feet. Each of them wore a golden ring.

'We've got it off the sloop,' Digs murmured reassuringly.

'That was the easy bit,' Bayly whispered in reply. 'It's what comes next that worries me.'

He was no good at all this cloak and dagger stuff. It had seemed like a lark back on the *Diligence*, hiding little pieces of silver and gold in their pockets while they dreamed of a rich eternity in which they could spend it. But now they were back in Port Royal with the threat of discovery pressing in all around them, the huge bag of loot felt less like freedom and more like a ball and chain.

'We take what we need, and we stash the rest,' said Digs. 'Then when everything's calmed down a bit, we can slip away to the mainland and set ourselves up in style, for the rest of our eternal lives.'

'The mainland?' The bottom dropped out of Bayly's stomach. 'As in, on land?'

'We'll buy a plantation. Make a fortune. Be proper gentlemen.'

'On land?'

Bayly had found it surprisingly simple to adapt to life as a vampire – a splash of blood here, a quick murder there; not so different from being a pirate, really – but a life away from the sea held little appeal. The land was all right to visit, but he didn't want to be tethered there permanently.

'Yes, on land. Where else?' Digs said. 'It's not like we can grow sugar in the ocean. Use your head.'

Bayly took a mouthful of rum and swallowed it down with his protests. He didn't want a plantation. He definitely didn't want slaves. He didn't want to be around people much at all, in fact. He just wanted to buy a ship and sail the beautiful, treacherous Caribbean seas with Digs, away from the prying eyes of civilised society. He'd thought that was what Digs wanted too, but it was becoming clear now that when they'd imagined their futures together, each of them had seen a completely different picture in their heads.

'What we've got is plenty enough to buy us land in Charles Town,' said Digs. 'We just have to find somewhere safe to hoard it until then.'

'Where?'

'Bury it. I have a place in mind. I reckon we should split up, though, in case any of the old hands are keeping an eye on us.'

Bayly could see Digs's wheels turning. 'You have a plan?' he asked.

'One of us takes this bag—' Digs pushed a second bag forward with his foot. It held everything they owned that wasn't treasure. '—and they play the decoy, drawing off any unwanted attention. Then the other one goes off to bury the loot elsewhere.'

'You do it,' said Bayly. 'You bury it.'

'Are you certain?'

Bayly thought about the militia and the port authorities, not to mention the Spanish, the French and all the other pirates who might be waiting to get their hands on the treasure. Then a horrible thought occurred.

'Are there other vampires on the island?' he asked Digs. 'Do we have to worry about them too?'

'Can't you tell?'

Bayly's brow wrinkled. 'How would I tell?'

Digs sighed as though disappointed, and Bayly's wrinkles deepened. Bayly hated the dynamic that was emerging between them. Their time on the *Diligence* had been a paradise of diving and searching and messing around together in the water. There was something wonderfully freeing about knowing that you were immune to poison, to drowning, and that you'd even recover from a shark bite if one of them dared to get close. In the water, Bayly and Digs had enjoyed themselves, and each other.

But now they'd returned to Port Royal, there was a distinct edge of condescension creeping into Digs's tone. It seemed to Bayly that Digs was already tired of his company, and that he resented having to educate him about life as a vampire, as though he expected Bayly to pick it all up on his own. Every question was met with a sigh, every moment of ignorance was greeted with disdain or ridicule, and each negative reaction from Digs just made Bayly feel more insecure, more desperate to please him, but so anxious about putting a foot wrong that he deferred to Digs in everything, which just made Digs angrier still. The situation was cycling downwards at an alarming rate, but Bayly was powerless to change its trajectory.

'Listen to my heart,' said Digs. 'You hear how slow it is?'

After a moment's concentration, Bayly realised Digs was right. He should have noticed the difference between it and a human heartbeat. He should have been listening all the time, but his senses were so overwhelmed by the extra sights, sounds and smells that now flooded his world that separating them out was still a challenge.

'And yes,' Digs continued, 'there are other vampires in Port Royal, but don't you worry about them. You can scupper a vampire the same way you do a human: drain their blood and they'll be too lubberly to fight you. But be sure and get them before they get you. Surprise is your best bet.'

Bayly swallowed nervously and said, 'You bury it,' with even more conviction than he had previously.

Digs muttered something under his breath that sounded like *caitiff*. Bayly pretended he hadn't heard it as Digs pulled the bag of their inexpensive possessions up onto the table.

'Here,' Digs said, scratching something into the bag's leather flap before shoving it towards Bayly. 'This is where it'll be buried, just in case something should go awry.'

'What?' Bayly asked. 'Where are you going?'

'Nowhere, but best I not return here this evening. I'll find you tomorrow.'

'Truly?'

Digs took his hand under the table again, turning Bayly's gold ring with his fingers.

'I swear it,' he said, then clasped Bayly's hand tightly. Bayly clasped Digs's hand back, the closest to an embrace that they could risk in this place, then Digs was pushing Bayly out of his seat towards the tavern door. He didn't look back, but he felt the eyes watching as he left.

It was only later, when Bayly returned to their sordid lodgings on the waterfront after weaving around the town, that he took the time to study the indecipherable marks Digs had left in the leather.

HM Plsds †

To Bayly, the marks meant nothing at all. He couldn't read.

Two days after Jane started searching for the *Diligence*,

Bayly follows her to Charleston harbour. She boards a cruise ship to the Caribbean, looking like any other tourist with her short shorts, her sunglasses and her garish red lipstick, but Bayly knows she's not on a sight-seeing trip. She's going to Jamaica to track down the things he left buried there.

And she's not alone.

Ten minutes after Jane embarks, a familiar, bearded, long-haired man walks up the ramp to the ship.

Five minutes after that, the third kid shows up.

This is going to complicate things.

Bayly doesn't bother to buy a ticket. He knows enough about ships that he can find his way aboard without using the gangplank, then set himself up beneath a parasol on the sun deck with a ridiculous Hawaiian shirt and a cocktail he has no intention of drinking. No one knows how to make good rum anymore. It's from this perfect vantage point that he watches the kids' various attempts at subterfuge dissolve.

Penny is a poor spy. Within two hours of the ship's departure, she seems to have forgotten what she's doing there. Instead of keeping track of the other two, she's entering – and winning – a wet T-shirt contest on the lido deck. Brandon, walking past on his way to the 24/7 buffet, yells, 'What are you doing here?'

Penny's answering tirade, chastising Brandon for cutting her out of the treasure hunt, is enough to attract the attention of the entire ship. Bayly is sure that Jane will have spotted them too.

'Hello, Bayly,' she says.

The third kid is sitting next to him. He's criticising Penny and Brandon for their undercover skills, but here he is letting her creep up on him. Somehow, in all the confusion, he missed her scent.

It's the nerves. This treasure hunt of theirs is stirring up the memories, and he's letting them get the best of him, but he's not that fresh young vampire anymore. He knows what he's doing, and he knows better than to get riled up by a few lucky breaks. He needs to get composed and stay that way, so he shrugs off his anxiety and reapplies his swagger.

'Good morning,' he says. 'I was starting to think I might have to enter the wet T-shirt contest myself before you'd spot me.'

Bayly can see through Jane's sunglasses well enough to know that she's bought his blag. Good. Let her think that he's always one step ahead, that she'll never catch him out, and maybe she'll give up and go home.

Please, God, let her just go home.

She pushes up her sunglasses, takes a swig of her own cocktail and settles back in her chair.

'So,' she says. 'You were a pirate.'

Bayly gives no response except a faint grunt.

'You were fake-executed with Stede Bonnet's crew.'

Another grunt.

'But before that, you crewed on a sloop called the *Diligence*, salvaging Spanish gold from Pedro Cays.'

This time, Bayly gives no response at all.

'I saw the port records,' she goes on. 'I saw your papers, too. There's no point denying it.'

'And why should you care, Miss Doe?' She seems surprised that Bayly knows her name. 'Oh yes, I know all of you, well enough to know that you're not the greedy type. Chasing treasure feels out of character. Care to explain?'

'No,' she says.

'Answer my question,' he says, 'and I'll answer one of yours.'

She hesitates for a moment, then says, 'I don't know why. I don't remember.'

'I'd heard that about you. I wasn't sure it was true.'

'Well, it is.' She looks away, pulling her sunglasses back down over her eyes. 'I can't remember my own name, but for some reason I can remember the biography of every pirate ever to grace the shores of Charleston. I know Stede Bonnet's life better than I know my own. I think his crew buried his treasure somewhere in the Caribbean, and I know I need to find it.'

'He had nothing to bury,' Bayly says softly. 'Everything Stede had he frittered away.'

'But the *Diligence* found gold, didn't it? So what did you do with that treasure?'

'*My* treasure, you mean?'

'Hah,' Jane says triumphantly. 'So it *does* exist.'

'Not anymore,' says Bayly. 'We spent money like water in old Port Royal. If you know pirates, then you must know the stories.'

'One tavern for every three citizens. Sex and rum and general debauchery, right?'

'Something like that.'

'Sounds like fun.'

'Right,' says Bayly. 'Lice and gonorrhoea are tons of fun.'

'I bet you had fun getting them. I read the old papers from when the city sank into the sea. They said it was God's judgement on the city.'

Bayly grunts noncommittally.

'Divine retribution for its sin,' Jane prods.

'Sure,' Bayly snorts. 'Because God hates drunken sodomites like me and has no problem at all with the rich bastards who made their fortunes on the sugar plantations they were bribed with by the kings and queens back home.'

'I didn't—'

'We were having a nice boozy time, buggering no one but

each other, and the church-going white people just *hated* that. But they couldn't see anything wrong with slave owners who tortured and murdered their supposed *chattels*, and buggered up *everything*, and enjoyed punishing their slaves so much that instead of just executing them, they skewered them to the ground and surrounded them with small fires so they could literally roast them to death. But sure, it was the sailors and their syphilis that lowered the tone of Port Royal. That seems right.'

Jane blinks at him. 'Have you been drinking?'

'This piss?' He looks askance at the terrible cocktail. 'You've got to be kidding.'

He's letting the memories rile him up. He's letting *her* rile him up, and that's no good. She's just a kid. She wasn't there. She doesn't know what it was like, so how can she possibly understand? She's not the real target of Bayly's anger. He needs to change her mind about this little adventure of hers before she gets caught in the crossfire.

'You should go home, Miss Doe,' he says. 'There are worse things than bad memories buried on Jamaica.'

'You don't scare me, Bayly.'

'I should,' he says seriously, but she pays no attention to his tone. 'This obsession will take you nowhere good.'

She hesitates for a moment before steeling her resolve.

'I'm going to find that treasure,' she says. 'Because it's real, isn't it? If it wasn't, then you wouldn't be here. You're guarding something. Why else would you follow me on a cruise all the way to the Caribbean?'

'Maybe I just felt like a holiday.'

'I don't think so.'

'I'll tell you this: I've never buried any treasure in my whole, long life. You're not going to find what you're looking for in Port Royal.'

Jane gives him a level look, meeting his gaze for a second, then looks away dismissively.

'Oh, I think I will,' she says. 'You're a terrible liar. But don't worry, I've brought an extra suitcase, because I have no intention of coming back to the States empty-handed.'

'Miss Doe, if you don't return home—'

'Jane!' The yell comes from the deck below their seats. It's the idiot pirate lookalike. 'You found him! Did you find the treasure?'

'Shut up,' Jane hisses at him.

'Oh, hey!' Penny yells, joining Brandon. 'Have we got a treasure map, then?'

Heads are turning. Jane stands from her chair and rushes to the railing at the edge of the sun deck.

'Will both of you shut the fuck up?' she says to them. 'And fuck off, too. That would be good.'

Bayly wishes they'd all fuck off. It's time for him to make his exit. He smiles at the kids and says, 'Enjoy your cruise,' then slips away into the bowels of the ship before any of them can follow.

Damn it. This is not going to plan.

The Palisadoes, Jamaica, June 1692

After the night Digs buried the treasure, his relationship with Bayly plummeted like it was tied to the anchor of a first-rate warship. Bayly asked where the loot was stashed, time and again. Time and again, Digs simply told him it was not time.

In truth, they were only staying together because of their shared stakes in the loot, and because of their shared stakes in a future that Bayly was dreading. Digs was negotiating the land sale in Charles Town. It would be any day now, and Bayly felt the weight of each one as though it were his last.

He could feel Digs pulling away too, little by little. Whatever they promised each other in the dead of the night, Bayly was certain that they would not be leaving the island together. Both of them knew it, and yet they stuck together like barnacles on a hull. It was an excruciatingly drawn out ending to what had once been a spontaneous romance.

Still, Bayly waited, though not with any optimism. He was resigned and ready when Digs crept out of their latest lodgings – higher rates, fewer rats – slipping from their shared bedroom late one morning carrying his boots and a pre-packed bag. Digs left through the door. Bayly followed through the window.

They went in circles through the streets of Port Royal for a short while, past the *Swan* in the dry dock, past the fruit market on the High Street where Digs picked up his breakfast, and past the synagogue on New Street. Eventually, Digs walked up Thames Street, past Fort Rupert, out of town, and by then Bayly knew where they were heading.

The citizens of Port Royal buried their dead beyond their walls, on a thin strip of sand and scrub that joined the city to the rest of the island. As Digs made his way there, Bayly walked into the ocean and kept pace by swimming alongside. Digs wouldn't hear his heartbeat in the surf, or if he did, he might think Bayly was a dolphin or a shark. In any case, it seemed that Digs was now too intent on his task to be vigilant. When he reached the graveyard, he didn't dally. Instead, he made his way to one particular grave, whose occupant had been in the ground only four years. Where better to bury their privateer booty than in the grave of Jamaica's most notorious privateer?

Bayly watched as Digs dug. He made short work of it, and in no time at all he was hauling a lead box out of the sandy ground and prying it open. While he did so, Bayly rose quietly from the surf and approached Digs from behind.

'Son of a bitch,' Digs muttered, looking into the empty box. Then his back went rigid. He turned and sighed. 'Where's the loot, Bayly?'

'I bought a ship,' Bayly replied, shaking off the water. 'A little sloop. Then I fitted it out. And the rest... well. I'm saving that for a rainy day.'

'How did you find the spot?' Digs said.

As Digs got to his feet, there was a tremor in the sand, but neither of them paid it any mind. Bayly had been resident in Port Royal on and off for years now and he was accustomed to the way that the earth sometimes shifted beneath his feet for no apparent reason. He was so used to it that he ignored it in much the same way as he ignored the rolling of a deck beneath his feet: it was simply part of life in the Caribbean.

He pulled the leather bag flap from his pocket and showed it to Digs.

HM Plsds †

'Henry Morgan, Palisadoes graveyard,' Bayly said. 'It's easy to decipher when you can actually read the letters, which you knew I couldn't. Not until recently, anyway. You were always planning to take it all for yourself, weren't you?'

There was another tremor, stronger this time.

'You should have surprised me,' Digs said with quiet menace. 'I'm older and faster than you.'

He was right, but Bayly had needed to see Digs's reaction, not just for the satisfaction of the ruse but so that he would know absolutely, certainly, that Digs had intended to betray him. Well, now he had his answer. It was time to stop playing games.

'I have the loot,' Bayly said. 'How are you going to find it if you kill me?'

'I'm not planning to kill you.' Digs stalked closer as he spoke. 'I'm planning to seal you up in the ground for a time and give you a chance to think about your choices.'

The ground shook again, enough to make it seem as though the ocean was sloshing like water in a cup, and this time it didn't stop. Digs was still advancing towards Bayly when the land beneath his feet started bubbling and spurting, slicked into quicksand by water forced out of the earth by its shaking. By the time Digs realised that this quake was different, it was too late to get out of its way. The ground sucked at his feet, wedging him into the sand, an act of God that saved Bayly from falling under Digs's teeth once more.

Divine retribution.

Digs's eyes met Bayly's with a plea.

Bayly could hear the screams from within the city walls now and could only guess at the destruction that was heading their way. He had scant seconds to act before he was sucked into the sand himself, along with the rest of the city.

But God was on his side.

At the southern edge of Kingston harbour, there's a highway that runs along a narrow strip of land to what was once the bustling seventeenth-century metropolis of Port Royal. The road is lined by rocks but beyond them, on the seaward side, there's a small area of dark sand and scrubby grass that was once a graveyard.

Bayly expected that everything buried here would stay that way forever, sucked down into the earth by the same disaster that claimed Port Royal, but what he didn't account for is that Caribbean islands like Jamaica are rather prone to disasters. Sitting at the point where two tectonic plates meet, the tombolo joining Port Royal to the rest of the island has been battered by so many earthquakes, hurricanes and tsunamis over the past three centuries that the shifting sand on which it stands has now shifted enough to divulge even its deepest secrets.

Against all odds, Jane has dug one of them up. There's a lead box at her feet, about a yard along each side. She's almost got it open.

'You're early,' she says to Bayly as she leans on her shovel.

'And you shouldn't be here at all.'

'I admit I was hoping to be done before you showed up. Finders keepers?'

'You don't want what's in that box, Miss Doe,' Bayly warns her, but she doesn't listen. She's crouching beside it, using the point of the shovel to pry up the seal and release the lid.

'Where are your friends?' Bayly asks.

'Brandon and Penny?' She scoffs. 'They couldn't follow a trail if it was laid in neon paint. I lost them two hours ago.'

'Did you, now?'

Jane looks up at Bayly and, out of her line of sight, he sees two desiccated fingers reaching out through the gap under the box's lid.

'I might be new to the vampire thing,' she says, her attention focussed on Bayly, 'but I'm not as green as I look. I can shake a tail when I have to, and I wasn't going to share this find with them, was I?'

She seems pretty pleased with herself, until Bayly says, 'So no one knows you're here?'

She sees the teeth in his smile at the same moment that the fingers from the box close weakly around her wrist. She has enough time to scream, but Bayly doesn't need to take her by surprise. He's old, and fast, and strong. She is a sugarcane in a hurricane.

After the digging is done, Bayly rinses his hands in the surf and walks back along the sand to the highway, wiping the blood from the corners of his mouth.

Neat and tidy, that's how Bayly likes things.

He has two secrets now, both wrapped up in one neat box, and each is known only to the sea.

Cara Mia

THIS IS HOW the end started. This is how the world began to die: with love.

It wasn't epic love, or tragic love, or forever love, not to begin with. At its core it was mundane and unspectacular: the everyday, ordinary love that glues the world together, a miracle only to its protagonists. To everyone else it was so pedestrian as to be almost inevitable, predictable in its characters and cues.

Until it was coated in silver and blood, and turned into a beacon.

Leo had known her all of his life. Their houses were next door to each other and, despite the wide lots and spacious farm land surrounding them, they'd grown up stepping on each other's toes. Well, she'd stepped on his, anyway.

He was only nine months older, but that small gap felt significant when it had put her a year below him as she followed him through the same kindergarten, the same elementary school, and then finally through the same high school.

While they were younger it hadn't mattered so much. Their parents had taken it in turns to walk them to kindergarten and then drive them to elementary school, sharing the work of shepherding them around. More often than not they'd also stayed together when they got home, going out to play in the yard, watching TV or building dens in each other's homes. For Leo, it wasn't so much a matter of choice as it was one of inaction. The little girl, her blonde hair plaited into pigtails, had followed him everywhere. He hadn't thought to send her away.

He hadn't analysed it, and he wouldn't have known how to articulate it even if he had, but the truth was that he had enjoyed the attention. His sister was ten years older than him and, as he had started school, she had seemed more interested in boys and music than in him. It had been a blow to a child used to having a sister and a mother who both doted on him.

So he had let the little girl be his audience while he conquered video-game villains, had tried to scare her with horror films and had let her trail him through the woods and fields of Oklahoma as he poked through the scrub for insects and eggshells. After all, it had been useful to have someone to carry the boxes and jelly jars for his finds.

But that tolerance had only lasted until they reached school, or until he had a real friend over to play. After all, she was just the neighbour kid.

Then, the summer he turned twelve, everything had changed. His sister was already married and had moved away to South Carolina. There had been a falling out, some disagreement about her husband, and so when their mom had died she hadn't come back for the funeral.

He'd been left with just his dad, a carpenter who had always communicated better through his work than he had with words. He had done his best, and he was a kind and loving man at heart, but he had struggled to manage the grief of his pubescent son along with his own.

Leo had spoken to her about it after it happened, talked about the depression that had driven his mom to alcoholism and, eventually, suicide. He had told the girl in hushed tones how he had found her, lying in the bath with the razor blade resting in her bloody hands, how the colour had filled his head until he could see nothing else, closing his eyes and screaming to push the red from his mind, fading to burgundy, fading to black.

But after a few weeks, it had been clear that he wasn't coping, and that she didn't know what to say to make it better. She saw less and less of him that summer, then by the time school rolled around again they felt like strangers to one another, too much time and emotion passed in the interim for them to know each other still. Now he took the bus to high school, while her mom drove her to elementary school alone. That distance coupled with the vanity of high school, the weight of reinvention eclipsing his conscience, drove a wedge into their concord.

Eventually, it was fragile enough that it only took one day to shatter it utterly.

He'd tested their friendship in the past, daring her to steal cookies and eat worms, and she'd done it all without much complaint, almost as though her own curiosity pushed her to it. And somehow, she'd always managed to get him back twofold. If she'd spent one afternoon grounded, some apparently innocent suggestion of hers would see him stuck inside for three days by the end of the week. Somehow, she always came out on top, and it infuriated him.

That summer, with all the turmoil bubbling inside him, it made him bitter and spiteful.

She had tried to see him those first couple of weeks of the

semester. In truth, she was lonely without him. She didn't have any siblings and he was the only kid her age in walking distance of the house, so without him she would be playing alone or reading, and she was getting to the age where games held little amusement. For the first time, it had seemed to matter what he thought. It had mattered that he wouldn't talk to her, that he wouldn't tolerate her presence any more.

She had consoled herself with the fact that he didn't seem to hang out with any friends at all, and her mom had told her it would take time. So she had felt betrayed when she had watched him getting off the school bus with a new friend.

A girl.

A pretty girl.

She had known for a few years that she herself was not a particularly pretty girl. She had pretty blonde hair, and pretty blue eyes, but her lips were too small for her face, her nose too big.

But this girl, the girl Leo had brought home with him, she had rich, dark skin and big brown eyes, her lips full and her nose small and neat. And, as she had discovered when she trailed them silently into the woods out behind his house, the girl was what her mother would euphemistically have called a 'lost' girl.

She had crouched with her knees in the dirt and watched as the lost girl pulled a packet of cigarettes from her pocket. The lost girl had passed him one and lit it for him, his green eyes fixed on her brown ones as she held a flame between their faces, and an unpleasant sensation writhed in the watching girl's stomach. She had listened for a moment as they talked about people she didn't know and music she'd never heard of, and she had felt a gulf opening up between them, a world of experience unshared and unknown.

It had made her feel young and ignorant, silly for ever

having thought that she knew the boy and unsure why the realisation hurt her so much.

Confused and mournful, she had seen enough. She'd raised herself to her feet, as soundlessly as she could manage, and made to move away. But she had not been quiet enough. As she'd turned to leave, Leo had looked over his shoulder and caught her eye. A sneer had spread across his face, dismissive and belittling. He'd raised his eyebrow at her and then, slowly and deliberately, reached out to take the hand of the pretty girl, his fingers twining in hers.

Oblivious to their voyeur, the lost girl had smiled at him. He had smiled back.

By the time she started high school the following year, they were no longer speaking to one another. They didn't acknowledge each other in the halls, their age gap an excuse for them to be perfect strangers. Every day, they waited for and boarded the bus together in silence, a single year of estrangement outweighing eleven years of companionship. It wasn't logical, but it was the way it had been for them.

Their lives grew apart through high school, she an excellent student and he not so much. He had been on a downward trajectory every day since that first, illicit cigarette: ditching classes and staying out late with the pretty dark-eyed girl, and with his other lost friends. She watched him as he spiralled down and away from her, pitying him but no longer hoping for his friendship. She mourned it instead.

Her pity only made him more vitriolic. As far as he was concerned, she didn't understand him or his world, the good girl from next door who'd never had a single thing go wrong. She showed him a shadow of the life he could have had, a reflection of what he might have been. She was technicolour, brave and bright because she had nothing to fear, because she didn't know the world. She hadn't lived.

He had lived too much and too quickly, in a monochrome of blood red.

But still, they watched each other.

His dad got sick in his last year of high school. Leo dropped out and took a job bussing tables to help cover the medical bills, but in the end there wasn't much point; it wasn't more than a month before he found himself on his own. She went to the funeral, the whole family did, but he didn't speak to her. He was coiled in on himself, a darker, hollowed version of himself that she found it hard to recognise. When she tried to meet his eyes he looked away, snatching his gaze from hers and blocking her out.

But he couldn't help himself from watching her when she wasn't looking, the colours drawing him in.

Her bedroom window overlooked the backyards of their neighbouring houses. More and more frequently he'd find himself out in the dark in the evening, smoking in the shade of the trees as she moved from her desk to her dressing table, from her dressing table to her bed, pulling the drapes across the glass to block out the night. It became a routine for him in the final months before she left for college: catching those last few glimpses of her shining through the darkness at the end of the day.

He felt like a creep for watching, but after the first accidental glimpse he started to establish a routine he found difficult to break. The more he watched, the less invasive it seemed, and the more acceptable it became to him. After all, it wasn't as though he was some stranger breathing up against her windows. He was looking out for her. He cared about her. And, once upon a time, they'd meant something to one another.

Some days he could even fool himself into believing that she knew he was there. The way she paused in front of the window, her fingers trailing across the glass as she looked up at the moon. It felt posed, like she was putting on a performance just for him. Other days, he just hated himself for hovering on the fringes of her life.

By now, he knew that he was the one who was broken, and that surrounding himself with other broken people would never make him any less so. He might seem less broken by comparison, but they couldn't fix him. They couldn't make him whole. On the other hand, he couldn't break them, either. Not like he'd break her.

Now that she was leaving, he knew what she had been to him: she wasn't a shadow of opportunities lost; she was a light of hope. Regardless of his misfortunes, she was the life he could have. She had never turned him away. He had been the one to push her out, when he should have held on.

He knew all of this, but he also knew that he was still broken. How could he make himself good enough for her? What right had he to infect her with that misery, to ask her to take him on with the darkness he trailed in his wake?

Then she was gone, and he was too scared to follow.

'You're home!'

Her mom gathered her up into a rib-crushing hug that took her breath away. It was surprisingly forceful for such a small, soft woman.

'Mom,' she gasped, 'calm down. It's only been a couple of months.'

'You look thin. Have you been eating right?' her mom took her hands, concern lighting her expression for a moment, then turned and shouted up the stairs behind her. 'John! She's home! Come help with the bags!'

There was a grunt of acknowledgement from upstairs, but her father didn't appear.

'John!' her mom shouted again.

'Mom, it's okay, I can carry my own…'

'John! Your only daughter comes home after months away and you don't even have time to come say hello?'

'For god's sake, Helen,' his rumbling baritone sounded distant. 'Give a man a moment of privacy, will you? I'll be down when I'm done.'

'I'll take the bags up,' she said.

'Oh no,' her mom insisted, 'you leave them right there and your father will see to them. Now come on out back. Your Aunt Louise is here with your cousins.'

She stifled a groan, badly. After hours on the road, that was the last thing she wanted to deal with.

'I know,' her mom said.

'How can you expect me to talk to Taylor after what she did to Rosa? And all Dee wants to do is talk about her boyfriend. It's just boring.'

'I know, but they're family. And anyway,' she added in a whisper, 'Taylor got fat.'

'She did?'

'Come see. Best behaviour, now.'

It was still boring. She smiled and nodded for twenty minutes straight while Dee told her all about the college courses she and her boyfriend were taking, how clever her boyfriend was, how popular, how athletic, how handsome. She was about ready to slap the smug smile off her face when her dad came to join them.

'Fresh lemonade, anyone?' he said, putting the tray down on the patio table. He was a short man who had been athletic in his day, but his waistband had run up the white flag some years ago, followed shortly by his hairline.

'Hey, cookie,' he said.

'Hey, dad. Did you remember the sugar this time?'

'Of course,' he replied, but he looked a little unsure. 'How's college?'

'Fine,' she said as he pulled her into a hug. 'How's work?'

'Fine.'

'Good.'

There was a pause.

'So we're all caught up.'

'Looks like.'

She smiled at her father. He smiled back before walking over to the side of the terrace to get the grill going. Apparently she was getting a welcome home cook out.

The temperature was finally starting to drop as the afternoon segued into the evening, but it was still hot enough that the lemonade was welcome, and her dad had remembered to sweeten it after all. Her mom was talking to her while the steaks grilled, catching her up on all the local news, but she couldn't stop her eyes from straying over the fence. It didn't go unnoticed.

'He's been away,' her mom said, following her gaze.

'Huh?' she said.

'Leo. He's been away visiting that sister of his in Charleston. You know.'

'Oh.'

It wasn't that she'd been hoping to see him while she was home, it was just that, well, she'd been expecting to. That was all.

'How is he?' she asked, casually.

Her mom shrugged.

'Never see the boy. He's always out of the house or shut away in there in the dark. Very quiet, that child. Keeps to himself, since his father passed.'

She wished her mom had more news, some reason to keep talking about him, even though it hurt. It had been half her lifetime ago since that day in the woods, but it still hurt. She couldn't put her finger on why. Maybe it was because she'd been humiliated by him, or maybe because it had made her feel worthless, a betrayal by someone she had thought of as her best friend in the world. Maybe it was simply because she missed him.

But, unwilling though she was, she let the conversation move on to other friends and news. After all, there was nothing else to say.

He got back from his shift late and angry. His boss's attitude was that he should be grateful to have a job at all after skipping town to go see Jenny, and the guy had made his day as awful as possible to teach him a lesson. Leo thought it was a stupid way to get him to appreciate his crappy lot in life. He hadn't been happy about Leo wearing the shades either, convinced that his excuse of 'conjunctivitis' was just a euphemism for 'hangover'.

But anyway, it didn't matter now. Everything had changed. He'd changed. Now, for the first time in his life, he felt powerful. Just a couple more weeks, and he'd be out of here.

He walked straight through the house and out of the back door, grabbing a beer from the otherwise empty fridge on his way. Not long, he thought.

He sat down in the chair on the scraggly lawn, dry and untended, and swigged from the bottle as he stretched his long legs out in front of him to catch the evening sun.

Then he heard it.

That lilting voice, the gentle cadences singing through the still air. It was a voice he recognised, one he'd heard countless times before, but not with these ears. Now the tones were magical in their purity, tinkling into place with a musical clarity that had him holding his breath, waiting in silence for the next note.

She was here. She was home.

Was he good enough for her now, he wondered, now that he had changed himself?

He pushed himself up and out of the chair, silently creeping towards the tall, wooden fence that separated the two properties. There was a gap in the slats, just a sliver of space wide enough to see a narrow column of next door's yard. He put his eye to it, squinting against the setting sun, and looked for her.

She was here. Her blonde hair blew loosely around her bare shoulders in the breeze, the neckline of her sleeveless top cut modestly high to balance the shortness of her skirt. She was golden, glowing in the warm light of the evening as it hit her limbs. He almost imagined he could smell the salt on her skin from the heat of the day, together with a scent that was indefinably hers, a scent he had learned to recognise through years of stomping around the fields with her at his side.

Pressure filled his body and spread out through him, blossoming hotly across his skin and fizzing through his eyeballs with an electric sensation. It was unlike anything he'd ever felt before, and he didn't understand it, but with it came an uncontrollable desire that he couldn't deny. He knew exactly what he had to do, with perfect clarity.

There was a rush of air, a crash of breaking glass, and in a second she found herself gasping for breath in a dark room. She was pressed up against a wall by the warmth of a body and, as she registered the proximity, she started to panic.

'It's me,' he said quickly.

She raised her hands to the bulk in front of her and pushed a little. He moved away, letting her sway his body backwards, and she realised she wasn't trapped.

'Leo?'

'Yes. It's me.'

His voice was deeper. She'd watched his face change as he'd grown, the jaw and cheekbones squaring out, the softness leaving his eyes. But his voice… It had a richness to it, a deep rumble that hadn't been there when they'd spoken last.

'What just happened?' she asked.

Her breath was still coming fast and uneven, and she was feeling dizzy from the…whatever it had been.

'I didn't mean to scare you,' he whispered. 'I'm sorry.'

'Where are we?'

'At my dad's house.' He paused. 'My house.'

She looked around and, in the scant daylight creeping through the gaps in the drapes, she recognised the shapes of the old furniture around them. There was the big dining table they used to hide under as kids, the wooden coffee table still marked by their crayons, and the shelving against the wall creaking under the weight of a new TV.

'How did I get here?' she asked.

'I brought you. Carried you.'

'What? How?'

'It's sort of a long story.'

He leaned away from her to let the light reach her face, then followed the lines of her features with his eyes, tracing the curve of her eyebrows and the bow of her mouth. His gaze fixed on it, on those lips he had watched so many times as they set with determination or pursed with concentration. He started to reach out his hand towards her, to touch her face and feel her skin on his fingertips, but he stopped himself and prised his eyes back up to hers.

'Leo?' she said as she took his raised hand in her own. 'What's wrong?'

He looked different. That harsh veneer he'd worn since his teenage years was gone, replaced with something vulnerable and fragile. He looked like a little boy, but not the one from their childhood. That one had been bossy and confident, oblivious of other people's opinions, particularly hers. And there was something up with his eyes, something shining there like a circle of light around his pupils.

He looked away.

When they spoke again, they did so at the same time:

'What's wrong with your eyes?' she asked.

'I think I'm in love with you,' he said.

There was silence for a moment.

'What?' she asked.

'I'm in love with you,' he repeated, turning back to face her.

Her heart flipped in her chest.

He searched her face, waiting for her to say something, looking for any hint of her own feelings. But her expression was frozen, her mouth open in surprise.

She stared at him.

After so many years apart, she couldn't believe what she was hearing.

'You don't know me anymore,' she said numbly.

He shook his head.

'That's not true. I know you better than I know anyone.'

She couldn't believe it. It was surreal, like someone had jumped her to a parallel universe where his mom hadn't died, where he'd never shut her out, where they'd been childhood sweethearts and lived happily ever after. But that hadn't been their lives. There was a gaping hole in them, a chasm that their shared happiness should have filled. They'd lost track of each other. You couldn't come back from that, she thought. Could you?

'People don't stay the same,' she said quietly. 'You changed. I changed.'

He shook his head again, more forcefully this time, as though trying to dislodge the words from his brain.

'Not that much,' he said. 'Not enough to change this.'

He gestured between them, describing a bond, a thread between their hearts. To him, it was so real he could feel its pull, feel it tugging him closer to her with every breath.

'How do you know?' she asked. 'We haven't even spoken in years.'

'Maybe not,' he conceded, 'but I didn't stop thinking about you. We were still together, even though we were apart. Weren't we?'

But he sounded uncertain, as though his conviction had been shaken. Doubt and confusion crossed his face, and it occurred to her that this meeting today wasn't something he had planned. It had just happened. And despite all the time that had passed, she realised that she wanted it to be real.

She wanted to believe him. She wanted to be special, to be adored. She wanted to erase the agonising indignities of the past by explaining them away like this: he loved her, so he'd behaved like an idiot. He'd only shunned her to make her jealous, make her feel his absence, because at the root of it all he was crazy about her.

That was a line she could sell herself. That way, she came out on top and her pride was preserved. She'd like to think of herself as the kind of girl that could drive a boy like him crazy.

More than that, she wanted to buy into the story that they

were meant for each other, soul mates separated by the cruelty of circumstance and tragedy. Star-crossed lovers. There was something so romantic about it all.

But the wrongness of the situation itched under her skin.

She wondered what he'd been taking, whether this whole performance was a result of some drug spinning him out. She had too many questions, too many suspicions pushing the feelings away. Until she knew what was going on, she wasn't going to expose herself to ridicule by talking about her own emotions. If this was all just some joke, then the humiliation didn't bear thinking about.

She shuddered.

'Are you going to explain this to me?' she asked. 'How did I get here? What's with your eyes? And where do you get off telling me you love me after ignoring me for a decade?'

So he sat her on the couch, and he told her.

'You promise you'll hear me out?' he asked. 'You promise you won't freak out.'

She eyed him cautiously.

'Okay,' she said.

'Okay.'

He took a deep breath and let it out slowly.

'So,' he said, 'I went to visit Jenny.'

'Yes…'

'Well, so, this thing happened, and I met this guy who she didn't know, but her husband does, and…' He paused and pushed his hair back from his face in exasperation. 'I'm telling this wrong,' he said.

It struck her that she could recognise a lot of the boyhood Leo in his mannerisms. With her trailing him around all the time as a kid, she'd seen him exasperated frequently in the past. His gestures and expressions were still the same to her, still such a familiar part of him.

'Start at the beginning,' she prompted.

'We were in a bar,' he said, closing his eyes briefly as though he were picturing the scene. 'I know I shouldn't have been, being underage and all, but there was a barman there. He's maybe five years older than us, I guess, and he was a real good looking guy. Had this brooding thing going on, all dark hair and tattoos, and all the girls were hot for him. But it turns out that he's friends with Matt, Jenny's guy, and so he gives me a pass for the night. Then after the place closes up, he invites us back to this party. Now, Matt doesn't want to come because he's got Jenny to worry about at home, but he and this barman guy are real chummy and the barman, his name's Alex, he says I can stay over at the party house so Matt's not to worry about me, and he'll bring me home the next day. So I go off with him ready to party like crazy.

'Then things get a bit, well, fuzzy. I remember getting to the place, this massive plantation house with these huge grounds, and a pool, and people everywhere having a great time. There must have been hundreds of them: girls wandering around in bikinis, guys with kegs and board shorts, then people in formal wear and stuff. It was like a very weird dream.

'So, yeah, we joined in. We had some beers and then pretty soon I was alone talking to this guy in what looked like a library. And I'm telling you, he was scary. He had this look in his eye like you were nothing to him, like he was playing nice with you for the moment but he could get bored of you any time and then just, I don't know, whatever.'

He leaned forward in his seat and rested his elbows on his knees, his forehead in his hands.

'And this is where you have to stay with me, okay?'

He lifted his face and looked at her, meeting her eyes.

'Okay,' she said uncertainly.

'It's going to sound crazy, but you stay with me?'

'Okay, Leo. I said okay.'

He took another deep breath.

'He told me about the Silver,' he said.

'The what?'

'The Silver. They're sort of, and don't freak out, they're sort of vampires.'

'Vampires?' she asked incredulously. What had he been taking, she wondered?

'Sort of. They're not what you think, though. They're strong, and fast, and indestructible, but they don't mind the sun, or garlic, or silver. Actually, it's like they've got silver in their blood, and you can see it in the blood vessels in their eyes.'

'You're one of them,' she said immediately, watching his shining eyes and knowing it for a certainty.

'Yes,' he said. 'It's how I got you here so fast. Pretty cool, right?'

'You kill people?' she asked, an edge of fear creeping into her voice.

'God no,' he said, horrified. 'No. We don't need to do that. I don't need to do that. I mean, some people do, but you can control it, and you don't have to. I don't have to. I haven't even bitten anyone. Not ever.'

She looked at him, her eyes tracing his features and trying to mark the changes his new state had made. He looked harder, more angular, but she wasn't sure whether that was just because he was older now than he had been the last time they were this close.

'So you're practically indestructible?' she asked.

'Practically. But there's this thing that happens when the Silver fall in love. They call it 'silvering'. It's like a life-link thing that means the death of the person we love will kill us, but it also means we can heal our lover if they're injured. You can see when someone silvers because you get silver bits in the irises, not just the whites of the eyes. And there's more to it: if the person we love loves us back, the silver turns gold.'

Something changed in the air and she felt the silent question hanging between them. She had to admit there was a connection that was almost palpable, but she still wasn't quite ready to take him seriously, despite the evidence to support his words.

'So what happened next?' she asked.

'Not sure,' he said. 'I think I passed out, then there was pain. A lot of pain. Pain like I've never experienced before in my life. Then I woke up and everything was different, and I was like this.'

'And me?' she asked inelegantly, needing to know whether what she was seeing in his eyes was real.

He looked away for a second before he found her face again.

'This evening, when I saw you out back, I silvered for you. I could feel it, and you can see it, can't you, in my irises? I think I've always loved you,' he said quietly. 'I just never thought, you know, with everything that happened… Well, I thought, now, with this, that maybe I might be good enough.'

And she saw that, at some point in the story, the magic had taken over. She could see the silver in his eyes, but it was now tinged with yellow, golden in the dimming light.

So she loved him too, she thought.

She thought briefly about her family, thought she should tell them she was okay, but somehow she couldn't bring herself to leave him. After all, who was she to argue with this kind of predestination? Magic had picked her a man, a superhuman man, and here he was. It was just like the fairytale she'd always wished for. Well, a darker fairytale than she might have imagined, but a fairytale nonetheless.

And she got to be the princess, for once.

She'd never had a boyfriend before. It wasn't that she couldn't have had one if she'd wanted, it's just that no one had asked her and her pride wouldn't let her look for herself. She'd kissed a few boys, but it had meant nothing, so when Leo reached forward to take her cheek in his hand, she wasn't quite sure what to expect. She certainly hadn't expected the intense electric thrill that coursed through her when his lips brushed against hers.

She felt as though she were being cocooned with warmth and perfume, sunshine wrapping around her and warming the bare skin of her legs and arms in the cool, dark room.

'Leo,' she whispered against his mouth.

'I love you,' he whispered back, then he pulled her body close against his and kissed her.

His lips moved desperately, pressing his mouth to hers as though he couldn't get enough of her taste, as though he were trying to compensate for the years they'd lost. She was swept away by him, her head spinning from the raw exhilaration he elicited with his touch. His fingers were trailing over her naked legs, raising chills of excitement across her skin, exploring further and further until he was tickling the sensitive skin of her inner thigh.

She hadn't known it before that day, but it was definitely a sweet spot for her. Her head dropped back against the headrest of the couch as she lost herself in the heady sensation, the kisses forgotten as his touch took precedence.

He saw her reaction and moved smoothly to his knees on the floor in front of her, replacing his hand with his mouth as he kissed his way along the inside of her thigh. He licked the skin, conscious every second of the artery pulsing there beneath his mouth. She writhed, her hips kicking to the side as her muscles clenched. Encouraged, he nibbled a little at the tender flesh.

She moaned. She'd never moaned like that before in her life, but she couldn't help it. The noise escaped from her lips before she could stop it, but she didn't have time to get embarrassed about it. Responding with his own groan of pleasure, Leo took hold of her hips and bit harder, his teeth slightly piercing the delicate skin.

She screamed.

But it was a good scream.

Nonetheless, he pulled his face away and raised his eyes to hers.

'Is this okay?' he asked, pretty sure it was rude to drink a girl's blood without her permission. Particularly when the girl in question was the girl he loved.

'Are you kidding me?' she gasped. 'Don't stop!'

He'd been struggling to keep his teeth out of her since the moment he'd brought her back to the house, so there was no hesitation. In a second, he felt the blood flowing over his tongue, the rich, floral scent of her flooding into him, and he groaned again, sucking harder to draw out the rush of warmth. He was lost to the sensation, to the thrill and the intensity of the deed, his head spinning as he suckled at her skin.

He lifted his head and licked his lips, the smell of blood and excitement on the air. Then he saw her face, her head drooping forward onto her chest and hanging limply from her neck.

She wasn't breathing.

'No,' he murmured, rising from the floor and taking her

by the shoulders. 'No. Wake up! Come on. Come on.'

Panic dropped a weight into his stomach. He pressed his fingers to her neck and tried to find a pulse. There was a single, weak thud. The empty seconds stretched out, but her heart didn't thud again.

'No!' he yelled. 'I'm not losing you. You can't go.'

He grabbed the hem of her T-shirt and ripped it up from the bottom, pulling it open as he laid her body down sideways on the couch. Then, acting on instinct rather than knowledge, he sat down next to her and pressed his palm flat to her stomach as his other hand probed again for the pulse in her neck. The sensation shot through him, a crashing energy that discharged through the point where he touched the exposed skin of her stomach.

She didn't move.

He tried again, lifting his hand before pressing the palm down again on her skin, more firmly this time. But there was no energy, no connection to make.

She was gone, taking the bond with her.

And that bond isn't just in the eyes of the Silver. It wraps around the heart, a fist with thousands of fingers woven through the flesh, ready to squeeze and crush and clamp into an intractable bundle of metallic threads. When one thread is pulled, it doesn't unravel. It just tightens the knot, strangling the life within.

The death of one means the death of both.

'Cara,' he whispered.

The fist clenched.

The two Silver stood outside the front door and knocked. When there was no answer, the man knocked again before forcing the lock.

'Leo?' he called into the dark house. 'It's Al and Jessamy.

You missed your pick up.'

'Jesus Christ,' Sam said as she followed him inside, 'what the fuck have you been doing in here, Leo? Smells like something fucking died.'

They turned the corner into the lounge and took in the scene.

The blood.

The bodies.

'Fuck,' Sam said as she pulled a phone out of her pocket. 'Is he fucking dead? How is he fucking dead? Aw, fuck, we're going to have to scrub this shit.'

Al stepped closer to the couch, prodding the inert boy to roll him over onto his back.

'Look.'

He pointed at the silver handprint glimmering on the girl's stomach, the mark of the healing power Leo had used in his attempt to save her. If the humans saw that, then how were the Silver supposed to keep themselves in the shadows? Some of them were going to be seriously displeased.

'Jesus fuck!' Sam yelled. 'What the fuck do we do now?'

'Well you could start by keeping your voice down. Give me that phone. I'll call it in. You sweep the house.'

Al was still talking to the man himself when Sam came back into the room carrying a laptop computer.

'You've got to look at this shit,' she said, opening the screen and putting it down on the dining table. 'Leo was one sick fuck. There's a fucking camera out back, and he's been taping this girl for fucking years. And for some reason she fucking loved the creep, like some Stockholm Syndrome fuck.'

'Yessir,' Al said into the phone, waving Sam down to get her to shut up. 'Sir?'

He took the handset from his ear and covered the

microphone with his finger before turning to her.

'Sam, you shut your foul mouth. Get the camera, get the laptop, and get the bodies. We're out of here. He's got a plan.' He smiled, his eyes twinkling with excitement, and she knew the day they'd been waiting for had finally arrived.

'It's time?' she asked.

A grin split his lips open, baring his teeth in an evil smirk.

'We've got a plan.'

This is how the start ended: with love, and with death. For one race it was a battle cry, for another a requiem. For both it brought the world to its knees and set the Revelation in motion.

But still, it was only the start.

BELLA DONNA

I THINK I loved him. I knew he didn't love me, but there was something there, and it was enough to make me hope that it might grow into something more meaningful for him too.

He lied to me about it, though, told me it was special. Well, I think we lied to each other, really. But it had to be special, because otherwise what was the point? What were we doing with each other if it meant nothing? There was a desperation there, I guess. Maybe that was what we had in common, at the end of the day.

We were lonely.

We were bored.

We wanted to feel something, so fiercely that we convinced ourselves we'd found it in each other. At least, that's what I think it was all about for me. He had other reasons to push us together, reasons I didn't know about at the time.

To me it was like we were teenagers, with all the drama and excitement that comes along with it. It was like a drug, and I couldn't give it up. I'm not sure how much it actually had to do with him, to tell the truth. I just wanted to feel that intensity of emotion.

Hormones, isn't it? Addictive chemistry.

I always had a bit of an addictive personality. I love the adrenaline, the rollercoaster, the fall, the knife, the needle, the speed and the thump of the beat in my chest. I love the rush that rolls your eyes back in your skull the second before the pain hits, the second after flesh slams into flesh, and the second before you topple over the edge and drop.

It's magic.

But most of the time life just isn't like that. It's dull, predictable and meaningless, and I fucking hate it. If it's a choice between boredom and risking the pain, I'd take the pain every day. Hell, I'd probably take it even if it were guaranteed, just to keep things interesting.

So I tend to put myself out there a lot. I wear my heart on my sleeve, and I get crushed, but I'd rather be crying over loves lost than sitting around like a fucking zombie. And, you know, practice makes perfect. Every time I get my heart broken it seems to get stuck back together a bit stronger.

That's what I tell myself, anyway, but maybe I'm just getting numbed to it through exposure. Maybe I need a bigger high.

I'm not sure anything's ever going to top him for that.

He isn't like me. The first few months I knew him it was like he was slowly coiling further and further in on himself, like he was shutting everything out. That should have given me a clue, but I'm not so smart when I get a plan in my head, and for some reason he became the plan.

Well, like I said: I was bored. But let me start at the beginning.

He started it, of course.

She opened the fridge door and stared at the shelves for a few seconds before pulling out each of the drawers in turn and rifling through their contents.

'You got any beer?' she asked, looking over her shoulder at the young man seated at the kitchen table on the other side of the countertop. He inclined his head towards the door leading to the garage. It was on the other side of the kitchen-diner, next to the door that led into the small lounge.

The layout of the house was a bit kooky, but not in a deliberate, designed fashion. The floors were all at different levels, connected by a step or two here and there, and the rooms were all oddly shaped, the product of multiple ill-planned extensions over the years. It made furnishing a bit of a nightmare, but the structure had a lot of character in a town that was mostly full of new-build, cookie-cutter houses.

She slammed the fridge closed and made her way across the room. He discreetly watched her every movement, tracing her progress with his gaze.

'I like this place,' she said. 'It's not what I would have expected from you.'

He feigned distraction, flicking his eyes down to the papers spread across the table in front of him and pretending to read.

'Hmm?'

'You know,' she continued as she opened the garage door. 'It's cosy. It feels like a family home or something, not a bachelor pad. I mean, it's just you here, right? Other than the gardener, of course.'

'Mm hmm,' he replied, his attention fixed on the page he wasn't reading as he tried to control his nausea.

'See, it's just not very you.'

There was an electric clicking sound as the fluorescent lights in the garage flickered into life, and then he lost sight of her as she crossed the space to reach the second fridge-freezer. He heard her boots clopping away from him on the poured concrete floor, but he waited until he heard the seal of the fridge door releasing before he tried to move.

The ropes were cutting into his wrists even without his applying any pressure. There was no give in them at all. His arms were looped through the struts on the back of the chair, so he couldn't move without taking it with him. No time for that yet, he thought. So instead he started to rub his bound wrists along the chair back, searching for the protruding nail or shard of wood that he knew wasn't there. After all, it was one of his own kitchen chairs, and he couldn't recall there being any sharp edges. He took pride in his home, and he wouldn't have tolerated them. But still, futile though it was, he had to try something.

There was a clink from the garage, followed by the muffled thud of the fridge door closing, and then those footsteps were clomping back towards him. The sound of the first few paces was slightly different this time: a tacky, viscous noise following each heel strike as her feet peeled away from the floor.

He grimaced to himself.

Time's up.

Sticky footprints marked her path across the oak floorboards as she walked back to the counter. She set a line of bottles on the side and twisted the top off one, swigging from it noisily as she pushed her long, blonde hair back from her face and over her shoulder. It flowed down her back and brushed the curve of her backside, swishing gently from side to side as she tipped her head back to drink, pushing her chest forward and exposing her neck.

He lowered his head and looked up under his brows surreptitiously, his eyes raking her body. Her arms were bare and the satin of her thin-strapped top draped loosely across her breasts, dipping tantalisingly between them. He didn't have to work very hard to imagine her naked, her jeans so tight he could see every curve of her hips. An involuntary thrill rushed straight to his shorts.

He hated her, was terrified of her (much though it hurt his pride to admit it), but dear god did he want to fuck her.

This evening was not going the way he had planned it. Not even a little bit.

He screwed his eyes shut and exhaled heavily through his nose.

'So,' she said, leaning back against the counter.

So, where to start, where to start…?

Okay.

Now, we're not talking that long ago, here. Maybe January? Not long ago at all, really.

I've got this crappy job I took at the university doing crappy office admin at this crappy research building where all the scientists look down their noses at me because I don't know science or any of that crap. I'm not stupid or anything, and I can organise an office like a demon, but I'm just not a genius. And I'm mostly doing okay, and the money's not awful, but I keep getting in shit for messing up tiny things that wouldn't matter in any other lab. They're hyper-sensitive about security, so every time I forget to shut a door or step away from the front desk for a second without getting cover, there's a drama about it.

So, there's this one professor, and he's actually nice to me most of the time and seems like he's a human being. We've become sort of friends, even though he's ancient, because he helped me out when the office manager was yelling at me for some imagined failing of mine. But anyway, one day he brought in a new research student.

This guy walks in the door, and he looks like a fucking

movie star. I mean: sandy-blond hair, square jaw, bright blue eyes, chiselled abs, the whole deal. Seriously, I had to press my lips together to stop myself from drooling at him.

Then he opens his mouth and there's the accent too. God knows where it comes from, but it must be European because it has a sort of Italian lilt to it.

She put one empty beer bottle on the countertop and hopped up next to it, so she sat facing him with her legs dangling against the kitchen cupboards below. Her heels left dirty, red smears on the varnished doors as she kicked her feet gently back and forth, thudding softly onto the wood. She screwed the cap off a second bottle and swigged from it noisily.

'So, yeah,' she said. 'It was pretty much like when you saw me, right?'

She laughed callously; a sharp, barking sound of pure disdain. He could feel his cheeks heating up under the pressure of the gag, but he wasn't sure whether it was from anger or embarrassment.

She had him bang to rights.

Dollar signs had lit up behind his eyes when she'd walked into his office that morning. He'd clocked the understated but well-made clothes, the massive handbag, the impractical shoes and, most of all, her youth. She looked like she was barely out of her teens, and he didn't get many kids looking for property in the price ranges he offered. He tried to keep up with celebrity in his line of work in this part of town, because a failure to recognise often caused offence that could lose him a sale, but he hadn't recognised her. Was she a new internet sensation, he'd wondered, or maybe a trust fund kid, or a sugar daddy's prize? Maybe, he'd thought as he'd followed the line of her necklace down into her cleavage, she was a really successful porn star.

But then, of course, he'd have recognised her.

She'd been on the phone as she was ushered towards his desk, her voice cutting sharply across the open plan space. He'd stood to greet her, but had been met with an imperious finger to indicate that he should wait. She had been wearing sunglasses, but he could see from the light glinting behind them that she hadn't even looked at him.

He'd taken the opportunity to look at every inch of her. In detail.

The telephone conversation had been a couple of minutes long, the content businesslike and apparently focused on property specifications, as though she had been taking instructions.

Maybe a billionaire's PA, he'd thought, but it still didn't fit. Her attitude was entitled rather than subservient.

When she'd eventually finished on the phone and acknowledged his presence, he'd shown her a few places. She was looking for something multipurpose and of a considerable size: living space, office space and party space all in one complex. She'd been particular and critical about virtual irrelevancies, and he was left with the distinct impression that she didn't know what she was doing, but that might just have been because she'd turned down all the properties he'd shown her for one reason or another.

He would have been more irritated if she hadn't been so hot, but as it was he'd decided to cut his losses and just enjoy the ride, so at the end of a fruitless day viewing incredible realty he'd asked her back to his for a drink. He knew he was a fairly good-looking man, and he worked out to keep his body in top shape. In reality, he was a lot older than her and looked it, but he was arrogant enough that he hadn't been as surprised as he should have been when she'd accepted.

In his case, pride was definitely going before a fall, and a big one at that.

They'd stopped off on the way at a bar. He'd told her he was going to order a martini, expecting her to follow suit, but she'd asked for a beer instead. Not from him, either; she'd ignored him completely and sashayed up to the bar, propping her elbows on its edge and jutting out her hip as she flirted with the barman.

He wasn't used to being made to feel invisible.

There was something about it, that complete indifference, that had riled something in him. It wasn't anger. It had been a challenge issued and accepted, and he'd relished every second of the competition, the dance.

He'd thought he was finally winning when she'd agreed to come back to his place, but the moment they'd walked in the door her demeanour had changed. Initially, the disdain had seemed contrived, a deliberate attempt to engage his interest, but as soon as the front door had opened to her the illusion retreated. The sunglasses came off and he saw the silver filaments threading through the whites of her eyes.

It took her seconds to incapacitate him, to tie him to his own furniture. After that there had been noises, a scuffle and a gurgle from the garage before she'd shut the door behind her and joined him in the kitchen, delicately wiping the corners of her mouth. Then he'd remembered that today was the day the gardener came.

He didn't know what she was, but he didn't think he'd be getting laid tonight. Not in a way that he'd enjoy, anyway.

'He wasn't like you,' she said. 'He was… What's the word I'm looking for? Shiny, I guess. He was sort of radiant, like there was something extra in him that you could see from the outside. Of course, he was hiding it then. Trying to manoeuvre himself so he had everything he wanted.'

Her face changed, twisting into a shape that was harsh and sharp. Quicker than he could follow, she raised the half-full beer bottle above her head and smashed it down forcefully onto the tiled kitchen floor, shattering it into a blossoming cloud of slick glass shards that detonated outwards. They cut through the cloth of his thousand-dollar suit, slicing through the silk-blend to embed themselves into his shins and calves. He cried out plaintively into the tea towel gagging him.

'That didn't include me, of course,' she sneered bitterly. 'He didn't want me, in the end.'

Her gaze flickered quickly to him, to the liquid that was dripping down his legs. He couldn't tell whether it was beer or blood, and he didn't want to look and see the scale of the damage. He could feel the pieces sticking into his skin, stretching the flesh open and making it gape.

He moaned as the shivers of the scratching, twisting pain rippled up his legs.

'Oh, stop whining,' she muttered as she picked up the next beer bottle in the line and broke its top off on the side of the counter. As the jagged edge touched her lips it drew blood, a red line that ran down her chin and dripped onto the ivory satin of her top. She caught his eye and, making sure she had his attention, wiped her chin with her index finger then sucked it into her mouth, her eyes fixed on his as she drew it back out clean.

She licked her lips.

He groaned. He was hard again.

She laughed that horrible laugh of hers.

'You wouldn't last ten seconds with me,' she said. 'See for you, everything's about the superficial. You want to possess things, but only for what they say about you, not because you actually want them. You're all about the car, the house, the watch, the fucking. Nothing's actually meaningful. You don't know what it is to want something to be yours forever, so much that it sticks and twists in your blood and your flesh.'

There was a pause as she drank again, staring through him as she licked away the blood once more to reveal clear, unbroken skin beneath.

'Forever's a long time for me. I don't know. Maybe I'm just being naïve. Maybe I don't really understand what it means yet, but I really did think we'd be together forever, me and him.'

She drained the beer and threw the bottle casually over her shoulder, where it shattered against the wall behind her. Was she drunk? He thought she probably should be given the amount of beer she'd had before they'd even left the bar.

He just had to wait. Wait until she passed out, or was drunk enough for the alcohol to slow her down a bit.

'Apparently that was just me, though,' she added quietly.

He made it easy for me to fall for him. Deliberately, of course. All's fair in love and war, and all that. I suppose this is a war, for them. Well, us.

So, anyway, after that first time, he was in the lab a lot. I saw him maybe three or four days a week for the next couple of months. He worked long and late, and because this place is a secure facility they like to have someone in the admin office the whole time the lab's open. We do it in shifts, but mostly I used to try to take the day shift. Suddenly I found I didn't mind so much covering the odd evening here and there when the others were busy, or had things planned. I haven't got that many friends round here honestly, not since I came back from college, so I didn't have much to do with my Friday nights and weekends anyway. As it turned out, I didn't mind spending them with him.

Well, in a manner of speaking anyway. Yes, I was working in the office, and he was working in the lab, but they have to come out to use the kitchen and the bathroom, and obviously the lab is accessed through the office part of the building, so I got to see him a fair amount.

Now that I think about it I know that sounds a little crazy, but it really didn't seem that way at the time. It's not like I was stalking him. It's not like I was watching him from behind the water cooler or anything, I mean he stopped to talk to me every time. And not just for a few seconds and a hello, I mean we talked. We talked about The Big Questions, you know? We talked about life and love and what it means to be human.

Ironic, really, when I look back.

But it felt real, every second of it, and that's always what I'm looking for. I got the sense that he was as bored and trapped as me, and that he was looking for some kind of release from that.

We never talked about his work. I assumed it was because he felt that our time together was a break from it. That should have rung alarm bells, given how much time he devoted to working, how consumed by it he was. His reluctance to discuss it makes more sense now in retrospect. Everything does.

To him, manipulating me was part of the mission, part of the job. He distracted me, and I let him break in and take it all.

He started asking me if I wanted him to pick up lunch or dinner for me. Then he started asking if I wanted to join him to go pick up food and bring it back to the office. Finally, he started just asking me to go out to eat with him. As it turned out, his place was pretty close by and, well, one thing led to another.

At work, I stopped paying attention when it was just the two of us in the building. If I was working late, sometimes I'd step out for an hour or so and leave him there. I trusted him, and he took advantage of that in so many ways.

What's shocking about it is that no one noticed. I only know about it because he told me, after he'd already done this to me, after it was already too late for me to object. He knew I would have been sacked if I'd told anyone about the security breaches on my watch, but he didn't think that was enough. He wanted much more effective leverage over me, so he engineered it.

He made me one of them. He put me on the other side of this fight. It's not about who you are, or what you believe, it's about what you are. And he made me into one of them, turned me into this. He made me a defector, because I have no other choice now but to join them.

'Can you imagine what that feels like?' she asked.

She grabbed another beer and cracked it open. He'd lost count of them by now, but she was showing no sign of slowing down. More worryingly, she was showing no overt signs of inebriation either. There was plenty of emotion, but he was beginning to think that was all she was feeling.

'I don't mean the whole transformation thing, because you're going to get to experience that first hand. Well, you know, that's why you're here after all.'

His stomach dropped.

She had a purpose for him.

There was no getting out of this. He thought tying him up might have been fallout from the break-up from hell. He'd been quietly praying that it was some kind of kinky sex game. Otherwise, he'd thought that maybe it was a control thing and that he might have been able to slip away unnoticed when she went to collect more beer.

No such luck.

He was the focus here. She had her own mission, and apparently it involved doing to him whatever had been done to her. A transformation. It didn't sound promising, certainly not if her behaviour was anything to go by.

'I mean the gut-wrenching emotional pain,' she continued. 'To have someone you love do that to you, control you so lightly, without a thought for your feelings? And you know the worst thing about that, the thing that twists in my stomach, is the fact that he didn't think my loving him was enough to make me want to support him. I mean, this was a man I practically lived with. I would have done anything for him, would have broken all the rules for him, if he'd just asked. Hell, I would probably even have let him turn me into this, I might even have thought it was appealing, if it had meant being with him.

'But then, of course, that was never what he had wanted from me. After it happened, the change I mean, he took me back to this massive place in the middle of nowhere, and there were loads of them there. It was like the Playboy fucking mansion, only with guys too. Most of them were new like me, and most of them had stories like mine. We'd been played, turned and dumped there, waiting around until they needed us. Can you imagine that?'

Her tone was tense as she tightened her grip around the bottle in her hand until it collapsed, crushing the glass into her fist. Drops fell and pooled on the countertop into a pink puddle of beer and blood.

'No, of course you can't. You've never had a real emotion in your life, which is why you're just perfect to help me with this little experiment of mine. I mean,' she said, leaning forwards from her perch to lower her eyes to his level, 'you're not exactly going to be a loss to the world if this goes wrong, are you?'

His eyes widened, his gaze jumping erratically from her face to her bloody boots to the bloodstained glass dropping from her hand to the floor.

He didn't want to die. There were so many things he wanted to do. He was having trouble thinking of anything that didn't involve sex or money, but he knew there were things he hadn't done. He thought he was a good man. He'd never done anything actively evil. He didn't think he deserved to die.

He looked up at her pleadingly, silently begging her not to do whatever the hell she was going to do.

'Oh, relax. How hard can it be? Besides, I was betrayed by the man I love. I'm just a girl you want to fuck. It's not like you have anything to complain about here.'

He turned up there yesterday, you know, at the mansion. We've all been waiting there, waiting for something to happen, to be told what to do, and then yesterday they all came back.

I had to know, then. Despite the others, and despite everything that had happened since the days in the lab, I couldn't believe what we had wasn't real.

So I asked. I asked him if he'd ever loved me. But it turns out that's all I ever was to him: an access key and a soldier. The shithead made me feel like this about him then turned me into this... Whatever this is.

Maybe I should thank him. I don't know yet. Maybe it will have been worth it in the end.

I know it gets better, because it always does. I know that pain will go away, and one day I won't miss him. One day, I'll wake up in the morning and not think about him. I'll stop checking my phone for his calls and messages, stop checking the post box for letters, as if anyone even sends them anymore.

And I know it's for the best that it's over, I do. I know that it's pointless to pour your efforts into something that's never going to matter, and you can't pretend it does once you know the truth. No one's that delusional, not even me. It was a good thing, really, that things came out the way they did. I needed that push to get me off the hook, to stop me coming back for the next fix. I needed him to tell me how little I meant to him so I could move on. There's nothing like wounded pride to drive a wedge between people. One day he'll be no one to me, just another person I used to know.

So, you know, that should be some consolation.

One day.

One day I won't look back and wish I hadn't asked the question in the first place. If I hadn't pushed it, then maybe it wouldn't have mattered. Maybe it would have grown into something after all.

And not just for me.

'But, hey,' she said, sliding down from the countertop where she had been perched, 'enough about me, right?'

She ripped his shirt away from his neck and rubbed the skin with the bottom of her satin top, polishing it like an apple.

'Let's talk about you.'

Ciao Bella

BELLA LOOKED AT the chair-bound zombie and sighed.

He hadn't magically recovered overnight, then. Instead, he'd tipped over the chair to which he was tied and cut himself on the glass that littered the kitchen floor, so now there was blood everywhere too.

'You're a pain in the ass,' she said, kicking his chair. 'You know that, right?'

The zombie didn't reply. He didn't even groan. He just lay on the floor, tugging ineffectually at his bound wrists and ankles, and looked up at Bella with big, sad eyes.

'Don't give me that look,' she said, cracking open the last intact bottle of beer. 'Maybe if you'd made a little effort, we wouldn't be in this mess.'

He was supposed to be a vampire, of course, like her.

That had been the plan: take him to a bar, soften him up a little, then bring him back to his place and do the deed. The vampire-turning deed.

Apparently she hadn't softened him up enough, though, because here they were. She'd softened herself up plenty. They'd been drinking last night, and she'd got a little melancholy. When that happened she was liable to throw things, hence the glass. She felt like throwing things again now.

'I was right about you,' she said to the prostrate zombie, kicking the chair again. 'You never had a real emotion in your life. If you had, if you'd actually cared about me *at all*, then it would have worked, but you're all the same, aren't you? Fucking men.'

She kicked the chair one final time, a little too hard, and it splintered apart into so many pieces that the zombie began to free himself.

Bella rolled her eyes. 'You are *such* a pain in the ass.'

Then the doorbell rang.

Bella had a moment of sheer panic. This was the zombie guy's house. She wasn't supposed to be here. And it was seven in the morning. Who the hell went visiting at seven in the morning? People only rang other people's doorbells this early if it was bad news, or if they knew each other *really* well. Either would be unwelcome right now.

There was another ring, followed by a knock.

Only a short corridor separated the front door from the kitchen. If she answered the door with zombie guy shut in the kitchen and he stumbled out, or if whoever was at the door had a key and came inside looking for him…

'Shit,' Bella muttered, then she grabbed the zombie by his bound hands and dragged him across the kitchen floor to the side door that led into his garage. There was a beer fridge out there that she'd steadily emptied over the past twelve hours, and a chest freezer she'd filled with the gardener who'd rudely interrupted their party last night, and next to both of those appliances a sturdy tool rack was drilled into the wall. It looked strong enough to hold a rhino, and a quick tug confirmed that even Bella – with her superhuman strength – would have trouble shifting it.

Whoever was out front knocked again. They were

persistent, all right.

The tool rack would have to do. She found a coil of chain under a workbench and used it to secure the zombie to the wall.

'Don't move,' she hissed at him, then she stopped to rinse her bloody hands and arms in the sink before going to answer the damn door.

The man on the other side looked surprised to see her for a moment, then his eyes trailed inexorably down to her cleavage. True, she was wearing a satin top, and yes, it had got a little wet in the blood-rinsing process, but it was still pretty fucking rude to be staring at a stranger's assets at seven am without permission, particularly if you were a crusty old guy with thinning sandy hair and rheumy eyes.

'What?' Bella said, crossing her arms. It didn't help with the cleavage situation.

'You're a… um… You're a friend of Steve's, are you?' he said, licking his lips as his gaze fluttered between her face and her chest.

'Yes,' she said. Best not to elaborate.

'Well, I'm Randolph Carter the Third,' he said haughtily, as though that should mean something to her. 'I live over the way, and I couldn't help but notice that our gardener's truck is parked in the driveway there,' he said, pointing at a large green truck that was indeed parked in Zombie Guy's drive.

'Yeah?' Bella said.

'Thing is, sugar, Tuesday morning is my yard work slot. First one of the day. Always has been.'

'Okay, well, the gardener's not here.'

'He's not?' Randolph said, looking pointedly at the truck.

'No,' Bella insisted. 'He's not. I don't know why his truck's here, but he isn't.'

'Oh,' said Randolph, but he wasn't letting it go. 'Can I

speak with Steve?'

'Not right now,' Bella said. 'He's in the shower. Now, if you'll excuse me.'

'If you could tell him to come see me when he's—'

'Yeah, sure. Bye,' said Bella, then she slammed the door in his face.

She had bigger problems to deal with right now.

Back in the garage, the erstwhile Steve was hanging from the tool rack like a marionette.

It really wasn't fair. All Bella had wanted to do was turn one little human into a vampire. She told herself she'd just wanted to prove that she could do it, but the truth was that she'd wanted to prove it to *him*.

To Enzo.

He was the one who'd turned her, months ago now. She'd thought they were in love. The other vampires said that was a necessary factor, that you needed to make the human feel something for you to make them turn, and Enzo had certainly made Bella feel something for him. He hadn't done that just to turn her into a vampire though; he'd done it to get unfettered access to the lab where they'd both worked so he could steal a formula about which she'd rather not speculate. Turned out the place was run by vampires, and they'd been cooking up some very strange and valuable stuff, valuable enough to kill for. That's why Enzo had turned Bella into a vampire: to buy her silence afterwards, and so ensure his safety.

When she'd found out yesterday that he was not only in a relationship with someone else, but that he was actually gay, she'd had a slight meltdown.

Hence the broken bottles. Hence the broken Steve.

But she'd been careful about her own choice of test subject. She'd chosen Steve in particular because she'd thought he'd turn easily, a shallow kind of guy who cared about tits and ass and not much else. Easy to win over, easy to excite, or so she'd thought. Plus, Bella was playing to her strengths. She had tits and ass. She had *incredible* tits and ass.

But her choice had been about more than that. The truth was, she didn't want to be like Enzo. She didn't want to make someone feel genuine feelings for her just to use those feelings to turn them into a monster. She'd wanted to pick someone who'd deserve what they got. Maybe that was the problem: she'd picked someone so shallow they weren't capable of feeling anything at all.

The whole thing had been doomed from the start.

Or maybe not…

Maybe there was something at the lab that could salvage Steve.

By the time Bella got back to the house, Monty was already on the phone, stressing out as usual.

'Where are you?' he demanded, ever the bossy prick. He'd appointed himself as commander of the new vampires currently congregating in South Carolina, and he was always pulling this shit.

Well, Bella didn't answer to him. She didn't answer to anyone anymore.

'It's none of your business where I am,' she said, closing the front door behind her. She went straight to the garage, where she found Zombie Steve just as she'd left him.

'You don't know what you've got there, Bella,' Monty warned her. 'That vial you took from the lab is dangerous. If even a drop of it comes into contact with one of us, we'll go up in smoke.'

Bella scoffed down the phone at him. 'Nothing kills us.'

'What's in that vial will.'

'Then why did the doctor I stole it from say it was a cure?'

'Because she's using it to *make* a cure. For itself. What's in that vial *is* the poison.'

'Sure, Monty,' Bella replied sceptically.

She pulled the little vial out of her massive handbag – which she flung down against the wall – and held it up against the fluorescent lighting of the garage. The liquid inside almost seemed to glow. It was like lava, coiling and swirling in ripples of black, orange and red. One moment it flared into glorious colour, and the next it was extinguished by a wave of darkness.

Zombie Steve was looking too, his otherwise vacant eyes following the movement of the colours.

'I'm serious,' Monty said. 'It'll kill you.'

'Uh-huh.'

'Really.'

'Then I won't go drinking it. Will that make you happy?'

'No,' Monty said, his voice sharp and irritated now. 'I'll be happy when you bring me the vial – the *whole* vial. Or tell me where you are, and I'll come get it myself.'

'Goodbye, Monty,' she said, pulling the phone away from her ear.

Monty was still yelling when she hung up on him. She turned off her phone and chucked it in her handbag. Let him ring and ring if he wanted. She wouldn't be answering again.

'All right, Steve,' she said, shaking the vial at him. 'Let's see what this cure can do.'

Ten minutes later, things weren't looking good for Zombie Steve. She'd dosed him with the contents of the vial – an easy manoeuvre when he was slaw-jacked and hog-tied to the wall – and he'd immediately begun to change. But instead of turning into a vampire, or even changing back into a human, Zombie Steve had started to go a bit, well, scary.

His eyes weren't just bloodshot, they were actively bleeding. He wasn't slack-jawed anymore, but alert and almost watchful, and the way he moved… It was weird. Creepy, even. Instead of the jerky, mindless movement that Bella had seen from zombies created by previous failed turnings, Zombie Steve's movements had become sinuous and fluid, predatory and keen. It was as though he were dancing around her, waiting for an opening, then shying at her approach.

Whatever he was looking for, it wasn't her.

Then someone rang the doorbell.

'Christ, aren't you supposed to be at work?' Bella said. 'You get a lot of Jehovah's Witnesses round here or something?'

Creepy Zombie Steve looked back at her with calculation in his eyes. That wasn't normal, and it worried her. She wrapped another loop of chains around him, making extra sure that he was properly secured. He was twisting away from her the whole time.

The doorbell rang again. Bella hurried to answer it, depositing the empty vial on the kitchen counter as she went, but when she opened the door there was no one behind it, just a pink minivan parked in Steve's driveway behind the gardener's truck.

'Mr Purdue!' came a voice from inside the garage. 'It's Mariella's. Are you home? I used the side door key.'

Inside the garage.

Bella slammed the front door and ran back through the house as fast as she could while still maintaining the pretence that she was human. She was halfway through the kitchen when the voice said, 'Oh, Mr Purdue! What happened?'

By that time, of course, it was too late. Bella abandoned the pretence and moved the rest of the way at Silver speed, only to find Creepy Zombie Steve chomping down on the neck of a small, brown-skinned woman wearing a T-shirt emblazoned with a logo for *Mariella's Maids*. Bella should still have been able to save the woman – zombie bites weren't normally fatal – but that wasn't what happened. Instead, the woman screamed for a moment, then her eyes turned bloodshot and began to run with bloody tears. Within a second, she was moving in the same strange, undulating way as Creepy Zombie Steve, her eyes tracking every move Bella made.

'Holy shit,' Bella murmured. 'It's catching.'

Bella had just got the woman from the maid service chained up to the wall next to Creepy Zombie Steve when the doorbell rang yet again.

It was Randolph Carter the Third.

'Heard someone hollering,' he said, peering into the house over Bella's shoulder. 'I thought I should come and check it out, in case someone might be hurt. Like maybe my gardener, which would explain why he still hasn't turned up to do my lawn. I notice his truck's still in the drive.'

'But he still isn't here, Mr Carter.'

'Hmph,' Carter said disapprovingly. 'Steve still not available either, I guess?'

'Right.'

Carter looked at Bella with his brow creased, as though he were contemplating something. Bella decided she didn't want to know what it was.

'Never did get your name,' he said.

There was a noise from the garage.

'Bella,' she replied loudly, trying to cover it up. 'My name's Bella.'

A leering smile rose to Carter's wet lips. 'Bella,' he murmured, that contemplative look back on his face. 'Suits you.'

The noise from the garage was getting louder.

'If you don't mind, Mr Carter,' she said, starting to close the door. 'I'm a bit busy.'

'Well, if there's anything I can help with, then—'

'No, thank you,' Bella said forcefully, slamming the door shut in his face.

She heard him chuckle on the other side of the door. He called, 'Ciao, Bella!' before wandering slowly back across the road to his house.

Trust Creepy Zombie Steve to live in Creepy Neighbour Central.

When she got back to the garage, two zombies had somehow become three. Steve and the woman from Mariella's were chained up where she left them, but there was a man in a T-shirt advertising HVAC repair walking sinuously towards the garage door, with a bite on either side of his neck and eyes that dripped blood down to his chin.

'How the hell did you get in here?' Bella asked, bewildered, but of course the HVAC zombie didn't answer. She wasn't expecting him to, not with half his throat missing.

She got him chained up alongside the others, then she found the open door. Through the house, through the kitchen, past the sitting room and through a utility area to a garden room, there was a set of glass doors that led out into the back yard. It turned out there was parking down the side of the house as well as in the drive, and that was where the HVAC guy had left his truck, out of sight.

'Fuck!' Bella yelled.

Then the doorbell rang again.

Frantic now, Bella locked the back doors, then rushed through the house to the garage to lock the side door, before finally going to the front to answer the door.

'Package for you, ma'am,' the UPS woman said. 'Can you sign?'

'Sure, sure,' Bella said distractedly.

It was only when she was already holding the little electronic pen in her hand that she realised there was still blood on her fingers from chaining up the HVAC guy. She signed the tablet quickly and returned it, hoping the woman wouldn't notice. Apparently she didn't, because she slipped the pen between her teeth to hold it as she juggled the large parcel and the tablet in her hands. The moment the blood hit her tongue, the pen dropped from her mouth, the parcel and tablet fell to the ground, and her eyes went bloodshot and began to bleed.

'Oh, for *fuck's* sake!' Bella yelled.

She hooked the UPS woman around the neck, hauled her into the house and slammed the door.

'Four creepy zombies, chained up to the wall,' Bella sang. 'Four creepy zombies, chained up to the wall. And if one creepy zombie, should accidentally get hit in the head with a bottle of scotch—'

Creepy HVAC Zombie ducked out of the way as though he'd anticipated the throw.

'You see,' Bella said, leaning back against the opposite wall, 'you shouldn't be able to do that. None of the others could. They were just human-chasing machines, and they only bothered doing the chasing if humans were actually in sight. This thing you're doing, with the dodging, and this swaying thing? You shouldn't be doing that.'

Bella picked another bottle up off the ground, vodka this time. She'd found Steve's liquor stash in the sitting room in one of those corny globes that had a hidden bar inside. It was just the kind of shit that shallow old Steve would have loved. Bella was almost missing him at this point, but it was clear that he was never coming back.

What a shit show. She couldn't exactly call Monty now, could she? She was supposed to be returning triumphant, having proved herself by turning a new vampire. She was supposed to be showing Enzo just how much he was missing out on, because here she was turning handsome – if greasy – realtors into vampires with no effort at all, *that's* how fucking gorgeous she was, and he was stuck with one mediocre-looking man for the rest of his life. She was winning, and he was a loser.

Things hadn't gone her way, though, had they?

Now what would she say? *I used the vial to create a zombie super race who can turn humans into zombies with a bite, or even with a drop of blood.* That wasn't just a failure, it was a catastrophic one.

Bella was busy drowning her sorrows in the vodka bottle and contemplating her next throw when she was interrupted by a squeaking sound. She put the bottle down quietly and, watched by four creepy sets of bleeding eyes, made her way across the garage to the far wall. She thought that was where the noise was coming from, but she couldn't pinpoint its source. Was there a mouse in the walls or something? She strained to hear more closely, opening her vampire senses to all the sounds in the immediate area, and heard a heartbeat. A human heartbeat.

Shit.

With a last glance back at the zombies – all safely stowed

for now – she strode to the side door, stepped outside and almost walked straight into the source of the noise: a window cleaner, squeegeeing the high garage windows.

'Morning, ma'am,' the woman said.

'What are you doing?' Bella asked.

The woman looked from Bella to the long handle of the squeegee in her hand, confused, then said, 'Washing your windows. You had a booking, ma'am. The office would have sent you an email yesterday to confirm?'

'Right,' Bella said. 'Well. We don't need them washed after all, thank you.'

'You sure?' the woman asked, looking sceptically at the filthy water coming off the dirt-covered glass. 'Might as well do them now I'm here. You'll be charged either way.'

Bella was torn, wondering if sending the window cleaner away would raise suspicions. The woman looked pretty damn suspicious already and besides, what was the worst that could happen? It wasn't like she could see into the garage, and there was no way for her to spot the zombies from any other room in the house. There was the blood and glass in the kitchen, of course, but the blinds were drawn and Bella could clear up the mess before the woman got to that side of the house anyway.

Panic made her indecisive.

Then the fucking doorbell rang again.

'Just…' Bella hesitated, but she couldn't ignore the door. 'I'll be right back.'

She strode around the corner of the house to the front yard, passing the gardener's truck and the maid service van. The window cleaner had parked at the side of the house behind the HVAC guy, but if anyone else showed up they were going to have to pull up at the curb. The yard was turning into a parking lot.

'Mr Carter,' she said, hurrying to where the man was waiting at the front door, leaning impatiently on the doorbell. He didn't look happy.

'Miss Bella,' he said, turning to her with barely-restrained irritation.

'It's just Bella.'

'Is it not enough that you've lured away our gardener? Do you really need to monopolise our maid service too?'

'Excuse me?'

'Fifteen minutes late,' Carter said, tapping his expensive-looking watch. It was massive, and the gold chain hung heavily around his bony wrist. 'Mariella's comes to us on the hour, every Tuesday, without fail. I don't know what Steve thinks he's playing at, but I'd like to give him a piece of my mind.'

'He's busy just now, Mr Carter, and so am I, so if you'll just—'

'No, young lady, I will not.'

'Oh, fuck off, Randy,' Bella said. 'I'm busy.'

It took Randolph Carter the Third a moment to process the words she'd just said, as though his brain wouldn't comprehend the idea that she might have sworn at him. When reality finally penetrated his thick skull, his cheeks and nose flushed red, and he began to vibrate with rage.

'Right,' he said, then he turned on his heel and started marching back across the road. 'Let's see what the police have to say about this.'

'The police don't care that your cleaner's late!' Bella yelled after him.

'And my gardener!' he yelled back. 'Something sinister's going on in that house, and I'm going to find out what. You see if I don't!'

That nosy little asshole was going to be a problem.

But he wasn't the most immediate problem Bella had to deal with. She hurried back around the side of the building to find the window cleaner nowhere in sight.

'Hello?' she called. 'Um, window cleaning person? Are you in the back yard?'

Then Bella noticed that the side door was open.

'Just doing the inside of the windows,' the woman called. 'What the—'

Bella burst back into the garage just in time to see the window cleaner rushing towards the zombies, muttering, 'Oh my lord, let me help you,' and that was the end of that.

More blood. More chains.

The tool rack was getting decidedly crowded.

Five creepy zombies, and one frozen gardener.

If Carter really did call the police – and in the unlikely event that they gave enough of a shit to come out and check the house – that's what they'd find. Maybe Bella should let them find it all, just wash her hands and walk away from this mess. But Monty and the others wouldn't let her get away with that. Leaving the zombies here would put all their plans at risk, and they'd make her pay for it.

It was time she gave up and called for help.

The doorbell rang again. By this point, Bella was about ready to pull the damn thing out of the wall. For a moment, she ignored it, wishing the latest caller away, but then someone yelled, 'Security Patrol! Answer the door, please, ma'am,' and started hammering with the door knocker.

Of course this stupid neighbourhood had a security patrol. It was practically a gated community, all manicured green lawns and swept driveways. There were probably ordinances that mandated it. And of course that nosy crank Carter had called them when the police told him where to go.

This just wasn't her fucking day.

Bella went to answer the door. She was a little slower getting there than she should have been, but even if she'd been quicker, she doubted it would have made a difference.

She opened the door to find a uniformed man staring at a small cut on his hand. His eyes went bloodshot. Bella sighed and turned to look at the door knocker, which was streaked with a smear of partially-dried blood. The UPS woman must have grabbed it when Bella hauled her into the house, leaving a booby trap right there on the front door.

'Fuck my life,' Bella moaned, then she pulled the security guard inside to add to her collection.

She backed along the corridor, dragging the man along behind her by his underarms to the kitchen. His heels left trails through the glass on the kitchen floor on their way to the garage, where they came to an abrupt and unexpected stop. Between the squirming zombie in her grip and the relentless fuckery of the day, Bella was a little distracted, so she didn't notice that Carter had broken into the garage until she literally backed into him.

'My god,' he breathed, looking in horror between the five zombies chained to the wall and the new one in Bella's arms, who was now lunging towards him with snapping jaws. 'What have you done?'

'You couldn't just mind your own business, could you?' Bella said.

Carter's rheumy eyes were as wide as silver dollars, his previously-florid skin as pale as paper. He said nothing for a moment, then he pressed his lips together in indignation and started moving towards the side door.

'I'm calling the police,' he said. 'And they'll come this time, you betcha. Don't try and stop me!'

The security patrol zombie was straining in Bella's arms

now, despite her Silver strength, desperate to get at Carter.

That's when she snapped.

It had been a long morning, she hadn't drunk a thing since she'd bitten Steve last night, and she was exhausted. There didn't seem to be any point in fighting it.

'Just eat him already,' she said, and then she let the zombie loose.

Seven creepy zombies, chained up to the wall.

It was time Bella faced facts: she was out of options. She had to call Monty.

She could almost imagine what he'd say.

I told you the vial was dangerous, but you didn't listen. I told you that a single drop would send a vampire up in smoke, so why did you think it would do any good for a zombie?

The thing Monty didn't understand was that she hadn't believed him. He kept stuff from them all the time, so how was she supposed to know when he was telling the truth or not? Really, this was his fault. She'd had a good plan, but the situation had got way out of control. She'd fucked up a bit, sure. They all fucked up a bit. Monty had fucked up plenty of times, and he was still around.

Maybe the punishment the others cooked up for her wouldn't be so bad.

But she still couldn't bring herself to make the call.

It didn't help that the consequences of her bad decisions were all lined up against the opposite wall, staring at her through bloody eyes. Probably she just needed a break to clear her head, so she riffled through some pockets, locked the house up firmly behind her – all three doors – and went to distribute the zombies' vehicles around the neighbourhood.

Part of her hoped they'd be gone when she got back, or that the police would have arrived, but no such luck. Everything was just as she had left it.

She really should have called Monty then, but she still couldn't face it.

More clean up, then. Between the glass and the blood, the kitchen was a state. She could do something about that.

In a moment, though, because right now she was just overwhelmed by it all; by the mess on the floor, by the chaos in the garage, and by the staggering scale of her failure. She took a deep breath in and let it out again slowly, leaning back against the kitchen countertop. After a few more breaths, she shifted the position of her hands on the tiled surface, and flinched when something sharp lanced into her palm.

Fucking hell, there was glass *everywhere*. Broken beer bottles. Her fault, of course, because she had to admit she'd been a little out of control last night when she'd hatched this manic plan in the first place, but could the world not cut her a break, just once?

But no, of course not, because here she was bleeding onto the floor. She wanted to cry, but instead she ran the cut under the kitchen faucet, pulled out the foreign object, then squinted at the shard that had been embedded in her skin. It didn't look like bottle glass. It was finer, transparent, and curved like a thin tube.

Or a vial.

As she watched, a tiny speck of colour on the point of the shard bloomed from black, to orange, to red.

Oh, *shi—*

If you enjoyed the *QuickSilver* series, why not read *Dead Road*? They're serialised sequel episodes to the *QuickSilver* series, following a load of new characters as they navigate the zombie apocalypse.

***

Join my Readers' Club and receive a FREE short story

www.josiejaffrey.com/subscribe

***

Please leave a review!

If you enjoyed the *QuickSilver* series, I'd be so grateful if you would please review it. Book reviews can make a huge difference to the success of a novel, particularly those of self-published authors like me. If you have time to leave a review, even if it's just a sentence or two, then I'd really appreciate it.

***

Explore the rest of the Silverse…

This book is just one small part of the Silverse, a whole world of vampires that's waiting for you to explore. There are more novels, short stories, serialised story episodes, and even audio drama podcasts. They're all interrelated, although each series stands alone.

Find out more on my website at www.josiejaffrey.com

Acknowledgements

The QuickSilver series has been a decade in the making. It pulls together threads of story littered over hundreds of years' of world-building, and spread across three other separate novel series and a stack of short stories. Finding those threads and lining them up properly to write this central puzzle piece of the Silverse apocalypse has been an absolute undertaking, and one I would never have been able to manage without the unfailing support of my editor Adie Hart. She goes above and beyond to make sure that I haven't borked the continuity or introduced inconsistencies that will tie me in knots later, and she does so with the kind of enthusiasm that keeps me writing when nothing else would. Thank you so much, A, for everything you do.

Huge thanks also to Jen Sugden, my personal cheerleader and bookseller, and wonderful fellow author. I would not have been able to become an audio fiction writer without your support, and I can't wait to explore the podcast world further with you. Big love.

Thanks also to my author buddies Ali Clack and the UKYA Authors Instagram group for their company and support, and to Rachel Bowdler and the Swords & Sapphics Discord for writing with me. Without the sprints channel in that Discord group, I seriously doubt that this series would have been completed so quickly, and I certainly wouldn't have had as much fun doing it.

And thanks to my street team the Silverse Squad, for their unfailing support in promoting my books. I am so grateful.

Finally – and always – thank you to my husband and son, for everything.

CONTENT WARNINGS

<u>QuickSilver Books</u>

General warning for violence/murder.

General warning for extremely graphic blood/gore, including consensual and non-consensual blood drinking, description of injuries, dead bodies, undead body horror, forensic investigation.

Sexual content (mostly consensual, some dubiously consensual due to coercive control).

Some swearing (up to and including 'fuck').

Cannibalism and ritual murder/dismemberment.

Cult-like community with coercive control.

Emotionally abusive/coercive relationships, including family.

Self-inflicted knife injuries (but not mental health-related self-harm).

Memories of child neglect and abuse.

Uncomfortably sexual behaviour with a quasi-father figure.

Dubiously consensual voyeurism.

Graphic description of being burned, by sun and by arson.

Discussion of immortal characters buried alive.

Discussion of historical piratical crimes.

Mentions of slavery and killing of enslaved people, both in real/historical context and fantastical/modern context, including keeping humans imprisoned for use as a blood bank.

Zombie apocalypse.

<u>QuickSilver Short Stories</u>

<u>A Shanty in the Key of F You</u>: General warning for violence/murder; General warning for graphic blood/gore, including blood drinking, description of injuries and venereal disease, amputation; Some swearing (up to and including 'fuck').

<u>Dolce Evita</u>: General warning for violence/murder; General warning for graphic blood/gore, including non-consensual blood drinking; Some swearing (up to and including 'fuck'); Discussion of historical piratical crimes and historical slavery; Mentions of historical misogyny and racism.

<u>Ex Marks the Spot</u>: General warning for violence/murder, including detailed depiction of public execution by hanging; General warning for graphic blood/gore, including blood drinking, description of injuries; Some swearing (up to and including 'fuck'); Implied homophobia; One graphic reference to the torture and murder of enslaved Black people; Depiction of death by drowning.

<u>Cara Mia</u>: General warning for violence, death, murder; General warning for consensual blood-drinking gone wrong; Graphic description of suicide of a close family member; Discussion of grief; Stalking (in person and by recording), presented as romantic by stalker.

<u>Bella Donna</u>: General warning for violence, injuries, death,

murder; Mentions of drug addiction and usage; Kidnapping and restraining victim.

<u>Ciao Bella</u>: General warning for violence, death, murder, including supernatural gore.